ENEMIES OF

Rebecca Dean is a Yorkshire girl of German extraction who now lives in London with her husband and four small dogs.

Visit www.AuthorTracker.co.uk for exclusive updates on Rebecca Dean.

REBECCA DEAN

Enemies of the Heart

HARPER

This novel is entirely a work of fiction.
The names, characters and incidents portrayed in it are
the work of the author's imagination. Any resemblance to
actual persons, living or dead, events or localities is
entirely coincidental.

Harper
An imprint of HarperCollins*Publishers*
77–85 Fulham Palace Road,
Hammersmith, London W6 8JB

www.harpercollins.co.uk

A Paperback Original 2008
1

A catalogue record for this book
is available from the British Library

ISBN-13: 978-0-00-726099-7

Set in Sabon by Palimpsest Book Production Limited,
Grangemouth, Stirlingshire

Printed and bound in Great Britain by
Clays Ltd, St Ives plc

For Carol Smith

ONE

Berlin, June 1909

'You can't possibly decide to marry a man you haven't yet met.' Vicky Hudson's voice held an underlying trace of North Yorkshire vowels – and a wealth of affection and amusement.

Her American-born cousin, five years her senior, looked at her through an ornate dressing-table mirror as her maid put finishing touches to her elaborate chignon. 'I can when he's heir to a steel empire that makes the Pennsylvanian steel empires back home seem child's play in comparison,' she said drily, uncaring that a chambermaid was also present and that she was talking about the eldest son of the house in her hearing. 'My father says Harald Remer has one of the finest financial brains he's ever come across, which is why he was so insistent that Uncle Arthur pay him this visit.'

Vicky walked across to the nearest of the large windows that looked down over the tree-lined Unter den Linden. Zelda's father was a New York banker and his assessment of Harald Remer's financial abilities was, presumably, based on hard evidence.

It was early evening and carriages and smart motorcars thronged the already gas-lit boulevard. Because she was not

1

husband-hunting – and wouldn't be interested in a heel-clicking, stiffly formal German even if she were – Harald Remer's eldest son's eligibility was of little interest to her. For Zelda, widowed three years ago when she was twenty-three, the situation was different.

Zelda's father was rich on a scale that far exceeded her own father's comfortable lifestyle as a Yorkshire mill-owner. As a matter of course Zelda had married a man of enormous wealth and, now that she was a widow, had no intention of marrying anyone whose fortune didn't exceed her own. Even within mega rich New York society this narrowed the field of possible husbands – and something that narrowed the field even further was the unfortunate manner of her husband's death.

After an evening dining at Delmonico's, Harry Gould had committed suicide by throwing himself into the East River from the central span of Brooklyn Bridge. As there was no obvious cause for his action – no financial catastrophe, no sordid scandal attached to his name – rumour had whispered that perhaps his exotically beautiful wife was the cause of the despair that had driven him to take his life. Though nothing was ever said to Zelda directly, she was aware enough of the gossip to have welcomed the opportunity of leaving New York for a trip to Venice, Florence and Rome as part of Vicky's twenty-first-birthday celebrations.

Now, for the first time, it occurred to Vicky that Zelda might have had a part to play in their detour to Berlin.

Zelda glanced down at the diamond-encrusted watch on her wrist. 'Be an angel, Vicky, and say goodnight to Paul for me, would you? I haven't decided what gown to wear and Germans are so obsessive about time I daren't run the risk of being late – not if I want to be considered daughter-in-law material.'

Already dressed for dinner in a powder-blue silk gown that skimmed her satin evening shoes and fell into a small train, Vicky turned away from the window. 'Yes,' she said agreeably,

2

not understanding how Zelda could delegate such a precious ritual. 'Of course I will.'

As she left the room she reminded herself of how modest her own lifestyle was in comparison to Zelda's. Their late mothers, Georgiana and Christina Harland, had been sisters, but whereas her mother had lived all her life in the peaceful serenity of the Yorkshire Dales, Zelda's mother, Christina, had gone to New York, married a merchant banker and lived a life of ostentatious luxury.

Zelda had never lived in anything other than a vast Fifth Avenue mansion and she was accustomed to Paul occupying his own nursery suite and being in the care of not only his nanny, but a shoal of nursery maids. She certainly wasn't accustomed to his travelling with her. That he was doing so now was to please Vicky and her uncle.

The corridor that led towards the suite of rooms allocated to Paul and his nanny was walled and floored in dark red marble. Zelda thought it pleasingly grandiose. Vicky thought it oppressive and ugly. As she circumvented a life-size statue of Hercules she wondered if the other mansions on the Unter den Linden were equally overwhelming and gloomy.

Entering the nursery and seeing Paul seated in the centre of a vast high bed, his face rosy from his recent bath, his dark hair curling damply, was a welcome contrast to all the museum-like statuary.

'Goodness, Paul,' she said, laughter in her voice as she crossed acres of floor to reach him. 'You remind me of the fairy story of the princess and the pea.'

He giggled. 'Is that the story of the princess who could feel a hard lump in her bed no matter how many mattresses she slept on?' he asked as his Scottish nanny, accustomed to Vicky's bedtime visits, left them on their own.

'It is.' Vicky hitched up her evening gown and clambered onto the bed beside him. 'And because she was able to do so the handsome prince, who was looking for a wife, decided she must be a very special princess, a really royal princess, and that she was the princess he would marry.'

'Tell me it again, Aunt Vicky.' He cuddled up against her, smelling of soap and shampoo. 'Tell me it from the beginning.'

'Once upon a time . . .' she began, putting her arm lovingly around him, wondering for the first time if, like Zelda, she too should be thinking of looking for a husband. It would be nice to have children of her own – in fact, she couldn't think of anything nicer. The trouble was she'd never met anyone she could even begin to imagine living with for the rest of her life. All the eligible young men she had met so far had been the hale and hearty sons of Yorkshire mill-owners, their only interests the wool industry and the brass to be made from it.

None of them had appealed to her. She wanted a different kind of husband, a husband who would take pleasure in the things she took pleasure in: music and books and flowers and gardens. Most especially she wanted a husband who would take pleasure in family life, not one who would regard his family duty fulfilled simply because the home he provided was grand and the lifestyle enjoyed in it was luxurious.

There was a tap on the door and a maid entered. 'Excuse me, Fräulein,' she said, accompanying the words with something that looked embarrassingly like a curtsey. 'Dinner is about to be served.'

Vicky gave Paul a kiss. 'I must go, sweetheart,' she said reluctantly. 'Goodnight. God bless.'

'Night,' he said. As she slipped from the bed, he snuggled down against mammoth goose-feather pillows, saying sleepily, 'I love you, Aunt Vicky.'

'And I love you,' she said, her throat tightening with emotion.

She closed the door gently behind her and hurriedly made her way along the long corridor and down the marble and bronze stairway to the reception room, finding with relief that Harald Remer and her father and Zelda were still there and that she hadn't disgraced herself by being late. With them were two young men.

Harald Remer made the introductions.

Josef Remer was introduced to her first and, as he clicked his heels and bent low over her evening-gloved hand, her immediate impression of him was that he was, in almost every way, the image of his father. Handsome in a way that didn't appeal to her, he had the same short Prussian haircut, the same hard blue eyes, the same thin-lipped mouth beneath an immaculately clipped moustache.

Berthold Remer looked nothing like him and, as he too heel-clicked and bowed, she reflected that Zelda would be vastly relieved he wasn't the elder of the two brothers. Not very tall, with mousy hair parted unflatteringly in the centre and wearing thick-lensed spectacles, he lacked the forceful presence of his father and brother.

As he raised his head, she saw with a stab of surprise that the expression in his light-coloured eyes wasn't merely one of Teutonic politeness, but was genuinely warm and welcoming.

'Is it true that Count Zeppelin's airship nearly crashed on its record-breaking flight when it came in to refuel?' her father asked Harald Remer with interest.

'At Stuttgart, yes,' his host said, obviously not best pleased at being reminded that Germany's magnificent achievement had had its hiccups. 'But it was nothing, Herr Hudson. The only consequence was that Count Zeppelin was unable to fly on to Berlin and be received here by the Kaiser.'

He frowned suddenly, seeing something at the far end of the reception room that violently displeased him. Reverting to German he harshly snapped an order at the manservant standing nearest to them.

The manservant ran off in haste and scooped a little

dachshund into his arms. The dog, offended by the action, wriggled furiously.

'It belonged to my late wife,' Harald Remer said apologetically to his guests as the still-struggling dog was carried from the room. 'An annoying animal that never knew its place, even when she was alive.'

Vicky saw Berthold Remer's mouth tighten, but whether it was because he was as annoyed as his father, she wasn't sure.

The small-talk conversation she had interrupted in the reception room continued as they went in to dinner where, to her relief, she found herself seated between Berthold and her father while Zelda, at the far side of the massive dining table, was seated next to Harald and Josef.

'Though Count Zeppelin didn't have the pleasure of meeting with the Kaiser when his airship landed,' Harald Remer said as turtle soup was served, 'I had the honour of being among those invited to the planned reception.'

'To the reception at which the Kaiser would have been present?' There was nothing feigned about the vibrant interest in Zelda's sloe-dark eyes.

'The House of Remer plays a large part in the economy of our Fatherland,' Harald Remer said pompously. 'And I have often had the honour of entertaining Kaiser Wilhelm at Schloss Niedernhall, my family home in Baden-Württemberg.'

Zelda was suitably impressed and Vicky knew exactly what her cousin was thinking. Schloss Niedernhall would be even more vast than the Berlin mansion. Schloss Niedernhall would be palatial on a breathtaking scale.

As if reading her thoughts Berthold leaned towards her slightly. 'It's a two-hundred-room castle perched on a high crag, Fräulein Hudson,' he whispered. 'And quite, quite hideous.'

Vicky fought the desire to giggle, glad that his English was so flawless; glad that, unlike his father, he possessed a sense of humour.

'No one has been able to live in it for years,' Berthold continued as, for her father's benefit, his father launched into a tediously detailed account of the differences between the German Navy League and the German Colonial League. 'It is built entirely of steel and stone with cavernous rooms as high-ceilinged as steeples, and no one has ever been able to devise a satisfactory method of heating it. My late mother always referred to it as the biggest mausoleum in the world.'

The corners of Vicky's mouth dimpled in a smile she couldn't suppress. 'And the gardens?' she asked. 'It must have enormous gardens.'

'It has, but they are the worst kind of Italianate. All gravel and statuary.'

Vicky shuddered and this time it was Berthold's turn to smile. He had, Vicky decided, a very sweet smile.

She said confidingly, 'At my home in Yorkshire my father grows roses – and he doesn't grow them the fashionable way, in neat and tidy beds. They rampage up the sides of the house and into trees and scramble down the banks of the river we look out on to.'

'*Wunderschön*. And whereabouts in Yorkshire is this paradise? Is it in the Dales or on the edge of the moors?'

'You're familiar with Yorkshire?' She was so surprised she abandoned toying with the carp fillets that had long since followed her soup.

He flashed her his sweet smile once again. 'I finished my education at Oxford. As a result I have a great affection for England and the English countryside.'

It explained his excellent English and Vicky was just beginning to settle down to an enjoyable conversation with him, telling him of how her home, Shuttleworth Hall, was in Wensleydale – and of how pretty Wensleydale was – when she was interrupted by Harald Remer exclaiming loudly: '*Ja, natürlich*, Herr Hudson. *Natürlich*. Remer factories are not only one of Germany's biggest producers of steel – second only to the House of Krupp – but we are also next to the biggest producer of clothing for the army and the navy. If Yorkshire wool is as superior as you claim, we will put large quantities to good use. Isn't that so, Berthold?'

As Berthold was drawn reluctantly into the general conversation, Vicky felt a rough little tongue lick her ankle. Reaching down beneath the overhang of the lace tablecloth she touched the top of the dachshund's silky-smooth head.

Knowing how speedily the dog would be removed if Harald Remer were made aware of its presence, she didn't attract attention to it, hoping that if Zelda noticed the uninvited guest she would also say nothing.

On the far side of a giant silver epergne, Zelda was showing no sign of being interested in anything other than Harald Remer's conversation. As she listened to him with flatteringly rapt attention, she too was being given undivided attention. Not from Harald Remer, but from Josef.

Vicky could quite understand why, for Zelda's looks were striking. Though she didn't like it spoken of, her paternal grandmother had been a Native American, an Iroquois, and Zelda had inherited not only her high cheekbones and cat-like eyes, but also her flawless olive skin and night-black hair. The vivid yellow gown she was wearing had been made in Paris and was cut in the very latest neoclassical style, low at the bosom and falling daringly straight to her feet. It was the perfect foil for her voluptuous beauty, and Vicky was well aware that her own gown was unfashionably provincial in comparison.

She was happily uncaring. When it came to clothes and jewellery, competition with Zelda was impossible. The five-string choker of diamond-clasped pearls and the dazzling array of diamond bracelets on Zelda's wrists and arms were, for instance, no ordinary pieces of jewellery. Zelda had dressed to impress, wanting the Remers to be in no doubt she was a member of New York's most exclusive social elite – a social elite that was at home mixing with kings, presidents and, given the opportunity, kaisers.

She also realized something else. The food on Berthold Remer's plate was disappearing fast – and not because he was eating it. As he continued to take part in the conversation that now included his brother and her father, his hand would, every so often, move across his plate and then drop beneath the table.

Laughter fizzed in her throat.

The dachshund had known exactly whose feet to sit beside.

'*Wiener Schnitzel* seems to be a very popular dish, Herr Remer,' she said impishly. 'Almost as popular as the side dish of little dumplings.'

'Ah, those are called *Nockerl*. They are an Austrian dish much loved by north Germans.'

Once again he discreetly fielded a titbit beneath the table.

With the laughter now thick in her voice, she said: 'And is that where your small friend comes from? North Germany?'

'But, yes.' There was answering amusement in Berthold's voice. 'My friend, as you call him, is a little Dackel. A typical north German dog. His name is Wastl.'

'Perhaps I could tempt Wastl with something?'

In utter complicity their eyes met.

'There will be chocolate finger biscuits with the dessert, Fräulein Hudson. I think you will find Wastl very fond of them.'

As their eyes held, Vicky forgot about the dachshund at their feet. Behind his spectacles Berthold's eyes were smoke-grey marked with gold flecks. They were the nicest eyes she had ever seen. They were the eyes of a man who could be trusted. The eyes of a man who, unlike his father, had not a shred of pomposity about him. A man who was decent and kind. Beneath his trimly clipped moustache his mouth was just as pleasing, firm and well shaped.

A distant part of her brain registered that the conversation at the table had now turned to culture. Opera was being discussed, or was it ballet? She didn't know and didn't care. As Berthold asked her if she had a dog of her own, the most extraordinary things began happening inside her tummy.

'My father has three,' she said, aware that, close to, his hair wasn't mousy at all. Beneath the lights of the chandeliers it was almost blond.

'And what kind of dogs are they? Are they like Wastl, small and friendly, or are they big and fierce?'

The smile in his eyes sent excitement spiralling in her tummy as if she were on a roller-coaster. 'Harry is a Yorkshire terrier and is as small as Wastl,' she said, knowing he was teasing her, but not minding because it was teasing in the nicest possible way. 'I'm not sure if he is as friendly, though. He's full of what Zelda calls "pep". The other two dogs are spaniels and are wonderfully affectionate.'

Dimly, she was aware that the conversation on the other side of the dinner table was again about royalty. 'I thought the King of England looked quite splendid in German military uniform when he visited Berlin in February,' Zelda was saying, trying to lure Harald Remer into speaking of the Kaiser again. 'Being American I tend to forget how close the relationship between Germany and Britain is, but then I also tend to forget that King Edward and Kaiser Wilhelm are uncle and nephew.'

What Harald Remer's response to Zelda's last remark was, Vicky didn't know. All her attention was focused on Berthold – on how much she liked him and on the extraordinary effects his gold-flecked eyes and sweet smile had on her. She'd never been in love, but she wondered if she was falling in love now. Could it happen so suddenly? And with someone so unlikely?

As the dessert was served with accompanying chocolate finger biscuits, Berthold quirked an eyebrow inquiringly in her direction and Vicky decided that it could – and that it had.

Giddy at the speed of events, wondering if Berthold reciprocated her feelings in even the tiniest way and wondering what on earth Zelda would say when she told her, she slid a finger biscuit beneath the table to Wastl, her heart singing like a bird's.

'Dear Lord, what a bizarre evening!' Zelda said the minute they were in the privacy of her bedroom. 'Only six of us for dinner. *Six*.' Though she had seated herself at her dressing table, she shooed her hovering maid away. 'It would be unheard of in New York. And do Germans always discuss business affairs in front of ladies? Every time the conversation touched on anything remotely interesting, Harald Remer brought it back to the subject of Yorkshire wool!'

Vicky picked up her skirts and climbed onto Zelda's elaborately carved bed. 'I think dining *en famille* was a compliment, not an insult,' she said, wanting Zelda to be in a good mood before she shared her delicious secret with her. 'And my father was quite as much at fault as Harald Remer when it came to the subject of Yorkshire wool. It is, after all, why he's here. It's a little odd, don't you think, that the Remer textile factories only make military clothing? How much military clothing can a country at peace need?'

'I don't know and I don't care.' Not bothering to call back her maid, Zelda pulled the ivory combs out of her hair and shook it free so that it fell in a rippling black waterfall to her waist. 'Thank heavens Josef lived up to expectations. He's quite a beau and would make a swell husband. The Remers entertain German royalty. They're not only stupendously rich, they're members of the social elite. It would mean living in Berlin – and I would *love* to live in Berlin. Just think of it, Vicky darling. No more New York. No more murmurs in Rockefeller and Vanderbilt drawing rooms about my pedigree

11

not being quite the thing. And no more hideous gossip about the nature of Harry's death.'

She swung round to face Vicky, her near-black eyes brilliant. 'I've made up my mind I'm going to have him,' she said decisively. 'He may be stiffly formal – all Germans are as buttoned-up and contained as hell – but a new life in Europe is just what I need. And I like the idea of acting as my father-in-law's hostess and entertaining German royalty.'

'But how do you know that Josef Remer is even looking for a bride?' Zelda's certainty that all she had to do to have Josef Remer as a husband was to crook her little finger, astounded her. 'And if he were looking for a bride, why should he choose to marry an American? English aristocracy fall over themselves where American heiresses are concerned, but that's because they're so often in need of American dollars. The Remers aren't.'

'No, and they're not English aristocracy either.'

Vicky blinked, totally confused.

Zelda said impatiently, 'So many New York heiresses have married into the English aristocracy that if I did, my history would soon be as well known in London as it is at home. You may think my grandmother's Iroquois blood glamorous, but take it from me, in England it wouldn't be regarded as *chic*. Here, in Berlin, no one will be aware of it – and I shall take great care no one ever becomes aware of it.'

'And is that how you feel about Harry's death too? That it is something you could put behind you in Berlin?'

'Of course I could put it behind me if there was no gossip about it. And as no one in Berlin knows that Harry threw himself into the East River, there will be no gossip, will there?'

'No,' Vicky said slowly, realizing that Zelda was in deadly earnest about acquiring Josef Remer as a husband. 'But we're only in Berlin for a few days, Zelda. How can you get a proposal out of him in only a few days?'

'I don't suppose I can, but I can make an impression and I

already have. He's never met anyone like me before and he's hooked. I just know he is. And when we return from Italy, I won't re-cross the Atlantic. I'll stay in Europe – and I'll make sure he knows where to find me.'

It was all so calculatingly thought out – and so bereft of romance – that Vicky was no longer bursting to confide her own news. Zelda wouldn't understand about love at first sight – or love at very nearly first sight. And she wouldn't be able to explain to Zelda just why she was so certain she was in love. Saying she instinctively knew she and Berthold were kindred spirits would mean nothing to Zelda and she didn't want the precious emotion he had kindled in her to be dismissed or, even worse, ridiculed.

She slid from the bed. 'I'm tired, Zelda,' she said truthfully. 'Goodnight, God bless.'

'Night, Vicky darling.'

As Zelda rang for her maid, Vicky crossed to the door, opened it and paused. There was something she had forgotten to say.

'You're wrong about all Germans being buttoned-up and contained,' she said. 'Not all of them are. Berthold isn't.'

As Zelda's eyebrows rose nearly into her hair, she closed the door.

The next morning, much to Vicky's pleasure, Berthold breakfasted with them. To Zelda's annoyance, Josef did not.

'Instead of accompanying your father on his visit to the clothing factory this morning, why don't you let me show you the Tiergarten and the Zoological Gardens?' he said, speaking to them both.

As Zelda sucked in her breath, about to refuse, Vicky said hurriedly, 'Oh, that would be lovely, Herr Remer.' She smiled at him sunnily, so happy she could hardly breathe. 'The Tiergarten is a park, isn't it? We have lovely parks in

Yorkshire. One of them, in Bradford, is within sight of the mill.' She was aware of Zelda rolling her eyes to heaven and didn't care. 'Can Paul and his nanny come with us? Paul would love the zoo.'

'Of course he can.' He beamed back at her, the morning sun catching on the lenses of his spectacles. 'We can't leave the little chap behind. In an hour's time, then? That won't be hurrying things too much for you, will it?'

'No,' Vicky said, certain it was going to be one of the most perfect mornings of her life. 'An hour won't be hurrying things at all.'

'How *could* you, Vicky?' Zelda said crossly as they went upstairs for hats and parasols. 'Paul's nanny is quite capable of taking Paul to the park or the Zoological Gardens on her own. It's what nannies are for.'

'But it will be so much nicer if he is with us. And didn't you think it wonderfully kind of Berthold Remer to agree he could come? I think he's an *exceptional* person. Quite, quite special.'

Zelda came to a halt as they reached a spacious landing, home to an enormous marble statue of a Greek goddess. 'Are you losing your mind, Vicky? Only a man verging on the witless would take someone else's child – a child he is not acquainted with – on an excursion. Can you imagine Josef Remer doing such a thing?'

'No, I can't.' She didn't add that she couldn't do so because she didn't think Josef Remer nice enough for such a gesture.

The conversation between the two of them didn't improve as they waited for Paul's nanny to bring Paul to them.

'My instincts tell me Berthold Remer is a disappointment to his father.' Zelda tilted her wide-brimmed hat, laden with peacock feathers, to a more seductive angle. 'He quite obviously takes no interest in the Remer steelworks or in any other aspect of the family's vast holdings – and the little I overheard of his conversation with you yesterday evening was pathetically unsophisticated. Josef was telling me of how, on his visit to Baden-Baden last month, there were more crowned heads in the casino than at King Edward's coronation. I doubt Berthold ever visits Baden-Baden.'

Vicky doubted it as well, and was glad of it. She didn't want to be in love with a man who thought it important to be seen in the company of European royalty.

Not wanting to discuss Berthold any further with Zelda she adjusted her broad straw hat with its decoration of artificial pink roses and picked up her white lace gloves. Her dress was white too, high at the throat, fashionably hobble-skirted and prettily trimmed with broderie anglaise. She didn't look as breathtakingly sophisticated as Zelda, but it didn't matter. Berthold wasn't interested in sophistication. He was interested in the things she was interested in, and also – and this she knew with happy certainty – he was interested in her.

Three days later, Berthold asked her father for his permission to propose to her.

'Great Scott, Vicky! I could hardly believe my ears!' her father said to her later that evening when he spoke to her in the privacy of her room. 'Naturally, I told him it was far too soon – not at all the thing. Still, he'd be a grand catch. Much better than Amos Ramsbotham's son at Ilkley, or William Priestley's son at Keighley. And though you would expect his father to be opposed to his marrying a non-German – and to someone not of their own elite social set – that isn't the case. Herr Remer knows of his intentions and has raised no objections. Considering all the advantages such a marriage would bring to you, it calls for serious thought. That being the case I told Berthold to approach me again in six months' time, when it is possible I might give him a different reply.'

'You told him *not* to propose to me?' Panic bubbled in

Vicky's throat. 'But I *want* him to propose to me, Papa! I don't *need* to give it serious thought. I don't want to wait another six months before you give him permission to speak to me. I want him to propose to me now! Tonight!'

The next morning, with her father's permission, Berthold took her into the mansion's vast, glass-enclosed winter garden.

'I would very much like it if . . . I would be very honoured if . . .' He ran a finger round the rim of his stiff wing collar, so nervous and awkward she could hardly bear it. 'I would be very honoured if you would become my wife,' he managed at last.

Then, before she could give him her reply, he said pleadingly in a rush of such emotion all her heart went out to him: 'Do love me a little, *Liebchen*, because I love you so much.'

He looked so anxious, so terrified she would turn him down, that she flung her arms around his neck, saying passionately, 'But I already love you far more than a little, Berthold! I love you lots and lots – truly I do!'

For a second there was disbelief in his eyes and then relief flooded them. He gathered her into his arms, saying in a voice cracking and breaking with the force of his feelings, 'I'll always love you, Vicky. Always and for ever.'

He was holding her so close she could smell his skin and feel his heart beating against hers. With sensations she had never before experienced flooding through her, she raised her face for his kiss, closing her eyes, knowing it was a moment she would remember always, a moment she would never forget, no matter how long she lived.

His kiss was long and sweet and, as she had known it would be, utterly perfect.

The ring too, when he gave it to her, was beautiful beyond description.

16

'It was my mother's,' he said simply, slipping a huge solitaire pink diamond onto the third finger of her left hand. 'I never thought I'd find anyone I loved enough to give it to.'

Then, hand in hand, her head resting against his shoulder, they walked back into the house to break their news to his father and to Zelda.

'What do you say has just happened, Vicky darling?' Zelda was lying on her bed, resting. 'Berthold has proposed to whom?'

'To me, Zelda.' Vicky was fizzing with joy. 'To *me*!'

Zelda sat upright so quickly a comb flew out of her upswept hair. 'But you've only known him a matter of days!'

'I know, isn't it magical? I'm so in love with him, Zelda. He's everything I want my future husband to be. He's kind and decent and he makes me laugh and –'

'And he wears pebble-thick spectacles and is as homely as grits.'

And then Zelda saw the enormous pink diamond on Vicky's left hand and immediately regretted her unkind words. What did it matter if Vicky thought the homely Berthold as handsome as a prince? What *did* matter was that via Vicky she and the Remer family would be permanently linked. There would be lots of opportunities for her to work her charm on Josef Remer, heir to the Remer steel fortune. There would be the wedding, for one thing, when she would be Vicky's matron of honour and Josef would be Berthold's best man.

Sliding quickly from the bed she threw her arms around Vicky, hugging her tight, laughing the carelessly spoken words away. 'And I'm only joking about Berthold being homely. He's quiet, though. Too quiet for me, but perfect for you. Does Josef know yet? Is everyone meeting downstairs to toast the two of you with champagne?'

'Probably.' Though Zelda's remark had hurt, Vicky wasn't going to brood on it. Zelda was so outspoken she couldn't help but be unintentionally hurtful sometimes.

As Zelda released her hold of her and began cooing over the spectacular engagement ring, Vicky said happily, 'It was Berthold's mother's ring. It's beautiful, isn't it?'

'It sure is, but shouldn't –' Zelda was about to say 'but shouldn't it be Josef's fiancée who will one day wear it?' but common sense kicked in. The ring had obviously been one of his mother's dress rings, not her engagement ring. 'Shouldn't we go downstairs?' she finished instead. 'I'm sure the champagne will be on ice by now.'

It was. Harald Remer, Josef Remer, Vicky's father and Berthold were all gathered in the cathedral-like drawing room.

With shining eyes and blushing cheeks Vicky took her place by Berthold's side. Champagne was poured. Harald Remer made a speech of congratulations and then, as champagne bubbles tickled Vicky's nose and Berthold tenderly drew her free hand into the crook of his arm, he said, 'The announcement will be sent to the Berlin newspapers. As for English newspapers, which is appropriate, Herr Hudson? The *Daily Telegraph* or *The Times*?'

'Both, I think.' Vicky's father was visibly dazed at the speed of events. 'In England it is customary for the bride's mother to attend to the engagement and wedding announcements. As Vicky's mother is sadly no longer with us, I will attend to it. It's simply a case of "The engagement is announced between Herr Berthold Harald Remer, elder son of Herr Harald Erich Remer and the late Frau Lisl Remer of Schloss Niedernhall, Baden-Württemberg, and Victoria Hudson, only daughter of Mr Arthur Hudson and the late Mrs Georgiana Hudson of Shuttleworth Hall, Little Ridding, Yorkshire," isn't it? Or would the Berlin address be preferable?'

Before either Harald Remer or Berthold could make a

18

response Zelda said with a laugh in her voice to cover up the embarrassment of his *faux pas*, 'You're in error, Uncle Arthur. Josef is the elder son, not Berthold.'

The Remers stared at her as if she had grown two heads.

'*Nein*, Frau Gould,' Harald Remer said stiffly. 'It is you, I am afraid, who is in error. As to the address for the announcements, Herr Hudson, I think both the Baden-Württemberg and the Berlin address should be inserted.'

Vicky felt as if her chest was about to explode. If Berthold was the elder then nothing was going to be as she had imagined it would be. The day would come when Berthold would have huge responsibilities. Would she, when Berthold was head of the Remer steel dynasty, have to entertain German royalty at the monstrous-sounding Schloss Niedernhall in Baden-Württemberg? It didn't bear thinking about.

As she swayed, a fraction away from fainting, she saw the expression on Zelda's face.

If she was appalled, Zelda was poleaxed. Perfectly immobile, she stood as frozen as one of the mansion's many statues.

'I think I had Berthold and Josef's relationship a little confused before we arrived here, Zelda,' her uncle said to her, aware an apology was due. 'If I caused you similar confusion, I'm sorry. The main thing is, no harm's been done, eh?'

Zelda didn't even attempt to make a response. Her fingers tightened on the stem of her champagne flute until the knuckles were white.

Watching her, terrified that the fragile glass was about to shatter, Vicky knew that her father had never been more wrong.

A great deal of harm had been done.

Harm that was, quite possibly, incalculable.

TWO

Berlin, September 1910

The scent of the massed lilies in Berlin's Kaiser Wilhelm Memorial Church was so overpowering that Vicky, seated between her father and Berthold, felt giddy with nausea. Because she was heavily pregnant no one, apart from Zelda, of course, had wanted her to attend the wedding, but how could she not have done? She and Zelda were as close as sisters and she had been determined that nothing, not even the fact that her baby was due at any moment, was going to prevent her from seeing Zelda marry into the family she herself had married into ten months earlier.

'Are you all right, *Liebchen*?' Berthold asked anxiously, aware she was far paler than was normal.

'I'm fine, darling.' Vicky squeezed his hand reassuringly and smiled up into his concerned face.

In serried ranks behind them were other family members plus three hundred guests drawn almost exclusively from the worlds of politics, finance and government. Gold lacings on uniforms glittered. Orders and jewels shone. Nearly everyone was craning his or her head for a view, not of Josef, standing at the altar rail with his best man as he awaited the arrival of his bride, but of the Kaiser, the guest around whom the entire wedding had been arranged.

It was because of the Kaiser that the date of the wedding, set at the time of Zelda and Josef's engagement at Easter, had been impossible to change, even though it had soon become apparent that Vicky would be too heavily pregnant to act as matron of honour. She had been disappointed, of course, but had tried hard not to show it.

Looking at the ramrod-straight figure of Count Ernst Schulenburg she still didn't understand why he, and not Berthold, was standing at Josef's side.

Neither did her father.

'But Germans are sticklers for etiquette!' he had said shortly after his arrival in Berlin for the wedding. 'How can Josef *not* have his only brother act as his best man? I've never heard the like of it. Surely it will cause talk?'

Vicky slid her net-gloved hand inside her satin purse in search of a peppermint to ease the nausea she was feeling, knowing there probably was talk. Why Harald Remer had sanctioned Josef's choice of best man was a mystery – and it wasn't the first mystery she had been faced with. Why, for instance, had her father-in-law agreed so easily that she and Berthold be married in Yorkshire and not Berlin? At the time she had thought he was simply being kind to her and bowing to the tradition that the wedding take place in the bride's parish church. Now she wasn't so sure. For one thing, kindness was a quality she no longer thought of in connection with Harald Remer, for though Josef could do no wrong in his eyes, he most certainly wasn't kind to her beloved Berthold.

This wedding in Berlin's most prestigious church and with the Kaiser in attendance was a case in point. Anyone not knowing differently would assume it was the wedding of the elder son of the family – and in every way, big and small, that was exactly how Harald Remer treated Josef. When she and Berthold had returned from their honeymoon in the Lake District, she had been shocked to discover the disregard with which Berthold was treated by his father and brother.

'But Josef and I are very different,' he had said when she had first dared to mention her feelings. 'I wasn't brought up to take an interest in the steelworks, Josef was. My father took him with him on inspections of the steel plants when he was only twelve – and down a coal mine when he was thirteen. I never went. I didn't want to go. Because they share the same passion for the steelworks it naturally makes my father and Josef very close. And think how uncomfortable our lives would be if I were his favourite, not Josef. I doubt we would have been able to marry in Yorkshire with only family and friends present – and they were real friends, weren't they, *Liebchen*? I doubt if Josef will know half the guests who have been invited to his and Zelda's wedding.'

As the organist launched into the Wedding March from *Lohengrin* and as all heads, hers included, turned for a first glimpse of the bride, Vicky wondered if Josef would have been allowed to propose marriage to a Yorkshire girl of no great fortune only days after meeting her, and knew that he would not. It had not been magnanimity that had prompted Herr Remer to be so happily accepting of her as a daughter-in-law. It had been something else – and that she didn't yet know what that something was, deeply troubled her.

As Zelda began her progress down the aisle on her father's arm, Berthold sucked in his breath. Vicky didn't blame him. Wearing a blue silk dress that fell into a long train behind her and carrying a spray of crimson roses, Zelda looked magnificent. Her wide hat, tilted at a seductive angle and the same lavender-blue as her dress, was veiled and wreathed in roses identical to those in her spray.

'Being a widow, I can't wear white and so I shall have

Monsieur Worth create me something utterly wonderful,' she had said at the time of her engagement, and her Paris gown, adorned with exquisite hand-embroidery in patterns of peacock feathers decorated with seed pearls, was certainly that.

Walking behind her, flushed with excitement at being his mother's trainbearer, was Paul.

As Zelda took her place at Josef's side, Vicky knew that Zelda had achieved her aim. Amid the grandeur of the surroundings and the ceremony necessitated by the presence of the Kaiser, her progress down the aisle attended solely by Paul had been a masterpiece of understatement and good taste.

The backache she had been feeling all morning intensified and Vicky arched her spine to try to relieve it, reflecting that Zelda's determination to speak German fluently as quickly as possible was all of a piece with her fierce resolve to cut all links with America. Though her father had crossed the Atlantic in order to give her away, no other members of her family had been invited to make the journey with him and no invitations had been extended to family in England other than to her uncle Arthur.

The wedding had occasioned a happy reunion between her father and Zelda's father who, separated by the Atlantic, rarely saw each other. 'Zelda really is my sister now,' she whispered to him. 'Which is lovely, because it is how we've always thought of each other.'

He patted her hand, knowing only too well how close she and Zelda were, and she wondered if he knew just how deeply she missed him – and not only him, but Yorkshire too. She had taken advantage of her honeymoon by spending it at home, and had fully expected Zelda to do a similar thing and to honeymoon in America, at Niagara or somewhere else close to New York.

'Landsakes, Vicky! And risk socializing with someone who would tell Josef the sordid details of Harry's death?' Zelda had said when she had voiced surprise that Vienna was to be the honeymoon destination. 'Or, nearly as bad, have him discover that my paternal grandmother was an Iroquois Indian? No, thank you. My days of being gossiped about on those counts are in the past. As is America. From now on I'm a Berliner.'

Dearly as she loved Berthold, Vicky knew she would never be able to think of herself as a Berliner. In her ten months of living in the museum-like mansion on Unter den Linden, her heart hadn't warmed to Berlin. She was a country girl, a Yorkshire girl, and the grandiose architecture of Berlin left her cold. She ached for the lush sweeping valley that was Wensleydale; for small villages with weekly markets; for woods and waterfalls; for the River Ure that tumbled through the grounds of her home; for the jigsaw pattern of drystone walls; for sheep dotted everywhere; and for the exhilarating sight, always, in the distance, of high bare moorland.

'Are you uncomfortable, sweetheart?' Berthold asked, covering her hand with his.

She nodded, grateful for his gentleness and sweetness.

'You'll be able to rest soon. It isn't customary in Germany for the bride and groom to remain long at the reception and as soon as they leave for their honeymoon, you will be able to excuse yourself.'

'Won't my doing so be seen as bad manners?'

Behind his pebble-thick lenses his eyes were amused. 'Not considering your condition and the length of this wedding service.'

As the first notes of Mendelssohn's Wedding March rang triumphantly out and the happy couple began to make their way down the aisle as man and wife, Berthold leaned towards her again, saying in her ear, 'I much preferred our wedding in

Yorkshire, with the snow falling and only family and real friends wishing us well.'

The Kaiser began to make his way down the aisle and Vicky rose to her feet with the rest of the congregation. Once the baby was born she and Berthold would be able to make plans for a return trip to Yorkshire. They might even be able to spend their wedding anniversary there. Suddenly, she didn't feel quite so nauseous. The future was full of things to look forward to. Her baby would soon be in her arms, and once Zelda returned from honeymoon she would have her companionship constantly, for Zelda and Josef would be living for most of the year in the mansion on Unter den Linden.

Walking out of the church between her husband and her father, another thought occurred to her. Because Berthold was so little interested in his father's steel empire and because he had so little to do with the running of it, perhaps they would be able to move to Yorkshire permanently. It would mean their baby growing up in the home she had grown up in, a home as different to the Remer mansion as it was possible to imagine.

At the thought of cream-papered walls patterned with roses, instead of walls covered in blood-red silk, and of window seats looking out over undulating lawns towards a river and woods, instead of windows so heavily swathed in dark velvet hardly any sunlight permeated, her throat tightened so that she could hardly breathe. To live with Berthold at Shuttleworth Hall would be very heaven.

As the royal carriage and then Zelda and Josef's carriage rattled away down the Kurfürstendamm in the direction of Unter den Linden and the chauffeur handed her into Berthold's Austro-Daimler motorcar, she thought of nothing else.

Her stomach muscles were tight with excitement. That

evening, when the reception was over and she and Berthold were on their own, she would speak to him about it.

When they arrived back at the Remer mansion her stomach muscles were still tight so she knew the cause was something more than excitement.

'I don't think I'm going to be able to last out the reception, Berthold,' she said, leaning against him heavily. 'I feel most peculiar and most uncomfortable.'

One look at her face and alarm rushed through him.

'Is the baby coming? Should I send for Dr Soller?'

Aware that the baby probably was coming, but not wanting the doctor sent for before it was absolutely necessary and not wanting to cause any disturbance just as Josef and Zelda were beginning to receive their guests, she said, 'There's no need to call Dr Soller just yet. I do want to lie down, though. Give my apologies to Zelda, will you, Berthold?'

Leaving him under the impression that all she needed was a short rest she left him to enter the flower-filled, white and gold ballroom alone and made her way upstairs, Wastl at her heels.

When she asked for Indian tea, Josephine, her snub-nosed, freckle-faced, Yorkshire-born maid, stared at her with almost as much alarm as Berthold had. 'Certainly, ma'am, but don't you think I should also call for a doctor?'

'I don't think so, Josephine. Not yet.'

She eased her feet out of her cream kid shoes and lay down. Very faintly, she could hear the sound of music and chatter floating up from the ballroom. It meant Josef and Zelda had finished receiving their guests and that the refreshment part of the reception was now under way. Despite the fact that she was now very definitely having contractions she smiled to herself, hoping that her father and her uncle were enjoying themselves and, as the only non-Germans, were managing to hold their own socially.

'Though I shan't be seeking out business contacts with any of Harald's friends,' her father had warned her when they had had supper together on the evening of his arrival. 'Truth to tell, Vicky dear, my business arrangement with Harald is proving a little embarrassing.'

'Because he's my father-in-law?' she'd said, bewildered.

'Because the wool I ship to him is wool used exclusively for government contracts – and those contracts are for military clothing, not civilian clothing.'

'And does that matter?'

'It would if Germany were to go to war. And you have to bear in mind that the Kaiser is a bully. France and Russia don't like it, and they especially don't like the way Germany is building up her navy. It's a disturbing situation, Vicky, and not one I want to profit from.'

'But there isn't going to be a war between Germany and Britain, is there?'

Her alarm had been so naked he'd reached across the table and grasped hold of her hand.

'No, of course not,' he'd said reassuringly. 'Germany's relations with Britain are different to those she has with other countries. We have a shared history – our monarchs are closely related. Goodness, if I'd thought you were going to come to such a conclusion I would never have mentioned my doubts about the Kaiser's military intentions.'

He'd turned the conversation to family matters and they'd talked of his pleasure in the reunion he and his brother-in-law were enjoying and her pleasure that Zelda would soon be her sister-in-law as well as her cousin.

Now, lying on her bed and listening to the growing noise of the wedding reception, she wondered what Harald Remer's reaction would be if her father declined to send him any more wool. Even though the Remer clothing factory was of small importance compared to the industrial giant that was the Remer steelworks, she was sure he would be furious.

A contraction totally different in nature to the ones she had been having banished all thoughts of her father-in-law. As Josephine entered the room, a tea tray in her hands, she said with urgency, 'I do need the doctor, Josephine. I need him as soon as possible.'

Seated at the centre of the splendidly ornate top table, the Kaiser on one side of her, her husband on the other, Zelda was brimming with radiant self-satisfaction. Though she hadn't married the elder son as she had intended when she had first arrived in the Remer mansion as a guest, she had certainly achieved a great deal. She was, for instance, now on social terms with an emperor, and how many Fifth Avenue grand hostesses could claim the same? The answer, as she well knew, was that none of them could.

As the Kaiser leaned towards her slightly, complimenting her on the speed with which she was learning German, she wished with all her heart the Vanderbilt, Whitney and Astor matriarchs, who had never let her forget she had Iroquois blood in her veins, could see her now.

'Ugly old dragons,' she said with fierce feeling beneath her breath, remembering the rumours they had helped to spread in the wake of Harry's suicide.

'Excuse me?' The Kaiser looked startled.

Her luscious lips curved into a seductive smile. 'I was thinking out loud about dachshunds, sir. Like all things German, I find them delightful.'

The gleam in the Kaiser's eyes told her that he, like many other men, found her exotic beauty fascinating.

That her looks were so striking, especially in a country where the women were predominantly fair-haired and blue-eyed, was something that both pleased and infuriated her. It pleased her to be admired, but she found it infuriating that

28

with her night-black hair and dark eyes she could never look typically German. Making the matter worse was that Vicky, who had no desire at all to be mistaken for a German, was as golden-haired and sapphire-eyed as a Rhine Maiden.

'It is time to cut the cake, Zelda,' Josef said in his habitually brusque manner.

Her smile deepened. Many people found Josef intimidating, but she didn't. She found his dominating personality intensely arousing – especially when it came to love-making.

As she and Josef cut the cake to applause, Zelda wondered what was keeping Vicky away from the reception for so long. Berthold had said she'd needed to rest, but that had been nearly two hours ago and she still hadn't put in an appearance. Could it be that the baby was on its way?

Thinking that her father-in-law might have been told something she looked towards him to see if he was displaying any signs of unusual tenseness. Shock stabbed through her. He looked ill. *Was* ill. She continued to hold her cake-cutting pose for the photographer who, his camera on a tripod, his head under a cloth, had yet to take the first photograph. As she nerved herself for the mini explosion and flash, Harald Remer let out an agonized cry and, clutching at his chest, pitched forward across the table, sending wine glasses and china crashing to the floor.

For a split second no one moved and then there was uproar as footmen, waiters and the guests closest to him all rushed to his aid.

'Fetch a doctor!' Josef shouted to the family's horrified butler. 'Immediately!'

Her uncle was on his feet almost as quickly, striding not towards Harald Remer, but towards Paul.

Amid a great deal of clamour her husband helped Berthold and Ernst Schulenburg lift the semi-conscious Harald Remer away from the table and lay him on the floor, and it occurred to her that there were going to be other disruptions to her wedding arrangements, for how could she and Josef leave for their honeymoon when his father's collapse had been so public?

'I suspect he's had a heart attack,' her father said to her grimly. 'It doesn't look good, Zelda.'

The Kaiser was long gone, having been whisked away by his entourage within seconds of Harald Remer's spectacular collapse. Speculation was rife. Where was the doctor? How was it possible that with over three hundred people in the ballroom, not one of them was a medical man? Was it a heart attack or was it a stroke? Was he still breathing or was he, perhaps, already dead?

As someone voiced this last possibility in her hearing, Zelda sucked in her breath. If Harald Remer were dead then Berthold – ineffectual, uninspiring Berthold – would be head of the Remer steel dynasty.

The blood pounded in her ears. Nominal head. That was what Josef had told her and it was ludicrous to think of Berthold as being anything else. The real head of the House of Remer would be Josef.

'I think he is coming round,' she heard one guest say as someone else shouted that the doctor had arrived.

She pressed her lips together tighter than ever and closed her eyes, fervently praying they were both wrong.

'Where is the doctor? Why isn't he here yet?' Vicky's voice was filled with panic. 'I know first babies aren't supposed to come quickly, but this one is!'

Though she wasn't much older than Vicky, Josephine had assisted at the births of her sister's children and was well aware that Vicky wasn't exaggerating.

'He'll be here any minute,' she said with a confidence she was far from feeling. Where was everyone? No matter how

30

long she rang the bell to summon help, no one responded. 'I don't like leaving you, ma'am,' she said with deep feeling, 'but if I'm to get someone to hurry the doctor up, I'm going to have to go downstairs.'

'Then go now,' Vicky said on a gasp. 'But be quick, Josephine. And please find Berthold. Please tell him the baby is coming.' Her face was sheened with sweat, her hair clinging damply to her forehead.

Josephine, knowing she had no alternative but to leave her alone and wanting to do so for the very shortest time possible, sprinted for the stairs.

Within seconds of running down them she realized that something was very wrong. There was no music coming from the direction of the ballroom. No sound of speeches or laughter. No buzz of celebratory conversation.

A group of footmen stood in the hall, muttering anxiously between themselves.

With her hand slipping and sliding on the banister rail she hurried down the last few steps, calling out breathlessly as she did so: 'Where is the doctor? He's needed urgently. Will one of you please go and tell him there's not a minute to lose?'

They turned towards her. 'The doctor is here,' one of them said in careful English. 'Has been here for some time.'

'Where?' Josephine's head was spinning. Foreign ways weren't English ways, but if the doctor had arrived why wasn't he with Vicky? Had he, without even determining how far on in labour Vicky was, gone into the wedding reception to enjoy a glass of champagne? The very thought of such a possibility sent the Yorkshire blood boiling through her veins. 'Where?' she demanded again. 'Where is he?'

'In the ballroom, with Herr Remer,' the young footman said, looking at her as if she had taken leave of her senses.

Josephine was uncaring of the strict rules that permitted only certain servants to enter certain sections of the mansion, the ballroom being most definitely out of bounds to her. She headed straight for it.

The minute she entered it she knew that whatever was wrong in the house was not a small thing but a major catastrophe. Hardly any guests remained. The musicians had gone. Zelda was seated at a table with her father and Vicky's father. There was no sign of the bridegroom. No sign of Berthold. No sign of anyone who looked as if they might be the doctor. And no sign of Harald Remer.

With her heart beating like a piston she crossed the ballroom floor.

'Excuse me, Mrs Gould,' she said, forgetting in her anxiety that she should now be addressing Zelda as Frau Remer. 'But where is the doctor? I sent word for him nearly two hours ago and –'

'*You* sent for him?' Vicky's father stared at her in a way not dissimilar to the way the footman had stared at her.

Zelda rose swiftly to her feet. 'Oh, Lord,' she said unsteadily. 'It's Vicky, isn't it? The baby is coming?'

'Yes, ma'am. I gave orders for the doctor to be sent for and I'm told he's here, but –'

'He is, but he thought he'd been called to attend to Herr Remer, who has been taken ill.'

Josephine let out a deep breath, finally understanding all that had been puzzling her. 'Can someone tell him that Mrs Remer also needs him?'

Zelda's eyes flew to the closed doors of a small salon leading off from the ballroom.

Aware of what she was intending to do, her father said bluntly, 'You can't walk in on whatever is taking place in there. When Harald has been taken to hospital then, and only then, can the doctor attend Vicky.'

Zelda hesitated and then, ignoring his opinion, walked towards the closed doors. When she opened them all she could see was a sofa on which the comatose figure of Harald Remer was laid, with Josef, Berthold, Ernst Schulenburg and Dr Soller in attendance around it.

'I'm sorry, Josef,' she said as they all swung to face her, hope that the ambulance had finally arrived clear on their faces. 'Vicky's baby is coming and she is in urgent need of a doctor.'

She was aware of Berthold's distraught intake of breath and then Josef said, 'And you want Soller?' The incredulity on his face was total. 'My father's condition is critical. Soller can't be spared, not for a moment.'

He turned his back on her and, having seen her father-in-law's grey, sweat-sheened face close to, Zelda didn't argue with him. She looked at Berthold, expecting him to leave his father's side in order to go upstairs with her and be with Vicky until the doctor arrived. He didn't move.

'I'm sorry, Zelda,' he said, his face agonized as he read the expectation on her face, 'but I can't leave my father when he is so ill. Please tell Vicky I will be with her once my father's condition improves.'

Zelda held his eyes for a moment, giving him the chance to rethink the choice he had made, and then, as he turned his attention back to his father, his face a mask of misery, she left the room.

As she closed the doors behind her she said to the anxiously waiting Josephine, 'How far on in labour is Mrs Remer?'

'It's hard to say because I've never seen anyone go into labour so hard and so suddenly, but she needs a doctor – and at the moment there's no one with her apart from the dog.'

Her deeply worried father and uncle strode up to Zelda and she said, 'You were right, Pa. Soller can't be spared. I'm going upstairs to sit with Vicky, but we need another doctor and we need one fast.'

'Don't worry,' her father said capably. 'You'll have one.'

Grateful he was there, knowing she could rely on him, she wasted no more time. As fast as the train of her wedding dress would allow, she hurried out of the ballroom and towards the stairs, Josephine hard on her heels.

Never in her life had Vicky been so glad to see anyone.

'I'm trying to hold back till the doctor arrives, but I can't, Zelda! I just want to push and push!'

'Landsakes!' Zelda, who had expected to find her in labour, but with hours to go before the actual birth, stared down at her, appalled. The baby was quite obviously on the verge of being born and she was sickeningly aware there was no one to deliver it apart from herself and Josephine.

She never panicked and she didn't panic now.

'Hot water, fast!' she said to Josephine, gathering her scattered wits, knowing she didn't even have time to change out of her wedding dress. 'And towels and scissors and string. And get that darned dog out of the room.'

Vicky let out a deep groan, her eyes glazed with pain. 'Where is Berthold?' she gasped. 'Is he worrying? Please tell him not to worry, Zelda.'

'Never mind Berthold. Berthold can take care of himself. Can you push yourself a little lower down on the bed, Vicky? That way I can be centre-on to you, not standing off-side.'

As Vicky struggled to comply, Zelda pushed every available pillow behind her so that she also had support.

There was a gush of fluid and Josephine, hurrying into the room with everything Zelda had asked her to collect, hastily thrust a towel towards her.

Zelda spread it on the bed, saying tautly, 'The baby's head is showing. I can see its hair. Don't push any more, Vicky. Hold my hand tightly and pant, darling. *Pant!*'

Seconds later the baby's head crowned.

Vicky screamed.

Zelda barely heard her. Never before had she been so excited and exhilarated.

'Oh, God, Vicky!' she gasped. 'It's coming! *It's coming!*'

Bending low, she stretched out her hands and seconds later, as easy as shelling peas, her nephew slithered into them.

He was covered in mucus and blood and she didn't care. He had all his fingers and toes and, eyes screwed tight, was bawling as lustily as a New York stevedore.

Never in her life had Zelda felt so emotional, not even when her own son had been born. Never. Tears streamed down her face. 'Darling, darling Vicky,' she said as the baby squirmed slipperily, 'you have a little boy. You have a son.'

Sobbing with joy, Vicky pushed herself up against her pillows so that she could look at the miracle lying between her legs. 'Oh!' she gasped, her face radiant. 'Isn't he wonderful, Zelda? Look how perfect he is! I want to hold him. I want to hold him right now.'

Josephine draped a large soft towel around the still-bawling baby and then, with utmost care, Zelda placed him in Vicky's arms.

As Vicky gazed rapturously down into the red, wrinkled face, Zelda said unsteadily, 'Didn't we do a marvellous job, Vicky darling? Who would have thought I'd be acting as a midwife to you on my wedding day?'

She looked down at her dress, unable to believe she was so uncaring of the damage that had been done to it. Even if the blood and mucus stains came out of the fabric, the hand-embroidered seed pearls would never be the same again.

'I'm going to call him Maximilian.' Vicky's voice was thick with joy. 'Maximilian Berthold.'

It was such a big name for a little baby that despite the deep emotions she was feeling, Zelda's dry humour surfaced. 'That will go down well in Yorkshire,' she said, vastly amused.

Seeing the joke, Vicky giggled. 'It's a pity he wasn't born in

Yorkshire, then he could have played cricket for the county.'

'Never mind.' Zelda was all mock sympathy. 'Perhaps the next boy you have will be born in Little Ridding.'

Bantering at a time like this was incomprehensible to Josephine and she said a little hesitantly, 'Are you going to cut the cord now, Mrs Remer?'

'No.' Zelda shook her head, knowing her limitations. 'I'm going to let the doctor do that.'

Right on cue there came a brief knock on the door and Dr Soller walked in.

Vastly relieved, Zelda stretched out her aching back. 'While you're being attended to, Vicky, I'm going to bathe and change and tell Paul he has a cousin.'

Vicky didn't reply because she wasn't listening. She was smiling down into the face of Maximilian Berthold, joy singing through every fibre of her being.

Berthold stumbled out of the small salon, thinking of nothing but the crushing burden now on his shoulders. It was a burden he'd feared as long as he could remember. A burden he'd hoped wouldn't be his for another twenty, perhaps even thirty, years.

Blindly, he made his way upstairs, wondering how he was going to break the news to Vicky, wondering if Vicky would even begin to realize how drastically their lives would now change.

Entering the room like a man whose world has come to an end he barely registered how radiant and exhausted she looked and was oblivious to the cot by the side of the bed.

As she said ecstatically, 'Oh, Berthold! Do come! Do look!' he collapsed on the nearest chair, his words cutting across hers as he said starkly, 'He's dead, Vicky. My father is dead. From now on life is going to be different. From now on it's going to be insupportable.'

THREE

Berlin, June 1911

Vicky sat on a park bench in the Tiergarten, Max in his perambulator beside her, Paul happily playing with a whip-and-top a few yards away. Other than the children and Wastl, who was sunning himself on the grass at her feet, she was completely on her own.

'You'll be mistaken for a nanny,' Zelda had said tartly when she had first begun taking Max for walks in his pram by herself. 'Either that or someone embarrassingly middle class.'

She had been uncaring. Now that she was five months pregnant again it was highly unlikely she would be taken for a nanny and besides, unlike Zelda, she enjoyed spending time with her son and didn't see why Max's nanny should have all the enjoyment of him when she was perfectly capable of looking after him herself. He was nine months old now and beginning to crawl. Sometimes when they were in the Tiergarten – and she knew this would appal Zelda and horrify his nanny – she laid him on a blanket on the grass. Today he was in his perambulator and, shaded by a parasol, was lying on his back fast asleep.

He looked utterly content. Watching him as he slept she

wished that she too were as untroubled. She had tried to be rational about her growing stirrings of unhappiness, telling herself they were due to her constant homesickness for Yorkshire. While this was true, it wasn't the whole truth. Other, more serious things were causing her disquiet.

There was Josef's assumption that though Berthold was now head of the House of Remer, he, not Berthold, would be the acting head where administration was concerned. It was an assumption a vastly relieved Berthold had happily gone along with – and the doubts she had expressed when he had done so had perplexed him deeply.

'But surely that's what you want, *Liebchen*?' he had said to her with a puzzled frown. 'You've always said you didn't want to be married to a man who thought of nothing but business – and it is impossible to run an industry as vast as the steelworks without giving every second of the day to it, especially when, unlike Josef, I've never had personal experience of all the different aspects of steel production.'

Everything he said was true and she should, she knew, have been just as grateful as Berthold that Josef was taking the huge responsibilities of the House of Remer from his shoulders. Perversely, though, she wasn't.

Among her many muddled feelings was resentment at Josef's patronizing attitude towards Berthold. She was offended by the inference that it wasn't so much that Berthold didn't want to step into his father's shoes, as that he wasn't capable of stepping into them. She didn't like seeing his mild manner mistaken for inadequacy. And if all those troubled emotions weren't clouds enough, there was also her disappointment at how little time she and Zelda were spending with each other.

Within days of Harald Remer's funeral Zelda and Josef had announced that in future they would be carrying out all major entertaining at Schloss Niedernhall. 'Men like shooting and the shooting in Schloss Niedernhall's woods is excellent,' Zelda had said when announcing their decision.

As she and Berthold had not the slightest desire to spend long weekends killing animals and birds, increasingly long periods went by without her having Zelda's lively companionship. And without Zelda's companionship, Berlin weighed heavy on her.

Vicky hated its military trappings. She disliked the Column of Victory, its shaft made of cannon captured from the enemy in German victories over Denmark, Austria and France. It indicated an enthusiasm for war that left her feeling deeply unsettled, especially when she remembered her father's remarks about Germany's bullish attitude towards France and Russia and the sinister way in which the country was building up its naval strength.

It wasn't only monuments that were a constant reminder of Germany's love of all things military. Foot Guards, Grenadier Guards, Dragoons and Fusiliers regularly marched or galloped through the streets. Zelda regarded such parades as part of the glamour of Berlin life and revelled in them, just as she revelled in the brass fanfares that announced the arrival of the Kaiser whenever he rode down Unter den Linden.

'It's the most vibrant city in the world,' she said time and again to her. 'How can you hanker for village life in Yorkshire, Vicky, when you have so many opera houses, concert halls and art galleries on your doorstep? If it wasn't for the *cachet* of being able to entertain on an even grander scale at Schloss Niedernhall than I can in Berlin, I swear I'd never leave it.'

Paul broke her train of thought by walking up to her, his whip-and-top in his hands. 'Have you some coloured chalks with you, Aunt Vicky?' he asked. 'I want to chalk a new pattern.'

He was wearing knickerbocker trousers with a sailor-suit top, his shining dark hair cut short, his hazel eyes solemn.

Obligingly, she opened the bag she had brought with her

and took a cardboard box of chalks out of it, reflecting on how much of a Berliner his mother had become.

'Thank you, Aunt Vicky,' he said, sitting down cross-legged at her side, Wastl running rings around him.

As he rubbed the old pattern off his top with a handkerchief and a little spit, it occurred to Vicky that Zelda hadn't so much become a Berliner, as that by character and inclination she had always been one. Like the city, she glittered with a hard, shameless glamour. Her direct manner, uncompromising tongue and scepticism were all typical Berliner traits. All Berliners looked at life without illusions, living it to the full, sparing no one in the process. Only Berthold, of everyone she had met, seemed the odd one out. Dearest Berthold, whom she loved with all her heart.

With a sigh she returned her attention to her bag, taking a paper cone of mint humbugs from it. As she offered one to Paul he smiled and thanked her for it and, not for the first time, she noticed that his smile didn't reach his eyes.

She watched him as, hampered by Wastl, he began chalking a new pattern on his top. A year or so ago he hadn't always been so solemn. A year or so ago he had been as light-hearted and boisterous as any other little boy.

'You're looking very serious, Paul,' she said, deciding that now was as good a moment as any for them to have a heart-to-heart talk. 'Is anything the matter?'

'No,' he said, not very convincingly. 'I'm fine, Aunt Vicky.'

'That's good.' She waited a minute or two and then said, gently probing, 'It must be strange having a new German papa. Germans can be very stiff and formal sometimes, can't they?'

He nodded in agreement and then said, 'But Uncle Berthold isn't stiff and formal. And though step-Papa Josef *is* stiff and formal it doesn't really matter too much because he hardly ever spends any time with me. I can't remember my proper papa, but I think he would have done, wouldn't he?'

Vicky felt her throat tighten. 'Yes, darling,' she said, aware that her eyes were smarting. 'I'm sure he would have spent time with you.'

Paul put down his chalks. 'Berlin is a strange place to live, isn't it, Aunt Vicky? It's not at all like Yorkshire. And though it's a city, like New York, it isn't like New York either.' He shifted position, sitting back on his heels. 'I think it's the language,' he said after a little pause. 'It's such hard work trying to understand German – and apart from you and Uncle Berthold, everyone speaks to me in German. Even Mama.'

Vicky, who already knew this – and disapproved of it, remained silent.

'And my tutor only ever wants to teach me about German history, not American history.' A look of disgust came over his face. 'I don't think he *knows* about American history or British history. And he doesn't ever find things funny. When I referred to the Kaiser as Kaiser Bill he told Mama and I was punished.'

He flinched at the memory and Vicky's lips tightened.

'And what I really don't understand,' he said, the floodgates opening, 'is having to speak German to Mama. I shouldn't have to, should I? I'm an American.'

'You most certainly are,' she said emphatically. 'And I'm from Yorkshire. It's something we must never forget.'

He grinned, the solemnity vanishing from his eyes. 'It's as if we are in a secret society, isn't it, Aunt Vicky? Even though everyone *thinks* we are becoming more and more German, we know differently, don't we?'

'We do indeed,' she said, taking out the bag of sweets again, resolving to speak to Zelda about Paul's unhappiness at the first opportunity. 'Have another mint humbug, pet lamb, and then we'll walk over to the lake and you can sail your boat for a little while.'

*

'It's a chance we must seize with both hands, Zelda.'

As a heavily pregnant Zelda sat at her writing desk, Josef walked up and down their vast bedroom, his hands clasped behind his back. 'For the last nine years, ever since Fritz Krupp bought the old Germania shipyards at Kiel, the building of ships has been the preserve of Krupps. To be offered a contract to build two battleships for the navy is a wonderful opportunity for the House of Remer. A great opportunity.'

Well accustomed to his discussing business affairs with her, she said, straight to the point as usual, 'But we have no shipyards.'

He grabbed hold of a spindly legged gilt chair and dragged it across to her desk, flicking his coat tails aside before sitting down.

'Oh, but we have.'

Her beautifully arched eyebrows rose.

Josef seldom smiled, but he did so now.

'My father knew years ago, when Krupps began making berths big enough for battleships, that the Kaiser intended building a navy equal to that of the British navy – and that the day would come when even Krupps' vast output would need supplementing.'

'And without making it public knowledge he bought a shipyard?'

Josef nodded. 'And excess waterfront in which to expand.'

'Where?'

'Hamburg.'

In mutual satisfaction their eyes held.

'And what about Berthold?' she asked after a little pause. 'Is he happy about the House of Remer building battleships?'

Josef gave a snort. 'Berthold has had no part in the negotiations – and the less he knows, the better.'

'But his name will be on the contracts?'

'Of necessity, yes. It won't be a problem, Zelda.'

'No. I know.' She regarded him with sensual pleasure, loving the barely restrained power she always sensed about him. 'And what do you think Vicky's reaction is going to be when she knows the family firm is building battleships?'

'Little Bo Peep?' Josef gave another snort. 'Why should she ever know? She married into the family eighteen months ago and to the best of my knowledge thinks the wealth she enjoys comes solely from the manufacture of steel-plating. That we actually *make* things with the steel we produce hasn't occurred to her.'

'No, but it will. You underestimate Vicky, Josef. She isn't stupid, only young and still naive. And she won't like the idea of Remer shipyards building battleships, even if the battleships in question are for defensive purposes.'

He said nothing and at the expression on his face, her eyes widened. 'They *are* for defensive purposes, aren't they?'

'But of course.' He shrugged. 'A strong navy is the best defence any country can have. Look how well a strong navy has served Great Britain. All Germany intends is to reach parity with Great Britain and end Great Britain's long run of naval supremacy.'

He rose to his feet and stepped behind her chair. 'Battleships are like armaments, Zelda. They are a product, just as the ovens we make are a product. Making them doesn't mean they will be used.'

Before she should retort that the ovens the House of Remer produced were used in kitchens all over Germany, he bent over her slightly, slipping his hands beneath the loose bodice of her tea gown, caressing her with skilful fingers.

She caught her breath, sexual need flooding through her. For the last few weeks, ever since her pregnancy had become so advanced, they had not made love. 'Soller says it could bring on premature labour,' he had said and, as always when Josef made a decision, he had not moved from it.

He removed his hands from her breasts and straightened up. 'I must go,' he said. 'I have a meeting at the Admiralty in half an hour with two purchasing board officials and a government minister.'

Her flesh felt scorched from his touch and her eyes followed him as he crossed the room, picking up his hat and cane. When the door closed behind him she bit her lip, passionately hoping he was speaking the truth about going to the Admiralty and that he hadn't acquired a mistress, however temporary.

'Another few weeks,' she said fiercely as she heaved herself cumbersomely to her feet, 'and then there'll be not the slightest risk of his looking at another woman.'

Confident of her ability to keep him sexually enthralled, she crossed to the window. In a few minutes, he would step from the house and into his waiting Daimler Mercedes and she always loved watching him when he thought himself unobserved.

Even from a distance there was an air of power about him. As he walked to the motorcar his hat was still in his hand, and in the late afternoon sunlight his fair hair gleamed the colour of ripe wheat.

She rested her hand on the bulge of her belly. Life was good, and when Berthold renounced his position as head of the House of Remer in favour of Josef, it would be even better. That Berthold would very soon be taking such an action she knew because Josef had told her he would be doing so. And when it came to managing his elder brother, she trusted her forceful husband utterly.

The next morning, when she was certain that Josef had left the house, Vicky made her way to Zelda's bedroom.

'Have a cup of *Schokolade*, Vicky darling,' Zelda said, pushing herself up against her pillows, a scarlet ribbon holding her waist-length hair away from her face. 'And to what do I owe such an early morning visit?'

Vicky sat down on the edge of Zelda's bed. 'I want to talk to you about Paul.'

'Ah. I knew you took him to the park yesterday. Did he misbehave?'

'Paul? Don't be ridiculous, Zelda. He never misbehaves, not on any serious level.' Taking advantage of the spare cup and saucer on the breakfast tray, Vicky poured herself a hot chocolate. 'And why do you talk to me in English, when you don't talk to Paul in English? He hates you speaking to him in German, and I don't blame him. He gets enough practice in German in his school lessons.'

'No, he doesn't.' There was no doubt at all in Zelda's voice. 'Germany is now Paul's home. Both Josef and I believe it is essential that as he grows older people think of him as being German and not American, and that *he* thinks of himself as being German.'

Vicky took a sip of hot chocolate and said, 'But why should he? He's an American. He was born in America. His father was American. You are American. Until he was five years old he lived entirely in America. Trying to make him into something he isn't, simply isn't fair, Zelda.'

Zelda tilted her head a little to one side and regarded Vicky quizzically. 'I think it's very fair. It will make sure he fits in – and that's important in Germany.'

'But it's making him unhappy. There has to be a middle way, Zelda.'

Zelda pushed her breakfast tray away. 'This is Berlin, Vicky, and we are Remers. There *isn't* a middle way. Think how impossible it would be for Max to inherit the Remer steelworks – and all that goes with the steelworks – if he only spoke German with a Yorkshire accent and spent more time in Yorkshire than in Berlin. It would be impossible. No one

45

would wear it, not the Committee of Management, not the workers, no one. And though Paul will never, of course, inherit the steelworks, I do intend that he will grow up feeling a part of the family business and that he will have a responsible part to play in it. And *that* is why I speak to him in German.'

Vicky stared at her, appalled. It wasn't Zelda's hopes for Paul's future in the House of Remer that appalled her, though she was quite sure they would horrify Paul, it was being so abruptly faced with the realization that Max would have no choice as to his future. He would one day inherit the steelworks and, even before he did so, would be expected to make them his life.

Reading Vicky's feelings in her eyes, Zelda was more than satisfied at the direction she had steered their little tête-à-tête. When Berthold handed over his position as head of the House of Remer to Josef, both she and Josef were determined it would be on the understanding that Josef's firstborn son would inherit after him.

Aware she had sown the first seed to that end, she changed the subject, saying, 'When will you be visiting Yorkshire? If you wait until after the baby is born it will be nearly two years since you were there, and as you won't want to take a newborn baby across the Channel and won't want to go without it, by the time you are in Little Ridding again it will be nearly three years since your last visit.'

'I know. I've decided I'm going now, even though it means I won't be here when your baby is born.'

'As I plan for the baby to be born in Baden-Württemberg you wouldn't be with me anyhow. Not unless you move into Schloss Niedernhall for a few weeks.'

Vicky shuddered and Zelda, not wanting the conversation to veer off in another direction, said, 'Will you be taking Max with you to Yorkshire?'

'Yes. Of course.'

'Would you like to take Paul with you as well?'

It was such an unexpected offer, Vicky's eyes widened.

Zelda gave a shrug. 'You said Paul was unhappy, Vicky. Even though I know I'm right about what is best for him, I don't like the thought of him being unhappy. A holiday in Yorkshire will do him good.'

'And will mean he is well out of the way when his half-brother or half-sister is born?'

'That too.' There was amusement in Zelda's voice. 'And the baby is going to be a boy, Vicky. Don't wish a daughter on me. I don't want one. Not yet.'

Five days later, accompanied by Max, his nanny, Paul, Josephine and a mountain of luggage, Vicky boarded a train en route for Ostende and the ferry to Dover.

Saying goodbye to her, Berthold was nearly in tears. 'If you waited another few months, *Liebchen*, I could go with you,' he said as the whistle blew. 'It wouldn't look so bad then, my leaving Berlin. Now is a difficult time. Josef has a major contract with the navy to put into operation and wants me to show my face at lots of meetings with admirals and government ministers.'

'In another few months we'll have another baby,' she said, half hanging out of the train window as he reached up to grasp her hands. 'And babies are like wine, Berthold, they don't travel well.'

She was near to tears too, at parting from him, but her craving to have Yorkshire air in her lungs was so deep she didn't even come close to changing her mind about her trip. She had to go to Yorkshire. She *had* to. Then, after a few weeks of life at Shuttleworth Hall, she would be able to face living in Berlin once again.

The whistle blew a second time and, amid billows of steam, the train began edging along the platform.

'*Auf Wiedersehen, Liebchen!*' he shouted as their hands were torn apart. 'I love you!'

'I love you too!' she called back. 'Goodbye, Berthold darling. God bless!'

Only when his figure was no longer discernible did she move away from the window.

'Uncle Berthold will be lonely without you,' Paul said, slipping his hand into hers as she seated herself next to him.

'Yes, he will.' Tears of guilt burned the backs of her eyes. 'But it's only for a few weeks, Paul, and he will have lots of things to keep him busy.'

'Seeing admirals?'

'Seeing admirals,' she said, wondering what on earth admirals had to do with a major contract for steel.

'Welcome 'ome, Miss Hudson! Welcome 'ome!' the elderly stationmaster at Little Ridding said jovially as she and her little party descended from the Harrogate train. 'And who's this grand little chap?' He beamed down at Paul. 'It's never Mrs Gould's little lad, is it?'

Paul beamed sunnily back at him. 'Yes, it is.'

The stationmaster clapped his forehead with a gnarled hand in pretend wonderment. 'Well, I nivver. Tha's growed so's I'd nivver 'ave known thee.'

'I'm not Miss Hudson any longer,' Vicky said, not wanting the stationmaster's misunderstanding to continue. 'I'm Mrs Berthold Remer now – and Mrs Gould is Mrs Josef Remer.'

'And this is my cousin,' Paul said proudly, indicating Max, cocooned in a shawl in his nanny's arms. 'He's nine months old and it's his first visit to Yorkshire.'

'Then 'e's a lucky little chap an' e's very welcome.'

'He most certainly is,' boomed another, very different voice. As her father strode across the platform towards them, Vicky

48

gave a gasp and, uncaring of being pregnant, ran to meet him, throwing herself into his arms.

'Welcome home, dear girl,' he said gruffly, his arms closing around her. 'You've been absent for far too long.'

His tweed jacket was rough against her cheek and smelled of cigar smoke. Overcoming the desire never to lift her head from it again she looked up at him, saying thickly, 'It's wonderful to be home, Papa.' Tears sparkled on her eyelashes. 'Berthold would have come with me if he could, but he has vast responsibilities now. Josef does a very great deal, but there are some things only Berthold can sign and some people it would be inappropriate for Josef to meet without Berthold also being there.'

'Well, of course there are, Vicky,' he said as the stationmaster and the station's one and only porter carried the luggage out to the waiting motorcar. 'Berthold is now responsible for one of the biggest industrial enterprises in Germany and we'll talk of how he's coping as head of the House of Remer a little later on. For now I want to say hello to my grandson.'

He walked over to where Max's nanny was standing and gently eased the shawl away from Max's sleeping face.

For a few seconds he was silent and then he said emotionally, 'My, but he's a grand little boy, Vicky. He has your mother's eyes and my nose. Keep bringing him to Shuttleworth Hall every year and I promise you I'll make a Yorkshireman of him.'

Minutes later they were all in a magnificent motorcar adorned by a mascot on its radiator, a silver figure of a woman looking as if she was about to take flight.

'She's called the Spirit of Ecstasy,' Vicky's father said to Paul as he drove along the winding lanes skirting the glistening River Ure.

Vicky thought the silver figure beautifully named. She gave a deep contented sigh. She was home. For the next few weeks

49

she wouldn't be living in a vast mansion in the most glittering, sophisticated city in Europe. She would be living in the home built by her grandfather, a substantial country house built of mellow stone, honey-coloured woods and soft grey slate. Instead of streets jammed with motorcars and horse-drawn carriages and controlled by white-gloved, spike-helmeted policemen carrying sabres, there would be the pleasurable bustle of village life in Little Ridding and the rolling calm of the surrounding Yorkshire countryside. Countryside that was among the most beautiful in the world.

Later that evening, when she had read a bedtime story to Paul and seen Max settled into the nursery that had once been hers, she stood at the window and looked out over the gardens. Her father's dogs, Harry, a Yorkshire terrier, and Coco and Charlie, two cocker spaniels, were asleep on the terrace. The heat of the day still hung in the air and her father's roses gleamed milkily pale in the blue-spangled dusk. She could hear birds gathering for the night and the sound of the river as it flowed over its rock-strewn bed. Her throat ached with the beauty of it all. How, when she loved being at Shuttleworth Hall so much, was she ever going to truly think of Berlin as being her home?

'I just don't see how it's possible,' she said to her father an hour later as they dined together. 'I've tried, truly I have, but I always feel a foreigner.'

'Well, that's because you *are* a foreigner,' her father said with Yorkshire bluntness, helping himself to another slice of ham.

Aware that he didn't realize how deep her sense of alienation in Berlin was, she laid down her fork and said, 'Zelda is a foreigner too, but she doesn't feel like one.'

'Ah, well. Zelda wouldn't.' He helped himself to more pickle. 'Zelda is a typical member of her caste. Like many others belonging to New York's social elite she has the will power to always adapt to her immediate surroundings.'

Seeing that she still looked deeply troubled, he said gently, 'And you mustn't forget, my dear, that Zelda is accustomed to living in the hurly-burly of a big, sophisticated city. Berlin isn't as different to her, as it is to you. And I don't think city-bred people have the same strong sense of place that people born and brought up in the country have. Give it time and you'll acclimatize just as Zelda has.'

Not wanting her father to become concerned about her, Vicky merely nodded, keeping her doubts to herself.

'And now tell me how Berthold is enjoying being an industrial tycoon,' her father said, broaching the subject he was most eager to know about. 'Has it been a smooth transition period for him?'

Vicky paused, wondering how she could best explain to her father that Berthold loathed every single aspect of his position as head of the House of Remer and that it was Josef who, in everything but name, had stepped into Harald Remer's shoes.

'He relies very much on Josef,' she said evasively.

Her father helped himself to more mustard. 'With the European situation as unstable as it is at present he needs to keep a firm hold of the reins. I would hate to see the House of Remer becoming as heavily involved as the House of Krupp where the manufacturing of armaments is concerned.'

Vicky smiled. 'The House of Remer doesn't manufacture armaments, Papa.' She laid her knife and fork side by side on her plate. 'If it is as hot tomorrow as it has been today I'm going to take Paul for a picnic down by the river, and perhaps now he's seven we could find him a bicycle to ride.'

The next afternoon, when she and Paul returned from the banks of the Ure with an empty picnic hamper, a small bicycle was propped against the stone balustrade of the terrace.

'I was talking with Adam Priestley this morning in the Wool Exchange at Bradford,' her father said, his thumbs tucked into the pockets of his waistcoat. 'He's William Priestley's son and has grown up to be a fine wool man, just like his father. I mentioned our need of a child's bicycle and he had this spanking-new BSA sent from Keighley.'

'How wonderfully kind of him.'

Vicky remembered Adam Priestley from tennis parties and occasional dances they had both attended. Like his father he was a typical Yorkshire man, tall, broad, big-boned and, which was not so typical, with a distinctive thatch of red curly hair. He was also, she now knew, kind.

On 5 July a telegram came informing them that Zelda had given birth to a boy at Schloss Niedernhall. 'They've named him Claus Heinrich,' her father said. 'What Zelda's father is going to think about a grandson with such a Prussian name, I can't imagine.'

'When the baby begins to talk, will he only talk in German, Great-Uncle Arthur?' Paul asked, worry in his voice.

'Of course not.' Vicky's father laughed at the very idea. 'He's your little half-brother and he's half-American. He'll grow up speaking German and English, just as you are beginning to do.'

Paul looked vastly relieved. Vicky, well aware of what Zelda's intentions were for her second son, kept prudently silent.

The next few weeks were deeply restorative for Vicky. Though she missed Berthold and felt guilty whenever she thought of how lonely he must be without her, she knew that the respite she was taking from Berlin was utterly necessary to her.

The weather was hot, though not with the stifling oppressive heat she had become accustomed to in Berlin. In Yorkshire there was nearly always a light breeze and, when there wasn't, there was always the river bank to escape to. While Paul scrambled in the rocky shallows, ceaselessly building dams and re-routing the flow of water where possible, she would sit in the shade of a tree, Max kicking chubby legs on a blanket beside her. Sometimes she would take her shoes and stockings off, hitch her skirts up and, like Paul, would wade into the deliciously icy, crystal-clear water, enjoying the sight of dragonflies and damselflies as they darted across the river's glittering surface.

There were birds too. Yellow wagtails and dippers and, most beautiful of all, kingfishers. Water voles were a regular sight, and on one very special day they even caught sight of an otter.

Some mornings before they set off for the river Paul would go into Shuttleworth Hall's kitchen and help the cook bake Yorkshire teacakes and curd tarts. Other times, especially if it was market day, he would accompany Josephine into Little Ridding. Vicky's father even took him into Bradford and gave him a personal tour of the mill.

'It was very frightening, Aunt Vicky,' he said to her the next day. 'The machines were so big and so noisy they were like huge monsters and you had to shout at the top of your voice to be heard. If Great-Uncle Arthur suggests taking me again, could you please tell him I don't want to go?'

In the evenings, in the hour between suppertime and bedtime, he worked on a scrapbook. 'It's going to be for pictures of the new king,' he said. 'I'm doing it for Max to look at when he's older, because he's too little to know he has a new king now.'

From then on every newspaper and periodical that came into the house was carefully searched for pictures of King George V, and when any were found Paul would carefully cut them out and stick them into his scrapbook with flour-paste. It was a whole new kind of life for him. Instead of a relentless routine of tutors and lessons and of only enjoying pleasures, such as walks in the Tiergarten, if his marks in his schoolwork were exceptionally high, he was able to enjoy a freedom he had never enjoyed before, not even when he had been living in New York.

'He's a fine little chap,' Vicky's father said to her the day before they were to return to Berlin. 'I'm going to miss him when he's gone.'

'He'll miss you too. And so will I.'

'But not so much that it is going to make you as unhappy as it has in the past. We've agreed on that, Vicky dear, haven't we?'

Seeing the concern in his eyes, she smiled. 'Yes,' she said resolutely. 'We have.'

It was true. Her weeks at Shuttleworth Hall had worked their magic. She longed to be with Berthold again and felt rested enough to start afresh where her relationship with Berlin was concerned. She was going to work harder at her German conversation and, happy in the resolution she had made to visit Yorkshire at least once every year, she was determined that from now on she was going to gain as much enjoyment from the city's opera houses, concert halls and art galleries as Zelda did. If marriage to Berthold meant her becoming a Berliner, then she was going to try her very hardest to become one.

The next morning, adjusting her hat in front of her dressing-table mirror as her luggage was being taken downstairs to be loaded into the motorcar, she resolved that from now on nothing was going to faze her. Not Josef's patronizing attitude towards Berthold. Not the alien sound of trams clanging and swaying everywhere, nor the even more alien roar of the city's elevated railway. Not the sombrely grandiose mansion that no amount of lovingly arranged flowers ever seemed to cheer. She had a husband she loved with all her heart and she was going to allow nothing – absolutely nothing – to mar their happiness together.

FOUR

Berlin, August 1911

Nearly the first thing Berthold said to her after they had rapturously kissed and hugged, was: 'Josef has secured a wonderful new contract with the navy, Vicky. It's going to mean work for thousands of men.'

They were still on the station platform, still in each other's arms. She put her net-gloved hands on his chest, staring up at him bewilderedly.

'A contract with the navy? For steel-plating?'

'No.' He shook his head, the late August sun reflecting on the pebble-thick lenses of his spectacles. 'It's for ships.'

He tucked one of her hands in the crook of his arm and began leading her down the platform to where Paul, Max, Max's nanny and Josephine were already being ushered into a waiting motorcar.

'Ships? You mean the House of Remer will be building ships?'

'Yes, *Liebchen*. It's a huge contract. The biggest the House of Remer has ever had.'

He beamed down at her.

Vicky didn't beam back. Her mouth felt dry and her throat felt tight.

'What kind of ships?' She was remembering her father telling her of how the Kaiser was building up his navy and of how the action brought with it a terrible threat of war.

'Battleships.'

She stopped dead.

'What's the matter, *Liebchen*?' His good-natured face was concerned.

'No.' Her eyes were urgent. 'Berthold, you must find a way out of this contract. Building battleships is no different to making armaments and that is something the House of Remer doesn't do.'

She knew then, as she saw his expression, how very wrong she was, how stupidly ignorant and pathetically naive she had been. The blood drained from her face.

'Please tell me we don't produce armaments, Berthold,' she said hoarsely. 'Please.'

'We don't produce them in huge numbers,' he said evasively. 'We don't dominate the industry as Krupps do – and we make lots of other things. Ovens and agricultural machinery and cash registers and –'

She wasn't interested in ovens and agricultural machinery and cash registers. 'What kind?' she asked urgently. 'What kind of weapons do we make?'

'I'm not sure.' He was looking more and more uncomfortable, and more and more unhappy. 'Guns . . . cannon. These things don't get *used*, Vicky darling. Every country in the world has armaments. They're a safeguard. A kind of currency.'

They were still on the station platform. Another train had pulled in and people were streaming past them in order to board.

'Let's go home, *Liebchen*,' he said pleadingly. 'I'll explain to you later . . . I'll ask Josef to explain to you later . . . when you are not so tired from travelling.'

As the chauffeur pulled out into a maelstrom of motorcars, horse-drawn carriages and trams, she pressed her fingers to her throbbing temples. Only minutes ago she had been on top of the world, head over heels with happiness at being reunited with Berthold, full of fierce determination to turn herself into a true Berliner. Now all she could think of was that if Germany went to war it might very well be war against Great Britain, and in such a war Remer armaments would kill and maim British soldiers and Remer-built battleships would be responsible for wholesale slaughter on the high seas.

By the time she reached the sanctuary of their bedroom her hands were trembling.

'You're tired, sweetheart,' Berthold said tenderly, lifting her flower-bedecked hat from her hair. 'There're only another seven or eight weeks before the baby is due to be born. You should be resting all day, every day, not crossing the Channel and then travelling hundreds of miles on a train.'

'The Channel was like a millpond.'

She seated herself on her dressing-table stool and took hold of his hand. 'Berthold. Please listen to me. My father thinks the Kaiser is building up his navy because he intends to go to war. All the British newspapers think so too. If the House of Remer provides him with guns and cannon and battleships – and if there is a war – we will have the blood of thousands of men on our hands. You must tell the navy Remers don't have the facilities for shipbuilding and you must renege on all existing contracts for guns and cannon.'

To her horror he looked aghast.

'You don't understand, Vicky.' With his free hand he ran his fingers through his hair. 'These are not contracts for private companies. They are state contracts. They've been signed by government ministers and by the President of the Ordnance Board. To try and cancel them or renege on them would be the end of the House of Remer. It would be ruination.'

'Then let it be our ruination,' she said fiercely. 'Far better that, Berthold, than the name of Remer becoming as linked with war as the name Krupp is.'

He broke free of her hold and sat down on the edge of their bed. 'To be as mighty as the House of Krupp was my father's and my grandfather's dream, Vicky.' He buried his head in his hands. 'It's been Josef's dream too. I can't rob him of it. It isn't possible, *Liebchen*. Don't you see?'

There was a tight band crushing her chest. She did see. For the first time since their marriage she was seeing things clearly. She was seeing Berthold as others saw him. A kindly, endearingly hopeless man who was head of a steel dynasty, but had no steel in him.

The band around her chest grew tighter. It was, of course, what she had wanted in a husband. Mildness. Gentleness. A lack of threatening masculinity. In the situation they were now in, though, she desperately needed him to summon up other qualities as well. She needed him to be strong. And surely him being strong wasn't too much to expect? She thought of her father. Like Berthold, he was kind, rarely angry, never quarrelsome – and yet he wasn't weak. And in this situation Berthold could not be weak either.

Josef could not be allowed to plunge the House of Remer into the moral morass of full-scale armament production and Berthold was the only person who could prevent him from doing so. Though Josef had organized all the contracts Berthold had spoken of, he wasn't head of the House of Remer. Berthold was. And as the head of the House of Remer, if he wanted to bring it to ruination, that was, surely, his prerogative.

She took in a deep, steadying breath. As Berthold was so reluctant to confront Josef then she would have to do so on his behalf.

'Are Josef and Zelda here, or at Schloss Niedernhall?'

He lifted his head from his hands. 'Here, *Liebchen*,' he said eagerly, vastly relieved that the previous subject appeared to be miraculously at an end. 'And Claus Heinrich is a wonderfully healthy baby. He's not as big as Max was when he was born, but he's sturdy and . . .'

There was something so pathetic about his relief, something so childlike, that she felt a stab of despair. How could he believe a subject of such monumental importance could be shelved so easily? For the first time it occurred to her that those who thought her dearly loved husband inadequate were very probably right.

The instant the thought came, she closed her mind to it. She couldn't think of such a hideous possibility now. For now all she could cope with was how ineffectual he was being. And she was going to help him overcome his ineffectuality. She was going to show Josef that even if he could ride roughshod over Berthold, he most certainly couldn't ride roughshod over her.

'I need a couple of hours' rest before dinner, Berthold.'

It wasn't the truth. What she needed was a couple of hours on her own in which to think.

He rose to his feet, smiling sheepishly. 'It's good to have you home, Vicky. I've missed you every single minute of every single day.'

It was so obviously the literal truth that tears pricked the backs of her eyes. He loved her so very much, and with terrible certainty she knew that her love for him had undergone a profound change. She still loved him, of course, but not in the unquestioning way she had before she had left for Yorkshire. Then, she had thought him perfect. Now, she knew he was weak.

'I missed you too,' she said, hoping he would never know that his dependence on her was far greater than her dependence on him.

59

He touched her cheek gently, bent his head and kissed her and then left the room.

She sat still for a long time, wondering if she would ever be able to recapture the mood of fierce optimism with which she had left Yorkshire. Then, she had been determined to become just as much of a Berliner as Zelda. Now, the prospect of doing so seemed as far away as ever.

When she dressed for dinner, she did so carefully. Paris fashions and jewels had never been as important to her as they were to Zelda, but tonight she wanted Josef to be aware that she was someone he was going to have to take notice of. Until now she had been criminally uninformed about Remer steel plants and factories. She was going to be so no longer.

As Josephine helped her into a floor-length midnight-blue silk dress that had been cut low at the bosom to help draw attention away from her advanced pregnancy, she wondered just how much Zelda knew about Remer contracts and armament production, fairly sure it would be a lot. And yet Zelda had never raised the subject with her and there could be only one reason for her not doing so. Knowing what her reaction would be, Zelda had wanted to keep her in the dark.

It was not a nice thought.

Josephine was just fastening a sapphire and diamond pendant around her neck when the door burst open and Zelda whirled into the room.

'I've just been told you've been back for hours, Vicky. I'd no idea. How *can* you have been back for hours and not visited the nursery to take a look at Claus Heinrich?' She kissed her effusively. 'He's an absolute joy. Every inch a German. All blond and blue-eyed – a miracle when he has such a raven-haired mama.'

Dressed for dinner in a ravishing sea-green gown that emphasized her luscious curves, she seated herself on one of the spindly legged gilt bedroom chairs. 'You look tired, Vicky darling. You shouldn't have stayed so long in Yorkshire. It's *Wundervoll* to have you back here again!'

Faced with Zelda's blazing pleasure at seeing her again, it was impossible to hold on to her suspicions of a moment ago. She decided not to bring up the new steel contract but instead wait and confront Josef at the dinner table. She would take him by surprise.

'Take me to see Claus Heinrich now,' she said, taking hold of Zelda's hand and rising to her feet. 'And tell me how you managed to get your figure back so quickly. You don't look as if you are the mother of one child, let alone two.'

Minutes later, as she stood looking down at Claus Heinrich in his lavishly draped cradle, Vicky had to admit that a baby so blond-haired when his mother was so dazzlingly dark-haired was, indeed, some kind of a miracle.

'He's beautiful,' she said, knowing how much Zelda had longed for a baby who would possess none of her grandmother's Iroquois characteristics.

'Isn't he just?' Zelda glowed with self-satisfaction. 'Josef says he wants another six just like him.'

'Then tell Josef to have them,' Vicky said drily.

Zelda's laughter lifted Vicky's spirits as nothing else could have done. Whatever the hideous state of affairs of the House of Remer steel plants and factories, she and Zelda were as they had always been – as close as sisters. And with her strength behind Berthold – a strength she knew was going to surprise everyone – the House of Remer would extricate itself from the nightmare Josef had plunged it into.

'Let's go down to dinner,' she said, slipping her hand into Zelda's just as she had been in the habit of doing ever since she had been a two-year-old and Zelda had been seven.

With no intimation that it was the last time she and Zelda would ever be so close – that it was the last time she would have even the faintest optimism that what had gone so wrong could be put right – they left the nursery together, walking down the grand marble and bronze staircase, her midnight-blue gown a perfect contrast to the shimmering sea-green of Zelda's Poiret-inspired creation.

The dining room was candlelit and Berthold and Josef were already waiting for them, glasses of brandy and soda water to hand.

For a fleeting moment Vicky was hopeful that Berthold had reconsidered his defeatist attitude of earlier and had already begun a discussion with Josef as to the best way of approaching the Admiralty with news that the two promised battleships would not now be built – at least not by Remers.

And then Josef walked towards her, greeting her with the heel-clicking formality with which he would have greeted a stranger. There was no tightly controlled fury in his eyes, no burning resentment, and she knew with stinging disappointment that Berthold had said nothing.

'You are looking well, Victoria.'

She looked into eyes as chilly as the Baltic, wondering why Zelda was so besotted with him.

'Thank you.' She hated his habit of always referring to her by her full Christian name. No one else ever did. Now, though, was not the time to make an issue of it.

Biding her moment, she curbed her patience as other meaningless, polite trivialities were trotted out. Not until they were seated at the table and the soup had been served, did she say coolly, 'Berthold tells me you have secured a mammoth contract from the navy, Josef. A contract for two battleships.'

'Yes.' If he was surprised or annoyed by her comment he didn't allow it to show. 'And the House of Remer has also acquired a new coal mine in Lorraine. We have cause for great celebration. Perhaps we should be drinking champagne, not this rather fine Riesling.'

Berthold dabbed nervously at his mouth with a napkin. 'I think Vicky is eager to talk to us about Yorkshire. You had a wonderful time there, *Liebchen*, didn't you?'

'Yes, but I don't want to talk about it now, Berthold.' She laid down her soup spoon. 'I want Josef to know how unhappy you are about the navy contract. I want him to know that as head of the House of Remer you are going to renege on it.'

Zelda's soup spoon clattered into her plate. Berthold choked into his napkin. Josef remained perfectly motionless, his soup spoon in mid-air, and then he began to laugh.

Vicky regarded him steadily. 'It isn't a joke, Josef. Berthold doesn't want his family name to become synonymous with war. He's aware there will be a heavy price to pay in compensation, but –'

'The House of Remer's business affairs are nothing to do with you, Victoria,' he said, still visibly amused. 'As for you, Berthold. Are you too inept to keep her in order?'

Vicky's nails dug deep into the palms of her hands. 'Berthold isn't inept. He's simply allowed you too much authority in House of Remer affairs. From now on he's going to take charge of things himself and the first thing he is going to do is to extricate the House of Remer from all armaments contracts.'

Josef quirked an eyebrow. 'Really? You think so, do you?'

'Yes,' she said curtly. 'I do.'

'Then perhaps you need a little educating.'

Despite the insulting smile, the Baltic eyes were still icy. Seated beside her, Berthold remained paralysed in horrified silence. Opposite her, Zelda bit her lip so hard she drew a fleck of blood.

'Even if Berthold were to choose to take charge of things himself,' Josef continued silkily, 'it would not be possible for him to do so.'

'Why not?'

There was a change of atmosphere in the room that she didn't understand. Berthold was screwing his napkin into a ball. There was perspiration on Zelda's upper lip.

Signalling that the maid who had been waiting on them should leave the room, Josef pushed his chair away from the table and rose to his feet. Resting his hands on the table and leaning towards her slightly, he said, 'Because, though at my father's death Berthold became the formal owner of the House of Remer, he has never, as Chairman of the Board, been anything other than a figurehead. And because, though he is continuing to be a figurehead, he is no longer the owner of the Remer steelworks or any Remer factory.'

Vicky stared at him, her bewilderment total.

Josef smiled.

'In your absence, Victoria, a great deal of legal paperwork was undertaken. The House of Remer became a limited liability company, though a private one. All shares are held principally by myself, the others being divided between Berthold and Zelda. Berthold has renounced all claim to the House of Remer steelworks and factories and I am now the sole legal owner, and Claus Heinrich will be the owner after me. Berthold is entitled to twenty per cent of House of Remer profits. As well as being a Board Director he also has a seat on the Committee of Management, though without any particular responsibility. Does that answer all your questions?'

As she looked at her husband's face and Zelda's face, Vicky knew there wasn't the faintest possibility that Josef was bluffing. The enormity of the inheritance Berthold had given up – an inheritance that would, in turn, have been their son's – stupefied her. She couldn't begin to make any sense of it, because there wasn't any sense to it.

'Why?' she asked, turning towards Berthold, her face bloodless. 'For the love of God, Berthold. *Why?*'

'Because it was easiest, *Liebchen*.' He took off his spectacles and rubbed his forehead. 'The provisos with which the steelworks and factories were left to me meant that I would never have had complete control over them. My father had always intended Josef would have control. The only reason the House of Remer was even nominally left to me was to prevent rumours flying. In families like ours it is traditional for the family business to be left to the eldest son. Any other arrangement would have caused too much speculation.'

'Speculation?' Vicky felt as if she were drowning in treacle. 'What kind of speculation?' She looked around the table, aware that something was known by all of them which was totally unknown to her.

'Tell her,' Zelda said, wiping away the perspiration on her upper lip.

'I don't think it's my position to tell her.' Josef eased his hands from the table and stood upright. 'It is Berthold who should tell her.'

The blood was pounding in Vicky's ears like the waves of the sea.

Slowly, clumsily, Berthold rose to his feet.

'I'm sorry, *Liebchen*, I never wanted you to know this.' The napkin was still in his hands and he was still screwing it into knots.

He licked his lips. 'My father believed my mother was unfaithful to him shortly after they married,' he said unsteadily. 'And he believed me to be the result. He never truly accepted I was his son.'

'Oh, God.' Vicky began to tremble. 'Oh, *dear* God.' Things that had always puzzled her about Harald Remer's attitude towards Berthold now became crystal clear. And what was also crystal clear was that because of Berthold's unpardonable weakness in not fighting for what was rightfully his, the House of Remer, under Josef's control, would continue to produce armaments and would begin building battleships. There was nothing she, or Berthold, could do that would prevent it.

'Would you like me to get you a brandy, Vicky darling?' Zelda asked in deep concern.

Vicky looked across at her. Her sense of being betrayed by both her husband and her cousin was enormous. How long had Zelda known? Had she known ever since she had married Josef? Had she, perhaps, known even before then? Had she known as far back as when she, Vicky, had married Berthold?

She rose to her feet. 'No,' she said in a voice she scarcely recognized as her own. 'No, you can't get me anything, Zelda. And now if you will all excuse me, I want to be alone.'

She remained alone for a long time, sitting in Max's lamplit nursery, watching him as he slept.

In not fighting for what was rightfully his, Berthold had also not fought for what was rightfully Maximilian's – and she wasn't sure if she would ever be able to forgive him.

A few weeks later, at the end of September, she made a momentous decision. No matter what Berthold's feelings were on the subject, this child was going to be born in Yorkshire.

Berthold, conscious of how badly damaged their marriage now was, agreed to her decision with deep unhappiness and acute concern for her welfare and the welfare of their unborn child.

Zelda, well aware of Vicky's still-simmering rage over the machinations that had taken place in Berlin during her last trip to Yorkshire, said bluntly, 'Is this your way of getting back at Berthold? Ensuring his second child's nationality will be British, not German? Because if it is, I think you should be ashamed of yourself.'

'Do you?' Vicky's clear eyes held Zelda's sloe-dark ones

unflinchingly. 'Where shame is concerned, Zelda, I think you should first look to yourself.'

For once Zelda didn't swiftly retaliate. She sucked in her breath, colour mounting in her cheeks. From then on nothing more was said about her decision to leave Berlin for Yorkshire.

In the third week of October, at Shuttleworth Hall, she gave birth to a second son and named him Hugo. Fighting the temptation to remain in Yorkshire, as soon as she and the baby were strong enough to travel she returned to Berlin. Then, in the spring, she was back at Shuttleworth Hall again, this time both her children were with her. Paul, who would love to have gone, was not given permission to do so.

When she returned at the end of the summer, it was to find that life in Berlin had become one endless military parade. The Kaiser and his six sons, all resplendent in uniform, plumes decorating their spiked steel helmets, were to be seen regularly at the head of great processions. In the autumn, the rumbling trouble in the Balkans intensified as the Turkish army reeled under an assault by Bulgaria and her Serbian allies.

Though she read every newspaper report she could lay her hands on concerning the precarious political situation in Europe, it was a subject never discussed between Berthold and herself. To talk of the growing possibility of a war that would see Germany and Britain camped on opposite sides was to raise the subject of the armaments being produced by the House of Remer, and that was a subject both of them now avoided.

In April the following year, Berthold travelled with her to Yorkshire and this time, as well as their own children accompanying them, so did Paul.

As always when she was at Shuttleworth Hall, her father discussed the contents of the day's newspapers with her every evening, shaking his head at the way Europe was being divided into two camps, with Germany, Italy and Austria on one side of the divide, and France, Russia and England on the other.

'What will you do, my dear, if war comes?' he asked her sombrely one evening as Berthold was reading a bedtime story to Max. 'Will you stay in Berlin, as Zelda almost certainly will stay? Or will you come home to Yorkshire until the world regains its senses?'

'And not see Berthold again until it does so, Papa?' She hugged her arms to her chest. 'It's too hard a question for me to answer. All I can do is pray the situation never arises.'

All through the winter the build-up of arms continued. In the spring, as the arms race threatened to run out of control and as photograph after photograph appeared in German newspapers of the bemedalled Kaiser on military manoeuvres with his senior officers, Vicky finally raised the subject with Berthold.

'If there is a war, what will we do? How can I stay here, in Berlin, if Germany is at war with England?'

'But you must stay here!' His face was agonized with distress.

She was pregnant again and knitting a shawl. She laid her needles down. 'If I went to Yorkshire, would you come with me?'

'How could I?' His voice was despairing. 'I would be interned as an enemy alien.'

Their eyes held, the hideousness of their situation starkly clear to them.

'And if you went to Yorkshire,' he said, breaking the silence, 'would you take the children with you?'

It was a needless question. Both of them knew that she would never leave Germany without Max and Hugo.

'I think we must pray, *Liebchen*,' he said at last, his voice raw. 'It is all we can do.'

Their prayers were in vain. On 28 June, a Bosnian Serb, Gavrilo Princip, assassinated the heir to the Austrian throne in Sarajevo.

From then on, with Austria calling for a military response against Serbia and the Kaiser promising Germany's full support if she were to take action, it was obvious war was only days away.

'I'm leaving for England before the borders close,' she said to Berthold, tears stinging her eyes at the pain she knew she was causing him. 'I can't remain in Berlin.'

'And I can't leave it, *Liebchen*.'

For both of them, it was the most terrible moment they had ever endured.

'Put your arms around me,' she said hoarsely. 'Hold me close, Berthold. For the next few hours, let's not think of what the future holds.'

FIVE

Yorkshire, July 1914

Seeing Berthold saying goodbye to his children at the train station was so heart-rending it took Vicky all her strength to keep her composure.

'Won't you change your mind, *Liebchen*?' he asked pleadingly as she stood in the circle of his arms.

'I can't, Berthold.' She touched his cheek lovingly, fighting back her tears. 'But we won't be separated for long. Papa says the whole hideous business will be over by Christmas.'

The whistle, which had already blown once, blew again.

'I must go, Berthold.' The tears she had so successfully held at bay until now began streaming down her face.

'Take care of yourself, *Liebchen*,' he said, his voice cracking slightly. 'You need plenty of rest from now until the baby is born. Promise me you will rest. Promise me that you will look after yourself.'

'Of course I will,' she said, aware that minutes were now running down into seconds. Josephine was already aboard the train with the children, Max highly excited at the prospect of a train ride and then a sea journey. Grateful that he was too young to understand the nature of this parting from his father, she raised her face one last time for Berthold's kiss.

It was, as always, loving and gentle and tender. She closed her eyes tightly, wishing that it were not. She yearned for a kiss that expressed raw need of her. Deep passion. Despair. And Berthold, because of his diffident nature, could not respond to her in the violent way she wanted, just as he had not responded to Josef's takeover of the steelworks and factories in the way she had wanted.

Confused as always by the mixture of love and disappointment he aroused in her, she reluctantly stepped away from him and onto the train. Dreadful as this parting was, there was one consolation. Zelda had suggested Paul leave Berlin with her.

Unlike Max, Paul was old enough to understand the nature of their leave-taking and he too was tearful.

Together they stood at the open window of their compartment, blowing kisses as the Pullman began to ease down the platform. Outwardly, it was just like all the other goodbyes when they had left for Yorkshire. In reality, even ten-year-old Paul knew how different it was.

'And so Zelda's taken out German citizenship, has she?' her father said to her as they had dinner together on the night of her arrival. 'I'm glad you never did.'

'I couldn't. I don't feel remotely German. I'm English down to my toes.'

He laughed. 'You're *Yorkshire* down to your toes,' he corrected. 'And as Yorkshire is God's own country, it isn't surprising you haven't transplanted well elsewhere.'

The next morning, the main story in *The Times* was of how Serbia had rejected Austria's ultimatum.

'Isn't it odd we might soon be at war with Germany all because of a country so small I can hardly find it on my globe?' Paul said, lying on his tummy on the drawing room's faded Aubusson carpet. The globe from her father's study was in front of him and with his weight resting on his elbows Paul spun it around until he was looking at Europe. 'The word "Balkans" isn't even written on here,' he said plaintively. 'But look how big Austria-Hungary is, Aunt Vicky. And when it's joined with Germany, it's enormous.'

'But not as big as Russia,' Vicky said, not wanting him to have bleak thoughts about Britain's prospects. 'And Russia has a huge army.'

He nodded, frowning. 'Do you think boys in Berlin are doing the same thing? Looking at globes and atlases to see which countries are the biggest and which side is likely to win if there is a war?'

'Probably.' Vicky found it hard to speak. The thought of Berthold's friends' sons poring over maps, whipped up into a hatred of all things English by propaganda, was hideous. Even more hideous was the prospect of Berthold's friends being maimed and slaughtered by young Englishmen who felt obligated – or were conscripted – to fight. Young Englishmen such as Adam Priestly and his friends.

When Max had gone to bed she stepped out onto the terrace, her head aching. The heat of the day was still coming out of the ground in waves and scent from her father's roses hung heavily in the air. She pressed her fingers to her throbbing temples. Berthold had told her that if Germany went to war, neither he nor Josef would be called upon to fight. 'Our patriotic duty will be seen as being to the steelworks and factories,' he had said when she had expressed her terrible fears. 'Please do not worry about me.'

Not to worry, though, was impossible. Looking across the dusk-darkened lawn she closed her eyes, praying fervently that Austria would step back from the brink of war and that sanity would prevail.

It did not do so. Three days later, Austria declared war on Serbia. Four days afterwards, Germany declared that she was at war with Russia and, two days later, that she was at war with France and Belgium also. On 4 August, Britain entered the fray.

'It's happened,' her father said brusquely, dropping a copy of the morning newspaper onto her lap.

The headline 'BRITAIN AT WAR!' was spread over the entire front page in huge red capital letters.

Vicky felt as if iced water were pouring through her veins. Despite the August heat she began shivering, goose pimples on her arms.

'You need a cup of tea,' her father said gruffly. 'And I need a brandy.'

As he tugged on the bell-pull to summon the maid, Vicky's thoughts were in Berlin where she knew the streets would be thronged with exultant, flag-waving crowds. Zelda and Josef would most likely be among them, but Berthold wouldn't. Berthold, like her, would be heartsick.

For the first few weeks of the war she was too busy to brood. Among other things, Paul had to be found a place in a suitable school and a nursery maid engaged to help her and Josephine care for Max, Hugo and also, in due course, the new baby.

'Adam Priestley tells me he went to St Dunstan's in Harrogate when he was a boy,' her father said, as aware as Vicky that Zelda would not want Paul attending a local elementary school. 'It has a good preparatory department and the boys don't have to board full-time. They can board on a Monday to Friday basis and spend the weekends at home.'

'Then we'll go and visit it. Does Adam have a son there?'

Her father shook his head. 'No. Adam and his wife have no children. Have you seen this?' He stabbed an arthritic finger at the morning newspaper. 'Police in London have rounded up over three hundred Germans and detained them as spies, and there have been wholesale arrests in other parts of the country. I shudder to think what might have happened to Berthold if he had come to Yorkshire with you.'

She made no response, but inwardly she was shuddering to think of what might be happening to Berthold in Berlin. Without her presence at his side there was little chance of him distancing himself from the steel plants and factories under Josef's control. Even though Berthold didn't want to be involved, he was a Remer. He would have to be involved.

The thought was unbearable. 'I'm going to make an appointment with the headmaster of St Dunstan's,' she said, forcing herself to think of other things. 'The sooner Paul is having lessons again, the better.'

'I'm not sure about this, Aunt Vicky,' Paul said unhappily as they walked up the steps of St Dunstan's. 'I think I'd much rather go to school in Little Ridding. Then I wouldn't have to board at all. Not even Monday to Friday.'

'The school in Little Ridding wouldn't be suitable, darling.' She took hold of his hand. 'In another few months, we'll be back in Berlin and you'll be going to one of the city's leading academies. The school in Little Ridding couldn't prepare you for that kind of an education. At St Dunstan's you will be able to keep up with your Greek and Latin and possibly start taking French.'

'But why do I need to start French when I've been studying German for nearly three years?'

'Because in England learning German is now seen as being unpatriotic. Even if it was once on St Dunstan's syllabus, it won't be now.'

She was quite right in her assumption. St Dunstan's very affable headmaster told them there was no German, but there was French, Latin, Greek and, where games were concerned, rugby, cricket and tennis. 'We don't have any other American boys at St Dunstan's at the moment,' he also said to Paul, 'but that doesn't matter. It's a friendly school. You'll soon fit in and feel at home.'

After a reassuring tour of the playing fields and classrooms, the chapel and refectory, Paul began to look more cheerful. Vastly relieved, Vicky made a detour on the way home, taking him to the tea rooms in Harrogate.

'The headmaster thinks my mother is in America, doesn't he, Aunt Vicky?' he said as a waitress set a pot of tea and a cake stand laden with iced fancies in front of them.

'Yes. Not because I've told him so. It's just the assumption he made.'

'And is it an assumption I should let everyone make?'

His hazel eyes were troubled and she stretched her hand across the table, taking hold of his. 'Yes. I think it wisest, Paul. Anyone German or having connections to Germany is being treated very badly at the moment. It wouldn't go down very well if it became known that your mother was living in Berlin and had become a German citizen. What truly counts is that you are an American. And that is all anyone needs to know.'

He nodded, understanding but not happy about it, as she was not happy about it.

Aware of how difficult all the enormous changes in his life must be for him, she was just about to comfort him by telling him of how he would soon be making lots of new friends, when he said suddenly, 'There's a soldier coming towards us, Aunt Vicky.'

Vicky turned her head. A handsome broad-shouldered man in an officer's uniform was making a beeline towards them.

'Vicky Hudson! It *is* Vicky Hudson, isn't it?' he said in an attractively deep voice as he came to a halt by their table.

'It's Vicky Remer now. I'm sorry, I –'

'Adam Priestley.' He took his cap off, revealing unforgettable flame-red hair as curly as a ram's fleece. 'We met once or twice a few years ago at tennis parties.'

Vicky's smile lit up her face. 'Of course! How nice of you to come across and introduce yourself.' She looked from Adam to Paul. 'Paul, this is the gentleman who sent you your bicycle – and who used to go to St Dunstan's when he was your age.'

'And how old is that?' Adam Priestley asked Paul.

'Ten, sir.' Paul was pink with pride at being spoken to in public by an army officer. 'And thank you for the bicycle. It's super.'

'My pleasure, young man.'

'Are you a captain, sir? Or a colonel?'

Adam Priestley's mouth tugged into a smile. 'Neither yet, Paul. I'm a lieutenant.'

'With what regiment?' Paul asked, too unfamiliar with British regiments to be able to tell from Adam Priestley's cap badge.

'The Alexandra Princess of Wales's own Yorkshire Regiment.'

'Won't you sit down and join us?' Vicky asked, aware that Adam was enjoying his conversation with Paul almost as much as Paul was.

'I'd love to, but I'm on my way to meet my wife from the York train.'

Though he didn't sit down he still made no move to leave. 'And are you about to become a St Dunstan's boy?' he asked Paul.

If Paul had had even the faintest shred of doubt about attending St Dunstan's, he had it no longer. 'Yes, sir,' he said eagerly. 'I've just been accepted. I'm to start next week.'

'Congratulations. You'll enjoy the rugger. I did. It's a splendid game.'

He turned his attention back to Vicky. 'It's been nice running into you again, Vicky. Let me know how Paul gets on at St Dunstan's. Perhaps when I'm back from France I'll be able to watch him play for the school.'

'You're going to France? To the Front?' For Vicky, the happy carefree atmosphere was wiped out at a stroke.

'Of course.' He quirked an eyebrow quizzically. 'We can't let the Germans take Paris, can we? Give my regards to your father. And make sure this young man has a decent pair of rugby boots in his kit when you send him off to school.'

'Gosh,' Paul said, watching in wide-eyed admiration as Adam Priestley took his leave of them. 'Do you think he'll come back a hero? With a medal?'

'I don't know, Paul,' she said, rather suspecting it was Adam Priestley's intention to do so. 'The important thing for his family will simply be that he comes back alive.'

'I'll bet he's a captain, or maybe even a major, the next time we see him.' Paul helped himself to a cream cake. 'I hope if he does come to watch me play rugby that he wears his uniform. He looked swell in it, didn't he?'

'Yes, he did.' Wondering if Adam Priestley would get to the station in time to meet his wife's train and wondering why she felt so oddly unsettled, Vicky poured the tea.

Though the war was only weeks old, the news from the various fronts was already bad. German troops had swept over most of Belgium forcing an Allied retreat to the Marne, the last barrier before Paris. If that was where Adam Priestley was heading, he would be right in the centre of a battlefield hell.

Over the next few days she tried to put the dark thought out of her mind by keeping even busier than usual. She took Paul to York where he was fitted out with his school uniform and sports kits. Then she spent hours marking his name in everything they had bought and in his underwear, handkerchiefs, towels, sheets and pillowcases as well.

She also interviewed several local girls for the position of nursery maid, finally selecting a dark-haired, merry-faced girl whose parents owned Little Ridding's only haberdashery shop.

In October she gave birth to a daughter.

'And what is her name to be?' her father asked, highly delighted to be a grandfather for a third time.

'Nancy.'

It wasn't a Hudson family name and didn't sound to him as if it was a Remer family name either.

'Why Nancy?' he asked, bemused.

'Because I like it,' she said simply.

'. . . and so I have named her Nancy,' she wrote to Berthold.

I hope you approve. Her hair is fair, like Hugo's, and her eyes, though blue, are a very indistinct blue. She is very pretty and already showing a strong will of her own. I wish you could see her, my darling. I wish this hideous war was over and that we were together again.

The letter, like all their correspondence, was sent via Zelda's father in New York.

She waited for a reply with mixed feelings. Berthold would be both overjoyed at knowing he had a daughter and anguished at not being able to see and hold her. When they had parted it had been in the belief that if war came, it would be over by Christmas. Neither of them had imagined that they would be parting for years. The Front had shifted from France to Flanders. Ghent, Bruges and Ostende had fallen. The Belgian government had fled to France and the nature of the war had changed from one of movement to one where both sides were deeply entrenched. It was not a situation hopeful of a short, sharp victory.

Berthold's Christmas letter to her mercifully escaped the attention of the censor.

Dearest *Liebchen*,

Christmas without you is not Christmas at all. Give all our darling children a big hug and a kiss from their loving

78

papa. I have carved Max a wooden horse big enough for him to ride on.

I would like to think I will soon be giving it to him here, in Berlin, but, despite all the propaganda we are being ceaselessly exposed to in Germany, the war news is grim. Those who told us the war would be over by Christmas were fools. The trenches now stretch from Switzerland to the North Sea. How can any decisive battles take place when both sides are permanently and miserably dug in? Josef thinks the answer lies in the use of big guns – and if big guns should bring an end to things speedily, perhaps he is right. I'll say no more about it, *Liebchen*, because I know how painful you find any reference to munitions production.

Domestically, things are well with Zelda and Josef. She is expecting another baby in the summer. Perhaps this time it will be a girl and, if it is, there will be very little age difference between her and Nancy. Perhaps in a year's time they will be sharing a pram together as you take them for a walk in the Tiergarten.

All my love, dearest darling.

Your lonely Berthold

Only after rereading it several times did she put it in the sandalwood box in her dressing-table drawer with all his other letters.

That evening she said to her father, 'Berthold writes that Josef believes big guns are the answer for a speedy ending of the war. What does he mean by "big"? Does he mean cannon?'

'I don't know, my dear.' Her father looked deeply worried. 'But even with letters being sent via New York he shouldn't be mentioning in them things that, were they to be opened and read by the censor, could have disastrous consequences for

79

you. So far it has escaped official notice that you are married to a German but if it became known, and especially if the connection was made that your husband is the Berthold Remer of the House of Remer, you would be immediately interned. Caution Berthold never to mention arms of any kind ever again. Things are bad enough at the moment without them being made worse.'

It was advice she took to heart. The number of Germans living in England who had been interned ran into thousands. On the streets anyone with a German surname, even if British-born, risked being attacked by anti-German mobs. That she had been spared any such hideousness was, she knew, only because she lived in a village where she had been known since birth and where her father was greatly respected.

'And because you came straight home,' Josephine pointed out to her pragmatically. 'Yorkshire folk aren't daft. They know where your loyalties lie and that's all that matters to them.'

By Easter, with Paul well settled at St Dunstan's and Jenny, the new nursery maid, proving to be a great help to Josephine, Vicky's thoughts turned to ways in which she could help the war effort. All over the country women were doing work that previously only men had done, in order that the men could be freed for fighting.

She thought of Shuttleworth Hall's long terrace and of the many French windows that opened out onto it. Beds could easily be wheeled out there on summer afternoons and, with the view down to the river, there could be no better place for rest and recuperation. She would have to engage qualified nursing staff, of course, and the conversion of the east wing into wards would take a lot of work. It could be done, though. And once it was done, she would have the satisfaction of knowing she was contributing to war work just as much as anyone else.

The next morning, after telling her father her plans and

having his full support for them, she telephoned Violet Ramsbotham.

'Dearest girl, of course I remember you,' Violet rasped. 'And I knew you were back at Shuttleworth Hall with your children after leaving . . . well, we won't go into where it was you left. What is it I can do for you?'

'I want to convert Shuttleworth Hall into a convalescent home, but I'm not sure how to go about it.'

'Then I shall tell you,' said Violet robustly. 'First, it helps if it's run under the jurisdiction of the Red Cross. Second, you need to become a member of the Voluntary Aid Detachment. Third, you need to obtain the services of an experienced ward sister and two fully trained nurses. Fourth, you need to obtain the services of three or four VAD workers other than yourself. Fifth, you need equipment. Medical equipment, of course, and beds that can be wheeled and plenty of wheelchairs and masses of linen. If you like, I'll drive over to Shuttleworth Hall and assess what is needed in a more detailed way.'

When she told her father of the impending visit he paled. 'Great Scott, Vicky! You didn't agree to the suggestion, did you? You'll have to deal with her yourself. I'd rather face the Kaiser's hordes than Violet!'

Intimidating though Violet undoubtedly was, she was also frighteningly efficient. Within a few short weeks Shuttleworth Hall was transformed and, by midsummer, was fully functioning as a convalescent home for wounded soldiers.

'Poor beggars,' Arthur Hudson said after making his initial acquaintance with them. 'I doubt many of them will ever work again, never mind fight.'

Vicky, too, wondered what the fate of her patients would be when the war was over. Nearly all of them had lost a limb. For the luckier ones it was an arm or a hand that had been blown into eternity. For the less lucky it was a leg – and sometimes it was both legs.

'The Krauts have big guns, miss, see?' a youth who had lost both legs to gas gangrene said to her as she bathed his stumps. 'They're so big they can lob shells weighing nearly a ton. It's like an express train coming at you. The fort me and my mates were in was supposed to be able to stand up to anything, but the Krauts' big guns flattened it – and us – as if we were beetles.'

She'd had to ask another nurse to finish her task, not because she could no longer bear the sight and smell of his wounds, but because the fear that the guns had been made by the House of Remer was so intense she knew she was going to vomit.

July brought with it the news that Zelda had given birth to a daughter and had named her Lotti.

'A pretty name,' her father said approvingly. 'Not too obviously German. At least not if you add an "e" to the end of it.'

In September, when his beloved roses were flowering only intermittently and the Michaelmas daisies were in full bloom, Arthur announced that he'd lunched with William Priestley and that Adam was home on leave.

She had been dangling Nancy on her lap and, a little unsteadily, she set her down on the sheepskin hearthrug.

'Will he be home for long?' Even to herself her voice sounded odd and tight.

Her father shook his newspaper open. 'I doubt it,' he said, as Nancy began tottering away from them on uncertain legs. 'He's a captain now and they never get long back in Blighty. Though in Adam's case, of course, things might be a little different.'

She stared at him. 'Why do you say "in Adam's case"? He's not injured, is he?'

'No, but his wife is in poor shape. TB, I believe. Great heavens. Have you seen today's headlines? The Allies have smashed through German lines around Loos. Now will this force the Germans into a retreat, do you think?'

She didn't know. Having reached the door and not being

able to go any farther, Nancy had fallen on her bottom and begun to wail. Vicky hurried across to her, scooping her into her arms, too appalled at Adam's situation to be able to reflect on the war news.

'You and Max are coming to watch me play in the house team in the Inter-School Competition, aren't you, Aunt Vicky?' Paul said, striding into the room via the French windows, accompanied by a blast of chill autumn air and three dogs. 'It's going to be a spiffing game.'

Despite the pain she was feeling on Adam Priestley's behalf, her lips twitched in amusement.

Paul's forehead crinkled. For the life of him he couldn't think what it was he had said that was funny.

'Yes, of course we will be at the match, and I'm amused because, for an American, you are beginning to use some very English expressions.'

He grinned. 'It's going to be a swell game, then. It's important I play really well because I'm hoping to make Junior School captain next year.'

Her father's newspaper rustled slightly and Vicky knew what he was thinking. In another year, the war would, with God's good grace, be over. And when it was, Paul would be twelve and back in Berlin with his mother and stepfather, attending a school that would be different in every way from St Dunstan's.

On the day of the Inter-School Competition she dressed warmly, having had previous experience of just how cold it was possible to get watching a game of rugby.

As always at St Dunstan's there was a good turnout of spectators, comprised mainly of devoted parents, grand-parents and fond aunts and uncles.

'I'm going to play for the school when I come to St Dunstan's,' Max said to her, his gloved hand tucked in hers. 'It won't be long now, will it, Mama?'

She squeezed his hand, knowing that Max would settle into preparatory-school life as easily as a duck taking to water. He was a gregarious little boy, making friends easily and possessing none of his father's diffidence. Rugby, too, would come easily to him. He was a natural ball player, swift on his feet and, thanks to years of boisterous, friendly scraps with Paul, unfazed by close physical tussling.

As Paul's team ran out onto the field, eyes glowing and young faces set with determination, a large maroon-coloured motorcar drew to a halt in close proximity to the playing field.

Seconds later, a distinctive red-haired figure stepped out of it and assisted a beautiful-looking woman, heavily swathed in furs, to do the same.

Next to his magnificent physique she looked frighteningly frail.

On the pitch, the two teams were lined up, about to kick off.

Vicky was oblivious.

She was watching Adam Priestley as he slid his arm around his wife and, tenderly supporting her, walked her slowly towards the touchline.

Somewhere behind Vicky the whistle blew for the start of play, and as it did so Adam Priestley's eyes met hers and his face lit with pleasure.

He inclined his head to say something to his wife and she too looked across at Vicky, her mouth curving in a slow, gentle smile.

They began walking towards her and as it was obvious how difficult Adam's wife was finding the uneven ground Vicky had no option but to narrow the distance and walk towards them.

'My wife, Elise,' Adam said as they met in a little group. 'And darling, this is Vicky Remer, Arthur Hudson's daughter. It is her nephew we have come to see play.'

Close to, Elise Priestley was even more beautiful than she had looked at a distance. Beneath her sable hat her features were as delicate as porcelain, her skin almost translucent.

'It's lovely to meet you, Vicky,' she said, her voice a little breathless. She proffered a kid-gloved hand so small-boned Vicky hardly dared shake it for fear of crushing it. 'Adam tells me he suggested St Dunstan's to your father as being a suitable school for Paul. I'm so glad it has worked out for him.' She stopped speaking suddenly, turning aside to cough.

It wasn't a short cough, it was long and racking and, as his arm tightened around Elise, Vicky saw a pulse begin pounding at the corner of Adam Priestley's jawline.

After what seemed an eternity his wife finally raised her head, her face deathly pale against her richly coloured furs. 'And is the little boy you were standing with, one of your children?' she asked.

Vicky turned swiftly, terrified in case Max was no longer where she had left him.

She needn't have worried. Uncaring that she had walked away from him to speak to people he did not know, he was jumping up and down on the touchline, his cheeks flushed with excitement as he shouted at the top of his lungs: 'Come *on*, Paul! Pick up the ball and *run*!'

'Yes,' she said, relaxing in relief. 'Max will be starting at St Dunstan's in September.'

'And you have other children?'

'I have another two.' Knowing of Elise's childlessness, Vicky felt uncomfortably guilty at her good fortune.

'You are very blessed.'

'Yes.' A lump was forming in Vicky's throat. 'Yes. I know.'

Adam's attention was on the game and the difficult moment was ended as he shouted, 'Paul's got the ball! He's going to make a break for it! Oh, good Lord, he has done! He's away!'

Amid a roar of applause and approval, Paul, head down, the ball tucked under his arm, legs pumping like pistons, stormed down the field to score a try.

Elise Priestley clapped her hands delightedly.

Adam grinned down at her. 'Happy, darling?' he asked.

'Oh, yes!'

She clasped hold of his hand and kissed it, and when Vicky saw the expression in Elise's eyes she looked away, overcome by the same realization that had overcome her so often when she had been in Zelda and Josef's company. As a married couple, Adam and Elise shared something she and Berthold didn't.

That night, sleep wouldn't come. She counted sheep and, when sheep failed her, she counted her blessings. She had a loving, kind-hearted husband, three splendidly healthy children, a nephew she loved as if he were her own son, a father who doted on her and a wartime occupation that challenged her to the utmost. Why, then, her growing feeling that there was something lacking in her life? She'd been aware of it before, in Berlin, but never to this extent.

She turned her pillow over, pummelling it fiercely, knowing the answer and not wanting to face it.

The turbulent, unsettled feeling troubling her had stemmed from one very precise moment. The moment when she had looked across the tea rooms in Harrogate and seen Adam Priestley walking towards her.

The self-knowledge the realization brought filled her with anguish.

She no longer felt as if she were the same person who had left Berlin a little over a year ago – and she most certainly wasn't the same person who had so naively married in Little Ridding's church nearly six years ago.

Somewhere along the way she had turned into someone else. Someone she didn't recognize. And if she didn't recognize herself how, when the war was over, would Berthold be able to do so?

SIX

Yorkshire, Christmas 1915

'... and so I'm already pregnant again,' Zelda wrote in distinctive purple ink.

I'm not over the moon about it and can only hope it will be another boy. Lotti is more tiresome than any baby I've ever known. C is now attending a military preparatory school. Even though he's only four he loves army routines and all the shouting and marching. He also shows every sign of being scholastically brilliant. Paul will be old enough for Harrow next year and I don't want him to remain a day longer than necessary at St Dunstan's. It's far too minor a public school and I can't understand what possessed you to send him there. I see very little of J. He works constantly. B isn't much help to him.

All love,
Zelda

'Well, at least she's being careful,' her father said when Vicky showed the letter to him. 'She's used an initial when the name in question was unmistakably German and her mention of a military preparatory school could be taken to mean an American military preparatory school.'

He gave the letter back to her without saying anything about Zelda's reference to Berthold. Berthold's docile handing over to Josef of all House of Remer steelworks and factories had so appalled him he now very rarely mentioned Berthold's name. 'If he'd behaved differently, Germany wouldn't have quite so many armaments and battleships. He was in a position of great responsibility and he should have shouldered it and not walked away from it,' was all he ever said on the subject.

It was how she felt herself, but wifely loyalty ensured she never said so.

'You're not going to take any notice of her nonsense about Paul, are you? He's well settled at St Dunstan's. It would be a shame to move him,' her father said.

'I should take notice of her wishes. She is his mother after all.' She paused and then added mischievously, 'I rather think, though, that Harrow may not take him, Papa. Not when they know his mother is a German citizen.'

Arthur's bushy eyebrows shot high and then he bellowed with laughter. 'No, indeed. Clever thinking, Vicky. It's a trick almost worthy of Zelda herself.'

On Christmas Eve, all the able-bodied patients helped Paul, Max and Hugo decorate an enormous Christmas tree.

'Who's going to put the angel at the top of the tree?' Hugo asked as even the patients in wheelchairs joined in the fun, decorating the lower branches with glittering baubles and tinsel and holly.

'I'll hold you up, laddie, then you'll be able to reach,' a thirty-year-old veteran of Mons said with a grin.

Even at four years old, Hugo knew when he was being teased.

'Silly,' he said, giggling. 'You only have one arm.'

'Well, if I'm ready to give it a go, I don't see why you aren't. What do you think, Mrs Remer? Shall I hoist him high?'

'I think that might be a tad unsafe, Will,' Vicky said, laughing. 'What you could do, though, is to take a plate of hot mince pies round to everyone.'

'Can I do it with him, Mama?' Hugo was always eager to show that, like Max, he was a big boy too.

'Yes, of course, but let Josephine put mince pies on a smaller plate for you. Then you'll be able to carry it a little easier.'

'And then are we having carols?' Max asked, tinsel streamers garlanding his neck.

'We are. And you and Paul are going to sing "Away in a Manger" as a duet. I know you've been practising. Grandpa told me.'

'I'm going to put the angel at the top of the tree!' Paul called out, climbing a strategically placed stepladder one-handed, the angel held tightly in his free hand.

As Vicky watched him, her heart in her mouth, Hugo said innocently, repeating information contained in his father's last letter to him, 'The idea of Christmas trees comes from Germany. They're pretty, aren't they?'

'Aye, and Big Bertha and Long Tom come from the same place, and they aren't,' a grizzled man in a wheelchair, old before his time, said savagely.

Vicky saw the blank incomprehension on Hugo's face and, before anything else unkind was said to her son, she crossed swiftly towards him, saying with a wide smile, 'Josephine has a plate of mince pies ready for you now, sweetheart. And ask people if they want a slice of cheese with them, will you?'

'Yes, Mama,' he said, still looking confused. 'Mama, who are Big Bertha and Long Tom and why doesn't Sergeant Smith like them?'

'Later, darling. You don't want the mince pies to get cold, do you?'

As he trotted off with them she wondered how she could explain that Big Bertha and Long Tom were not people, but giant guns that could fire shells fantastic distances, nine miles in the case of Big Bertha. They were Krupp-made guns and whether the House of Remer was manufacturing anything remotely similar she didn't know. Hoping that Hugo would forget what had been said to him and that no explanations would be necessary, she led a round of applause as Paul, wobbling dangerously, placed the angel at the top of the tree.

Sergeant Smith's remark had been ill timed. Tonight, Christmas night, she wanted no reminders of the war.

As Josephine supervised the handing round of glasses of mulled wine she reflected on how lucky they were that the war so rarely intruded on their daily life. Being deep in the Dales they suffered no Zeppelin raids, and though food was now short in the towns it wasn't short at Shuttleworth Hall where vegetables, fish and game were plentiful. Most of the local farmers had Land Army girls seconded to them and their familiar green-smocked figures in the fields were often the only reminder of the ghastliness taking place in northern France.

There the armies were paralysed in a terrible deadlock it seemed nothing could break. Adam Priestley had long since returned to his regiment, but where his regiment now was, she didn't know. She could only pray that William Priestley would not join the hideously growing ranks of her father's friends sporting black armbands.

'Excuse me, Vicky, but Sister has an emergency,' Josephine said to her apologetically. 'Jonathan Rouse's stump is leaking and it needs two hands to put a new drainage tube in. I'd help her myself but she'd prefer you. You have steadier hands.'

'Take over here for me, then, Josephine. The next thing on the agenda is the carol service. Paul and Max are to sing "Away in a Manger" as a duet.'

Minutes later, as she helped Shuttleworth Hall's nursing

sister insert a new drainage tube in the mangled stump of an eighteen-year-old boy's leg, the rousing strains of 'Once in Royal David's City' could be clearly heard.

Were her German family singing carols? Was Berthold with Zelda and Josef and their children? There was very little difference in age between Hugo and Claus, and Nancy and Lotti.

Emotionally, she wondered how long it would be before Berthold held Nancy in his arms. The great autumn campaign that had opened in September with such a fanfare had petered into the familiar situation of stalemate, with the fronts swaying backwards and forwards in offensives marked only by losing or recapturing a few miles of devastated, shell-pocked wasteland.

'Let this be the last year,' she prayed fervently. 'Let the war be over by Christmas 1916. Please, Lord. Please.'

In the spring, she became aware of a change of tone in Zelda's letters. Writing in her flamboyant purple scrawl she no longer seemed to care whether or not the censor got his hands on them.

When are the French and British going to come to their senses and realize that the Kaiser is in complete command of this war? Generals Joffre and Haig are donkeys and the Russians are even worse, unable to come up with any scheme Germany can't easily dislocate. The only course open to the Allies is to surrender.

'Good God in heaven!' Arthur Hudson said, his eyes bulging. 'What on earth is she thinking of? If this was to be opened and read we'd be facing a firing squad!'

His legs gave way beneath him and he sat down abruptly. 'Fetch me a pen and paper, Vicky. I must write to her father at once. From now on he must open and vet every letter he is asked to send on to us. And unless there's nothing in them but harmless domestic chatter, he must burn them!'

For a long time there was no communication from Zelda, though Berthold's letters continued to arrive without interference. She received one on 1 May.

> My dearest Vicky,
>   I worry desperately that you are suffering the kind of food shortages being suffered by others. Not by myself, of course, or Z and J. The situation elsewhere is, I believe, quite acute. How are our darling boys and my little Nancy? Is she walking yet and saying 'Mama'? I think of you all ceaselessly and pray the day will soon come when we will all be together again.
>   Your loving husband, B

'Not a word about Claus and Lotti,' Arthur said, 'but at least he's now a little more circumspect and it isn't littered with German names. His references to food shortages are obviously as far as he could go in letting us know what the situation is like in Berlin. According to *The Times* there were riots there a month or so ago. I hate to say it, but it's all to our good. A loss of public morale in Germany might help bring the war to a close.'

Vicky made no comment, certain that the bitter tone in the last letter from Zelda had been because the war was beginning to go badly for Germany and life in Berlin, even for a Remer, was no longer so comfortable. She wished Berthold's letter had given a little information about Claus and Lotti – especially Lotti.

Even when Zelda's letters had been suitably restrained and only about domestic matters, there had never been much information about Lotti. It had always been about Claus.

'Hope the little mite is all right,' her father had said, trying to read between the lines as to why Zelda so rarely referred to her daughter.

Vicky didn't need to read between the lines. She was willing to bet that Lotti was a dark-haired, dark-eyed dazzler. And if she were, Zelda's disappointment in her would be intense.

All through May and June the weather was hot. Day after day, beds were trundled out onto the terrace and the sound of male voices, laughing and bantering, could be heard as far as the river.

That her patients were able to enjoy such perfect surroundings gave her deep satisfaction. Even the blind were given pleasure, for her father's roses were in full bloom and the air was heavy with scent.

Climbing high all along the walls of the house was Zéphirine Drouhin, a Bourbon rose covered in wonderful clusters of rosy-pink blooms, and intertwining with it was Veilchenblau, an orange-scented rose whose small flowers were so dark as to be almost magenta when they opened, but then turned to a heavenly violet-blue streaked with white. Neither rose had thorns and their clusters of flowers bobbed in at open bedroom windows and hung in cascades around the French doors.

Whenever anyone asked her what it was called, she didn't give it its German name. 'Blue Rosalie,' she would say, hoping Herr Schmidt, its breeder, would forgive her. 'It's a rambler and the bluest rose I think there is.'

'This is a little piece of heaven on earth, Mrs Remer,' Will Patchett said to her as she changed his dressing. 'If I still had two arms I'd ask if I could stay on here as a gardener.'

Vicky put his soiled dressing in a bag for disposal and then helped him back into his shirt. One sleeve, the sleeve he no longer had cause to use, was permanently safety-pinned so that it wouldn't flap. It was his left sleeve.

'With a little practice I imagine rose pruning can be carried out with one hand, Will. Would you like to give it a try?'

'Not half, I wouldn't!'

She grinned. 'I'll go and get Paul's pruning knife. He's almost as mad about roses as he is about rugby and my father gave him a very neat knife for a birthday present.'

A month later and the war news was, if possible, worse than it had ever been.

'Dear God in heaven,' her father said devoutly, staring at the front page of *The Times* with disbelieving eyes. 'Just listen to this, Vicky. Just listen to this and weep:

'They came up to the Front during the night singing a music-hall tune. It was the biggest British army yet sent into battle, 26 divisions on a 15-mile front. At 7.30 a.m. they went over the top in waves, their aim to seize 4,000 yards of enemy territory. In the first five minutes of the battle thousands were cut down by relentless enemy fire. By nightfall many battalions numbered barely a hundred men. The success was limited to a few miles. British casualties were 60,000.'

He stopped reading, his voice choked. 'Sixty thousand, Vicky. In one day. And that is only the first day of the campaign. How many dead and injured are there going to be by the time it ends?'

Overcome with emotion he shielded his eyes with his hands and then, not speaking again, rose to his feet and unsteadily left the room.

The agony of the Somme ground on all through the summer and into early autumn, and when it was over British casualties numbered 450,000. All that had been gained was a tiny tongue of ground just over a mile deep.

Whether Adam Priestley was one of the many thousands who had endured the horrors of the fruitless campaign she had no way of knowing. She only knew he hadn't died during it, for if he had, Violet, a close friend of Adam's parents, would most certainly have told her.

Berthold's Christmas letter was despairing.

Dearest darling,

How can it be that we have already been separated for over two years? There is no good war news, only bad. Zelda had another daughter a few months ago and she and all the children are at SN. J works ceaselessly. I do my best to be a support to him, Wastl my only companion. Write me news of the boys and Nancy. Is Paul still captain of his House rugby team? How is Max enjoying St Dunstan's? And is Hugo still being patient with Nancy and not cross with her when she follows him everywhere? I miss you more than words can say.

Your loving and lonely husband, B

She put it with all his other letters in her sandalwood box, wondering what name Zelda had given her new baby, knowing it must be a very German name for Berthold to have been so mindful of the censor to have included it. The censor's looming presence made all their letters to each other inadequate and stilted. He could not call her his *Liebchen* and nor could he tell her any real news. She wanted to know what he was doing to 'support' Josef. She wanted to know what Josef was doing. And the only real information she had was the useless fact that Zelda and her children were sitting out the war at Schloss Niedernhall.

Work was her salvation. As a convalescent home, Shuttleworth Hall never had an empty bed.

None of the patients with her was ill in the sense of being

sick. All were recovering from the loss of limbs or attempting to adjust themselves to blindness. Right from the beginning she had worked hard to create an atmosphere of camaraderie, almost – though she knew it would seem strange to some people – a house-party atmosphere. Paul, Max and Hugo had never been shielded from the hideous injuries some of the men had sustained. They simply accepted the patients as they were, disabilities included. Pity was not an emotion she allowed. She was fiercely convinced her patients didn't need it.

'They need to feel normal,' she said time and again to her little band of staff. 'They need to feel they still fit into society; that their lives aren't over. Pity isn't a help to them, so please don't give it.'

In April came news she had been both praying for and dreading. America entered the war.

'It will speed up the end,' her father said as they heard cheers coming from the direction of the wards and knew that the news had already spread. 'America's potential force in manpower and material is limitless. Her young men will be fresh and enthusiastic. Perhaps the war really will be over by Christmas.'

'I hope so.' Her hands were clasped so tightly in her lap that the knuckles showed white. 'And for that reason I'm glad that America has joined the Allies, but there will be no more letters, Papa. Berthold and Zelda won't be able to send post to America any more. The children's contact with Berthold and Paul's contact with his mother will be over completely.'

'But not for ever, for the day will come when the war will end.' Arthur Hudson's voice was gruff, for he, like her, could not imagine quite what was going to happen to her little family when that day finally came. He couldn't imagine her returning to Berlin any more than he could imagine Paul returning to Berlin, and nor could he imagine Little Ridding's reaction if Berthold were to come and live with them.

At the knowledge that she and Berthold could have no further contact with each other until hostilities ended, Vicky's desolation was enormous. Even though the love she felt for him was now purely platonic, he was still her loving companion and dearest friend and the thought of how desperately he must be missing her distressed her deeply.

In June, the King ordered all members of the royal family to drop German names and titles.

'We're no longer to be ruled by the House of Saxe-Coburg-Gotha,' Will Patchett said to her wryly as he pruned a rose growing in a lead urn on the terrace. 'From now on Saxe-Coburg-Gotha becomes Windsor and Battenberg becomes Mountbatten. What's this rose called, Mrs Remer? It's a pretty little thing.'

'Its botanical name is Rosa Richardii,' she said, wondering, not too seriously, if she should also change her surname. 'Its common name is "Holy Rose of Abyssinia". It's been grown on Christian tombs in Abyssinia for over fifteen hundred years.'

'Is that so?' Will was impressed. 'And what about our English dog rose. How old is that?'

As he was talking he was expertly continuing to prune, doing so just as well with one hand as her father did with two.

'I don't know.' She tucked a strand of blonde hair back into the bun set low in the nape of her neck. 'Ancient, I expect. Paul might know. He's always reading my father's botanical books.'

'P'raps he'll be a gardener, like me.' He grinned at her, showing a cracked front tooth.

She grinned back, happy that his future was safely assured.

'I'm sure we can always find enough work for him,' her father had said, when she'd told him of Will's ambition. 'Sister says she's about to discharge him so he'll need to find somewhere to live close by.'

She had found him lodgings with Jenny's parents and, though it was early days yet, was hopeful that a romance might flourish between him and Jenny.

In July, Violet Ramsbotham paid one of her regular visits.

'Just want to see how you are getting on, dearest girl,' Violet said in a voice like the sound of a hacksaw blade.

As Arthur scurried for cover, Vicky led Violet through the downstairs rooms and towards the French windows leading out onto the terrace, wondering how old she would have to be before Violet ceased referring to her as a girl.

'I'm twenty-nine,' she said casually as Violet came to a halt at the open French windows.

'And I'm fifty and you'll always be a girl to me,' Violet said, knife-sharp as to why the remark had been made. 'And everything looks as splendid as always, Vicky. Absolutely splendid.'

Twelve beds, their occupants all lying back against snowy-white pillows, were lined up on the terrace. Shuttleworth Hall's nursing sister was by the side of one bed, changing a dressing. One nurse was writing a letter for a man who had lost three fingers on one hand and two on the other; another was leading a blind man towards the summer house. On the lawn, in little groups around tables, were several men in wheelchairs. Some were playing dominoes. Other men were down by the river, managing very ably on crutches. Others had the assistance of a VAD girl. Slung between two trees was a hammock in which a young man was noisily snoozing.

'What is that child doing with that dog?' Violet asked as two of the men on crutches suddenly roared with laughter.

Looking towards them Vicky saw that Nancy was pushing one of her father's spaniels around in her doll's pram, and the dog was wearing one of her sun hats.

'She's pretending it's a doll. The dog is so daft it lets her do anything she wants with it. Yesterday, she dressed it in an army shirt and cap and we all had to salute it.'

Violet snorted in amusement. 'Did she, indeed? Well, she's certainly keeping the men entertained. Is that another of your children over there, playing draughts with that young man?'

'Yes. Max and Private Callaghan have struck up quite a friendship. Are you staying for tea, Violet? It's due to be served very soon and Josephine has baked her secret-recipe curd tarts.'

'Well, I will stay, but not until I've carried out a rather painful task.' Her amusement at the sight of Nancy and the dog faded from her face. 'Amos thought you and your father should know that Elise Priestley died yesterday.'

Vicky sucked in her breath and tried to speak, but no words came.

'It was expected, of course,' Violet continued. 'She'd been ill a long time – was ill when Adam married her.' A spasm of emotion crossed her face. 'Even though he's now a captain, he still won't get compassionate leave. Not with the state things are in at the Front. Dear Lord, when is it ever going to end? All the latest offensive seems to be yielding is an unending procession of wounded and dying men.'

Not commenting on Elise's death, Vicky wondered if she should go to the funeral, aware that as she had met Elise only once it might look rather odd.

'The funeral is to be private,' Violet said, admiring the drawing the man in the bed nearest to her was doing. 'William thinks it's for the best as Adam won't be able to attend. That's an excellent drawing, young man. Absolutely champion.'

The drawing was of the scene before them. The lawns rolling down to the river and the trees beyond.

'Would you excuse me a moment, Violet?' Vicky knew she

had to be on her own, even if it was only for a few brief minutes. 'There's something I've remembered I have to do.'

Not waiting for Violet's response she walked swiftly back into the house, her pulse racing.

Where would Adam be when he received the news? In a trench, knee-deep in mud? On a battlefield? And without the wife he had so deeply loved, would he care any longer if he lived or died?

In the peace and quiet of the nursery she prayed that he would not grow careless. That when the war ended he would return to Keighley and pick up the pieces of his shattered life.

She took in a deep, steadying breath. She would write a letter of condolence that evening to William Priestley. And she would write one that just might find its way to Adam.

She smoothed her skirt and straightened her belt and then, outwardly serene and inwardly in turmoil, went back downstairs to play hostess to Violet.

Though she and her father avoided all mention of the war in front of Hugo, the situation with Max was different. Now that he was attending the preparatory department at St Dunstan's he was surrounded by boys his own age who could talk of nothing else.

'Papa isn't a German pig, is he, Mama?' he asked her miserably one morning when he was home for the weekend.

She had been rolling bandages. She stopped what she was doing and folded her hands in her lap so that he wouldn't see they had become unsteady.

'No, darling. Of course he isn't. Has someone said he is?'

'No. I don't know why, but no one seems to think Remer is a German name. P'raps it's because they know Paul is my cousin and he's an American, and the chaps at school just think Remer is the same kind of funny name that lots of

Americans have. Everyone says all Germans are pigs, though, and when they say it I don't know what to do. Because if I don't do anything, I feel I am being disloyal to Papa. And if I were to say anything – well, I don't know what would happen, but I do know it would get very sticky. I might even have to leave the school and I don't want to. I want to go into the Upper School, like Paul.'

He looked so dejected, her heart hurt. She put an arm around his narrow shoulders, saying gently, 'You must always act with common sense, Max. And until now it has been common sense not to volunteer information about Papa. That doesn't mean you can't, though, if your silence is making you feel uncomfortable and disloyal to him.'

'And what if there are such ructions that I'm asked to leave the school?'

Vicky thought of St Dunstan's sensible and fair-minded headmaster.

'I don't think that will happen, darling, but if it does, you will be able to leave knowing you have nothing to be ashamed of.' With her arm still around his shoulders, she hugged him a little closer to her. 'What was it Papa once wrote in a letter to you? "Never do anything common or mean, or underhand or cruel just because it is easier to do so or because someone else does so." And though he didn't say you must always be brave, I know he would want you to be so.'

He nodded, feeling better, and then said, 'I wish I could remember more about when we lived in Germany, but I can't. I can only remember the big statues in the house we lived in and sailing my boat on the lake in the Tiergarten and Papa taking me to the zoo. Hugo doesn't remember anything.'

By February there were several grim reports in the newspapers as to the conditions in Berlin.

'Martial law has been declared,' Arthur said, diligent as

ever when it came to delivering regular news bulletins. 'Apparently, it's because of a lot of strikes by Spartacist socialists – communists, the lot of them. According to this account the local army chief has ordered them to return to work or be shot.'

It wasn't news that made her feel good. Though House of Remer workers were concentrated almost entirely in the Ruhr, it conjured up hideous pictures of what might be happening to them there.

'I'm going out,' she said. 'I'm going to give the dogs a long walk.'

'In the snow?'

'It isn't so deep – and besides, they like the snow.'

'Silly animals,' her father said, and returned his attention to *The Times*.

Wearing a chocolate-brown wool coat with black velvet frog-fastenings, a black fur hat crammed on her head and covering her ears, her hands deep in a matching muff, Vicky set off across the snow-covered lawn in the direction of the river. Nursing in winter was not as easy as nursing in the summer. There were fewer distractions for the disabled and despite all the many games by the beds and in the communal sitting room – draughts, dominoes, chess, mah-jong, cards – they still grew bored.

She had a new set of VAD workers and, under the nursing sister and two staff nurses who had been with her from the beginning, nursing care ran like clockwork. It was physiotherapy care that grew more difficult.

Once down by the semi-frozen river, with the dogs skittering at her ankles and kicking up clouds of snow, she trudged on for a good two miles before turning for home.

Though it was only three in the afternoon the crisp cold air was beginning to smoke with dusk, and when she saw someone striding towards her from the direction of the house, at first she thought it was Will. Then she saw that the man carving new tracks through the snow was wearing an officer's cap and a military greatcoat.

She stood still, her heart pounding.

The dogs ran in circles around her and then, ever friendly, raced off towards Adam, barking at full throttle and with tails wagging.

He stopped a few feet away from her. Though she hadn't noticed, it had started to snow again and there were snowflakes on his cap and eyelashes.

'I'm sorry,' she said simply. 'So very sorry.'

He cleared his throat and then said, 'Thank you. I got your letter. It was kind of you to write.'

She didn't know what else to say. He looked terrible. His strong-boned face was drawn and haggard, his eyes bleak.

In the end she said, 'Have you been to the house? Have you spoken to my father?'

He nodded, and as she began to walk again he fell into step beside her. 'Yes. You've done a remarkable job. Your father gave me a tour of the wards. All your patients sang your praises.'

A flush of colour touched her cheeks. 'They all just need somewhere in calm surroundings where they can adjust to the reality of what has happened to them. Most of them will never be able to work again, or certainly not in the way they used to.'

She didn't mention his DSO or congratulate him on it. Somehow she didn't think he would want her to. Instead she said, 'Where have you been fighting?'

Beneath his cap, hair the colour of fire curled low in the nape of his neck. She wondered how long he had been on leave.

'Flanders,' he said. 'Ypres.'

She said nothing, because there was nothing she could say. She knew from her nursing experience that the horrors experienced at the Front were so beyond all imagining they couldn't be shared with anyone other than a fellow Tommy.

Compacted snow crackled beneath their booted feet and every now and again a powdering of snow fell from the branches of near by trees.

'Your father tells me it's known at St Dunstan's that your husband is German.'

'Yes.'

He wasn't looking at her. They had come to the part of the river that ran through Shuttleworth Hall's parkland and as they turned away from it, beginning to walk towards the snow-covered lawns, he said, 'That must have been difficult for Max.'

'Yes,' she said again.

He came to a halt.

'Have you thought how difficult it's going to be when the war is over, Vicky?'

She stopped a yard or so in front of him and turned to face him.

'In what way?' she asked, noticing there was a deep scar running through his left eyebrow. A scar that hadn't previously been there.

'For your husband.'

Her eyes widened, startled.

'He's a Remer of the House of Remer, isn't he?'

She nodded, aware of a bubble of fear beginning to rise in her throat.

He was looking at her now, his eyes holding hers. 'The Allies are going to win this war, Vicky, and when it's over there will be war trials. Have you thought of that?'

'War trials?' She took her hand out of her muff, brushing snow away from her face. 'But war trials won't affect Berthold. He isn't a soldier . . . isn't a general . . .'

'He's a member of the House of Remer and so a producer of armaments. It will be enough.'

She sucked in her breath.

'I heard it spoken of and thought I should warn you. Prepare you.'

The shock was so overwhelming she swung away from him, stumbling.

He caught hold of her arm.

She half fell against him, her distress so great at the thought of Berthold standing in a dock alongside war criminals that tears streamed down her face. 'He's a kind, gentle, vulnerable man,' she said in a choked voice as he steadied her. 'Nothing so bad could happen to him. God wouldn't let it happen.'

She knew the instant she said it, what a foolish thing it had been to say. None of the millions maimed and dead had deserved what had happened to them. The war wasn't of God's making and neither were the consequences.

Struggling for self-control she turned away from him, beginning to walk as quickly as the snow would allow, glad that he'd had the sense not to make a response to her idiotic outburst.

As they stepped onto the terrace he said, 'I won't come in again. Give my best wishes to your father and to Max and Paul.'

She fought the temptation to throw her arms around his neck. Instead, she said stiffly, 'Yes. Of course I will. Goodbye, Adam. Good luck.'

He hesitated, as if about to say something, and then merely nodded and turned away from her, walking across the terrace towards the path leading to the drive, his hands deep in the pockets of his snow-covered overcoat, his broad shoulders hunched.

In March, Russia sued for a separate peace with Germany and in April, Germany hammered the Allies at Arras. One weekend, when Paul and Max were home, the little flags on the large map moved constantly. And not in the right direction.

'We're being pushed back towards the Channel,' Vicky

heard Paul say bleakly, and then Max said in an uncertain voice, 'I suppose . . . I suppose that Papa and Uncle Josef will be pleased.'

In July, her father stood brooding over the map and then said to her, 'We're no longer moving backwards, Vicky. We're moving forwards. Blow me, but I think this bally war might be moving to a conclusion.'

Paul thought so too. 'The Germans are withdrawing from the Marne,' he said, repositioning flags with the aid of the latest information in that day's *Times*. 'I think we've got the Kaiser on the run, Aunt Vicky.'

He was right. Suddenly, the mood in the country became fiercely optimistic. Talk of the 'final push' was on everyone's lips.

With American forces pouring into battle in huge numbers and fighting with great heroism, the flags on Paul's map which represented the German army ebbed backwards farther and farther.

August gave way to September and there began to be rumours of a surrender. By the end of October, Germany was living in the shadow of defeat and Austria's empire was disintegrating fast.

On 11 November, in a railway carriage in the forest of Compiègne, Germany signed an armistice.

All over the country church bells rang and people went mad with relief and joy. Paul and Max cycled through Little Ridding's streets with the local Boy Scouts, sounding the all-clear for the last time on bugles and sirens. Everyone was out of doors, cheering, waving flags, letting off fireworks and dancing cakewalks. At Shuttleworth Hall there was a blaze of flags and bunting and her father, well prepared as always, opened up crate after crate of celebratory beer for the men and, for her, a bottle of champagne.

She shared it with him, knowing she was perhaps the only person in the country who was celebrating with such mixed emotions. The war was over and the killing had stopped, and for that blessing her heart was full and overflowing. It was not full and overflowing, though, at the thought of what was possibly happening in Berlin. Was Berthold perhaps only hours away from being arrested by Allied Military Police? And if he were to be arrested, how would she know? How would she get news?

SEVEN

Yorkshire, November 1918

Dear Vicky,

It is my painful duty to inform you that Berthold has been arrested by the Allies and that Josef's arrest is possibly imminent. Zelda and the children remain in Baden-Württemberg where they are safer. The situation in Berlin is chaotic. Food shortages have reached critical proportions and influenza is rampant. People are dying in their hundreds. Getting further news to you as to where Berthold is being held and how long he is likely to be held before trial is not going to be easy, but I will do my best to keep you informed.

Yours respectfully,

Ernst Schulenburg

Vicky stared at the unfamiliar signature. Her first thought was that without Adam's warning that such a thing could happen, she would be falling to pieces entirely. Her second thought was to wonder why it was Ernst who had written to her and not Zelda. Or was Zelda, in Baden-

Württemberg, ignorant as to what was happening in Berlin? Perhaps she too was just receiving news from Ernst of Berthold's arrest.

'I'm leaving for Berlin,' she said to her father as she showed him the letter. 'I can't simply sit and wait for news. I have to be on the spot. I have to try and visit him.'

'Absolutely not!' It was the first time in her life she had ever known her father be angry with her.

With his beloved newspaper still in his hands he rose to his feet, his face a mottled red. 'There are no means for you to travel to Berlin. The war may technically be over, but Allied shipping is still blockading Germany. Ferries and trains will be full of prisoners being repatriated. Whatever the situation in Berlin when Schulenburg wrote to you, it will be worse now the Kaiser has fled to Holland. The whole country will be in an uproar. If it isn't safe for Zelda to return to Berlin, it most certainly isn't safe for you to go there.'

'But I must! There will be Allied authorities I can speak to. British authorities. They need to know that Berthold hasn't been behind House of Remer armament production and the building of battleships. They need to know that Josef is head of the House of Remer, not Berthold!'

'Let Schulenburg deal with them. Let him tell them.' ·

'Ernst is German, Papa. Why should they believe him? I'm the person that needs to contact British authorities.'

Arthur Hudson thrust his newspaper onto the chair behind him. 'If you insist on going, then I am coming with you, for you'll be walking straight into a revolution, Vicky. The streets won't be safe and an Englishwoman with the name of Remer will most certainly not be safe.'

'You're trying to emotionally blackmail me, Papa, and I won't allow you to.'

She turned away from him, walking swiftly towards the door.

'Where are you going now?' he asked, distressed. 'What are you going to do?'

She didn't pause long enough to turn and face him; she simply said over her shoulder, 'I'm going to pack a travelling bag.'

Packing the bag was easy. Travelling anywhere with it, wasn't. Within hours she discovered that her father was right and that crossing the Channel was an impossibility.

'But it's a situation that has to change,' she said to Josephine, 'and until it does I'm going to write ceaseless letters to Mr Lloyd George and see if he can do anything for Berthold.'

Josephine regarded her in consternation. 'The Prime Minister? But he's called an election. He'll be too busy to respond to personal letters – especially personal letters about a . . . about a . . .'

'About a German,' Vicky finished for her. 'Maybe so. But I have to try, Josephine. I have to try everything.'

She wrote letters to every member of the Allied High Command, the Armistice Commission and the Red Cross. Only the Red Cross responded and they were unable to be helpful.

Finally, just when she had given up on Zelda, she received a letter.

Dear Vicky,

Thanks to Allied injustices Germany is hell on earth. I shall never step foot on American or British soil again. Never. As for France I'll go in rags in future rather than patronize a Parisian fashion house.

Josef has undergone the most terrible time. Work stopped in the steel plants and factories even before the armistice was signed. A Social Democratic Republic has been proclaimed in Berlin and all Josef's enemies are now in power. The Socialists say they are going to nationalize the House of Remer. The Allies say they are going to destroy it. God knows who will win, but Josef will be the loser either way. In early November, he was on the point of being arrested but the Allies had second thoughts. Hundreds of other people, however, have not been so fortunate. He has plans to launch a new production programme, but Bolsheviks have occupied the factories and workers' committees – the same as those in Russia – insist they have a say in the running of the firm. Coupled with the fact that coal is almost unobtainable it makes things well-nigh impossible. Food is short. I stand in food lines like a peasant AND I WILL NEVER FORGIVE IT.

It is all the fault of the Allies. The fighting has stopped but their naval blockade continues. No food can get to Germany and people are dying of hunger. I believe you have had a very good war in Britain. Plenty of food and no hardship. The British always come out of things smelling of roses, but this wasn't a war they won on their own and the peace treaty the Allies are cobbling together is a disgrace. Alsace-Lorraine to be handed over to the French? It's monstrous. I wouldn't hurry back to Berlin if I were you, Vicky. As an *Engländerin*, your life would be in danger from the mobs. Zelda

PS Berthold was imprisoned for a short while but is back in the house on Unter den Linden. Josef has moved into the Adlon. After experiencing conditions in Berlin I have returned to Schloss Niedernhall.

Vicky put the letter down, sick with relief. Berthold was no longer under arrest. He would now be able to write to her. Hard on the heels of her relief came outrage at Zelda's bitter, hostile tone. What Allied injustices was she thinking of? It hadn't been Britain which had been thirsting for war, with a king always dressed in military uniform and wearing a steel helmet complete with a vicious spike sticking out of the top of it. As for Zelda's indignation at having to stand in food lines – didn't she realize that British women had had to queue endlessly for food too? And her remark about Britain always coming out of things smelling of roses, as if Britain hadn't suffered at all, was unforgivable.

Also unforgivable and quite, quite incredible, was the way she had barely mentioned Berthold and had only mentioned his release in a hastily added postscript.

'Zelda is Zelda,' her father said placatingly when he read the letter, keeping his thoughts to himself. 'She always speaks before she thinks and obviously writes the same way too. If Josef has lost control of the House of Remer he will be facing a very uncertain future. She's writing from a position of great stress. We have to make allowances.'

Vicky didn't feel so magnanimous. Zelda wasn't a fool. She had brains and, as far as Vicky was concerned, it was unconscionable of her not to use them.

'So will Papa now come and live with us?' Hugo asked her at teatime, unaware of the danger his father had been in.

She ruffled his silky-straight hair. 'I don't know, darling. Maybe. Or maybe, when things have settled down, we will go and live with him.'

He blinked. 'In Germany? We can't go and live in Germany. It's full of all the people we've been fighting against. And don't tell me that I'm a German, which is what Max says when he wants to annoy me, because I'm not. I know I'm not. If I was a German I'd speak German and I don't. Just because Papa is a German doesn't mean that I'm a German, does it? I'm English, aren't I? Just like Grandpa.'

'Because you were born in Britain, you're a British citizen,' she said carefully, not wanting to get too embroiled in the question of his nationality and wishing with all her heart that Max had also been born in Yorkshire.

A week later she received her first letter from Berthold.

Meine Liebchen,

How wonderful it is to be in contact with you again! I know that Ernst wrote to you and that you must have been worrying dreadfully, but lots of people were arrested who have now been set free. Not Gustav Krupp, though. He, it seems, will almost certainly stand trial.

I cannot wait for us to be together again as a family, but the situation in Berlin is even worse than it was before the fighting stopped. You mustn't think of returning here, *Liebchen*. Not yet. Not till things calm down. Naval mutineers are occupying the Imperial Palace, demanding money from the state. They are browbeating and bullying everyone. Government ministers. Military personnel. Civilians. Gunfire can be heard almost hourly and there is constant looting and housebreaking. The Tiergarten is being used as a military camp, but no one knows whether the soldiers are on the side of the mutineers or on the side of the government. Zelda and the children are at Schloss Niedernhall. Josef is sometimes here, more often at the Adlon.

Tell my very dear children that when the madness dies we will be together again and I will once again be their very loving papa, taking them for walks by the lake in the Tiergarten and to the zoo. As for yourself, *Liebchen*, I kiss your picture every night and pray that you remain safe.

Your loving husband,
Berthold

'I hope you won't think badly of me for saying this, Aunt Vicky,' Paul said as he came in from toboganing, stamping snow from his boots, 'but I'm rather relieved we can't go back to Berlin yet. I'm enjoying Upper School and I don't want to leave. I know when we go back you're going to ask my mother if I can finish off my schooling in Yorkshire, but somehow I don't think she'll say yes. For the moment, though, it doesn't matter, does it? We can just go on enjoying life as usual, with the added bonus of knowing soldiers aren't dying in battle any more.'

'We can indeed, darling,' she said, aware, not for the first time, that she and Paul nearly always thought the same way about things.

Though she didn't admit it to anyone, she also felt relief that any question of an immediate return to Berlin was being postponed. When the day came that she and Berthold were reunited there were going to be too many issues to resolve for it to be an occasion to look forward to wholeheartedly. Though she had tried to prepare Hugo for the possibility of again living in Berlin, it wasn't something she could actually imagine herself doing. Her fierce hope was that it wouldn't be necessary and that no matter what Josef's plans for the future, Berthold would feel free enough of all connections with the House of Remer to live with her at Shuttleworth Hall.

As Easter approached, Max said to her, 'You and Grandpa must come early to end-of-term prize-giving so that you get seats at the front because I'm going to be presented with the Inter-House Rugby Trophy and Hugo will be receiving a certificate for having come top of his year in English and maths.'

'Don't worry, sweetheart, we'll be there so early we'll have seats in the middle of the front row.'

'That's good,' he said, well pleased. 'And will you wear

114

your new-length lilac suit, the one that shows your ankles, and the lilac hat trimmed with violets and your long sable stole?'

Aware that Max wanted her to be in what he called 'full fig' and to look as grand as possible, she said, 'If that's what you want me to wear, then I'll wear it.'

'Good,' he said again, 'because you'll look spiffing.'

The next weekend when Paul, Max and Hugo were again home from school, Paul said to her, 'It's splendid news about Max winning his trophy for rugby, isn't it? I wish when I'd won it I'd been presented with it by Captain Priestley.'

'Captain Priestley?' She had been writing out a list of needed medical supplies and her hand came to such a sharp halt ink spilled in a huge blot.

'Captain Priestley, DSO,' he said, thinking she had been prompting him to add mention of it. 'All the chaps think it's ripping news he's going to be presenting the prizes. They're hoping he'll talk about how he won his Distinguished Service Order, but I bet he doesn't.'

Vicky didn't think he would, either. Not only that, but if Adam were to be giving the prizes, she didn't want to be seated conspicuously in the middle of the front row. She had never deliberately disappointed Max, but when it came to at least one of his requests, she had every intention of doing so.

When prize-giving day dawned it was as warm and as sunny as midsummer.

'But it won't last,' her father said, adjusting his gold watch chain across his waistcoated chest. 'The thermometer is already falling. You're going to need that sable stole.'

Ridiculously, she felt as if she was also in need of a drink – a brandy, for preference.

As she waited for Jenny to bring Nancy downstairs she knew very well why she was so nervous. It was because the last time she had been in Adam Priestley's company she had come perilously near to letting her feelings for him show in her eyes. Even just thinking about the moment when his arms had closed around her, to steady her, caused her cheeks to flush with heat. Whatever happened today, she couldn't allow such a response to him to arise again. It would be too shaming. Too embarrassing.

Her hope of arriving late enough to have lost all chance of sitting near the front were dashed as Max darted up to her, saying breathlessly, 'Thank goodness you've arrived! I've had a jolly hard job keeping seats in the front row for you. Hugo put a pile of books on one chair and an umbrella from Lost Property across the other two, but it isn't a wheeze that would have worked for much longer.'

'I'm going to come here when I go to school,' Nancy announced to the world at large, looking approvingly around at St Dunstan's magnificently impressive Great Hall.

'You can't, silly,' Max said, as his mother and grandfather seated themselves on the chairs he had saved for them, his mother a little reluctantly he thought. 'Only boys can come to St Dunstan's. You're going to have to go somewhere else.'

'Well, I won't.' For a four-year-old, Nancy had very definite ideas and a very strong will. 'If I want to come here, I will.' She wriggled onto her chair, saying to Vicky. 'Tell him I'm coming here, Mama. Tell him.'

'I see the headmaster has lost no time in adding DSO after Adam's name on the Old Boys' Board of Honour,' Arthur Hudson said, wondering for how long his bulk was going to be comfortable seated on a wooden chair. 'William will be pleased. These things matter to a man with an only son.'

Suddenly, a line of gowned and mortar-boarded figures began to make their way onto the platform and, as everyone in the main body of the hall rose to their feet, Vicky saw Adam step onto it with them. He was in uniform, his medal clearly displayed.

116

St Dunstan's Upper School pupils were seated in a long phalanx down the left side of the hall and the Preparatory School pupils in a similar phalanx down the right side. At Adam's appearance there was a rustle of excitement from their ranks and murmurs of admiration.

He took his place next to the headmaster. His hair was shorter than it had been when she had seen him last, but was still visible beneath his cap. Against the black of the gowns and mortar boards the red was so distinctive it seemed to sizzle.

The opening hymn was William Blake's 'Jerusalem'.

'And did those feet, in ancient time . . .' she sang, trying to avoid catching his eye.

She failed.

He gave a nod of recognition and a hint of a smile.

'Walk upon England's mountains green . . .' she sang, her heart fluttering somewhere up in her throat.

As the hymn came to an end and the prize-giving proper got under way, she fiercely reminded herself that she had experienced a similar kind of foolishness once before. On the first evening of her twenty-first-birthday trip to Berlin, Berthold too, with his sweet smile and gentle manner, had had the most extraordinary effect on her. Those awakenings of passion had, however, never fully flowered. Much as he loved her and she him, deep sexual need had never played a part in their relationship. Theirs had been a young love, inexperienced and naive – and because of Berthold's passive nature it had remained inexperienced and naive.

Where Adam Priestley was concerned things would be very, very different. Except, of course, not only was she married to a man she would never willingly hurt, she was also innately honourable. As was Adam Priestley. And as well as instinctively knowing that he was not the kind of man to pursue an affair with a married woman, she knew that he had loved his wife deeply and was still grieving for her.

'And Captain Priestley will now present to Max Remer, Captain of North House, St Dunstan's Inter-House Rugby Trophy,' the headmaster announced to a storm of applause.

'He's popular, then, our lad,' her father said to her, flushed with pride.

Aware that she had been in danger of missing her elder son's moment of glory, Vicky dragged her thoughts to the occasion in hand and joined in the enthusiastic clapping.

Max proudly walked up onto the platform and Adam presented him with a trophy so big Max could hardly be seen once he held it aloft.

Fifteen minutes or so later it was Hugo's turn to walk up to Adam and receive a certificate for scholastic achievement in English and maths.

'And one day I will walk up there and get a big silver cup *and* a certificate,' Nancy said, her stocky little legs jutting straight out in front of her. 'And the cup will be for playing rugby even though Max says girls can't play it.'

Despite all her emotional turmoil Vicky's mouth twitched in amusement. Nancy was such a tough little character that, where her future was concerned, nothing would surprise her mother.

Later, as schoolmasters mingled with parents, glasses of sherry in hand, and as pupils scurried about euphoric at the prospect of three weeks' Easter vacation, Adam strode through the throng towards her.

She was ready for him. Neither her smile nor her eyes betrayed the nature of the feelings his nearness aroused in her.

'You carried off your task with great panache,' she said lightly, as if he were a brother or a cousin.

For a moment there was a jolt of surprise in his eyes and then he said in a tone of answering affability, 'Thank you. It isn't something I ever imagined myself doing when I received the Inter-House Trophy at Max's age. It was Harrogate's mayor who presented it to me and, as far as I can remember, I thought he was as old as Noah.'

'I doubt Max thinks the same of you. He was thrilled when he knew you would be doing the presentations.'

Her facial muscles ached with the effort of keeping a carefree smile on her face. They were being jostled on all sides, for nearly every woman there wanted to have a few words with him and all the men were eager to shake his hand and congratulate him on his decoration.

'You look very well,' he said. 'I take it there's been no bad news from Berlin.'

'No. Berthold was arrested, but then released.'

'Good. You must be vastly relieved. When will the two of you be reunited?'

'Probably not for ages. The situation in Berlin is dreadful. Berthold says there are riots in the streets and Bolsheviks are occupying the Remer factories. He's told me not to even try and join him until things are safer.'

A couple knocked into them, trying to get a closer look at Adam's medal.

He smiled courteously, allowed them the closer look and exchanged a few polite words with them. When they had gone on their way, he said, 'It's too crowded in here to talk properly. Let's go outside.'

Vicky looked over the sea of heads, saw that Nancy was safely with her grandpa, and allowed herself to be ushered out of the Great Hall and into the school grounds.

The pressure of his hand beneath her arm made her feel faint. She was aware of curious – and envious – glances in their direction. If Adam noticed them, he showed no signs of it.

'That's better,' he said, as they stepped out into the crisp fresh air. 'I'd like to know more about your husband's position; it sounds complicated.'

119

'You mean in reference to the factories? It isn't really.'

They'd come to a halt beneath a large beech tree. The breeze was chilly and she adjusted her fur so that it lay closer to her throat.

'Berthold was arrested because of the general belief that he is head of the House of Remer. But he isn't. Even before the war started he handed over control to Josef, his younger brother. And it was Josef who involved the House of Remer in armaments contracts and shipbuilding, not Berthold.'

'I see. He must be quite a man to have relinquished a business empire of that scale for pacifist principles.'

Considering his own gallant war record, his attitude to a man he thought a pacifist was remarkably generous.

She said uncomfortably, 'It wasn't quite like that. Berthold simply didn't want the responsibility of managing the steelworks and factories and, unlike Josef, hadn't been brought up to do so.'

'And so there was pressure brought to bear on him?'

'Yes,' she said, remembering her father's insistence that if Berthold hadn't given in to that pressure, the German army would have had fewer munitions and the German navy fewer ships.

Beneath his officer's cap, Adam's brows pulled into a slight frown and she knew that he was reviewing his opinion of Berthold and probably thinking exactly what her father had thought. If his face wasn't quite as haggard as when she had last been with him, it still bore the marks of his loss. There were shadows beneath his blue eyes and deep lines about his mouth. Neither the signs of sleeplessness nor the lines detracted from his physical attractiveness.

'He's right about it not being safe for you and the children to return to Berlin,' he said, moving his cap back a little so that it sat at a rakish angle on his curly hair. 'There's a Red revolution going on in central Europe at the moment. With its

120

army no longer operative, Germany could fall either way. Did Berthold fight? Is he now in the Freikorps?'

'The Freikorps?' She was beginning to feel as ignorant as she had once been about the goods the Remer factories produced.

'The Freikorps is the nearest thing Germany now has to any organized body of men opposed to the communists. It's comprised mainly of former front-line soldiers. I thought it was something your husband might be involved in.'

'No.' She didn't say that though Berthold wasn't a paid-up pacifist, he most certainly wasn't a fighter. Berthold's kind of inadequacies weren't something a man like Adam Priestley would be able to understand. She wondered what his DSO had been awarded for, knowing that for ranks below Lieutenant-Colonel it was awarded only for gallantry just short of deserving the Victoria Cross.

Lots more people were now spilling out of the school and into the grounds and it was obvious their little island of privacy would soon be invaded.

He said with reassurance in his voice, 'Things might be sticky for Berthold for a time when he joins you, but not too seriously. People are too relieved the war is over to persist in violent anti-German behaviour.'

The rakish tilt of his cap was making her feel sick with desire for him. Wondering for how much longer she could keep her feelings from showing in her voice and in her eyes, she said, 'I don't think it's Berthold's intention to come to England.'

She hadn't said it to provoke a reaction from him. It had just been a plain statement of fact.

There was a reaction, though. One he couldn't hide.

'Good Lord,' he said explosively. 'You've been separated for over four years! How can he not go through hell and high water to be with you again?'

121

It was difficult to say which of them was the most taken aback by his outburst.

For a stunned moment their eyes simply held and it was impossible for her to maintain a merely friendly expression in hers – and for him to conceal from himself any longer what the motivation behind his questioning had been.

'Vicky, I . . .'

'No. Please no, Adam.' She put up a hand to ward him off, knowing that if he narrowed the few inches separating them and touched her, she would be lost.

'I have to go.' Her words were rushed, her voice unsteady. 'Nancy . . . my father . . . the children . . . they'll be wondering where I am.'

His eyes were dark with heat and as he made a movement towards her, she turned swiftly, beginning to run. Scores of heads turned in her direction and she knew the gossips would be having a field day for years. She didn't care. Her emotions were in chaos, one half of her absolutely appalled at what had so nearly happened between them, the other half so exultant she thought she would die with the joy of it. He felt the same way about her as she did about him. He might have only just realized it, but the realization had struck deep. She knew it had, because she had seen it in his eyes. Though his grief for Elise was still raw he cared about her just as violently as she cared about him.

'Mama, what on earth is the matter?' Max asked, sprinting to meet her. 'Has there been an accident?'

She came to a halt, sucking in great breaths of air. 'No, darling,' she said when she could speak. 'I was just walking in the grounds and a fox startled me. It was stupid of me to have run. Where are Grandpa and Nancy? Is Hugo with them?'

That night, in bed, she resolved never to speak to Adam alone again and never to seek out opportunities to see him.

The prospect of never doing so caused heartache so intense

it was a physical pain. There was other heartache also. Incredibly, until Adam had put the thought in her mind, it had never occurred to her that as it wasn't safe for her and the children to go to Berlin, Berthold should have announced his intention of journeying to Yorkshire just as soon as civilian travel made it possible for him to do so.

And he'd made no such suggestion.

Maybe it was because he was unwilling to face any hostile anti-German feeling. Maybe not. Whatever the reason, the bottom line was that he wasn't urgently making his way to be with her.

During the following months, with a scaled-down staff, she cared for the remainder of her patients until they were fit enough to be discharged. Then she turned her attention to the task of converting what had been a convalescent home back into a family home.

Paul, now a head and a half taller than her, gave what help he could at weekends and Will, now engaged to Jenny, helped as well.

'Adam would come and give a hand if we asked him,' Paul said as the three of them struggled with the dismantling of the sluice room. 'He gives rugby coaching on Saturday mornings, so I see him regularly.'

'But he's not at the school full-time, is he?' she had asked, startled. 'He isn't now one of the masters?'

'Don't be daft, Aunt Vicky,' Paul said, imitating her Yorkshire way of talking. 'He has a mill to run. Priestley's employ even more workers than Hudson's now.'

She had had to make a very firm resolve not to keep asking him for news of Adam. It was a resolve she didn't always keep. Adam was always in her thoughts and she could only presume she was always in his, for both Paul and Max would say on a weekly basis, 'Captain Priestley's been asking after you.'

123

'I told him we'd just dismantled the sluice room,' Max said on one occasion, chattily. 'It's nice he's so interested in us all, isn't it?'

A month later he telephoned.

The sound of his voice made her weak at the knees. She leaned against the hall wall for support, the receiver slippery in her hands.

'Will you have lunch with me, Vicky?' His rich, dark voice was urgent. 'Tea with me? Anything. We were friends before I so stupidly frightened you away. Let's be friends again. I promise I'll say and do nothing to cause you offence. I just want to see you again. I have to see you again.'

'No . . . I can't . . .' The words were strangled in her throat. She felt utterly panicked, longing to see him again with all her heart but knowing that if she did so she wouldn't have the will power to ignore the electrical excitement that always spiralled between them – and that he wouldn't either.

'Please don't telephone me again, Adam. And don't continue trying to maintain contact via Paul and Max. They think it's just friendly courtesy, but it isn't fair to them.'

'This isn't fair to me, either,' he said with a fierceness that made her heart somersault. 'You haven't seen your husband for five years. He could be with you now, and he isn't. Life is too short to live without love when it's there for the taking. Believe me, Vicky. I know.'

'No,' she said again, stunned by his frankness, feeling as if there was a knife in her chest that was plunging ever deeper. 'You deserve something better than a cheap affair with a married woman.'

'It wouldn't be a cheap affair.' His voice was so authoritative she almost believed him. 'Nothing you ever did could ever be cheap, Vicky. And you wouldn't be a married woman for long. Not if I had my way. Not unless you were married to me.'

It was all too much to handle, and she wasn't handling it well. 'No,' she said for a third time, her voice little more than a whisper. 'Don't telephone me again, Adam. Don't try and contact me.'

And then, without even saying goodbye to him – knowing she couldn't say goodbye to him – she put the receiver down.

In the spring of 1920, fifteen months after the war ended, Berthold at last suggested she return to Berlin.

It's still a devastated city, *Liebchen*, but we must do our best to ignore the riots still taking place and make a new start to our lives. As Max is now nearly ten, perhaps he would like to consider going to one of the academies that specialize in technical subjects. Hugo's school we can discuss when you arrive. As for Nancy, the Auguste-Victoria School on the Nürenbergerstrasse would be ideal. I will wait until you arrive and then we can make the decisions together.

With love and longing.

Your impatient husband,

Berthold

Her reaction was not as euphoric as she knew it should have been. There was all her long-felt reluctance to live in Berlin. There was her profound reluctance to leave the garden she had begun creating. And, though she had never broken her self-imposed vow not to see him alone again, there was her deep reluctance to have the Channel separating her from Adam.

Zelda was also back in communication with her. A letter about Paul's educational future was as abrupt and terse as all her letters had been since the last years of the war.

Dear Vicky,

Paul has been so long in England I cannot imagine him fitting into Berlin life again. I think it best he remains at St Dunstan's and that he then goes to an English university.

Things have changed here so drastically that if it were known Josef has an American stepson, life would be even more difficult for him than it is already. He's gained control of the steelworks and factories again, but reaching full production is an uphill task. So many machines and workshops were smashed to smithereens that rebuilding is taking a long time and as yet only two of the blast furnaces in the Ruhr are in operation.

Berthold tells me you are finally returning with the children. Please ensure Paul understands that, for him, the return will be a visit only. From now on he will have to board full-time at school. If all this sounds unwelcoming, I don't mean it to, but I have endured more these last few years than you can ever imagine. When you see conditions here, you will understand.

Zelda

'I take it Ma has written the same kind of letter to you as she has to me,' Paul said, too happy at the prospect of being able to remain at St Dunstan's to be concerned by his letter's lack of effusive maternal love. 'Why don't you ask Max and Hugo if they'd like to change to being full-time boarders as I did? They'd be able to have rugby coaching on Saturdays, them. I bet they'd much prefer it to going to school in Germany. Any German either of them knew they've long forgotten and, besides, I wouldn't want to be an English boy in a Berlin school. Not with the height of feeling there is about the Peace Treaty.'

The Versailles Peace Treaty was, as everyone knew, a

nightmare, with many German delegates refusing to sign it. Once again, Paul was voicing exactly what she felt herself. That Berthold had even suggested Max and Hugo should attend schools in Berlin had taken her breath away, for the bullying they would be exposed to would be horrendous. And, as Paul said, neither of the boys any longer spoke even a word of German.

With an unpleasant lurch of her stomach she wondered if Berthold was under the impression Max and Hugo had been receiving lessons in German all through the war years? That she, perhaps, had regularly talked to them in German?

With a dreadful feeling of foreboding she unearthed the two large trunks with which she had travelled from Berlin in 1914 and, with very mixed emotions, started the mammoth job of packing for her return.

EIGHT

Berlin, May 1920

Leaning out of the carriage window he was the first thing she saw as the train hissed into Berlin's main railway station.

'Berthold! *Berthold!*'

He was standing at the barrier and as she waved furiously towards him his face lit with joy.

'Is that Papa? Lift me up, please, so that I can see him,' Nancy demanded imperiously, tugging on the skirt of her lilac suit.

As the train juddered to a halt she flung the carriage door open and, leaving Josephine to shepherd the children onto the platform, began running as if she were a young girl and not a mature woman of thirty-two.

In a way she was to remember with pleasure all her life Berthold behaved totally out of character. Instead of waiting for her to reach him at the barrier, he pushed through it, running to meet her.

Her first thoughts in the seconds before she reached his arms, were that he looked much smaller than she remembered, and much older. His hair had thinned and everything about him seemed, somehow, to be diminished. She was uncaring.

As his arms closed around her she was aware only that whatever her emotional chaos where Adam was concerned, her family was at last reunited.

'Vicky, *meine Liebchen*!' As they hugged tight, his cheek against hers was wet with tears. 'I thought this day was never going to come!'

'And I was beginning to think I would never be called *Liebchen* again,' she said, laughing through reciprocal tears as she drew away from him so she could look up into his face.

For a long perfect moment they simply beamed at each other, and then a little dark-haired tornado hurtled towards them.

'So *you're* my papa!' Nancy shouted exultantly, throwing her arms around Berthold's legs and hanging on to them like a limpet.

As he transferred his attention from Vicky to the daughter he had never previously seen, Paul, Max and Hugo walked up to them, Paul with easy confidence, Max with curiosity and Hugo hesitantly.

'Hello, Uncle Berthold,' Paul said as Berthold succeeded in lifting Nancy away from his legs and into his arms. 'It's nice to see you again. You're looking well, sir.'

It wasn't strictly true. Though Berthold didn't look ill, he looked far older than his thirty-four years.

'And you look . . . *Wundervoll*!' The change from the ten-year-old boy who had left Berlin nearly six years ago, to the six-foot-tall sixteen-year-old shaking his hand, was so great Berthold looked positively dazed.

'And I'm Max . . . sir,' Max said, deeply uncomfortable at meeting in such a public place the father he scarcely remembered.

Berthold set Nancy back on her feet and gazed at the dark curly-haired nine-year-old who looked nothing like him.

'And I'm Papa,' he said gently and, sensitive to Max's

awareness of the many people around them, didn't cause him more embarrassment by hugging him, but simply held out his hand.

Max shook it and then, recovering his equilibrium as swiftly as always, said, 'And this is Hugo, Papa. He doesn't remember Berlin, but I do.'

Reluctantly, Hugo stepped forward. 'Hello, Papa,' he said shyly, keeping very close to Vicky.

'Hello, Hugo.' Berthold bent down to him, recognizing himself in Hugo's slight build, pale straight hair and uncertain manner. 'Welcome to Berlin. I've missed you a great deal these last six years. We've a lot of time to make up for, haven't we?'

Hugo nodded, still reluctant to talk to his strange, German papa.

Berthold straightened up and, his eyes still moist, said to Vicky, 'I think it is time to take our little family home, *Liebchen*.'

'But not without Josephine.' There was laughter in her voice. 'And certainly not without our luggage.'

Standing in a little family group they waited for Josephine, who was making her way down the platform towards them, heavily laden porters on either side of her.

'It's good to see you again, Josephine,' Berthold said as porters and luggage came to a temporary halt.

'Likewise, sir. It's been a long six years.'

'It has indeed, Josephine.'

With Vicky at one side of him, her arm tucked in his, Nancy at his other side clinging tightly to his hand, and with his two sons and his nephew walking a few feet behind him, Berthold led the way out of the station to two chauffeured motorcars.

As the luggage was loaded Paul, trying not to sound too disappointed that his mother hadn't been at the station to meet him, said, 'Is my mother in Berlin or Baden-Württemberg, Uncle Berthold?'

'Berlin,' Berthold said, resting a hand in a comradely fashion on his shoulder. 'She is at home, waiting for you. German ladies don't like to have emotional reunions in public.'

There was a pause in which a pin could have been heard to drop and then Paul said, 'My mother is American, Uncle Berthold.'

It was said pleasantly but Berthold froze in awkwardness and Max sucked in his breath.

'Paul is forgetting that Zelda took out German citizenship before the war,' Vicky said, smoothing the moment over by behaving as if nothing awkward had happened. 'Now, how are we going to divide up? Would you three boys like to go in the car taking Josephine, while Papa and I take Nancy with us, in the second car?'

'That's a good idea.' Max shot his mother a look of relief, hoping to goodness his father wasn't going to start referring to her as a German Frau.

Once in the second of the cars with Nancy seated comfily between them, Berthold said, 'I didn't realize Paul would be so unaware of how Zelda thinks of herself. In everything but birth she is German now. And she will expect him to speak German.'

'Then her expectations will be disappointed, Berthold. None of the children has had the opportunity to continue with lessons in German. The minute war was declared German was taken off every school syllabus in England – and it still hasn't been reinstated. And though Paul hasn't lived in America since he was a small child, he is still very American – and proud of being so.'

He frowned in concern. 'Being American – or British – is still difficult in Berlin. The sooner Paul, Max and Hugo get to grips with German again, the easier they will find living here.'

Aware they were heading towards a conversational

minefield she wasn't yet ready for, she changed the subject, saying, 'The city has altered so much, Berthold, it's hard to recognize it.'

Shops that had once glittered expensively now had windows displaying only shoddy goods. Peeling billboards were everywhere. One large poster, ripped and defaced, depicted a giant red fist smashing into an assembly at the Reichstag, the words 'Vote Spartacus' emblazoned across it in giant lettering. Everywhere people were walking aimlessly, seemingly without purpose. The frenetic activity, so much a part of Berlin, was shockingly absent.

'Things still haven't settled down,' Berthold said, his voice strained. 'A few months ago a peaceful political demonstration turned into a bloodbath. There's bad public feeling about the number of war criminals awaiting trial – and how Josef and I are not among their number is a miracle – and there's growing bad feeling about the Jews and the amount of influence they have.'

'Do they have a lot of influence?' Vicky asked, seeing another political poster, this time with the word 'Juden' written in large letters.

'I don't know.' He flashed her a wry smile. 'I only know that I don't have influence any more, not even in Remer factories.'

She didn't want the subject of the steelworks and factories to mar their reunion until later and she was deeply grateful when he didn't pursue the subject.

Their car sped through the familiar leafy acres of the Tiergarten towards the Brandenburg Gate and she noticed that even the Tiergarten no longer seemed a happy place to be.

'We're nearly home,' he said to her, across the top of Nancy's curly hair.

She smiled, trying not to let her growing panic show. How,

132

after the life they were accustomed to living at St Dunstan's and Shuttleworth Hall, could Max, Hugo and Paul adapt to living in what had become not only a desperately impoverished city, but also a brutal city? And how could she allow Nancy to grow up in it?

'Where are the sheep?' Nancy asked, as if on cue. 'We have sheep at home. And we have a river.'

'We have a river here as well, *Liebling*. It's called the Spree.'

'And will I be able to paddle in it? Does it have otters in it?'

'No, *Liebling*. It has cement embankments. But look how pretty the trees are – aren't they a pretty green?'

Accustomed to the greenery of the Dales, Nancy was not as impressed by Unter den Linden's lime trees as Berthold had hoped she would be.

And nor was she impressed as their car swung through giant iron gates and she realized her new home was one without any countryside in sight.

'Shuttleworth Hall is much prettier,' she said to him with North Yorkshire bluntness. 'I'm glad we're not going to live here for always. I wouldn't like it.'

Moments later, as he helped Vicky out of the car, Berthold said, 'I can see it is going to take time for the children to get accustomed to their new life in Berlin. We simply have to be patient, *Liebchen*.'

Knowing that the conversation about their future was going to have to take place as soon as there was the privacy for it, Vicky stepped into the mansion's mausoleum-like entrance hall, feeling as if she were stepping into a prison.

As Berlin had grown shabby, so had the interior of the house. The dark red marble walls and floors were dull and, in several places, cracked. On the ceiling, gold filigree was flaking.

Several dozen yards away, at the foot of the bronze and

133

Marble grand stairway, stood Zelda. Behind her, several stair-treads up the staircase, sat a small boy she knew must be Claus. Farther up still, sat two small girls.

Eager as she was to make their acquaintance, Vicky's entire attention was on her cousin. In the past it had always been Zelda who, after long partings, had rushed up to her, fizzing with energy and vitality, dark eyes blazing with the pleasure of seeing her again.

Now the too-thin figure at the bottom of the stairs didn't move.

Neither did anyone else, not even Paul.

Vicky's heart began to pound. She ran a tongue nervously across her bottom lip and then, feeling as if she were stepping off a precipice into an unknown void, she moved swiftly forward, opening her arms wide.

'Zelda! Oh, Zelda! How I have missed you!'

It was true. Suddenly, all the crossness she had felt at the crass and clumsy remarks in Zelda's letters was forgotten. She was aware only that Zelda had always been the person closest to her in the whole world. That she was the sister she had never had and that she was overjoyed at being with her once again.

For a terrible second, as her arms closed around her, Vicky thought Zelda wasn't going to respond – and then Zelda was hugging her fiercely, saying in her familiar cracked-ice voice: 'The war hasn't aged you, Vicky. You got the best deal. I got the short straw.'

'Later,' Vicky said gently, mindful of the many little pairs of ears listening to them. 'For now just enjoy your reunion with Paul. It's going to be hard for you to recognize him, he's grown so much. And do speak English to him, Zelda. He hasn't been able to keep up with his German. And then, later, you can introduce me to Lotti and her little sister and I want you to meet Nancy.'

Zelda looked beyond Vicky to where a tall, dark-haired young man was standing next to Berthold.

'Landsakes!' she said, shocked into using an Americanism for the first time in years. 'Are you Paul?'

''Fraid I am, Ma,' Paul said, walking towards her with easy self-assurance and a wide grin. 'Six years has this effect on ten-year-olds. They grow.'

'Like Redwood trees, it would seem,' Zelda said with a glimpse of her old dry humour. She hugged him and kissed him and then held him away from her appraisingly, saying, 'You've been away too long for me to feel comfortable having you refer to me as Ma. Why don't you call me Zelda? I'd prefer it.'

His eyebrows rose, but he said equably, 'If that's how you want it, Ma . . . Zelda . . . that's fine by me.'

Determined though she was to do everything to recreate the closeness that had once existed between herself and Zelda, Vicky was already cross with her again, certain that Zelda wanted Paul to refer to her by her Christian name so that no one outside the family would know he was her son. An English cousin was something she couldn't hide, not when the cousin in question was married to her brother-in-law, but an American son was something Zelda had obviously become too *berlinerisch* to want to admit to.

'Who are those children?' Nancy asked, tugging at Berthold with one hand and pointing to Claus and his two sisters with the other. 'Why are they staring at us like that? Why don't they speak?'

'They're your cousins, *Liebling*. Claus, come and say hello to Paul, Max, Hugo and Nancy. And you as well, Lotti and Ilse. Come downstairs and make friends.'

As Zelda's children did as he asked, Vicky saw with a shaft of amusement that she had been right about Lotti. Where Claus and Ilse were as fair-haired as their father, Lotti was all

135

Zelda in colouring, dark-haired and dark-eyed and, if the expression in her eyes was anything to go by, as full of lively impudence as Nancy.

'Claus, this is Nancy,' Berthold said, squatting down by Nancy's side. 'Nancy, this is your cousin, Claus. He is eight.'

'Pleased to meet you,' Nancy said forthrightly, feeling very grown-up and important.

'*Freut mich*,' Claus said stiffly.

Though Vicky couldn't have sworn to it, she thought she saw a look of satisfaction on Zelda's face.

'Now then, Claus,' Berthold said reprovingly. 'Remember what I told you – and what I've taught you – now your cousins are here, you must speak English as well as German. And they will speak German as well as English.'

Max and Hugo shot each other panic-stricken glances.

Paul cleared his throat. '*Ich heiße Paul*,' he said, doing his best to help things along and hoping he wouldn't be required to say much more until he'd had the chance for a bit of swotting.

He held out his hand to Claus. Claus took it, clicking his heels as he did so.

It was a step too far for Paul. 'Can't do that, I'm afraid,' he said cheerfully. 'How about you say hello to Max and Hugo?'

'*Ich heiße Lotti*,' Lotti said to Nancy, uncaring of her Uncle Berthold's request that she summon up the English he had taught her. '*Und das ist Ilse*,' she added, dragging her little sister by the hand behind her.

Nancy was not a child who was ever stumped for long and she liked the look of this cousin who was so near her in age. 'Ik iza Nancy,' she said, and clicked her heels.

There was smothered laughter from Paul, Max and Hugo and Claus said sternly, 'In Germany, girls do not click heels.'

Nancy regarded him witheringly, aware that where boys

were concerned Berlin was no different to Yorkshire. 'Maybe not,' she said bullishly, 'but if I want to, I will.'

Before Claus could make any kind of a response a small animal charged into the hall, barking frenziedly.

'Wastl!' Paul cried, as the dog made a leap into his arms. 'Look how he's remembered me, Uncle Berthold! He has, hasn't he?'

By the way Wastl was frantically licking Paul's face, it was obvious to everyone that the elderly little Dackel had a memory as long as an elephant's.

'Let's leave the children and Wastl to it,' Zelda said to Vicky. 'We've things to talk about and we can't do it standing in the hall.'

'And these introductions among the children can't continue in the hall,' Berthold said, standing upright again and taking hold of Nancy's hand. 'I'm going to take them all into the drawing room where they can have tea and cakes.'

'*Tee und Kuchen?*' Max said, never having forgotten such an important word as cake and entering into the spirit of the thing. 'Jolly good, Papa. Let's go.'

As Zelda and Vicky walked into Zelda's vast bedroom the first thing that met them was the sight of themselves in a huge, heavily carved mirror.

Zelda came to an abrupt halt.

'There,' she said. 'Now do you see? Now do you understand just how much I have suffered?'

Vicky stared at their reflections. Always, Zelda had been the one who had turned all heads wherever they had gone. Now, innately modest as she was, even she knew she was the head-turning one. She was wearing the ankle-skimming lilac suit and long sable stole she had worn on her last meeting with Adam. Her small hat, trimmed with closely packed violets, hugged her head, flattering the gold of her hair. Though laughter lines were visible at the corners of her eyes, there were no other signs she was now in her early thirties.

Zelda, five years her senior, was not so lucky. The hardness there had always been in her nature now showed in her face. Her high cheekbones no longer gave her face a sculpted look, instead they emphasized a gauntness that had never previously been there. Her figure had also lost its luscious curves and, as if conscious of the fact, she was wearing a dark-coloured silk dress that did nothing for the dramatic impact of her night-black hair.

'You need to put a little weight back on, Zelda. That's all,' she said a little awkwardly, taking off her hat and laying her stole over the back of a familiar, spindly legged chair.

'And I will.' The words were said vehemently and her dark eyes flashed fire. 'And I'll get my looks back, by God I will!'

For a heart-stopping moment Vicky was reminded of Nancy, who was always saying 'I will' with equal fierceness. Perhaps Nancy, when she grew up, was going to be as strong-willed – and difficult – as her aunt. It was a thought she couldn't quite cope with and she thrust it to the back of her mind.

'You may have been on short rations in England,' Zelda said, picking up a long ebony holder from her dressing table and putting a small black Russian cigarette into it, 'but you didn't go hungry. I can tell that by looking at you.'

She lit the cigarette, inhaled deeply and then blew smoke out through her nose. 'Thanks to the naval blockade we went hungry in Berlin. In Berlin we *starved*.'

She moved across to one of the long windows that looked out towards Unter den Linden's lime trees. 'I know by your letters that after the Armistice life in Britain just went back to being normal. There were no revolutions for you, in Yorkshire, were there? Your army didn't collapse like a deck of cards, did it? Your king didn't go scurrying off to Holland, did he?'

Slowly, Vicky came and sat opposite her.

Zelda gave a harsh, mirthless laugh. 'God, you've no idea what it was like here, Vicky. There were riots in the streets, Bolsheviks in our factories and Allied army personnel barracked here, in the house. And though Josef has more or less gained control of the Remer factories again, other things haven't improved. In February, the police turned machine-gun fire on a crowd demonstrating outside the Reichstag. Machine-gun fire! Can you imagine? I could see people from here, dammed up against the Brandenburg Gate, shouting and screaming.'

She shuddered and took another deep draw on her cigarette. 'There is no sense of order in the country, no sense of control. Germany needs a leader and hasn't got one. The Fatherland is dying. Britain isn't dying, is it? Britain, as usual, is simply going from strength to bloody strength.'

Vicky hugged her arms to her chest. 'I'm sorry life has been such hell for you,' she said sincerely, 'and I'm sorry you feel so bitter at my having left Berlin when war broke out. But my going, and you staying, were the choices we made, Zelda. What matters now to us as a family, is the future. And we need to be friends and our children need to be friends.'

Zelda gave an unladylike snort. 'German children, English children and an American child? What kind of a mix is that? Berthold may have taught Claus a little English, but take it from me, the words will be sticking in his throat. As for Paul . . .' She averted her eyes from Vicky's and looked out towards the lime trees. 'I once thought I would be able to make a German out of him, but those days are long gone. I don't even feel as if I'm his mother any more. He's become more your child than he is mine.'

As Vicky started to protest, she waved her into silence with her cigarette-holder. 'I'm not upset about it, Vicky. I'm relieved. Life in Berlin is difficult enough without my parading an American-born son everywhere. I take it that Paul will be returning to St Dunstan's?'

'If that is what you want, Zelda. It's certainly what Paul wants.'

'And Max and Hugo?'

Vicky hesitated and then said, 'I still have to discuss Max and Hugo's future with Berthold.'

'Good luck to you. Discussions with Berthold are usually totally futile. Ask Josef.'

The contempt in her voice was naked, but with great self-discipline Vicky didn't rise to it. She said, 'Where is Josef? Is he in Berlin?'

'He's in the Ruhr, trying to prove to Allied inspectors that all tools in Remer factories used for making armaments have been destroyed. Tell me how you see Max and Hugo's future.'

'I see it as being in Yorkshire – and in Yorkshire with their papa. I want Berthold to live with us at Shuttleworth Hall.'

Zelda's sleek eyebrows rose high. 'Berthold is under the impression you have all just arrived here in order to stay for good.'

'I know. I'm hoping he'll see things differently when I've talked to him.'

Zelda rose to her feet and crossed the room, stubbing her half-smoked cigarette out in the ashtray on her dressing table. 'I hope you're successful, Vicky,' she said with feeling. 'Because it would be the best thing for everyone if you did so. You didn't fit into Berlin life before the war and, like Paul, there's no chance at all of you doing so now. As for the children, even if they got to grips with the language they'd never be accepted. After six years in England they're always going to speak the language with an unmistakable English accent. They'll be bullied horrendously in school and socially ostracized out of it. For their sake, and yours, return to

Yorkshire as soon as possible. And for Josef's sake,' she added, her tongue as tart as ever, 'take Berthold with you.'

That night, alone in the bedroom they had shared together before the war, Vicky finally had the opportunity she had been waiting for. 'We need to talk, Berthold,' she said, looking at him through her dressing-table mirror.

Her waist-length hair was unpinned and she was wearing a cream silk nightdress edged in coffee-coloured lace.

Standing a few feet away from her, Berthold was unfastening his white piqué bow tie.

'I know, *Liebchen*,' he said, avoiding her eyes as he fumbled with the tie. 'I know you're nervous. It's been a long time and I'm nervous too. Perhaps tonight it would be best if I didn't attempt to . . . to . . .'

As she realized what it was he had assumed she wanted to talk about, she flushed scarlet, not out of embarrassment at the thought of their resuming marital relations again, but with shame because such a thought had been the last thing on her mind.

'I want to talk about the children, Berthold,' she said swiftly, putting down the heavy silver-backed hairbrush she had been holding. 'And about Berlin.'

Relief crossed his face to be speedily followed by concern. 'What about the children and Berlin?' he asked, struggling now to remove the stud from his wing collar.

She turned around on her stool so that she was no longer looking at him through the mirror, but face to face.

'I think living permanently in Berlin is going to be too difficult for them, Berthold. And that it is going to be too difficult for me. What we would like is for you to live with us in Yorkshire.'

'*Unmöglich!*' It was an indication of how distressed he was that he reacted in German.

'But why is it impossible? Berlin is still devastated by the consequences of the war. Little Ridding isn't. The boys enjoy the school they go to in Yorkshire – and it is a good school. Under the present circumstances, school life in Berlin will be nearly impossible for them. Everything would be so much easier if you would only live with us in Yorkshire, instead of us living with you in Berlin.'

Slowly, he sat down on the edge of the bed, his hands clasped between his knees. 'But you and the children returning to Berlin is what we have both been planning and looking forward to for so long, *Liebchen*. And everything is going so well. Max and Hugo are already remembering a little German and Nancy doesn't seem to need German to make herself understood. She and Lotti are already as thick and thieves and Ilse is following Hugo around in exactly the same way you said Nancy used to do when she was a toddler.'

She rose to her feet and moved across to him, sitting by his side. 'The plan for the children and me to return to Berlin has always been your plan, Berthold dear. Not mine. And not the children's. We are just here because we so longed to see you again and because we want to be a reunited family again. It would be easiest, though, to be a reunited family in Yorkshire. Surely you can see that, Berthold?'

'It isn't what I want,' he said stubbornly. 'I want my children brought up as Germans – even if they will be Germans who also speak English.'

'At the moment, they *only* speak English,' she said, trying to humour him into seeing the situation sensibly. 'Your English is so flawless there won't be the language problems for you in Yorkshire that there will be for the boys in Berlin. And in a village like Little Ridding you won't meet with violent anti-German feeling, whereas the boys will certainly meet with anti-British feeling here.'

He groaned, holding his head in his hands, and then he

looked towards her, saying, 'If I promise that by the end of the summer I will think about leaving Germany for England, will you promise that until then you and the children will live here as Berliners, as Zelda and her children are Berliners?'

His eyes were so pleading that much against her better judgement she said, 'I promise, but only until the end of the summer, Berthold. Only until the start of St Dunstan's Michaelmas term.'

Once again there was relief in his eyes and once again it was fleeting.

'About bed, *Liebchen*,' he said nervously. 'I'm not sure that I . . . It has been a long time and I –'

She raised one of his hands and pressed it against her cheek. 'Let's go to bed grateful we can lie in each other's arms again,' she said gently. 'There's no need for us to rush this part of our reunion. We can just be content to be together again.'

An hour later she lay in their vast double bed, struggling for sleep. It wouldn't come. Having Berthold sleeping by her side felt too strange, as did being back in the house she had always disliked so intensely. Another thing she found strange was that neither Max nor Hugo seemed to share her aversion for the Remer mansion. They seemed, in fact, to relish it.

'There's a whopping great statue of Hercules on the first floor,' Max had said to Hugo after his first exploratory expedition. 'It's an absolute whizzer, come and see.'

Nancy too, once Lotti had introduced her to the enormous nursery, had soon forgotten the mansion's lack of parkland and river. 'There's a giant rocking horse and lots and lots of dolls and Lotti is now my best friend and she says I can have however many of her dolls as I want for my own,' she'd said breathlessly when Vicky had gone in to say goodnight to her. 'And I like Papa,' Nancy had continued. 'I like his spectacles and his moustache and the funny way he parts his hair in the

143

middle. And I like Claus too. He's teaching me German and I can already count from one to ten. *Eins, zwei, drei, vier, fünf, sechs, sieben, acht, neun, zehn.*'

It had been quite a performance and it had left Vicky with very mixed feelings. It was good, of course, that her children and Zelda's had become friends so quickly and easily and that they were already beginning to be able to communicate with each other. The problem was she didn't want them to adapt too completely to life in Berlin. She didn't want them to become Germanized in case, if they did, they became strangers to her.

'It's only for the summer,' she said reassuringly to herself, 'and then next summer, Claus, Lotti and Ilse can come and stay at Shuttleworth Hall.'

She closed her eyes, certain she could at last sleep.

Adam's image burned the backs of her eyes.

She opened them again swiftly, tormented by her mental unfaithfulness. Staring into the darkness she was forced to face the knowledge that her feelings for Adam were too deep ever to change. Though she and Berthold were reunited, her heart still belonged to Adam Priestley – and always would do.

By the end of the summer, when it was time for Vicky and the children to return to Yorkshire, the change in her and Berthold's relationship had become something they both knew was not going to be reversed. Platonic friendship and deep affection suited Berthold. It was something he was good at, and for the first time Vicky realized what a strain the sexual part of their marriage must once have been for him.

It was a knowledge that freed her to speak to him about her feelings for Adam.

'Another man?' His bewilderment was total. 'You're not asking for a divorce, *Liebchen*, are you?' His distress was almost childlike. 'I couldn't bear the thought of a divorce.

What would happen to the children? What would happen to us? How could we still be such loving friends?'

He grew so agitated she had to take his hands firmly in hers. 'Nothing is going to change between us, Berthold. We will always be each other's dearest friend. And I'm not asking for a divorce. I just don't want to have secrets from you. When I came here, at the beginning of the summer, it was to be a wife to you again – if you had wanted me to be. But it hasn't been like that, Berthold, has it?'

Her eyes pleaded for his understanding. 'And because it hadn't been like that – and because we are both happy that it hasn't been like that – I want to be free to give my love to Adam.'

He cried, but he didn't suggest that their own relationship became sexual again, and by the time she and their children again stepped on the train on their way to Ostende, he was talking about visiting them for Christmas just as if their conversation had never taken place.

NINE

Yorkshire, August 1924
Paul strolled out of Shuttleworth Hall and, hands thrust in the pockets of his grey flannels, strolled along the terrace and round to the rear of the house where his great-uncle's latest pride and joy, a Lanchester, was garaged in what had originally been the Hall's carriage-house.

Today was a red-letter day in his life. He'd been twenty for all of a week and his American grandfather was making a special visit to Yorkshire to spend time with him. Not only that, but his great-uncle Arthur was allowing him to drive the Lanchester down to Little Ridding's station in order that he could meet his grandfather from the Harrogate train.

As he entered the carriage-house and drew the Lanchester's keys from his pocket, he was whistling. Since he was five, he had met his grandfather only twice, and on those visits, he had formed an affectionate relationship with him. Relationships were something he was good at. He even managed to enjoy a good relationship with his difficult and complex mother.

He slid behind the wheel and turned the key in the ignition. Just as he was fond of his grandfather, but didn't know him well enough to love him as he loved his great-uncle, so he was fond of his mother, but didn't love her in the way he loved his aunt. His awareness of this disparity in feeling didn't cause him guilt. Ever since he could remember, Vicky had been more of a mother to him than Zelda had ever been – and there was also the inescapable fact that Vicky was intrinsically lovable and Zelda, though it pained him to admit it, wasn't.

As he drove the Lanchester down the tree-lined drive, he pondered the mystery that was Zelda. The present situation at Shuttleworth Hall was a case in point. All his German half-siblings were, as usual, spending their summer holidays at Shuttleworth Hall as was a school friend of Lotti's, a quiet, grave-eyed child by the name of Hester. Berthold was there too, but Zelda, despite Vicky's urging, was not.

'I vowed in 1918 I would never set foot on British or American soil and it's a vow I intend keeping,' she'd said to him tartly when he'd told her how much everyone wanted her to be with them.

Little Ridding's stationmaster, who had been elderly for as long as Paul could remember, was now stationmaster in name only and, as his slim-shouldered grandson officiated for him, he spent his days seated on a bench outside the waiting room, watching the world go by.

At the sight of Paul, his eyes lit up. 'Well, then, young fellow-me-lad, how's tha' doing?' he said, greeting him with all the familiarity of an old friend as the train steamed into view. 'Who is it coomin' 'ome now? Ah'd think Shuttleworth Hall was full to bustin' already, what with all them young German tykes 'ere agin.'

'They do make the place a little crowded,' Paul said with a grin, knowing there was no rancour in the remark. 'And I'm here to meet my American grandfather. He's visiting as part of my twentieth-birthday celebrations.'

'Americki, is it? Then 'e's coomin' a long road. He'll be needin' a good pint of Yorkshire tea when 'e gets 'ere.'

At the thought of his grandfather drinking from a thick china pint pot – which was the way Yorkshire workingmen drank their tea – Paul's grin deepened.

He'd been fourteen, when, in the heady days after the end of the war, his suavely sophisticated grandfather had previously crossed the Atlantic to visit him. It was a visit that had been a success. Three years later, in the company of a friend of his great-uncle's who was making a business trip to New York, he had travelled to America to spend his long summer holidays with his grandfather.

The ostentatious and ornate Fifth Avenue mansion had been disconcertingly similar to the Remer mansion on Unter den Linden and, for the first time, he had been able to understand why his mother had always felt so at home there. His own reaction had been the exact opposite, as it had been when living in Berlin. Both he and his aunt Vicky found that grandiose luxury gave them claustrophobia.

He'd left America when only five but he was well aware that in looks and manner there was still something decidedly American about him, something that set him apart not only from his half-brother and half-sisters in Berlin, but also from his Yorkshire cousins. That something wasn't, though, enough to make a New Yorker out of him. If he was ever to settle in America he knew it would be in up state New York, or Vermont or New Hampshire, somewhere there were woods and rivers and small townships. For the moment, however, he was happy to be living in Yorkshire and happy to be welcoming his grandfather back to it.

With the train now puffing to a halt a solitary carriage door opened. The figure that emerged was splendidly majestic, for with his portly build and immaculately trimmed goatee beard, Charles Wallace resembled the late King Edward VII. But instead of the homburgs Edward VII had favoured he was wearing a stylish grey trilby set at a jaunty angle. His suit was grey too, his waistcoat criss-crossed by a heavy silver chain. In one kid-gloved hand he carried a silver-topped walking cane and in the other a half-smoked cigar.

'Welcome back to Yorkshire, Grandfather,' Paul said, striding to meet him.

'Wonderful to be here, my boy.'

As the porter began speedily removing brass-cornered travelling cases from the train onto a trolley, Charles passed his half-smoked cigar into the receptive hand of the aged figure seated on the bench and gave his American-born grandchild a warm handshake and a pat on the back that was almost a hug.

Then, not troubling to retrieve the cigar, he walked with Paul out of the station and towards the waiting Lanchester.

His beetling eyebrows rose slightly. 'What's this? Has Arthur finally said goodbye to his Rolls?'

'Last year. The Lanchester is a wonderful-looking car, though, don't you think?'

'It is. Where is its chauffeur?'

'You're looking at him.'

As the porter loaded the luggage, Paul saluted and opened the front passenger door.

Charles chuckled and stepped into the car.

'Good as you might be at it, chauffeuring is never going to be part of your future, Paul. And it's your future, particularly your financial future, that I've crossed the Atlantic in order to discuss.'

Certain his grandfather was about to announce he was financing him through college, Paul gritted his teeth. He'd managed to delay the ticklish subject of Oxford for two years by making himself useful to his aunt and Will in the nursery garden. Now it seemed as if all delay was over.

'I didn't intend getting into such a heavy subject so quickly, Grandfather,' he said as he settled himself behind the wheel.

'But if you're talking about Oxford, it's only fair to tell you I don't want to go. Academia bores me.' He gunned the engine into life. 'Like Aunt Vicky, I like to be out in the open air. I don't want this to come as too much of a shock, but I want to become a rose-breeder. It's something Aunt Vicky and Will Patchett have been trying their hands at for a few years now and it's something I'd like to go at whole hog.'

He eased the Lanchester away from the station, waiting for his grandfather's wrath to fall on him in full flood.

It didn't do so.

'Interesting,' was all his grandfather said and then, after a little pause, 'It never occurred to you that I might have plans for you to step into my shoes on Wall Street?'

'At the bank?' Paul was so disconcerted he nearly drove the Lanchester into a ditch. Hurriedly righting the wheel, he said, 'Good grief, no! I'd be no use whatsoever in a bank!'

'No,' his grandfather agreed, not seeming too overly distressed. 'You wouldn't. Which is why I have never made any such plans – and don't intend making them.'

Paul looked across at him. 'And you're not annoyed at the thought of me ducking out of Oxford?'

'Not if you've carefully thought it through. How had you planned to subsist, though, as a rose-breeder? It's a long-term occupation, isn't it? You'll have no financial return for years.'

'Probably not, but I don't have to worry about a roof over my head. Shuttleworth Hall is my home for as long as I want it to be. Aunt Vicky made that clear from day one. Naturally, though, I shan't want to live on her and Great-uncle Arthur's generosity and I thought I'd hire out as a general gardener.'

His grandfather made an explosive snorting sound and when he could trust himself to speak said vehemently, 'A rose-breeder I'll just about accept, but no grandson of mine becomes a jobbing gardener!'

Paul winced. 'It would only be until I'd established a name

for myself as a breeder,' he said defensively, 'and it would be a necessity. I receive nothing from my father's will until I'm thirty.'

'I'm aware of that, my boy.'

The road was following a curve in the river and Charles looked at the view appreciatively and then said, 'The main reason for my visit is to tell you I've cut your mother out of my will and have made you my heir. There will be something for my Remer grandchildren, of course, but as your mother seems determined to bring them up as if they had no American blood whatsoever, the amounts will reflect that circumstance. I feel fit and dandy enough to last for at least another couple of decades, so you won't be a wealthy man tomorrow, but you will always be able to draw down on some of what is coming to you. I've specifically arranged that. And now let's change the subject. What changes are there at Shuttleworth Hall?'

'The main one is that Josephine has married a local man and has a home of her own in Little Ridding. She still helps out with the cooking, though.' He flashed his grandfather a grin. 'There'll be curd tarts for tea, just as always.'

Only much later that day was Paul sufficiently over the shock to be able to think straight and to say, 'I know you don't want to talk further about making me your heir, Grandfather, but there are questions I need to ask, things I need to know.'

It was mid-evening and dinner had not yet been served. Nancy, Ilse, Lotti and Lotti's friend, Hester, had had supper and were enjoying a last half-hour before bedtime, playing a riotous game of 'tag' on the lawn. Claus was down by the river. Max and Hugo were seated at a garden table on the terrace and playing chess, watched by Berthold. Vicky was nowhere in sight and Arthur Hudson was in the drawing room, enjoying a pre-prandial whisky and soda.

'I'll give you twenty minutes, no longer,' Charles said, as if

Paul was a banking client. 'And we'll walk over to the summer house to talk.' He nodded in the direction of Max and Hugo, saying drily, 'Little pitchers have big ears.'

As they walked across the grass together Lotti could be heard squealing, '*Nein!* You can't tag me here, Nancy. I'm on a cluster of daisies and *everyone* knows that clusters of daisies are home!'

'Thank goodness the Berlin contingent now speak excellent English,' Charles said, pausing to watch as Lotti and Nancy prepared to battle the issue out. 'It's a circumstance that owes nothing whatsoever to your mother and everything to your aunt. Without her efforts, I would still be conversing with them only with the help of an interpreter.'

He resumed walking towards the summer house and Paul fell into step beside him, refraining from pointing out that the language ability worked both ways and that Max, Hugo and Nancy now spoke pretty good German.

'Now, what are all these things you need to know?' his grandfather said, getting to the point. 'It's nothing to do with the financial side of things, is it? The executor I have appointed will take you through that particular minefield, as – at the appropriate time – will the financial advisors you will find yourself surrounded by.'

'It isn't the money – or not as it applies to me.'

'Then why,' his grandfather demanded testily, 'have we trekked out here to speak in privacy?'

'Because I don't feel comfortable inheriting an amount different to that Claus, Lotti and Ilse are to receive. And then there's my mother's situation,' he added as they stepped into the summer house. 'She's your only child. She should be the major beneficiary, not me, especially considering how precarious Germany's finances are.'

His grandfather seated himself in a wicker chair. 'The inflation that brought the country to its knees has now, thanks to the issue of the new Reichsmark, been brought under control.' He spoke with all the certainty of his profession. 'And even when the nightmare was at its height, the House of Remer wasn't in danger. Your stepfather took advantage of it to buy large quantities of machinery with borrowed money – money that had lost its value by the time he came to pay it back. My information is that between the beginning of 1921 and the end of 1923 he almost doubled his fortune. So no more worries about your mother's financial situation.' He continued, his voice suddenly hard, 'I made my decision in May 1917 on the day a Remer-built battleship sank an American merchant ship with the loss of a hundred and fifty lives. Is that clear enough for you?'

Paul nodded, not wanting to speak. In the six years since the war had ended, Vicky had worked so successfully at binding the English and German halves of their family together again that the more hideous aspects of the loyalties that had divided them had been almost forgotten – at least by him. Now, however, his grandfather was forcing him to confront them yet again and it wasn't a pleasant experience.

From where they were sitting they had an uninterrupted view of the vast lawn rolling down to the river. The game of tag was still going on, though now it wasn't only the girls who were playing it. Berthold had abandoned being a spectator to Max and Hugo's game of chess and, jacketless, was chasing Nancy in order to tag her, while Ilse, Lotti and Hester shrieked in delight at his involvement in their game. He watched the happy scene for a few minutes and then said stubbornly, 'And Claus and Lotti and Ilse? They are just as much your grandchildren as I am. I'd be far more comfortable if we were all treated equally.'

'Would you, indeed? Well, my boy, you're just going to have live uncomfortable, because I'm not going to do so. I'm going to leave the bulk of my wealth to the only grandchild I have who is an American – and who I happen to know is proud of being an American.'

He rose to his feet. 'And if you don't like the arrangement,' he said in a voice that indicated the subject was now very definitely at an end, 'I'll leave every damned dollar and cent to the New York City Dogs' Home!'

When Paul was twelve, Vicky had decided he was old enough to join her and her father every evening for dinner, even when guests were also dining. It was an arrangement she applied to Max and Hugo and one they were now well accustomed to. Claus, who had never in his life dined in the evening with his parents, was pink with nerves at the prospect of doing so with his American grandfather.

'Can I sit next to you, Paul?' he asked as they entered the dining room.

Paul slid an arm reassuringly around his young half-brother's shoulders. 'Of course you can, but I expect Grandfather will ask you to sit next to him as well. He'll be wanting to take every opportunity to get to know you better.'

'But I find it so *strange* having an American grandfather,' Claus whispered as everyone began taking their seats. 'And English and American etiquette is so different to etiquette in Berlin.'

'It's certainly more informal,' Paul agreed, knowing that in the mansion on Unter den Linden the kind of family chatter now taking place at the table – Max and Hugo discussing their game of chess, their great-uncle chuckling at something their grandfather had said, Vicky teasing Berthold about his joint-carving abilities – would never be allowed.

'Sit next to me, Claus,' Charles boomed. 'I want to know all about your schoolwork and I want to know how much you know about American history. Are you familiar with the name of Thomas Jefferson?'

154

'He wrote the Declaration of Independence, Grandfather,' Claus said, deeply grateful for the way Paul had primed him as to the kind of questions his grandfather was likely to ask.

Charles made a sound of satisfaction.

Vicky turned her attention away from her husband, saying to her uncle, 'Has Claus told you he came first in the Berlin under-fourteen ski championships? It's a brilliant achievement. Isn't it wonderful he's such a good athlete, as well as such a good scholar?'

'It most certainly is.' Excellence of any kind always deeply gratified Charles Wallace. 'Tell me all about the ski championship, Claus. Where was it held? We have excellent skiing country in western America. Perhaps we can persuade your parents to allow you to visit me in New York and then together we can make a trip to Utah.'

Realizing that, thanks to his aunt, his grandfather had now abandoned the American history inquisition, Claus shot her a look of deep gratitude and then said, 'It was held in southern Germany, at Garmisch-Partenkirchen, Grandfather. All our year at school went and we slept in wooden huts and at night we had log fires and it was all very *gemütlich* and great fun.'

Charles flinched slightly at the lapse into German, but bearing in mind that Claus had called him 'Grandfather' and not '*Opa*', as Lotti persistently and annoyingly did, he overlooked it.

Paul, as aware as Claus that pigs would fly before Josef and Zelda allowed him to visit Utah, listened in as Claus managed to steer the conversation in other directions, reflecting that everything his aunt had said about his half-brother was true. Claus was not only a natural athlete but highly intelligent, which was just as well as Josef had already made it perfectly clear that Claus was destined to one day be head of the House of Remer.

As soup was served Paul reflected how fortunate he was no

such future had been marked out for him. He was a free agent and, thanks to his grandfather, one without money worries. He was also very close with his aunt, and his great-uncle regarded him as if he were his grandson, not his nephew. His relationship with Max and Hugo was like that of brothers.

With Claus, things were a little different. Claus had a stumbling block over their difference in nationality, mainly, Paul suspected, because it was a reminder to him that their mother – now totally German in every respect but her looks – was American by birth. It was something Claus obviously found very difficult to grasp; that he had an American grandfather was, Paul knew, a concept Claus found even harder to come to terms with.

He was doing all right now, though, talking quite freely to his grandfather about the youth movement he belonged to. 'We go hiking and camping,' he was saying to him, clearly enthused about both activities, 'and we have a uniform and sing songs and –'

'A uniform?' Charles Wallace interrupted in some concern. 'What kind of uniform? And what kind of songs?'

Paul held his breath, knowing from his Easter visit to Berlin that Claus's youth movement wore a paramilitary-style uniform and that many of the songs they sang were fiercely patriotic.

'A uniform like a Boy Scout's uniform.'

Paul could tell from Claus's voice that he wasn't trying to deceive their grandfather; the idea of their grandfather not approving of the youth movement he belonged to hadn't entered his head. 'You have Boy Scouts in America, don't you, Grandfather?' he continued innocently. 'And the songs we sing are folk songs and –'

Before Claus could say 'patriotic songs', Paul said hastily, 'Would you pass the peas, Grandfather? And what do you think about the new Olympic record that was set in the four hundred metres last month? Pretty impressive, wasn't it?'

His ploy worked. Suitably diverted, his grandfather gave his opinion of Eric Liddell's stupendous run and a general discussion followed as to how much help Liddell's experience as a fast-running international rugby player had been to him.

From the other side of the table, Max suddenly said: 'Do you think Lotti's friend is shy, Paul, or do you think she's stand-offish? I can't get a word out of her.'

Hugo, who rarely spoke, uncharacteristically pitched in before Paul had the chance to reply. 'Hester is shy,' he said flatly. 'And asking her all that stuff about why the Jewish Sabbath is a Saturday and not a Sunday, and what sort of a meal they have for it and why, was a bit much if you don't mind me saying so. How would you like it if you visited her family and they immediately started asking you questions about the Church of England?'

'Well, if they did, I'd be a bit stuck,' Max said with his usual disarming frankness. 'All I know is the Henry the Eighth bit and that some of the hymns are pretty good. Are we going to go on a picnic to Fountains Abbey while Great-Uncle Charles is with us?' he asked, directing the question to his mother. 'Fountains Abbey is always a good bet for a family day out. Even Grandpa likes it there.'

His grandfather was deep in conversation and oblivious to the suggestion. 'Adam Priestley, Charles?' Paul heard him saying. 'Yes, I see him quite often. He's a good wool man. Priestley's was always a fine mill, but since his father's death Adam has turned it into an exceptional one.'

'And is he still the most eligible widower in Yorkshire?' Charles Wallace asked with interest. 'Or has he by now remarried?'

'He's still the most eligible widower in Yorkshire, much to the frustration of the local matriarchs who have been trying to

157

secure him as a son-in-law and, it must be said, to the intense disappointment of their daughters.'

Their conversation turned to that day's news report of the discovery of remains of an ancient civilization in the Galapagos Islands. Paul ceased to listen.

He was watching his aunt as the dinner plates were cleared and the pudding – a baked jam-roll – was placed on the table. She, like him, had overheard the conversation and there was a touch of heightened colour in her cheeks.

Anyone noticing it would probably assume the steaming pudding to be the culprit. He knew differently.

That his aunt and Adam Priestley were in love was something he had known for about three years. Before that, like Max and Hugo, he had thought Adam's asking after his aunt whenever they ran into him at school rugby matches, and his aunt's reciprocal queries as to whether they had seen Adam lately, had been merely neighbourly good manners.

The change in his understanding as to the true nature of their relationship had taken place in the summer of 1921. It had been a blisteringly hot day and he had gone to Scarborough by train.

It was there, within minutes of leaving the station, that he saw them. They were strolling along the promenade towards him and there was absolutely no chance of their seeing him, for they had eyes only for each other.

They were arm in arm and she was leaning in towards him as they walked, looking adoringly up at him as he looked lovingly down at her. Not even to an inexperienced seventeen-year-old could they have been mistaken for two people who were merely casual friends.

Shock had rooted him to the spot

The promenade was broad and had been busy with holidaymakers. As they had drawn near to him he had turned his back for a few moments and then, when they were safely past, he had again turned to watch them in disbelieving fascination.

Three years after that day in Scarborough he could still remember the incredulity he had felt. Since then, Adam had become a regular visitor to Shuttleworth Hall. Ostensibly, he came to visit Arthur Hudson and many mill and wool matters were discussed. Afterwards, though, he would spend time with Vicky, and while they were both far too careful to gaze at each other with the expressions he had seen on Scarborough's promenade, they would walk across the lawn together and down to the river, Arthur Hudson's aged spaniels at their heels.

It had become such a common occurrence that he knew no one but himself even wondered about the nature of their relationship – just as no one but himself ever seemed to think it odd that although Vicky's bedroom boasted a large double bed she always moved out of it whenever Berthold visited, in order to share a twin-bedded guest room with him.

Even to a twenty-year-old virgin like himself, it indicated that all was not quite normal within his aunt and uncle's marriage. Yet as he looked at them now, across the table, it was impossible to imagine them divorcing. His aunt would, he knew, find such an act far too distressing for Max, Hugo and Nancy. Besides, even if they no longer enjoyed marital relations – and he very much doubted that they did – they were most certainly still good friends. Their friendship showed in the gentle teasing that took place between them, as when, at the beginning of dinner, his aunt had teased his uncle about his joint-carving ability.

Even though they were terribly old to be lovers – his aunt was, he knew, thirty-six and Adam was possibly even forty – he still thought it all very romantic.

He wasn't able to continue thinking about just how romantic it all was, as his grandfather suddenly said in a loud voice, 'And so are the rumours we are hearing in New York correct, Berthold, and is this Hitler person going to be paroled long before he's served his five-year prison sentence?'

Vicky, who never encouraged political talk when children were present, cleared her throat.

Her uncle was oblivious to the signal he was being sent, as, apparently, was Berthold, for he said in his habitually pedantic manner, 'Yes, Mr Wallace. When his prison sentence was handed down to him last April, Herr Hitler was told specifically he could expect to be paroled in nine months' time.'

Charles Wallace gave a snort of disgust. 'What kind of a sentence is that for a charge of treason? He did make a farcical attempt to seize power from the legally elected Bavarian government, did he not?'

'He attempted a putsch,' Berthold responded, always a purist where language was concerned.

'What's a putsch?' Hugo asked, beginning to listen with interest.

'An attempt to seize power by armed force,' Max said knowledgeably.

Vicky cleared her throat again, but it was too little, too late.

'The fellow's a madman,' her father said, screwing up his napkin and tossing it down beside his now empty pudding plate. 'He should have been shot – and would have been shot if he'd been sentenced anywhere else but Bavaria.'

Paul was suddenly aware that the room was no longer stifling with late evening heat. The muslin curtains at the open French windows had begun rustling in a chill breeze and the Michaelmas daisies in urns on the terrace looked more storm-tossed than milkily serene.

A small voice said stalwartly: 'My father doesn't think Herr Hitler a madman.' Claus's face was set and pinched. 'My father thinks Herr Hitler is exactly the kind of man Germany needs. He thinks he is a new Messiah.'

160

There was a silence that could have been cut with a knife. It was Vicky who broke it.

Pushing her chair away from the table, she said a little unsteadily, 'I think it's time we went into the drawing room for coffee. And even though it's so soon after dinner, I think it's time the boys went to bed.'

Everyone began rising to their feet and it was then Paul saw the expression on Berthold's face and the look that flashed between him and Claus.

He stumbled, wondering if he had read it aright. Surely Berthold, the most meek and mild of men, could not be in sympathy with the kind of ruffians supporting Hitler? It seemed so highly unlikely as to be ridiculous, but then he remembered how Berthold had always followed wherever Josef led. If Josef had become a Hitler supporter – and from what Claus had just said, it was obvious he had – then it was more than possible Berthold was also in sympathy with Hitler's rabble-rousing tactics.

It was a grim thought and, as he walked from the dining room and as thunder rolled from somewhere across the river, he found himself hoping with all his heart that his instincts were wrong.

TEN

Berlin, May 1928

Nancy bounced into exuberant wakefulness. She was in Berlin again and she loved Berlin. It was so much more exciting than boring, uneventful Little Ridding. Jumping from the bed – it was so high she would have had to be six foot tall instead of five foot nothing not to have done so – she ran to the nearest window.

May was her favourite month to be in Berlin, but it was one that she wasn't often able to enjoy there, because of school. Easter was the more usual time she and her brothers came to visit, but this year Max and Hugo had gone down with measles just before Easter and, though in the normal way of things they would have now been back at St Dunstan's, they'd been excused for a month on the grounds they were recuperating, and as she was always brilliantly ahead in her schoolwork, her mother had leniently decided it would do no harm if she too spent May in Berlin.

With a delicious shiver of anticipation she flung the window open and, as she had known it would, the heady scent of linden blossom filled the air.

With her hands splayed on the window sill she leaned dangerously far out and announced to the world at large:

'It's going to be a *wonderful* day. Absolutely spiffing!'

There was so much delightfulness lying ahead of her, she didn't know which event to look forward to the most.

There was Claus, of course. Ever since she could remember, looking forward to being in Berlin had meant looking forward to being with Claus. Not that he ever spent much time with her. There were only three months' difference in age between him and Hugo, and ten months between him and Max, and because of this closeness her brothers monopolized most of his time – especially when Claus visited Yorkshire.

In Berlin, though, things were sometimes a little different, for here there were far more interesting things for her brothers to do than to press-gang Claus into games of cricket or, with other friends, rugby. In Berlin there was far more chance of her having her favourite cousin to herself.

There was also Hester to see. Though technically speaking Hester was Lotti's best friend, when they were all together Hester spent most time with her. The reason was simple. Hester's parents were very conservative, very mindful of what was proper and not proper – and they wanted their only child to be exceedingly proper. Which, as a good Jewish girl, Hester was. It was, however, very difficult for her – or anyone else – to remain well behaved when in Lotti's company.

Lotti was turbulent mischief personified. If there was trouble to be found, then Lotti found it. Last night, for instance, within a half-hour of their arrival, Lotti had sat cross-legged on the high bed and announced she was going to dragoon Max into taking her to the famous Romanische Café, near to the Memorial church.

'It's where all the artists, actors, actresses, dancers and writers go,' she had said, 'and now Max is nearly eighteen he'll be able to take me there. He might even meet and fall in love with a beautiful actress. I bet he doesn't get to meet many beautiful actresses in Yorkshire.'

163

Though Nancy had privately liked the idea of going to a place where writers met, she'd had no intention of making Lotti feel cleverer than she already did. Lotti was, after all, almost a year younger than she was. If any kow-towing in admiration was to be done, it should be being done the other way around.

'You're not even thirteen,' she'd said crushingly. 'You'll stand out like a sore thumb and if Max were to meet a beautiful actress, you'd cramp his style.'

'No, I wouldn't.' Lotti's curiously attractive face – in which eyes that were a shade too large and a mouth that was far too wide fought for living space with a nose that was anything but classical – was fiercely determined. 'I'd be very entertaining company and she might tell me how to get a job as a dancer. Because that's what I'm going to be. I'm going to wear feathers and sequins and have a jolly good time.'

Aware that it would mean Max wouldn't be spending time with Claus if Lotti *did* manage to coerce Max into taking her somewhere so blatantly unsuitable, Nancy had clamped her mouth tight shut and said nothing.

Leaving the window still wide open she turned back into the room now and took out the first dress her hand touched when reaching inside the enormous wardrobe. This was a favourite ploy of hers. It meant she never had to make a decision about what to wear and there was always an extra surprise to the start of her day. The maid who had unpacked and hung up her clothes for her, had done her a favour. Her dress for the day was one of her favourites, a rose-pink polka-dotted silk with a sweetheart neckline and a quite grown-up low waistline, even if the length was too childishly long.

When she had washed and dressed and brushed and re-plaited her hair, she looked critically at herself in the cheval glass. Because she was short and stocky she never looked quite as she would have liked to look, and her mother's refusal to

164

allow her to have her fair hair cut short until her sixteenth birthday – which was years away – didn't help.

Her hair was thick and too naturally curly to ever plait sleekly and in Berlin she had got into the habit of plaiting it in one long thick braid, much to her aunt's approval. 'You suit a Brunnhilde look, Nancy,' she had said in her distinctive cracked-ice voice. 'It makes you look every inch a Berliner.'

Because she admired her aunt so much, the approval had meant a lot to Nancy. Aunt Zelda was *exactly* the sort of woman she wanted to be when she grew up. Aunt Zelda never suffered fools gladly and nor did she attempt to hide her intelligence. Claus had once told her that his mother was as much the head of the House of Remer as his father was, and she had never forgotten it.

Whether she would ever be able to look as glamorous as her aunt, was doubtful, she knew, but one thing she was determined on and that was that she wouldn't spend her life pottering in a garden as her mother did. She would become a professional woman – a journalist.

As she headed out of the room and made her way down the sweeping stairway to the Remer mansion's cavernous breakfast room she mentally added a rider to her last thought. When she became a journalist, she would become a journalist in Berlin, perhaps for the *Neue Berliner Zeitung* or the *Berliner Tageblatt* or even the *Berliner Börsen-Courier*.

'Good morning,' Josef Remer said tersely as she entered the breakfast room.

'Good morning, Uncle Josef,' she said dutifully, wishing there was someone else at the table. Where was her father? Where were Max and Hugo? Where were her aunt and Claus and Lotti and Ilse?

As usual in the Remer mansion, there was no sideboard from which she could help herself to bacon, eggs or sausage.

165

Instead, a maid dressed in black and wearing a lace apron and a coronet of a cap, waited on her.

She asked for hot chocolate and for eggs served with *Bratwurst* and fried potatoes.

Her uncle did something unheard of. He put down the newspaper he had been reading and looked across at her.

Nancy wasn't to know it, but he was curious. His habit was to ignore the annual visits Berthold's children made to Berlin and to never exchange more than half a dozen formally polite words with them.

That he was on the verge of breaking this habit – at least where his niece was concerned – was because Zelda's partiality for her had become impossible for him to ignore. 'She reminds me of me,' she had said the previous evening. 'She's got grit and a stubbornness mountains couldn't move.'

Watching his niece tuck into a breakfast that would have satisfied a German farmer, he was well aware that Zelda could not possibly have been talking about a similarity of looks. Berthold's daughter was sturdy enough and fair-haired enough to pass for a Bavarian peasant. It made the suspicions Zelda's words had aroused in him seem ludicrous. His wife could not, in a million years, be priming him for the suggestion that Berthold's daughter would make a suitable daughter-in-law.

Satisfied that he had been letting his imagination run away with him, he said abruptly, 'Do you feel German, Nancy? If your mother hadn't returned to England when war broke out, you would have been born in Germany and been just as German as your cousins.'

His manner was intimidating, but as Nancy never let anything intimidate her she laid down her knife and fork and gave the question due consideration. 'No,' she said at last, knowing it wasn't the answer that was wanted, but being blisteringly truthful as always. 'I've too much Yorkshire in me ever to feel all-German. I like the fact that I'm half-German,

166

though I don't actually think of it quite like that. I usually think of myself as being half a Berliner.'

'Do you?' Despite himself, Josef was intrigued. There was a no-nonsense forthrightness about his niece that was immensely appealing and he was beginning to see why Zelda had long ago taken such a shine to her.

'And what does that mean to you? Being half a Berliner?'

Nancy flashed him a smile that transformed her from being a plain girl into a pretty one. 'It means that though I was born in Yorkshire and live in Yorkshire and love Yorkshire, I'm not a parochial Yorkshire girl. I'm a city girl. I like to be where things happen. And they happen in Berlin. Which is why I will live here when I've gained experience on the *Yorkshire Post*.'

'The *Yorkshire Post*?'

'A very prestigious local newspaper. I'm going to become a journalist when I leave school.'

'And what will you do when you come to live in Berlin?'

Nancy pushed her plate to one side and clasped her hands on the table. 'I shall be a journalist for a Berlin newspaper. That will mean I shall know absolutely everything that is going on.'

'You mean everything that is going on in the world of fashion and homemaking?'

Nancy stared at him, dumbfounded he imagined her interests and capabilities to be so narrow.

'Absolutely not,' she said when she had recovered from her shock. 'I shall write about politics.'

Josef choked on his coffee.

'I shall write about inflation and unemployment,' she continued, not sparing him, 'and assassinations and criminality and theatres and art and . . . and even about the stock exchange.'

He was just about to ask her what the devil she knew about the stock exchange when she looked beyond him and he knew by the way her face lit up that Claus had entered the room.

A second later he became aware that Claus hadn't entered the room alone and that Max and Hugo were with him.

Abruptly, he rose to his feet. Breakfast with his niece he could just about stomach and had, this morning, positively enjoyed. Breakfast with his nephews was another matter entirely, however, and he had no intention of enduring it.

'Politics!' he said disbelievingly to Zelda when, instead of leaving the house to meet with one of his bankers as he had intended, he went back upstairs to speak with her. 'Why would a thirteen-year-old girl imagine herself to be interested in politics – and especially in the murky world of Berlin politics?'

Lifting her breakfast tray to one side, she swung long shapely legs from the bed and stood up. Reaching for a cream silk peignoir she slipped her arms into its sleeves and said, 'You like her, though, don't you?'

'Why does my liking her matter so much to you?'

'Because she's family and the older I get the more important family is to me.'

He stared at her, suddenly uneasy. 'Are you regretting never visiting your father? Regretting never accompanying the children when they visit Yorkshire?'

She crossed to her dressing table and picked up a silver cigarette case. 'I regret my father cutting me out of his will,' she said drily, taking one of the small black Russian cigarettes she favoured out of the case and clicking it shut. 'And I miss Vicky.'

'She could be here now, if she wanted to be,' he said irritably, not wanting Zelda to begin joining Berthold on tediously regular visits to Shuttleworth Hall.

Zelda made no response. Instead, she lit her cigarette and drew heavily on it, knowing very well why Vicky wasn't now with them in Berlin. Max, Hugo and Nancy were old enough to travel from Yorkshire to Berlin without her and in their absence – and with her father spending most of his time at his mill or at his gentlemen's club in Harrogate – Shuttleworth Hall was a rare oasis of privacy. And for Vicky and her lover, Adam Priestley, privacy was too precious a commodity to be lightly squandered.

'May is a busy month in the garden,' she said to Josef, who hadn't a clue as to his sister-in-law's secret love life. 'It's why Paul isn't here. It's the prime time of year for crossing roses and grafting onto rootstocks.'

At the thought of a grown man spending his time conveying pollen from one rose to another and then growing the resultant seed in the hope of producing a worthwhile new variety of rose, a trial and error process that required many thousands of cross-breedings and could take years, Josef raised his eyes to heaven.

Deeply grateful that his stepson had no German blood and that his being in Yorkshire throughout the war years had effectively put paid to Zelda's earlier ambition that he be involved in the running of the steelworks, he seated himself in a wing chair near to one of the windows.

'I'm going to see Kirchner today, in fact I should be with him now.'

The name of their leading banker immediately caught Zelda's attention.

'Why?' she asked, crossing the room towards him. 'We don't have a problem, do we?'

He pinched the bridge of his nose with his forefinger and thumb. 'The repayments the government are demanding on the profits we made out of government loans during inflation are biting deeply and there are some old deals we still have to pay out on.'

'And you think the Nazi Party would put an end to these kinds of demands?'

'Yes. Hitler is on the right track. He wants an end to endless bureaucracy. He wants an end to unnecessary Socialist strikes. He knows who is to blame for all Germany's troubles and he knows how to make Germany great again.'

She sat down on his knee, her face full of doubt. 'But he's such a rabble-rouser, darling. And his Nazi Party is such a little political party. Tinhorn is the word they'd use for it in the States.'

It was a remark he would have slapped down if it had come from anyone else.

He slid his arm around her waist. The perfume she had worn yesterday lingered on her skin, musky and exotic. Even more pleasurable was that after seventeen years of marriage she was still light enough to sit easily on his knee. Nearly every woman of the same age that he knew was built like a dray-horse. Zelda was as slender and supple as a scantily clad cabaret dancer.

'You're wrong, *Liebling*,' he said without annoyance. 'The Nazis will come to power sooner or later and when they do there will be no more House of Remer repayments, no fear of the Communist Party coming to power and taking over the factories, and no more being beholden to Jewish bankers, either.'

Aware of how hard he'd worked to ensure that the House of Remer was still one of Germany's major steelworks, she kept to herself her thoughts that the Nazis were far too oddball an organization and far too socially unacceptable ever to come to power.

Changing the subject, she said, 'As Claus is going to disappoint Nancy when he tells her he has to attend school today, I think I will take her and Ilse to the Zoological Gardens. Exotic creatures always give pleasure.'

'They most certainly do.'

The throb in his usually hard, clipped voice, told her he was referring to herself.

As he lovingly shooed her off his knee in order that he could meet with Kirchner, he did so conscious that he was as dazzled by her now as he had been nineteen years ago, when they had first met. The government might be corrupt and inept, the spectre of unemployment for the masses might be growing by the minute, his steelworks might still be banned from producing armaments, but he did have one security and that was his marriage. Built on a rock of physical desire that never waned, it never disappointed him and he found it inconceivable it ever would.

Keen as Nancy's disappointment was at not spending the day with Claus, she had enjoyed her day at the zoo.

'My aunt looked like a gorgeously plumed South American bird,' she said to Hester the next day as they swung on a hammock together in the Dresners' garden, catching up on things over a jug of lemonade. 'Her dress was turquoise silk and she wore a long string of pearls with it and slave bangles on her upper arms. Can you imagine it? Slave bangles *in the day time*?'

Hester couldn't and wished she'd been at the zoo to see the sight herself.

'And we had Ilse with us which was nice, but she's still such a child.'

Hester looked disconcerted. There was almost the same difference in age between her and Nancy, Nancy being ten months her senior, as there was between her and eleven-year-old Ilse. It made her uncomfortable. She didn't want Nancy thinking she was a child as well.

'Afterwards, we went to a *very* smart café for chocolate ice creams – all of which Lotti missed because she disappeared for the day with Max.'

Nancy didn't tell Hester that Max and Lotti had probably gone to the Romanische Café – a café so worldly it hadn't even occurred to her aunt to take her and Ilse there.

171

'And what about Hugo?' Hester asked. She liked Hugo. Unlike the super-confident, gregarious Max, he was quiet and studious and he always went out of his way to make her feel part of things – as if she too was a Remer.

'Hugo spent time with Pa.'

'It must be odd,' she said, 'seeing your father only two or three times a year.'

Nancy shrugged. 'Not really, because we've never had the experience of seeing him more often. All families are different and it's just the way ours is. Pa lives in Berlin and we live in Yorkshire. Though Pa likes visiting us in Yorkshire, he wouldn't like living there. Yorkshire is almost a country of its own and Pa's not very adventurous. He doesn't like new experiences.'

'I don't think many Germans do,' Hester said sagely, thinking about her own parents, who most certainly didn't like new experiences and for whom present-day Germany was becoming very difficult.

She said tentatively, broaching the subject she'd wanted to broach ever since Nancy's arrival, 'My father has hardly any work now. All his patients are going elsewhere.'

Nancy looked disbelieving. 'I think you must have got that wrong, Hester. Your father's a children's doctor. Children's doctors always have work, because people are always having babies.'

'Well, he does still have some patients, because Jewish mothers still bring their children to him, but he's lost nearly all his others. It's not very easy to be a Jew in Berlin. There's too much anti-Jewish feeling. People don't like us any more.'

The swinging of the hammock was beginning to make Nancy feel a little queasy and she jumped down from it, sitting on a garden chair instead. The table with the jug of lemonade was near by and she refilled her glass.

'If you're talking about horrid brown-shirted storm-troopers, we ran into a group of them at the zoo yesterday and

Aunt Zelda said they were rabble and that we weren't to take any notice of them – so you mustn't take any notice of them either.'

Hester chewed the corner of her lip. It was all right for Nancy to be so off-hand about stormtroopers. She didn't live in Berlin, she only visited it and, even more to the point, she wasn't Jewish. She was, though, usually quite knowledgeable about things, or liked to think she was.

'Did your aunt tell you that Jews now get blamed for everything?' she said, persisting even though the subject was distressing her. 'Even the war is said to have been our fault.'

'Well, there you are, then! My aunt was right. Taking any notice of such a statement is downright ridiculous and you shouldn't do so.'

'But there are fights in the streets, Nancy. Jews are being beaten up just for being Jews.' Hester couldn't believe that Nancy was so unaware of what was happening.

Nancy couldn't believe it either. She drained her glass of lemonade, determining to speak to her father about the *Sturmabteilung*, which was the correct name for the brown-shirted stormtroopers. And if the facts were as Hester said they were, she would speak to Aunt Zelda and, if necessary, disabuse her of her presently held opinion that they were people it was possible to ignore.

Zelda stared at Josef in blank disbelief. 'Lotti being friends with Hester Dresner can have no possible repercussions on a family like ours. How *dare* Heinrich Kirchner make such a suggestion to you? And no, I will *not* ask Lotti to cease seeing her.'

They were alone in the dining room, Berthold having taking his children and theirs to a Russian restaurant for a treat.

For once, Josef didn't pay her any heed.

'Kirchner isn't a fool, Zelda,' he said tightly. 'Lotti's friendship with a Jewish girl may seem trivial, but it's been noted. If it hadn't been, Kirchner wouldn't have mentioned it. When the next elections are called the National Socialists are going to gain a huge majority. You may think they are a negligible party. Men like Kirchner don't. And as Hitler's star rises, so will the House of Remer's – if we play our cards right. And if playing our cards right means my becoming a party member and ensuring that my family have no social relations with Jews, or any other racial riff-raff or miscegenates, then so be it.'

They were dining by candlelight. As always she had changed into an evening dress for dinner. It was silver lamé and the neckline was cut on a slant, boldly asymmetrical.

She put her wine glass down a little unsteadily. 'Miscegenates? Just who, exactly, falls into that category?'

'Anyone of mixed race,' he said, sure she knew and was merely being annoying. 'People with Negro or gypsy or Indian blood in their veins.'

'Indian blood?' Her voice had taken on a very odd quality, one he couldn't place. 'Native American Indian blood?'

'Damn it all, Zelda, yes! Of course someone with Native American blood in their veins would be a miscegenate! But how many people, outside of a circus or a burlesque show, have such a background?'

She sat very still. In nineteen years she'd given hardly a thought to her third-generation Iroquois blood. In her New York days it had infuriated her that Stuyvesant and Vanderbilt matriarchs had looked down their noses at her because of it, but fury was very different to shame.

Shame was something she had never felt and was not about to start feeling now.

Josef's question still hung in the air.

Knowing it was a Rubicon that, once crossed, there could be no retreating from, she looked him straight in the eyes and said coolly, 'I do, Josef. I do.'

ELEVEN

Yorkshire and Berlin, July 1931

Vicky stood by the banks of the River Ure, her thoughts and emotions in such chaos she didn't know where to begin untangling them. She was forty-three and she was pregnant.

She knew what Adam's reaction was going to be when she told him. Though he'd be concerned for her well-being – she was, after all, anciently old to be having another baby – he would be over the moon with joy. It had always caused her deep guilt that because of his love for her he had not married and raised a family with one of the countless young women hopeful of becoming his second wife. Now at last he would be a father for the first time.

She stood looking deep into the river, knowing that at any moment she would hear his dear, familiar long stride as he walked towards her over the grass. His joy, and hers at being able to give him such joy, were one side of the coin, but what about the other?

Ever since the autumn of 1920, when she had returned from Berlin, she and Adam had been lovers. For her, in the early years, it had been a passion fraught with guilt. She wasn't used to deceiving people, and deceiving her children and her father,

175

as well as friends like Violet Ramsbotham, as to the true nature of her and Adam's relationship had not come easily to her.

Time had eased her mental distress. Marital relations had never been resumed between her and Berthold and he had been pathetically relieved when he had discovered his inability made no difference to her loving affection for him. Two years later, when she had told him that she and Adam were lovers, he had been anguished about it, but it had been anguish he had slowly overcome.

The children were spending a week in Berlin before returning with their cousins to spend the rest of the summer at Shuttleworth Hall and she would have to tell them.

How would she do so?

How *could* she tell them?

That Adam would demand she now divorce Berthold and marry him, she didn't have a doubt. And that Berthold, when he was told the situation, would reluctantly acquiesce to a divorce, she also didn't doubt. But it would take time. If Berthold were to divorce her for adultery it wouldn't be granted till long after the baby was born, and if either of them were to divorce the other on the grounds of desertion, the wait would be even longer. In the meantime, Adam's child would be born out of wedlock and she would be the talk of Yorkshire.

Not, of course, that she would let that trouble her. It was how the gossip would affect Max, Hugo and Nancy that was concerning her. Paul, she was quite sure, would take it in his stride, but then Paul was her nephew, not her son.

What about Max, newly embarked on a career in banking? And Hugo, still at Oxford?

A kingfisher flew low across the river and she watched it, unable to resolve how to go about tackling the difficulties that lay ahead, even wondering if she would, perhaps, have to leave Shuttleworth Hall and live elsewhere.

Suddenly, she heard the sound of him walking towards her

176

over the sun-parched grass. She sucked in her breath, her pulse racing.

For Adam this was going to be a life-changing moment and, in the certain knowledge he was always going to love and cherish both her and the child she was carrying, she turned around, troubled no longer.

'I have news,' she said, and began running towards him. 'I have wonderful news, Adam! Incredible news!'

As his arms closed around her, she said, her face radiant, 'We're having a baby, Adam. I'm three months pregnant.'

His handsome face was almost comical in its stupefaction, and then he gave a roar of delight that had every bird in the vicinity taking to flight.

'Great heavens! That's astounding! That's the best news I've ever heard in my life!'

Alight with joy, he swung her off her feet and round and round so that they only narrowly missed falling into the river. 'And now you'll *have* to get a divorce and marry me,' he said, as they collapsed breathlessly on the grass. He kissed her eyelids, her mouth, her throat and then, gazing down at her with eyes blazing with love, said, 'So when are you going to leave for Berlin, sweetheart? Today or tomorrow?'

'But I don't want a divorce.' Berthold looked dazed. 'I thought we were happy as we were?' He took off his spectacles and began polishing them furiously. 'And why should your having a baby cause talk in Little Ridding? You're married to me. People will think it is our baby.'

It was so true that for a moment she didn't know what to say. Their relationship had been asexual for so long it had simply never entered her head that there were people who would naturally assume the child she was carrying was Berthold's.

'And have Max, Hugo and Nancy think that also?' she asked, knowing it was something she could never do. 'Have them believe that you are the baby's father? And have the baby growing up believing that? Have the baby never knowing that Adam is its father? And have Adam unable to acknowledge his child?'

As he read the tone of her voice and the expression on her face, he shielded his eyes with his hand. 'I'm sorry,' he said inadequately. 'I hadn't thought . . . It's just that I was happy with the way things were. Seeing you and the children at Shuttleworth Hall every Christmas and for weeks at a time during the summer, the children being here for Easter –' He broke off, too distressed to continue.

She slipped to her knees in front of him and took hold of one of his hands, pressing it close against her cheek. 'Where you and I are concerned nothing is going to change, Berthold. We will still be loving friends. I will still want you to spend the summer and Christmas at Shuttleworth Hall. Our children will still visit you every Easter. Hugo is sitting the Foreign Office examinations when he leaves Oxford in the hope he can work at the British Embassy in Berlin. Nancy wants to be a journalist in Berlin. We will still all be a family – a family you will see more and more of, not less and less. But I love Adam, Berthold. He's loved me for a long time, and because he loves me he's denied himself one opportunity after another of marrying and having a family. Now, in a few months' time, he will have a child. I want him to be able to acknowledge that child openly. I want him to experience all the joys of fatherhood, just as you have. I want this child to grow up knowing who his father is and being proud of him.'

'Yes. Of course.' There was defeat in his voice and he added plaintively, 'It would all have been so different, *Liebchen*, if you had returned to Berlin for good in 1920.'

She hesitated, sorely tempted to point out that things could have been very different if he had left Berlin to live with her at Shuttleworth Hall.

The temptation passed. It was too late for such remarks and they could serve no purpose.

Instead, she said, 'I'm going to break the news to Zelda. She is back from Schloss Niedernhall, isn't she? I spoke to her on the telephone before leaving England and she said she would be returning to Berlin so that we could spend some time together.'

'Yes, she's back.' He lowered his hand away from his eyes and she was aware of how fast and prematurely he was ageing. 'I don't know why she spends so much time in Baden-Württemberg. Josef only leaves Berlin now in order to visit the Ruhr and the steelworks, and the children are nearly always here. Zelda used to love Berlin, but now she seems to have taken an aversion to it.'

'For once in his life, Berthold has come to a correct conclusion,' Zelda said waspishly, minutes after their reunion. 'Berlin isn't the city I fell in love with before the war. That was a city of imperial pomp and splendour and culture. Now it's a city of demonstrations and street fighting and arm-saluting Nazis.'

Vicky was quite aware of what kind of a city Berlin had become and she was also aware that Josef was a fully paid-up member of the Nazi Party. That Zelda was not supporting Josef to the hilt could mean only one thing.

'What's wrong between the two of you?' she asked.

The drawing room they were in was exquisitely decorated and furnished in the art deco style Zelda favoured. She looked around it and then, as if deeming it not private enough for what she wanted to say, said: 'Let's go for a drive out to Wannsee. Then I'll tell you.'

Escaping from the city to the wooded shores of Lake Wannsee was always a pleasure for Vicky. When the children had been much younger and she had accompanied them on their visits to Berlin, picnics beside the lake had always been her favourite way of spending a day out.

179

Zelda drove out of the city unusually quiet and tight-lipped. Vicky, having more than enough to think about, didn't try to make conversation. She was too busy wondering how to prepare Max, Hugo and Nancy for the bombshells she was about to drop – and which to drop first. Was it best to tell them that she and their father were divorcing before she told them of her long-term love affair with Adam? Or should she tell them about the divorce after she had told them about Adam? As for the coming baby – she still couldn't even imagine how she was going to break that news.

'Let's walk on the promenade,' Zelda said as they stepped from the car. 'There will be a nice cool breeze blowing in from the lake.'

Willowy and graceful, she was wearing an apple-green silk dress, her hair coiled in a twist beneath a straw hat dyed the exact colour of her dress, its brim saucily upturned and pinned in place by a white silk rose. Her mouth was a deep glossy red, her eyebrows and eyelashes a glossy blue-black. She was forty-eight and looked all of thirty-two. Vicky, wearing a cream-coloured linen dress, its matching loose jacket hiding her condition, was well aware she looked frumpy in comparison.

'So what is it?' she asked bluntly, hoping it was simply that Zelda had tired of Josef's autocratic humourlessness.

'It's this idiotic, anti-Semitic drivel the National Socialists continually pump out,' Zelda said savagely. 'It's so rife you can practically smell it in the air and the damage it has done to my relationship with Josef is enormous.'

They were approaching a seat positioned to give a scenic view of the lake. Zelda sat down on it abruptly and began searching in her lizard-skin handbag for her cigarette case, holder and lighter.

'Josef believes that if Hitler comes to power he'll ride roughshod over the Versailles Treaty and implement full-scale rearmament, so he's a party member. If the House of Remer is to ever go into armament production again, and enjoy all the profits that will come from such production, he has to be. But being a party member means he has to be seen to be in agreement with all this hating-the-Jews nonsense.'

She rammed a Sobranie into its short ebony holder.

'And the nonsense includes other racial groups besides Jews. Gypsies are considered to be something less than human. Poles and Russians are completely personae non gratae. Anyone who can be described as a miscegenate is a social pariah.'

'A miscegenate?' It was such an ugly word, Vicky knew it was going to have an ugly meaning.

'It means someone of mixed blood. Someone with Jewish blood in their veins. Or Romany blood. Or –' she inhaled deeply and then blew smoke out through her nose – 'or Native American Indian blood.'

Vicky's eyes widened in shocked understanding.

Zelda gave a mirthless laugh. 'The instant I told Josef he might as well include me in his list of social undesirables he went into a frothing-mouthed manic fit of fury worthy of Hitler himself. That was three years ago. He's calmed down a good deal since, but he's terrified of anyone finding out. And whereas he was once proud of the way my looks turned heads, he now lives in fear his Nazi Party cronies will mistake me for a Jewess. So to spare him embarrassment I spend more and more time at Schloss Niedernhall and he see-saws between still not being able to keep his hands off me and railing at me for something I can't help.'

'And what about the politics of it? What if the National Socialists don't get an avalanche of votes at the next election? Won't that mean their rise to power is severely curbed? And if it's curbed, won't Josef and the bulk of other Nazi Party members become disenchanted and hitch their wagon to a different star elsewhere?'

181

'Maybe.' Zelda's voice was no longer angry, it was merely taut and tired. 'Whatever the outcome of the September elections, the damage where Josef and I are concerned has already been done. And there's been damage to his relationship with Lotti, for she's still firm friends with Hester Dresner and he won't allow Hester in the house.' She shot Vicky a wry glance. 'It makes things a little awkward when Hugo is with us.'

'Hugo?' Vicky looked startled at the new direction the conversation had taken. 'I imagine Max and Nancy would find Hester not being made welcome just as offensive as Hugo does.'

'Oh, I'm sure you're right.' Zelda, as always, was recovering her equilibrium fast. 'But Max and Nancy aren't in love with Hester, are they? Hugo is.'

On the lake two yachts were tacking, leaving white spumes in their wake. Looking at them with the sun in her eyes, Vicky blinked.

'Rubbish,' she said uncertainly. 'They're just good friends. Hugo is only nineteen and Hester is still a child.'

'She's sixteen.' There was amusement in Zelda's voice. 'And in Berlin, Vicky, sixteen is quite old enough to fall in love.'

Well aware that Zelda didn't often come to wrong conclusions, Vicky was silent, wondering how she felt about the thought of Hugo being in love with the quiet, grave-eyed Hester. Hester was far too young, of course, to be seriously in love – and there was the fact that, as a non-Jew, Hugo would hardly find favour in Hester's parents' eyes – but if they ever decided they did want to marry, it was a marriage that would have her approval. Hester's integrity shone from her. She would be a daughter-in-law to be proud of.

'Let's walk down the promenade to the nearest café and have a couple of cocktails.' Zelda removed her half-smoked cigarette from its holder and crushed it beneath a lizard-skin shod foot. 'And since I've had a couple of pieces of earth-shaking news for you, what have you got for me?' There was dry sarcasm in her voice. 'Has Little Ridding's vicar run off with the Sunday collection money? Has Violet Ramsbothan turned Presbyterian?'

'No,' Vicky said, completely deadpan, 'but Berthold has agreed to divorce me and I will be giving birth to Adam's baby in six months' time.'

Zelda's stupefied reaction was so glorious Vicky forgot all about the nightmare of telling her children the same news and began giggling.

Within seconds, Zelda was giggling just as helplessly and by the time they reached the café they were laughing hard enough to bust a gut.

It was laughter that did her the world of good; laughter that enabled her to get everything into perspective. Though her children's shock was going to be painful to bear, they were, after all, now adults. Whatever the future held for them, they would no doubt live through it without too much concern as to whether or not they had her wholehearted approval.

And from now on, she was going to live the same way. At forty-three, her life was about to become wonderful. She was going to be a mother again and she had always adored being a mother. And when the divorce Berthold had agreed to was finalized, she would marry Adam.

Full of confidence now for the family council she was about to hold, she was disconcerted, when she and Zelda returned to Unter den Linden, to find that Hugo was at the Dresners', that Max had taken fourteen-year-old Ilse to the Schöneberger Volkspark and that Nancy had badgered Berthold into taking her to a political rally.

Hoping the rally was on behalf of the Social Democrats and not the National Socialists, Vicky did something she did very rarely when in Berlin. She set off alone to take a long walk through the city.

Walking always soothed her. In Yorkshire, she walked for

miles, though no longer with the dogs she had grown up with. When her father's two spaniels and Yorkshire terrier had succumbed to old age and been buried beneath the shade of the trees in Shuttleworth Hall's parkland, she had bought herself a little Norfolk terrier and named him Tinker. Wherever she went, Tinker went too. In Berlin there was no such companion. Wastl had died in 1921, shortly after her first post-war visit to the city, and Berthold hadn't had the heart to try and replace him.

With no destination in mind she walked down Unter den Linden in the direction of the Brandenburg Gate and from there into the familiar leafy acres of the Tiergarten. The Tiergarten was where she had often come when Max was a baby and Paul a small boy, and at the thought of Paul she smiled wryly. Though he and Zelda had a satisfactory relationship, it was one that most people wouldn't have recognized as being that of mother and son. Always quite pleased to see each other, they never went out of their way to do so. During all the years Shuttleworth Hall had been Paul's home, Zelda had never troubled to visit him there, and as Paul had grown to adulthood his visits to Berlin had become more and more infrequent. Like Vicky, he was always deeply uncomfortable in Berlin.

She began walking without any thought of where she was going, wishing her sons shared a little of Paul's antipathy. Berlin had always possessed a hard, smart, glittering and cynical atmosphere, but now other ingredients had added to the mix, ingredients she found deeply repellent.

The sidewalk cafés where, before the war, she and Zelda used to enjoy a morning coffee, were now the haunt of rouged and bedizened transvestites. The Kurfürstendamm, where they used to shop, was littered with prostitutes. In beer gardens and nightclubs, pleasure was pursued frenetically, the sensation of barely reined-in hysteria emphasized by Hitler's screaming rants at Nazi Party rallies.

That her children regarded such a city as being their home,

just as Little Ridding was their home, deeply disturbed her, but there was nothing she could do about it. Their father was a Berliner. Max had been born in Berlin. Whenever possible she had brought her three children on long, regular visits to the city and the result was that they all spoke German with an unmistakable Berlin accent. What she hadn't anticipated, though, when she had instigated their yearly visits to see Berthold, was that the day would come when Hugo and Nancy would want to live and work in Berlin. And she had never anticipated that – if Zelda's reading of the situation were correct – Hugo would fall in love with a Berliner.

She had reached the Victory Column, or, as the rest of her family referred to it, the *Siegessäule*. She turned away from it. By now Max, Hugo and Nancy would have returned to the Remer mansion and it was time for her to return to it too.

Tired and hot, she flagged down a gold-striped black taxi. The next hour or so was going to be the most difficult she had ever lived through and afterwards – for her children – nothing would ever be quite the same.

'And so you see, darlings, now that you are all adults and living independent lives of your own –'

'Nancy isn't living an independent life of her own,' Max said reasonably, wondering what on earth his mother was leading up to.

'I am. And working,' Nancy chipped in indignantly. 'Being a cub reporter on the *Yorkshire Post* means I'm just as independent as you are.'

They were gathered in the bedroom always allocated to Vicky on her Berlin visits. She was seated on her dressing table stool, but facing away from the dressing table. Nancy was sitting cross-legged on the bed. Max was leaning nonchalantly against the door, his arms folded, one foot crossing the other at the ankle. Hugo was seated on a spindly legged gilt chair

185

and, without much respect for its fragility, had tipped it back against the wall so that it was balanced on only two legs.

'You're a junior reporter,' Max responded crushingly to Nancy's interruption, 'and only earning peanuts.'

Before a full-scale verbal battle broke out, Vicky clasped her hands a little tighter together and said, 'Now that you are all old enough to come to terms with changes of circumstances and to understand just how complex life can be . . .'

'What's the matter, Mother? You're not about to tell us that you and Pa are getting divorced, are you?' Max's voice was full of teasing laughter.

Nancy giggled at the thought.

Hugo smiled.

Vicky cleared her throat, gripping her hands together so tightly that the knuckles shone white.

'Yes,' she said, struggling to keep her voice steady. 'Yes. I am.'

Max's eyes flew wide open, all laughter vanishing. Nancy looked bewildered. Hugo jerked his chair back onto all four legs, the blood draining from his face.

'If this is a joke, Mother, it isn't a very funny one.' Max's voice was as terse as the crack of a whip.

'It isn't a joke, darling.'

Their eyes held. Of her three children, he was the handsome one. His hair was darker than either hers or Berthold's and was thick and curly and worn a trifle too long. His eyes were blue, like hers, but a hot, electric blue and were as thick-lashed as a girl's. There was nothing girlish about his physique, though. At nearly twenty-one he was tall and slim-hipped and had the shoulders of a young man at ease and at home on a rugby pitch.

They had never, as far as she could remember, ever had a serious disagreement about anything. From the expression in his eyes, she knew they were about to have one now.

'If it isn't a joke, then it ought to be,' he said tersely. 'What reason could there possibly be for the two of you to divorce?'

As she licked dry lips, Nancy said with hard-headed practicality, 'Well, they don't live together, do they? They've never lived together.'

'That's no reason for them to divorce!' The words erupted out of Hugo as explosively as balls from a cannon. 'Mother prefers living in Yorkshire and Pa prefers living in Berlin. Their not living together is simply a sensible arrangement, that's all.'

His eyes begged her to agree with him.

'No,' she said gently. 'There is more to things than that, Hugo. Though your father and I love each other and always will, we are loving friends who are no longer in love with each other and haven't been for many years.'

'Balderdash!' Never before had Max had spoken to her in such a way and he made no apology for it. 'Absolute poppycock!' He strode across the room, coming to a halt in front of her, a pulse pounding at the corner of his jaw line. 'You're our parents and you love each other and you're married and that's all there is to it. If the two of you have had some sort of a quarrel while you've been here, then I'm sorry. But talking of divorce is overdramatic and ridiculous.'

As she remained silent, wondering how best to respond to him, Nancy said perceptively, 'Is it because Papa won't live in Yorkshire? Is that why you want to divorce him?'

'No, Nancy. That might have been the cause if we had divorced many years ago, when we should have done, but it isn't the cause now.'

'Then what is?' Max was as taut as a coiled spring. 'If you're going to say that Pa loves another woman then I don't believe you. Pa couldn't be a womanizer if he tried.'

Aware of the unwitting irony in his last remark, Vicky said, 'It isn't that Pa loves another woman, Max. It's that I love another man.'

Max came to an abrupt halt.

Hugo made a small, agonized sound.

Nancy's jaw dropped.

'It's quite reasonable that I should do so,' she continued, not daring to stop now the truth was so nearly out in the open. 'Your father and I haven't lived together as a married couple for seventeen years and for a long time now I've been in love with someone else – someone who loves me as I love him. And your father and I are divorcing so that I can marry this . . . other person.'

Max stared at her, stunned.

Hugo looked sick.

Nancy looked interested.

'Christ!' Max made a sudden, uncertain movement, like a vertigo sufferer who sees the world tilt crazily before his eyes and can only pray for the dizziness to pass. 'And when are you going to introduce us to this . . . this *person*, Mother?'

'I don't need to introduce you, Max. You already know him.' Suddenly, her voice was steady and she felt completely calm. 'It's Adam,' she said simply. 'Adam Priestley.'

The blood drained from Max's face.

Hugo struggled to his feet, knocking the chair over as he did so. 'I don't believe it.' His voice was raw. 'I *refuse* to believe it. And if all this . . . this *stuff* . . . has been going on for such a long time, why do you have to marry him now? Why can't you just continue as . . . as you have been doing?' The words choked in his throat.

'Because I've always wanted to marry him. And he's always wanted to marry me – and because I'm having a baby.'

No one moved. No one spoke.

At last, Max said unsteadily, 'I can't deal with this. I can't cope with it.' Looking like death, he turned away from her and made a beeline for the door.

As it slammed behind him, Hugo said, 'I feel ill. I think I'm going to be sick.'

Aware that it was no idle threat, Nancy scooped a fruit

bowl from a small table, tipped the fruit onto the floor and thrust it towards him.

As he retched she turned to her mother and said, with a maturity far beyond her sixteen years, 'Don't feel too badly, Mama. They'll get used to having Adam as a stepfather. They've always liked him and they're not going to be able to stop liking him just because he loves you, and you love him. And I think it's smashing news about the baby. I didn't know people your age could still have them. I hope it will be a girl because, when the chips are down, men can be pretty useless.'

'I know your mother is annoyed at my calling on you so late, but I had to see you. I had to.'

It was nine o'clock at night and Hugo was standing with Hester on the lamplit front step of the Dresners' imposing-looking family house in Haberlandstrasse.

'What on earth is it?' Hester's concern was immediate. 'Are you ill? You look ill. Do you want to come inside? I know my mother won't mind if I explain.'

'No.' Hugo shook his head, a lock of fine, mouse-brown hair falling low across his brow. 'I just need to talk to you . . . need to be with you.'

He was so distressed he was on the verge of tears.

At the drawing-room window a curtain twitched.

Well aware of the scrutiny they were under, Hester took hold of his hand. 'Let's walk round the side of the house and sit on the garden swing. We won't be able to be seen there.'

Uncaring of what Hester's parents might make of such a move, Hugo nodded. He was done with worrying about whether he upset people or not. His mother hadn't worried about upsetting him and Max and Nancy when she had become pregnant with Adam Priestley's baby. At the thought of what his gentle, mild-mannered father must have felt when he had been told the news, he felt ill.

'What is it, sweetheart?' Hester's delicately boned face was fraught with anxiety. 'What has happened? Has there been an accident? Is your mother all right?'

They were out of sight of the drawing-room windows now and he pulled her towards him, burrowing his head in the smoke-black cloud of her hair, sobbing like a child.

Horrified, certain that someone was either dead or dying, she propelled him towards the garden swing.

'It's my mother,' he said, as she pulled him down next to her. 'She's going to divorce my father and marry Adam Priestley – and she has to marry Adam because she's having his baby.'

In the deepening dusk he could see Hester's eyes widen in stark disbelief.

'I know it's incredible, Hester, but it's true. And the worst thing is, the truly terrible thing is that, though she was uncomfortable telling us, she wasn't *unhappy* about it. She wasn't full of guilt or shame or . . . or any of the things you would think she would be.' He ran a hand agitatedly through his hair. 'And when she marries Adam, she won't move into his home. His mother is still alive and she won't want another woman moving into her house, will she? It will be Adam who will move into Shuttleworth Hall, and when he does I will have to move out. To remain there would be just too excruciatingly embarrassing.'

There were no more sobs. His voice was under control again, but it was so bleak, her heart hurt.

She slid her arm around his neck, hugging him close.

He groaned, clinging to her as if she were his only remaining reality.

'I can't believe your mother would do anything dishonourable,' she said after a little while. 'Your mother and father have never lived together, have they? Not since you were very small. Perhaps, so as not to hurt you and Max and Nancy, she's waited a long time to divorce your father and marry

190

Adam. And if she is going to divorce him and marry someone else, surely you're pleased it's someone you all like? I know I don't know him as well as you all do, but whenever I've met him I've always thought him a splendid kind of person.'

'He *is* a splendid kind of person! But that isn't the point, Hester. The point is he and my mother are in their *forties*. What are people going to think? What are they going to say?'

She slid her arm down from around his neck and looked steadily into his eyes. 'Is that all that is truly bothering you, Hugo?'

He shook his head, grateful for her good sense; grateful for the inner calm that never deserted her. 'No,' he said, lifting up her hand and kissing it. 'I just don't like to think of Adam and my mother –' He stopped, unable to go on.

'Making love?' she asked. 'But then you probably wouldn't want to think of your mother and your father making love.' She gave a tiny chuckle. 'I know I wouldn't want to think of my parents making love.'

He made a sound in his throat that could have been halfway to an answering chuckle.

'I'm glad you're beginning to feel a little better about it.' She leaned against him, her head on his shoulder.

'If I am, it's only because of you, Hester.'

The dusk had merged into night and in the darkness she smiled, content.

He was silent for a long while, soothed by her nearness, by the fresh lemon fragrance of her hair and the sound of her gentle breathing.

'This has all put a lot of things in perspective for me,' he said at last, with quiet certainty. 'It's made me see there's no point in taking mind of what other people think or feel. My mother certainly hasn't, has she? And I don't think we should either, Hester.'

She pulled away from him slightly, looking up into his face, a face she loved with all her heart. 'I'm sorry, sweetheart,' she said, puzzled. 'I don't know what you mean.'

'Well, we love each other, don't we? And because you're only sixteen we have to pretend to everyone that we're just good friends – though after tonight, I think your parents are going to realize differently, and not allow you to see me any more – and I don't see why we have to continue pretending.'

'But how can we stop pretending? If my parents knew we loved each other they'd be frantic about the fact that you're not Jewish. When I'm eighteen, *then* we'll tell them, because by then, no matter how much they object, they won't be able to stop me seeing you as they'll be able to stop me seeing you now. That's what we agreed, Hugo, isn't it?'

'Yes.' His voice was suddenly so authoritative as to be completely out of character and for a fleeting moment she was reminded of his uncle, Josef Remer. 'But that was then, Hester, and this is now.'

He took hold of her shoulders, his eyes burning with purpose. 'We don't have to put up with your being forbidden to see me any more. We don't have to put up with waiting until you're eighteen before we tell people we're in love. You're coming to Shuttleworth Hall for Christmas with Claus and Lotti and Ilse, aren't you? It's all arranged, isn't it?'

She nodded, not knowing what he was going to say, but knowing that whatever it was she would go along with it; knowing she loved him with all her heart.

He said with fierce urgency, 'When you come to Yorkshire, bring your birth certificate with you.'

Her eyes rounded. 'But why?'

'Because we're going to go to Gretna Green.' He grinned, dizzyingly happy. 'We're going to elope, Hester. We're going to get married!'

TWELVE

Berlin, October 1933

Lotti sat before one of the chaotically disarrayed dressing tables in the Guido Theilscher's Revue dressing room. For the first time in her life she was truly nervous before a performance. Max had often come to see her when she had appeared in small-time clubs off the Ku'damm, but then she had always been relatively decently clothed. Guido Theilscher's Revue dancers were some of the most famous in Berlin and their exotic costumes were scanty in the extreme.

She added more kohl around her eyes, telling herself that Max had never sat in judgement on her and wasn't likely to start now. Of all her cousins, he was the one she had the most in common with; the one who, to use an English term, was her best chum.

'I've ripped my tights!' the girl at the next dressing table suddenly wailed. 'And not just a little bit. They're totally *kaputt*!'

Lotti, whose routine called for black stockings and suspenders, scrabbled in the bag at her feet and withdrew a scrunched-up pair of fishnets.

'Here,' she said, handing them to her, happy to bail her out.

'Thank you, thank you, *thank you.*' The girl blew her a kiss.

Lotti grinned, enjoying the sensation of backstage camaraderie.

With the kohl in place she began putting on batwing eyelashes. Because her eyes were already a tad too big for her face, they made her look like a startled lemur – though that was not what Max called her. His nickname for her was Monkeyface and had been ever since his visit to Berlin after the war, when he had been nine years old and she had been four.

'*Mords!*' a six-foot transvestite on the other side of her suddenly shrieked. 'My saxophone! Where is it? Where *is* it?' He was a member of the orchestra and beneath his toweringly high blond wig and garish make-up his face was panic-stricken.

This time, Lotti could be of no help.

As bedlam continued all around her she fluttered her eyelashes, relieved to see she had got them on evenly.

When she had telephoned London, which was where Max now lived and worked, and told him she was no longer a small-time chorus girl, but a big-time chorus girl, his congratulations had been instant. Which meant she was worrying unnecessarily about his reaction when he saw her on stage in twenty minutes' time. Max knew his way backwards around Berlin's nightclubs. Though other members of her family would probably have heart attacks if they saw her on stage, bicycling her legs slowly in the air, wearing only a sequinned bolero and skin-tight black satin shorts, Max wouldn't. It would be something he could take in his stride.

She painted her wide, full mouth a vibrant red and then smeared a touch of Vaseline on her lips.

Hugo had once come with Max when she was dancing in a club on Leipzigerstrasse and had been most unhappy at what he had seen.

'You are a Remer, Lotti,' he had said bewilderedly. 'You've

been well brought up. How can you dance half naked every night? The other girls probably need the money, but you don't.'

'Well, first of all, no one knows I'm a Remer,' she had said, unrepentantly. 'I have a stage name. Lotti Lennartz. And I do it because I enjoy doing it. I like plastering stage make-up on and wearing sequins and feathers and being applauded. It's exciting. And I need the money just as much as anyone else, because *Vati* has totally given up on me. I'm barely welcome beneath the family roof these days and I definitely get no allowance.'

He hadn't looked any happier, but then nightclubs and revue bars were not places Hugo was at home in. He'd been posted to the British Embassy in Berlin just over a year ago and could, if he had wanted, have been enjoying the kind of social life that went with such a posting. Instead of which, he and Hester lived very quietly in a small flat in Kaiserallee.

She took one last look at herself in the mirror, liked what she saw, and bounced to her feet, reflecting that Hugo and Hester probably lived quietly so as not to draw attention to Hester's Jewishness. To be a Jew, now, was to live in a constant state of anxiety and fear. It was one reason she loved the tawdry glitter of the clubs. They were the one place Hitler was never likely to be seen.

From the stage, Max couldn't be seen, either. The spotlights were so bright Lotti couldn't see anyone seated beyond the pool of light following her wherever she went. As a chorus girl she was one of the line-up that acted as backing and eye-interest to whoever was centre-stage – the comedians, the top-of-the-bill singers, the skits. She had her own moment of glory, though, as did several other girls. Hers was a zippy, erotic act that involved her doing cartwheels, splits and, last but by no means least, what had become her signature routine: bicycling her legs slowly in the air to a storm of gratifying applause.

'You were truly unforgettable, Monkeyface,' Max said two

hours later as they strolled companionably down the street in the direction of the small club that was his regular haunt whenever he was in the city. 'Better not tell Hugo about the bicycling, though.'

There was laughter in his voice and she laughed with him, happy as she always was when they were together.

'Will one of your girlfriends be joining us when we reach the club?' she asked, knowing that if there was she would at least be someone who would be good company, unlike Claus's girlfriends, who were all complete bores.

'Not tonight. I'm meeting up with a friend. He's in the SA so try not to show your aversion.'

She flashed him a sidelong look, on the verge of saying something. Thinking better of it she simply pursed her lips. What Max got up to when he was in Berlin was none of her affair. Hobnobbing with a Brownshirt was a bit unsavoury, though. Max wasn't aware that she knew it wouldn't be the first time he had done so, for she had seen him some months ago deep in conversation with a Brownshirt in a beer garden on the Marburgerstrasse. And what had been truly odd about *that* incident was that neither she, nor anyone else in the family, had known he was in Berlin at the time.

She shrugged the mystery away. It wasn't important. All that was important was that, unlike Claus, Max wasn't a Nazi.

'Do you think Claus is only a party member because he's concerned about the future of the steelworks?' she asked as they walked past the burned-out shell of offices where communist newsletters had once been printed.

'Well, he'd be pleased about that,' he said, glancing towards the blackened building. 'If the communists had gained power, it would have meant the end of the House of Remer. So the answer is yes. I can't think of any other reason for his being a Nazi, can you?'

'No,' she said emphatically. 'He isn't a Jew-hater. He

doesn't see a lot of Hugo and Hester, but he does see them. They sometimes have dinner together at Hugo and Hester's flat, sometimes in a little restaurant near to the flat.'

'Do you ever join them?'

'For dinner? Not when Claus is with them. He hasn't quite cut me off as completely as Josef has, but he's certainly not best pleased at having a sister who dances in revue bars.'

Max, who saw far more of Claus than Lotti realized, suppressed a grin, well aware that the expression 'best pleased' didn't quite do justice to Claus's feelings where Lotti's choice of profession was concerned.

She slipped her arm into his. 'Tell me the latest news from Shuttleworth Hall,' she said, knowing that there was going to be little chance of exchanging such gossip once they were in the club and his friend was with them. 'Do you manage to spend many weekends there, or are you always in London now? How is Paul? Is he any nearer to breeding his perfect rose? And is baby Emily Elise walking yet? She was still refusing to get off her bottom when Ilse and I were last there.'

They had reached the doorway of the club and paused as a group of noisy drunks exited from it.

'I was there last weekend,' he said, his voice indicating it had been a pleasurable visit. 'Paul thinks he's nearly finished the groundwork for a perfect white rose to be named after my mother and the plant nursery is going great guns. It must be one of the biggest in Yorkshire. As for my little half-sister, she's toddling all over the place.'

'And doing so with curly red hair?' she asked, a giggle in her voice.

'And doing so with *flaming* red hair,' he said, noticing that all the drunks were sporting swastika badges in their lapels. 'Adam couldn't deny her if he tried.'

'And the gossip?'

'Rampant,' he said as they began to walk down the steps

197

into the smoke-filled, noisy club. 'But my mother has never been a social butterfly and no longer being on Harrogate high-society guest lists is no hardship to her. Adam, of course, hasn't been cut from anyone's guest list – though as he refuses point-blank to go to any social function without my mother, he may as well have been. As to his reaction to all the gossip – he's indifferent to it.'

He shot her a wry grin. 'Which is the kind of reaction you'd expect from a man awarded the DSO for courage under enemy fire. They have the Ramsbothams as close friends and they have each other. It's all they need. And once they are married, the scandal of Emily Elise being born out of wedlock will soon be forgotten, as will my mother's divorce. If the husband she had been divorcing had been a Yorkshireman, memories would be a little longer. Divorcing a foreigner will be seen in a different light, and even if it isn't, my mother will be oblivious. She may not look unconventional, but you have to remember there's a deep streak of unconventionality in her. Only someone unconventional would have married a German. It would have made her the source of a good deal of gossip when war broke out in 1914 but I never remember her mentioning it. She would have been as unheeding of gossip then, as she is now.'

He gave a nod in the direction of the bar. 'That's Fritz over there. Good behaviour, Monkeyface. I want him to talk, not you.'

Wearing shiny high boots, breeches and brown shirt with swastika armband, Fritz was built like a stoker, with brutal shoulders and a corpulent, but powerful body. Disliking him on sight, Lotti took care that her feelings didn't show on her face. Nor did she let her feelings show when, within minutes of their joining him at the bar, she realized Fritz had no idea Max had an English mother, had been brought up in England and lived in England.

'The English are pigs,' he said expressively as Max bought

a round of drinks and the man next to him at the bar called out for a bottle of champagne, his appalling German blighted by an unmistakable English accent.

As Max made a sound that his friend took to mean agreement, Fritz turned his attention to Lotti.

It would have been hard for him not to. She had shrugged off her coat to reveal her revue costume. A bra now brought a shred of decency to the tie-fastened sequinned bolero, though did little to hide the voluptuousness of her breasts, and a black wrap-around satin skirt now revealed the satin shorts only when she crossed her legs – which she did with studied slowness, out of sheer force of habit.

Fritz raised his foaming glass of beer towards her, eyeing her leeringly.

'I don't think you've met my girlfriend before, have you, Fritz?' Max draped an arm proprietorially around her shoulders. 'Lotti, Fritz Schenck. Fritz, Lotti Lennartz. And now have we to move away from the bar and find a quiet corner somewhere? I want some Berlin gossip to take back to Munich.'

Lotti kept her eyes firmly on the glass in her hand. If he wanted her to act the part of his girlfriend, that was fine by her. It meant there would be no lecherous advances by Fritz, which was presumably why the lie had been told. Keeping surprise out of her eyes over his remark about Munich was a little more difficult. Munich was a city she'd never heard Max mention, and though the bank he worked for in London gave him generous holiday time, she couldn't imagine his leave would be long enough for him to be spending time in Munich as well as in Berlin.

'And are you also from Munich?' Fritz asked, managing to brush against her breasts as they walked over to a booth at the rear of the club.

She glanced across at Max, read his eyes and, certain he had no need for a lie, said, 'No. I'm a Berliner.'

'And so life is more interesting for her than for me,' Max said as they seated themselves on the shabby red banquettes of a corner booth. 'All Communist Party organizations have been smashed to smithereens in Munich, but it seems that here, in Berlin, there is still work to do.'

'Bollocks!' Fritz gave a roar of laughter. 'Göring runs things in Berlin and he runs them well. In Berlin, communists are with anyone else who is troublesome – in Dachau.'

Most people in the club were now giving their attention to the hatbox-sized stage where a blonde stripper was going through her routine, a bored expression on her face.

'I thought Dachau was for political prisoners?' Max took a deep drink of his beer and wiped his mouth with the back of his hand. It was an uncouth gesture Lotti had never seen him make before.

'Dachau is for anyone.' Fritz was grinning broadly, showing a gold molar. 'It is for Jews, for the bourgeoisie, for anyone who is proving themselves a nuisance.' He began laughing again. 'And you, who live on its doorstep, have to come to Berlin to find that out!'

The girl on the stage had now divested herself of everything but a G-string and silver nipple tassels.

Lotti began paying professional interest. She was a chorus girl, not a stripper, but whenever she was given the opportunity of a solo routine, it was a routine nearly always performed almost naked. She had never worn nipple tassels but now thought they could be a very good idea.

'Are the charges always the same?' Max was asking Fritz, his voice showing little real interest. 'Fighting with storm-troopers, illegal consorting with German girls by Jews – that sort of thing?'

'Sometimes, but not always. We're living in a world without regulations or rules, Max, my friend. Charges are no longer necessary.'

Lotti registered the remark with a shudder. If anyone could be picked off the street and disappear into Dachau, or a camp like it, what safety was there now, in Germany, for anyone?

The girl on stage was coming to the high point of her act. The nipple tassels were shaken vigorously, to noisy appreciation. Then, as Lotti's eyes widened, the girl began moving in such a way that the tassels began circling in opposite directions. The audience let out a collective gasp. Lotti didn't blame them. It was something she had never seen done before – and it was something she had to learn how to do.

'Excuse me,' she said to Max as the girl stepped down from the stage to enthusiastic applause. 'There's someone I have to speak to. I won't be long.'

'Was the someone you had to speak to as useful to you as Fritz was to me?' Max asked a couple of hours later as they walked at an unhurried pace through the early morning streets.

'Hard to say, as I don't know in what way Fritz was useful to you and can tell you don't want to tell me,' she said, her coat collar turned up against the chill dawn air. 'But I've made a new friend and will shortly be learning a new skill. Does that satisfy you?'

'It will have to,' he said, grinning across at her.

They turned into an alley heaped with pyramids of empty wine bottles.

'Wouldn't you rather be living on Unter den Linden?' he asked, moving a bottle out of the way with his foot.

'And have my father aware of the times I come and go? And what I wear? No. Sharing an apartment with other dancers is far preferable.'

They turned out of the alley and into a street of shabby four-storey houses. Somewhere near by a tram squeaked on its tracks.

'You're welcome to come in for a coffee,' she said, coming

to a halt outside a house fronted by a short flight of stone steps. 'The girls won't mind.'

'Not this morning. I've got a busy day ahead of me and I need a little sleep. Give my regards to the girls. And to the boyfriend.'

She looked startled, but only for the briefest of moments. 'Ah, yes,' she said, smiling sunnily. 'Him. Of course I will.'

There was no need for him to say he'd be seeing her again while he was in Berlin, because for both of them it was a given.

'*Auf Wiedersehen*,' he said, and kissed her on the cheek.

'Give my love to my brother,' she said, knowing he was scooting back to Unter den Linden to spend time with his father and that he would also be seeing Claus. She turned away from him and began walking up the steps, adding as an afterthought as she reached the front door, 'And tell him one Nazi in the family is enough. We don't need two.'

When the door was closed behind her, she leaned against it, suddenly exhausted. She'd nearly given herself away when he'd asked her to give his regards to her boyfriend. It would never do for him to know there wasn't one. She had her reputation as a sexily decadent chorus girl to preserve.

She slipped off her high heels and began the long climb to the fourth floor. The lack of boyfriends wasn't because of the lack of offers. She spent her life knee-deep in men and could have her pick. The problem was that after the first couple of dates they all lost their appeal. The only time she never got bored with a man was when that man was Max – and the problem there was that not only was he her cousin, he was also her best buddy. When it came to sex, Max went elsewhere – and if the number of different girlfriends she saw him with was anything to go by, did so frequently and with great variety.

Although Lotti's apartment was a good distance from Unter den Linden, Max didn't trouble to try and find a taxi. The city

202

was beginning to stir with early morning noise and activity. Cleaning women were everywhere, hurrying off to offices and private homes. The occasional bus passed by him. Trams could be heard more frequently. Shouting could be heard as well. In any other city it was shouting that would have struck a discordant note – that would perhaps indicate police sirens might soon be heard. In Berlin it was shouting that attracted barely any attention. There was always violent shouting; always the sound of brawls and fights.

A squad of stormtroopers zipped past him in a truck. The shop window he was approaching had been defaced by an ugly placard on which was written, in scarlet paint, 'DON'T BUY FROM JEWS.' A little farther along the pavement were marks that looked suspiciously like dried blood.

He slid his hands into his trouser pockets. Though he intended spending the day with Claus – whose high-ranking Nazi friends were of even more interest to him than Fritz – he was also anxious for a tête-à-tête with Hugo. Hugo, he knew, was trying to persuade Hester that the time had come for her to leave Germany for good.

'Transferring to a different embassy is no problem for me, Max,' he had said every time the subject had come up between them. 'The problem is Hester's parents. They resolutely refuse to even consider leaving Germany. And unless they leave, Hester won't.'

The shouting suddenly came to an abrupt, sinister end. Max's mouth tightened. He was extremely fond of his gentle-natured sister-in-law. Far too fond of her to want to see her end up in Dachau.

Lotti faced Hester across the checked tablecloth. 'And so I put this red streak in my hair this morning. What do you think of it? Do you like it?'

'It's attention-grabbing,' Hester said with utter truth.

They were having lunchtime coffee and cakes in a small café near to the Kaiser Wilhelm Memorial Church.

'It is.' There was immense satisfaction in Lotti's voice. 'I got the idea when I was with Max last night, talking about Emily Elise.'

Hester's amusement deepened. 'But Emily Elise's hair is Titian. The streak you've put in yours is the colour of a British pillar box!'

'I wanted it to match my lipstick and nail varnish – and it does, perfectly. It also looks sensational with my astrakhan fur.'

The fur was draped over the back of her chair and it was true, the red did look sensational against it.

'I sometimes think Hugo should have sought a position with a bank, instead of with the Foreign Office,' Hester said, reaching for a macaroon. 'I've never known anyone have so much time off work as Max manages to get.'

It wasn't a statement that needed a response and Lotti didn't make one. She had her own idea as to why Max was able to spend so much time in Germany – and it was an idea she had no intention of putting into words.

Hester glanced down at her watch. 'It's nearly time for me to be back,' she said regretfully.

Lotti pushed her coffee cup to one side. 'I'll walk with you to the shop.' She signalled to the waiter that they were ready for the bill. 'Don't you get bored working in a florist's all day, Hester? Don't you ever long for something a little more exciting?'

'Such as dancing in feathers and sequins every evening?' The amusement Lotti always aroused in her was thick in her voice. 'No. I prefer flowers to feathers and as for the dancing bit, I don't think I could do one of your routines in front of Hugo, let alone a revue bar full of strange men!'

With arms linked, both giggling, they walked from the café, Hester the epitome of respectability in a streamlined grey coat, matching trilby-style hat and low-heeled shoes and Lotti looking far from respectable in astrakhan coat, Cossack hat and teeteringly heeled high boots.

'If Max is in Berlin, perhaps he'll come to the apartment for dinner one evening with you and Ilse. He's very fond of Ilse, isn't he?'

It was a rhetorical question. Ilse was the baby of the clan and, sweet-natured and shy, had always been treated with great protectiveness by all the males in the family, Max included.

Lotti was just about to point out that, though Ilse was still treated by everyone as if she were a child, she was less than two years younger than herself, when a truck full of SA men hurtled past, screaming to a halt fifty yards or so in front of them.

Hester stopped abruptly, the blood leaving her face.

'It's OK, Hester,' Lotti said reassuringly. 'It's only the usual office or shop rampage. We'll cross the road if they make you nervous.'

Hester made no response. The stormtroopers piled out of the truck, pistols on their hips, truncheons in their hands. A house door was rammed in and as they charged up the stairs beyond it, a woman began screaming.

Aware that this was something more horrid than the routine destruction of an office used by a subversive political party, Lotti said tautly, 'Let's go back the way we came. Let's take another route.'

'And turn our backs on it?' Hester's face was as white as a sheet. 'Pretend it isn't happening?'

Men were being dragged out of the house and into the street, vainly trying to shield their heads as blows from the truncheons rained down on them.

On the far side of the street a group of bystanders was forming. Other pedestrians, businessmen and women with shopping baskets simply continued walking, neatly stepping out of the way as the men were herded into the back of the truck.

'Jewboys,' a portly man carrying a briefcase said dismissively to Hester and Lotti as he walked past them. 'The street won't stink so much now they've gone.'

Lotti was just about to make a savage response when Hester clutched her arm. 'No, Lotti! Don't draw attention to me!'

Appalled at how different the situation was for Hester than for herself, Lotti shut her mouth abruptly.

The truck revved up, about to move off. As it did so, an elderly woman rushed out of the house and began running dementedly after it, screaming abuse.

'Oh, God.' Lotti's face was now as white as Hester's. 'Oh, Christ!'

The truck slowed. Two stormtroopers leapt down from it, truncheons raised.

Some of the bystanders finally averted their gaze, hurrying away.

Lotti didn't hurry away.

As the woman fell beneath the blows, she tore herself from Hester's grasp and began to run.

The stormtroopers, satisfied with their work, vaulted back into the truck, and by the time Lotti reached the crumpled body the vehicle was roaring out of the street and towards the Ku'damm.

The woman was conscious, bleeding from a blow to her head.

'Can you move? Can you get up?' Lotti asked urgently, kneeling at her side.

As she tried to lift her into a sitting position, she heard the sound of Hester running towards them.

'We need to get her back into the house,' she said as Hester came to a floundering halt, gasping for breath.

Bending down, Hester put an arm around the woman's waist and together, with difficulty, they hauled her to her feet, holding on to her to keep her upright.

No one came to help them. Most of the bystanders had now disappeared, though a couple of them remained, standing on the opposite side of the street, watching.

'She needs a doctor,' Lotti said as she and Hester half-carried the woman out of the street and across the pavement.

'It will have to be a Jewish doctor. No other doctor will want to come.'

As they gained the doorway Lotti fiercely hoped Hester wasn't known to any of the bystanders watching them. Informing had become a national pastime. Giving aid to a victim of SA brutality would, if reported, be interpreted as interfering with SA activity. And a Jewess charged with interfering with SA activity would be dealt with far more severely than she would be.

'I know of someone. And if he won't come, my father will.'

Lotti had forgotten all about Hester's father's profession.

'Let's hope there's a phone in the house,' she said grimly as the woman's head fell against her chest, smearing her astrakhan coat with blood.

The sitting room was in chaos. Tables and chairs were overturned, crockery smashed. The phone, however, was still connected.

They laid the groaning woman down on a sofa and it was only then, when she was no longer supporting the woman's weight, that Lotti felt her knees give way with delayed shock.

She slumped down against a corner of the sofa, her knees up to her chin. She needed a cigarette. Hell, she needed a brandy.

As she heard Hester make telephone contact with a doctor she clasped her hands around her knees to stop herself from shaking, wondering what pit of hell her country was hurtling into.

THIRTEEN

Yorkshire, Christmas 1933

Nancy drove down to Little Ridding's station in a state of high elation. Christmas was always a special time of year because it was when the Berlin contingent, as Paul referred to them, became part of their family life in Yorkshire.

Her one fear, when she knew her parents were to divorce, and especially after Emily Elise had been born, had been that her father would no longer make his annual Christmas visits to Shuttleworth Hall. It had been a fear that had proved groundless.

As far as she could discern, nothing much had changed in her parents' relationship – which, as she had once said to Hugo, showed that their marriage had never been all that it should have been.

Adam wasn't living at Shuttleworth Hall, of course, and wouldn't be until he and her mother were able to marry, which wouldn't be for another few months. Their not living in sin was a vestige of respectability that made little sense when it was common gossip that Emily Elise was Adam's child, but it was a vestige her mother was stubbornly clinging to. Adam was, however, a regular visitor and after Emily Elise had been born it had been unthinkable for him not to be with them over Christmas.

The previous Christmas she had geared herself up for what she had anticipated would be the appalling difficulty of seeing her mother, her father, Adam and Emily Elise all in the same room for the first time. It had been yet another needless worry.

Her father and Adam had been pleasantly courteous to each other, and her father – who loved children – had speedily taken Emily Elise on his knee and become a great favourite with her. Her mother had behaved as if it was quite usual to have her aged father, her husband, a lover, her husband's adult children and her lover's child all under the same roof and around the same dinner table and had been just as openly affectionate to Berthold as she had always been. Everyone had been put at ease. Everyone had had a wonderful Christmas.

This Christmas would, she knew, be just as enjoyable. It was snowing and Shuttleworth Hall always looked blissfully beautiful under snow. Will Patchett had cut armloads of holly and he and Paul had set up the most enormous Christmas tree in the drawing room. Her grandfather had expressed a fancy for seeing a pantomime in Harrogate and Hester, who had arrived with Hugo two days ago and who had never been to a British pantomime, had been so keen to go with him that Adam had made a family block-booking for all of them.

What Claus was going to say when he found out he'd been roped in to enjoy an evening of Aladdin and Widow Twanky custard-pie humour was anyone's guess, but he'd go along with it. Everyone always went along with everything at Shuttleworth Hall. It was why being there was always so special.

At the prospect of Claus spending a whole ten days in Yorkshire she negotiated Little Ridding's snow-covered streets singing 'We Three Kings' at full belt. Her father, Lotti and Ilse would be with him and she was looking forward to seeing all of them, but Claus was different. For her, Claus had always been different. As a child she had been his shadow, never letting him out of her sight. As a teenager, she had decided she would marry him when she was old enough and, now she was nineteen, was happily aware she was old enough any time now.

The really glorious thing about her ambition was that it was an ambition shared, for his mother had made no secret of her belief that as Claus would one day inherit the House of Remer, a wife who was already a Remer would be far more suitable than a fortune-hunter who wasn't.

She skidded slightly on the ice, drove into the skid unpanicked and straightened the car. The nature of her relationship with Claus was such that she had also made no secret of her belief that she would make him an ideal wife. Playing things cannily simply wasn't in her nature.

Four months ago, when she had last been in Berlin, they had become lovers. She had been the one who had deliberately set out to change the nature of their relationship. To her, it had been an obvious thing to do. She was going to marry him and, as it wasn't likely he would ask her to marry him if he continued viewing their relationship as Max and Lotti viewed theirs – that they were intensely close cousins and nothing else – she had determined a dramatic step needed to be taken. And had taken it.

They had been out for the evening to the opera and had returned home to find the vast drawing room deserted.

'Everyone must be either out, or in bed,' he had said, switching on lamps and taking off his bow tie.

She had stood very still, knowing what it was she was going to do and knowing that if he didn't respond to her as she prayed he would, her life might as well be over.

'Are you off to bed as well?' he had asked.

'Yes,' she had said. 'I think so.'

Still wearing his white dinner jacket, his evening shirt now open at the throat, he had walked towards her to kiss her goodnight, as she had known he would.

It had always been a kiss on the nose. It had been a kiss on the nose when she had been six and he had been nine.

Putting his hands on her shoulders he had lowered his head and had kissed her on the nose.

Instead of responding with a smile and wishing him goodnight, God bless, and going off to her room, she had laid her hands slowly on his chest and lifted her head so that her eyes met his.

'Kiss me properly,' she had whispered.

There had been shock in his eyes and then agonized indecision.

'I can't,' he had said, his voice strangled. 'If I did . . . there'd be no going back, Nancy.'

'I know,' she had said, feeling triumph seep into her very bones. 'And I don't want there to be any going back, Claus.' The sexual attraction that had sizzled between them unacknowledged for so long, had been almost unbearable. She had slid her arms up and around his neck. 'I want you to make love to me. I want it more than I've ever wanted anything else, ever.'

Still he had paused, his mouth only a millimeter from hers. She had known what was holding him back. Always a realist, he had been considering what would happen if their new relationship as lovers should one day come to an end and their old relationship be impossible to recapture.

Always a romantic and viewing it as being a needless concern, she had raised herself on her toes, pressing her lips against his. From that moment on, there had been no need for her to take the lead again. He had kissed her as she had longed for him to kiss her – and the knowledge that there could be no going back had filled her with joy.

Snow was still falling as she parked at the back of the

station. In a pair of sensible boots she had bought in Berlin a year ago and a capacious tie-belted trenchcoat, she stepped from the car.

She'd forgotten to wear a hat or a headscarf and by the time she gained the cover of the waiting room her fair hair was speckled with snowflakes.

'Bah gum, lass. Is that confetti in yer 'air?' a wizened figure, hunched comfortably over a coal fire asked.

'No, worse luck.' Nancy regarded Little Ridding's stationmaster-in-name-only with something like disbelief. 'How come you're still alive?' she asked with her usual crushing directness. 'You must be at least a hundred.'

'A 'undred and one,' he said with satisfaction. 'I got a telegram from't King last year, but I doan't suppose I'll get anything this year.'

'Yes, you will.' Nancy warmed her hands in front of the fire. 'I'm going to do a piece on you for the *Yorkshire Post*. "A Hundred-and-One and Still Going". It will make a lovely caption. You don't mind if someone comes to take your photograph, do you?'

'Not so long as I 'ave mi teeth in.'

'You're on,' Nancy said, finding it a reasonable stipulation. 'Has the snow delayed the trains? The Harrogate train should be coming in now.'

'Aye, well. Mebbe it will be and mebbe it won't. Is that yon rose man's coit. It looks as if it'd fit 'im.'

'My coat is my own. If it was Paul's it would be trailing on the ground.'

'Aye, well . . .' The old man was just about to say that it wasn't far from doing so when there came the sound of a train approaching.

Nancy headed out of the waiting room like a shot from a gun.

As the train hove into view, she could see someone leaning out of a window and knew it would be Lotti.

She began waving, thinking how wonderful it was to be part of such a united, extended family. And it *was* a united family even though they were of different nationalities – American, British and German – and had totally different interests – who, for instance, could be more dissimilar than Paul and Claus, with Paul passionate about roses and Claus passionate about the Remer steelworks and factories? Or her and Lotti, with Lotti spending her life hurtling from party to party and nightclub to nightclub, while she spent her life as a cub reporter on the *Yorkshire Post*, reporting on births, deaths, fetes and traffic accidents? There were even more glaring disparities when one took into account Claus's Nazi Party membership and Hester's Jewishness.

As the train steamed nearer and she could see Lotti clearly, she gave her head a sharp shake, not wanting to think about Claus's Nazi Party membership. Though the family knew why he had joined the party, his continuing to be a member, now that Hitler was showing his true colours, was becoming a problem to everyone apart from his father.

The problem was an especially big one for her, for she'd no intention of marrying a Nazi, which meant that Claus was going to have to face up to a very difficult situation where the House of Remer was concerned. Personally, like nearly everyone else in the family, she didn't give two hoots about the vast wealth that came from the steelworks. Her mother hadn't touched a penny of House of Remer money for decades. Lotti had cut herself off from it when she had outraged Josef by becoming a chorus girl. Ilse, she suspected, never gave House of Remer wealth a thought. As for Max and Hugo, neither of them was materialistic and had never, to the best of her knowledge, expressed hopes that a fortune might one day come their way via their father.

Claus, though, was of a different stamp. Claus had always known he was destined to one day take over the steelworks and it was a destiny he'd never had any problem accommodating himself to. Neither had he ever had any problem in accommodating himself to being an exceptionally wealthy young man who would one day be wealthy on a vast scale. He had a passion for fast cars. He owned a powerful speedboat that was berthed at Wannsee and a small plane for when he wanted to fly down to the Alps to ski. Though she could happily live without Remer wealth – and would prefer to live without it – Claus would not be able to. It was a problem and she didn't yet know how she was going to solve it.

'Nancy! *Nancy!*' Lotti shouted, saving her from thinking any further about it as she waved furiously with one hand and held on to an astrakhan, Russian-styled hat with the other.

Nancy's grin nearly split her face in two. God, but she loved her family. Lotti was the sister she'd never had. She was totally irrepressible. Always outrageous. Always fun.

'Merry Christmas, Lotti!' she yelled as the train slid to a halt. 'It's snowing! Isn't it marvellous?'

The train door opened and Lotti tumbled out onto the platform.

As she ran towards her, Nancy saw Ilse step out of the carriage followed by Berthold and then, last because he was in charge of their luggage, Claus.

Lotti hurtled towards her, hugging her and enveloping her in a cloud of musky scent. Nancy responded enthusiastically, eager for the hug to be over so that she could give her attention to Claus.

'*Mein Gott*, but it's good to be back in Yorkshire!' Lotti's beaming smile was radiant. 'I can't wait to tuck into Josephine's Christmas cake and mince pies.'

'And I can't wait to tuck into some *Stollen*. You have brought one with you, haven't you?'

'*Stollen, Schokoladen, Schnapps*. We've brought everything but the kitchen cooker.'

'Kitchen sink,' Nancy said, wondering how Lotti could still get Yorkshire sayings muddled.

She disentangled herself and as Claus was still not looking towards her but was ensuring Little Ridding's young porter had all the luggage safely out of the carriage and onto a trolley, she gave her attention to her father and to Ilse.

'Goodness, you look wonderful, Father,' she said, hugging him tightly so that he couldn't look into her eyes and wouldn't know she was exaggerating. Though Berthold looked *well*, he certainly didn't look wonderful. His innate gentleness had long ago become indistinguishable from the kind of passivity usually apparent only in the elderly – and he wasn't elderly. He was forty-seven. Adam was three years his senior, though she didn't know of anyone who would believe it.

Her future stepfather had retained his good looks. There was no fat on him, only well-toned muscle. His hair was still spicily red, still thick and curly and he still possessed the kind of vigour that ensured it was obvious he was Emily Elise's father, and not her grandfather.

'Your hair is wet with snow,' Berthold said, trying to brush the snowflakes from it.

'It's fine, Father.' Not wanting him to fuss she turned to Ilse, registering with astonishment just what it was Ilse was wearing. 'Gosh! What are you doing wearing fox furs, Ilse? Aren't you a little young for furs?'

'Evidently not.' Ilse's mouth curved into her habitual slow, sweet smile. 'Papa bought them for my seventeenth birthday. They're all the rage in Berlin. One of my favourite actresses wears as many as five at a time.'

'And the actress in question also wears a monocle, so just be grateful Ilse hasn't gone the whole hog,' Lotti said as Claus, satisfied they'd left nothing on the train, slammed the carriage door closed. 'I'm just disappointed Ilse didn't have the sense to have asked for a serious fur. Mink or sable. Then I could

215

have borrowed it. I can't borrow the fox. The colour clashes with the streak in my hair.'

'So does your blue nail varnish.' Though she was speaking to Lotti, Nancy wasn't looking at her. She was looking at Claus.

He was wearing the kind of clothes that few Yorkshiremen could have afforded and that none would have been seen dead in – a pearl-grey silk suit and, draped around his shoulders, a deep-grey cashmere overcoat with a black sable collar. With his striking fair hair and trimly clipped moustache he looked absolutely splendid, the epitome of sophistication and handsome enough to commit suicide for.

As Berthold and Lotti headed out of the station he fell into step beside her. 'I hope there's a traditional Yorkshire tea waiting for us,' he said. 'Toasted teacakes and sticky parkin and curd tarts?'

'Is food the only thing you Berliners think about?' she teased, happy as a sandboy as his arm slid around her waist. 'The first thing Lotti said was that she couldn't wait to tuck into Christmas cake and mince pies.'

The banter was the kind of banter that took place between everyone in the family. The look that passed between them was of a far different nature.

Now, as they walked out of the station towards the car, in answer to her teasing, he said, 'Food is most definitely not the only thing I think about – as you well know.'

She blushed furiously and as her father stepped into the front passenger seat and Claus held one of the rear passenger doors open for Lotti and Ilse, she was aware of Lotti looking across at her questioningly.

She put the aged Lanchester into gear, her grin deepening. Telling Lotti she was on the verge of becoming her sister-in-law, as well as her cousin, was something she was looking forward to.

*

'But that's ... amazing.' Seated on the bed in the guest bedroom she always occupied when at Shuttleworth Hall, Lotti was, for once, almost lost for words.

'I think the world to be used is "wonderful",' Nancy responded chidingly. '"Amazing" would mean it's something you'd never even have dreamed of and as I've always known this would happen, it's not quite the case.'

A journalistic precision with words wasn't Lotti's forté.

'It's amazing,' she said again, taking off her hat and running her hands through her dark, sharply bobbed hair. 'I know it's what *you've* always wanted, but I always thought the cousin thing would put Claus off.'

'Why on earth should it?' Nancy saw no reason to admit that until she'd forced Claus into seeing her as someone other than a cousin, the close familiarity of their cousinship had, indeed, been something of a handicap. 'Cousins can marry. It will all be perfectly legal.'

'Yes.'

There was an expression in Lotti's eyes and voice that Nancy couldn't quite pin down. It was almost as if a thought had occurred to her that had never occurred before.

'And so it means that when we get married my relationship to you will be like our mothers' relationship to each other. We'll be cousins who are also sisters-in-law. Don't you think that's cosy?'

'It's weird. You'll be in exactly the same position as your mother was when she married your father. You'll be the English wife of the heir to the Remer steelworks. And that may be quite complicating for you, Nancy. Especially as things are in Germany at the moment.'

Hearing a car approach, Nancy crossed to the window just in time to see Max's MG sports car turn into the long drive. 'It's only Hitler who's complicating things,' she said, her straight eyebrows drawing together in a slight frown. 'And Claus will find a way of ensuring the steelworks stay under Remer control without his having to continue being a party member.'

Lotti's arched eyebrows rose. 'The two of you have talked about this, then, have you?'

'Not exactly. When we were last together, I was too busy getting him to fall in love with me to talk about the steelworks and the Nazis. We'll be talking about things like that over the next few days, while he's at Shuttleworth Hall. Max has just arrived, and by the look of it he hasn't got a girlfriend with him, thank goodness. The last one he brought with him from London was a horror. A debutante who seemed to think Yorkshire was Outer Mongolia.'

If Lotti's reaction had been oddly thoughtful when she had broken the news as to the change in her and Claus's relationship, her mother's reaction was even more of a surprise. In fact, it wasn't a surprise at all. It was a shock.

'But it's unthinkable, Nancy, love!' she said, putting down her cup so sharply that the tea slopped into the saucer. 'An infatuation is one thing – I know you've always been infatuated with him. But for Claus to lead you on and to take advantage of your feelings . . . it's almost beyond belief.'

'He hasn't led me on, Mother.' Stupidly, her disappointment in her mother's reaction to the news was so intense she felt tears burning her eyes. She blinked them away. 'We're *in love* with each other. He's going to ask me to marry him and –'

'So he hasn't asked you yet?' Vicky's relief was so overwhelming she couldn't keep it from showing in her voice.

'No, but he will.' As yet she hadn't told anyone of her secret hope that his Christmas present to her was going to be an engagement ring and now was clearly not the moment to do so. 'I don't understand why you're reacting like this, Mother.' She dug her nails into her palms, trying not to sound plaintive. 'You like Claus. You're just as fond of him as you are of Lotti and Ilse. It means our family will be even closer than ever and it means that the Remer steelworks will one day pass down to Father's grandchildren, and that will mean a lot to him.'

Her mother sucked in her breath, her face paling.

'And it means that you will become part of a heritage – the House of Remer steelworks – that I've tried for nearly twenty years to distance myself from,' she said unsteadily. 'What will you do, Nancy, if, as happened to me, you one day discover that the House of Remer is manufacturing armaments destined to be used against Britain?'

Nancy bit her lip. Mentioning the likelihood of the steelworks one day passing down to her father's grandchildren had been a grave tactical error, especially as she had no interest in perpetuating a House of Remer steel dynasty and was hoping that Claus would find a way of eventually dissociating himself from it.

'I appreciate that Claus and I will have difficulties to face,' she said stiffly, aware it was the first time in her life her mother had been so curiously unbending towards her, 'but we love each other and we're going to overcome our difficulties together.'

Hopefully, she waited for her mother to put her arms around her and to tell her she was sorry if she had upset her and that she was happy she and Claus were in love. Just as she thought such a move was about to be made, Paul came into the room, Emily Elise toddling in his wake and, as her mother scooped Emily Elise into her arms, the moment was lost.

'I never realized how difficult snatching private moments was going to be for us,' Claus said, doubtfully eyeing the door and the chair jammed beneath the doorknob.

It was early evening and they were lying on his bed, semi-dressed. He was wearing slacks, his shirt unbuttoned, his chest bare. She was naked apart from a rose-pink underslip and matching, lace-trimmed cami-knickers.

219

'You're worrying needlessly, darling. A herd of elephants couldn't dislodge that chair.' Serenly unfazed, Nancy played her fingers slowly across his chest and down towards his stomach. 'And anyhow, no well-mannered person ever walks into someone else's bedroom without first knocking. And everyone is well mannered at Shuttleworth Hall.'

Her hand slid beneath the waistband of his slacks. He looked towards the door again. Having their family know they were in love was one thing. Making love practically within earshot of them all was quite another and he knew he wasn't going to be comfortable doing so.

Gently, he removed her hand.

She gave a sigh, accepting the restrictions he was imposing on them. 'We'll simply have to book into the Queen's Hotel at Leeds,' she said practically.

'Don't you mean the Queen's Hotel in Harrogate?'

She shook her head, moving her leg up and across him. 'Absolutely not. I'm known at the Queen's Hotel in Harrogate.'

His erection was so urgent, it hurt.

Well aware of the agony she was putting him through, she smiled, brushing his mouth with her lips, saying softly as she did so, 'It wouldn't be like this, if we were married.'

'Then marry me,' he said thickly, taking hold of her and rolling her beneath him.

She hooked her legs around his. 'When? We could see the vicar tomorrow, have the first of the banns called on Sunday and marry in three weeks' time.'

His hand, sliding up the warm flesh of her thigh, came to a sudden stop. 'Without my parents? They'd never forgive me.' His hand began moving again. 'You could pack up your job on the *Yorkshire Post* and travel back with me to Berlin. We could marry in the Kaiser Wilhelm Kirche.'

'And your Nazi Party membership?' Her breath was

coming in short gasps as with his free hand he unbuttoned his trousers. 'Will you be able to relinquish it before we marry?'

'No,' he said, having no intention of lying to her.

Her eyes, which had been half closed with desire, flew wide open. With an anguished cry she twisted away from him, drawing her knees up to her chin and hugging them tight.

He slammed a clenched fist hard down on the bed and then moved equally quickly, fastening his trousers and springing to his feet. 'If withdrawing from the party is going to be a condition of our getting married, then we're never likely to get married,' he said frustratedly, tucking his shirt in his trousers.

He crossed to the dressing table, taking a cigarette from his cigarette case, lighting it and inhaling deeply. 'It just shows how hopelessly naive you are, Nancy.' He blew a stream of smoke out through his nose. 'Hitler is doing wonderful things for Germany. The communists are no longer a threat to our industries, and as for the anti-Semitism, that's merely a political tactic to please all those who believe Jews are responsible for everything that's wrong with German society. Once Hitler's securely in power, once he's not just Chancellor but Head of State, all that nonsense will come to an end.'

'I don't believe you.' Beneath her straight emphatic eyebrows her eyes were fierce. 'I don't believe Hitler would have sanctioned laws allowing public meetings to be banned, phones tapped and private homes searched, if he intended backtracking. And he can't become Head of State, Claus. Hindenburg is Head of State.'

He took another deep draw on his cigarette, then said, 'The people I associate with in the party are not thugs, Nancy. If they were, no matter what the advantages to the House of Remer, I wouldn't be allying myself with them. It's the Brownshirts that are the thugs and even though Hitler is technically their supreme commander, in practice it isn't working that way. Ernst Röhm trained and organized them and it is Röhm who is really in control of them.'

He remembered her profession and hesitated. 'This information isn't public knowledge, Nancy – and hasn't to become public knowledge. Do you understand me?'

She nodded, aware that her journalistic impulses were going to have to be suppressed.

'Word is that control will soon be taken from Röhm, and when it is there will be a big difference on the streets of Berlin. The lawlessness generated by his thugs will be at an end. The emergency decrees will be repealed. Do you believe me?'

'I believe that you believe it,' she said cautiously.

'And do you believe that I love you?'

She nodded. 'Yes,' she whispered. 'And I love you.'

He crushed out his cigarette, she slid off the bed and they met in a passionate embrace in the middle of the room.

'Give it time, *Liebchen*,' he said hoarsely. 'I promise that within a few months you'll see a difference in Germany. A change for the better. A change you'll be able to live with without demanding actions from me that would jeopardize everything my father and grandfather worked so hard to build.'

She wound her arms around his waist and with her head on his chest, closed her eyes tight. She wanted to believe him – and half did so.

The bottom line, though, was that they wouldn't be marrying in three weeks' time in Little Ridding's village church and her Christmas present from him wasn't going to be an engagement ring – at least, it wasn't going to be so this year. And unless the political climate in Berlin changed drastically in the way he had predicted, it was unlikely to be so next year either.

FOURTEEN

London, Yorkshire and Berlin, June 1934
From where he was seated Max had a bird's-eye view of the far side of Whitehall and the Cenotaph. The man facing him across the giant expanse of a mahogany Biedermeier desk, said courteously, 'Cigar, Remer?'

Max shook his head. 'No, thanks. I don't.' He withdrew a cigarette case from his inside pocket and quirked an eyebrow for permission to take one.

'By all means,' his Controller said, leaning back a little more comfortably in his leather-padded swivel chair. 'Now, what's the state of play with regard to what the Nazis describe as "mild reform centres" and Röhm? Is he likely to soon find himself visiting one of them?'

'My cousin thinks so. He sees Röhm's Brownshirts as having become a handicap to Hitler. In numbers, they now exceed the number of men in the German army – and a paramilitary organization of that strength is liable to become as much of a danger as it is of an asset. That's one side of the coin. The other – and this is Claus's take on things – is that the street violence which served Hitler so well before he became Chancellor is now an embarrassment to him. He believes

Hitler wants to be perceived as being respectable. Which means he'll have to get rid of Röhm, before Röhm decides it's time to get rid of him.'

'When he gets rid of Röhm, he'll have to get rid of all high-ranking Brownshirts at the same time. It will be a bloodbath.'

'Yes, sir. It will.'

His Controller swivelled his chair around so that he too had a view of the Cenotaph. 'And what do you think will be the outcome of such a purge? Are we going to see Hitler become more tractable?'

'There's a section of German society that believes once Röhm is gone, and the men he organized and trained are disbanded, things will change for the better. The view I've heard expressed is that street violence will de-escalate and Hitler will begin paying more attention to mainstream political matters, and put anti-Semitism on a back burner.'

His Controller swung back to face him. 'And what do you think, Remer? Do you think it likely?'

'That anti-Semitism will cease to be the driving force behind National Socialism? No, sir. I don't.'

'Good. Because neither do I.' He took a cigar from the box on his desk and cut the end from it. 'Tell me about the camps. Are we to believe the propaganda being put out? Are they only for the imprisonment in protective custody of all communists and other members of outlawed political parties?'

'Dachau is the main camp and anyone is at risk of being sent to it if they publicly oppose the status quo. For Jews the situation is far worse. Any kind of trumped-up charge will serve to send a Jew to Dachau.'

His Controller puffed on his cigar for a minute or two and then said queryingly, 'And your cousin's side of the family tree? Any Jewish blood there?'

'No, sir. The Remers haven't any Jewish antecedents and my aunt is American – and not Jewish.'

He wondered whether to add that his sister-in-law was Jewish and decided against it. As Hugo worked for the Foreign Office, MI6 would already know all it needed to know about Hester.

'And your sister? I understand she's now living and working in Berlin?'

'Yes, sir. Nancy moved there some months ago. She's working as a junior reporter for the *International Herald*.'

'Excellent.' His Controller took the cigar out of his mouth and gave him a beaming smile. 'Another useful contact, eh, Remer?'

'Yes, sir.'

'And you find the cover of being an employee at Barings Bank works well for you?'

'Yes, sir.'

'Good. Well, that's all for now, Remer. Keep up the good work.'

With the interview at an end, Max rose to his feet and made his exit.

He had two days in hand before he was due to leave for Germany again and though two days wasn't long enough for a really enjoyable visit to Yorkshire, it was better than nothing.

As he stepped out into Whitehall he looked at his watch. The 12.10 for York via Harrogate left in just over an hour. He had plenty of time to take a cab to his Albany flat and pick up an overnight bag.

He didn't trouble to let anyone know he was arriving because lately, whenever he did so, his mother or Adam insisted on driving down to Little Ridding to meet him from the Harrogate train. Instead he took a taxi from the station, exchanging a few words with his old friend the stationmaster before he left.

The drive through Wensleydale, the river skirting the road, was such a peaceful, beautiful contrast to Berlin it would have been easy for him to believe he was on a different planet. The sheep on the hills still had lambs at their sides and the edges of the narrow roads were thick with cow parsley and wild dog roses.

It was at times like this, loving Yorkshire so much it hurt, that he found it hard to accept he wasn't Yorkshire-born. By birth, he was a Berliner. His passport was that of a German citizen. It was a dichotomy he'd struggled with for years and one he still hadn't resolved, for it wasn't as if his ties to Germany had ever been broken, or ever could be broken. His love for his father was far too deep for that to happen, and he had far too many cherished childhood memories of Berlin – his father taking him to the Tiergarten and the zoo, on little excursions to the Schöneberger Volkspark and on long day expeditions to Wannsee – for him ever to be able to view the city dispassionately.

Knowing he wasn't likely to resolve all his complex feelings about Berlin on this particular trip to Yorkshire he settled back to enjoy the sight of the fast-flowing Ure and to relish the sense of relaxation that came over him whenever he was about to spend time at Shuttleworth Hall.

The minute he stepped across the threshold he knew he'd arrived on no ordinary day and that something special was being celebrated. The lavender-waxed furniture was always polished to a glass-like sheen and there were always bowls of flowers everywhere, even in winter. Today, though, vases of white roses crammed every available surface.

Musingly, he walked through the drawing room towards the French windows and, as he did so, there came the sound of laughter and a champagne cork popped.

He knew then, even before he saw them, that he'd arrived home on his mother and Adam's wedding day.

He stepped out onto the terrace, a smile on his face.

'Congratulations,' he said, genuinely pleased for them. 'You make a beautiful couple.'

At a large round table on the terrace were seated his mother and Adam, his grandfather, Paul, Josephine, Violet Ramsbotham, Will and Jenny. The table was covered with a glistening white damask tablecloth and in the centre of it was a two-tier wedding cake surrounded by yet more white roses.

Adam, splendidly handsome in a dove-grey three-piece suit, rose to his feet, the fizzing champagne bottle still in his hand.

'Fantastic timing, Max!' he said ebulliently, pouring Max a glass of champagne.

Vicky pushed her chair away from the table. 'Oh, darling! This is so wonderful! But you're not cross that we didn't let you or anyone else know, are you?'

Joy at his walking in on them so unexpectedly and concern that his feelings might be hurt fought for supremacy as she ran across to him.

'No, I'm not cross,' he said easily as she stood on tiptoe to kiss him lovingly on the cheek. 'But why the secrecy? You're going to have quite a bit of explaining to do to Hugo and Nancy and the Berlin contingent.'

'I know.' With her hand in his she walked him towards the table. 'But we didn't want a big-number wedding. Under the circumstances we felt it would have been totally inappropriate. And if we'd told you and Hugo and Nancy, we would have had to tell Claus and Lotti and Ilse. And then what would I have done with regard to your father? Although he's accepted the situation he would still have felt deep hurt at seeing me marry Adam, and it was equally unthinkable for everyone else to be here and not him. So this seemed the best way.'

'Yes,' he said as Adam pressed a glass of champagne into his hand. 'I can see that. I'm glad I'm here by accident, though, if only to see what a beautiful bride you are.'

Vicky blushed and Paul laughed.

'It's true, Aunt Vicky,' he said, his cane chair pushed a little away from the table, his legs crossed at the ankle.

Though Vicky was no longer wearing the flower bedecked hat she had worn at the Register Office there were flecks of confetti in her flaxen-blonde chignon. Her dress was of oyster silk, the skirt perfectly draped into a river of tiny, impeccably executed pleats. Three long strands of pearls – pearls he had never seen before and which he assumed were a wedding gift from Adam – hung from her neck at precisely the right depth of the softly draped neckline. Her lipstick was a soft rose pink and her lightly mascaraed eyes were a deep, cerulean blue.

'And how long are you here for, my boy?' his grandfather asked as Max sat down beside him in a chair Will Patchett had hastily gone to fetch.

'Two days. Then I'm off to Berlin.'

Everyone was so accustomed to his regular jaunts to Germany that no one made any remark on the fact that it wasn't so long since he'd last been there.

'I think it's time Vicky and Adam cut the cake,' Violet said authoritatively, a large corsage of roses adorning her magnificent purple-swathed bosom, a Box Brownie camera at the ready.

Max settled himself comfortably to enjoy the rest of the wedding celebrations, seeing with amusement that Emily Elise, oblivious to her parents' nuptials, was playing on the lawn with Tinker, who was sporting a huge pink satin bow around his neck in honour of the wedding and was allowing himself to be pushed around by Emily Elise in a toy wheelbarrow.

The harmony and contentment that eased into Max's soul whenever he was at Shuttleworth Hall, eased into it now in full abundance. It was an atmosphere that was, he knew, due solely to his mother; an extension of her own contentment with life and her serene nature.

As he watched her cut her wedding cake with the man she

so obviously loved with all her heart, he was well aware that many people in the North Riding would think his mother a very lucky woman to have snared such a wealthy, personable, war-decorated widower. As far as he was concerned, though, it was very much the other way around.

It was Adam Priestley who was the lucky one.

And if his stepfather was an exceedingly lucky man, his father had been an exceedingly foolish one.

As he thought of his mild-mannered father, he couldn't help feeling a surge of exasperation – exasperation he knew his mother must have often felt in far greater measure. Why, when it would have been so easy for him to do so, had he always refused to leave Berlin to live with them, as a family, in Yorkshire? Surely, if he had done so, his parents' marriage would have survived?

As slices of wedding cake were passed around the table, he reflected that the person most to blame for the breakdown of his parents' marriage was his uncle. He'd been aware for years that it was Josef who had always brought pressure to bear on Berthold to remain in Berlin.

'Josef needs me,' his father would say, pathetically unable to see that his younger brother didn't need him in the slightest; that his younger brother had never done anything but manipulate him to his own advantage.

In the past, as a schoolboy, he had often secretly felt grateful for that manipulation, for if Josef had never bullied his father into handing over control and ownership of the steelworks, he, Max, would have been heir to the House of Remer, not Claus. And that he wouldn't have liked at all.

Freedom from inheriting such a burden was, for him, a good consequence of Josef's unpleasantly domineering personality. The disturbing side of it was the way he had ensured that Berthold thought exactly as he did with regard to National Socialism.

That Claus had become a Nazi was bad enough – but Max could at least understand what his cousin's motivation had been. The House of Remer was Claus's legacy and he wanted his legacy be in good order when he inherited it. To that end he had long believed the only real opponent to communism in Germany was National Socialism. And in that he had, of course, been proved right.

Claus would, he was sure, eventually see that one evil had been prevented only by the perpetration of an even greater evil. He doubted that his father would ever see such a light, or certainly not until Josef saw it first.

'Photographs,' Violet said, heaving her mighty weight to her feet. 'I want one of the bride and groom and Emily Elise first. Then one of Vicky with her father. Then one of the happy couple with Max and Paul. And then a group photograph with everyone in it.'

'Great Scott, Violet! It isn't a royal wedding!' Arthur Hudson protested, well knowing that his protest was going to be in vain. 'The next thing you'll be wanting is a photograph of Vicky and Adam with Tinker!'

'Thank you for reminding me, Arthur. I most certainly do want a photograph of them with Tinker. Max? Are you going for Emily Elise? Please make sure Tinker comes back with you, will you?'

His two days at home were extremely joyous ones and when it was time for him to leave, Vicky insisted on driving him to Little Ridding herself.

'It's great to see you so happy, Ma,' he said as she drove at a decorous thirty miles an hour beside the banks of the Ure.

She turned her head, flashing him a wide, sunny smile. 'It's great to be so happy.'

They motored on in silence for a little way and then she said, 'Is there no young lady in your life, Max? There is

230

usually a girlfriend with you when you come to Shuttleworth Hall.'

He grinned. 'They're not really girlfriends, Ma. Not steady girlfriends at any rate. They're more ships that pass in the night.'

She gave an exclamation of mock outrage at his flippancy and then said, 'I really would like it if there was someone a little more permanent in your life, Max. Hugo and Hester are very happy.'

'I know they are – and they're also exceptionally young to be married. Hugo is still only twenty-two and Hester is only nineteen. I don't think you're going to have the satisfaction of seeing me married off for another decade at least.' He hesitated and then said, 'Are you giving similar advice to Nancy, where Claus is concerned? Or is that a different kettle of fish entirely?'

She didn't look towards him, but he knew that her face had clouded over. 'Nancy doesn't listen to advice from anyone, you know that. And she's unhappy, Max – and I wish that she wasn't.'

He frowned. 'Are you telling me that her living in Berlin and seeing more of Claus isn't working out?'

'How can it?' she asked as she drove into the outskirts of Little Ridding. 'She's living with Lotti and her friends and, much as I love Lotti, her lifestyle isn't exactly an organized one, is it? And Nancy likes life to be ordered. The real problem, though, is that she's discovering Berlin is a very different city to live in than to visit. And she's a political animal. Whereas someone else in the same position might be able to turn a blind eye to the hideousness of what is taking place in Germany now Hitler is Chancellor, Nancy can't. Writing about it is her bread and butter. She's attending Nazi rallies and instead of turning her back on all the viciousness, she's going out of her way to witness it in order to be able to

231

write about it. It's causing great tension between her and Claus. Until it's resolved there will certainly be no wedding between them.'

'And you're relieved?'

She turned her head, her eyes once again meeting his. 'Yes,' she said with utter frankness. 'I'm relieved.'

He was silent and she returned her attention to the road ahead of them. After a little while, she said, 'Nancy's situation is too like the situation I was in when I was her age. She's a Yorkshire girl in love with a Berliner who is heir to one of Germany's biggest steelworks. If she marries him she's going to be tormented by a great division of loyalties. For me, the division became too great when war broke out and the House of Remer began producing armaments, which I knew were to be used against Britain and her Allies. Though we're not now facing another war with Germany, I know from the little I've gleaned from Berthold that the House of Remer is contravening the Versailles Treaty and is producing armaments again. If Remer is, then bigger steelworks such as Krupp will be doing so as well – and on a far vaster scale. It isn't a situation Nancy could ever comfortably live with. And that's why I'm relieved there's been no marriage yet and why I hope there won't be one.'

She drew into the small car park behind the station. 'Let's change the subject,' she said, not wanting to say goodbye to him on such a bleak note. 'Have you heard the news about Ilse? It seems she's a little girl no longer. She's been going to parties given by Hugo's embassy friends and has got herself an admirer, Count Nicholas Schulenburg, Ernst Schulenburg's son – Ernst was best man when Zelda married Josef – as well as another type of admirer. A very influential one.' She switched the engine off and turned towards him, wanting to see his face when she told him. 'Gustav Gründgens is taking an interest in her.'

His face, as she had known it would be, was a picture of incredulity.

'Gustav Gründgens? The Gustav Gründgens who has just taken over as director of Berlin's Staatstheater?'

'If the Staatstheater is Berlin's principal theatre, then yes. The very one.'

'Good God!' He was utterly appalled. 'Gründgens will have her on his stage in the blink of an eye!'

'So Ilse is hoping.' There was merely amusement in Vicky's voice. 'She wants to be an actress. Apparently, her ambition was to be a pupil at the Max Reinhardt Theatre School, but as Reinhardt – and most of the actors and actresses who worked for him – have left Germany for the United States, Gründgens is now the most influential man in the world of Berlin theatre. I imagine that at the moment he's simply been bowled over by her beauty and is now waiting to see whether or not she can act.'

'And Josef and Zelda are allowing this?' Max ran a hand through his thick thatch of curly hair. He wasn't often stupefied, but no other word could describe his reaction to his mother's news. 'How come their attitude to Ilse going on the stage is so different to their attitude towards Lotti being on the stage?'

His mother regarded him fondly. 'For an intelligent, worldly, sophisticated young man, you can be quite dim at times, darling. Lotti is a cabaret artiste and, as such, her lifestyle is exceedingly rackety and bohemian, as I am sure you are well aware. Ilse wants to become a classical stage actress. There is a world of difference between the two. Even more to the point, though she's only eighteen, Ilse is a lady from the top of her head to the soles of her feet. She's begun moving in the kind of social circle that is light years away from the social circle Lotti moves in. Nicholas Schulenburg, for instance, is a scion of the ex-reigning House of Hohenzollern.'

Max tried to look suitably impressed and failed. He was far from being a fuddy-duddy, but he would have preferred Ilse to be going off to university rather than being stage-struck and partying with the likes of Nicholas Schulenburg.

As he kissed his mother goodbye it occurred to him there was an upside to the news he had been given. Via Ilse, he would now have entrée into yet another of Berlin's social circles – one he wasn't yet on intimate terms with and one which, when he was, would be exceedingly useful to him.

Max flew into Tempelhof and then took the train to Friedrichstrasse. It was a beautiful day and, a change for Berlin in midsummer, not too hot. A light breeze was blowing and as he walked out of the station he unbuttoned his shirt at the neck, loosened his tie and then, his jacket hooked on his thumb, he slung it over his shoulder and strolled along Friedrichstrasse in the direction of Unter den Linden.

The familiarity of the city made his arrival in it seem almost like a homecoming – almost, but not quite. He paused at a news-stand to buy a copy of the *International Herald* and, for professional purposes, *Der Stürmer*, reflecting that if it hadn't been for his mother's insistence on giving loyalty to Britain throughout the war years – and then remaining in Britain – Berlin and the mansion on Unter den Linden would truly have been his home.

He glanced down at the front page of the *Herald*. The headline was fairly innocuous: 'Mussolini Watches as Italy Wins First World Cup in Europe'. Accompanying the news report was a photograph of the Italian football team giving the Fascist salute before beating Czechoslovakia 2–1 in Rome. British news was that fierce fighting had broken out at a rally held at Olympia by Sir Oswald Mosley's black-shirted Fascists, and in the United States six billion dollars in aid had been voted for farmers in drought-stricken areas.

The only reference to events in Germany was the news that the Reichsbank had put a six-month moratorium on German loan payments. There was nothing about the arbitrary arrests taking place in Germany; no mention of the civil liberties being taken away from Germany's Jewish population; no mention of the way German society was becoming completely Nazified.

As the *Herald* was one of the most conscientious of newspapers it indicated how little true awareness there was, outside Germany, of just what was going on inside it.

Der Stürmer, he knew, would be far different, but he didn't want to be sickened as yet by the contents of *Der Stürmer*. He would read Streicher's anti-Semitic, vile and vulgar rag later, when he had a glass of brandy to hand to help wash the taste of it away.

Tucking both papers under his arm he turned left into Unter den Linden and, as always, instead of keeping to the pavement he headed towards the wide gravel walk that, flanked by a double row of linden trees, led down the centre of the boulevard.

It was, he thought, the most beautiful walk in the city, probably the most beautiful walk in any European city. The buildings on either side were all magnificently neoclassical in style, as was the Remer mansion. He paused before leaving the gravel path to walk towards its great, gilded gates, wondering for how much longer Josef and Zelda would be able to retain it as a family home. Many of the other mansions that had once kept it company were now no longer family-owned.

That his uncle had managed to steer the House of Remer so successfully through the great financial upheavals that had beset the country since the war years was, he had to admit, something close to an act of genius. And if it was true that the House of Remer was again covertly producing armaments, this time for a Nazi government, then it was no wonder his uncle and Claus were wearing gold and black swastikas in their lapels, for the profits to be gained would be enormous.

When he entered the house it was to find his aunt was fully appreciating the lovely day. Lying lazily in a hammock slung between the low-growing branches of a giant cedar, she turned her head at his approach, a smile curving her glossy red lips.

'Max! How lovely!' She sat up, swinging long legs over the edge of the hammock, but making no attempt to jump down from it. 'Pull up a garden chair or sit on the grass. It's a perfect day for grass sitting.'

She was quite right and he dropped his jacket to the impeccably mown lawn then sat down beside it, his legs crossed in front of him Indian-fashion.

'I was hoping you'd be here and not down at the Schloss,' he said, wondering how a woman who was touching fifty, or was even, perhaps, a few months over fifty, could look so sensual. If her hair wasn't quite as blue-black as it had been when she had been younger, it was still glossily dark and cut so that it fell dramatically forward at cheekbone level on either side of her face, accentuating a fringe that came down to her eyebrows. Her afternoon garden wear was a sleeveless, loosely flowing silk-georgette dress in sizzling yellow. A scattering of appliquéd silver leaves decorated the skirt and she was wearing one of her favourite, heavily embossed silver bracelets.

'I'm hardly ever in Baden-Württemberg these days,' she said wryly. 'Not since Josef began using the Schloss for entertaining the Nazi hierarchy. You're looking rather wonderful. I like it when you wear your hair a little longer than is quite proper. It makes you look like a pirate!'

He laughed. He'd always known that he was a favourite with his usually acid-tongued aunt, for Zelda had never made any secret of it. 'Hugo reminds me of your father,' she had once said to him. 'Not in character – he's not a weakling – but in looks. He has the same fine, straight hair and reserved manner. I prefer a roustabout look and, if I may say so, you have that in spades, young Max.'

'You're her favourite because she delivered you when you were born,' was his mother's opinion, pleased at the closeness that existed between at least two of her children and Zelda.

A maid came across the lawn towards them to see if they required anything. 'Two vodkas with Kahlua,' Zelda said, not troubling to ask Max what he might like to drink. 'And a jug of ice and some biscuits.'

Turning her attention again to Max, she said, 'I had a telephone call from your mother on the day of her wedding, so don't think you're about to give me news I haven't heard already. I don't suppose the wedding will stop Yorkshire tongues wagging about the two of them. Little Ridding must have been goggle-eyed when Emily Elise was born with flame-red hair.'

'It was certainly a talking-point,' he said with a grin. 'But what's happening here? Is Claus in Berlin, or down at the steelworks?'

'At the steelworks. He's spending more and more time in the Ruhr.' Her voice had altered slightly and her hands had tightened on the edge of the hammock, the knuckles beginning to show white.

He said carefully, 'How are things with the steelworks? Is Claus having to tread very carefully with the present regime?'

'It's swings and roundabouts,' she said, the odd edge to her voice now even more apparent. 'Hitler has gone out of his way to assure the House of Remer that he's not going to interfere with its property or profits. As he's smashed the power of the trade unions, neither Josef nor Claus have that aspect of industrial relations to worry about and because of new arms and munitions contracts that have been given to Remers, both

237

Josef and Claus feel that any concessions they're called upon to make are worth it.'

The maid came with a tray on which were two Black Russian cocktails, a bottle of vodka and a bottle of Kahlua so that more cocktails could be made, a jug of ice and a doily-covered plate of fancy biscuits.

'Don't worry about bringing a garden table over,' Zelda said to her. 'Just put the tray on the grass next to Herr Remer.'

When the maid had done so and departed, Max said, 'What kind of concessions?'

Zelda took a sip of her drink and then said, 'Some financial. Some moral.' She held her glass towards him so that he could drop another ice cube into it. 'The House of Remer has had to pledge united support for Hitler in his fight for military equality with every other nation. Part of that support is to contribute to what is known as the *Hitler Spende* whereby major businessmen contribute to Nazi Party funds. It buys immunity from the attentions of the Gestapo and the violence of the stormtroopers. That's the financial side and the payment the House of Remer makes is huge. The moral side has been the dismissal of all the House of Remer's Jewish workers.'

'And does Nancy know about that?'

Zelda handed him her empty glass so that he could mix her another Black Russian.

'No. Claus tells her as little as possible and, because I want things to eventually work out between the two of them, I tell her nothing.'

Well aware that Nancy, with her zealous passion for truth, would find out all she needed to know from other sources, he said, 'And Lotti? How is the crackdown on licentious entertainment affecting her?'

A flicker of amusement touched Zelda's ruby-red lips. 'She's turned to singing, which is quite remarkable, because she actually can't sing. What she does, though, is look provocatively sexy and huskily growl her way through Billie Holiday-type numbers.'

He grinned and then said, sounding far more casual about it than he actually felt, 'And Ilse? I understand she's become a protégée of Gustav Gründgens?'

'She's attending a drama school run by him, a drama school on the same lines as the one Max Reinhardt ran for so long before the Nazis forced him from the country.'

'And Gründgens is more amenable to Nazi control when it comes to his work?'

Zelda shrugged a narrow shoulder. 'He must be. More to the point, he isn't a Jew.'

'And Josef?' he asked finally. 'Did you say he was down at Schloss Niedernhall?'

'He has been,' she said, the odd, taut note back in her voice again, 'but he's back in Berlin at the moment.' She glanced down at the diamond-encrusted watch on her wrist. 'In fact, at this very moment, he's in a meeting with Hermann Göring. Among all his many other responsibilities, Göring is Minister of the Interior and has direct control of the police. I imagine he is updating Josef on new laws and regulations as they apply to House of Remer workers.'

'Is the House of Remer capable of fulfilling the new contracts that have just been signed, Herr Remer?'

Though a Bavarian by birth, Göring's upper-middle-class accent was immaculate.

'Of course, Herr Reichsminister,' Josef said, grateful to be dealing with a man he regarded as being socially, as well as politically, acceptable, but puzzled as to Göring's interest in House of Remer business matters. 'We have sufficient furnaces. Our steelworks are the equal of any in Germany. Every single House of Remer factory is geared to the kind of production required.'

'And it is your desire to see the Fatherland armed and the military equal of all other nations?'

'Good God, yes!' Josef's affront at even being asked such a question was genuine and deep. 'Chancellor Hitler and President Hindenburg have my wholehearted support. I took out Nazi Party membership as long ago as 1928.'

Göring walked to the window, looked out, pondered a moment and then walked back to his desk, sliding his rump onto it, one jackbooted leg swinging free.

'And your desire is for a racially pure Fatherland?'

'But of course,' he said emphatically. 'No Jew now works in any capacity for the House of Remer.'

'And miscegenates?' Göring asked silkily.

The room was very still. Through the open window Josef could hear a tram creak and a car horn blare.

'And miscegenates – when miscegenation is known, of course,' he said, keeping his voice steady with difficulty, certain, now, of what it was Göring wanted with him.

The panic he felt was overwhelming. He could feel sweat on his forehead and fought the desire to reach for his handkerchief.

'The contracts in question are huge, Herr Remer,' Göring continued musingly. 'They are worth millions and, as you can appreciate, could only have been agreed upon with an Aryan-owned company.'

'But of course. Naturally.' To prevent his hands from shaking, Josef put them on his knees.

'Would it surprise you to know, then, Herr Remer, that we have evidence of non-Aryan blood in your family tree?'

Josef swallowed hard. 'It would be more than a surprise,' he said, unable to think of any course of action other than continuing to try and bluff things out. 'It would be an impossibility. The Remers' Aryan bloodline is traceable, untainted, as far back as the fifteenth century.'

240

'Oh, until recently it was, Herr Remer. It was. A careless marriage can, however, bring dung to the best of families and, when it is brought in, it must be rooted out.'

'There is absolutely no instance of any such marriage within my family . . .' Josef began, panic beginning to bubble in his throat.

Göring picked up a sheet of paper from his desk and handed it to him.

It was a copy of Zelda's father's birth certificate. Under the entry for mother's name were written, in brackets, the words 'Reservation Indian'.

'Exactly,' Josef croaked, as if Göring had kindly proved a point. 'My wife's family are one hundred per cent American. There is no Jewish blood whatsoever . . .'

'There is Native American Indian blood, which is enough. It changes the situation with the House of Remer, making it impossible for the government to be seen to be doing business with it. However, taking into account your loyalty to the Nazi Party and that you were, presumably, ignorant of your wife's bloodline at the time of your marriage, I am going to offer you a deal.'

'A deal?' Josef felt as if the world were shelving away from his feet. The sweat on his upper lip was salty on his mouth. 'But surely no kind of a deal is necessary? My wife is not even half American Indian. She comes from one of the most respected families in New York. Her father, Charles Wallace, is a merchant banker of international reputation.'

'And the House of Remer has an international reputation. And there is the problem. The House of Remer is representative of the new Germany and, as such, must be unsullied by rumours of miscegenation. Your wife's dramatic looks have ensured there have been many rumours – hence the investigation that was made.'

'Then issue a report saying only that the investigation has

proved my wife has no Jewish blood!' Agitatedly, Josef clenched and unclenched his hands. 'She isn't a Jewess and surely that is all that matters? And she never represents the House of Remer in public. Only my son does that and no one could believe Claus to be anything other than one hundred per cent Aryan. He's as blond-haired and blue-eyed as a Nordic god!'

He was on the verge of hysteria and making himself ridiculous, but he couldn't help it. He couldn't lose the contracts for armaments. He couldn't. He had kept the House of Remer flourishing through nightmare years of inflation and depression. There was hardly another industrialist, apart from the giants, who had prospered as he had prospered. And his early, passionate espousal of National Socialism had been a prime example of his long-sightedness. When others had slightingly referred to Hitler as the 'Bavarian corporal', he had had faith that Hitler would one day come to power and had given him unstinting support.

It was support that had had its reward in the mammoth contracts for armaments – and now he was on the verge of losing those contracts. It was unspeakable. Unbelievable.

'I quite agree that your son is a fine physical specimen of new German manhood,' Göring said equably. 'And I have had the pleasure of meeting your younger daughter, who is, in every respect, the prototype of German beauty. Your elder daughter is, I understand, out of the country.'

Josef blinked and then, realizing that Göring's informants had no idea that Lotti Remer was Lotti Lennartz, said rapidly, 'Yes, Herr Reichsminister. You have been informed correctly.'

'Your children's lack of any appearance of mixed blood, coupled with the great respect that the Chancellor has for you, is what is enabling me to offer a deal,' Göring continued urbanely.

This time Josef didn't suggest a deal was unnecessary. This time he knew it was his only hope.

'Then let me hear what it is,' he said, well aware that no matter what the huge amount of money demanded of him, he would find it.

'If the contracts are to remain with the House of Remer, then your wife must be expunged from the Remer family tree,' Göring said, matter-of-factly. 'No similar action will be demanded where your children are concerned.'

'Expunged?' Josef blinked, trying to grasp just what it was that Göring meant. 'But how . . . ? In what way . . . ?'

'You will divorce her and have no further contact with her,' Göring said, as if the request was a mere trifle. 'And when she disappears – as disappear she must – you and the rest of your family will accept her disappearance without question. Now, can I have your answer, Herr Remer? Is it to be yes? Or is it to be no?'

FIFTEEN

Berlin, September 1934

Ilse wound the heavy blonde braids of her hair in a circlet around her head and secured it in place with pins. The effect, in the soft lamplight of her bedroom, was reminiscent of a halo.

She smiled at the thought and ran a hand over the shiny smoothness of her gold satin evening gown. It was halter-necked, the bias-cut of the long skirt accentuating the perfection of her flawless young body.

Still seated at her dressing table she reached for her perfume, spraying *Je Reviens* onto her throat and wrists, deeply happy. Tonight was going to be a lovely evening, for Max was in Berlin and was taking her to the club in which Lotti was singing. They wouldn't be on their own because, before Max had contacted her, she'd arranged to spend the evening with Prince Vladimir Ovelensky, a White Russian émigré she had met at a British Embassy ball. Not wanting to rudely cut Vladimir, and feeling sure Max would enjoy the prince's company, she had suggested he join them for the evening.

She opened her jewellery box and took out a pair of drop-pearl earrings that her mother had given her when she had moved out of the house for good.

'We're going to move into an apartment in Charlottenburg,' her father had said, grey-faced. 'It will be more suitable now I've retired from public life. As the new head of the House of Remer Claus will remain here, in the family home – a family home that is, of course, now his.'

Schloss Niedernhall hadn't become Claus's property, though, or at least she didn't think it had. The problem was the difficulty in understanding exactly what had taken place over the last few turbulent weeks. First there had been the incredible murder of Ernst Röhm and the arrest of hundreds – some said thousands – of his stormtroopers. Rumours and counter-rumours were still rife, with the only certainty being that the Brownshirts existed no longer. Because of her father's sudden collapse of health, Ilse, though, had been unable to give the event the attention she knew it deserved.

At first she thought her father had suffered a heart attack for she could think of nothing else that would account for both his ghastly pallor and the frantic haste in which he signed over ownership of the House of Remer to Claus. Then her father had dropped the bombshell that he and her mother were moving out of the Unter den Linden mansion and into an apartment at the far side of Berlin, in Charlottenburg. Finally and equally incredibly, Claus had told her that Schloss Niedernhall was off limits to the family as a high-ranking Nazi minister and his family had moved into it.

It had been like being on a roller-coaster ride and one of her hopes for the evening ahead was that Max, who always seemed to know what was going on, would be able to cast a little light on things that still mystified and troubled her.

Ilse surveyed her reflection in the glass, knowing it was perfect and, because she had very little vanity, not being much impressed by the fact. Instead of thinking about herself she was wondering if Max would be staying at the Unter den Linden mansion and spending time with his father while he was in Berlin. At one time there would have been no question but that he would have been staying in what was, after all, his family home. Over the last couple of years, though, he had begun staying in other places as well. Sometimes he stayed with Hugo and Hester. Sometimes he stayed a couple of nights with Hester's parents, the Dresners, enjoying suppers of fried chicken and potato latkes. Sometimes he stayed with friends of dubious character, such as his friend Fritz, a former Brownshirt. He had friends all over Berlin and they came from every circle of Berlin society. When he had rung her to say he was back in Berlin he had totally surprised her by saying he was doing so from her parents' new apartment in Charlottenburg.

Sometimes – and her tummy muscles tightened at the thought – he stayed with Lotti.

She rose to her feet and crossed the room in order to take her evening bag from one of the shelves of her wardrobe.

Even though she knew Max and Lotti were only good friends – best friends – she couldn't help the panic she felt at the prospect of that friendship turning into something deeper, as Nancy and Claus's friendship had. The idea of being jealous of her much-loved sister was too unbearable to contemplate.

She put a lipstick, a compact, an embroidered handkerchief and a small phial of *Je Reviens* into her handbag and snapped it shut.

She mustn't think of Max falling in love with anyone. She must just be glad he was once again in Berlin and that at any minute he would be taking the steps of the mansion's bronze and marble staircase two at a time in order to tell her he had arrived and it was time for them to be leaving.

It wasn't Max who arrived first, though; it was Vladimir.

The butler led him into the grand drawing room and, by

the time she joined him, he was halfway through a whisky and soda.

'You look – breathtaking,' he said as she welcomed him.

Ilse gave him the benefit of her slow, sweet smile. Everyone told her she looked breathtaking, but her looks meant very little to her except in so far as they were useful where her classical acting ambitions were concerned. Unworldly about things as she often was, even she knew Gustav Gründgens would not have taken such an interest in her if it hadn't been for her extraordinarily angelic looks.

'You don't mind my commandeering our evening by arranging to go with my cousin to the club my sister sings in?' she asked, concerned about his feelings.

'Of course not,' Vladimir said sincerely. 'He's Hugo's brother, isn't he?'

She nodded.

'Then in that case, I'm delighted to be having the opportunity to get to know him. Is he in the Foreign Service, like Hugo?'

'Goodness, no. Max works for Barings, a British bank. He's often in Berlin transacting business on their behalf – or here simply because this is where he was born and half his family are here – but he has no connection with diplomatic life.'

Vladimir, who had lots of connections with diplomatic life, continued to show interest. He knew Hugo well, and liked him. He also knew Nancy Remer slightly and though her bluntly expressed fierce anti-Nazi remarks had startled him, he had liked her as well, especially as her fearless opinions were so identical to his own. If Max Remer were in the same mould as his brother and sister, he would be congenial company.

'Will any other family members be at Ciro's tonight?' he asked, wondering if Hugo would also be there.

'No. Claus is in the Ruhr and Hugo and Hester don't nightclub much.'

'Not even to enjoy a Lotti Remer performance?'

Ilse's seductive smile touched her mouth yet again. 'Lotti doesn't sing as Lotti Remer. It would cause too many family problems. Her stage name is Lotti Lennartz.'

Sophisticated from the soles of his feet to the top of his immaculately groomed head, Vladimir was not in the habit of displaying ignorant surprise, but he did so now, almost choking on his whisky.

'Great heavens! I had no idea! She's splendid, absolutely wonderful. But she doesn't look remotely like you and Hugo. I'd never have realized she was your sister in a million years.'

'Well, she is. The oddity actually is not that Lotti is dark, when Hugo and I are so fair, but that any of us are fair at all, for my mother is very dark-haired.'

'Yes. Of course.' Vladimir cursed himself for a fool. Zelda Remer's exotic looks could easily be interpreted as being Jewish, and drawing attention to them had been a crass thing to do, even though Ilse seemed oblivious to any embarrassment.

'It's good to have such close family, isn't it?' Vladimir, whose family connections weaved through most of the ex-reigning houses of Europe, actually thought it rather odd that the Remers had no other extended family. His own family ramifications ran into the hundreds.

'Oh, it is – and there's Max now. I can always recognize his footsteps.'

As she finished speaking, the door opened and Max entered the room. He was wearing an immaculately cut white dinner jacket and his thick dark hair was, as always, curling a little too long in the nape of his neck. He moved with the grace and toughness of an athlete and Vladimir's eyebrows rose slightly. Being friends with the rather self-effacing Hugo had not prepared him for this blazingly handsome, utterly self-assured and confident man.

His next surprise was Ilse's reaction to him. Instead of

merely greeting him with careless cousinly affection, she ran towards him as if she were a small girl about to be swung up into his arms.

He wasn't to know it, but Max was almost as taken aback as he was.

Ilse was the baby of the family and that was how he had always treated her. His best chum was Lotti, but it was Ilse he had always taken out on treats such as circus and theatre and cinema visits. Though there were only six years between them, they were an important six years. When he had become a young adult, she had still been a child playing with dolls. When he had been recruited into the British Intelligence Service, she had been a schoolgirl. Three months ago, when he had last been in Berlin, she had clearly been a schoolgirl no longer, but neither had she been the ravishingly poised and beautiful creature that now, incredibly, was about to throw herself into his arms and hug him.

A cloud of expensive perfume assailed him. His arms closed around her. The satin of her dress was slippery beneath his touch. It was the dress of a worldly young woman, a sophisticated young woman, a young woman with an exceptionally beautiful body and a young woman who wasn't shy of showing it off.

'How wonderful that you're back in Berlin!' she said happily as he kissed her on the cheek. 'Do come and meet Vladimir. He's a good friend of Hugo's and he knows Nancy as well.'

Slipping her hand into his she walked with him across the vast art deco-furnished room to where Vladimir was waiting for them, an odd expression in his eyes.

The expression was circumspectly extinguished before Ilse began making introductions, but not before Max had seen it and known exactly the kind of prurient speculation going through the other man's head.

'Max, let me introduce you to Prince Vladimir Ovelensky. Vladimir, my cousin, Max Remer.'

This time it was Max's turn to have to try and hide stunned surprise. He had assumed Ilse's escort for the evening to be Nicholas Schulenburg, the admirer both his mother and her mother had spoken of.

As he joined Ovelensky in a glass of whisky and soda and trivial politenesses were trotted out, Max tried to work out what the devil was going on. Had his sweet guileless cousin become a floozy or was she unaware that the new men in her life were intent on becoming something other than mere friends?

Once at Ciro's it became clear that Ovelensky and Schulenburg were not the only moths being drawn to Ilse's flame. Axel Hewel, a Swiss attaché Max knew slightly, came across to their table to say hello to him. His eyes, however, never left Ilse for a moment – nor did the eyes of many other men. And then Nicholas Schulenburg entered the nightclub with a party of friends and, at Ilse's request, the entire group progressed no farther than their table.

It was obvious to Max that Vladimir was well aware Nicholas was a rival for Ilse's affections and that beneath his urbane, indifferent exterior, he was annoyed. Max didn't blame him, because he was annoyed as well. What he had been looking forward to was squiring the baby of the family to a nightclub – perhaps her first nightclub – and sharing in her pleasure at her excursion into a whole new, adult world.

What he hadn't expected was that she would already be happily familiar with that world and a centre of attention in it. As Ilse laughed at something Nicholas said and as one of Nicholas's friends ordered more champagne for the table, he felt himself to be absolutely unnecessary to her. It wasn't a feeling he liked.

Ilse, delighted Max had the opportunity to make friends

with the people she now spent most time with, was totally oblivious as to what was going through his mind. Nicholas and Vladimir were, if not already friends, at least old acquaintances and both she and Vladimir knew practically everyone in Nicholas's party. The laughter and conviviality now taking place around their large and crowded table was such a welcome joy after the political stresses and strains of the last few months it never occurred to her that Max wasn't taking quite as much of a leading part as was normal for him.

'I think it decidedly clever of Hitler to have let the title of President die when Hindenburg died,' she heard Nicholas say to Vladimir. 'Styling himself Führer and Reich Chancellor, instead of President, means he doesn't have to take a vow upholding the constitution, as Hindenburg did.'

'Which gives him far more power than any former Head of State has ever had,' Vladimir said, seeing Nicholas's point immediately.

'And the oath now exacted from all members of the Armed Forces is to him personally, not to Germany,' one of the girls in Nicholas's party added drily. 'It puts quite a new slant on the title of Supreme Commander.'

Ilse sighed. Fond as she was of Nicholas she wished he hadn't steered the conversation on to politics. Politics made laughter impossible. She was just wondering how she could put an end to such seriousness when Max leaned towards her and said quietly, 'I was a bit thrown when I walked in the house to find Vladimir with you. I was expecting your escort to be Nicholas.'

'Nicholas?' Ilse blushed. 'I do spend a lot of time with Nicholas. He's an exceptionally nice person, but going to drama school and, thanks to Hugo, being invited to lots of embassy parties has meant I now have lots of other friends as well.' Her smile was as innocent as a child's. 'And Vladimir is one of them.'

'So I see,' he said, wanting to ask exactly what kind of a relationship it was she had with Nicholas – since she had blushed when he had mentioned his name – but, under the circumstances, not being able to.

As he listened with half an ear to the conversation going on around them, he wondered if his uncle and aunt knew of the extent of Ilse's new social life, or if their self-imposed seclusion in Charlottenburg meant they were largely unaware of it.

'It was an amazing spectacle,' said Count Giuseppe Bennazzo, one of Nicholas's friends who was with the Italian Embassy in Berlin, referring to the Nazi Party conference he had attended a week earlier in Nuremberg. 'You Berliners may be used to such sights, but I wasn't. There were scores of thousands there and the applause and cheers were deafening. When the Gauleiter of Bavaria declared that Hitler's Reich was going to last a thousand years I thought the roof of the hall was going to lift off.'

'Führer,' said the pretty girl who had taken part in all the political conversation, amused chastisement thick in her voice. 'You can't continue referring to Hitler as Hitler, Giuseppe. Disrespect will get you carted off to a camp. His title is Führer.'

Nicholas Schulenburg snorted in disgust and another member of Nicholas's party took a hasty look around to make sure no one at near by tables was listening in to them or inadvertently overhearing them.

Max didn't blame him. Though nothing overtly disloyal had been said, the *way* things had been said had left him in no doubt that Ilse's upper-crust friends were, without exception, fervently anti-Nazi and anyone listening to them would, no doubt, come to the same conclusion. As reporting anyone guilty of disloyal talk had become something of a way of life, it didn't do to speak carelessly in public, not even in the kind of nightclub no card-carrying Nazi was likely to patronize.

252

'Why is the present Reich referred to as the Third Reich?' Ilse asked, intrigued enough to finally join in the conversation.

Nicholas Schulenburg's well-shaped mouth twitched in amusement at her ignorance. 'Because it makes a powerful symbolic link to the greatness of the past, *Liebchen*,' he said, his eyes and voice softening as he looked towards her. 'The First Reich refers to the rule of Charlemagne. The Second Reich to the rule of Bismarck.'

His use of *Liebchen* went unnoticed by everyone but Vladimir and Max, for it was a term of endearment often used carelessly.

Max knew that in this instance, however, it hadn't been used carelessly and, by the look on his face, so did Vladimir. There was no time for either of them to ponder it, however, for Lotti was hurtling towards them, dressed and made-up ready for her performance.

'Darlings, how *wonderful* there is such a big party of you!' The smile splitting her face sizzled. 'Max! I didn't know you were back in Berlin! Why didn't you phone?' She kissed and hugged him and then turned her attention to Nicholas Schulenburg. 'And Nicky! How blissful you're here again, but be warned that I haven't changed my repertoire. I'm singing the same songs as Monday night and so you'll just have to die of boredom.' There were more kisses and hugs as she greeted the friends who had come with him and who she already knew. Then she turned the full blaze of her attention on Vladimir.

Ilse did the honours. 'Lotti, Vladimir Ovelensky. Vladimir, my sister, Lotti.'

'I saw you perform at Kakadu a month ago,' Vladimir said, bowing low over her hand and kissing it. The scarlet streak in Lotti's turbulent dark hair was the exact shade of her glossy lipstick. Her batwing eyelashes were the longest he'd ever seen in his life and her petite, voluptuous body was poured into an evening gown consisting of nothing but scattered sequins on a background of sheer black gauze, the skirt split to the thigh. 'You were sensational,' he added, visibly dazed.

'I was good, wasn't I?' Lotti's throaty chuckle took all immodesty from her words. 'And now I have to dash because I'm almost due to go on. I'll join you all afterwards, though, if I may?'

The last few words were directed at Max and he grinned. 'You may indeed, Monkeyface,' he said affectionately, 'and whether you sang it last Monday or not, sing "Mack the Knife".'

As Vladimir blinked, wondering if he could possibly have heard Max Remer's nickname for Lotti correctly, he saw her give her cousin a wicked wink and then, like a human tornado, she darted towards the podium-like stage, not bothering to go backstage again but, as intro music played and a spotlight zeroed in on her, merely stepping on it to clamorous applause.

'Your sister's got quite a following,' Nicholas Schulenburg shouted across to Ilse as whistles added to the din.

'I know!' Ilse's smile was radiant. 'And she's not really a singer at all. She's a dancer.'

'Now that,' Giuseppe Bennazzo said to the table at large, 'I would really like to see.'

As Lotti launched huskily into a jazzed-up version of 'You're the Cream in My Coffee', Ilse felt nothing but pleasure and pride in the admiration and attention Lotti was receiving. All she wanted was for those she loved to be happy – and that Lotti was happy being the star attraction at Ciro's was clearly obvious.

She looked across at Vladimir and knew, by the besotted expression on his face as he watched Lotti sing, that he was completely dazzled by her. The knowledge gave her pleasure. Though Lotti had countless men-friends, none of them, in her opinion, were worthy of her. Vladimir, however, was not only extremely eligible, he was also an extremely nice person and he would make a delightful brother-in-law.

She was aware that Max too had registered Vladimir's change of interest and as he looked down at her to see her reaction she smiled sunnily, not wanting him to think she was the slightest bit jealous or put out, for she wasn't.

Lotti continued with Irving Berlin's 'Always' and then with 'Falling in Love Again' from the film *The Blue Angel*.

'Anything Marlene Dietrich sings, Lotti sings to perfection,' she whispered to him.

'She sings it better,' he whispered back, drily. 'Marlene is always cynical. Lotti's sexiness is never cynical. Her sense of fun is too strong.'

Their chairs were close together and her shoulder was lightly touching his. She wondered what his response would be if she were to pluck up her courage and ask if his close friendship with Lotti was likely to turn one day into something deeper.

Lotti's backing band, the Weintraub Syncopators, a jazz band that played in clubs all over Berlin, launched into the opening riff of 'Mack the Knife'.

It wasn't something she could ask. It wasn't something she should even be thinking about. All that mattered, right here and now, was that she and her friends and Max were in a carefree group watching Lotti perform, and when Lotti had made her second appearance of the evening they would all go in a large group to the Schwanneke Artists' Club or the Romanische Café for a noisy, boisterous supper.

She wondered, if she telephoned Hugo and Hester and Claus and Nancy, whether she would be able to tempt them into joining them. Then she remembered that Claus was in the Ruhr and, even if he were not, there was no way she could bring him into contact with her friends, for if she did so their uninhibited conversation would immediately freeze. The small circular swastika badge Claus habitually wore in his lapel would see to that. As for Hugo and Hester – neither of them were night owls. Only Nancy would be up for a late-night supper invitation.

A storm of applause brought her out of her reverie. After following 'Mack the Knife' with a huskily sultry version of 'Stormy Weather' and an even sultrier version of 'Smoke Gets in Your Eyes' Lotti had finished her first set with Irving Berlin's 'How Deep is the Ocean'.

'*Wunderbar!*' Vladimir was shouting, beating Max, Nicholas and Giuseppe to be the first up on his feet and applauding. '*Wunderbar!*'

Lotti blew him a kiss. Vladimir gave a whoop of delight.

As Lotti ran trippingly from the stage, the band began playing dance music and Nicholas Schulenburg leaned across the table towards Ilse. 'May I have the first dance?' he asked, uncaring of Vladimir, who was still on his feet and still clapping with gusto.

'In a moment. I'm just going to telephone Nancy and ask her if she'd like to join us for supper. Where do you think we'll be going? Schwanneke's or the Romanische?'

'I think we'll be going anywhere you want to go.'

'Then we'll go to the Romanische.' Picking up the little gold evening bag that matched her gown she left the table and made her way across to the phone booths.

'The Romanische? Tonight?' Even though it was nearly midnight, Nancy's voice was as bright and crisp as always. 'I'd love to, but I can't. I've been to another God-awful Nazi rally and have to write a piece about it by morning. Sorry, sweetheart.'

'Never mind, but let's try and meet up another time while Max is in town.'

'Definitely. There's a lot I'd like to talk to my brother about. Have a nice evening, coz. I'll speak to you again soon.'

Ilse put the telephone receiver on its hook and walked back through the crowded nightclub, drawing admiring male glances every step of the way.

Vladimir rose to his feet at her approach and strode towards her. 'As I'm your escort for the evening, Nicholas is going to have to wait his turn for a dance,' he said, beginning to lead her away from their table. 'And as it is a foxtrot, you're going to find that I'm almost Fred Astaire standard. Something Nicholas most certainly is not.'

As he led her out onto the dance floor and took her in his arms she saw, over his shoulder, Nicholas spreading upturned hands in an expression of amused, rueful despair. She shot him her bewitching smile. If this dance was a foxtrot, the next was bound to be a waltz. And she knew Nicholas would far prefer to waltz with her than foxtrot.

Max watched the proceedings through narrowed eyes. Outwardly, he looked completely at ease, even a little drunk, his chair pushed away from the table, one leg nonchalantly across the other, a hand resting on his ankle.

The talkative girl who had joined the table with Nicholas and his friends, and whose name he hadn't registered, kept looking meaningfully across at him and he knew she wanted him to ask her to dance. She was a pretty girl and, under normal circumstances, he would have done so automatically. Tonight, he didn't do so. Tonight, he watched the cousin he had always regarded as the baby of the family turn all heads as, light as a feather and beautiful as an angel, she danced in the arms of Prince Vladimir Ovelensky.

When the music changed to a waltz he saw her gently insist to Vladimir that they leave the floor. Nicholas was immediately on his feet, not even allowing her to sit down before he waltzed away with her.

The nightclub's dance floor was too small for the kind of extravagant waltz Nicholas was no doubt capable of and Max

257

found his hands clenching as he watched them barely moving to the music, intimately close and deep in conversation.

'I saw your parents walking along the promenade together at Wannsee last weekend,' Nicholas was saying, blissfully unaware that the person he was making jealous wasn't Vladimir, but Max. 'It was quite extraordinary. They didn't see me, because they had eyes for no one but each other. One could have almost believed they were a honeymoon couple.'

Ilse smiled up at him. 'I know. It *is* extraordinary, isn't it? And it's all happened over the last few weeks. I'm sure they've always been happy together, but it wasn't very visible, if you know what I mean. And then for quite a few years Mama lived mostly at Schloss Niedernhall, while Papa was always either in Berlin or in the Ruhr. And now, since Papa has taken retirement, they are completely wrapped up in each other again.'

'And Claus and Nancy?' he asked. 'Are wedding bells in the offing yet?'

A cloud passed over Ilse's classically beautiful face. 'No. There are too many issues between the two of them.'

She didn't say any more; she had no need to, for Nicholas knew very well the kind of issues marring Claus and Nancy's romance.

'Some people are beginning to make compromises,' he said at last. 'Especially now Röhm is out of the picture and Hitler is presenting a more respectable face to the world.'

'And are you now making compromises?' she asked, tilting her head slightly so she could look into his eyes.

He shook his head, his face grave. 'No. For me, compromise of any kind isn't an option.'

Ilse felt a shiver run down her spine. Nicholas was a special friend, so special that, if it were not for the way she felt about Max, she could have almost imagined herself a little in love with him. She didn't want him to come to the attention of the authorities as being an enemy of the state. She didn't want anything awful happening to him and when he changed the subject, saying, 'Will you have lunch with me one day next week, Ilse?' her response was unhesitating.

'Yes,' she said, her eyes smiling into his. 'Yes, Nicholas. I'd love to.'

Watching them, Max's eyes narrowed even further. It was impossible for him to have any idea as to what they were saying to each other, but the way they were looking at each other spoke volumes.

When the waltz came to an end, they left the dance floor hand in hand. Vladimir, who had been dancing with the girl who was a member of Nicholas's party, remained on the floor with her as the music changed to a rumba rhythm.

Max remained with one leg carelessly across the other as Ilse sat down again next to him.

Within seconds, Giuseppe Bennazzo asked her to dance.

After that, Axel Hewel asked her, and then Vladimir asserted his rights as her escort again.

By the time Lotti appeared for her second set Max had abandoned the champagne and was nursing another whisky and soda.

Nicholas, who had heard that Max was usually the life and soul of any social gathering, looked at him oddly a few times, but no one else seemed to notice he wasn't dancing or keeping the table in fits of laughter with wise-cracking jokes.

As they waited for Lotti to join them after her performance had come to an end, Vladimir again led Ilse out onto the dance floor.

Max drained his glass of whisky and then, his evening shirt unfastened at the throat and his bow tie hanging loose, he rose slightly unsteadily to his feet.

Nicholas quirked an eyebrow in his direction, wondering if Max was finally going to ask the girl who had been eyeing him all evening, to dance.

He didn't do so.

Instead he strolled out onto the dance floor and cut in on Vladimir.

Nicholas saw a second's surprise flash across Vladimir's face and then an expression followed it that he couldn't quite work out. It was almost as if Vladimir had been half expecting Max's action.

On Ilse's face there was nothing but startled pleasure.

Seconds later, Vladimir threw himself angrily down in the chair next to him. 'You want to look to your laurels, Nicky,' he said tautly. 'Some Remer family relationships are far closer than is decent.'

Nicholas looked from Vladimir back to the crowded dance floor. Ilse, her gold evening dress shimmering as she danced, her braided hair a gleaming coronet around her head, was totally absorbed in what Max was saying to her. With the first intimations of disquiet he wondered what it was. His disquiet grew as he saw the expression on her face when she replied to him, and he wondered what she was saying.

'What? Leave now?' As she looked into the intensity of Max's electric-blue eyes, she was more startled than ever. 'Without waiting for Lotti?'

'Without waiting for anyone,' he said fiercely, his arm around her waist where it had ached to be all evening. 'I want to be on my own with you. I want to alter our relationship just as Claus altered his relationship with Nancy.'

As her eyes widened and her lips parted in incredulity, he lowered his head to hers and, uncaring of whoever was watching, kissed her deeply, full on the mouth.

SIXTEEN

The Ruhr and Berlin, Easter 1935

It was a brilliantly warm day for mid-April and Claus pushed his chair away from his magnificent hand-carved desk and walked across to the massive windows that looked out over the Remer steelworks. The area they covered was vast. From giant furnaces and chimneys steam and smoke rose in unbroken dense clouds. Production was at full pelt, and with Germany's mammoth rearmament programme now no longer a secret but a source of international contention, was likely to remain so for the foreseeable future.

He pinched the bridge of his nose to relieve the beginnings of a headache. Ever since he could remember he'd been brought up with the knowledge that he was heir to the House of Remer. All his education – his years at technical college studying engineering and steel-making – had been geared to that end. What he had never expected, though, was that he would find himself the sole proprietor of the House of Remer so suddenly or at such a young age.

'So – you're only twenty-three?' his father had said testily when he had dropped the bombshell that he was not only retiring but reverting the company from being a joint-stock company into one of single proprietorship and that the proprietorship was now Claus's. 'So what difference does that make? Running the management of the House of Remer is something you've been brought up to do. Every head of every administrative department is absolutely capable and totally loyal, as are all the engineers and all the workforce. All that is needed is control. And you are more than capable of exerting that control.'

That had been true and he had known it, false modesty not being something that ever troubled him.

What did sometimes trouble him was how Max felt about things, for if Berthold hadn't voluntarily relinquished control of the House of Remer in 1911, it would have been Max who was heir to the House of Remer, not him.

It wouldn't have worked, of course. Not because Max was like his father and wouldn't have been capable of such responsibility – he sometimes thought that despite Max's apparently relaxed exterior he was capable of anything – but because there was no way a House of Remer workforce would have accepted him after England became his home – and the present government would certainly not have accepted him.

At the thought of the Nazi hierarchy and Max in deep discussion about House of Remer armament production he felt a flare of amusement. Even if Max had remained in Berlin and been educated in Berlin, it was unlikely he would have become a Nazi – and Hitler didn't deal with anyone not totally loyal to National Socialism.

It was so warm he wanted to open a window, but knowing how acrid the air then entering the room would be he resisted the impulse. Though it was essential for him to spend long periods of time in the Ruhr, he was never there longer than necessary. As far as he was aware his father had never done so either, except for the period when, for reasons still unknown to him, his father's relationship with his mother had been under strain.

That strain was, though, now a thing of the past. It was as if relinquishing proprietorship of the Remer steel empire had righted whatever was wrong between the two of them, which was odd, because for as long as he could remember his mother had been as fiercely ambitious for the House of Remer as his father had always been.

He looked down at his watch. He'd arranged to have a one o'clock lunch with the director in charge of mining and armaments, but it was still only twelve-thirty.

Restlessly, he walked back to his desk and sat down again. If he'd been in Berlin he would have been anticipating lunch with Paul, for his half-brother was making one of his rare visits to Berlin. As he stared broodingly at his telephone he wondered if Paul's visit had been occasioned by anxiety over their mother so suddenly and inexplicably opting for life in an apartment in Charlottenburg, instead of in the family mansion on Unter den Linden. Whatever the reason, Zelda would be pleased to see him. Though she never said so, he rather thought she regretted her vow to never again step foot on English or American soil. It had meant she hadn't seen as much of Paul when he was growing up as she otherwise would have done; neither had she seen as much of Vicky as she could have.

That she had caused herself so much heartache in the past and continued to suffer it for the same reason even now, was, he knew, due to nothing else but stubborn pride.

His mouth tightened.

That kind of stubbornness – the refusal to change any stance or opinion once taken – was one that ran in the family. Lotti could be as stubborn as a mule, but even Lotti's brand of stubbornness was nothing compared to Nancy's.

From outside the closed windows there came the sound of sirens indicating to Remer workers that the hour's lunch break had begun. As a sea of men began streaming towards whichever canteen was nearest to them, Claus remained at his desk, his eyes still on his telephone.

He glanced down at his watch again, saw that he was now ten minutes late for his lunch and rose to his feet. He wouldn't ring Nancy. Why should he? She was the one who was at fault. She was the one who was *always* at fault. There were times when he didn't know why on earth he needed her so much. He certainly didn't need anyone else. Like his father, he was hard-headed, coolly self-sufficient and, if the occasion arose, merciless.

Tight-lipped, he strode towards his private dining room, hoping he wouldn't need to be merciless with his mining and armaments director. Production at the House of Remer needed to escalate and, if it was to please the Nazi hierarchy, it needed to escalate fast. Closing his mind to his personal problems, focusing on production figures and output, he entered the dining room intent on putting the fear of God into a man old enough to be his father.

Nancy hauled an overnight bag from the bottom of her wardrobe and threw it on one of the twin beds in the room she shared with Lotti. Then she went into the bathroom they shared with two of Lotti's friends and scooped all her toiletries into a toilet bag. At high speed she headed back to the bedroom, dropped the toilet bag into her overnight bag and yanked open a drawer. A second or so later there was a change of underwear in the bag, a pair of pyjamas and – as an afterthought – an uncrushable and very pretty turquoise silk dress.

Slightly breathless, she stood and looked down at the packed bag.

Why was she doing this? Claus hadn't phoned to apologize for their appalling row of three days ago. He certainly hadn't thought to suggest she take a train to the Ruhr and join him so they could spend a night together and make up.

She chewed the corner of her lip.

What he had done was to behave abominably.

With violent suddenness she seized the bag and tipped the contents onto the floor.

She wasn't going to go running to him when he couldn't be bothered even to pick up the phone to talk to her in order to make things right between them again.

Fighting back tears of rage and frustration she walked swiftly into the kitchen and put the kettle on for a cup of tea.

As she waited for the water to boil she continued to fume. Why couldn't he see what was staring him in the face? Why couldn't he admit that monstrous injustices were taking place in Germany and that they would continue to take place as long as Hitler and his cronies retained power? Why, in the face of all the bullying repression being suffered by the Jews, did he persist in insisting that Hitler was good for Germany?

'Is there any street fighting now Hitler has put paid to Röhm?' he had demanded furiously when she had tried to make him understand just how bad things were for people like Hester's parents. 'No, there isn't.'

They had been in the grand drawing room at Unter den Linden and he had begun striding up and down it, hardly able to control his anger. 'And there isn't any mass unemployment any longer, either,' he had shot at her, his face taut with the force of his feelings, his eyes blazing. 'All that is thanks to Hitler. And it's thanks to Hitler that this country is no longer plunging headlong towards civil war.'

He had continued his pacing. 'You weren't living in Berlin during the 1920s, Nancy. You may think you know what it was like here when the Bolsheviks were gaining the upper hand, but in reality you haven't a clue.' He had come to a halt in front of her. 'And you haven't a clue as to what it was like when inflation was rampant. That this family still has a steelworks is due to Hitler. And don't you ever forget it!'

'That *you* still have a steelworks is due to Hitler!' she had snapped back at him. 'I don't have a steelworks. I don't take a penny piece from the steelworks and neither does my mother, nor Max nor Hugo.'

'Your father does!' he had flung back at her, his blond hair falling low across his forehead. 'Your father has always taken a large share of the profits and has done so without contributing a day's work towards them!'

It had been a hideous, unproductive, savage row and the worst thing about it had been that even when she was hating him for his pig-headed obduracy, as she watched him stride the room, slim-hipped and handsome, she had been aching with longing for him.

She was aching with longing for him now.

The kettle boiled. She took it off the heat. If it were not for the steelworks she was certain Claus would not be a National Socialist. He might well believe that Hitler had done a good job where unemployment and inflation were concerned and that a one-party state was preferable to living with the fear of civil war, but the Claus she had known since childhood and who had been her lover for well over a year was a sophisticate who hated crudity and vulgarity.

On that score, if on no other, he would never in normal circumstances have given his political support to a party who published such obscenities as *Der Stürmer* and had a leader who ranted and raved and promised the gullible that when Jews were driven from public life their problems would all be over.

The reason she and Claus could not be happy together was not because of their political differences. It was because of the House of Remer. If the House of Remer were taken out of the equation, Claus would not be flaunting a swastika in his lapel. Instead, he would be of the same mind as Lotti and her friends, wanting no part of the new, hateful Germany Hitler was creating. That was what she believed. It was what, for the sake of her sanity, she had to believe.

As so often in the past, the conviction it was still possible for everything to be all right between her and Claus swamped her. His kowtowing to Nazism was only out of concern for the future of the steelworks, a concern that was mainly on his father's behalf. His father had, however, divested himself of ownership of the House of Remer and abnegated all interest in it. That being the case, surely Claus could now do likewise, if he so wished?

She thought of the loss of family wealth that would be attendant on such an action. It would be vast, but whose wealth would it be? As she had pointed out so passionately in her last quarrel with him, her mother hadn't touched a penny piece of it for decades and neither she, Max, nor Hugo were remotely interested in living off the back of an industry that had made arms during the Great War and was doing so yet again. Lotti had also long since spurned the idea of living off House of Remer wealth, which left only her father, Uncle Josef, Aunt Zelda, Ilse and Claus who were still doing so.

She pursed her lips, deep in thought.

Ilse was so obviously destined to marry into money she doubted if she would mind too much what happened to the House of Remer. It was certainly impossible to think of her battling with Claus if he were to announce he was relinquishing it. It would be different with her uncle and aunt, of course. Until recently, the House of Remer had been their life's work and though her uncle had signed over the proprietorship to Claus it was unlikely he had ever envisaged living life uncushioned by House of Remer wealth.

The idea of Claus living without such wealth was also unrealistic, but when it came to divesting himself of the House of Remer, he could surely do so in a way that would still leave him and his parents exceptionally wealthy. Private wealth was not something Nancy approved of, but if Claus had to have wealth, exceptional wealth was an improvement on monumental wealth.

All she had to do was to present her case to him yet again, this time taking into account the new set of arguments.

In a flood of certainty she ran from the kitchen and back into the bedroom, grabbed a key, scooped her things from the floor, crammed them again into her bag and hurtled out of the apartment.

Forty-five minutes later, still breathless with haste, she was seated on a train as it pulled out of Berlin heading in the direction of the Ruhr.

Claus tried to concentrate on the discussion in hand but his usually razor-sharp brain kept straying. How long were he and Nancy to continue with their fractious on/off affair? Marriage was quite clearly out of the question. Though the Nazi hierarchy were well aware that his cousins had an English mother and had been brought up and educated in England, and that Hugo and Nancy had been born there as well, it had never yet become an issue. It would become an issue, though, if he were to marry an English cousin. Especially an English cousin who expressed the kind of virulent anti-Nazi views Nancy insisted on giving vent to.

'This is the proposed new turret design,' his mining and armaments director said, passing yet another sheaf of papers across to him.

Claus studied it. The turret was a tank turret. Knowing the furore there would be if Nancy were ever to catch a glimpse of it, he nodded his approval. The director began elaborating on the design and, though Claus was listening to him, his thoughts were again on Nancy.

All that was necessary for the continuance of his affair with her was that she kept her opinions to herself and abandoned her journalism. It was, under the circumstances – and considering the kind of issues at stake – very little to ask.

There was a knock at the dining-room door and his secretary entered. 'These photographs arrived by special courier, Herr Direktor,' she said deferentially. 'I thought you would like to see them.'

He thanked her and took them, knowing very well what they were. On his last night in Berlin before leaving for the Ruhr he had been one of a highly select group of major industrialists invited to dinner at the Chancellery.

Against the background of a giant flag of the black swastika in its white circle, impossible to avoid, Göring had addressed them, urging the necessity of increased armament production in order that the Reich would not only reach parity with Britain in regard to warships and planes but would supersede her. Other members of the Nazi hierarchy had been present. Himmler, bespectacled and mild-mannered, looking more like a schoolmaster than one of the most powerful men in the country. Wilhelm Keppler, Hitler's gimlet-eyed economic adviser. Dr Schacht, the corpulent and genial Reichsbank president. And then, as the evening drew to a close, Hitler had made an unscheduled appearance.

His doing so was, of course, a great honour, but Claus's heart had sunk, for it meant an evening he'd already found over-long would simply become even longer. It hadn't been quite as bad as he had feared. Instead of launching into one of his long, excitable diatribes, the Führer had simply mingled among them socially. Heinrich Hoffmann, his favoured photographer, had been called. Photographs taken.

Not for the first time, Claus had been struck by the Führer's lack of inches. A commanding presence, whether standing on a speaker's platform before thousands or in a small room nursing a glass of something non-alcoholic, but the power he exuded had nothing to do with physical stature. And it was a tangible thing. Even from several yards away, Claus had felt the forcefulness of Hitler's personality snake across his nerve ends like a live thing.

He put the photographs to one side. Though one of them would no doubt find its way onto the wall of his office, where it would impress his visitors, they weren't important. What was important was an impending visit by the Armaments Inspectorate.

'Are we ready for the visit?' he asked his mining and armaments director. 'If there are problems, or potential problems, I want to know now.'

There were potential problems and he spent the rest of his day trying to iron them out.

By the time the siren went, signalling the end of the working day for House of Remer day-shift workers, Claus still had hours of paperwork ahead of him. As his night-shift workers streamed into the giant industrial complex, heading for foundries and factories, he packed files and folders into a bulging briefcase. It was work that could be continued in the comfort of his near by apartment.

Thirty minutes later, before he had even put his key in the lock, the door opened.

She was wearing a turquoise dress that clung too tightly to her slightly plump, sturdy figure to be elegant, but which he found erotically arousing. Her dark-blonde hair, usually a mass of untidy curls, had been brushed into gleaming submission. The grey-blue of her eyes had been defined by eye shadow and her full wide mouth was shiny with pink lipstick. Usually she was careless about her appearance, nearly always having a pencil tucked behind her ear, or ink marks on her hands. Tonight there were no signs of either. Tonight Nancy had made an effort and his heart hurt with love.

Behind her, lamps glowed softly. A bottle of Schwartz-riesling and two crystal glasses stood on a low glass-topped table and on the gramophone Bing Crosby was singing 'Try a Little Tenderness'.

He put his briefcase down, allowed the door to swing shut behind him and said simply, 'I'm sorry, *Liebchen*.'

Even though she knew he wasn't saying sorry for his political opinions, only for the way he had expressed them and then, having done so, for not having put things right between the two of them, she gave a cry that sounded as if it had been torn from her heart and threw herself into his arms.

His arms closed around her, strong and hard. He didn't attempt to take her into the bedroom; didn't even attempt to cross the few feet to the sofa. Instead, with passionate urgency, he swung her round so that her back was against the door and then, as she moaned with need, pressing her face into his neck and knotting her fingers tightly in his hair, he slid his hands high above her stocking tops and, seconds later, in an orgasm of explosive intensity, took her where she stood.

For a long time afterwards they simply clung together, weak-kneed and trembling, and then, hearts still hammering, they collapsed on the sofa, their arms still entwined.

'I think,' she said at last, unsteadily, 'that I would like a glass of wine.'

'I think,' he said, looking down at her with unfettered pleasure, 'that that is a very good idea.'

Gently he disentangled himself from her, reaching for the bottle on the near by table.

She lay back against the sofa's many cushions, watching him, taking infinite pleasure in the hard, exciting line of his cheek, the slightly arrogant, sculpted mouth, his silkily straight, well-cut blond hair.

He poured the wine. The crystal glass sparkled with a myriad of tiny flashing lights as he handed it to her.

'Happy?' he asked.

She nodded, a smile tugging at the corners of her mouth as

she assessed the damage done. The shoulder of his immaculately cut dark-blue business suit was covered in make-up. The silk French knickers that had been one of his many presents to her the previous Christmas, were torn beyond repair.

Fleetingly, she wondered if now was the moment to broach her suggestions for the future – a future that did not include the House of Remer steelworks and factories.

'Let's go to bed,' he said, rising to his feet, his tie loose, his shirt open at the throat. 'Let's make love in comfort this time.' The expression in his slate-blue eyes as he looked down at her sent heat once again racing through her veins.

Discussion could wait.

Love-making was far more important.

This time both of them were languorously and sensually unhurried. When he moved to enter her she stayed him with her hand, rolling from beneath him and easing herself on top, sitting astride him and leaning forward so that her breasts brushed his tautly muscled chest.

'I love you,' she said huskily, using all her self-control to move with exquisite slowness.

'I know,' he said, his voice breaking as he fought to hold his orgasm back for just a few seconds longer.

As his face contorted with the effort, she felt so much joy at their mutual pleasure she thought she was going to die.

At that moment it was impossible to think of anything ever dividing them. It was impossible to think of anything but of how very much she loved him.

'I love you, Claus,' she whispered again, bending towards him, her mouth a fraction away his. 'No matter what. Always and for ever.'

Their bodies were slippery with sweat, their orgasms simultaneous. Afterwards, satiated and deeply exhausted and amid a tangle of sheets, they fell asleep in each other's arms.

A little after two o'clock he woke, remembering the work he still had to do. Raising himself up on his elbow, he gazed down at her.

She stirred, opening her eyes.

'Go back to sleep,' he said gently, tucking the sheet over her naked shoulder. 'I'm going in the sitting room to finish some paperwork. I won't be long.'

She made a mewling sound of protest, but there was no fire in it. Even before he had gone from the bed, her eyes were again closed, her breathing rhythmic.

He shrugged himself into his dressing gown and padded barefoot into the sitting room. Picking up his briefcase from where he had dropped it at the door, he carried it across to the coffee table and delved into it for the file he deemed the most urgent. Other files, together with the hard-backed envelope containing the photographs his secretary had handed him, he put to one side.

Over the last year, bureaucratic paperwork had swollen from a torrent of red tape to a positive Niagara. A single business transaction could entail as many as forty different forms, and industry was bound by so many rules and regulations that it needed an army of lawyers to keep track of them all. Unfortunately, someone had to keep track of the lawyers and where the House of Remer was concerned, he was that person.

Ignoring the half-full bottle of wine, he poured himself a whisky, settled himself comfortably on the sofa and began the tedious task of checking the latest armaments contract, a copy of which had been requested by the Minister of Economics.

One file led to another and by the time he was finished the night sky was pearling to grey. Putting the files back in his briefcase and leaving unnecessary ones on the coffee table, he went back to bed, sliding his arm around her. In the morning,

273

they would have to talk. She had to be made to understand that her career as a journalist couldn't be continued, that there were too many people eager to report anti-Nazi remarks to the Security Service.

She was lying turned away from him and he kissed the nape of her neck. She hadn't been too obdurate to travel from Berlin in order to make things right between them again. She wouldn't be too obdurate when, in a few hours' time, he finally made her understand just what was necessary if they were to have a life together. And they were going to have a life together, of that he'd become certain.

It was just after seven o'clock when she woke. Claus was still deep in sleep and, vaguely remembering that sometime during the night he had told her he was going to go into the sitting room to do some paperwork, she didn't disturb him.

Slipping on his dressing gown, she headed for the kitchen to make a pot of coffee.

As she crossed the sitting room she paused to pick up their two empty wine glasses. There were other things on the glass-topped table, files and a large, stiff-backed envelope.

Snooping was as far from being a vice with her as stealing. Under normal circumstances she would never, in a million years, have looked at anything not meant for her eyes. The envelope was open, though, and the glossy photograph spilling from it showed Adolf Hitler, arm outstretched.

To be confronted by a glossy photograph of Adolf Hitler was not normal circumstances. With her heart beating somewhere up in her throat, she slid the photograph farther from the envelope.

It was a line-up similar to many she had seen before, only then the photographs had been grainy press photographs. This was a personal photograph and the reason it had been sent to Claus was obvious.

In front of a mammoth swastika-emblazoned flag, stood an array of dinner-jacketed men flanking their Führer, arms outstretched in the Nazi salute.

Himmler and Göring, Hitler's key players, stood at either side of him. Himmler, camera reflection dancing off his round rimless glasses, looked extremely pleased with himself. Göring looked slightly drunk. There were three other men in the line-up. One she didn't recognize and two she did.

One of those she recognized was Dr Schacht, President of the Reichsbank. The other was Claus.

In a split second she was aware of her whole life changing course. Until then she had never realized how much of a romantic she was. Now she did. Only a romantic would have believed there was a future for her and Claus that did not include politics and Berlin and the House of Remer. It had been wishful thinking. A castle in the air. A pipe dream.

Now she was faced with reality. Reality was the sight of Claus standing shoulder to shoulder with Jew-hating fanatics. With men like Hermann Göring and the Head of the SS, Heinrich Himmler. How long had Claus been on such close terms with the Nazi hierarchy? For how long had he been attending private functions – and the nature of the photograph showed quite clearly that this had been a private function – at which Hitler had been present?

She had no way of knowing because he had never spoken to her of such things. She actually knew nothing about the life he led when he was not with her. Looking down at the photograph, seeing him no longer as the man she loved, seeing him no longer even as her cousin but as a committed Nazi, his arm rigid in the Nazi salute, the swastika on the enamel pin in the lapel of his evening jacket clearly visible, her gorge rose. Here was a man she had not known at all.

No longer a romantic but now a realist, she knew her belief that he would give up the House of Remer for her had been infantile. The House of Remer was as much his life as, until recently, it had been his father's life.

Her heart felt as if it would never be whole again. It was over, and all that was left now was to tell him so.

When Claus woke to find she was no longer next to him he immediately assumed she was making breakfast. Breakfast was a meal he never usually bothered with, but on this occasion he welcomed the prospect. It would give him the opportunity of doing some straight talking.

Picking up the dressing gown that had been thrown carelessly across the bottom of the bed and not, if he remembered rightly, by him, he shrugged it on and strolled into the sitting room.

She was seated on the sofa as primly as if in a dentist's waiting room, back straight, knees together, hands clasped.

She was also fully dressed and by her feet was the travelling bag she had brought with her.

He didn't need to ask why she was leaving so suddenly.

The photograph lay on the glass-topped table. Hitler and his cronies. Hitler and his cronies and Claus Remer.

'It isn't what you think,' he said, standing perfectly still, his hands deep in his dressing-gown pockets. 'It was a dinner at the Chancellery for a group of major industrialists. Alfried Krupp was there; August Diehn, of the potash industry was there; Georg von Schnitzler, a director of I G Farben, the giant chemical cartel was there. None of us knew Hitler was going to make an appearance. We were there at Göring's invitation.'

Her eyes held his, tortured and bleak.

'I came here to ask you to rid yourself of the steelworks and the factories, just as your father has rid himself of them. I thought that his action would make it easier for you to do so. I thought that if you were no longer head of the House of Remer you wouldn't need to be a Nazi. And I believed that if you were no longer a Nazi we could be happy. I was wrong, wasn't I?'

'Wrong in that we could be happy?' He gave a twisted smile. 'No, Nancy. There has always been the possibility that we could be happy. All you have to do for that to happen is to change your opinions.'

She didn't even bother responding to his last remark. Instead, she said, 'If I'd asked the question I came here to ask, your answer would have been "no", wouldn't it?'

He nodded. 'Of course. Only a child could have asked such a question expecting any different reply. The Remer steelworks is not a *Lebensmittelgeschaft*, Nancy. It is a steelworks of national importance. Which is why I was at the Chancellery alongside men like Alfried Krupp and August Diehn.'

'And men like Himmler and Göring.' She rose to her feet. 'It would have been better if the family business had been a grocery shop, Claus. If it had been, we would all have been happier.'

She picked up her bag and still he made no move towards her.

She knew now that he wouldn't; it had come to an end for them.

'I shan't stay in Berlin,' she said, feeling dead inside. 'Berlin holds nothing for me now. Like my mother, I've come to hate it.'

'I love you,' he said, his voice matter-of-fact and without any plea in it. 'Remember that, will you?'

'Yes,' she said, knowing there was to be no goodbye kiss; knowing it would have been beyond the endurance of both of them. 'I'll remember.' Turning away from him she walked towards the door, opening it and closing it behind her without a backward look.

SEVENTEEN

Yorkshire, Christmas 1935

'Only two more days to Christmas,' Vicky said rapturously, rolling over in bed so that she was on her side, snuggled up close against Adam. He was lying on his back and she slid her hand onto his chest. 'It's my favourite time of year, especially when it's snowing, as now.'

'The curtains are still drawn. How do you know it's snowing?' There was amusement in his voice and she undid a button of his pyjama top and kissed a chest that was still broad and well-muscled.

'I can tell by the light. Even when the curtains are drawn the light is always different in a room if it's snowing.'

He chuckled, raising himself on his elbow to look down at her, heat in his eyes.

'No,' she said firmly, knowing very well what he had in mind. 'I've far too much to do today to spend the morning in bed, making love.'

Before her will power should weaken she swung her legs from the bed and stood up, her lace-trimmed nightdress falling to her ankles. 'And so have you, my love,' she said, walking across to the washstand. 'Will isn't around to help Paul haul

278

a tree into the house. He and Jenny have gone to Northumberland, to relatives, for Christmas, remember? It's a difficult job to do single-handed and Paul is going to need some help.' As she spoke she was pulling her nightdress over her head. 'Also, I'd like you to buy a sledge. Emily Elise is quite old enough now to enjoy sledging down a gentle slope.'

'Not by herself, she isn't. She's only four.' His alarm at the thought of his precious daughter indulging in any activity in which she might come to grief was so great it even intruded on the pleasure he always felt at seeing his wife naked.

Vicky didn't trouble to continue the conversation until she'd washed and brushed her hair, then, pinning it into a heavy golden coil, she said chidingly, 'If Emily Elise had been a boy, you would have been *encouraging* her to do adventurous things.'

She began to dress. It was going to be a day of baking and putting up decorations and the skirt she stepped into was a honey-coloured tweed that had seen better days. 'And if she does fall off the sledge,' she continued, zipping it up over the generous curve of her hips, 'she'll land in snow and so there'll be no harm done.'

'Only if it's snowing heavily enough for a soft landing,' he said sheepishly, aware of how overprotective he was where Emily Elise was concerned. 'And you haven't drawn the curtains back. For all you know, it may not be snowing at all.'

Vicky pulled a cinnamon-coloured sweater over her head, added a matching cardigan and, in loving exasperation, crossed to the window and pulled back the curtains. The world outside was white, with flakes falling steadily from a heavy, pearl-grey sky.

'Why,' she said, throwing a pair of socks towards him as he swung his feet to the floor, 'do you never believe me?'

'Why,' he asked in mock annoyance, 'are you always *right*?'

She walked across to where he was sitting on the edge of

the bed and dropped a kiss onto his still thick and curly fox-red hair. 'It's because I'm a wife,' she said, love and amusement in her voice. 'And it goes with the territory. You should be used to it by now.'

He pulled her against him and for a contented moment they simply held each other close and then, aware of all the work there was to do if the house was to look suitably festive, he gave her a light pat on the bottom. 'Into the kitchen with you. I much prefer your mince pies to Josephine's and well you know it.'

Once in the kitchen she put some porridge on for Emily Elise's breakfast and then, a mackintosh around her shoulders and Tinker close behind, she went out into the garden to put food out for the birds, enjoying the sensation of the snow settling on her hair.

Over the next two days all her children, as well as her much-loved daughter-in-law and one of her nieces, would be with her. That her family and extended family came to her for Christmas, staying several days, was the reason she liked Christmas so much. They came in ones and twos at other times of the year, but Christmas was an opportunity for them all to be there at the same time.

She put a handful of nuts and seed onto the tin tray Adam had hung from the low branch of a tree, reminding herself that this year the opportunity was not going to be fully taken, for neither Ilse nor Claus were going to be with them.

'Claus isn't coming out of consideration for me,' Nancy had said, telephoning from London. 'Because if he were at Shuttleworth Hall, I wouldn't be. I couldn't be. It would be too much for me to bear.'

'And I am in a play, Aunt Vicky,' Ilse had said, telephoning from Berlin, her lovely voice full of deep disappointment. 'It's not in performance on Christmas Day, of course, but it is being performed both the day before and two days afterwards.

I'll be thinking of you, though. And I'll be in Yorkshire for Easter, I promise.'

Berthold had also decided against coming to Shuttleworth Hall for Christmas. 'It isn't as if I don't see the children at other times of the year,' he had said, sounding apologetic and defensive, even though there was no reason for him to be either. 'Because of his living in Berlin, I probably see more of Hugo than you do and, until a few months ago, I saw more of Nancy than you did. As for Max, he's always in Berlin. I don't know why Barings don't transfer him here permanently.'

'Will you be spending Christmas with Josef and Zelda?' she had asked, concerned that his Christmas should be pleasant.

'Er, no,' he'd said, sounding uncomfortable. 'I shall be spending it in Potsdam . . . with a lepidopterist friend.'

She'd known that Berthold's interest in butterflies had escalated over the years and that he had begun spending a lot of time with people of a like mind, but hadn't realized he'd forged any real friendships within Berlin's Lepidopterist Society. That he apparently had done so pleased her. What she hadn't thought to ask until it was too late, was if his friend was male or female.

Her thoughts were interrupted by the sound of someone shouting, 'Cooee!'

She turned to see Josephine at the open kitchen door.

'Sorry I'm late, Vicky!' Josephine shouted. 'I didn't like to bicycle when there was so much snow on the road. The egg-man gave me a lift in his van. Do you want me to crack on with icing the Christmas cake or is that something you want to do?'

Brushing snowflakes from her eyelashes, Vicky began walking back to the house, Tinker at her heels. 'You do the Christmas cake, Josephine,' she said as she neared her. 'I'll do the mince pies. The snow looks as if it's going to be with us for days yet, which means we're going to have a gloriously beautiful white Christmas.'

*

Nancy was the first of her chicks to arrive home. By the time the taxi dropped her off, mid-morning, the snow had stopped falling and the sky was no longer grey but a pale icy blue.

'The main roads aren't too bad,' she said, entering the hall and throwing the bag she had brought with her onto the nearest chair. 'They've all been sanded. The taxi driver wouldn't bring me up the drive, though. He said the snow was far too deep.' She took off her coat and dropped it on top of her bag. 'What are you going to do about it? I thought Paul and Will would have cleared some of it by now.'

Vicky gave her a hug and a kiss, hiding the concern she felt at Nancy's appearance, for though Nancy's voice was as brisk and no-nonsense as ever, her face was pale and there were deep circles carved beneath her eyes. 'Will isn't here,' she said, wishing she knew how best to comfort her. 'He's gone to Northumberland for Christmas.'

'Well, Paul and Adam, then. Where are they both? And are those freshly baked mince pies I can smell? I'm starving. There wasn't a buffet car on the London train.'

Avoiding her mother's eyes, grimly behaving as if she hadn't a care in the world, Nancy headed for the kitchen.

Not fooled for a moment, Vicky followed in her wake. 'Paul is out searching for a suitable Christmas tree,' she said, her heart hurting at seeing her daughter so bitterly unhappy, 'and Adam has gone to buy a sledge for Emily Elise.'

'Good. I love sledging. Happy Christmas, Josephine. The cake looks smashing. Did Emily Elise help ice it?'

'I did, *I did*,' Emily Elise abandoned the pastry Josephine had given her to roll and hurtled across the large kitchen, flinging herself into her half-sister's arms. 'Your hair is all tickly and wet,' she said as Nancy scooped her up off the floor, hugging her tight. 'And you smell of smoke, Nancy. You don't smoke cigarettes, do you? Mummy doesn't smoke cigarettes. She doesn't like people smoking them.'

'It's smoke from the train,' Nancy said, lowering Emily Elise back to ground level and resolving to have a little chat with her about tact. 'Did you put the snowman on the Christmas cake?'

'Yes.' Emily Elise's blue eyes shone. 'And I made those little marks to show where he's walked across the cake. I did them with a fork. And then I ruffled up the icing to make a little hill for him to stand on.'

'Here's your cup of tea and two mince pies,' Josephine said, handing Nancy a steaming mug and a plate. 'Now tell me about this new job of yours in London. You're still a journalist, aren't you? No change there, then.'

By the time Max arrived, just before lunch, Paul, Adam and Nancy were busy shovelling snow from the drive so that cars could navigate it without becoming snow-bound.

'Get yourself a pair of wellingtons,' Paul said to him as a giggling Emily Elise pelted him with snowballs. 'There are spare shovels in the potting shed.'

'So why isn't Pa coming this year?' Max asked an hour and a half later as, weary with shovelling, they sat around the huge kitchen table, enjoying home-made chicken soup and freshly baked bread.

'He's had an alternative offer.' Vicky passed a napkin to Emily Elise, who was finding her soup spoon difficult to manage. 'He's spending it with a lepidopterist friend.'

'Male or female?' Josephine asked, cutting to the heart of the matter with Yorkshire bluntness.

'I don't know.'

'It would be nice if the friend was female.' Nancy carved herself another wedge of bread. 'He might marry again.'

'Then if he does, we'd better hope she isn't a Nazi,' Max said drily. 'Three in the family is already three too many.'

There was an awkward silence. That Berthold had years

283

ago followed in Josef's wake where admiration of Hitler was concerned was something they all had difficulty with.

Not wanting Max to begin talking about Claus – certain Nancy would not be able to cope if he did – Vicky changed the subject. 'As soon as we've cleared away the lunch things, we'll put the house decorations up,' she said decisively. 'I want Shuttleworth Hall to be at its Christmassy best by the time Hugo, Hester and Lotti arrive.'

Later that afternoon, Nancy spent time upstairs with her grandfather. 'I can still get downstairs,' Arthur Hudson said to her as he sat in a chair by the window, looking out over the snow-covered lawns to the river, 'but at the moment I'm saving my strength for Christmas Eve and Christmas Day.' He struggled with his breathing for a few minutes and then said, 'And what about you, Nancy? Why are you in London and not in Yorkshire? You could have gone back to reporting for the *Yorkshire Post*, couldn't you?'

'I could, Grandpa, but I didn't want to.' She tucked his blanket a little tighter around his knees. 'It would have seemed too much like going backwards instead of forwards.'

He looked at her with rheumy eyes, seeing how the light had gone out of her, sensing her misery.

'It wouldn't have worked out for the two of you, lass,' he said gently. 'Not as long as there's a House of Remer steelworks making armaments. It didn't work for your mother and it wouldn't have worked for you.'

'I know.' Her eyes were bright with tears. 'I know, Grandpa. But it doesn't make it any easier to bear.'

'Time will heal the hurt,' he said, trying to offer comfort. 'It always does.'

From downstairs there came the sound of Vicky laughing and Emily Elise squealing with joy as Adam swung her high onto his shoulders.

She squeezed his gnarled hand, grateful for his love and concern, certain history wasn't going to repeat itself in the same manner. She couldn't know for sure, but she didn't think her mother had loved her father in the way that she had loved Claus and she couldn't even begin to imagine loving someone else.

Pain bit deep into her heart, so forcefully she didn't know how she was bearing it. It was the first Christmas, since she could remember, that they hadn't been spending together. He had always been a part of her life, and trying to live life without him was proving to be almost impossible for her to manage. She had known even before the door of his apartment had closed behind her that she couldn't continue living in Berlin, knowing he was near by, knowing she might see him unexpectedly at any moment. And she had known too that she couldn't return to life at Shuttleworth Hall, working for the *Yorkshire Post* or the Bradford *Telegraph & Argus*, for Shuttleworth Hall was filled with just as many memories of him as Berlin was.

So she had gone to London and, though wild horses wouldn't have made her admit it to her family, London wasn't working for her. Despite having made friends with a couple of fellow journalists, her social life hadn't got into gear. Life was dull. In Berlin, hideous though the political situation had been, at least it had kept the adrenalin flowing and she had been in the thick of things.

She wanted to be in the thick of things again and had got into the habit of going to Speakers' Corner on a Sunday, listening to the left-wing agitators and finding herself in sympathy with them. Only they, it seemed to her, had the sense to see Hitler's New Germany for what it really was. Even though Hitler had now nailed his colours to the mast, declaring a few months ago at Nuremberg that all Jews were to be deprived of citizenship and no longer had any legal rights, many British newspapers were still clinging to the opinion that, overall, because of the improvement he had made to the German economy and because his Nazi troops were acting as a bulwark for the rest of Europe against communism, Hitler was a good thing and the unpleasantness being meted out to the Jews was something that would eventually die down and that would, while it lasted, simply have to be lived with.

They, though, were not the ones living with it, and she had found it almost impossible to get her colleagues in London to understand the enormity of the violence or just how terrifying life now was for Germany's Jews.

Hugo, Hester and Lotti arrived next day in the middle of the afternoon, having journeyed from Berlin together.

'And we did all manage to squeeze into one of Little Ridding's taxis together,' Hugo said, leading the way into the hall and stamping snow from his shoes, 'squeeze being the operative word, because I've never seen so many parcels and packages as Hester and Lotti have brought with them.'

As Hester and Lotti struggled from the taxi to the house, weighed down with Christmas-wrapped gifts, he gave his mother a fervent hug.

'God, but it's good to be back in England,' he said, his face looking almost as strained as Nancy's. 'Life in Berlin is getting grimmer by the minute.'

'Presents!' Emily Elise shouted gleefully as Hester and Lotti crossed the threshold, so heavily laden they could hardly see where they were going.

'Merry Christmas, you three,' Nancy said, heartily glad to see them and not at all abashed that, unlike them, she had barely given present-giving a thought.

'Don't close the door, Max,' Lotti said as he moved to do so. 'There are stacks more things to bring in yet.'

As Max walked out to the taxi to begin bringing them in, Lotti dropped all her packages onto the nearest chair and opened her fox fur-coated arms wide for Emily Elise to run into them.

'My goodness, but you've grown!' she said, swinging her round and round until the two of them were both dizzy. 'And I've brought you so many presents that when Santa Claus sees them he'll think you don't need any more and he'll leave your Christmas stocking empty.'

'No, he won't,' Emily Elise said, giggling, knowing she was being teased. She nuzzled her face against the fox fur. Of all her half-siblings and cousins, Lotti was her favourite because Lotti always let her dress up in her clothes, and they were such fun to dress up in. Nancy's clothes weren't any fun at all. Apart from a turquoise dress that Nancy wouldn't allow her to even touch, all her clothes were sensible suits and blouses, and her shoes were always sensible too.

Lotti's shoes weren't sensible. Lotti's shoes were all dizzily high-heeled and some had black satin flowers on them and others had red spangles. Her clothes were always glittery and spangly as well and she had lots of long, elbow-length satin gloves and, her favourites, black lace gloves that had no fingers in them.

She supposed that if she asked, Hester would let her dress up in some of her clothes, but though Hester's clothes were pretty they weren't spangly. And Ilse's clothes were all white and pale beige silks and chiffons or, in the wintertime, cashmere. Even at four years old, Emily Elise knew there was no fun to be had in dressing-up in clothes that spent their wardrobe life wrapped in tissue. The risk of getting into troubling for spoiling them was far too great.

Only allowing Lotti to take off her fox-fur hat and shrug herself out of her coat before she grabbed her hand again, she skipped along at her side into the drawing room where there

287

was a log fire roaring in the grate and a huge spice-scented fir tree waiting to be decorated.

'We put up all the paper-chains and the holly yesterday,' she confided as they bagged a comfy corner of the sofa, 'but Mummy said we must wait till you and Hugo and Hester arrived before we decorated the tree.'

'So how are things in Berlin?' her cousin Paul asked Hugo.

Paul was in his favourite armchair, his lean, big-boned frame far too lanky to look comfortable in it unless, as now, he draped one leg over the arm.

Emily Elise always thought it very strange that someone who was an adult, like her daddy, was also her cousin or, in Hugo's case, her half-brother. 'Why aren't they my uncles?' she had constantly asked her mother and Josephine when she had first discovered that the cousins and brothers of little girls her own age, were children also. 'No one else I know has grown-up cousins or a grown-up half-sister and half-brothers. And why is Nancy only half my sister and Hugo and Max only half my brothers?'

Her mother had explained to her that Nancy, Max and Hugo had a different daddy, which had only perplexed her more. Her own daddy was so nice, she couldn't understand why they should have preferred to have a different one. There were, though, lots of thing she didn't understand. The conversation taking place now, for instance. It was Christmas and yet, for some reason she couldn't fathom, everyone had become very serious, even her ebullient cousin Lotti.

'There's going to be a war,' Max was saying, his face grim, his tone matter-of-fact. 'Why else the rearmament programme? Why else the fevered building of battleships and submarines? German naval personnel has tripled over the last couple of years. The army has trebled in strength and House of Remer order books are full to bursting. And the orders are all for armaments.'

288

No one looked towards Nancy, but everyone was aware of how her hand tightened on the gin and tonic she had poured herself.

'War with who?' Lotti asked, her legs curled up beneath her, Tinker resting comfortably against them. 'France? Britain?'

'Not Britain. Not if Hitler can avoid it.' It was Hugo who answered her. He was seated on the opposite sofa, next to Hester. 'The Foreign Office are taking the line that it's Germany's neighbours to the east who are most at risk of German aggression. Britain also has army and navy expansionist plans under way.'

'Forgive me for being dim,' Lotti said, her voice indicating she didn't think she was dim at all, 'but why is Britain so unexcited by all this German rearmament?'

'Because Britain is giving Germany the benefit of the doubt,' Hugo said wearily. 'When Hitler says Germany has no intention of being anything other than friendly towards Britain, our Prime Minister and Foreign Secretary believe him.'

'And you don't?' Adam asked, puffing on a pipe.

'No. Like everyone else in this room, I'm too familiar with what is going on in Germany to put any trust in anything he says. Baldwin and Eden may think they are dealing with a fellow statesman who honours agreements and treaties, but they aren't. Hitler is a dangerous opportunist.'

'Hitler is a barbarian,' Hester said quietly, her face pinched and pale beneath the soft cloud of her dark hair.

Hugo looked around at his family. 'I'll give you an update on what is happening to people like Hester's parents when little ears aren't listening in. I don't want to give Emily Elise nightmares.'

Hearing the tension in his voice, Vicky felt her heart contract. Germany was no longer a country she wanted those she loved living in and the minute she was alone with Hugo she intended wringing a promise from him that he would ask for a transfer to an embassy somewhere else. Until then, the obvious thing was for Hester and her parents to leave Germany for England. There was plenty of room for them at Shuttleworth Hall and whatever the legal paperwork where Hester's parents were concerned, Hugo, with all his Foreign Office expertise, was well equipped to handle it.

The opportunity came that evening as Hester, Lotti, Emily Elise, Max, Paul and Nancy were all decorating the tree.

As there were already sufficient pairs of hands at work, Vicky was seated on one of the sofas, a glass of sherry in her hand.

Hugo, who had been helping Adam bring in a fresh batch of logs for the fire, sat down beside her.

'It's good to be home, Mother,' he said with deep feeling. 'The contrast between life here and life in Berlin – for people like the Dresners – is almost surreal.'

'They don't have to stay in Berlin,' she said quietly. 'And nor should they. I know the Dresners have been hoping that things would eventually get back to normal for them, but it isn't going to. At least not in the immediate future. And before things get worse – though now all Jews have been deprived of their German citizenship it's hard to see how much worse things can get – they should leave. There's plenty of room for them here, at Shuttleworth Hall. And it goes without saying that Hester should be living in England – and as she's married to a British citizen there's absolutely no problem on that score.'

'The problem,' Hugo said, strain once again showing on his face, 'is that though Hester's parents are Jews they are also Germans and they love Germany. Solomon Dresner fought so fiercely for his country in the Great War that he was awarded an Iron Cross. He doesn't see why he should leave the country

290

he was born in and that his father and grandfather were born in, simply because it is now in the hands of racial maniacs. He won't leave. I've asked him. I've pleaded with him. And he won't budge.'

'And Hester?'

'You can cease worrying about Hester. I'm being transferred to London. Faced with the choice of living with me in London, or her parents in Berlin, I'm relieved to say Hester's chosen to live with me in London. It wasn't an easy choice for her to make, though. And if she knew I'd actually asked for the transfer, it's a choice she may not have made.'

'Then thank God she doesn't know.'

The tree was now so festooned with glass crystals and baroque angels that hardly any pine needles were showing. Aware that their few moments of privacy were fast coming to an end, Vicky rose to her feet.

'Mulled wine, anyone?' she asked, knowing that everyone would want a glass. 'And no, Emily Elise, you can't have one. You'll have your mug of hot cocoa as usual.'

The next morning Hugo and Hester took Emily Elise sledging, Paul took Max for a look around the rose nursery's glass houses, Nancy took Tinker for a long walk by the river, Josephine embarked on a mammoth baking session, Adam spent time with Arthur Hudson and Vicky went into Little Ridding with Lotti for last-minute food shopping.

As always on Christmas Eve morning, there was a long queue at Tom Payne's, the greengrocer's, but it was a friendly, chatty queue, for in Little Ridding everyone knew everyone else.

'Two pounds of Brussels sprouts, a pound of leeks, three pounds of parsnips,' she said when it was finally her turn to be served.

'What on earth are the leeks for?' Lotti asked, squeezing in by her side, her fox-fur coat and hat an exotic contrast to the plain serviceable coats and headscarves of the other customers.

'There's bound to be lots of leftover turkey. I thought I'd use it up in a flan with leeks and cheese.' She turned her attention back to Tom. 'And a couple of pounds of carrots, a swede, a bag of potatoes, a box of dates and two dozen tangerines.'

'Good job I came, or you'd never have managed to carry this little lot out of the shop.' Lotti took the already heavy shopping basket from Vicky and held it out so that Tom Payne could rattle the loose carrots on top of the leeks and parsnips.

Her nail varnish was midnight-blue and Tom didn't flinch, though the woman waiting her turn immediately behind Vicky, did.

When the rest of Vicky's shopping had been squeezed into a second basket Lotti picked up the bag of potatoes, blew Tom a kiss and led the way out of the shop, wishing everybody a cheery Merry Christmas as she did so.

'I need to check with Jack Wilkinson what time I can expect the turkey,' Vicky said, easing the handle of her cane shopping basket so that it sat a little more comfortably on her arm. 'Last year it wasn't delivered till late afternoon and I don't know whose panic was worse, mine or Josephine's.'

The queue at the butcher's was even longer than the queue at the greengrocer's had been and Jack Wilkinson, seeing her at the back of the shop, simply shouted: 'Mid-morning, Mrs Priestley! And it's a reet grand bird!'

'Paul or Hugo or Max would have come into Little Ridding for the veg, if you'd asked them,' Lotti said as they made their way towards where Vicky had parked the car, the settled snow scrunching beneath their feet.

'I know they would, but I enjoy shopping on Christmas Eve morning. In fact, I like everything about Christmas Eve, especially the carol service at church this evening. Violet will be coming with us. I don't think you've seen her for a long time, have you?'

'No, but I don't imagine she's changed, which is fine by me even though she is always wonderfully rude about the way I dress.'

As they neared the car, Vicky said tentatively, 'I thought you might have brought someone with you this Christmas. Boyfriends are always welcome at Shuttleworth Hall, as you well know.'

'I do know.' Lotti thought of Vladimir and dismissed him as not being worthy of mention. 'And if there was anyone special I would have brought him. Only there isn't.'

She lowered the basket and bag she was carrying to the ground as Vicky unlocked the car. 'And it's no use trying to marry me off, Aunt Vicky. As a cabaret artiste, the only men I meet are either homosexuals or Nazis. And though I much prefer the homosexuals to the Nazis, they aren't brilliant husband material.'

Vicky's lips twitched in a smile. 'No,' she said, as she slid behind the wheel and Lotti opened the front passenger door, 'I don't imagine they are.'

'And speaking of trying to marry people off,' Lotti said when seated, 'what news is there of a girlfriend in Paul's life? He must have one, surely? He inherited squillions when his grandfather died – and I say "his" grandfather, because Grandfather Wallace could never get along with the fact that the rest of us had German blood, and his legacies to us were only nominal. So . . . as squillions of cash always makes a man highly eligible, Paul must have a girlfriend. Who is she? Why do we never see her?'

'There usually is a girl in his life, but they only ever stay the course for a year or so. After that, they fade away. Mainly, I suspect, because they want a ring on their finger and Paul never shows any signs of being interested in that kind of commitment. Roses are the love of his life – everything else comes a very poor second.'

The road out of Little Ridding had been heavily sanded, but was still icy. As her wheels began to spin, Vicky eased her foot off the accelerator. Not until the car was again completely under her control did she continue the conversation.

'I see very little of Max these days,' she said as they left the village behind them. 'He's nearly always either in Berlin or in London and, like all sons, when I do see him, he never tells me all I'd like to know about what is going on in his life.'

She looked across at Lotti as she finished speaking, but Lotti didn't meet her gaze and, unusually for her, made no comment.

Vicky changed gear and turned into the road that hugged the left-hand bank of the river.

'I'm not very sure of my facts here,' she continued, trying to sound as if the subject wasn't of much importance, 'but I believe he's forsaken his usual string of girlfriends and is now spending all his free time with Ilse.'

It wasn't couched as a question, but it very obviously was one.

'He always has spent a lot of time with Ilse,' Lotti replied neutrally, still keeping her eyes on the glistening snow-covered banks of the Ure. 'When Ilse was younger he took her to the Zoological Gardens and the Schöneberger Volkspark. Now that she's older, he takes her to restaurants and nightclubs.'

As Lotti was quite obviously not going to be voluntarily forthcoming about the nature of Max and Ilse's present relationship, Vicky was reduced to Yorkshire bluntness. 'Are they in love? Because if they are, I'd like to know. I'd like to be prepared for it.'

Lotti finally looked towards her. 'Because it would distress you? Because you would be disapproving, as you were disapproving of Nancy's love affair with Claus?'

Vicky took a hand off the wheel and tucked a stray strand of gold hair back into its heavy coil. 'No,' she said at last. 'I was disapproving of Nancy and Claus's affair for reasons over and above my belief that they were not right for each other.'

She looked away from the road, her eyes meeting Lotti's. 'And so is Max in love with Ilse? You are the person who has always been the closest to him. If anyone knows, you must do.'

'Yes.' Lotti broke eye contact with her. 'Yes,' she said again, her face inscrutable, 'Max is in love with Ilse.'

'And is Ilse in love with Max?'

'Oh, I imagine so. I imagine she's been in love with him for a long time.'

There was an odd note in Lotti's voice. A note Vicky couldn't place.

They could see Shuttleworth Hall in the distance now and Lotti said, sounding more like her usual self, 'There is another man in Ilse's life. Whenever Max isn't in Berlin, she spends a lot of time with Count Nicholas Schulenburg, and Nicky Schulenburg is deeply in love with her.'

'Is he?' Vicky's eyebrows flew high. She returned her attention to the road. She knew all about Nicholas Schulenburg and liked him. 'It would be a wonderful match,' she said musingly.

'Because he's wealthy and titled?'

'Because he's a fine young man and because of the long friendship Josef enjoyed with his father.'

'But wealth and title are an issue with Ilse, aren't they?' Lotti said with stunning bluntness. 'She doesn't think they are, of course. If you asked her, she would say she didn't care about being rich or being a countess – and she would say that her being in love with Max proves that.'

Vicky slowed the car to a snail's pace, not wanting the

journey to end before their conversation should do so. 'And you don't think that's the case?'

'I think Ilse has no idea at all of what it would be like to live on a restricted income. And Max's income is restricted, isn't it? He's never likely to be super-rich, the way that Claus is super-rich, or the way that Nicholas is super-rich, is he? Ilse is used to being pampered and spoiled. It's not a role Max could easily fulfil, is it? And even if he could fulfil it, I don't think it's a role that would make him happy.'

'No,' Vicky said quietly. 'It isn't.' She turned the car off the road and into the narrow lane leading towards the river and Shuttleworth Hall. 'And so let's hope Nicholas Schulenburg is a persistent suitor,' she said wryly, 'because it seems to me that he, not Max, is the right person for Ilse.'

There was no response from Lotti, but there didn't need to be one. On this subject Vicky knew that Lotti was in full agreement with her.

'Jack Wilkinson says the turkey will be delivered by mid-morning – which is any time now,' she said to Josephine as she walked into the kitchen, setting her heavy basket of greengroceries down. 'I'm just going to have a cup of tea and a five-minute rest and then I'm going to take the Christmas-dinner tablecloth and napkins out of the linen cupboard and polish the epergne.'

Lotti plopped her basket next to Vicky's and lowered the bag of potatoes to the floor. 'Do you think everyone has Christmas tableware that's never used at any other time of the year?' she asked, taking off her hat and shaking her head so that her dark hair swung glossily forward against her cheeks.

'I expect so.' Josephine continued with what she was doing, which was making a trifle. 'When else would a dark red tablecloth and dark green napkins be suitable? As for the epergne – it's only used at Christmas and it's become Emily Elise's task to fill it with sweeties.'

Vicky put the kettle on to boil. 'Where is everyone?' she asked, taking cups and saucers out of a cupboard.

'Adam has helped your father downstairs. They are in the study, enjoying a quiet game of draughts. Hugo, Hester and Emily Elise are back from their sledging. I don't know where Hugo is now, but Emily Elise is upstairs with Hester and I think Hester is allowing Emily Elise free run of her make-up bag. Paul was chopping logs earlier, but I don't know where he is now, either. Nancy's taken Tinker for another long walk. I don't think Tinker wanted to go, but Nancy didn't give him much option. Max has gone into Harrogate to do some last-minute Christmas shopping.'

'And I'm going to take my cup of tea and enjoy it listening to a carol concert on the wireless,' Lotti said, peeping into the oven to see what it was that was filling the kitchen with such a heavenly smell.

'It won't cook properly if you keep letting cold air into the oven,' Josephine said chastisingly, whisking egg yolks, sugar, cornflour and vanilla extract. 'And if you want to know what it is, it's a raised game pie for Boxing Day tea.'

Deciding that the kitchen might not be the most peaceful place for a five-minute rest, when the tea had mashed and been poured Vicky carried her cup and saucer into the drawing room. All the sofas and armchairs were deeply cushioned and almost as soon as she sat down, her eyes closed. Dimly, she was aware of the kitchen doorbell ringing and registered that the turkey had arrived and then, despite all her good intentions of sorting out table linen and cleaning silver, she shifted position so that she was lying full length on the sofa, and fell asleep.

'It's hellishly grim, Paul.'

The fierce tone of Hugo's voice swam into her dreams.

'Without a British or an American passport, Jews desperate to leave Germany simply cannot do so, and even for the fortunate few who have such passports there are problems.'

The sofa was facing away from Hugo and Paul and Vicky knew they didn't realize she was there.

'Why?' Paul said, his voice unruffled and patient. 'I don't understand.'

Hugo's voice was taut with tension. 'No country, however sympathetic to their plight, is willing to grant entry visas to potentially destitute Jews. Without funds abroad, emigration is virtually impossible. They need sponsors. They need people to stand surety for them.'

'And you know people who are in this position? People who have passports but can't put them to good use because they need a sponsor?'

Hugo nodded.

Paul gave a shrug of broad shoulders. 'I'd be happy to stand as a sponsor and I'll do it for as many people as you can arrange.'

'Thanks, Paul.' It was what Hugo had been hoping for and his voice was choked with relief.

Vicky opened her eyes and pushed herself up into a sitting position so that they became aware of her presence for the first time.

'And I have another idea,' she said, as if she had been part of the conversation all along. 'As Jews aren't allowed to take money or valuables out of the country, I could do it for them.'

Hugo blinked.

Paul looked appalled.

'Because I have German family there's nothing at all odd about my visiting Germany regularly. And each time I return to England I can bring money or valuables out with me.'

'Of course you can't, Aunt Vicky!' Paul was no longer appalled. He was horrified. 'If Hitler's SS became aware of what you were doing, God only knows what would happen to you. You could end up in Dachau!'

He looked towards Hugo. 'For goodness sake, tell her it's out of the question, Hugo.'

'But it isn't out of the question.'

Never in his life had Paul been so badly let down.

Hugo was gazing at his mother as if he had never seen her before. 'It's an absolutely brilliant idea, Mother. You could travel to Berlin with Hester and me when we return after Christmas and then come back with someone's life savings a week or two afterwards. And if everything goes smoothly, it would be quite natural for you to be making another trip at Easter.'

'That's it, then,' Vicky said, ignoring Paul's horror-struck face. 'I shall be doing something really worthwhile and I can't wait to start.'

EIGHTEEN

Berlin, July 1936

Ilse was perched on a stool at the side of the stage, a well-thumbed copy of Friedrich von Schiller's *Intrigue and Love* clutched tightly to her chest. As the actors taking the parts of President Walter and his son, Ferdinand, rehearsed one of their key scenes yet again, she was mentally going over her own lines.

She had been given the part of the play's virtuous heroine, Louisa Miller, and was determined to put her stamp on it in a way that would make her name as an up-and-coming classical actress.

'Nein. Nein. *Nein!*' Gustav Gründgens exploded, but not, thank God, at her. 'President Walter is rich and powerful! Rich and powerful men move with authority, shoulders back and belly out! Again, please. Again.'

Her own character had to be both self-sufficient, for when she was dealing with President Walter and his dastardly plotting, and also heart-stoppingly vulnerable, for when the text demanded she swoon and faint – and there was a lot of swooning and fainting in *Intrigue and Love*.

'Nein. Nein. *Nein!*' Gründgens erupted again, storming down the main aisle of the auditorium towards the stage. 'The voice is all wrong. It is disastrous! It needs work. *Work*. We will do the poison-in-the-lemonade scene instead. On stage, if you please, Ilse.'

As the dejected actor playing Ferdinand's father left the stage, she walked onto it. The actor playing Ferdinand stayed where he was.

'We'll take it from "That letter. Prepare yourself for terrible disclosure." And remember that you are dying, poisoned by the man you love. When this scene ends, there mustn't be a dry eye in the house. OK, then. When you're ready.'

Ilse paused, mentally slipping out of her body and into that of the dying Louisa's. Her voice, when she began to speak, was the voice of a woman with only a precious few minutes left to live. Without conscious effort her fingers trembled with convulsive emotion.

'My hand wrote what my heart abhorred,' she continued, unaware that Nicholas Schulenburg had quietly entered the auditorium. 'It was dictated by your father! Oh, that sorrowful act! Ferdinand – I was compelled . . .'

The words came faultlessly. Not once did she have to refer to the text. In the seconds before she fell down dead, she heard someone clear their throat, but at no time did Gründgens shout, "*Nein*", or ask her to stop and repeat a line, or, worse, ask her to leave the stage.

As she picked herself up from the floor, Gründgens merely nodded, but there was satisfaction in his voice as he said, 'Right. Lunch. I want you all back here in an hour's time.'

'And I think you have a lunch date,' the actor playing Ferdinand said to her, indicating the presence of Nicholas as they walked from the stage. 'And you were stunning just then, Ilse. Absolutely magnificent.'

She could tell by his voice that he meant what he said and the knowledge that she had been good made her feel as if she were flying.

301

'I was just passing the theatre,' Nicholas lied smoothly when she joined him, 'and wondered if we could have lunch together.'

'That would be lovely.' She slipped her arm companionably into his. 'Max is in Munich this week. Barings seem to treat him almost like a commercial traveller. The week before last he was in Bremen.'

Nicholas had no desire to hear her talking about Max, especially when she did it with such love in her voice. 'I heard Gründgens say you had to be back in an hour,' he said, as they stepped out into the busy street, 'so perhaps we should settle for something light in a café, rather than a restaurant lunch.'

'Something light in a café would be lovely.'

She gave him her bewitching smile, happy to be with him, for she counted him one of her dearest friends.

Even today, dressed casually for rehearsals in an ivory silk blouse, nutmeg-brown straight skirt, her hair hanging in a single waist-length braid, she turned heads every step of the way.

As he looked across at her he positively ached with love. With her silvery-blonde hair, her creamy flawless skin and innate gentleness, she reminded him of a Botticelli angel. He loved her absolutely unconditionally and he lived in daily fear of her marrying Max.

As they went to the first café they came to that had tables set outside under an awning, he reflected that he loved her enough to have happily relinquished her to Max if he had thought Max would make her happy. Max, though, was a man who lived close to the edge – and not only because the times necessitated it, but because it was his nature – and a devil-may-care adventurer was not the kind of husband Ilse needed.

She needed someone like himself; someone who, in normal times, lived within the rules; someone who could provide her with the privileged lifestyle she had always been accustomed to. And though Max's profession as a banker was seemingly conventional, he doubted very much if Max's work for Barings was all it seemed.

Just as he and his close friends had a hidden and very dangerous agenda – plotting on how best to remove Hitler from power – so, he was sure, did Max. And though he didn't yet know what Max's agenda was, he was quite sure that in the very near future there would be full confidence between the two of them. A confidence that would work to both of their advantages.

As Ilse seated herself at the table and he sat down opposite her, he banished all thoughts of Max from his mind. They only had an hour and he wanted her to talk to him about things that were important to her.

'Tell me about the play,' he said when he had ordered a bottle of white wine. 'I'm not familiar with it. What is it about? Why did Ferdinand poison Louisa when he was obviously in love with her?'

Like a little girl, Ilse clasped her hands on the table. Her beautiful almond-shaped nails were unvarnished, buffed to a high, natural sheen.

'The play is set in 1776 and is the story of Ferdinand and Louisa. Ferdinand is the son of an unscrupulous nobleman, President von Walter, and Louisa is the daughter of a music teacher.'

She paused as the waiter came for their order. 'Sauerkraut salad with ham,' she said, bringing a flush to the waiter's cheeks as she gave him a smile that would have melted the hardest heart.

'Potato pancakes,' Nicholas said, knowing she was quite unaware of the effect she had on people. 'And what part in the story does the father play, Ilse? I take it he's the bad guy.'

'He's totally bad. He's trying to curry favour with his prince. First he tries to extricate the prince from a scandalous entanglement with a notorious lady by marrying the lady to

Ferdinand, but his scheme comes to nothing because Ferdinand is in love with me.'

'He'd be a fool not to be,' Nicholas said with great feeling, pouring her a glass of the chilled wine.

Ilse made no sign that she knew he was referring to her as herself, and not to Louisa. 'He hatches a new plot,' she continued, making no visible response as he handed her the wine glass and their fingers touched. 'He jails my father and tells me that the only way I will see him again is if I write a fraudulent love letter to the Lord Chamberlain. He then arranges for Ferdinand to find the letter, in the belief that Ferdinand will abandon me and instead marry the lady his father wishes him to marry. This plan also goes awry and the play ends with five lives ruined – and all for the sake of one avaricious man's political ambition.'

He grinned. 'It sounds likes a real roller-coaster ride.' He raised his glass. 'Here's hoping it's going to be a huge success.'

'Oh, I hope so, Nicky.' Her voice was fervent. 'Not only is it my first lead part, but it's a wonderful lead part. I couldn't have asked for anything better.'

The waiter served them with their order and when he had retreated out of earshot, Nicholas said, 'How is Nancy? Is she enjoying life in London?'

Ilse paused before answering, looking around at the tables near to them. No one was near enough to overhear what they were saying, especially as they were dining outside and there was a constant background hum of street and traffic noise.

'No, I don't think so,' she said, knowing she could trust Nicholas utterly. 'And she's not staying there. She's leaving for Spain at the end of the week.'

Nicholas stared at her. 'Dear God,' he said, profoundly shocked. 'Doesn't her newspaper realize how bloody the civil war there is going to be? There are already reports of atrocities being committed by both sides. It's no place for a woman.'

'Her newspaper isn't sending her there. She's going as a British Medical Aid Association volunteer.'

'To do what?' he asked, his potato pancakes forgotten.

'She's not sure. She thinks they'll probably use her as an ambulance driver.'

He was absolutely aghast and his feelings showed on his face.

'It's what she wants to do,' Ilse said simply, not aghast at all. 'Nancy needs a cause and, after her experience of living here, that cause is the fight against Fascism.'

There was a fierceness in her eyes he'd never seen before and utter resoluteness in her voice. With a stab of shock he realized for the first time that beneath his Botticelli angel's gentle exterior there lay a backbone of Remer steel.

On the far side of the street workers were putting up multicoloured bunting in readiness for the forthcoming Olympic Games. Berlin was *en fête*. The café they were having lunch in had a splendid collection of international flags on display. Thanks to a massive public relations clean-up, the signs 'Jews Not Welcome' had given way to signs proclaiming 'Welcome to Our Overseas Visitors'. For the length of time that the Games lasted there would, he knew, be no public persecution of the Jewish population. Thousands of foreign visitors would go home convinced that Hitler's brand of Fascism was not the evil it had been rumoured to be.

And they would be wrong. Nancy knew they were wrong. Nancy knew that Fascism was an evil that had to be fought wherever it was to be found and, in volunteering to help the Republican cause, she would be in the thick of the fighting.

As they sat in silence watching the bunting being hoisted high over shop fronts and street lamps he had to fight the temptation to unburden himself, to tell Ilse of the plans he and a small group of like-minded friends were making. Plans that would, he devoutly hoped, bring sanity back to Germany.

305

It was the kind of disclosure that could be made only to a wife – and maybe not even then. Determined not to let such dark thoughts spoil the last twenty minutes or so of his precious time with her he took a drink of his wine, smiled across at her and said, 'What is it to be for dessert? Chocolate cake or apple cake?'

They both opted for apple cake and when their meal was over and time had run out on them he walked her back to the theatre, asking her if she'd like to go with him that evening to Vladimir Ovelensky's birthday party. When she said she had already decided not to go to the party as Max wasn't in Berlin to go with her, he wasn't surprised by her refusal, but he was deeply disappointed.

At the theatre, when he said goodbye to her he did so without giving her a customary kiss on the cheek. She knew why he hadn't done so. It wasn't because he was cross with her. It was because a light kiss on the cheek would have been a torment for him when what he longed to do was to kiss her full on the mouth.

She felt vaguely out of sorts during the afternoon rehearsal. She had enjoyed having lunch with Nicholas. He was relaxing, easy company and, very important in the present political climate, utterly trustworthy. The problem was, though, that being with Nicholas always aroused in her anxieties about her relationship with Max. Anxieties she never shared with anyone.

When Gustav Gründgens hurled the expletive '*Dummkopf!*' at the actor she was playing a scene with and then stormed off amid clouds of cigarette smoke, leaving them to stay or go as they wished, she decided to go.

Not home, though. Since her parents had moved out of the Unter den Linden mansion, it had ceased to be a proper home to her. Claus still seemed quite happy living there, but she suspected that was only because he felt that, as head of the House of Remer, it was his duty to do so.

She walked to where her silver-grey Sports Cabriolet was parked, trying to decide what to do and where to go. In the past, whenever she had felt out of sorts, Lotti had always been her first port of call. Lotti, though, was now part of her problem.

She unlocked the car and slid behind the wheel, knowing that Lotti would be devastated if she knew why it was they weren't seeing quite as much of each other. Not in a million years could she admit to Lotti that she was still jealous of the close relationship that existed between her and Max, for it was a jealousy she knew was senseless. Max loved her, not Lotti. His relationship with Lotti was simply one of best buddies. She knew that – hadn't a shadow of a doubt about it. And to her deep and scorching shame, she was jealous of it.

Almost without thinking she began driving out of Berlin in the direction of Wannsee. It had been the favourite place for outings for all of them when they had been children and was still one of her favourite places for simply walking and thinking.

As she continued south-west, through the tree-lined roads of the elegant, wealthy suburb of Dahlem, a frown furrowed her forehead. She was a serenely happy person by nature and yet instead of being even happier now that she and Max were openly in love, she often found herself having to simulate happy radiance – as had happened with Nicholas, when Max's name had been mentioned.

She stopped short of Wannsee, pulling off the road into a wooded area through which the lake could be glimpsed. One of the things that most troubled her was how little she now saw of Max. Before the change in their relationship he had nearly always stayed at the Unter den Linden mansion when in Berlin. It was, after all, his family home. He had been born there. His father still lived there. Even when he had opted to stay with Hester's parents or with one of his many Berlin friends, he had still been in and out of the Unter den Linden mansion to see her parents and his father and Claus – and her – on practically a daily basis.

It hadn't been something she had expected would change. Max, though, had felt it inappropriate for them both to be sleeping beneath the same roof. As he wasn't remotely a prude, she had realized that it was the reminder of their family relationship that troubled him. He was the oldest Remer cousin, she the youngest, and all through her childhood he had behaved towards her as if he were not her cousin, but an indulgent uncle, rather as Paul, because of his age difference, had behaved to all of them. It was a relationship she knew Max now didn't want reminding of too strongly. And that it troubled him, troubled her.

It was early evening, but the July sun was still strong and the walk towards the lake, beneath the dappled shade of the trees, was pleasant. She discovered something else that was pleasant when she reached the lakeside. Because there were no cafés, as there were at Wannsee, there were also no jackbooted, black-uniformed SS men in view – and no Gestapo, either.

She sat down on a shallow bank where the trees gave way to sand, and hugged her knees to her chest. As if the complications with her relationship with Max weren't enough, she also had other difficulties to contend with.

Claus moved in very prestigious Nazi circles, Nazi circles that were aware of her existence in a way they were no longer aware of Lotti's existence.

'I've been invited to a Four-Year Plan celebration dinner on Friday,' Claus had said to her a few days ago. 'Göring is hosting it and he's expressed the desire to meet you. You don't have to stay long. I'll tell him you have a theatre performance that evening.'

She had known by the expression on his face that he found

the idea distasteful. Göring had a weakness for blue-eyed blondes, especially blue-eyed blonde actresses.

'I shall have to be at the theatre from very early on in the evening,' she had said, wondering for how much longer she and Claus could maintain even the outward semblance of a close brother and sister relationship when so much now divided them. 'Please give Reichsminister Göring my apologies.'

'I can't do that, Ilse,' he had said flatly. 'And you know it. It's becoming a little obvious that you rarely mix socially with the wives or girlfriends of the hierarchy. I don't want gossip to start. No other major industrialist has the potentially damaging family ties I have. I need your support, if only occasionally. If you were suspected of being an enemy of the state, the consequences would be disastrous.'

She'd known it wasn't an understatement and so, for his sake and for her father's sake, she had agreed to go.

She rose to her feet, brushed sand from her skirt and headed back to the car, unhappily aware that not everyone shared her political views. For a terrifyingly large number of people, Hitler's iron-fisted dictatorship was not a nightmare, but a vast relief. That the emasculating Versailles Treaty was now as dead as a doornail was something every German rejoiced over and was something even she felt satisfaction at. Sometimes she wondered if she too would have fallen under the mesmerizing glamour and theatricality of Nazi torch-lit processions and swastika waving, if it hadn't been for having a Jewish cousin-in-law.

Disturbingly, most people now no longer even paused to consider whether Jew-hating was rational. The barrage of Jew-hating propaganda had been so consistent and so relentless for so many years that now even the most patently absurd allegations about Jews were taken unquestioningly for fact. And when the harsh treatment being meted out to them did arouse concern, it was concern eased by the belief that the situation was too crazy to last for much longer.

She slid behind the Cabriolet's wheel and put the car into gear, wondering about Max. He was the man she loved and yet she knew far less about his political feelings than she did about Hugo's or Nicholas's. Even within the family, whenever the subject of National Socialism was raised, Max listened hard and said very little. Not only that, he was the only member of the family still truly close to Claus. When Nicholas had once asked her how much time Max spent with Claus she had said she didn't know, but thought it was very little. It hadn't been true. Whenever Max was in Berlin he spent time with Claus and, on many occasions, with Claus's high-ranking Nazi friends also.

Her head hurt with the puzzlement of it all and instead of turning the car around and heading straight back to Berlin she continued on the road towards Wannsee, intending to find somewhere on the lakeside where she could have dinner.

It was dusk now, but still pleasantly warm. The breeze ruffled her hair as she drove and she wished with all her heart that Max was beside her and that they were enjoying the lovely evening together. It would have been the perfect opportunity to speak to him about all the things causing her disquiet.

Just thinking about him made her heart beat faster. There were another four days before he was due to return to Berlin from Munich and the time stretched out endlessly.

As she turned off the road into the car park of a quiet-looking restaurant on Wannsee's outskirts she reflected wryly that an awful lot of her life had been spent waiting for Max to return to Berlin. As a child she had kept a calendar on her bedroom wall, ticking off the days to the next school holiday. Now, a decade later, she was still doing very much the same thing.

Smiling to herself, she stepped out of the car. The restaurant had a terrace overlooking the water; it was crowded with tables, all of them covered in bright-red gingham tablecloths. A string quartet was playing Strauss waltzes. Although there were several couples already dining, plenty of tables were still free and as she paused, wondering which one to head towards, she saw them.

Her heart rocketed against her breastbone.

They were dining alone, a bottle of wine on the table. Max was talking, probably telling some funny anecdote, for Lotti was giggling.

She tried to breathe, but seemed to have forgotten how.

He had told her he was in Munich. He had told he was going to be in Munich for another four days.

'Can I help you, madam?' a waiter asked. 'Are you waiting for someone, or are you dining alone?'

She didn't answer him. She couldn't. There was no air in her lungs. He was with Lotti when he should have been with her. He was talking to Lotti – sharing things with her – because he had always done so. Because doing so was second nature to him.

And he never did so with her. Not truly.

Blindly, she turned away, terrified of seeing him reach out and take hold of Lotti's hand; terrified of seeing something so painful she would never be able to live with it.

By the time she reached the car park again, she was running, her breath coming in harsh, shallow gasps.

What she had just seen had confirmed every fear she'd ever had.

She jammed the key in the lock of the car, her hands slipping and sliding on the door as she opened it. What was she going to do? Who was she going to turn to?

The answer came almost the minute her hands touched the steering wheel. As far as tonight was concerned, she was going to go home and shower and change.

And then, with a breaking heart, she was going to go to a birthday party.

NINETEEN

London and Berlin, May 1937

'You can't go back. Not by yourself. And as I can't get leave from the Foreign Office, it means you can't go to Berlin again until I do get leave.'

Hugo faced Hester across the width of their crisply made bed. Their flat was on the fifth floor of an elegant building a hand's throw away from Harrods and, as the window was open, subdued traffic noise could be heard. Both of them were uncaring of it.

On the floor beside Hester was a packed suitcase, and her handbag and a hip-length raspberry-red swagger jacket lay on the bed.

'I can't not go, just because you can't come with me.' Her low-pitched voice was fraught with tension. 'I'm needed, Hugo. Our friends can't both forge documents and deliver them. There has to be someone to break the chain in case of discovery. And there has to be someone to coach people given American or British documents on how they should behave at passport and visa controls so as not to arouse suspicion.'

Hugo ran a hand through his fine, straight hair, not knowing which of his emotions was uppermost: despair, fear

312

or fury at himself for being responsible for the present situation.

Struggling to keep his voice steady, he said, 'There are other people who can do deliveries, Hester. Lots of people. I transferred from Berlin to London to take you *out* of danger, not to expose you to *more* danger. And for you, as a German Jew, continually going in and out of the country is far more dangerous than when you were simply resident in it. It draws attention to you. Wait until we can both travel together.'

She shook her head. She hated quarrelling – and they hardly ever did so. Their disagreements were only ever over his concern for her safety.

'I can't, Hugo. You know I can't.' Her dark eyes were anguished. 'Lotti's phone calls make it quite clear that things are getting worse by the minute for my people. Anyone mentally or physically handicapped risks being sent away to a special centre for treatment, whether their families wish them to have treatment or not. Lotti says my mother's dentist's family, the Schimmels, are desperate because their youngest son is Mongoloid. If Miriam Schimmel is separated from him it will kill her.'

Hugo groaned. 'If the child is handicapped, there is nothing you can do, Hester. Even if the family have papers, there's little chance of any country accepting them. It's hard enough trying to get Britain and America to take the fit and healthy who have affidavits of support. The quotas are getting smaller and smaller. And a visa application for a child with such a disability is bound to come under even closer scrutiny than usual. Give up all thoughts of helping them. It can't be done.'

Her eyes held his. 'You don't mean that,' she said quietly. 'You're only saying that because you're too fearful of my safety to want *me* to be the person helping them.'

'I love you,' he said simply. 'I love you more than life itself, Hester. And that you have had to take risks in the past – that we have both had to take risks in the past – has been unavoidable. I could never have lived with myself if we hadn't helped to forge passports and visas. But that was when we were living in Germany. We're not living there now. We've done our bit – more than our bit. Anything we do now has to be done from this end of things – from London. You can't travel to Germany alone. It's too dangerous.'

Her eyes still held his. 'And what about your mother?' she asked steadily. 'Is it too dangerous for her as well?'

He flinched. His mother's journeys in and out of Germany had become a source of great concern to him, for she had made, and was still making, many more trips than he had ever originally envisaged. She had also – and this was something he doubted Max would ever forgive him for – become intimate friends with the small circle of people carrying out the passport and visa forgeries. It meant that if the forgery ring was busted, there was the risk his mother's name would be mentioned in connection with the smuggling of Jewish assets out of the country. And if that happened, even though she was a foreign national, the charge against her would be of being an enemy of the state.

'You know exactly how I feel about the number of trips my mother is now making, but at least she isn't Jewish, Hester. See sense. Wait until we can travel together.'

She shook her head. 'No, darling,' she said resolutely. 'I have to go. I have to sort things out for the Schimmels. Paul has already agreed to act as sponsor for them.'

She put her coat over her arm and picked up her handbag.

Swiftly, he rounded the bed towards her. 'One last time, darling,' he said urgently. 'Don't go.'

Silently, she stepped into his arms, raising her face for his kiss and then, when he finally drew apart from her, she simply picked up her suitcase and walked from the room.

*

314

'Good God! Of course you shouldn't have come!' Max said explosively when she walked into her parents' home to find him in the kitchen, enjoying a bowl of chicken soup with her father. 'Any Jew fortunate enough to get out of Germany should stay out of it. What the devil is Hugo thinking of, allowing you to come back here on your own?'

Hester put her suitcase down, kissed her father and said in a voice of sweet reason, 'I wish you wouldn't use the word "allow", Max. I'm not a child. No one need "allow" me to do anything.'

Max pushed his half-finished bowl of soup to one side and stood up. 'Would you excuse us, Solomon?' he said to her father. 'I want to talk to Hester alone, if that's OK with you?'

Solomon Dresner nodded. Max was, after all, his daughter's brother-in-law – and he was also a deeply trusted friend.

Putting a hand beneath her arm, Max propelled her out of the kitchen and into the minuscule room beyond that served as a parlour, a room far different from the spacious living accommodation the Dresners had previously occupied in their Haberlandstrasse home.

'I know you've been back to Berlin at least three times since Hugo was transferred to London,' he said the instant he closed the door behind them, 'but you haven't lived here. And because you haven't been living here, I don't think you realize just how much more dangerous Berlin is for you now.'

Hester slipped off her jacket and laid it over the arm of a sofa. 'It's because I realize how much more dangerous Berlin has become that I'm here. Good couriers and go-betweens are always needed, Max, and I'm good. Not only that, I'm here this time on a personal mission. Has my father told you about the nightmare situation his dentist, Mo Schimmel, is in?'

Max shook his head. Solomon Dresner said very little now about the plight of family and friends, and Max knew his silence was not due to lack of trust, but because Solomon found the present situation too unbearable to put into words.

Hester sat down on the sofa. 'The Schimmels have a Mongoloid son and have received notification he is to be sent to an unspecified treatment centre. It's a decision that can't be fought against – you know that as well as I do. The only way they are going to be able to keep their family together is to leave the country.'

There was quiet determination in her voice. Looking at her, even though her colouring was so diametrically opposed to Ilse's, he was reminded of Ilse. She possessed the same innate gentleness, the same quiet way of speaking – and beneath her sweet-tempered exterior there was the same strong-as-steel strength.

He slammed down hard on the thought. He mustn't start thinking of Ilse. Ilse was now engaged to Nicholas Schulenburg and the only way he could survive the pain of her abandonment was to force himself not to think of her. He said, concentrating on the matter in hand with great mental effort, 'Do they have relatives in America?'

Hester shook her head. Her dark shoulder-length hair was held away from her face with tortoiseshell combs and it swung as she moved, catching the light. 'No. Nothing so easy.'

There was a commotion in the street and he walked across to the window. She noticed he wasn't dressed in either a suit, or smart flannels and a jacket. Instead, he was wearing a pair of shabby trousers and his blue open-necked shirt was stretched tight across his muscled chest, making him look more like a labourer than a banker. Not for the first time, she wondered about the nature of his work for Barings – and if he actually worked for Barings at all.

'What's happening in the street?' she asked, almost certain she knew the answer.

'An arrest.'

The muscles in his arm were bulging and his fists were clenched.

She knew why. It was out of the sheer frustration of being able to do nothing, for interference on his part would mean increased brutality being meted out to the victim and would result in him being arrested also.

'Who is it?' She didn't go to the window to look. Looking was unbearable.

'It's an elderly man from the grocery shop, five doors down on the other side of the street.'

'The shop with the broken and boarded-up windows?'

He nodded.

There came the sound of a truck's engine revving and then the sound of it hurtling away over the cobbles.

The commotion was over – until the next time.

He turned away from the window, his face in slight shadow. It wasn't the face of a man to be trifled with. Always handsome, his handsomeness now had a hard, inscrutable quality that even she, who had known him since she was a schoolgirl, found intimidating. There was nothing of Hugo in him. In looks, though not in weakness of character, Hugo took after Berthold. Max didn't take after Berthold at all. And nor, since Ilse had left him for Nicholas Schulenburg, was Max any more the devil-may-care, affable personality he once had been. There was no laughter in his eyes any more. It was as if he had somehow turned in on himself. Always someone who kept his own counsel, now, as far as his private life was concerned, he was positively Sphinx-like.

'Wherever the Schimmels go, they'll need papers.'

'Papers aren't a problem.'

She considered the oddness of the fact that despite Max's continuing close relationship with Claus, neither she nor Hugo had any qualms about trusting Max with information. 'If it ever comes to it, Hester, you can trust Max with your life,' Hugo had once said to her, and she believed him.

'Has Hugo made any suggestions where the Schimmel family are concerned?'

She shook her head. 'No, but that's because he didn't want me getting involved with making arrangements for them. As the arrangements are going to have to be made speedily – and as the visa process always takes so long with America and Britain, I thought perhaps Switzerland?'

He gave a mirthless laugh. 'You can forget Switzerland, Hester. In order to prevent their labour market being flooded, the Swiss are refusing to grant any more permanent resident permits to German Jews.'

She didn't ask how he knew. If he told her it was so, then it was.

'Where are Jews to go, then?' she demanded tautly. 'Where are we to go when country after country is closing its borders to us? Even those countries accepting us as immigrants are lowering their quotas. Hitler is driving us out of Germany, but how can we go if no other country will take us in?' Tears of pain, frustration and anger filled her eyes. 'What are people like the Schimmels to do, Max? Are they to remain passively in a country where the Gestapo have unlimited powers of arrest? Where anyone can be taken into protective custody for any reason and be held for any length of time without a trial simply because it is thought that they *may* commit a crime? They've already been robbed of their livelihood. Mo Schimmel can't practise as a dentist any longer, just as my father can't practise as a doctor. Every Jew I know is fast being reduced to poverty. What a few years ago was discrimination is now full-scale persecution. How much longer will it be before it becomes state-condoned terrorism?'

He didn't tell her he thought the answer could be measured in months, not years. Instead, he said, 'Tell the Schimmels to try Trinidad.' He glanced at his watch, knowing he must be on his way. 'I've been told it's still relatively easy to get visas for the British West Indies. And tell them to move their son out of the house to somewhere safer.'

'You mean a Gentile home?'

He nodded. 'Lotti would be a good bet. And she'll be lively company for him,' he added, a glimmer of the old Max resurfacing. 'Meantime, be careful, Hester. When people are arrested now they don't reappear after a few weeks, as was once the case. They stay imprisoned. If you should need me in a hurry, Lotti usually knows where I am. And if Lotti isn't around, I can be contacted via Zelda. *Auf Wiedersehen* – and remember: be very careful.'

He left the room. She heard him say goodbye to her father and then the sound of his feet as he descended the stairs.

As the door leading onto the street closed behind him, she crossed to the window, watching him as he walked away. The part of Berlin her parents now lived in was a predominantly Jewish area and, since it was now next to impossible for Jews to find employment, it was also fast becoming run-down. In his faded shirt and shabby trousers and looking every inch a labourer, Max merged into the general street scene without drawing undue attention to himself. She wondered where he was going, whom he was going to see. She also wondered if Hugo knew the reason for Max being in Berlin so often – knew, and hadn't told her, because knowledge could now be such a dangerous thing.

She hugged her arms to her chest. Apart from Max and Vicky, no one else in the family knew of her and Hugo's involvement with the forgery ring and only the Yorkshire side of the family knew of the thousands of pounds' worth of jewellery Vicky so regularly smuggled out of the country for Jews who had emigrated, or who were about to emigrate. It didn't mean to say, though, that there weren't other secrets within the Remer family circle. Max telling her he could be contacted via Zelda, as well as by Lotti, had come as a complete revelation.

As he rounded the corner of the street and disappeared from view, she wondered if Max had always been close to Zelda Remer. Hugo, she knew, never had been. 'Uncle Josef is a grasping, manipulative, overbearing, dyed-in-the-wool Nazi,' he had once said to her, long before Hitler had ever come to power. 'At the end of the Great War he ruined my parents' marriage by bullying my father into remaining in Berlin instead of joining my mother in Yorkshire and Zelda backs him up in whatever he says or does. If I think of Berlin as my second home – and I do – it's because of the long years I've spent visiting my father here and because Claus, Lotti and Ilse are as close to me as Max and Nancy are.'

'And because you love the city,' she had added, knowing him even better than he knew himself.

'And because of that,' he had agreed, drawing her close. 'Especially the lakes in the Tiergarten and the wonderful stretches of open water at Wannsee.'

Broodingly, she remained at the window, looking down the street to where blood lay in the road outside the boarded-up grocery shop. Though Hugo was still as close to Ilse and Lotti as he was to Nancy, he was no longer close to Claus and hadn't been ever since the day Claus had begun wearing a small circular swastika badge in his lapel.

The very thought of Claus Remer raised gooseflesh on her arms. If he were to hear even a whisper of her and Hugo's activities, or of Vicky's involvement, and speak of them to one of his fellow Nazis, they, and everyone in the forgery ring linked to them, would be doomed. When Jews could be beaten to death for merely being in the wrong place at the wrong time, there could be only one fate for anyone accused of being an enemy of the state. They would disappear into the maws of a concentration camp and never be seen again. That a man on

320

speaking terms with Hermann Göring was a member of the family she had married into seemed unbelievable at times, but it was a cold, stark fact. And Max had just told her that if she were ever in danger and needed to contact him urgently, one of the two people to contact was Claus's mother.

It was a suggestion that made her head spin. Hoping fervently that she would never have to put Zelda Remer to the test, she turned her thoughts to her own mother. Wherever she was at the moment, she would be home soon and Hester didn't want to make contact with the Schimmels, or with anyone else, until she had seen her. She turned away from the window. Until her mother's arrival, she would keep her father company in the kitchen, and while she was in there she would make an apple cake.

'Hester! How wonderful to see you!' Ilse rose from the small table she had been seated at and hugged Hester close. 'But why isn't Hugo with you? Why are you back here alone?'

'I needed to see my mother and Hugo doesn't get leave for ages yet.' The café they had arranged to meet in was small and, at that time of the afternoon, uncrowded. 'And Vicky is over here as well, at the moment, isn't she?'

'Yes.' Ilse sat down again. 'She's staying with my parents in Charlottenburg. Berthold and Claus are both so pro-Hitler it makes staying at Unter den Linden difficult for her – and it's a house she's never liked.'

Hester sat down opposite her. 'Does it make it difficult for you as well?' she asked, taking advantage of the opportunity to ask a question she had often wanted to ask.

'No. Berthold is too mild-mannered to ever be objectionable about his loyalties and Claus . . .' She paused, looking deeply unhappy. 'Since he and Nancy said goodbye, he spends a great deal of his time at the steelworks.'

Hester was tempted to say, 'Except when he's in Berlin,

having meetings with Hermann Göring,' but didn't do so. It would only make Ilse even unhappier where her brother was concerned.

Instead she said, 'You're looking wonderful, Ilse. More like a film star than a theatre actress.'

Ilse laughingly pooh-poohed the idea, but it was true. With her barley-gold hair in a braided coronet and wearing an exquisitely cut white silk suit with a brown shirt tied at the neck in a cravat, she looked not only beautiful, but also stunningly elegant.

Hester slipped off her jacket and slid it over the back of her chair. 'Which of us is going to go first with our news? You or me?'

'You. I want an update on Nancy. I've tried several times to meet up with Vicky and get news from her, but have failed each time. When she's in Berlin, she's as busy as a bee. Let's order and then we'll talk.'

When they both had a glass of white wine in hand, Hester said, 'Nancy's stationed in a small hospital at Huete, almost on the Barcelona front. As there is just as much work to do outside the hospital as in, she works mostly on one of the hospital trains. It must be pretty gruelling. She writes of operations being carried out while bombs are falling.'

Ilse flinched, as aware as Hester that at General Franco's request much of the bombing was being carried out by German pilots in German planes. It had been Heinkels that had reduced Guernica to rubble and no doubt it was Heinkels bombing the area around Huete.

'Thank God,' Hester said quietly, 'that the House of Remer isn't involved in aircraft production. If it were and if anything should happen to Nancy, Claus would never forgive himself.'

She took another drink of her wine and, to her relief, Ilse changed the subject.

'How is Emily Elise?' she asked wistfully. 'I wish Vicky was

322

able to bring her with her to Berlin – or that I could get to Yorkshire as often as Lotti does. I can't, though. Ever since *Intrigue and Love* I've been in one play after another.'

There was no boastfulness in her voice. Hester knew quite well that Ilse didn't know how to boast. It was just a simple statement of fact.

'She's going to be a bridesmaid when you marry Nicholas, isn't she?' she said, sprinkling pepper on the omelette she had ordered.

Ilse, whose lunch consisted of a green salad and nothing else, laid down her fork. 'She is if the international situation is safe enough for her to do so. Nicholas thinks it may well not be.' An unhappy frown appeared on her forehead. 'He thinks war with Britain is only a matter of time. Hugo is in the Foreign Office. What does he think?'

'He also thinks war is only a matter of time.'

They stared at each other, each thinking the same thing: if there were war between Britain and Germany, when would they see each other again? When would Hester see her parents again? When would Ilse again be at Shuttleworth Hall?

'It couldn't happen twice, could it?' Hester said, thinking of how Hugo's family had been riven apart in 1914, thinking how much more dreadful it would be this time, when Hugo and Max would both be conscripted into the services – assuming they didn't volunteer first – and when the same thing, in Germany, would happen to Claus and Nicholas.

'I hope not,' Ilse's voice was devout, her face pale, 'but Nicholas thinks the bombing of Guernica was a test run to see how effective the Luftwaffe now is.'

Their eyes held. Neither of them spoke.

Four black-uniformed SS men came and sat down at a near by table.

Ilse said quietly, 'I'm so pleased to see you, Hester, yet this isn't a very jolly lunch, is it?'

Hester shook her head and opened her bag for her purse so that she could put sufficient money for the bill on the table and they could leave as speedily as possible. 'No,' she said. 'But nothing is jolly any more in Berlin, is it? Absolutely nothing at all.'

An hour later, as she neared the Schimmels' apartment building she found herself with an unexpected companion. 'Max told me where to find you,' Vicky said, falling into step beside her. 'I have some thoughts on Herr and Frau Schimmels' problem and thought I'd come with you.'

Hester stared at her mother-in-law in a mixture of relief and despair. Relief, because Vicky was always a comforting presence. Despair, because at every turn Vicky was becoming more and more involved in situations that could result in her arrest. Her thick fair hair was scooped back and gathered in a coil at the nape of her neck. She was wearing a pair of soft leather brogues and one of the tweed suits she favoured for her expeditions to and from Germany, though on this occasion there was no fabulous piece of Jewish jewellery masquerading as junk jewellery in her lapel. Her colouring made her look every inch a German. Only her clothing singled her out as being English.

As they came to a halt outside the door of the Schimmel's apartment building, Hester gave a cautious look up and down the street. There were no uniforms to be seen and no curious eyes watching.

Mo Schimmel opened the door to them and his eyes, when he saw Vicky, were immediately panicked.

'This is my mother-in-law,' she said swiftly. 'She can be trusted.'

Looking only slightly reassured, Mo Schimmel shook hands with Vicky and led the way upstairs. The smell of baking bread wafted to greet them and then a boy with slanting eyes and small, deep-set ears appeared at the top of the stairs, clapping his hands and beaming. He said something Hester couldn't understand, but which was quite clearly an expression of how pleased he was to meet them.

'My son, Heini,' Mo Schimmel said as they all congregated together on the landing.

Hester put out her hand to Heini, but instead of shaking it, Heini, who she judged to be about twelve or thirteen, enveloped her in a bear hug. She wasn't sure, but she thought he was saying, 'Pretty lady, pretty lady,' and then it was Vicky's turn to be nearly squeezed to death.

'Let's go in the sitting room,' Mo Schimmel said, and Heini immediately relinquished hold of Vicky in order to eagerly lead the way.

Hester was so entranced by Heini's disarming display of affection and his obvious happy nature that she didn't notice Miriam Schimmel enter the room behind them until her husband said, 'My wife, Miriam. Miriam, Frau Remer and . . . and Frau Remer's mother-in-law.'

'Please call me Vicky,' Vicky said, shaking Miriam Schimmel's hand and immediately realizing that here was a woman under immense stress. Though she smiled politely, everything about her was tight and drawn and, when her smile died, a corner of her mouth began twitching convulsively.

'We've come to talk about arrangements,' Hester said, not beating about the bush. 'Documentation won't be a problem. It's the country of destination that will be difficult.'

'But I thought America . . . ?' Mo Schimmel said, his anxiety palpable.

'Game,' Heini said, this time quite distinctly. He hugged Hester's arm, trying to pull her from the room, his small eyes alight with good humour and mischief. 'Game. Game.'

'American quotas are very tight and near impossible if you have no relatives there, Mr Schimmel,' Hester said, patting

Heini's hand and doing her best to stay put. 'Even with an affidavit of support – and Vicky's nephew, Paul, has taken out an affidavit of support for you – the waiting time would be too long when you have already been notified that Heini is scheduled to be sent to a special treatment centre.'

'What is a special treatment centre?' Vicky asked, looking from Mo to Hester.

Mo opened his mouth to answer, became aware that Heini was no longer intent on pulling Hester from the room to play a game but was instead now listening curiously, and said to his wife, 'Take Heini to his room for some quiet time, Miriam. There are some sweeties in his dressing-table drawer.'

Still beaming from ear to ear and waving goodbye to them, Heini compliantly allowed his mother to shepherd him from the room.

Returning his attention to Vicky, Mo shrugged. 'We don't know. And we don't know where it will be. It may not be in Berlin. It may be hundreds of miles away.'

'But even if he has to go before you are given authorization to emigrate, he'll be returned from the centre eventually and you can then leave the country as a family,' Vicky said, trying to look on the positive side of things.

Miriam Schimmel re-entered the room and closed the door behind her. 'Do you really think he will ever return?' There was barely reined-in hysteria in her voice. 'Do you really think if they take him away, we will ever see him again?'

Her husband tried to calm her by putting a hand on her arm, but she moved violently away from him. 'Do you think this government are sending my Heini away because they *care* about him? Do you think men who have passed laws saying all mentally handicapped people have to be sterilized for the public good, have my son's welfare at heart?'

She began wringing her hands together, tears streaking her face. 'If he goes to a centre he will never come back! *That* is what will happen to him and to all the others who are deemed to be of no use.' Her voice rose to a wail. 'They will disappear! *That* is what will happen!'

Her words hung in the air, the silence terrible.

At last Hester cleared her throat and said unsteadily, 'No one is going to take Heini away, Mrs Schimmel. One of the things I came here to suggest to you was that until you are able to leave the country, Heini move in with my husband's cousin. That way, no one will be able to find him.'

'Which cousin?' Vicky stared at her, bewildered. 'Ilse is still living at Unter den Linden and so is Claus, which makes it impossible. And Lotti is a cabaret artiste. How can Lotti look after him?'

'Claus? *Claus Remer?*' Mo Schimmel was rigid with horror.

So was his wife, but for a very different reason. 'A cabaret artiste?' she said to Hester, her distress increasing. 'You want my twelve-year-old Heini to live with a *cabaret* artiste?'

Hester ignored both Schimmels and said to Vicky, 'It was Max who suggested Lotti. There are other girls at the flat. One or other of them will always be in.'

Miriam Schimmel began to cry and Mo Schimmel was repeating time after time: 'Claus Remer? *The* Claus Remer? The Claus Remer who is friends with Reichsminister Göring?'

'It can't be done.' Vicky's voice, as she spoke to Hester, was adamant. 'It would be most unsuitable and the danger to Lotti would be immense.'

'But it *has* to be done.' The panic bubbling up in Hester's throat was clearly audible. 'If Heini stays here, he could be taken away at any moment – and what Mrs Schimmel says is true. They won't see him again. Trust me, Vicky.'

'Oh, I do.' Vicky tucked a stray strand of fair hair back into her bun. 'And I have a solution. *I* will take care of Heini. I will ask our friends to forge the necessary paperwork and I will take him with me back to England. I'm too well known at passport controls on my regular route and so I'll go a different way. Until Miriam and Mo are settled in some country that will take them, Heini will remain with me at Shuttleworth Hall.'

She turned to Miriam Solomon.

'Will you trust me to look after Heini for you, Miriam? I have a five-year-old daughter who will adore him. There is a little dog. A pony. Shuttleworth Hall is a children's paradise. And is utterly safe.'

Miriam Schimmel began crying again, but this time her tears weren't tears of desperation and fear, they were tears of relief.

'Oh, yes!' She grasped hold of Vicky's hands. 'Oh, *yes*! I can tell by your face that you are a kind person and that you will look after Heini and that Heini will be happy with you. When will you take him? Please take him soon. Please take him before the Gestapo take him away from me and I never see him again.'

'I will take him as soon as Hester's friends forge the necessary papers,' Vicky said. 'And that will be soon, Hester, won't it?'

'Oh, yes.' Hester tried to behave as if forging passports and visas was of no account whatsoever. 'And can I ask who is going to break this news to Max and Hugo? Is it going to be you, or me?'

'You dear, I think,' Vicky said serenely. 'Max and Hugo seem to do nothing but get cross with me these days. And now to other things. Heini said he wanted a game. We have time, I think, don't we?'

TWENTY

London, Yorkshire and Berlin, September 1938
'We have a Prime Minister who is a shilly-shallier, Remer,'
Max's Controller said, an expression of distaste on his
patrician features. 'He thinks the best of people and it robs
him of backbone. What I want is intelligence that will put the
fear of God in him and convince him that war with Hitler is
inevitable.'

Max glanced through the window to where the Cenotaph
could be seen, bathed in mellow sunlight. The transition from
the fevered war-mongering atmosphere of Berlin, swastika-
emblazoned flags fluttering from every building, to the
prosaic, unflurried atmosphere in London, always
disorientated him. If Hitler's behaviour of the last few months
hadn't put the fear of God into Chamberlain, then he didn't
see how he could do so.

What Chamberlain needed was to be among the masses
when Hitler gave one of his fevered exhibitions of
demagoguery. He needed to be deafened by the cheering of
thousands when the Führer harangued on the need for greater
living space, living space that could only come from conquered
territory. He needed to spend time among Germany's Jews.

He needed to see for himself what it was like to be robbed of citizenship in a country you had fought for; what it was like to be forcibly 'retired', to be barred from serving in government posts or from practising law or practising as a doctor or participating in any kind of cultural enterprise; what it was like to live in terror of being arrested and for no one – friends and family – to know of your whereabouts.

The chance of that happening was, of course, nil. Chamberlain would continue his policy of appeasement, believing that every demand Hitler made was his last, even though experience already showed otherwise.

He said, 'Everything I hear, from whatever source, is the same. Hitler is determined on welding all ethnic Germans into one huge nation – and he's going to let nothing stand in his way. He wants Czechoslovakia's German-speaking Sudetenland incorporated into the Reich and so, unless Britain and France are prepared to go to war over it, that is what will happen.'

'And what is the feeling of the man in the street? Is there real fear that war is imminent?'

Max thought of the round-the-clock production taking place in the House of Remer steelworks, the giant Krupp steelworks and Fritz Thyssen's vast United Steelworks, production that was nearly all militarily based. He thought of the euphoria with which the *Anchluss* with Austria had been greeted, euphoria in which the Austrians had shared. He thought of how even Zelda – who had as much reason to abhor Hitler as anyone – still grudgingly admitted he was making Germany into the strongest country in Europe.

'There is an expectation of war, but there's no fear of it. At the moment Germany is on such a high it seems inconceivable to Germans that any war they engage in could be detrimental to them. And if war with Britain and France is the price they have to pay for establishing a German nation that will stretch as far as the Urals, then it is one I think they are quite prepared for.'

His Controller's silvered eyebrows rose. 'You think Hitler might not be satisfied with the Sudetenland? You think he has his sights set on the whole of Czechoslovakia?'

'I think he has his sights set on the whole of central Europe. The word constantly on his lips is *Lebensraum*, more living space. He may be making out that his chief concern is for the welfare of Czechoslovakia's Sudeten Germans and that, in order to put an end to what he calls their "plight" as a minority group, he wants the Sudetenland handed over to Germany, but it's only a pretext. His real intent is to destroy the Czechoslovak state and incorporate all its territory into the Third Reich.'

His Controller said nothing. Still saying nothing he rose to his feet and crossed to the window.

Max waited, knowing what the move from desk to window signified. When the conversation resumed, the subject matter would be vastly different.

It was.

'Tell me,' his Controller said, his back towards him as he looked down over Whitehall, 'what the latest situation is with regard to the Jews. Has much changed since we last talked?'

'More and more are being arrested on little or no pretext and sent to camps which are ostensibly for political prisoners and enemies of the state. A large new camp is being built at Oranienburg, twenty miles or so from Berlin. My informant tells me that about a thousand inmates of a camp at Elmsland, near the Dutch border, have been transferred to take part in the construction.'

His Controller turned to face him. 'So he's begun using forced labour? And your informant on this point is reliable?'

Max nodded. Now a member of the SS, when it came to unwittingly giving information, Fritz Schenck was the most reliable informant he had.

'There is also deep anxiety about the special treatment centres the handicapped are being sent to. Families are given little or no information. Sometimes the only contact by the authorities is when there has been a death.'

He thought of Heini Schimmel, happily now part of the family at Shuttleworth Hall. Heini had been lucky. How many hundreds, perhaps thousands, of children hadn't been so lucky?

'And there are still the difficulties re emigration, I assume?' his Controller said, returning to his desk and seating himself behind it. 'Jews want to get out of Germany, Hitler wants them out of Germany and precious few countries – our own included – want to take them in.'

Max nodded. It was such an obvious statement he couldn't imagine what it was leading up to.

'The difficulty has, I assume, given rise to a large underground network of illegal activity,' his Controller continued impassively, steepling his fingers. 'Forgery rings, where passports and visas are concerned. Smuggling activity, when a family's wealth can't be got out of the country any other way.'

Again, it wasn't a question, merely a statement.

'Yes,' Max agreed, not betraying by a flicker how fast his heart had begun to beat. 'Some forgery and smuggling activity is very likely.'

He smiled disingenuously, furiously wondering for how long MI6 had known of Hugo's, Hester's and his mother's activities, fearful that if MI6 knew about it, the Gestapo might very well know about it too.

'I shouldn't think either activity is likely to have a long life span,' his Controller said, pushing his leather-padded swivel chair away from his desk, his usual signal that an interview was at an end. 'And in Nazi Germany there can be only one outcome for those involved.' Graphically, he ran a finger across his throat. 'If you know of anyone who needs such a warning I'd pass it on to them, Remer, if I were you.'

'Put the wireless on, sweetheart,' Vicky said to Emily Elise as she rubbed flour and butter into fine crumbs at the kitchen table. 'I want to hear the news.'

Emily Elise, who had been reading the latest William book, *William the Pirate*, at the same time as mixing sugar into a bowl of elderberries she and Heini had picked earlier that morning, did as she was bid.

'This is the one o'clock news,' a plummy voice said sonorously. 'In Czechoslovakia, Sudeten Germans are holding mass rallies to call for union with Germany. In his closing speech at the Nuremberg Party Rally, Herr Hitler has demanded the Czech government give justice to the Sudeten Germans and has declared that if the Czech government does not do so, Germany will intervene and will see to it that justice is given. In France, all army leave has been cancelled as tension grows over Czechoslovakia. In London, the Prime Minister, Mr Chamberlain, has announced his intention of meeting with Herr Hitler at Berchtesgaden in order to discuss a possible peaceful solution to the crisis. In Spain, General Franco has launched a heavy drive along the River Ebro in Catalonia. At the close of play yesterday, Australia suffered their first defeat outside Test matches for seventeen years when they were defeated by an invitation eleven at Scarborough, and at Edgbaston . . .'

'You can turn it off now,' Vicky said, not remotely interested in cricket scores.

'We are still going to Berlin next week, aren't we, Mummy?' Emily Elise asked, returning her attention to the bowl of elderberries. 'I am still going to be a bridesmaid to cousin Ilse, aren't I?'

Vicky added a little water to her flour and butter mix. 'Yees,' she said cautiously, forming the mixture into a ball. 'As long as the present situation continues, with Mr Chamberlain still seeking a peaceful solution to things, we will be going to Berlin.'

Seated in a rocking chair near to the Aga, Josephine, who was shelling peas, meaningfully cleared her throat.

It was a caution Vicky ignored.

'Ilse desperately wants you to be her bridesmaid,' she continued, beginning to roll out half the dough, 'and I just as desperately want to be there when she marries Nicholas.'

As subtlety was getting her nowhere, Josephine stopped what she was doing and said with Yorkshire bluntness, 'And if war breaks out while you're there? What then? You'll both be interned, and then where will we all be?'

'Mummy and I will be in Germany,' Emily Elise said with a giggle. 'And you'll be still in Yorkshire, Josephine.'

Josephine, well aware that a six-year-old child, no matter how bright, couldn't possibly realize the terrible seriousness of the present international situation, ignored her and said to Vicky, 'Adam isn't happy about your going, is he? And I know he's especially unhappy at the thought of Emily Elise going to Berlin.'

The merriment in Emily Elise's eyes died and she looked anxiously towards her mother.

Vicky suppressed a sigh of irritation. She loved Josephine dearly, but there were times when she wished Josephine wasn't quite so free at expressing her opinions when it came to family matters.

'I've promised Ilse we shall be at her wedding and it's a promise I intend keeping, Josephine.' She lined a pie dish with the rolled-out pastry, doing so with unnecessary vigour. 'If war is declared we'll know at least twenty-four hours beforehand and we'll have plenty of time to return home before the borders close.'

'Well, forgive me for saying so,' Josephine said tartly, not pulling her punches, 'but I think you're daft.' She resumed shelling the peas with sharp, angry movements. 'And I think Adam's daft for allowing you to go and I think Hugo and Hester are even dafter for going with you.'

Vicky passed the pastry-lined pie dish to Emily Elise, wishing she had a legitimate excuse to send her daughter out of the kitchen. There wasn't one and, as Emily Elise was far too intelligent to be fobbed off with a lame pretext, she simply gritted her teeth and said, 'Hugo works for the Foreign Office, Josephine. He's as clued up as anyone can be about the present situation.'

As Emily Elise began spooning the sugared elderberries into the dish, piling them up into a nice raised heap, Vicky began rolling out the rest of the dough, keeping her face carefully averted from Josephine's as she did so. She didn't want Josephine seeing the anxiety she knew was now showing on her face.

Despite the fact that she had decided to attend Ilse's wedding and to take Emily Elise with her, she hadn't wanted Hester to journey to Berlin with them. She, of all people, knew just how perilous a city Berlin was for a Jewess. Hester had been adamant, though.

'This is a family wedding and I'm now part of the family,' she had said firmly. 'Besides, it will give me an opportunity of seeing my parents again. If there *is* a war, it could be years before I get another opportunity.'

It was a statement that had sent time running down to nothing. It had stood still and then run backwards. She'd been twenty-six again, standing within the circle of Berthold's arms on the station platform with Josephine already aboard the train, Hugo in her arms, and Paul and Max leaning out of the open train window. Max and Hugo had been too young to understand the nature of the parting that was taking place, but Paul had known and he had been crying.

She had been crying too, hating the war that was dividing their little family.

And now there was a terrible possibility that their much bigger family was about to be divided by war yet again. And if it was, it would be far more terrible for them than it had been in 1914, for Max and Hugo would, she knew, immediately volunteer for one of the armed services, as no doubt would Claus and Nicholas.

The thought of her children and Zelda's children being on opposite sides in an armed conflict made her feel so physically ill that as she laid the rolled-out pastry over the top of the pie, her hands trembled.

Emily Elise didn't notice. 'Can I trim the edges, Mummy, and put the slits in the top?' she asked eagerly. 'And then can Heini and I take Tinker for a walk down by the woods? There's lots of blackberry bushes down there and if we take the pail we collected the elderberries in, we'll get enough blackberries to make both a pie and some jam.'

'Yes, but don't let Heini go too near the river. I know he can swim quite well now, but he still needs to have Daddy or Paul near by when he does so.'

As Emily Elise ran happily out of the room, Vicky crossed the red-tiled floor to the long window, its sill made gay with pots of late-flowering geraniums.

'You're taking a huge risk travelling as a family to Germany when war could be announced at any minute,' Josephine said, rising from the rocking chair and taking the bowl of shelled peas across to the sink in order to rinse them.

This time, with no Emily Elise in earshot, Vicky said quietly, 'I know, Josephine, but it matters very much to Ilse that we are all there and I feel the same as Hester – if war *does* break out it could be years before we are all together as a family again.'

She didn't add, 'If ever,' but she thought it as, hands clasped tightly, she watched Emily Elise and Heini running away from the house in the direction of the woods, Tinker at their heels.

'I'm agreeing to you taking Emily Elise only on certain conditions,' Adam said grim-faced as he sat beside her on the sofa in the drawing room that evening. 'The most important one is that you promise not to bring any Jewish life savings or jewellery out of the country with you on your return.'

His still handsome face was haggard with anxiety and she squeezed his hand. 'I promise. I promise I won't take any risks at all while I have Emily Elise with me. I won't get in touch with any of my Jewish contacts. I won't visit any of my Jewish friends, not even Hester's parents. This is going to be a purely family visit.'

'And you're going to stay there only forty-eight hours? It's going to be an in-and-out trip for all of you? Hugo and Hester included?'

She leaned her head against his shoulder and he slid his arm around her, hugging her close.

'We'll be there for only forty-eight hours and will be guests of the Schulenburg family all the time we are there. There's to be a large pre-wedding party at the Schulenburgs' mansion the evening we arrive. I'll have to unearth something full-length and grand to wear to it. Nicholas's family are vintage upper-crust. Lotti says the invitation list is a sea of minor ex-royals. The next day will be the wedding. And the day afterwards we return home.'

He sighed heavily, still not liking the thought of any of his family journeying to Germany at a time of such international tension.

'Would you feel happier if you came with us?' she asked gently. 'You were invited. Ilse wants you to be there.'

He shook his head. 'I can't go, darling. It's just not possible. I have to be in London to see the bankers about raising money for the new Huddersfield mill and the day of the wedding is the only time they can all meet together with me.'

She didn't argue with him. The new Huddersfield mill was important to him and, even if it were not, she knew how hard it would be for Adam to step on German soil when his memories of 1914 to 1918 were still so deep and searing. It was much better that he stayed at home. Trying to imagine him surrounded by a glittering array of bemedalled and bejewelled Hohenzollerns and Wittelsbachs was impossible, even for her.

'And so I'm still not going to meet Adam,' Zelda said as she and Vicky, minus Emily Elise who, as a bridesmaid, was with Ilse and Nicholas at the wedding rehearsal, walked arm in arm into the Schulenburgs' Charlottenburg mansion. There was both petulance and disappointment in her voice.

'You've been able to meet Adam any time you wanted to, for years now.' As always where Zelda was concerned, Vicky was both amused at her and cross with her. 'All you've ever had to do is come and stay at Shuttleworth Hall. Paul would love to be able to show off his rose nursery to you. He's one of the foremost rose-breeders in England now.'

'And he's still unmarried and fast disposing of his fortune,' Zelda retorted, genuine concern in her voice. 'He can't subsidize *every* Jewish family friend of the Dresners that wants to emigrate. It just isn't possible. He's going to be penniless.'

By now a housekeeper was showing them to their rooms and Vicky wondered if Zelda was always so careless about what she said and who she said it in front of.

Reading her thoughts, when the housekeeper left them Zelda said, 'Don't worry, Vicky darling, the Schulenburg household is *all* fiercely anti-Nazi and that includes the family retainers. The only people with whom conversation might need to be guarded, are Claus and Berthold.'

They'd gravitated into the room that had been assigned to Zelda and Josef. From the long corridor outside it came the sound of other arrivals: luggage being carried up the stairs, people who hadn't seen each other for a while squealing greetings.

Vicky sat down on the nearest elegant chair and looked across at Zelda. Whippet-thin and supremely elegant, she was standing at the window, looking down into the courtyard at the taxis and chauffeur-driven cars that were arriving in a long unending stream, laden with guests. Her mid-calf-length black tailored skirt was arrow-straight and her white hip-length jacket was belted at the waist with a crocodile-skin, silver-buckled belt. Her shoes were as suicidally high as always and her small white hat, dipping provocatively low over her forehead, crowned black satiny hair worn in the style that had become her trademark – a sharp bob with a low heavy fringe emphasizing her superb cheekbones.

'What about Josef, Zelda?' she asked, well aware she looked very unsophisticated in comparison. 'Are people going to have to be guarded about what they say in front of him this weekend?'

Zelda took a cigarette case, lighter and jade cigarette-holder from her crocodile-skin bag and tossed the bag onto the nearest available surface.

'Possibly, but not to the same extent,' she said, lighting up a black Sobranie and tossing the cigarette case and lighter in the general direction of her bag. She inhaled deeply and then said, 'Whatever Josef overhears he won't repeat it in Nazi hearing. He's too terrified of reminding the Nazi hierarchy of his existence and consequently of reminding them of my existence. This wedding is my first public outing in months.'

'Does Claus know why Josef handed the House of Remer over to him?' Vicky asked, curious. 'Does he know the veiled threats that were made where you were concerned?'

Zelda's mouth tightened. 'No – and the threats weren't so veiled, Vicky. They were pretty damned explicit. Josef had to either divorce me – and not care what happened to me after he divorced me – or give up the House of Remer. And if it wasn't for the fact that Claus is such a freak of nature and to all outward appearances such a magnificent example of Aryan manhood, the steelworks would have been lost to the family completely.'

She blew a plume of blue smoke into the air, her dark eyes hard and bitter. 'And the reason Claus doesn't know the reason behind the handover is that if he *were* to know, he'd be so incensed I doubt he'd be able to continue honouring contracts for the government; and if he didn't do that, the House of Remer would, most definitely, be lost to him and to the son I hope he will one day have.'

Their eyes held, both of them thinking of the person he had hoped would be the mother of his children. Both of them thinking of Nancy.

'She's the only person in the family, apart from Adam, who won't be at the wedding,' Vicky said, the constant anxiety she felt for her daughter's safety clear in her eyes.

'I shall miss her not being here just as much as you will.' Zelda stubbed out her barely smoked cigarette in a crystal ashtray. 'The upside of her not being here, though, is that it will make things easier for Claus. Though I guess you're glad that particular family love affair broke up, aren't you?'

Vicky felt her heart contract. There were still so many issues between her and Zelda, all of them to do directly or indirectly with the House of Remer, that it sometimes seemed to her they would never be able to enjoy a reunion without tension of one kind or another surfacing.

'Your son is a Nazi,' she said steadily. 'On that count alone I didn't want to see Nancy marry him. As for her becoming the wife of the head of a steelworks that devotes itself to making weapons of war – I feel no differently about that now than I did when I first repudiated the steelworks, decades ago.'

Zelda raised a hand. 'Pax, Vicky. I want a stress-free family wedding just as much as you do and under the circumstances – Berthold and Claus sporting lapel badges given to them personally by the Führer – it's going to be hard enough to achieve without us falling out into the bargain. What do you say we crack open a bottle of champagne? Ilse may be depriving me of Max as a son-in-law, but she is at least marrying someone I like. It's worth celebrating in a world where there's pretty little else to celebrate.'

'*Wunderbar*, Paul!' Wearing a nip-waisted black jacket with a peplum and a vivid emerald-green swirling skirt, Lotti hurtled towards him down a second-floor corridor of the Schulenburg mansion. 'Isn't it marvellous that all of us are together like this?'

Paul, big and raw-boned and looking every inch an American, gave his easy, lopsided grin and opened his arms wide to give her a bear-like hug.

'It certainly is,' he said as she squeezed him so tightly she nearly robbed him of breath. 'It reminds me of school holidays when we were children.'

'Except Nancy isn't with us.' He was so tall to her diminutive five foot two inches that despite her teeteringly high heels she had to take a step backwards in order to look up into his face. 'What is the latest news of her? The last we heard she was working in an army hospital in Barcelona.'

'That was our last piece of news as well.' He tucked her hand through the crook of his arm. 'The heaviest fighting at the moment seems to be along the River Ebro in Catalonia. My geography's a biz hazy, but I don't think it's near to Barcelona. Is your room on this floor or were you just noseying around to see who you could find?'

'Nicholas told me I'd find you on this floor. There's been a little segregation with the guest bedrooms. Most of Ilse's friends are on the first floor as are all female members of the family. Nicholas's friends and all other males are up here. It's a vast house, isn't it? Almost as big as the Charlottenburg Palace.'

'And only a tad bigger than the family mausoleum on Unter den Linden, and probably a tad smaller than Schloss Niedernhall.' They strolled companionably towards the main staircase, people they didn't know continually entering and exiting the rooms on either side of them as they did so. 'What's happening with the Schloss?' he asked. 'Is it still being used as a country retreat by Himmler or Göring or some other high-flying member of the government?'

Lotti wrinkled her nose. 'I believe it gets used mainly for high-ranking Nazi conferences and I haven't a clue who is in permanent residence. They're welcome to it, though. It's a hideous pseudo-medieval monstrosity. The only people who ever rated it were my parents. *Vati* handing it over for government use was surprising, to say the least.'

They began walking down the wide marble staircase and he hid the surprise he felt at her still referring to his stepfather as *Vati*. The diminutive of the word 'father' was not one he easily associated with Josef Remer's off-puttingly austere personality.

'I rather think Claus will offload the Unter den Linden mansion as well, when he gets the chance,' Lotti continued chattily, squeezing to one side to allow a giggling group of children to clatter past them. 'Now Ilse will no longer be living there, he and Berthold will be rattling around in it like two lonely peas in a drum. If he keeps it on it will only be because the house symbolizes a great deal to our parents.'

'Well, it has been the Remer family home for three or four generations now, hasn't it? It's hard to give up on something like that. Your father will want to see Claus handing it on to his son – when he has one.'

'*If* he has one,' Lotti said drily as they finally reached the grand entrance hall and walked out into warm September sunshine. 'Since Nancy ditched him there's always a glamorous blonde on his arm, but it's always a different one. I think it's safe to say marriage and a family no longer feature in his plans. All he thinks about are the House of Remer steelworks and the Berlin clothing factory.'

'Clothing factory?' Paul raised an eyebrow queryingly. 'What clothing factory? I didn't know there was one.'

Some yards away from them a Mercedes Benz drew up on the courtyard cobbles and an elderly gentleman stepped from it, his naval-uniformed chest resplendent with medals won in the Great War.

'It only manufactures military clothing.' Lotti no longer sounded pert and chirpy. 'And from something Claus let slip to Ilse, it would seem it's now in production day and night, just as it apparently was in 1913. And you can make of that what you will.'

The conversation had suddenly turned dark and Paul was just about to ask her if she thought Hitler really would go to war over the Sudetenland when another Mercedes rolled to a halt and Emily Elise tumbled out of it, Hester and Hugo close behind her.

'I've been practising to be a bridesmaid, Cousin Lotti!' she squealed, throwing herself into Lotti's opened arms. 'And my dress is a fairy dress. All pink and white with frills and ruffles *everywhere*. I must tell Mummy how pretty it is.'

As Lotti led the way back into the Schulenburg mansion, Emily Elise skipping along at her side, Paul fell into step beside Hugo and Hester. He was deeply fond of his cousin's wife and, because she and Hugo lived in London, didn't see as much of her as he would have liked. 'It's nice to see you, Hester,' he said, smiling down at her, well aware that being in Berlin again couldn't be easy for her. 'There are about a hundred guests already in residence here, most of them ex-royal Wittelsbachs and Hohenzollerns. Tonight's party is going to be quite an event.'

Hester's answering smile was as sweet and sunny as always, but she didn't respond with gay chatter. Her thoughts were on the surprisingly intimate conversation she had just had with the bride-to-be.

'I'm totally happy,' Ilse had said to her when the two of them had had a few moments alone at the church rehearsal.

'And so you should be,' she had responded, laughing. 'Tomorrow is your wedding day. No one would imagine you to be anything else but totally happy.'

'Oh, they might.' A faint shadow had touched Ilse's lovely face. 'Max will be here – and people have long memories.'

It was then she'd realized that this was a serious conversation; that there were things Ilse wanted to put into words before she married Nicholas.

'It's been over two years since you ceased being romantically involved with Max,' she had said tentatively. 'That's a long time, Ilse. You're not beginning to have doubts about that decision, are you? Because if you are –'

Ilse's response had been to cut her short with a vehement shake of her head. 'No,' she'd said with certainty. 'From the minute I realized it was Nicholas I should be marrying, not Max, I've never had a single moment's doubt. Not because of the incident that triggered that realization, but because of all the things that I suddenly saw clearly in the months afterwards; things had only been vaguely troubling up to then.'

'What things?' she'd said, deeply intrigued.

Ilse had looked to where Emily Elise was being shown where she would be standing once their bridal procession had reached the altar and said with startling candour, 'I was always jealous of Lotti. I was always terrified that Max loved her more than me and even if I was wrong about that – and I don't think I was – I realized that the kind of matey camaraderie they enjoyed would always exclude me. It simply wasn't something that had ever existed in my relationship with him. All through my childhood I had adored him and he had been the attentive elder cousin, taking me out for treats and indulging me, but we had never been co-conspirators in the way he and Lotti had always been. And the very nature of my childhood relationship with him marred our relationship when he fell in love with me.'

'I'm sorry, Ilse,' she had said, totally out of her depth. 'But in what way . . . ? How . . . ?'

Ilse's eyes had met hers with stark frankness. 'We were in love, but we were never lovers, Hester. At the time I believed it was because he knew I was a virgin and his respect for me was such that he wanted me to be a virgin on our wedding day. Within weeks of my being with Nicholas I knew my reading of the situation had been far too naive – and I also realized that if Max and I *had* married, our sex life would have been in deep trouble.'

As she'd blinked in disbelief, unable to conceive of any sexual scenario Max wouldn't be master of, Ilse had said with a wry smile: 'I know I'm right, Hester. From the day our relationship became romantic, Max stopped staying at the Unter den Linden house and I think that was because his being there, in the house where we had always been family together, was too disturbing to him once we were romantically involved.' Her smile relaxed and deepened. 'I've never been so happy as I have been these last two years. Nicholas is right for me in a way that Max never could be. Sometimes, with Max, I had to pretend to be far happier than I actually was. With Nicholas, I never have to pretend about

345

anything. We're perfect for each other and I love him with all my heart.'

'This is quite an event, isn't it?' Vicky said that evening to Paul as, hands aching after being introduced to a veritable army of Schulenburg aunts, uncles and cousins and an even larger army of related-by-marriage Wittelsbachs and Hohenzollerns, they finally sat down to a very formal meal in a grand dining room as vast as a ballroom.

'And what a relief that all the uniforms being worn are unfamiliar 1914 vintage,' Paul said, as the aged admiral he and Lotti had seen arriving earlier took his seat on the opposite side of the long table, not far from them.

It was an expression of feeling Vicky was totally in sympathy with. Despite the glittering array of military decorations pinned to aged male chests, there wasn't a Nazi uniform in sight. As she looked around the enormous, flower-filled dining room it occurred to her that there hadn't been a family celebration so magnificent since Zelda had married Josef – with Nicholas's father as his best man – and the Kaiser had been in attendance.

'I thought my tiara would be over the top,' Lotti said, leaning in front of Paul in order to speak to Vicky, 'but I'm completely underdressed. Do you think all the jewels in the room are real?'

'Mine are,' her emerald-laden mother said tartly from where she was seated directly opposite her, flanked by Josef and Berthold. 'And yours could have been if you'd had the sense to have asked to wear Remer family jewellery and not deck yourself out with chorus-girl paste.'

Lotti was completely unfazed. 'What about you, Aunt Vicky?' she asked impishly. 'This must be one occasion when you don't want people thinking your pearls are paste.'

'Absolutely,' Vicky said, fingering the beautiful pearl

346

necklace that had been Adam's gift to her when they had married.

'Nuff said, Monkeyface,' Max said warningly, in a voice only she could hear. 'We may be among friends and family, but walls can have ears.'

He was seated at the other side of her, his handsome face tense and strained. He was a man used to projecting an easygoing, wise-cracking facade few people ever saw past. This, though, was an occasion that was stretching his talent for deception to the utmost. There had been a moment in time when, if he had set the date, Ilse would have married him without a second's hesitation, and he had allowed that moment to slip through his fingers. Somehow he had lost her – and he hadn't a clue as to how or why.

The odd thing was, though, despite his gut-wrenching sense of loss, his bewilderment and – he was honest enough to admit to himself – his wounded pride, he was also certain that Ilse had made the right decision. He would always have treated her as if she were a piece of fragile porcelain – he had simply never been able to bring himself to treat her any other way. Nicholas would take great protective care of her too, but he would also treat her as a woman.

Looking at them, he knew they were already lovers. Sex, an area of activity that had never previously been a problem to him, had become a problem where Ilse was concerned. He had found he couldn't forget the almost avuncular relationship that had existed between them throughout her childhood. Though he hadn't realized it at the time, their relationship had never been as honest and as intimate as it should have been and it had been Ilse, far less experienced in the ways of the world than he, who had been the one to realize it.

He took a deep drink from his wine glass, fixed his habitual easy-going smile on his face and turned his attention to the long, funny complaint Lotti was making about Ilse's choice of sugar-pink chiffon for the bridesmaids' dresses.

'I shall look like something that's stepped off the top of a Christmas tree,' she said in mock resignation. 'And if Nancy had been here Ilse would never have got her into sugar-pink. She would have had open rebellion on her hands.'

It was so true that Vicky laughed and then, seeing the taut expression on Claus's face, her laughter died. He was seated directly opposite her. Like Berthold, with whom she had so far had little conversation, Claus was flaunting his gold swastika pin, engraved on the back with Hitler's signature; it glinted in the lapel of his evening jacket.

She averted her eyes from it and turned her attention to Berthold, who was seated on the other side of the table next to Zelda. It wasn't the happiest of seating arrangements but he seemed to be making the best of it.

'This reminds me of Zelda and Josef's wedding, Berthold,' she said, her voice full of gentle affection. 'And now here we are, about to attend the marriage of their daughter to the son of their best man. It's very satisfying, isn't it?'

'It is indeed, *Liebchen*,' he said, using his old endearment for her. 'The only thing marring the occasion is that our daughter is not here to be a bridesmaid.'

Under the circumstances, with Claus seated in such close proximity to them, it was not the most tactful of remarks.

'And how is Nancy, Aunt Vicky?' Claus said, destroying her hope that he hadn't overheard. 'I've heard rumours the International Brigade is to be withdrawn from the fighting and repatriated. Are there rumours to that effect in London?'

Vicky shook her head, knowing full well that even if there had been, it was unlikely she would have heard of them in Yorkshire.

'What about you, Hugo?' Claus persisted, his pale blond hair gleaming beneath the lights of the chandeliers. 'Do you

348

know if there's any chance Nancy will soon be home from Spain?'

Hugo, well aware that Hester's eyes would be fixed on Claus's swastika badge and nowhere else, said coldly, 'I've heard nothing to that effect. And even if she were to leave Spain, I doubt she'd return to England – not unless there was a war and she joined the armed forces.'

Vicky could practically feel family gaiety seeping away. 'No more mention of anything to do with the international situation,' she said swiftly. 'We have the rare opportunity to be together at a happy family occasion. Don't let's spoil it.'

Much to her relief, it was advice that was taken. Though the tension and strain never left his face, Max began cracking jokes and behaving as if the pre-wedding dinner was an ordinary event instead of being part of the wedding celebrations of the woman he loved. Claus also made great efforts to behave as if there were no great political and ideological differences between him and nearly everyone else present. By the time the evening came to a close it was nearly possible for Vicky to believe that they were a normal family with no very great tensions dividing them.

Almost, but not quite, for by the end of the evening the personally engraved swastikas in Berthold's and Claus's lapels gleamed and glimmered just as brightly as they had done at the beginning of it.

TWENTY-ONE

Yorkshire, London and Berlin, August 1939

'Elderberries,' Violet Ramsbotham said, triumph in her voice as she deposited a basket full of them on Vicky's kitchen table. 'They're a little early. My trees aren't usually ready to be picked until the beginning of September, but this lot are beautifully ripe and I thought you might like to make some wine with them.'

Vicky stopped what she was doing, which was making a pot of tea, and stared at the elderberries as if she had never seen any before.

'What's the matter?' Violet demanded, her rocking-horse nostrils flaring. 'If the bunches hadn't been ready to pick, they would still have been upright on the tree and they weren't. They were hanging down. I've already made a couple of good jellies with them.'

'I can see they're ripe, Violet. It's not that. I was just overcome by a strong sense of déjà vu. This time last year, when elderberries were in season, we were on a knife-edge in case war broke out over Hitler's demand that the Sudetenland be handed over to Germany. And here we are again, in just the same kind of situation, only instead of

Czechoslovakia being the country about to be overrun, it's Poland.'

'And this time there will be no Mr Chamberlain waving a piece of paper and promising us peace for our time,' Violet said grimly. 'This time, if Hitler does what he's threatening to do, there really will be a war. It's unavoidable.'

Vicky, fully sharing Violet's pessimism, gave a heavy sigh. If the future had looked nightmarish a year ago, it looked twice as nightmarish now. A year ago, it had generally been believed that Hitler would be content with being handed the Sudetenland and that he would make no more territorial demands. Then, six months ago, his jackbooted armies had invaded what was left of Czechoslovakia.

'And the rest of Czechoslovakia isn't German-speaking and never has been,' Hugo had said to her over the telephone, his voice raw. 'This time he's occupying territory not inhabited by people of German race and so you can forget the "he's only trying to weld all ethnic Germans into one huge nation" argument, because it won't wash. And what he's done once, he'll do again. Danzig will be his next demand, on the grounds that before Versailles it was a German city, but even if Danzig were returned to Germany he wouldn't be content with it. It's Poland itself he's after.'

She pushed the memory away, not wanting to dwell on it. 'Let's take our cups of tea and drink them in the sunshine, on the terrace,' she said, adding a plate of biscuits to the tea tray. 'I assume you've already been approached about accepting evacuee children? My letter arrived this morning. I've been told that in the event of war at least six children will be billeted here.'

Violet made a snorting sound as she followed her out of the kitchen. 'Have you, indeed? And have you room for so many now that Heini is permanently here and you've got two Jewish families in the west wing of the house?'

'At a squeeze.'

'Take my advice and don't tell the authorities. They'll billet another half-dozen on you and it's not accommodating them that will be the problem. It's the looking after them that will be the hard work.'

They walked out onto the terrace and Vicky put the tray down on a circular wrought-iron table. 'It's reminiscent of when we turned our houses into convalescent homes, isn't it?' she said as Violet arranged her prodigious weight on a chair that was far too small for her. 'Only this time, instead of being inundated with wounded soldiers, we'll be inundated with children.'

'And not only children,' Violet said darkly as Vicky poured the tea, 'because I suspect some of the little blighters will have mothers in tow – and how East End Londoners will fit into our kind of country lifestyle I can't begin to imagine.'

Vicky couldn't imagine it either, but was certain she would be able to cope. Coping was something she was good at.

'When this war that is hanging over us is finally declared, will Nancy come back to England?' Violet asked, changing the subject abruptly.

'She says not.' Vicky looked down over the vast rolling lawn to the river, wishing Nancy were striding along its banks, the warm August breeze tugging at her turbulently curly hair. 'She says she intends staying in Paris.'

'Not a very sensible intention,' Violet said flatly. 'I didn't understand why she went there when the International Brigades were repatriated. Has she developed some kind of a phobia for England?'

'No.' Vicky was not affronted, accustomed to Violet's blunt manner, a manner that had become even blunter now she was in her seventies. 'She simply likes to be in the thick of things and when she took up journalism again it was as a foreign correspondent based in France.'

'And there's no boyfriend on the scene?'

'No. Not that I know of.'

'A pity. It's been a long time.'

Vicky, knowing very well what Violet was referring to, said simply, 'Yes. It has.'

As Violet helped herself to a biscuit Vicky reflected on how hard it was to believe that in the four years since their affair had come to an end, neither Nancy nor Claus had embarked on another long-term relationship.

'You're never going to be a grandmother at this rate.' Violet brushed biscuit crumbs from her massive chest. 'I have fourteen grandchildren now. I'd have a word with Hugo, if I were you. Impending war or no impending war, it's time he and Hester thought of beginning a family.'

'Do you think Hugo and Hester haven't started a family yet by choice?' she asked Adam that night, as they lay in bed together, reading.

Adam put down Edgar Wallace's *The Thief in the Night*. 'I've no idea, sweetheart. It isn't something I'd be comfortable asking. Would you?'

'Probably not.' She slid a bookmark into Georgette Heyer's *Devil's Cub*. 'It's just that Violet mentioned it this afternoon and it started me wondering. I'd hate to think they wanted children and couldn't have them.'

He slid his arm around her shoulders and she nestled close to him, loving the sense of security he always gave her. 'I think if that was the case, Hester would have told you,' he said gently. 'They may have been married for seven years, but she's still only twenty-four and Hugo is only twenty-seven. They've got plenty of time. And Hester hasn't exactly been leading a stress-free lifestyle, has she? If war is declared, one thing I'll be thankful for is that it will mean a complete end to her illegal activities whenever she's in Berlin – and to your illegal activities too.'

Vicky bit her lip, well aware of the terrible strain she put him under every time she smuggled jewellery out of Germany. 'You're doing it too often, Ma,' Max had said to her at the time of the Munich crisis. 'Such a long run of luck can't hold. For all our sakes, especially Emily Elise's, call a halt to it.'

Since then she'd been to Berlin only twice, each time returning with jewellery belonging to two of Hester's cousins who, with their families, were now living in Shuttleworth Hall's west wing. With Paul's sponsorship they had legally entered the country as agricultural trainees and domestic servants, categories acceptable to the Home Office as long as they were funded and as long as they agreed to ultimate settlement elsewhere.

Hester's parents' age had meant no such entry into the country was open to them, and even if it had been, Vicky knew they wouldn't have taken advantage of it. 'We're Germans,' they said stubbornly every time she visited them. 'Hitler's madness has to end soon. Don't worry, Mrs Priestley. We'll draw no attention to ourselves. We'll be safe.'

'The war may put an end to Hester's activities with the forgery ring,' she said unhappily, 'but it will also put an end to her seeing her parents. That's going to be very hard for her to accept, Adam. It could be years before she gets news of them again.'

'She'll get news of them through Max and Paul,' he said reasonably.

She sat upright so abruptly she sent a pillow tumbling. 'What on *earth* do you mean?'

His eyes widened as he realized she hadn't taken on-board what was, to him, self-evident. 'Paul has an American passport. If there is a war, it will be a European war. If necessary, he'll be able to travel to Berlin, even though he'll have to do so via America and Switzerland. As for Max . . .

his father is German. He was born in Germany. I suspect his employers are going to take full advantage of that situation.'

She knew the word 'employers' referred to the British government, not Barings Bank, and she blanched. Accustomed as she was to living with danger – and knowing that members of her family were living with danger also – it had not occurred to her that Max's activities for MI6 might very well keep him behind enemy lines if war broke out. She clenched her hand, pressing it against her mouth.

'Vicky, darling, I'm sorry. I thought you'd realized . . .' Sick at heart he pulled her into his arms again. 'It may not happen,' he said, struggling to find words to comfort her. 'Just because Paul *could* travel to Germany doesn't mean he will do so. He isn't an unnecessary risk-taker. He survived from 1914 to 1918 without having contact with his mother, apart from letters, and I dare say he'll survive this coming war the same way. As for Max . . . who knows how – or where – intelligence officers will be used in a war? What I said was purely supposition, darling. Don't brood on it. None of it, not even the war, may ever happen.'

Tilting her face to his he kissed her tenderly and then with rising passion – passion she answered in full, losing her fears in her overpowering physical response to him.

Later, despite the deep comfort of their love-making, she lay awake long after he had fallen asleep. Her one consolation, amid all her anxieties, was that she no longer had to fear for Hester's safety. Hester was in London with Hugo, and if Hugo left the Foreign Office for active service she would no doubt come and live at Shuttleworth Hall.

The knowledge was a grain of solace in an otherwise grim scenario. Clinging to it, she eventually slept, but not until the sun had begun to rise, red-rimmed, above the trees beyond the river.

*

355

Hester set a boiled egg and a plate of toast in front of Hugo.

'What's the latest news?' she asked as he pushed the newspaper he had been reading to one side and smartly sliced off the top of his egg with a knife.

'Hitler has closed the border with Poland in Upper Silesia. The King is inspecting a hundred and thirty-three ships of the Auxiliary Fleet at Weymouth and France is calling up its reservists.'

'And there's nothing any more definite?'

He shook his head.

'Not even from the horse's mouth?'

His eyes held hers. It was a treasonable offence to reveal anything of what went on in his department at the Foreign Office and Hester had never before asked him to do so.

He said, 'Ambassadors and Dominion High Commissioners are flying in for talks with the Prime Minister. There's almost certainly going to be a war, Hester. Hitler didn't back down over the Rhineland. Didn't back down over union with Austria. Didn't back down over the Sudetenland. And he isn't going to back down over Danzig. He'll invade Poland and, when he does, Chamberlain will honour the military alliance Britain has with Poland and we'll be at war. And it won't be before time.'

There were thin white lines around his finely sculpted mouth. 'If we'd stood up to him when he first breached the Versailles Treaty – when he sent troops into the Rhineland – he'd have crumbled like dust. Instead of which,' he added, glancing down at his watch and rising to his feet, 'he's been able to consolidate his military power and embark on a reign of terror unequalled since the Middle Ages.'

'But that reign of terror doesn't often get into the newspapers, does it?' Hester said quietly, as he picked up his briefcase and bowler hat. 'The Night of Broken Glass got into the papers, but only because it was coordinated violence against Jews throughout the whole country. Hitler passes law after law stripping Jews of every basic human right and newspaper headlines are about someone in Peckham being killed because a branch of a tree fell on top of a bus, or that Pan American Airways' flying boat arrived at Southampton Water four hours late due to storms over the Atlantic.'

He put his briefcase down and pulled her towards him. 'There's going to be a war,' he said with quiet certainty, 'and when it's over, Hitler and his despicable racial policies will be no more. Cling to that thought, Hester. I do.'

She slid her arms up and around his neck. Hugo was an academic-looking man who looked his best when dressed formally and in his pinstriped three-piece suit, stiffly starched shirt and old school tie he looked incredibly sexy. 'I love you,' she said, hating the unbelievably long hours he was now working, knowing she wouldn't see him again until midnight or even later.

He gave her his gentle smile – his father's smile – and said, 'I love you too, Hester. More than life itself. But I daren't kiss you. If I do, I'll be more than minutes late getting to Whitehall. I'll be hours late.'

'Tough,' she said and, raising herself on her toes, she pressed her softly parted lips against his.

Later, when he had gone haring off to find a taxi and she had cleared the breakfast things, she knew that she too was going to be late for work. Her job in the book department at Harrods was important to her and she whirled around their bedroom, putting on powder and a dash of lipstick, pulling a comb through her shoulder-length hair, checking she had her door keys in her handbag.

She was just about to leave when the telephone rang.

For a second, she debated whether to answer it or not and then, aware it might be Vicky calling her, threw her handbag down onto a chair and lifted the receiver.

'Frau Remer?'

It was a woman's voice – and not one she was familiar with.

'Speaking,' she said a trifle breathlessly, automatically responding to *Frau*, by replying in German.

'I am Frau Debuss. I live in the apartment next to your parents.'

The voice was elderly and unsteady – and frightened.

Hester felt her blood run cold, felt her hand become suddenly slippery with sweat.

'What is it? What's happened?' she demanded, her voice sharp with fear. 'Has there been an accident?'

'No. No accident.'

The line was so crackly with static that the word '*Nein*' was barely intelligible.

'What is it, then, Frau Debuss? *What has happened?*'

'Your mother has been sick for days and your father has been nursing her, but now . . . this morning . . . he has collapsed. I think he has had a heart attack, Frau Remer, but I know no one else to call and the hospitals no longer accept Jews and –'

The line went dead.

Frantically, Hester pressed the rest repeatedly, but all she met with was the regular dialling tone.

She dialled the operator, looking at her watch as she did so. It was nearly nine-thirty. If she left immediately she could be on a cross-Channel ferry in less than two hours.

'Can I help you?' a female voice said tinnily in her ear.

'I received an overseas call from Berlin a minute or so ago, but was cut off. Can you trace the number for me?'

'It's doubtful, madam, but I'll try. Your number please?'

Hester gave it, already knowing she was wasting precious minutes. Even if by some miracle she were reconnected to her mother's neighbour, it would make no difference to the situation. Her mother was ill and her father was quite possibly dying, or dead.

'I'm trying to connect with the Folkestone exchange, madam, who will then connect me with the Bremen exchange who will then try to connect to the Berlin exchange –'

Hester slammed the phone down. She hadn't time to waste on what she was quite sure was a useless exercise.

She glanced at her watch again, her mind racing. With preparations for war going full ahead in Britain, France and Germany, boat and train services were most likely in a state of chaos. Certainly, they would be severely restricted.

As she was thinking she was running to the bedroom. She couldn't tell Hugo of the telephone call. For one thing, getting a personal call through to him at Whitehall was next to impossible, and for another, if he knew of her intention of leaving immediately for Berlin, he would physically prevent her from doing so.

She tugged a soft-sided bag from the top shelf of their wardrobe. She would leave a note for him, for when he returned home. By then, he would be unable to do anything. By then, she would be halfway across Germany.

She threw a change of underwear into the bag, some toiletries, a nightdress.

War, or no war, she wasn't going to allow her sick parents to remain in Berlin one hour longer than necessary. War hadn't been declared yet and, despite Hugo's certainly to the contrary, might not be declared at all. She had contacts who had been forging documents for nearly two years and they would certainly forge a couple of passports for her parents. Somehow or other she would get her parents into Switzerland and then, financially assisted by Paul, into either Britain or America.

She yanked open her dressing-table drawer, taking out the British passport she had acquired on her marriage to Hugo, and then she opened their bureau, taking out the emergency English and German currency always kept there.

Lastly, she scrawled a note for him.

Dearest darling,

Had a phone call, 9.28, from a Frau Debuss. Parents ill – *Vati* a suspected heart attack. Don't be cross, darling. I have to go. Max is in Berlin and will give me assistance. Love you with all my heart,

Hester

With her handbag in one hand and her travel bag in the other she paused for a brief moment at the door, gave a last look around the flat to make sure everything was as it should be – and five minutes later was in a cab, heading towards Charing Cross station and a train to Folkestone.

'Going the wrong way, ain't you, love?' the booking clerk at the ferry office said to her as she made enquiries about the next sailing to Calais. 'Old Hitler's about to finally upset the apple cart, or didn't you know?'

Forcing a smile and saying she was going to Paris, she bought a ticket for a boat about to sail and spent the voyage pondering what plan of action to take if she was prevented from entering Germany. The most obvious people to call would be Ilse and Lotti. Even if she couldn't get to her parents, Ilse and Lotti would be able to.

She stepped off the ferry at Calais wondering why she hadn't thought of contacting Ilse and Lotti before she had left London. The answer was pretty instant. It had been because she'd been panicked – and she was still panicked. What if her father was dead? How would her mother cope? What if even with false passports they couldn't get into Switzerland? What if war was declared before the attempt to enter Switzerland could be made and she, Hester, was trapped in Germany?

With fevered thought after fevered thought racing through her brain she boarded a train for Cologne. If she was refused entry into Germany at the border, she would simply have to somehow contact Ilse and Lotti and they would know how to contact Max. She knew enough about Hugo's family to know they wouldn't let her, or her parents, down. But *she* was the one who should be aiding her parents. And as war hadn't yet been declared, surely she wouldn't run into problems at passport control? Surely she would be allowed in?

Her anxiety was such she couldn't even see the irony of her situation. A Jewess terrified she wouldn't be able to get into Germany when millions of her fellow Jews within Germany were terrified they wouldn't be able to get out.

At the border, when she and everyone else had to disembark from the train, she struggled hard to keep her breathing steady. How did her mother-in-law manage, she wondered. Risking imprisonment and a probable death sentence every time she stood before a passport officer, a Jewish family's worldly goods pinned to the lapel of her well-worn tweed suit or draped around her neck as carelessly as children's glass beads.

There was an American in front of her, another American behind. The American passport was inspected, stamped.

'*Bitte?*'

She handed over her passport. There was the usual long, nerve-racking scrutiny. With icy control she kept her face and eyes perfectly impassive, not letting her reaction to his uniform and swastika-emblazoned red armband show.

'*Danke.*'

She followed the first American back onto the train, looking over her shoulder as she did so. The American who had been behind her in the queue looked to be having a hard time of it, for the border guard was deep in conversation on the telephone.

'These damn Krauts can make you feel uncomfortable for absolutely no good reason, can't they?' said the first American, seeing her slip her British passport back into her handbag. He sat down opposite her in the carriage, eyeing her admiringly. 'Still, their uniforms are pretty swell,' he added, wanting to prolong the conversation. 'I wouldn't mind a tricky black outfit like that myself.'

Her relief when she reached Cologne and was finally free of him, was vast. On the Berlin train she had no unwelcome companion. Her dark hair and eyes attracted mild attention, but she didn't look startlingly Jewish and she certainly didn't carry herself with the diffidence that Jewish women now nearly always did.

As the train roared towards Berlin she wondered what exactly it was her mother was sick with and why neither her father nor her mother had contacted her. They didn't have a telephone, of course. Luxuries like telephones had been left behind when they'd been forcibly removed from their beautiful house in Haberlandstrasse. Frau Debuss had managed to telephone her, though. And if Frau Debuss had managed it, surely her parents could have?

Flat monotonous landscape flashed past. She was oblivious to it. The task she had set herself wasn't going to be easy. She was going to need help and asking for that help was going to put others in great danger. Max was the person to help her, if she could find him. She remembered how he had once told her that if she needed to contact him in an emergency, Zelda was the person to go to.

She wondered if she dared risk that and knew that if neither Lotti nor Ilse knew of Max's whereabouts, she would have no choice. She would have to.

The landscape gave way to familiar suburbs. It was half-seven in the evening and the air was beginning to smoke with the first hint of dusk. In less than an hour she would be with her parents and would know the worst, whether they were too ill to be moved or whether she could go ahead with her plans to get them out of the country.

Before leaving the mainline station for the U-Bahn she darted into a telephone kiosk. The sooner she was in touch with Lotti or Ilse, the better.

Lotti's number rang and rang and then, when it was finally answered, it was by a voice she didn't know. 'Lotti isn't here,' a bored female voice said indifferently. 'She's already left for the club. Sorry.'

She rang Ilse's number, fervently hoping Ilse wouldn't be in a theatre performance. After only two rings the receiver at the other end of the line was picked up and Ilse's distinctively lovely voice said, 'Ilse Schulenburg speaking.'

'Oh, Ilse! Thank God.' Hester's relief was absolute. 'I was terrified you'd be out. I need to be put in contact with Max urgently.'

'Are you in London or Little Ridding, Hester?' Ilse was all immediate concern. 'Has there been an accident? What's the matter?'

'I'm in Berlin. At the railway station.' She cut across Ilse's exclamation of disbelief and horror. 'My parents are ill. One of their neighbours phoned me this morning. She thinks my father has had a heart attack and so I left immediately. I need to speak with Max, Hester. I've got to get my parents out of Germany before war is declared. It doesn't matter now whether they want to leave or not.'

'But you shouldn't *be* here!' The alarm in Ilse's voice was naked. 'What on earth was Hugo thinking of?' She made a valiant effort to remain calm. 'Put me on to Hugo, Hester. Let me speak with him.'

'Hugo isn't with me. He doesn't know I'm here. He won't know till he gets home much later this evening. I can't talk any longer, Ilse. I have to get straight to Mitte. Tell Max to meet me there as fast as he can.'

'Dear God, Hester!' Ilse's effort to be calm deserted her. 'Why didn't you phone me from London so that I could have checked on your parents? This is the last place on earth you should be at the present moment. Don't you know that there are –'

Ilse's protests were protests she didn't have time to listen to. 'Get Max to me, Ilse,' she said one last time and then, not even taking the time to replace the receiver back on its rest, she ran from the phone booth.

When she scrambled into a taxi she didn't speak German to the driver. The Mitte part of Berlin, where her parents now lived, had become predominantly Jewish and she didn't want him to suspect she was Jewish and to refuse to take her. As it was, even believing her to be a hare-brained Englishwoman, he refused take her any further than one of the main thoroughfares.

'*Juden*,' he said, using a word that even an Englishwoman would understand to indicate why he wasn't going to the street she had asked for. And then, to make quite sure she understood, he leaned his head out of the cab window and spat.

Slamming the taxi's door behind her, Hester began to run. If her father had had a heart attack, he had had it twelve hours or more ago. With her heart in her mouth, not knowing what she was going to find, she raced into the cobbled street that had once been generally working class and was now virtually a ghetto.

Even though the air was still claustrophobically warm, dusk was fast approaching. It gave a curious light to everything, and as she breathlessly entered the dingy apartment block she was aware of a curious stillness. There was no one on the stairs talking and passing the time of day. There were no children playing. No sounds coming from behind the doors she passed.

As she reached her parents' landing she saw that the door to their apartment was ajar. There was one brief second when she was aware that something was terribly, terribly wrong and then it was too late.

Calling out, '*Mutti! Vati!*' she flung herself into the apartment and came to a dead stop.

Even though it was not yet dark, there was a light on in the corridor that led from the front door into the sitting room. Pictures were askew on the walls as if there had been a struggle. There were smears of blood on the carpet.

And standing in the doorway of the sitting room were men in long, grey leather coats and felt hats.

Behind them, sitting on a chair, was a terrified, elderly lady.

She knew, even before Frau Debuss cried out waveringly, 'I had to do it! They told me I'd never see my husband again if I didn't do it!' that they were from the Gestapo and that her parents were no longer in the apartment. She knew the reason she'd had no problems at the border was because the border police had been expecting her. She knew that the American behind her in the queue had not been having a hard time, that the phone call being made had not been a query about him but was a call to Berlin alerting the authorities that she had entered the country.

And she knew why such lengths had been taken to lure her back to Berlin. The forgery ring had been busted. Like a fly into a spider's web she had been drawn back for the sole purpose of being arrested.

She didn't even turn towards the door and try to run for it. She knew that by now there would be another Gestapo agent standing only yards behind her.

Against a background of Frau Debuss's pitiful sobbing, she said in a voice she scarcely recognized as hers: 'Where are my parents? What have you done with them?'

'They are in Dachau, Fräulein Dresner,' one of the men, young and extremely good-looking, said. 'Where you soon will be.'

His use of her maiden name told her immediately she could hope for no help from the British Embassy. Though married to a British citizen, the fact was not going to be acknowledged.

Even though he was not in uniform, the silver death's-head insignia of the Gestapo seemed to shimmer in front of her eyes. Whatever had happened to her parents was her fault. The knowledge was something she was going to have to live with – and perhaps very soon die with. She thought of her darling Hugo walking into their London flat and finding the note she had left. He would come after her without even drawing breath – and he wouldn't find her. When the Gestapo took people away, as they were about to take her away, they didn't reappear.

As they moved towards her, her thoughts were all of Hugo, who loved her so very, very much, as she loved him. In losing her, his heart would be broken and she knew he would never find comfort.

'I'm sorry, my love,' she said in a whisper in English as her arms were wrenched cruelly high behind her back. 'Oh, God, my love! I'm so terribly, terribly sorry.'

She was bundled out of the apartment block with her feet scarcely touching the stone stairs.

Outside in the street was a large black car.

She was aware of people standing huddled in doorways, silently watching. There were no protests. How could there be? To protest would be to instantly share the same fate.

And then came protest.

A small expensive car hurtled into the narrow street and skidded to halt only yards behind the car she was being led to. With its engine still running, Ilse tumbled out of it, the golden plaits circling her head and her tailored cream suit incongruously elegant in the dusk-laden, dingy street.

'Stop!' she shouted, running pell-mell in high heels towards them. 'Frau Remer is a British subject. She has a British passport!'

With strength enough to break her neck, an iron hand thrust Hester's head down, forcing her into the car. Simultaneously, the Gestapo agent who had appeared behind Hester in the apartment sprinted towards Ilse, delivering a blow that knocked her reeling over the cobbles, stumbling and falling to her knees.

'Ilse! *Ilse!*' As she screamed Ilse's name, the powerful car surged away from the kerb. Certain Ilse was about to be shot, like a wild thing she fought the two men holding her. Briefly, through the rear window, she saw the Gestapo agent deliver a vicious kick to Ilse's stomach that sent her off her knees and sprawling backwards, and then the car zoomed round a corner and she knew with a sick lurch of terror where she was being taken. She was being taken to Gestapo headquarters at 8 Prinz-Albrecht-Strasse, the most feared address in Germany.

TWENTY-TWO

Yorkshire, Berlin and Munich, August 1939
Vicky was asleep when the ringing of the phone shattered the night-time peace and quiet of Shuttleworth Hall.

'What on earth . . . ?' She heard Adam say groggily as he disentangled himself from his sleeping position curled around her and struggled up against the pillows, fumbling for the bedside-light switch. 'Little Ridding 454 –'

He never finished giving their number. Instead he broke off, totally awake in an instant, leaping out of bed and saying as he did so: 'But Hester isn't in Berlin! She's in London. Is Ilse delirious? How badly has she been hurt?'

Vicky, aware that the call was from Berlin and couldn't possibly be about anything good, scrambled from the bed, reaching for her dressing gown.

'She's *what*?'

As Vicky saw the blood drain from Adam's face, icy fingers clutched at her heart.

He looked across at her and with the phone still held close to his ear, said to her, 'It's Nicholas. Hester has been arrested and Ilse is in hospital. He hasn't been able to contact Hugo yet.' Speaking again to Nicholas he said, 'Don't say any more. Not over the phone. It isn't safe. We'll contact Hugo.'

He put the receiver down and immediately began ringing Hugo's London number, looking across to their bedside clock as he did so. It was 11.45 p.m.

'But what was Hester doing in Berlin?' Vicky asked, her voice frantic. 'Does Hugo *know* she's in Berlin? And who has she been arrested by? The state criminal police or the Gestapo?'

He didn't ask what the difference was. He merely said, as the phone in Hugo and Hester's Knightsbridge flat continued to ring unanswered, 'I don't have answers for any of your questions, Vicky. I think we should get dressed, telephone Josephine to ask her to get over here so that your father isn't left on his own. She can babysit Emily Elise and Heini and that will enable us to set off immediately for London. I'll try and contact Hugo again from a phone box on the way. One thing is for certain: when he's told what has happened he's going to need family support. If we set off now, we'll be with him by breakfast time.'

Even while he was talking she was getting dressed, hurling her clothes on with feverish hands. At the back of her mind was the fear that, whatever Hester's reason for being in Berlin, her arrest had been in connection with the passport ring. And if Adam were to come to the same conclusion, there was no way he would let her go to Berlin to help find Hester. Though never having had any connection with the forgery of passports and visas, she had had connections with those who had received them. It would be enough to guarantee her own arrest.

As she thought of what could possibly be happening to her dearly loved daughter-in-law and of Hugo's distress, there was no doubt in her mind as to what she was going to do. Hugo's reaction would be to leave immediately for Berlin – and she was going to leave with him.

'I'm going to wake Paul,' she said, now fully dressed. 'He needs to know what has happened and where we are going. Did Nicholas say if he'd got in contact with Max?'

Adam tugged a sweater over his head. 'No. And I don't know if Lotti knows, either.'

Josephine had arrived, Paul had insisted he was coming down to London with them and they were all ready to go downstairs and leave the house when the telephone rang again. This time it was Hugo.

'I've just got home to find this insane note from Hester,' he said to Adam, sounding to Vicky and Paul as if he were on the verge of hysteria. 'She says she's left for Berlin, but I can't get through to anyone, not even Claus. Is she with you? Please say she thought better of it and that she's with you?'

Vicky took the phone from Adam's hand. 'We've been trying to get you on the phone for the past hour, darling. She did go to Berlin and Nicholas says she has been arrested. We're on our way down to London now. You can't do anything till the train and ferry services start in the morning. When they do start, Paul and I are coming with you to Berlin.'

Paul, seeing the expression on Adam's face and hearing Hugo's almost demented questions as to how Nicholas knew of Hester's arrest, took the receiver.

'It may only have been by the Kripo,' he said, referring to Germany's state uniformed police force, 'and it may be nothing life-threatening. Losing your calm now isn't going to do any good whatsoever, Hugo. What you need to be thinking about is who you know in the Foreign Office who may be able to throw some weight around and get information for you.'

As his conversation with Hugo continued, Adam said flatly to Vicky, 'You're not going. The borders could close at any moment. What would Emily Elise and I do if you were thrown into an internment camp? I can understand Hugo going. Hester is his wife and as he works for the Foreign Office there may be strings he can pull in order to find out where she's been taken. As for Paul – he has an American passport and even if war is declared between Britain and Germany, it won't affect him. Your presence isn't needed, Vicky. Where it's needed is here. At Shuttleworth Hall. With me.'

She pushed a deep wave of silver-flecked hair away from her face. 'Over the last couple of years I've taken enormous risks for people I scarcely know,' she said, holding his deeply worried eyes steadily. 'The least I can do is to take a risk for someone I love. I may always have abhorred Berlin, but I know it. The Jewish community trust me. If there's even a whisper of a rumour as to which camp she's been taken to – if she has been taken to a camp – it may filter back on the Jewish grapevine. If it does, I will be told. And if the boot were on the other foot, Adam, Hester would come looking for me, no matter what the dangers. I know that beyond a shadow of a doubt.'

Adam felt the familiar knot of utter helplessness he so often felt when confronting his wife over anything to do with the plight of Germany's Jews. That a woman so beguilingly feminine and tender in all her dealings could have a streak of such steel-like stubbornness and pig-headed tenacity, dumbfounded him no matter how many times he came up against it.

He understood, of course, why she felt as she did, even though he didn't think her reasoning logical. That she had once borne the name Remer, a name synonymous all through the Great War with arms production – arms used against Britain and her Allies – had inculcated in her a feeling of guilt that ran deep. Helping others, especially those persecuted by the government the House of Remer was still so closely allied to, was her way of expiating that guilt – that and the fact that, like her daughter, it was in her very nature to fight tooth and nail against injustice and tyranny and to do so with no thought for her own safety.

Behind him, Paul put the telephone receiver back on its rest. 'He's going to wait for us,' he said, his usually good-natured face grim, 'but only because there's no night train or ferry he can leave on. If we want to be in London before he leaves for Folkestone we need to go now.'

'I'll be right with you,' Vicky said. 'There's just one thing I have to do.'

And as Paul and Adam headed out of the room and down the stairs, she hurried along the landing into Emily Elise's bedroom to give her sleeping daughter a farewell kiss.

The private hospital room was dimly lit by a ghoulishly green light. A grey-faced Nicholas was seated at one side of Ilse's bed, Zelda on the other.

'How long until she comes round, do you think?' Nicholas asked, Ilse's hand held in his.

'After emergency surgery to remove a ruptured spleen? Hours, I should imagine. Probably not till midday tomorrow.'

With his free hand Nicholas wiped beads of perspiration from his forehead. 'I thought she was going to die,' he said, his voice choked. 'I truly thought she was going to die, *Schwiegermutter*.'

Much as she approved of her handsome, well-born and wealthy son-in-law, Zelda eyed him with displeasure. Being addressed as 'mother-in-law' was not something she relished, but now was not the time to tell him so. She said, 'She nearly did die. Internal bleeding on the scale Ilse was bleeding nearly always causes death. As it is, she's going to have to live without a spleen for the rest of her life and what the consequences of that are going to be is anyone's guess.'

Hatred for the Gestapo agent who had kicked her daughter so savagely she had nearly lost her life made her voice rasp like a rusty saw.

Taking his eyes momentarily away from his unconscious wife, Nicholas looked across at her. He had known her all his life. Even though the friendship between their two families had become distant at times, it had always endured, becoming

372

once again close when he had married Ilse. Zelda Remer was, though, still a mystery to him – as he suspected she was to her own children and to her niece and nephews.

Always dramatically beautiful and racehorse-slender, the slenderness was now close to gauntness. Tension was in every line of her body and however impossible it was to think of fear and Zelda in the same sentence, he suspected that she was afraid. And so was he.

If this kind of savagery could be perpetrated on someone as Aryan-looking and respectable as Ilse, then it could be perpetrated on anybody. In the Germany they were now living in, no one was safe. Even here, in the private hospital room paid for by Schulenburg wealth, he and Zelda could not speak freely to each other of what had happened.

In tacit understanding, while at Ilse's bedside, the word 'Gestapo' had not crossed their lips. Walls had ears. The entire country had become a country of spies and informants. Anyone foolish enough to say something risky or tell an anti-Nazi joke in company they were not utterly sure of, might get a knock in the middle of the night or a tap on the shoulder while walking along the street. And the result of that would be a trip to the Columbia-Haus, the prison centre in Berlin – and as screaming could often be heard coming from it, no one in their right minds wanted to risk being sent there.

Those wishing to ingratiate themselves with the regime they lived under, by informing on their fellows, could be anyone: a co-worker, a neighbour, the milkman, the postman, the old lady who lived across the street, the schoolboy in a near by apartment – and in a hospital it could easily be a nurse, a doctor or an orderly. Self-censorship had become a necessity and, in order not to bring further Gestapo attention to Ilse, the only politic thing to do was to stay silent and endure the charade that her ruptured spleen had been caused in a traffic accident.

It wasn't a charade he was enduring passively, though. For

the last three years, ever since it had begun to dawn on him, as a Foreign Office official, that Hitler was leading Germany towards a war it was almost sure to lose, he had been a member of a group of highly placed persons conspiring against him.

It had been – and was – an uphill task. Hitler controlled every aspect of German life. Not even in the smallest village or hamlet could anyone be in a club or society, not even a bowls club or a horticultural society, without also being a member of the Hitler Youth or a member of the Nazi Party. Only the army possessed the physical strength to overthrow him, and seeking out like-minded individuals in the upper echelons of the army was a nail-bitingly dangerous task.

It had been helped by the Night of Broken Glass, when what had previously been vicious harassment of the Jewish population turned into wholesale, murderous persecution, with over seven thousand Jewish business being destroyed in the one night, synagogues all over the country being simultaneously torched and Jews in their thousands being beaten on the streets and sent to camps. In the wake of such rabid anti-Semitism, resistance-group numbers had grown. Most of the new recruits were, like himself, young members of the old aristocracy. Some were former trade union leaders. A couple were clergymen. During the last year they had made several secret contacts with the British government, contacts in which Max had played a major part.

As a Foreign Office official, his role had not been to make an open break with the Nazis, but to work against them from within. It was how he had such accurate facts and figures with regard to the Night of Broken Glass. It was how he knew that no matter what concessions Poland might make with regard to Danzig, they would never be enough, for Danzig was merely Hitler's excuse for the war he had already decided to wage.

He said now to Zelda, 'I think you should go home and get

some rest. As you said yourself, Ilse's condition isn't going to change for several hours and tomorrow is going to be an exceptionally stressful day.'

Their eyes held and she knew by the expression in his that his last words hadn't been in reference to Ilse, but to Hester. Knowing that Hugo would be in the city by morning and would probably have Vicky and Paul with him, Zelda reluctantly rose to her feet.

'Goodnight, Nicholas,' she said, her voice fraught with weariness and anxiety.

'Goodnight, *Schwiegermutter*,' he said respectfully.

Zelda paused. Inappropriate time or not, she was going to have to say something.

'Zelda,' she said. 'I would prefer it if you would call me Zelda, Nicholas.'

And for the first time in her life, as she walked from the room she did so with the leaden tread of someone middle-aged.

None of them could remember the last time so many of their family had been gathered together in the Unter den Linden mansion. Hugo's face was haggard, his distress and the sleepless night he had spent clear for all to see. Paul, too, was looking obviously rumpled after the night-long drive to London, the early morning ferry crossing and the long train ride to Berlin. Only Vicky showed no sign of tiredness.

Beneath make-up applied more heavily than usual, Zelda's olive-toned skin was pale, her wine-red lipstick looking almost clownish. Josef, who hadn't left her side since they had arrived, looked grimly austere. In contrast, Berthold looked merely bewildered.

'Aren't we having any refreshments?' he kept asking plaintively. 'I always have a cup of tea at this time of day.'

Controlling her exasperation with difficulty, Lotti said

sharply, 'We've more on our mind at the moment than cups of tea, Uncle Berthold.'

Max looked directly across at Claus and said, 'I assume we can all talk freely in front of you, Claus?'

Claus, business-suited and smelling faintly of lemon-scented aftershave, his blond moustache immaculately clipped, flinched. 'This is a family matter,' he said savagely. 'Of course you can talk freely in front of me. I'm as concerned about Hester's arrest and her present whereabouts as any of you.'

'I bloody doubt that!' Every muscle of Hugo's body was as tight as a coiled spring. 'You're still wearing your bloody personally autographed swastika pin, aren't you? Having a Jewess in the family can't have done your standing any good with Göring and your other Nazi chums. How do we know you weren't party to any of this? How do we know you weren't behind the telephone call luring her back here?'

'Because however unwise I might have thought your marriage, I've always been perfectly courteous towards your wife and because an English cousin's marriage to a Jewess who is now a British subject and resident in England has never been an issue anyone has ever raised with me. Christ, Hugo! Have some sense! Whatever my reasons for being an admirer of the Führer, it isn't because I'm an anti-Semite. I've got more to fill my head with than that twaddle.'

'It isn't twaddle when people are dying because of it,' Max said steelily. 'But I believe you when you say you're concerned about Hester. And at bottom, so does Hugo. What you have to take into consideration is how desperate he feels at the moment. You know just as well as we do that when the Gestapo make an arrest there's no way of telling if that person is going to be seen again. Especially if the person in question is Jewish.'

Claus took in a deep, steadying breath. 'She'll be seen again,' he said with conviction. 'She's a British subject. She has a British passport.'

'Don't you know *anything* about what goes on in this country?' Hugo demanded, almost beside himself with frustration and fear. 'People *disappear*. Hester is *Jewish*. Reinhard Heydrich's goons in the Gestapo aren't going to give a damn about her British passport – not when Germany will probably be at war with Britain within days!'

'The situation with the Jews isn't as bad as you think,' Claus began pacifyingly. 'It's only those who are itinerant or disturb the peace or who are a danger to the state –'

It was too much for Hugo. Before Claus could say 'who are arrested and taken to camps' Hugo flew at him, punching wildly at his jaw.

Max and Paul immediately leapt forward to intervene, but Claus didn't need their intervention. Whereas Hugo's wildly thrown punch was futile, Claus's economical, but telling punch in return was not. Hugo went flying backwards, falling at his father's feet.

Lotti ran to his side, helping him to stand.

'Now you've both got that out of your system, can we settle down to the reason we're all here?' Vicky said, magisterially unruffled. 'Claus, I know Göring is no longer anything to do with the Gestapo, but you're on first-name terms with him and he, presumably, is on first-name terms with Heydrich. Find out all you can for us from the horse's mouth, will you? Max, I'm sure you've got plenty of ideas of your own as to what you can be doing.'

Max nodded agreement, intending to be in touch with Fritz within minutes of leaving the house.

'While Zelda goes back to sit with Ilse at the hospital, I'm going to speak to every Jewish contact I have. Someone may know something or have heard something.'

'You'll have a problem.'

The speaker was Josef and she turned towards him, startled. 'Jews are completely segregated in Berlin now. And they live under curfew. You'll be drawing attention to people who can't afford to have attention drawn to them.'

'*Vati* is right, Aunt Vicky,' Lotti said. 'There are people I can speak to, though. There are always Gestapo agents in the club I'm singing in. Being nice to them isn't something I generally do, but I can suffer it for Hester.'

'And Nicholas has his contacts in the Foreign Office,' Zelda said. 'The Gestapo aren't aware it was his wife who tried to interfere in Hester's arrest. Her name was never taken. The pigs simply left her in the street and drove off. It was only because she'd left a message for Nicholas before leaving for Mitte that he got to her before she bled to death. It means no connections will be made if he makes inquiries.'

'And me?' Paul said. 'What should I be doing?'

'Hang about Grunewald and Westhafen train stations,' Max said. 'I've heard rumours that Jews are beginning to be deported from there to various camps. The highest likelihood, though, is that she's still in Berlin and at Gestapo headquarters. I have a contact who owes me a favour and he may be able to find out for us.'

'Then let's stop wasting time,' Hugo said, his voice frantic. 'The British Embassy has already promised to do all it can. Somehow, someway, we've got to find her. We've *got* to.'

As Claus, Max, Hugo, Paul and Lotti began leaving the room, Berthold said plaintively to Vicky, 'I still haven't had a cup of tea, Vicky. I really can't understand why not.'

'Can't you?' Her voice was so waspish his jaw dropped. 'Perhaps it's because your Jewish daughter-in-law has been arrested by the Gestapo, Berthold. Perhaps it's because Hugo is out of his mind with worry. Perhaps that's why no one has given any thought to cups of tea.'

Over the years his eyes had grown increasingly myopic and his pebble-thick spectacle lenses had grown even thicker. He blinked at her owlishly through them and then said, 'Hugo

378

has only himself to blame. He shouldn't have married a Jewess. Jews aren't the same as us. They need to be kept separate from us.'

For a long, long moment Vicky neither moved nor spoke. For years she had clung to a vestigial feeling of sadness where the break-up of their marriage was concerned. She had wanted him to find happiness again, as she had found happiness. She had always been concerned about his welfare. Though she no longer loved him, she had always felt affectionate towards him and had always displayed that affection. Now she knew that not only love was dead, but affection was dead too.

'Vicky?' he said queryingly as she turned and walked away from him, sick at heart. 'What is it, Vicky? Why are you so angry?' And then, in growing frustration, he stamped his foot, shouting petulantly, '*And why won't anyone in this house bring me a cup of tea?*'

'I appreciate you giving me a few moments of your very busy time, Herr Reichsminister,' Claus said courteously, mindful of Göring's new rank. 'As I explained to your secretary when making this appointment, the matter is personal and nothing to do with House of Remer armament production.'

'I'm intrigued, Remer.' At Göring's uniformed neck was the Orden Pour le Mérite, the nation's highest award for valour, which he had won as a fighter pilot in 1917. Taking up his favourite position he perched his considerable bulk on the corner of his massive desk. 'And when you have disclosed to me your "personal matter", I would like to discuss with you the need for massively increased production where the Remer textile and clothing factories are concerned. The Führer is demanding that military uniform production be increased a hundredfold.'

'And it will certainly be so, Herr Reichsminister. The personal matter I wish to discuss with you is of a delicate nature. As you are no doubt aware, my uncle, Berthold Remer, was once married to an Englishwoman. The marriage ended in divorce many years ago but a child of the marriage, born in England and a British subject with a British passport, married a German woman in 1933. A Jewess.'

For Göring's benefit he made a moue of distaste. 'She has since become a British subject,' he continued when Göring made no attempt to stop the conversation there and then, 'and, like her husband, travels on a British passport. For reasons that are unclear to me, she returned to Berlin yesterday and was arrested by the Gestapo. I think it likely that there was a mistake over her identity – or that the arrest was made in order to facilitate her immediate deportation back to Britain. Either way, her whereabouts are now unknown and, with war imminent, it is a matter of great concern to her husband, who is, by the way, a British Foreign Office official.'

British Foreign Office officials cut no ice with Göring. 'I'm a Field Marshal, Commander-in-Chief of the Luftwaffe and Minister for Economic Affairs, Remer,' he said bluntly. 'Not a source of information on Jewish arrests. The Gestapo are not there to protect rogues, vagabonds, usurers and traitors. If people say that here and there someone has been taken away and maltreated, I can only reply: You can't make omelettes without breaking eggs. And that is my reply to you, Remer.'

The bonhomie with which Göring had greeted him was slipping away fast and Claus knew he was on exceedingly dangerous ground. The sensible thing for him to do was to now smilingly concur and resume the subject of increased military uniform production.

He said, 'I appreciate your comments, Herr Reichsminister, and am in complete agreement with them. I am also acutely aware of the irregularity of my coming to you on such a matter. If it were not for the fact of Hester Remer's British citizenship I would not have done so. A phone call will perhaps resolve the matter and it will be one less Jew to clog up the concentration camp or internment camp system.'

Göring, who, after the Night of Broken Glass, had ordered the elimination of all Jews from the German economy and their total exclusion from public places, even from parks and forests, was indifferent to how clogged concentration camps and internment camps might become. With anyone else his temper would have flared, but he thought of Claus as being a man after his own heart. A man not only of extreme good looks – it pained Göring that so many of Hitler's inner circle, men like Goebbels and Himmler, were so lacking in physical appeal – but a man of culture into the bargain.

'A phone call, then,' he said with a return of his usual hail-fellow-well-met bluff jollity. He slapped the flat of his hand against his massive thigh. 'And in exchange, not only increased textile and uniform production, but increased steel production too.'

When Claus stepped out once again into the Bendlerstrasse he did so fairly certain it would only be a matter of hours before Hester was released. He pushed a lock of hair away from his forehead, reflecting that Hugo now owed him in a big, big way.

Max had no intention of risking a phone conversation to Fritz. Instead, when he left the Unter den Linden mansion he made straight for the railway station and a train for Munich.

The newspaper he picked up before boarding the train did not make for comfortable reading. 'POLAND, LOOK OUT' warned a banner headline. 'ANSWER TO POLAND, THE RUNNER-AMOK AGAINST PEACE AND RIGHT IN EUROPE!'

There had been, of course, no foreign newspapers on sale at the kiosk. If there had been, Germans might have been able to read of how the rest of the world considered it was Germany that was running amok and putting the peace of Europe in jeopardy and that it was Germany that was threatening to attack Poland, not Poland that was, according to the newspaper Max was now reading, threatening Germany with armed invasion. That the German public believed such a ludicrous assertion was, to Max, beyond belief.

He went down to the buffet car and bought himself a cup of coffee and then, wishing he'd had the foresight to have brought something intelligent with him to read on the train, passed the long journey by reading the rest of the *Berliner Zeitung* from cover to cover.

'A contact in the Berlin Gestapo?' Fritz asked quizzically. 'And it doesn't matter whether it's an agent or a member of the clerical staff?'

They were seated in a quiet corner of Fritz's favourite beer-cellar, foaming tankards on the table in front of them.

Max flashed Fritz what he hoped would be interpreted as a wry smile. 'I'm trying to locate the whereabouts of a woman arrested two days ago in Mitte. As a private citizen I don't have the clout to find out that kind of information.'

'That's your own fault,' Fritz said, no real censure in his voice. 'I've been telling you for years to join the Gestapo. It was the best thing I ever did. I've signed up for twelve years and I get all the perks of a public employee, including medical insurance and a full state pension. I'll put in a word for you, if you want.'

'I'll bear it in mind,' Max said easily. 'And perhaps you can tell me which camp this woman I'm trying to trace is likely to be sent to? There're so many new ones now, it's hard to keep track.'

Fritz took a long drink of his beer, wiped his foam-fringed

mouth with the back of his hand and then said, 'At one time, especially if she has been arrested as *Volksschädling* – a public pest – it would have been down here, to Dachau. That was where all the antisocial malefactors, prostitutes, beggars, traffic offenders, homosexuals, found themselves. Now, though, it's likely to be one of the newer camps and one much nearer to Berlin. Sachsenhausen, at a guess.'

'And do you have contacts at Sachsenshausen?'

'No, but I could find one.' Fritz took a pencil and small notebook from the pocket of the green loden breeches he favoured whenever he was off duty. 'Here is the name of a friend of mine in the Berlin Gestapo. If you use my name, you'll be safe in speaking to him.'

Max took the piece of paper and put it in his pocket. 'And what if she hasn't been arrested as *Volksschädling*, Fritz? What if she's been arrested because she is guilty of treason to the state?'

Fritz roared with laughter, showing a mass of misshapen teeth. 'Then in that case, dear friend, you'll never hear of her again. She'll be dead within days.' He wiped tears of mirth from his eyes. 'Shall we get some schnapps to chase the beer down? Then you can tell me about your women. I miss Berlin women. Munich women are as big as carthorses.'

Lotti finished her set, stepping off the stage to loud applause and wolf whistles. Minutes later, still wearing the slinky, silver lamé gown she had performed in, she was seated with a Gestapo agent who had long been pestering her for a dinner date.

There was champagne in a bucket beside the table and a gleam of intense satisfaction in her dinner date's eyes.

'I've been looking forward to this for hours,' she said huskily, looking across at him smoulderingly from beneath batwing false eyelashes. 'Backstage has been absolute hell tonight.'

Her date, a personable-looking man in his early thirties, poured the champagne. 'In what way?' he asked, his eyes on the deep cleavage of her breasts.

Lotti gave a careless shrug, well aware that doing so ensured her breasts bounced erotically. 'One of the chorus girls was demented because a friend of hers had a run-in with one of your friends a night or so ago. Apparently, she was in an area of Mitte she had no reason to be in – lost, I expect. When she tried to interrupt a couple of Gestapo agents making an arrest they misconstrued the interruption and taught her how foolish it is to interfere when men are carrying out their duty. They hurt her pretty badly and, as the girl in question has to rely on her looks to earn a living, her friend is in despair about it.'

She gave another shrug to indicate that her interest in the matter was not very great. And waited.

'So she was a chorus girl. That explains a lot. I heard she was a looker.'

Lott felt her heart miss a beat. She took a languid sip of her champagne and, beneath the table, let her knee slip beneath his. 'Were the arresting agents friends of yours?' she asked, hardly able to believe her luck.

'Colleagues. The arrest was quite a coup for them. A German Jewess guilty of treason to the state, but a German Jewess with a British passport. She had to be lured back from England in order for the arrest to be made.'

With great effort and a fast-beating heart, Lotti drummed admiration into her eyes. 'And where is she now? Gestapo headquarters?'

'Maybe. I wouldn't know. I have a present for you.'

He placed a slim gold box on the table.

Lotti clapped her hands in apparent delight, her heart sinking at the prospect of the price she was going to have to pay for accepting it.

Inside the box was a mother-of-pearl necklace.

'Put it on,' he said.

She shook her head. 'No,' she said in a seductively teasing voice. 'You can put it on for me. Later.'

She saw almost unbearable sexual tension flare through his eyes and knew she had conjured up for him an image of herself naked, save for his gift. 'I expect if she has a British passport the British Embassy will intervene on her behalf,' she said musingly. 'It's sickening to think she may simply be returned to Britain instead of having to pay for her filthy crime.'

'You needn't worry on that score.' He dropped a hand beneath the table to fondle her leg. 'She has a British passport because she married a Briton, but she's been arrested under her maiden name and there is going to be no acknowledgement that she's anything other than a German Jewess.'

'And what will happen to her?' Lotti admiringly fingered the necklace in its box, as if her thoughts were on that and not on her question.

'Ravensbrück,' he said, cursing the width of the table between them. It meant his hand couldn't quite reach the soft enticing flesh at the top of her suspendered stockings. 'That's where high-grade women prisoners now go.'

'Ravensbrück? I've never heard of it.' She parted her legs to make his task a little easier. 'Where is it?'

'About thirty-five miles north of Berlin. It was only opened in May. Let's leave this damn club and go somewhere quiet. Somewhere we can get to know each other better. What about the Adlon?'

The Adlon not only had a superb dining room but, as it was a hotel, also had bedrooms within easy access.

Lotti suppressed a sigh of resignation. 'The Adlon would be lovely,' she lied, knowing she needed to keep him sweet until he could confirm whether Hester had, indeed, been sent to Ravensbrück.

And if she had?

As they left the club, his arm proprietorially around her naked shoulders, she felt sickening despair. Knowing Hester was in Ravensbrück would be one thing. Securing her release from Ravensbrück would be quite another.

'You know you've thrown your Foreign Office career away by travelling here at such a time without authorization?' The British Ambassador stared at Hugo as if he were a madman. 'This affair should have been dealt with through the proper channels in London. I'm up to my neck in what is possibly the deepest crisis of the century and I am simply not able to do anything for you other than go through the motions of formally complaining about the nature of your wife's arrest and requesting she be visited by a British official. At this moment in time, when the Führer is showing himself to be uncaring of the Prime Minister's assurance that Britain will go to war if Germany attacks Poland, I can assure you it is a complaint and a request that will go ignored.'

'With all due respect, this is my wife's *life* that is at risk!'

'With all due respect, your wife should not have travelled to Germany at such a time. It was arrant recklessness. Since early today, all radio, telegraph and telephone communication with the outside world has been cut off on orders from the Chancellery. I was informed an hour ago that the German Foreign Ministry has wired their embassies in Britain, France and Poland, requesting German citizens be asked to leave immediately by the quickest route. It is advice this embassy is now giving to British citizens in Germany. I appreciate the difficulty of your position, Mr Remer, and you have my utmost sympathy. However, as the borders could close at any time, my advice to you is to leave the country by tomorrow at the very latest. If – when – war is declared, your wife's name will no doubt surface on lists of those interned as enemy aliens. There may then be the opportunity of contact with her via the Red Cross. And that, I am afraid, is the only solace I can give you.'

For two days Paul's close watch on Grunewald and Westhafen station was fruitless. On the evening of the second day he began making his way back to the centre of Berlin, deeply dejected.

It was a warm and sultry evening and he walked for quite a long way, brooding over the impossibility of the situation he and the rest of the family were now in. Vicky and Hugo couldn't possibly stay for much longer in Berlin, not unless they wanted to spend perhaps years interned as enemy aliens, and drawing attention to the fact that a family member had married a Jewess – and a Jewess arrested by the Gestapo – was not going to do the Berlin side of the family any good.

He continued walking, pessimistically certain that even if they discovered Hester's whereabouts, securing her release would be impossible – especially if she had been arrested because her involvement with the passport ring had come to light.

Still deep in thought he walked into a station and boarded a Stadtbahn en route for Friedrichstrasse, the most convenient station for Unter den Linden. Had the family as a whole been criminally negligent in allowing Claus – who knew nothing about Hester's illegal activities – to speak to Göring about her? Nothing was now impossible in Nazi Germany and it wasn't beyond the realms of possibility that in openly acknowledging that Hester was related to him by marriage he too, if she had been arrested because of treason to the state, might find himself paying a visit to Gestapo headquarters.

Would the same apply to Ilse and Lotti, even though they were only Hester's husband's cousins? His head hurt with the grim thoughts pounding in it and then something happened that had never, in all his thirty-five years, happened to him before.

A young woman boarded the train and, before she could seat herself, she tripped slightly, dropping her handbag and spilling its contents. As he instinctively rose to help her collect her scattered possessions he looked into a heart-shaped face framed by a cloud of soft, light brown hair. Sea-green eyes met his and his heart stopped beating. It was a *coup de foudre*. A moment in which his entire life changed in an instant. Though he'd had girlfriends over the years, he had never been in love. He had never been close to being in love. At thirty-five, everyone who knew him assumed he was one of life's natural bachelors – and that, until now, was what he had assumed about himself also.

With his heart slamming against his breastbone he clumsily picked up a bunch of keys that had fallen from her bag and a pen that had rolled under one of the far seats.

'*Vielen dank*,' she said gratefully as he handed them to her.

She smiled as she spoke and he saw that there was a dimple at the side of her softly curving lips.

'*Bitte schön*,' he responded, and for the first time wished that his German was as fluent as Max's and Hugo's, both of whom spoke the language flawlessly, without even the slightest trace of an accent other than a Berlin accent. Like Vicky's, his German was excellent, a result of a lifetime of spending time in Germany, but it wasn't flawless and suddenly he very much wanted it to be.

With all her things now back in her handbag she sat down on one of the rattling wooden seats and he sat down opposite her, wondering how far she was travelling; wondering what he could say or do to ensure she remained with him.

The light coat she was wearing fell open a little and he saw she was in a nurse's uniform.

'You're a nurse,' he said, wishing he had Max's gift of the gab or Claus's smooth sophistication.

'Yes.' She smiled again. 'And I think that though you speak German with an English accent, you are an American.'

He grinned, aware that the ice was broken. 'I was born in New York, but I've lived in England – in Yorkshire – nearly all of my life. My name is Paul Gould.'

'And mine is Eva Ketzler.'

He wanted to take hold of her hand. She had lovely hands. Well-shaped and blessedly ringless.

'And do you live in Berlin, Fräulein Ketzler?'

She nodded and the light danced in the soft cloud of her hair. 'Yes. In Wedding.'

Wedding was a not very smart working-class suburb north of Tiergarten, which meant she wasn't on her way home, but was probably going to work. And if she was going to work it meant that when he plucked up the courage to ask her if she would have a tea or a coffee with him, she wouldn't be able to – in which case he would simply wait outside her hospital until her shift was finished and then take her for a tea or a coffee.

The train pulled into Alexanderplatz station and she made no move to stand up and to leave the train.

'Are you just going on duty?' he asked as the train continued towards Hackescher Markt.

She shook her head and again the lights danced. 'No. I'm going to visit an aunt who lives near Friedrichstrasse.'

'I'm getting off at Friedrichstrasse too,' he said truthfully, knowing he wouldn't have been doing so if she had been travelling farther, knowing that if she had been travelling to the end of the line, he would have been doing so too.

'Are you working in Berlin?' she asked as the train racketed on towards Friedrichstrasse station.

He shook his head, leaning towards her, his large hands

clasped loosely between his knees. 'No. I'm a rose-breeder. I have a large horticultural nursery in Yorkshire. I'm in Berlin because I have family here.'

The train pulled into the station. Simultaneously, they rose to their feet. Companionably, they stepped off the train and began making their way towards the turnstile. 'Would you have a tea or a coffee with me before you go to your aunt's?' he asked, knowing that his whole life depended on her answer.

She paused, looking up at him, her eyes the green of the River Spree. 'I'd like to do that very much,' she said, and as they walked through the turnstile and out of the station Paul knew that despite all the nightmares – the imminence of war, Ilse's beating, Hester's arrest – something glorious had happened.

It seemed crazy, but he was certain he had just met the love of his life. And he knew something else as well. He wouldn't be returning to England with Vicky and Hugo. He would be staying in Berlin. Any other alternative was now utterly unthinkable.

Wearing a black headscarf to cover her fair hair and the oldest, shabbiest black coat Zelda's cleaning lady possessed, Vicky made her way to what had been the Dresners' apartment block.

The tension on the streets was palpable. Uniformed men were everywhere, as were swastika-emblazoned flags. Troops in every kind of moving vehicle, vans, trucks, even grocery lorries, were pouring through the city, heading east, presumably in the direction of the Polish border. As she passed a newspaper kiosk she saw a copy of the *Voelkischer Beobachter* with the headline 'THE FÜHRER SAYS THE HOUR IS GRAVE!' Another newspaper proclaimed in headlines inches high: 'WHOLE OF POLAND IN WAR FEVER! POLAND MOBILIZES 1,500,000 MEN!'

There was no mention of the German troops rushing towards the border. No mention that any action of Poland's was in self-defence against naked German aggression. Aware there was no newspaper in Germany – and hadn't been for a long, long time – allowed to give the German people facts, not lies, Vicky reached the apartment block and rang the bell marked 'Debuss'.

It rang unanswered for several minutes and then the downstairs door was finally opened by a terrified-looking young girl.

'I'm Mrs Priestley, Hester Remer's mother-in-law,' Vicky said swiftly before the door should be shut in her face. 'I'd like to speak to Frau Debuss, if I may.'

The girl looked uncertain and Vicky said gently, 'It really is most important that I speak to Frau Debuss.'

Still looking very doubtful the girl turned and began to lead the way up the communal stone stairs.

Vicky felt her stomach muscles clench. What she was hoping to find out was if Frau Debuss knew of the reason for Hester's arrest. Had it simply been one of the senseless, arbitrary arrests carried out in their hundreds by the Gestapo, or had it been because Hester's association with the forgery ring had become known to them?

The air in the apartment she was led into was stale and sour and the blinds were drawn so that it was difficult to see clearly.

'She says she is Hester Remer's mother-in-law,' the girl said to a still figure seated on a sagging sofa. 'I thought there might be trouble if I didn't let her in.'

Vicky's eyes adjusted to the dim light. Frau Debuss was sitting in her coat, clasping a small cardboard box.

'I need to know if you know the reason for Hester's arrest,' she said, trying not to remember that if Frau Debuss hadn't given in to Gestapo pressure, Hester would still be safely in England. 'I need to know everything the Gestapo said to you.'

The eyes that met hers were blank with grief. She didn't even attempt to answer the question. 'They told me if I told Hester her mother was ill and her father had had a heart attack, that they would free my husband,' she said in the flat tones of someone who has suffered too deeply to be able to betray any more emotion. 'He was in Sachsenhausen. They told me if I did as they asked and if Hester came back to Berlin, I could go to Sachsenhausen and bring my husband home.'

Vicky nodded, understanding all too well the kind of hideous blackmail Frau Debuss had been under.

'They told me Hester was a traitor to the state and so, for my husband's sake, I did as they asked.'

Vicky felt her stomach muscles tighten into crippling knots. The answer was the one she had feared all along, and if Hester had been charged with treason the likelihood was she was already dead.

'And your husband?' she asked, aware that the apartment seemed empty but for themselves and the young girl. 'Is he here?'

'Oh, yes.' Tears began rolling down her face and splashing onto her coat. 'He's here. They gave him to me at Sachsenhausen's gates.'

And she lifted up the cardboard box containing his ashes.

'There can be no arguments,' Nicholas said. 'Not even from Hugo. You must all leave Germany at once. Tonight. Before England declares war on Germany and the borders are closed.'

This time the family conclave was being held in his and Ilse's home and neither Josef nor Berthold were present. Josef because he was at the hospital, sitting at his daughter's bedside, and Berthold because no one had thought it necessary to tell him of it.

'I can't leave,' Hugo said tautly. 'Not without knowing what has happened to Hester.'

'You have to.' Nicholas spoke with grave certainty and quiet authority. 'Secret coded dispatches have been humming over the wires all day at the Foreign Office. Because of my position there I can tell you that the British Ambassador has had yet another stormy meeting with Hitler this afternoon. The British government isn't going to give way over Poland. When German troops cross the Polish border Britain will declare itself to be at war with Germany. And I'm privy to the hideous information that German troops are going to invade Poland not within days, but within hours. So you have to leave, Hugo. Remaining here will mean internment, and if you are interned you will be able to do nothing towards finding out what has happened to Hester. You are simply going to have to leave searching for her up to myself and Claus.'

'And to me,' Paul said as the telephone rang and Nicholas went to answer it. 'As an American I can stay on and I'm going to.'

'We know now, from several sources, that it wasn't an arbitrary arrest,' Lotti said, her usually impish face pale and sombre. 'The forgery ring was busted and under interrogation someone gave her name.'

'But she wasn't a part of the inner forgery ring,' Hugo protested. 'She only helped people who had been given forged passports and visas know how to behave at passport controls. That isn't treason. It's a crime she may be imprisoned for, but it isn't a crime she could be executed for.'

Nicholas put the telephone receiver back on its rest and turned towards them. 'I have to go straight back to the Foreign Office. The attack on Poland is scheduled to begin within hours. This is it. This is when we have to say goodbye.'

Vicky turned to Zelda and hugged her tight. 'This is the second time in our lives this has happened to us,' she said thickly. 'Pray God our family isn't divided for as long as it was in 1914.'

'I know what you think of my allegiance to the Führer,' Claus said to Hugo, 'but I promise you this: I'll continue to do everything possible to find out where Hester is and to secure her release.'

Hugo nodded, not trusting himself to speak to him.

'What will you do, darling Hugo?' Lotti asked, tears brimming on her eyelashes at the terrible division about to rend the family apart.

'I shall join the air force – especially as I've probably shot my bolt with the Foreign Office.'

At the prospect of Hugo in armed attack against German pilots or, even worse, German civilians, everyone, even Zelda, flinched.

'Let's kiss each other and say goodbye,' Vicky said, her heart feeling as if it were breaking. 'And let's pray that even now, at the eleventh hour, there may be a miracle and war might be averted.'

All through the long, tension-strung, arduous night-time journey back to England, she prayed fervently that Hitler would come to his senses and that the German troops massing on the Polish border would stay on Germany's side of it.

They didn't do so. At daybreak German armies poured across the frontier and German warplanes blasted Polish troop columns and bridges, ammunition dumps and railroads.

Three days later, listening to the wireless hand in hand with Adam in the drawing room at Shuttleworth Hall, Vicky heard the words she had prayed she would never hear.

'This country,' Prime Minister Mr Neville Chamberlain said in deeply regretful, sombre tones, 'is now at war with Germany.'

TWENTY-THREE

Sachsenhausen Concentration Camp and Berlin, April 1940
It was 4.30 a.m. and, as always at 4.30 a.m., the guards' shouts of '*Raus! Raus!*' catapulted Hester into another unendurable, horrific, hunger-filled day.

She tumbled from the wooden bunk before a blow could fall across her head or her shoulders and hurriedly began to remake it. Remaking a bed comprising only of a hay-filled mattress on wooden boards and a rough, thin blanket was a mockery, but those were the rules. 'Beds' had to be made. As the bunks were three foot high and she was on a top one it wasn't an easy exercise. It did mean, though, that she could at least sit up in her bunk without hitting her head. The lower bunks were only high enough to crawl in and out of.

The elderly lady on the bunk beneath hers sagged against one of the metal supports, ashen-faced. With speed and dread Hester remade her bunk for her. The speed was because if she were to be seen doing so, punishment would follow. The dread was because when illness claimed a prisoner she disappeared, never to be seen again. And that this fate hovered over the woman whose bed she was now making was all too obvious.

There were fifty women in the barracks and as they washed

in cold water and then dressed in coarse-cotton prison dresses, none of them spoke to each other. It wasn't allowed.

Of all the rules and regulations designed to make their existence as miserable as possible, this was the one she minded the least. What conversation could possibly make the day that lay ahead even a smidgeon more endurable?

Silently, as she ate the thin porridge that was breakfast, she prayed, knowing that, incredible as it seemed, she had a lot to be grateful for.

For one thing she was alive – and she was convinced that her being alive was due only to a bureaucratic glitch. When she had first been arrested and taken to Gestapo headquarters for questioning – and after her British passport had been burned before her eyes – she had been told that as a traitor to the state, she was to be beheaded.

Then had come confusion. There were several other women being held in cells at Prinz-Albrecht-Strasse, all of whom were awaiting transportation to Ravensbrück, and when they were all herded out of their cells and into a truck, so was she.

The very thought of Ravensbrück made her want to faint. Death had stalked every day of being there. It was there she had first learned what real hunger was and that there were worse fates than being executed – that there were medical 'experiments' carried out in what was euphemistically termed 'the hospital wing'. Just when she was convinced she was about to be one of those selected to undergo unspeakable torture in the name of Nazi genetic experimentation, she was selected instead for cook and kitchen duties – and not at Ravensbrück, but at Sachsenhausen.

Sachsenhausen was twenty miles nearer to Berlin than Ravensbrück and a camp mainly for men. Shortly after she arrived there, so did thousands of communists, social democrats and former trade union leaders as well as nine hundred Jews. For them, the regime was just as brutal as the regime she had endured at Ravensbrück. There was excruciating hunger, slave-labour work in several adjoining factories and daily executions.

It was an existence she and the other women who carried out cooking and kitchen duties were spared. Their work was to prepare the food for the prisoners and for the SS guards and the soldiers guarding the camp. Heavy work was involved too. Carrying giant metal food containers almost as big as themselves from lorries into the kitchens.

And though they were spared many of the horrors they had endured at Ravensbrück, Sachsenhausen held one that was new to them.

Over and above their cooking and kitchen duties another service was expected of them. Even though they were all Jewish, this fact was overlooked by the rabidly racist SS guards when it came to sexual gratification.

Hester survived the sexual assaults on her body by remembering the so-called 'hospital wing' at Ravensbrück. At least at Sachsenhausen she had physical safety of a sort, and though she was sexually violated she was able by sheer mental will power to keep her inner self somehow untouched and untainted. She was also an exceptionally good cook and when this came to the Camp Commandant's attention, she was detailed away from preparing food for prisoners and guards and assigned the task of cooking for him alone.

It was for the mercy of the work she was assigned to, for the mercy of being beyond the reach of barbaric medical experimentation and for the mercy of still being alive, that she thanked God as she ate her paltry breakfast.

Through the day she never dared allow herself to think of Hugo or of Vicky and Shuttleworth Hall. To do so would be to bring her too close to breakdown and breakdown would mean being detailed back to prisoner and guard food-preparation duty – or even, perhaps, worse.

Thoughts of Hugo and Shuttleworth Hall were kept for the

night-time when, for a few precious hours, she could transport herself away from the horrors of reality and lose herself in sleep and dreams.

Last night she had dreamed she was bringing armfuls of deliciously scented lilac into Shuttleworth Hall for Vicky to arrange in tall, crystal vases. Tinker had been in her dream, no longer the fit young dog he had once been, but still gamely keeping up with her and trotting happily along at her heels.

There had been other delicious smells in her dream too. As well as lilac there had been the aroma of freshly baked bread and Josephine's sublime Yorkshire curd tarts. And there had been the scent of Hugo. The smell of the cologne he used after shaving. The lemon-clean fragrance of his hair when it was freshly washed. The tang of his sweat when they made love.

And then had come the sickening awakening. The shouts of '*Raus! Raus!*' And now another day lay ahead. Another day that was going to take her all her stamina and will power to live through.

Claus strode through the textile section of his Berlin clothing factory. It wasn't huge – woollens and worsteds still came in the main from other parts of the country – but it was an element of the factory he was keen to expand. As the clattering of looms almost deafened him he reflected wryly that the man he needed to speak to was Adam Priestley. Adam was a mill man down to his extremely capable fingertips.

The pity of it was that he didn't know Adam better. The years since Adam and Vicky's marriage had been years when he had rarely visited Yorkshire. Not because he hadn't longed to, but because there had been issues that had made him feel uncomfortable in doing so. There had been his early support of Hitler, for instance. It had been something his aunt had never been in sympathy with, even before Hitler's military aggression had become so nakedly apparent. And then there had been Nancy.

Though Vicky had never said so, he had known it was a relationship that had caused her deep disquiet. She hadn't wanted Nancy becoming what she had been: wife to the head of the House of Remer. Even more than Hitler, it had been the family steelworks that had marred his relationship with Vicky.

He walked out of the weaving sheds and along the stone-floored corridor that led to the building's offices. That he didn't now feel quite so euphoric about Hitler was not something he'd been able to share with anyone, not when his disquiet had been aroused by the government's cavalier attitude to private property.

The instant he was back in his office he took a bottle of schnapps from the bottom drawer of a filing cabinet and poured a good three fingers into a glass.

Once he had downed it he stood facing the window, gazing broodingly out over the factory yard.

Paul walked down the crowded street with long easy strides. He was on his way to the Charité hospital to meet Eva at the end of her shift, and they were then going to the cinema. Even though the war was now in its seventh month, his being in Berlin was causing him no great problems. Because he spoke with far more of a Yorkshire accent than an American one, he'd begun suppressing the Yorkshire and cultivating the American, and that, apart from constantly being stopped on the street by the police and being asked to show his passport, was the only inconvenience he had met with.

His only concern, other than his failure to have located Hester, was that the war looked like being a short one and the victor, Germany. Denmark had already been taken. Norway invaded. It meant that two countries which could have given

Britain aid, were now firmly in German hands. The thought of Britain following suit appalled him.

'But if the war continues, it will be even worse,' Eva had said to him when she had told him that she couldn't marry him. 'America will eventually join forces with Britain and France and then what would we do? You would have to leave Germany before she did so and I could not go with you. To leave my country at such a time would be unthinkable. And if you stayed, you would be imprisoned as an enemy alien and that I couldn't bear. When the war is over, then we will marry, Paul. And then you can take me to Yorkshire and to Shuttleworth Hall and I can meet your aunt and your cousins – and the little dog, Tinker.'

It was a rosy picture and he hadn't been able to bring himself to point out to her that if Germany were the victor in the war, Shuttleworth Hall would no longer exist, as it existed now. When he thought of jackbooted feet tramping over Vicky's lovingly polished oak floors and Wehrmacht or SS officers polluting the house with their presence, he felt physically ill.

It wasn't an emotion he shared with Eva. If Eva clung to the hope that a German victory would leave British towns and villages intact and Britons enjoying the same lifestyle they now enjoyed, he was not going to spoil their precious time together by taking that hope from her.

A smart black Steyr two-seater screeched to a halt at the kerbside just yards in front of him. The driver was Nicholas and as he stepped from the car, slamming the door behind him, Paul saw by the expression on his face that whatever the news he was in such a hurry to share with him, it wasn't good news.

He stood still as Nicholas walked towards him, hoping that the bad news was to do with the war and not family. Over the last few months he and Eva had become very close to Nicholas and Ilse. He had introduced Eva to Lotti the first week of meeting her and, much later and with many reservations, had even introduced her to Claus. It was when he had introduced her to Ilse and Nicholas, though, that he'd had the sensation of Eva becoming a part of the family, for she and Ilse had instantly bonded and, as the friendship between Ilse and Eva had deepened, so had his friendship with Nicholas.

Nicholas was a man he admired. He had a gravitas about him unusual for a man in his mid-thirties and his position at the Foreign Ministry was a responsible one. Via it he kept Paul informed of what was going on in the rest of the world, for a word-by-word record of all BBC news and other foreign broadcasts passed through his hands. Only thanks to Nicholas did he know that British troops had landed in Norway and that Norwegian resistance to Germany's invasion was intense.

'What is it?' he said as Nicholas reached him, fearing it was bad news with regard to British troops.

'Hester.' Nicholas said bluntly. 'Claus has just heard via Göring that she was sentenced to death within hours of being taken to Gestapo headquarters. The sentence would have been carried out almost immediately.'

Paul blanched.

A group of soldiers strode past them. A woman with a nearly empty shopping basket bumped into him. 'Why are we on food rationing if we're winning the war?' she demanded querulously. 'No butter, only a pot of jam a month. How far does that go?'

He didn't answer her. As she continued on down the busy street, still complaining aloud to anyone who would listen, he said to Nicholas, 'How can Hugo be told?'

'I thought a letter from you sent to him by way of one of your distant relatives in New York. It would have to be very innocent-sounding, though. Nothing the censor might pick up on.'

Paul tried to control the sick feeling surging in his stomach. He had been deeply fond of Hester. She had possessed an innate gentleness he had been very drawn towards.

With great difficulty he said, 'How? How would she have died?'

The skin was drawn tight across Nicholas's cheekbones and white lines etched his mouth. 'The penalty for high treason,' he said, 'is beheading by the guillotine.'

Paul swayed slightly and then swung away from him, rushing over to the edge of the pavement to be violently sick in the street.

TWENTY-FOUR

Berlin, June 1941

Even though there was an air raid in progress, Nicholas continued dressing for his and Ilse's evening appointment – dinner with the Radcliffs, an American couple they had met via Paul. Before being posted to Berlin, Robert Radcliff had for many years been with the US Embassy in Russia and Nicholas had high hopes that the evening would be an interesting one.

He continued wrestling with the collar-button of his evening shirt, wishing Ilse would emerge from the bathroom in order to help him and knowing that as long as the raid continued it wasn't very likely.

Because there was only a small window in the bathroom, Ilse had decided it was the safest room to be in when bombs were falling. That they would seek refuge in shelters only if caught out by an air raid when on the street or in a public place was something they had mutually decided upon long ago, but though he had nerves like steel, Ilse didn't. RAF air raids, especially of late when they had become almost nightly occurrences, shot her nerves to pieces.

With his stiff collar finally secured to his shirt he reached for his tie. As he tied a bow with practised expertise he wondered what Robert Radcliff's thoughts were on the fast-approaching complete breakdown of any kind of friendly relations between Germany and Russia.

'Does he know a German attack on Russia is only weeks, possibly days, away?' he had asked Paul.

'American Embassy officials know the Nazi–Soviet honeymoon is over,' Paul had said drily, 'but they find it hard to believe Hitler would stretch himself so thin as to invade a country the size of Russia when the war in the West is still blatantly unresolved.'

As if to remind him that it *was* still dreadfully unresolved there was a huge explosion. A bomb fell near to the apartment, mirrors and pictures fell off the walls and the floors shook.

'Dear God!' Ilse flew into the bedroom, wearing a white silk cocktail dress, her face ashen. 'Have we been hit? Are we on fire?'

Over the deafening thunder of answering flak guns, Nicholas shook his head.

'No. It fell in Wilhelmstrasse, I think. They will have been trying for a direct hit on government offices.'

She took a deep, steadying breath. 'Sorry for being such a craven coward, darling. It's just that I really did think we'd been hit and –'

He put his arms around her, pulling her close, uncaring that she already had make-up on and that he would get traces of face powder on his evening shirt.

'You're not a coward, darling,' he said thickly. 'Far from it.'

As she slid her arms around his waist, he thought of the danger his secret activities constantly put her in and of how staunchly she stood by him. An earlier plot to kill Hitler had already failed and he and his fellow conspirators were on the verge of carrying out another attempt. If this one failed and if this time his name and the names of others in the conspiracy became known, it would be the death penalty not only for him, but possibly for her also. And still she gave him her unstinting support. Though she failed to see it as such, it was courage of a high order.

'It's over,' he said as the hum of the bombers overhead began to fade away and the sound of flak guns became more and more intermittent.

'Thank God.' Her soft, smoky voice was unsteady with relief. Keeping her arms around his waist, she raised her face to his. 'Whenever there is a raid, I can't help wondering if Hugo is one of the pilots and of how he must feel if he is. Of how truly terrible it must be for him, dropping bombs on a city that he's always regarded as a second home, a city that his father and so many of the rest of his family are living in.'

'I suspect he's a fighter pilot, darling,' he said, trying to spare her the nightmare of her thoughts. 'He'll be flying a Hurricane or a Spitfire, not a bomber.'

She didn't say anything, for thinking of her cousin in the cockpit of a fighter plane was almost as bad as imagining him at the controls of a bomber.

Trying to focus her thoughts on something other than Hugo she looked around at the mirrors and pictures that had crashed to the floor. 'Let's clear up the worst of this mess before we leave for the restaurant. It's not fair to leave it for Dorie to do.'

Dorie was their live-in maid, who was out for the evening and who, hopefully, had been in an air raid shelter for the last hour and a half.

'Pour us both a steadying Martini,' he said, picking up one of the picture frames and shaking the broken glass from it, 'this job won't take long.'

*

Once at the restaurant he found it hard to keep his mind focused on the dinner-table conversation, amusing and interesting as it was. He even found it hard to appreciate the food, which was even more of a pity, because Horscher's was one of the finest restaurants in Berlin – and one miraculously free of food-rationing restrictions.

Aware that serious topics were unlikely to be raised because the Radcliffs were too bowled over at being out on the town in the company of a film star – which, with two films under her belt and another one due out in a month's time, was what Ilse now very definitely was – Nicholas pondered on the meeting he was due to have the next evening with Max.

Uppermost on his mind was whether Max would arrive in Berlin, from Munich, without incident. For twenty-one months, Max had successfully remained in Germany, but for how much longer he could do so was highly questionable. That he had been able to do so at all was due to his being Claus Remer's cousin and Berthold Remer's son – and to his being a German by birth and nationality. That he hadn't been conscripted into the army was thanks to Claus.

As soon as German armies had rolled over the Polish border and it had become obvious war with Britain was unavoidable, Max had told Claus he was in love with a girl from Munich and intended remaining in Germany. Whether Claus truly believed him was something even Max didn't know, for Claus – as always – kept his thoughts to himself. The important thing, though, was that he had certified Max was engaged on essential war work for the House of Remer, freeing Max from the tricky problem of military service.

'And this new film?' Robert Radcliff was asking Ilse. 'Is it historical, like your first two films?'

'I'm afraid not,' she said ruefully. 'There is far more propaganda in this film.'

Well aware that conversation was flowing easily without any

406

input from him, Nicholas returned his attention to thoughts of Max and their vitally important meeting tomorrow.

It would be the first time Max would meet all the key players in the conspiracy. The attempt on Hitler's life was to take place in five days' time and it was essential that Max, their direct link to the British government, knew in detail what their plans for an anti-Nazi government were. Though he, Nicholas, was utterly certain that with Hitler dead they would be able to come to satisfactory peace terms with Prime Minister Winston Churchill, other members of the conspiracy were not so sure and it was going to be down to Max to convince them.

'Are the Babelsburg film studios far from Berlin?' Elizabeth Radcliff asked Ilse, clearly as enraptured by Ilse as her husband was.

'Not too far. I travel by train to Babelsburg station and from there it's just a short walk through a wood to the studio.'

'But what if there was to be a raid?' Elizabeth Radcliff looked horrified.

'Daylight raids don't happen – not yet, at any rate. And I enjoy the early morning walk through the wood. It's possible to forget all about the war, and for a little amount of time the world seems to be just as it once was.'

'Ah,' Robert Radcliff said expressively, 'if only . . .'

Aware they were in a public restaurant where it was just possible they would be overheard, no one else said anything until Elizabeth Radcliff remarked, 'I'm amazed you have to travel to the studios by public transport. I can't imagine a Hollywood film star doing that. The studios send cars for them.'

'Some German actresses have studio cars,' Ilse said, black humour in her lovely voice, 'but only those who meet with the patron of the film industry personally, so that he can "get to know them a little better".'

Elizabeth Radcliff's mouth rounded on an 'oh' of understanding.

'And as the patron of the German film industry is Goebbels,' Nicholas said drily, 'you see why Ilse so much prefers to travel by train and walk in the woods!'

Lotti woke in the early hours of the following morning, her tummy a knot of nerves. Max was due to arrive in Berlin from Munich some time during the day, but whether she would see him or not she had no idea. And she wanted to see him. She wanted to see him so much it was a physical pain.

Her flatmates were still asleep as she washed and dressed. With dancing and jazz music forbidden they, like her, found club work hard to find and, like her, mainly worked as waitresses till late in the evening. The restaurant she worked in was an Italian restaurant, Roma. But she wasn't going to be working in it today. Today she had kept completely free in the hope that Max would contact her and they would be able to spend a little time together.

A drawback of their spending time together, of course, was that as he only ever treated her as a friend – his best friend – she was always kept abreast of what was happening in his love life. Though the story of his having fallen in love with a Munich girl had been a fabrication for Claus's benefit, there *was* a young woman in Munich whom he was regularly dating. A young woman she tried hard not to think about.

Standing before the bathroom mirror she dragged a hairbrush through her sleek, night-black hair. Her hair made it impossible for her to look fashionable, but then she'd never looked fashionable. What she had always looked was different.

Feeling quite certain that Max's girlfriend in Munich would look extremely fashionable, she gave up on her hair, well aware she should be grateful that the woman in his life was no longer Ilse.

The period of time when Max had been in love with Ilse had been the most difficult she had ever lived through. Ilse had been so deliriously happy at first and, loving her as she did, Lotti had wanted to be happy for her. She had found the task so hard as to be almost impossible.

The relief when, for some unfathomable reason, Ilse had ended her relationship with Max and become engaged to Nicholas, had been so vast she had cried with it. Being jealous of Max's previous girlfriends had been something she had accustomed herself to. Being jealous of Ilse had been a pain so deep it had nearly unhinged her.

Dressed but still barefoot she padded into the kitchen to make herself a coffee, or what nowadays passed for a coffee. Sun streamed into the kitchen, promising a day of heavy, languorous heat. It was the kind of day to be at Wannsee, sunbathing and swimming. As she waited for the water to boil she pondered on the risks of taking the train to Wannsee. Would Max realize where she had gone? And if he did and went to Wannsee, would he be able to find her?

Even in the same instant as asking herself the questions, she knew the answers. As children, Wannsee had been their favourite destination whenever the days were hot and long and free of schoolwork. When she wasn't to be found at the apartment or at the Roma, he would know where she would be and, despite the numerous beaches dotted alongside the lakeshore being crowded on a day like today, he would also be able to find her. Years ago, Vicky had found a swimming and picnicking place well away from the crowds that had become a favourite with all of them, even Zelda. Woods backed a silver crescent of sand and, though there had been no restaurant near by when they were children, there was one now. A pretty little restaurant where diners could eat overlooking the water. It was a restaurant she and Max often patronized and either it, or the secluded bay, was where he would instinctively assume her to be.

She went back into the bedroom and stuffed a swimming

costume and towel into her bag. The two girls she shared the room with didn't stir and leaving them still sleeping, she let herself out of the flat, hoping against hope that Max would join her at Wannsee, even if he couldn't do so for very long.

Soldiers and civilians were already on the streets, clearing up the rubble caused by the previous night's raid. Her area of the city hadn't been badly hit, but by the time she reached the train station it was obvious that the area around it hadn't been so lucky. Some shattered buildings were smoking and one or two fires still burned.

Praying that no one she loved had come to harm she entered the S-Bahn station, wondering if Max was striding through Anhalter Bahnhof, the station the trains from Munich terminated at.

He had told her enough for her to be able to guess at his reason for being in Berlin. It would be in order that he could meet up with Nicholas and other members of what she always thought of as the conspiracy. The plot.

How much Ilse knew about it, she didn't know. It wasn't something they ever spoke about.

She boarded the Potsdam, via Wannsee, train, aware of how ironic it was that she and Ilse – and everyone in the conspiracy – were aiding and abetting a British intelligence agent when they were all such loyal Germans.

That, though, was the crux of it. It was because they *were* such loyal Germans – because they loved their country so deeply – that they wanted to free it from Hitler's Nazi grip and form a new government. An anti-Nazi government that would restore individual freedom and be able to sue for peace with Britain before Hitler brought even further nightmares upon the country by engaging it in an invasion of Russia. And that was what Max wanted too. Despite his English upbringing he was, at heart, just as much of a Berliner as she was.

As the train pulled out of the station she wished he were

living in Berlin, and not Munich. 'I can't, Lotti,' he had told her regretfully when she had brought up the subject with him. 'Claus would be too aware of me and that could become dangerous. He may have become deeply disillusioned with National Socialism, but he's still very far from sharing Nicholas's sentiments. What his reaction would be if he were to discover the conspiracy is too problematic. Where Claus is concerned, it's best I keep out of sight.'

Thinking about Claus and the high-ranking Nazi company he kept was not pleasant and she wished she had brought a magazine with her so that she could focus her thoughts elsewhere. As she hadn't, she simply thought of happier times. Times when she, Ilse and Claus had gone to Wannsee to spend the day on the water, swimming and sailing with Max, Hugo and Nancy.

Today, she didn't sail. Until late afternoon she swam and sunbathed and swam some more and then, certain that all hope of Max joining her was gone, returned to Berlin, her disappointment intense.

There was a message waiting for her on her dressing table: *The singer at the Three Kings is sick. Can you stand in for her?* It was signed by Maria, one of her flatmates.

The only nightclubs still in business were those approved of by the regime and the Three Kings was no exception. It would, she knew, be packed to capacity with army and police officers. She sighed heavily. It couldn't be helped. Work was work and, as there was no message from Max, she might just as well be at the Three Kings as anywhere else.

The house where the key members of the conspiracy were meeting was in the leafy, lake-studded suburb of Grunewald. A white-painted chalet with a decorative wooden balcony running right round the first floor and, at ground level, a

411

veranda, it belonged to Peter Wasserman, a theatre-director friend of Nicholas's who, before the war had started, had left Berlin to try his luck in Hollywood. Ever since, the house had remained untenanted and, as far as Nicholas was concerned, it made the perfect trysting place. Whatever happened, there could be no comeback on Peter. He was long gone and far beyond the arm of any Nazi retribution.

Max was the last person to arrive and, by the time he did so, all the men he had come to meet were nervously on their second drinks. Though he had not previously met them, he knew them all. One of them was an ex-minister who had, four years ago, received the Nazi Party's highest decoration, the Golden Badge of Honour, for his services in shaping Germany's economy for war purposes. A devout Roman Catholic, he had broken with Hitler after the Night of Broken Glass had left him in no doubt as to the nature of the regime he had been serving.

Two of the others were army generals. Men who were vital to their plans. Another was a highly placed government minister and a member of the former aristocracy. There was a senior civil servant, a highly decorated Great War hero. The sixth member of the group was a young army officer Max instinctively knew was the person detailed to carry out the assassination. The seventh was Nicholas.

After the handshakes were over and they were all seated, Max said, 'I need to be able to inform London of the exact nature of your plans, gentlemen. Place, time. And the number of generals who, when the Führer's death releases them from personal oaths of loyalty to him, will openly support an anti-Nazi regime and sue for peace.'

'And we need an authoritative statement as to the way the new regime will be treated,' one of the generals said, steely-eyed. 'We need a guarantee that when Hitler is assassinated and a peace treaty is negotiated, it is negotiated on more generous terms than in 1918, when we got rid of the Kaiser.'

'Then let us put our cards on the table, gentlemen,' Max said, well aware that such a promise couldn't possibly be made and that he would have to tread very carefully if he were to avoid any senior members of the conspiracy getting cold feet and calling off the assassination. 'First of all, who is the man the British government will be directly dealing with in the immediate aftermath of Hitler's death?'

'Table ten want you to join them when you finish singing,' the manager of the Three Kings said to Lotti as she was about to step onto the club's small circular podium. 'They're celebrating in a big way and want some female company.'

'Then they should have brought some with them,' Lotti snapped, her green cat-eyes flashing fire. 'I'm a singer, not a prostitute!'

'Table ten after you sing, or you don't sing at all.'

The pianist was already playing the intro to her first song. With so few clubs now in existence Lotti had been looking forward to being able to sing, instead of waiting tables. Besides, it wasn't the first time she'd had to make herself agreeable to men she found disagreeable and she wouldn't have to do anything other than laugh and flirt.

'OK,' she said ungraciously, adjusting the T-strap of her knee-length, heavily sequinned black dress. 'But this isn't something I'm going to make a habit of.'

'Don't worry,' the manager snapped back. 'You're not going to be singing here often enough to be able to make a habit of it.'

Shooting him a look of contempt she stepped up onto the small dais in front of the band and launched into the popular 'Don't Ask How, Don't Ask Where'.

As she had known it would be, the club was full of uniformed officers. There were field-grey Wehrmacht uniforms, sinister black SS uniforms, even a sprinkling of grey-blue Luftwaffe uniforms. With a sinking heart she saw that the rowdy party at table ten were all SS men. Determining to stay at their table for no more than half an hour at the most, she sang the song she sang at every opportunity, Norbert Schultze's romantically wistful 'Lili Marleen'.

It brought the house down as it always did, and taking advantage of the good feeling she had aroused she sang Jerome Kern's 'The Way You Look Tonight' and then another American song, Cole Porter's 'Night and Day'.

When her set came to an end she left the dais to enthusiastic applause, so much so, she was sure the manager would have to eat humble pie and ask her to sing there again.

There was more noisy applause from the men at table ten when she joined them.

'So what is the celebration?' she asked, accepting a glass of champagne, knowing, as the men were SS officers, that there was every chance it would be good French champagne.

The officer nearest to her grinned and glanced down at his watch. 'In exactly an hour's time a group of German pigs planning to assassinate our beloved Führer are due to be arrested. It's a coup we've waited months for.'

Though Lotti's heart nearly stopped, her response was instantaneous. '*Wunderbar!*' she said gaily, somehow keeping a smile on her face, somehow managing not to break out in a sweat even though she was certain the German pigs in question were Max and Nicholas and their fellow plotters.

She moved from where she had been seated and sat provocatively on the officer's lap, sliding her arm around his neck.

'And will you and your friends get all the glory of making such an arrest?'

'No.' He said the word with heavy regret. 'The *Schweinehunde* in question are meeting in Grunewald.'

Lotti's heart began slamming so hard she was amazed the

young officer couldn't feel it through the black gabardine of his service uniform. Grunewald was a huge area. As well as leafy suburbs it encompassed forests and lakes – including Lake Wannsee.

For a hideous moment she wondered if Max's meeting was taking place at the restaurant they so often went to, then another officer at the table hiccuped drunkenly and, leering at her, said, 'They're meeting at the house of that homosexual Jewboy, Peter Wasserman. You never worked for Wasserman before he scooted off to America, did you, Fräulein Lennartz?'

Lotti gave a shudder of horror. 'No,' she said truthfully, relief making her feel giddy.

Ilse had worked for him. Before Wasserman left for America, Ilse and Nicholas had attended parties at Wasserman's secluded home in the Grunewald forest and, on one memorable occasion, she had been invited as well.

Was the telephone number still in her address book? If it wasn't, Ilse would have it, but would Ilse be at home? And how much time did she have left in which to phone the Wasserman house?

They had said the arrests were due to take place in an hour and the arresting SS unit would surely be in position around the house for twenty or thirty minutes beforehand. Time was running out so fast every second counted.

She moved suddenly, purposely spilling champagne down her dress, springing to her feet immediately she had done so. 'Now look what I've done,' she said in girlish despair. 'Will you excuse me while I go and change?'

There were loud demands that she didn't do so. One of the men offered to lick the champagne off the dripping-wet sequins.

'Five minutes,' she said, blowing a kiss. 'I'll be back in five minutes.'

It took her at least a minute to retrieve her handbag from

where she had left it at the side of the piano and to then lock herself into the Ladies toilet with it.

Feverishly, she rifled through the names in her address book. Wagner, Wahnfried, Warburg, Watzdorf. There was no Wasserman. Then, as sweat broke out on her forehead, she turned to the Ps. There was a long list of Peters. Peter Schaumberg. Peter Mertz. Pete Zeller. Pete Kempka and then, so low down the page it came under the Qs, Peter Wasserman.

She couldn't phone from the club. She would be seen. She had to phone from somewhere outside – and without being seen as she left. The window in the toilet was small and high, but she hadn't spent years working as a dancer for nothing.

Taking off her shoes, she stood on the toilet seat, opened the window as far as it would go and levered herself upwards, so that she could hang head first out of it. From then on it was just a case of wriggling until her chest was through the narrow opening as well, and then, with her hands on the sill for leverage, she jettisoned the rest of her body out of the window in a somersault that ensured she landed on her feet and not her head.

In the thick darkness of the blackout no one saw her spectacular exit, but how many minutes had it taken? Three? Four?

The area was one she knew like the back of her hand and she sprinted towards the nearest bar, descending the stairs that led to it with the agility of a cat.

Once inside and free of the blackout curtains, she made straight for the public phone booth. Only as she was dialling the number did it occur to her that the SS would have taken the precaution of cutting the telephone lines to the house. She gave a sob and then heard the sweetest sound she had ever heard in all her life. The connection tone and then Nicholas's voice, low and guarded as he repeated the phone number and waited for her to speak.

416

'It's Lotti.' Her voice was scarcely recognizable, even to herself. 'You're all about to be arrested! You must leave the house now! Immediately!'

He didn't even waste a second in speaking to her. He simply crashed the receiver back on its hook and she was left listening to nothing but the dialling tone.

With clammy, shaking hands, she replaced the receiver. She'd done it. She'd warned them. With luck – if an SS squad weren't already in position around the house – they would all get away. Max would be safe.

Her heart was beating so erratically it hurt. Would she be safe, though? When the SS discovered that their birds had flown they would know the men meeting in the house had been tipped off, and the men she had left behind her in the Three Kings would remember their careless talk and her immediate disappearance after it. She would be in a cell in Gestapo headquarters within hours.

Fleeing now, though, was no answer. If she didn't return to the Three Kings – and to the SS men on table ten – they would put two and two together even more quickly. So quickly that Max and the others might not be able to escape at all.

She took a deep, steadying breath, knowing what it was she had to do, praying that when her bluff was called and she was taken to Gestapo headquarters to be interrogated, God would give her the strength to survive whatever awaited her there.

TWENTY-FIVE

Berlin, June 1941

Backstage at the Three Kings Lotti hurled herself out of her black sequinned stage dress and into the red dress she had worn on her way to the club from home. The men at table ten were even noisier and drunker than when she had left them.

Feverishly, as she joined them she wondered how long ago that had been. Eight minutes? Ten minutes? Whatever the length of time, it had certainly been longer than the five minutes it would have taken her to step out of a champagne-sodden dress and into a dry one.

None of the men remarked on the length of time she had been away. Champagne was flowing. They were jubilant at the prospect of the glory about to come to their section for the capture of the high-flying Grunewald traitors, speculating recklessly as to who would be among their number, certain there would be a general or two, certain others would be members of the old aristocracy.

Lotti kept an admiring and provocative smile on her gamine-like face, her eyes straying almost constantly to her small wristwatch. Max and Nicholas and the other conspirators would be well away from Grunewald by now.

The SS swoop on the house was scheduled to happen in another five minutes. How long it would be before a message as to its failure was given to the men carousing around her she didn't know, but she did know it would be best for her if, by the time such a message arrived, she were long gone.

Other women joined the table and as the men erupted into a raucous rendition of the Horst Wessel song, she slipped from the knee she had been perched on and squeezed between the crowded, smoke-wreathed tables towards the rear of the club, leaving it as unobtrusively as possible. She had to get home. She had to collect money and personal items and disappear somewhere safe until she could make contact with Max.

The darkness of the blackout was all enveloping and as she hurried along the bomb-damaged streets she speculated ceaselessly as to what was happening now that the SS knew their birds had flown. How long would it be before they realized who it was who had tipped off the conspirators? And how long would it take them to find her?

Her relief, as she turned into her street and saw that no sinister-looking cars were parked in it, was immense. With the relief came another thought. For the men in the club to point the finger of suspicion at her, they would have to admit to their criminally careless drunken talk. And for all of them, the consequences would then be dire. That being the case, the likelihood of them saying nothing about it – and therefore saying nothing about her – was high.

With the heavy dread that had been weighing her down beginning to lift, she ran up the stone steps to the front door. The conclusion the SS would most likely come to was that whoever had told them of the Grunewald meeting had done so on the strength of rumour alone. That in actual fact there never had been such a meeting. And if that was the case, then she wasn't in the slightest danger at all.

Almost light-heartedly she turned her key in the lock and opened the door.

They were waiting for her.

Not SS men, but plainclothes Gestapo.

Behind them, wide-eyed with fear, were two of her flatmates.

'If you had not returned here,' one of the men said almost conversationally as he strolled towards her, 'we would have arrested them in your stead. Your friends have a lot to thank you for, Fräulein Lotti Lennartz.'

As they led her out of the house a large black car slid from around the corner, stopped in front of it and she was bundled into the back. The journey to Prinz-Albrecht-Strasse was so frighteningly swift she was there long before she had got her thoughts into order.

The car swept to a halt in front of the huge, grey granite building and as it did so she was still struggling with the dilemma of whether or not to tell them her real name was Lotti Remer and that she was the sister of Claus Remer, head of the giant Remer steelworks.

If Max hadn't been involved in the reason for her being there, it was what she would most certainly have done, for if anyone could get her out of the mess she was now in, that person was Claus – or one of Claus's influential friends.

The problem was that though the men at the club hadn't known the identities of any of those they had believed were about to be arrested, it didn't mean those senior to them didn't know. That a Remer was a spy for the British and a contact of those conspiring to kill the Führer was something that just might be known and, if it were, Claus might already be walking a perilous tightrope, albeit one he wasn't aware of.

Deciding that she posed far less danger to Claus and Max as Lotti Lennartz than she did as Lotti Remer, she decided to volunteer nothing about her real name until official paperwork brought it to light. Until then she would remain Lotti Lennartz. And she would remain emphatically bewildered as to why she was being questioned in Gestapo headquarters.

'You overheard that an arrest was to be made at a certain house in the Grunewald and you tipped off those about to be arrested.'

The room she was in was small, the window all boarded up. She was seated on a chair. Her hands were bound behind her back and there was a light shining in her face. A light blazing so fiercely it was hard to think straight.

'No,' she said for the umpteenth time. 'I warned no one. I got in touch with no one. What is it to me if someone in Grunewald was about to be arrested?' There was brazen indifference in her voice. 'I don't live in the Grunewald. I don't have neighbours in the Grunewald. I was drinking champagne and enjoying myself. That is all.'

She gave a careless lift of her shoulders.

A blow came out of nowhere, sending her reeling from the chair and crashing heavily onto the stone-flagged floor.

Unable to break her fall with her hands, her face caught the full impact.

'You tipped off those about to be arrested,' the voice from behind the arc light said again as she struggled to her feet. 'And that means that you know the identities of those who were about to be arrested. I need names, Fräulein Lennartz. And you are going to give them to me.'

'I can't give you what I don't know,' she said as she was forced back down onto the chair. 'I'm a singer.' She fought to keep her fear under control, not wanting to give him the satisfaction of seeing it. 'I was sent to join a table and I joined it. I didn't pay any heed to what was being said. Why should I? It was nothing to do with me.'

'You left the table. You made a phone call. And the result

421

of that telephone call was that no one was in the house at Grunewald when SS officers went to make their arrest. Now once again – who did you telephone? What is his name? What are the names of the friends who were with him?'

'I don't know. I didn't make a telephone call. I went backstage to change my dress. I can't tell you what I don't know and I don't know the names of those you say were about to be arrested.'

The dove-grey uniformed figure behind the arc lights didn't move, but from out of the darkness someone else did. The same man who had sent her crashing to the floor stepped towards her again, this time accompanied by a man whose presence she had been unaware of.

The chair she was seated on was fitted with straps and as one of the men unbound her hands, the other began buckling cold, unyielding leather around her waist and her legs. Her left arm was anchored behind her, her right arm was yanked forward, her hand slammed palm down on a table bare save for a black Bakelite telephone.

'Once again, Fräulein Lennartz,' the man behind the arc light said, invisible to her but for the gleam of the silver tabs on his uniform. 'The name of the man you telephoned at Grunewald. The names of his co-conspirators.'

As her hand was held in place by a vice-like grip on her wrist, the man who had strapped her to the chair took hold of her index finger. She knew what he was about to do; knew that her finger was about to be broken.

Steeling herself for the pain that would jackknife through her body, she said steadily, 'I made no phone call. I know no names. I know nothing of any meeting.'

Her finger was wrenched violently upwards, against the joint.

Despite her fierce determination not to, she screamed, convulsed with pain.

'One name will satisfy me, Fräulein Lennartz. Just one name and I will sign the order for your release. Who, among the men meeting at Grunewald, was your contact? Who did you telephone?'

She shook beads of sweat from out of her eyes. 'I know nothing of any meeting at Grunewald.' Her voice was so hoarse she scarcely recognized it. 'I have no contacts. I made no telephone call.'

Her second finger was taken hold of. This time she knew what the agony was going to be like. This time she knew they wouldn't stop until all her fingers were broken. And then what would they do?

As if reading her mind, her interrogator leaned forward into the light so that she could now see his face. 'You're being very foolish, Fräulein. Do you think any of the high-ranking men whose names you refuse to give would do the same for you? If you do, then you know nothing of what happens to men undergoing torture by electric current. They scream like animals and would incriminate their own mothers in order to have it stopped. Why suffer similarly when all you have to do to be able to walk out of here and go home, is to tell me the names of the men who met tonight in Grunewald.'

As he finished speaking he adjusted the arc light. For the first time the corners of the room were illuminated. There was a table similar to a massage table in one of the corners. A table fitted down either side with broad leather straps. Beneath it was a black box with wires coming from it.

This time no power on earth could have kept the fear from showing in her eyes.

'Just one name.' His voice sliced across her nerve ends. 'Just give me one name and I'll sign the order for your release. If not, when you have no more fingers left –' He lifted his shoulders expressively.

She was soaked in sweat and there was a terrific pounding of blood in her ears. 'I don't know any names,' she said again, pain roaring through her veins. 'I know nothing about any meeting. I made no telephone call.'

Her second finger was wrenched upwards and jerked backwards until the bone snapped.

She thought she was going to pass out. She wanted to pass out. She wanted to die so that it would be impossible for her to speak Max's name.

'Once again,' the implacable voice said. 'The name of the person you telephoned.'

Her hand hurt so much she wanted to vomit. 'I made no telephone call,' she said yet again. 'I know no names. I know nothing about any meeting.'

By the time her third and little fingers had been broken her voice was a whisper, and when she wasn't whispering that she knew no names, knew nothing about any meeting, she was retching.

'Wire her up.' The voice that now came from beyond the arc light seemed to be completely disembodied as it said dispassionately, 'But be careful of the voltage. We want her to talk, and she can't do that if she's dead.'

It was then, as she was dragged from the chair to the table and as they were strapping her down, that the telephone rang.

In the minutes after Lotti's telephone call, Max acted with ice-cool professionalism. His first priority was the safe abandonment of the Wasserman house. As it was likely that all the conspirators' identities were now compromised, he was emphatic that Nicholas didn't risk returning to his home, but that he went instead to a house pre-arranged as being safe.

'I'll contact Ilse,' he said. 'She'll be with you within half an hour. And then you're to lie low, Nicholas. If there are going to be any arrests, we'll know very soon.'

'And the assassination attempt?' Nicholas had been grey-faced. 'Can we risk going ahead with it?'

'Not as scheduled – and not in the future with the same group of people. Not till you know who informed on you.'

From then on, his concern had been Lotti. Where had she been when she had made her telephone call? Where was she now? And how had she become privy to the information that those plotting to kill Hitler were meeting at the Wasserman house and that all of them were about to be arrested?

Thankful there was no air raid, he went to the small restaurant she regularly worked at, only to be told that she had taken the entire day off in order to spend time with a friend she hadn't seen for a long time and who was visiting Berlin. Well aware he was the friend in question, he then made immediately for her flat in Lützowstrasse.

At first he thought no one was home and then, with the utmost reluctance, one of Lotti's flatmates opened the door to him.

'It's Max,' he said to the dishevelled-looking girl. 'Lotti's cousin. Where is she, do you know?'

'They've taken her.' The girl's fingers, as she held the door open a mere crack, trembled. 'They came for her about an hour and a half ago.'

'Gestapo?'

She nodded.

Fear fogged his throat. An hour and a half ago. It was just possible she was still waiting to be questioned. It was just possible she was still unhurt. Possible, but not very likely.

The door closed in his face and he swung round, looking down the darkened steps into the blacked-out street, saying savagely beneath his breath: 'Think, Max. Think!'

Lotti hadn't known about the Grunewald meeting from him or from Nicholas. Therefore it was something she had overheard and the only place Lotti was likely to overhear anything was in a club. A club these days meant soldiers on leave and SS men. He could quite easily envisage what the scenario had been and why the finger of suspicion had pointed at her so blatantly when the SS had descended on the Wasserman house and found it empty.

The line of questioning she would be undergoing at Gestapo headquarters was obvious and somehow he had to put an end to it. No matter what the risk to himself, he had to get her out of there.

Perspiration was cold on his forehead. No matter what they did to Lotti, she wouldn't talk. He knew that as surely as he knew he was still breathing. She would die rather than incriminate him or Nicholas. At the thought of Lotti dead, he felt like a man on the brink of an unspeakable abyss.

A world without Lotti and her dauntless buoyancy and irrepressible sense of humour was impossible to imagine. Ever since he had been ten and she had been five they had been inseparable on every possible occasion. She was his best friend. His chum. She was the one person in the world who knew him even better than he knew himself. She was his other half. His soulmate.

Realization hit him like a hammer.

Lotti was his life. Why had he never seen it before? Why had he never recognized what was now so blindingly, glaringly obvious? He loved her. He'd always loved her. And he didn't have to ask if she loved him. The answer was in her actions of that evening. She'd put her life on the line for him and was probably, at this very moment, undergoing the most barbaric kind of torture.

He sucked in his breath and began to run.

Every favour he'd ever done for Fritz was now going to be

called in for repayment – and every penny he could lay his hands on was going to go into persuading Fritz to make a vital phone call from Gestapo headquarters in Munich.

'Max? Max, my friend, what the devil of a time is this to wake a man up?'

Max could hear a muffled female protest as Fritz pushed himself up against the pillows and switched on a bedside light.

'I need a favour.' He knew that if the line was bugged Fritz would know of it and would immediately cut him short. To his unspeakable relief, he didn't do so.

'A favour? What sort of a favour can I do for a man with your connections?' There was good-natured humour in Fritz's voice. He'd been a farm labourer in the days before becoming an ardent National Socialist had changed his way of life for ever. Having a personal friend as educated and sophisticated as Max was a source of great pleasure to him.

'I'm in Berlin with a girlfriend and she's just been arrested on suspicion of making a phone call to warn off a group of anti-Hitlerites who were about to be arrested. It's a nonsensical situation. I was with her at the time she's supposed to have made this phone call and she's as loyal to the Führer as Himmler! She's been taken to Prinz-Albrecht-Strasse, though, and you know what that means. As someone in a reserved occupation I don't carry much clout with the Gestapo. If you could phone Prinz-Albrecht-Strasse from Gestapo headquarters in Munich, saying that under interrogation for something else entirely someone just brought in to you has admitted making the phone call warning the anti-Hitlerites to fly, it would get her off the hook.'

'Whoa!' There was no amusement now in Fritz's voice. 'That's not just a favour, Max. That's a request that could end up with someone being shot – and that someone would be me.

What happens when headquarters in Berlin ask for the prisoner to be sent to them?'

'You say he died while being questioned. You can do it, Fritz. But you have to do it now, immediately, or Lotti will be dead.'

'Lotti?' Fritz sat up so sharply a pillow tumbled to the floor. 'Lotti Lennartz?'

'The very one. I'll be so grateful if you get her out of Gestapo hands that I'll give you all my worldly wealth – and that's a lot, Fritz. Lotti will be so grateful she'll give you whatever you want – and I'll turn a blind eye.'

Fritz chuckled. He was being offered Lotti Lennartz on a plate and all for the sake of a phone call.

'Leave it with me,' he said. 'Pulling a fast one over those snobbish bastards in Berlin will give me great satisfaction.'

The line clicked and Max replaced the receiver on the hook with shaking hands. That there was no way Lotti would repay Fritz with sexual favours went without saying – and what Fritz's reaction would then be was anybody's guess. For the moment, though, it didn't matter. All that mattered was that whatever fiendish torture she was undergoing ceased immediately. All that mattered was that she was released. And all that mattered in the future was that she knew he loved her – and that he would love her always and for ever.

The ringing of the telephone reverberated around the small, stone-floored room. Lotti's interrogator answered it, and as he did so, one of the men fastened the last strap across her legs. He was bending down to the box with the wires protruding from it when the interrogator raised a hand, forestalling him.

'Yes, Major,' he said, sounding startled. 'Yes, of course. At once.' And then, before putting the receiver back on its rest, he added, 'Heil Hitler.'

428

He switched off the arc light and opened the door. 'You may not have thought this was your lucky day, Fraülein Lennartz,' he said drily, 'but let me assure you that it is. It's possibly the luckiest day you will ever know.'

To the two men waiting for further orders he said merely, 'She is to be released. The man who made the phone call to the Wasserman house is undergoing questioning in Munich. He'll be transferred here in the morning. Goodnight, gentlemen. Heil Hitler.'

When the straps were unbuckled and she was allowed to get off the table, her legs would barely support her. One-handedly and in agonizing pain, she struggled back into the clothes that had been torn from her. Who the man was in Munich who had falsely admitted to making the phone call she had made, she didn't know. She only hoped and prayed that it wasn't Max.

At the thought that it *was* Max, that this was something Max was doing in order to save her, she paused in her struggle to put on her dress. She couldn't let Max sacrifice himself for her.

She turned to her torturers, about to speak, and then realized the insanity of what she was about to do. Max was far too clever to simply put himself in her place. The man in Munich would be non-existent, and by the time the Gestapo discovered he was non-existent she would be somewhere safe. Max would see to that. Somehow he had engineered her release out of this hellhole and he would never allow her to be brought back to it.

The night sky was tinged with grey when she stepped out of the vast building and into Prinz-Albrecht-Strasse. On legs threatening to give way beneath her she began walking, struggling to decide where she should go. Her apartment in Lützowstrasse was no longer safe. She couldn't risk rearrest. Nicholas and Ilse's apartment, then? Or her parents' apartment in Charlottenburg?

429

The pain from her mangled, broken, tortured hand was indescribable. She needed painkillers. A doctor. A hospital.

She needed Max.

As she approached the corner with Saarlandstrasse, a two-seater black Steyr zoomed to a halt a few yards away. The car was Nicholas's, but the driver was Max.

Her joy and relief as Max vaulted from the car were so intense she reeled against the building she had been walking past, sagging against it, nursing her mutilated hand, tears flooding down her cheeks.

He sprinted towards her and, knowing he was about to seize her in a bear hug, she cried out urgently: 'No! My hand, Max! Please be careful of my hand!'

He stopped abruptly only inches away from her. The expression in his eyes, as he looked at what they had done to her, was one she knew she would never forget.

'Let me help you to the car,' he said thickly. 'I'm taking you to the hospital. To the Charité.'

Unable to hold her to him he gently tilted her face to his. 'Before we go, there's something I have to tell you. Something I should have told you long ago.'

She flinched, certain he was about to tell her he was going to marry his Munich girlfriend; that he had, perhaps, already married her.

'I love you, Lotti,' he said sombrely. 'I've always loved you and I've been too blind to know it.'

As she looked at him uncomprehendingly, he realized she thought he was speaking of family love, the kind of love he felt for all his cousins.

'I'm in love with you, Monkeyface.' His voice was thick with an emotion he'd never felt before, and beneath the thick tumble of his curly hair his eyes blazed the truth of what he was telling her. 'Will you forgive me for being such a fool as not to have realized it before? Will you try to feel differently

430

about me? To love me in the same way I so desperately love you?'

Lotti made a sound that sounded like a sob. 'I won't have to try,' she said, wondering how anyone in such pain could be so happy. 'I've loved you, the way you now love me, ever since I was fourteen or fifteen. You're the only person I've ever loved. The only person I ever will love.'

With exquisite tenderness, keeping his body away from hers so that it wouldn't even brush her hand, he lowered his head to hers.

She gave a small sigh and as his tongue slid past hers, her uninjured hand moved up to caress his neck, her fingers tightening in the coarseness of his hair.

From somewhere in the distance there came the sound of an early morning tram traversing Potsdamer Platz. Much nearer to them a pigeon squawked. It had been the most terrible night of her life and now it was the most wonderful morning she had ever known.

As he finally raised his head from hers, he said huskily, 'We can make love for the rest of our lives, sweetheart, but we need to get your fingers into splints as fast as possible.'

Despite the agonizing pain she was in she smiled loving agreement, her heart bursting with happiness as he slid his arm around her shoulders and led her gently towards the car.

TWENTY-SIX

Yorkshire, May 1942

Nestled next to Adam in their vast, brass-headed bed, Vicky woke early. She lay for a few moments, savouring the closeness and comfort Adam's body gave her. He was breathing deeply, still fast asleep. She moved away from him a little in order to look at the bedside clock, doing so carefully so as not to disturb him.

It was 5.30. There were no sounds from other parts of the house. Her evacuee children were, thank goodness, still sleeping as deeply as Adam. She wondered what had woken her so early and then realized it was the sound of a blackbird singing its heart out down by the river.

Aware now that sleep wasn't going to return she swung her legs from the bed and dressed, pulling on a hand-knitted Fair Isle jersey and a well-worn tweed skirt. Being so early it was still very chilly, but she didn't put on any stockings. Nylons were now nearly impossible to come by and not an item of clothing she regarded as essential.

Slipping her feet into a pair of comfortable flat shoes she let herself quietly out of the room and walked along the corridor to her father's room. At eighty-three, he was virtually bed-bound and often didn't sleep well.

'Are you all right, Dad? Would you like a cup of tea?'

'Not just yet, dear. Perhaps after you've taken Tinker for a walk. That is what you are about to do, isn't it?'

She nodded, blew him a kiss and continued on her way. At the foot of the stairs Tinker padded to meet her from his sleeping place by the Aga. The kitchen was the one room in the house that was always pleasantly warm and Tinker no longer cared for climbing stairs.

'Morning, Tink,' she said, as he waited to be scratched beneath his chin. 'Have we time to walk down to the river and through the woods?'

His tail wagged eagerly. The walks she took him on were always gentle-paced and he wasn't so old that he'd given up all hope of catching a rabbit or some other poor, unsuspecting creature when out on them.

Vicky, aware of his hopes and knowing there was little chance of his fulfilling them, walked out of the house and onto the broad terrace that fronted what had once been immaculate rolling lawns.

They were immaculate no longer. Because of Shuttleworth Hall's vast acreage of nursery gardens, now turned over entirely to the production of fruit and vegetables, the lawns had not, so far, been ploughed and furrowed. They had, though, been left untended. On the morning after the Japanese attack on Pearl Harbor, Paul had left Germany for America. Four days later, when Germany declared war on America, he had walked into a New York army recruiting office. He had written to explain.

Dearest Aunt Vicky,

I'm sorry the growing of fruit and vegetables for Britain's war effort is down to you entirely – though you'll get plenty of help from Will and the Berlin contingent, with no doubt a couple of Land Girls thrown in for good measure.

By the Berlin contingent he had meant Hester's two cousins who, with their families, were still living happily in Shuttleworth Hall's west wing after being given refugee status as agricultural trainees.

Paul had been right in thinking there was enough help on hand for her to be able to continue managing without him, but there wasn't so much help that time and attention could be given to luxury activities such as immaculate-lawn tending. Now, as she walked with Tinker in the direction of the river, some of the grass was knee-high and thick with buttercups.

Adam had been deeply gratified by Hitler's action in declaring war on America. 'It's the beginning of the end, Vicky,' he had said with confidence. 'It's Hitler's second great tactical error. The first was opening up a second front by invading Russia. No one has invaded Russia successfully, not even Bonaparte. This mistake is even crasser. Who knows for how long America would have remained stubbornly neutral if Germany hadn't declared war on her? And who knows for how long we would have been able to survive without America fighting alongside us? Now, though, we'll have American warships and warplanes and, very soon, her armies fighting on our side. Hitler has doomed himself. He doesn't stand a chance.'

That had been five months ago and though America's entry into the war had certainly boosted British spirits, it hadn't, as yet, showed any sign of putting a nail into Hitler's coffin. The war, now two-and-a-half-years old, still ground on.

Vicky tried hard not to think about it, but with her family and extended family involved so deeply – and on both sides – it wasn't an easy thing to do. Paul was stationed at an American army training camp in northern Ireland, which made her hopeful that the longed-for invasion of Europe was going to be sooner rather than later. Hugo was in Bomber Command, taking part in raids on naval facilities in the Atlantic and north Germany.

Nancy was back in London, still working for Reuters. Just short of a year ago, when Paul had still been in Berlin, she had received a letter from him via one of his American relatives, telling her that not only was he in love with a German girl, a nurse by the name of Eva Kestler, but that Lotti and Max were in love.

Knowing of how close they had always been it was something that hadn't surprised her in the least. It had flabbergasted Adam.

'Good God!' he'd said, his sandy eyebrows rising so high they nearly disappeared into the thick thatch of his curly hair. 'First he's in love with one cousin and then, when that doesn't work out, he falls in love with her sister! It's downright incestuous!'

'He was never truly in love with Ilse,' she'd said, unruffled, and feeling a deep sense of rightness about the news. 'He was just mesmerized by her beauty and deeply infatuated with her. Lotti is different. He and Lotti are soulmates and always have been.'

There was mist still hanging about in the hollows near the river and a smell in the air of a warm, sunny day to come. As she reached the river bank and turned left, to walk down towards the woods, she wondered where her much-loved elder son now was. Was he still in Berlin? Was he in Munich? Was he still living under the name Max Remer, or was he now living under an alias? And for how long, if he were still in Germany, would British Military Intelligence keep him there?

Her fear for his safety was compounded by fears for Nicholas and Ilse's safety. She knew very well that Nicholas wanted nothing more than to oust Hitler and, with those who thought like him, to bring the war to an end by coming to a peace agreement with the Allies. As the only way to oust Hitler was to assassinate him, wondering how deeply they were involved in such a plot left her in a state of permanent nervous tension.

One thing was certain: Claus wouldn't be one of the conspirators. Whenever she thought of her nephew sporting his Hitler-autographed gold swastika pin in his jacket lapel or, even worse, dressed in his Nazi Party paramilitary uniform, she felt heartsick. The war may have riven the Yorkshire and Berlin sides of their family apart, but that was a separation that would, God willing, end when the war came to an end. The chasm dividing Claus not only from the Yorkshire side of his family, but from the Berlin side of his family as well, was much deeper and was, she feared, unbridgeable.

She was in the woods now and bluebells spread out around her in a seemingly endless azure sea. She stood still for a moment, drinking in the sight and scent of them. They represented, to her, the very essence of England, and at the thought of all that England was fighting for, her heart felt as if it were going to burst.

'We're going to win this war, Tink,' she said fiercely as he sniffed the air for rabbits. 'And Germans like Nicholas and his friends, Germans who represent everything that is good and fine about Germany, are going to help us win it.'

Paul scrambled out of the early morning milk train into Harrogate. He had a forty-eight-hour pass and the only place he wanted to spend it was at Shuttleworth Hall.

'Mind me asking if you're stationed near here?' a young woman with peroxide-blonde hair asked cheekily as she came to a halt behind him at the ticket barrier.

'Nope,' Paul said good-naturedly as the return half of his ticket to Liverpool was handed back to him. 'Sorry.'

'So am I,' the girl said glumly. 'You don't have any chewing gum on you, do you?'

Paul obligingly fished in his pocket and handed her an unopened packet.

Her face brightened. 'Ta very much. It may have taken you Yanks a long time to get here, but it was worth the wait.'

As Paul walked away from her, he was grinning. Her last comment was one he, and all the other American soldiers now stationed in Ireland, were well used to. 'What took you so long?' was a favourite remark, usually given by a weary-looking Tommy on leave.

'There's no train today to Little Ridding,' he was told when he inquired after one. 'Don't you Yanks know there's a war on?'

Being referred to as a Yank all the time, when he'd grown up in Yorkshire, was something it was taking him a little while to get used to. Another thing he found it hard to reconcile himself to was the expression of savage hate not only for Nazi Germany – something he was in full accord with – but for every single German without exception.

He didn't tell people about Eva. Eva was too special and precious for him to want her name bandied about by people who couldn't understand that not every German was a Nazi.

'Well, if they're not, why don't they rise up and bury Hitler ten feet under?' Mitch, one of his buddies at camp had once asked him.

He'd tried explaining that in a totalitarian state, where people could be executed for even making a joke about the Führer, rising up against him wasn't the easy option people living under a democracy thought it was.

'Why not?' Mitch had said belligerently. 'I betcha I'd have done it.'

'Maybe you would,' he'd said to him, 'but it would have cost you your life and though you may have that kind of

437

bravery, the majority of people don't,' and he'd gone on to tell him of how, after Hitler had come to power in 1933, his first priority had been to ensure that everybody did as they were told – or paid the price. 'And that price was brutal beatings, torture and ritual humiliation, Mitch. One word of dissent and, pow – you were in Dachau.'

'Yeah, well. *Someone* should get rid of the son of a bitch. And it'd be easier for a German to put a bullet through him or a bomb under him than it would be for anyone else.'

'Don't worry,' he'd said grimly. 'Some Germans have been risking their lives for years trying to do just that.' He'd thought of Nicholas and Ilse and their friends. 'And one day soon they're going to succeed – and then this bloody war will be over.'

As he walked out of the station, deciding that as there wasn't a train to Little Ridding he'd have to hitch a lift there, he wondered if he was right in assuming that, with Hitler dead, the entire monstrous Nazi regime would also collapse. Surely what would actually happen was that Himmler would replace Hitler? Or if Himmler did not replace him, then Goebbels would.

He began walking out of the centre of Harrogate in the direction of the Little Ridding road, remembering a conversation he had once had with Nicholas.

'Once Hitler's death frees the army from their sacred oath of allegiance to him, its senior ranking officers won't give the same oath to Himmler. They loathe him. Which leaves as candidates Göring and Goebbels. Göring has long since alienated other senior Nazis with his ridiculous vanity – he's now taken to wearing make-up – and Goebbels is a realist. He'd know the Nazi regime wouldn't survive without Hitler and my guess is that, when he hears of Hitler's death, he'll commit suicide. Once he does so, there'll be no other contenders for the title of Führer and the way will be clear for the generals and high-ranking civil servants in the conspiracy to form an anti-Nazi government acceptable to the Allies.'

'And you reckon they'll do so with the backing of the armed forces?' he had asked, unable to keep the doubt from his voice.

Nicholas had nodded. 'There is more than one group of conspirators plotting to kill Hitler,' he'd said, revealing more than he'd ever revealed to him before. 'And every one of them is made up mainly of army officers. The SS, of course, is a different matter, but without Hitler and Himmler, the SS will crumble.'

'And the Luftwaffe and the Kreigsmarine?' he had asked, fascinated.

Nicholas had hesitated and then had said, 'The air force and the navy are more problematic. The air force owes its very existence to Hitler and will be slower to give its support. As for the navy . . .' His forehead had furrowed in a deep frown. 'There's bitter rivalry between the navy and the army and there may be difficulties there – but there won't be difficulties that can't be overcome, Paul. Of that I'm sure.'

A lorry slowed to a halt beside him. 'Looking for a lift, mate?' its driver asked.

'I am if you're heading towards Little Ridding,' Paul said, banishing all thoughts of what support, from within Germany, an anti-Nazi government would receive if one of the many plots to assassinate Hitler succeeded.

'Hop in,' the driver said. 'You're in luck,' and then, as Paul slammed the passenger door closed behind him, 'Got any chewing gum, mate?'

Adam rolled over in bed, expecting to come into contact with his much-loved wife. When he didn't do so, he opened his eyes and looked at the clock. It was still only half-past six.

He blinked, lay there for a minute or two and then, seeing

absolutely no point in staying in bed on his own, flung the covers back and swung his legs to the floor.

As he ran lightly down the stairs he could hear movement in the kitchen and the sound of a wireless.

'In Yugoslavia,' a BBC newsreader was saying in plummy tones, 'German reinforcements have arrived to fight Tito's partisans. In the Indian Ocean, British troops have landed on the pro-Vichy French colony of Madagascar.'

Avoiding the kitchen he walked through the drawing room and stepped out of the house via the French windows that opened onto the terrace. It was a beautiful morning. The laburnum that grew against the house wall was in full glorious-yellow bloom and near to it a wisteria was a haze of misty violet.

Deeply grateful that Shuttleworth Hall was never likely to be blasted to smithereens by a Luftwaffe raid and feeling profound pity for the poor devils that were not so lucky, he strode off in the direction of the river.

Vicky saw him immediately she stepped out of the woods. At the sight of him striding towards her over lawn that had become a meadow, she was overcome by an intense feeling of déjà vu, her memory of when he had first done so, way back in the winter of 1918, so vivid it made her giddy. Then, the ground had been covered in snow and he had been home on leave from the horror that was Ypres, still in grief after Elise's death. With his blue eyes and red hair, she had thought him the handsomest man she had ever seen.

Now, twenty-four years later, she still thought him the handsomest man she had ever seen. She loved the way the scar through his left eyebrow gave it a permanently attractive quirk. She loved his sheer masculinity. The firm, straight mouth. The slight cleft in his chin. The tough, uncompromising line of his jaw. She loved the fact that a man so physically strong could be so gentle. And most of all she loved his imperturbable good nature.

'Get up any earlier, my love, and you'll be down here in the moonlight,' he said, walking up to her and drawing her towards him.

She slipped her arms around his neck. 'Moonlight might be a good idea. Think how romantic it would be.'

'Hussy,' he said, amusement thick in his voice.

She giggled. One of the other things she loved about her husband was how young he made her feel. He was now fifty-seven and she was fifty-four. It didn't seem like that. Where loving each other was concerned, it was as if they were no older than they had been in 1918.

She tucked her hand in his as they walked through the deep grass towards the house. 'What's your schedule for today?' she asked. 'The Keighley mill or the Bradford mill?'

'The Keighley mill, though I might slip over to Bradford if time allows. What about you?' He shot her a smile full of love. 'Are you going to be gardening or marketing?'

'Both, I expect, now there's no delivering of groceries. Not that shops have much in them to deliver and you can forget all about choice. It doesn't exist. You just take what you're given and like it. If it wasn't for the vast amount of fruit and veg we grow I don't know how we'd manage.'

From the open French windows emerged a small boy dressed for school in a shirt and short pants. 'Wotcha, Missus!' he called, waving his arms excitedly, like a windmill. 'Yer've got a visitor! A Yank! A real live one!'

Vicky's heart gave a leap. 'It must be Paul.' She broke into a run. 'He must have leave.'

'Why does that particular blighter always call you Missus?' Adam asked, keeping abreast of her with ease. 'Why can't he call you Mrs Priestley or give you the honorary title of aunt and call you Aunt Vicky, like the some of the other children do. Even calling you Vicky would be better than Missus.'

'Jimmy Spinx thinks calling me Missus is the height of

politeness.' Vicky panted breathlessly. 'And it's a much better way of trying to attract my attention than the one he used to use.'

'Why, what was that?' he asked, preparing himself to be appalled.

'Oy, you!'

Seconds later, they ran into the house to find Paul in the kitchen, the centre of avid attention.

Vicky threw herself into his arms. 'Paul! Oh, Paul! What a wonderful surprise! Oh, it's so good to see you.'

As Paul hugged her so tightly she could scarcely breathe, Jimmy's mother said, with down-to-earth practicality, 'Have you any nylons?'

'I might have.' Paul reluctantly returned his attention to the other people in the kitchen.

'I'd be really 'ppreciative if you 'ave.' She smiled at him winningly, all thoughts of giving her son his breakfast forgotten.

Aware that her real reunion with Paul would have to wait until later, and aware that though the four children seated around the table had already finished their breakfasts, Jimmy hadn't yet started his, Vicky cleared her throat. 'If Jimmy doesn't have his breakfast now, he's going to be late for school, Ivy.'

Ivy Spinx gave a flounce of her shoulders and sauntered across to the cooker. Seconds later there came the sound of an egg being cracked into a frying pan.

'Eggs?' Paul asked, his eyebrows rising as he gave Vicky a hug. 'I thought eggs were as scarce as gold these days?'

'Not for people who keep hens. And no, I don't keep any, but Violet does. I supply her with fresh vegetables and she supplies me with fresh eggs. It's a system that works a treat.'

As another mother came into the room and tried to gather the children together in order to walk them down to the village school, Vicky put the kettle on to make a pot of fresh tea.

None of the children was eager to leave the kitchen. They milled around Paul, fingering his uniform and asking ceaseless questions.

'Why are you here? Are other American soldiers going to be coming here?'

'My mam says American soldiers are black. You ain't black. Why ain't yer black?'

'Have yer been to 'ollywood, Mister? Have yer met Roy Rodgers?'

And from Jimmy: 'Have yer killed any Jerries yet? My dad's killed lots of Jerries. My dad's bin killing Jerries for *years*.'

'Shut up and don't be cheeky,' his mother said crossly, annoyed that the existence of Jimmy's dad had been brought to Paul's attention.

Trying to ignore the mayhem, Adam clapped Paul on the back, saying regretfully, 'I'm going to have to be making tracks for the mill in another twenty minutes or so, Paul. We'll catch up on things tonight. How long a leave do you have? Twenty-four hours or forty-eight?'

'Forty-eight.' With relief, Paul saw that the children were finally being herded out of the room. 'And I'm not looking for any high life, so don't start telling me of village dances or thrashes in Harrogate. I just want to wander around Shuttleworth Hall and pretend that the war doesn't exist.'

'High life?' Ivy Spinx said as a parting shot from the doorway. 'You won't find any 'igh life round 'ere. All you'll find round 'ere is miles an' miles of boring countryside and soddin' sheep!'

When the door had safely closed behind her, Paul grinned. 'I take it Ivy doesn't appreciate country life?'

'She loathes it,' Vicky said, equally amused. 'The only thing she likes about Little Ridding is the fish and chip shop, though even that has its disappointments.'

'And why is that?'

443

'It doesn't also sell pie and mash. And without pie and mash – and dancing at the Empire Square ballroom – life isn't worth living for Ivy.'

When Adam had left for Keighley and after Paul had reacquainted himself with what had once been his rose nursery and was now nothing but furrow after furrow of vegetables, they walked into Little Ridding together.

'It's hard not having news of them, isn't it?' he said as a member of the Home Guard pedalled past them on a rusty bicycle.

She nodded, knowing it must be even harder for him than it was for her, for Paul had not only family to worry about, but the woman he loved, also.

She shifted her empty shopping basket a little higher on her arm, saying as she did so, 'At the beginning of the war I thought we wouldn't have to worry like this. I thought Berlin would be too far away for our bombers to reach it.'

'So did we all,' Paul said drily. 'Including Göring.'

Vicky managed a slight smile. Rumour had it that Göring had assured Hitler British bombers would never reach Berlin – on the morning of the very day that the RAF carried out a three-hour bombing raid.

'I just pray they are all safe,' she said, her smile fading. 'Every morning and every evening, and lots of times in between, I just pray that all our family – and Eva – are safe.'

TWENTY-SEVEN

Schloss Niedernhall and Berlin, April 1943

Claus stood at the entrance of the vast, throng-filled drawing room and tried to still the nervous tic jumping at the side of his right eye. Will power had no effect on it. The tic still jumped, betraying his inner tumult as he played the part of a guest in the Schloss that still, in name at least, belonged to him.

The artwork on the walls did not belong to him. It had come mainly from France and some had come from Poland. From where he was standing he could see a battle scene by Piotr Michalowski.

He averted his eyes. He had not hung it there. It was 'spare' plundered booty. Immediately Poland had been conquered, Göring had issued orders for the seizure of the country's art treasures. As with French artworks, the greater part of them went to augment Hitler's and Göring's private art collections. The rest were dispersed among favoured members of the Nazi hierarchy and German museums. Schloss Niedernhall, now not only the country home of a government minister, but also a government and military conference centre, had received a generous allocation of works deemed unsuitable for placement elsewhere.

This evening's event at the Schloss was a purely social one. A party to celebrate the minister's fiftieth birthday. His invitation to it had caused Claus great irritation. He had not the slightest desire to be there, but failure to show would have been regarded as 'unsupportive' and would not have been wise.

Viewing the familiar room from his vantage point at the doorway, he rather thought a majority of the people in it would have preferred to be elsewhere. Though French champagne – as looted as the artworks – was being served, the atmosphere of gaiety was decidedly forced. The war was no longer going well and everyone knew it. One word that would not be being mentioned by anyone was 'Stalingrad'.

He nodded a greeting in the direction of one of Göring's aides. Göring himself wasn't present, which was not surprising under the circumstances. The only hope for the Sixth Army besieged at Stalingrad had been the Luftwaffe – and the Luftwaffe, Göring's responsibility for so long, had failed spectacularly. The result had been one hundred thousand half-starved, frost-bitten soldiers and twenty-four generals being marched off over snow and ice to prisoner-of-war camps in Siberia. Not even Goebbel's massive propaganda machine could hide the fact that it was the greatest defeat ever suffered by a German army.

Closer to home the war news was equally grim. The US air force, as well as the RAF, was now bombing key German cities, the USAF by day, the RAF by night. Wilhelmshaven and Emden had suffered badly. In Dortmund, industrial and munition plants had been hit hard. In the Ruhr, Essen had been hit by a firestorm that in one night had devastated scores of engineering works, damaging part of the mighty Krupp factories. So far his own factories, south of Essen, were unscathed, but for how long that state of affairs would continue was anyone's guess.

Berlin too had become a nightmare to live in. He'd done his best to persuade his parents to leave for somewhere out of reach of the present bombing raids, the Black Forest or southern Baden-Württemberg. His father, who had begun to suffer with a heart condition, had flatly refused. His mother's only response had been to say tartly: 'Where do you suggest in Baden-Württemberg, Claus? The Schloss?'

He put his half-drunk flute of champagne on the tray of a passing waiter, saying tersely, 'Get me a brandy, please. A large one.'

A figure in the uniform of a colonel, a prestigious Knight's Cross hanging from his collar, excused himself from the small group of people he had been talking with and strolled across to him.

'Good evening, Herr Remer. My name is Todt. Colonel Christian Todt. We met briefly last year when I was in the company of your brother-in-law, Count Schulenburg.'

Claus forced a tight, polite smile. He remembered Todt – and the occasion. He had been dining at Horscher's when Nicholas and Todt had walked in and been seated at a near by table. Ever since Hester's death he had seen very little of Ilse and Nicholas, or of Lotti. For them, and him, it was easier that way.

He'd liked the look of Christian Todt when he had shaken hands with him. He was tall and lean and, unusual in a soldier, academic-looking. He and Nicholas were obviously close friends and, as Nicholas chose his close friends carefully, it was recommendation enough as to Todt's character.

'Nice to meet you again,' he said, pressing a finger against the corner of his eye to still the jumping nerve.

'I understand this castle was in your family's ownership until a few years ago?' Todt said, eyeing the cavernous room and its stunning chandeliers admiringly.

'It still is.'

Even as he said the words, Claus wondered if they were true. Even more to the point, if they were untrue, he wondered if he cared. Only his parents had ever taken pleasure in living for long periods at the Schloss. He couldn't imagine himself ever doing so and certainly no other member of the family would want to live there. Apart from the use it was now being put to, it was a white elephant on a gigantic scale. The mansion on Unter den Linden was also fast becoming an unnecessary encumbrance.

In the days before the Great War a privately occupied home on Unter den Linden had held a great social *cachet*. The Kaiser's palace had been on Unter den Linden. It had been the scene of constant parades and ceremonials. In the aftermath of the war – and the aftermath of the Kaiser's flight to Holland – the aristocracy had decided they preferred to live in Tiergarten palaces. His father hadn't followed their example. The mansion on Unter den Linden was the Remer family home and fashion, for his father, hadn't come into it.

The waiter approached with his brandy and, as he lifted the glass from the tray, he wondered why he hadn't ridden roughshod over his father's wishes long ago and moved into a modern palatial villa in Grunewald.

'I understand one of the Krupp factories was badly damaged on the sixth of March,' Christian Todt said conversationally. 'Did Remer factories suffer also, that night?'

'No.' Claus dragged his thoughts back to the conversation. 'We were lucky. So far the Remer steelworks have not been hit.'

'The labour problem must be difficult for you these days. I have my doubts as to the efficiency of the Russian prisoners of war being shipped in to man the factories. I know Krupp employs a large number of them. How satisfactory do you find them?'

The word 'employs' was a euphemism for slave labour and

he was quite sure Todt knew it. He took a deep swallow of his brandy. 'So far I've found them quite satisfactory,' he said in the distinterested voice he'd adopted long ago when hiding his true feelings.

The brandy burned his throat, but didn't take the bad taste from his mouth. With the war going badly and every available able-bodied male conscripted into the forces, he'd had no option but to accept Russian prisoners of war into his factories. It wasn't something he had wanted to do and it certainly wasn't something he felt right about doing. The use of prisoners of war in armament factories was a flagrant violation of the Hague and Geneva conventions.

'Alfried Krupp has several hundred Jewish women prisoners working for him,' Todt continued musingly. 'Is that a road the House of Remer will be going down as well?'

Claus felt the tic near his eye begin jumping again. Only a week ago he'd received a directive from Fritz Sauckel, the Plenipotentiary General for the Allocation of Labour, instructing him that Jewish women imprisoned at Sachsenhausen would be supplementing the workforce in his Berlin clothing factories and that they would be housed in a near by bombed-out work camp from which the previous inmates, British POWs, had been removed.

The directive had gone on to say that the women were 'to be treated in such a way as to exploit them to the highest possible extent at the lowest conceivable degree of expenditure'.

He'd known what that meant. It meant there was going to be no adequate, or even nearly adequate, food provision for them. And these women were German-born. They were as German as Ilse and Lotti. It was then he'd begun to be plagued by the nervous tic near his eye and by a permanent gut-wrenching feeling of sickness and self-disgust in the pit of his belly.

He signalled to a near by waiter that his brandy glass was empty.

'Probably,' he said stiffly. 'There's scarcely a factory now without such a supplementary workforce.'

'Ah, yes,' Christian Todt said lightly, his eyes anything but light. 'An unending supply of labour is one of the great benefits of our being the master race and holding the power of life and death over millions of Poles, Czechs and Russians. Though when we invaded Poland and Czechoslovakia, I must admit, Herr Remer, that I did not realize we were doing so in order that one half of their population could be shipped as slave labour to Germany and the other half, particularly the intellectuals, were to be simply "eliminated". Naive of me, I must admit.'

That Todt had deliberately steered the conversation in the direction it had taken, was obvious. Claus wondered what he hoped to gain by it and then, as a waiter approached with his brandy, Christian Todt clicked his heels and moved away from him, the expression in his eyes one of open contempt.

It was then that Claus knew why Todt had singled him out to speak to. As a highly decorated soldier, Todt's opinion of industrial tycoons who had no experience of battle would always have been low, but the use of prisoners of war as slave labour was something that quite obviously offended every military principle he had ever lived by – and the House of Remer was using such prisoners in their hundreds.

He downed the brandy, understanding the contempt in Christian Todt's eyes only too well. It was a contempt he also felt and, as his contempt was directed against himself, he wondered how on earth he was going to live with it.

After over three long years of imprisonment, Hester scarcely knew if she was alive or dead, except she knew that death would be preferable; that death would be a blessed release.

For spilling gravy when serving it, she'd been savagely beaten by the Camp Commandant and banished from all kitchen duties. She hadn't, though, been sent back to Ravensbrück. She was still at Sachsenhausen; still living in total terror.

While she had been on privileged kitchen duties for the officers and Commandant, nearly all her fellow Jews had been transported elsewhere. As rumour had it, to camps in Poland. In their place had come hundreds of Russians. As a German she was kept separate from the Russian women and her fellow prisoners were German Jehovah's Witnesses who had been sent to the camp when their husbands had been imprisoned for refusing to use their skills in aiding the Nazi war effort or to do military service.

She was now one of the longest-surviving among the female prisoners and for that she had her time in the kitchens to thank, for there she had been able to supplement her meagre food ration and keep up her strength. There was no way of supplementing it now. The daily bread ration was 350 grams and she and the women she shared a table with had to break up the loaf given them and divide it into pieces themselves. It meant the pieces were always uneven and that there was always a largest one.

Time after time she was grateful for their devoutly Christian nature, as when Detta Rödel had wisely suggested they share the largest piece by rota.

As day after day she endured the agony that life had become and the back-breaking labour of the work she was now assigned to in the camp's brickworks, Detta was an inspiration to her. Though she now looked to be easily sixty, Detta was only her own age. Married, with two small children, all Detta had to do to be released from the hell they shared, was to renounce her religion. And Detta resolutely refrained from doing so.

'Sachsenhausen is a test,' she said often to Hester. 'Do you remember the story of Abraham in the Bible? He was told to sacrifice his son and the scriptures tell us he was willing to do it. But then our creator, Jehovah, saw that he was willing and so he didn't allow it. He just wanted to test his faith. And that is what I believe is happening to me.'

Though Hester had a profound faith of her own, she didn't share Detta's attitude to their suffering, for to her it didn't make sense, not when those around them were losing their lives so cruelly. She did, however, come to admire the depth of Detta's faith. And she especially valued Detta's staunch, supportive friendship.

'Don't do it,' Detta had said to her fiercely one day when, in freezing sub-zero temperatures, they had been forced to stand for hour after hour in the prison yard, waiting for a roll call to be taken.

Aware that Detta had been reading her thoughts, she had dragged her eyes away from the electrified fence that ran round the camp a yard or so in front of the high brick walls. It was the last resort for those unable to bear their suffering any longer and the temptation to do as they had done, to commit suicide by sprinting across and grabbing hold of it, had been nearly overpowering.

Now, as under close guard they limped and dragged themselves back from the brickworks towards Sachsenhausen's barracks, wearing nothing but rags and roughly made clogs, Detta whispered to her, 'I've heard a rumour some of the Russian women are being detailed as labour to a factory in Spandau. A clothing factory. Perhaps, with luck, they'll include us. The work can't be as hard as it is in the brickworks.'

They both knew they wouldn't be able to survive the backbreaking work in the brickworks for much longer.

Not wanting to attract the guards' attention, Hester merely nodded. Spandau was in the suburbs of Berlin, about twenty miles away. The thought of Berlin brought back such memories of her life there, memories of her childhood home in Haberlandstrasse and of the flat in Kaiseralle she and Hugo had lived in, that she wanted to weep. She wondered if Nicholas and Ilse were still living in the city, if Lotti was still sharing a flat in Lützowstrasse with her friends, if they were all still alive. And last, but not least, she wondered if they remembered her.

'Prisoners Rödel, Dresner, Abt, Riedweg, Stangl and Tuja are to join the *Untermensch* labour force for Spandau,' the guard said next morning, walking down the crowded barracks and slamming each bunk he passed with his truncheon.

Untermensch was the way the guards always referred to the Russians. It meant sub-human, dross, dung.

'Take your blankets. You may be moving into a camp nearer the factory.'

As she folded up the thin coarse cloth that masqueraded under the name of a blanket, Hester's eyes met Detta's. Hopefully, this was going to be a move for the better. Hopefully, they weren't going to find themselves travelling east, as the majority of the Jews in the camp had done two years ago. Travelling east never to be heard of again.

They travelled by train, in freight wagons. Hester estimated there were well over two hundred of them, all Slavs except for the handful of German Jehovah's Witnesses and herself. She and the Jehovah's Witnesses had clogs on their feet but the majority of the Russian women were barefoot, their hair shorn, their sole clothing a sack with holes for their arms and head. As she saw open festering sores on their legs and feet she knew that, hellish and degrading as her and Detta's imprisonment had been, the treatment meted out to them had not been as bad as that meted out to those the guards called *Untermensch*.

453

They weren't taken straight to the factory. They were taken to a badly bombed-out, empty POW camp. The barracks that were still standing were fitted with bare bunks, though not enough bunks for two hundred women. There was no visible kitchen. No toilet block as such, only urinals. No sign of any access to water.

When one of the Jehovah's Witnesses bravely pointed out that there were not enough bunks, the guard simply snapped that the urinals would have to be used as sleeping places.

Once again Detta's and Hester's eyes met. It looked as if their living conditions were going to be as grim as those at Sachsenhausen.

'But the work will be better,' Detta whispered to her the next morning when, after a breakfast of watery-thin gruel, they were marched out of the old POW camp and the half mile to the factory. 'And at least we're in Berlin, even though it is a part of the outskirts of the city I'm not familiar with. Are you?'

Hester shook her head. She had never spoken much to Detta about her life in Berlin. Detta knew she was married to someone called Hugo, who, though he had a German father, had been born in England and had an English mother. She had never told Detta that the name under which she was imprisoned was her maiden name. For someone in her situation, the name Remer was best left unspoken.

The factory was large and sprawling and gave the appearance of being well run. As they were marched across the factory yard, existing workers stopped what they were doing and crowded the windows to stare down at them.

'Well may they stare,' Detta whispered to her bitterly. 'We look like the living dead.'

A foreman hurried out to meet them, giving the SS officer in charge of the prisoners a hasty 'Heil Hitler'.

'There are two hundred of them,' the officer said,

presenting a clipboard to the foreman. 'Have you the authority to sign or will Herr Remer sign for them?'

'As if we were parcels,' she heard Marta Tuja say bitterly.

Hester paid her no attention. She was too busy trying to stay upright, trying not to totter with sheer shock.

Was the Remer in question, Claus? Was the factory making use of half-starved, regularly beaten and degraded women a House of Remer factory?

Sensing that for some reason she was on the verge of fainting, Detta and Marta pressed close against her so that they were able to give her support without appearing to do so.

By the time they were marched into the factory itself Hester had recovered her balance, but her head was still spinning. Vainly, she tried to remember if Hugo had ever mentioned to her that his uncle had a textile factory in Berlin. She didn't think he had done, but then Hugo had hardly ever talked about Josef Remer. He had never been close to him. 'Uncle Josef is a dyed-in-the-wool Nazi' was one of the rare things he ever said about him, and few family occasions had ever included him.

Claus was different, though. In the early years of her involvement with Hugo's family, Claus had been as much a part of family life as Ilse and Lotti had been. His Nazi Party membership and his taking over ownership of the Ruhr steelworks and armament factories had put distance between him and Hugo, but there had never been a complete break. She knew they had always regarded themselves more as brothers divided by ideology, than as cousins divided by it.

And now she was faced with the prospect that if the factory was a House of Remer factory, Claus was responsible for the conditions in the bombed-out camp she and his other slave labourers would be returning to that evening. That there would soon be deaths among the weakened, severely brutalized Russian women was obvious – and that someone who was related to her by marriage would be responsible for those deaths was something she could barely comprehend.

The SS guards who had accompanied them from Sachsenhausen remained with them both in the POW camp they were now occupying and at the factory, and there were still beatings for the slightest misdemeanour. Talking when they shouldn't talk, slowing down in their work output when exhaustion became too much for them.

'But at least there are no punishment blocks here,' Detta said to her with deep feeling one night as they lay in cramped discomfort on their narrow bunks. 'And we're no longer in fear of being taken out on someone's whim and shot.'

Hester bit her lip. Being taken out and shot had never held any terrors for her. What had held terrors were rumours of the special room where prisoners were killed by a gallows adapted to hang three or four prisoners at the same time.

Over the next few weeks their lives took on a set routine. A water tap was installed in the camp. A kitchen of sorts was established, their food rations never exceeding the rations they had received at Sachsenhausen. Though the work at the factory was lighter than the work at the brickworks, the constant presence of the guards still ensured their days were full of fear and pain. As slave labourers they were completely segregated from the other workers. When the regular Remer workers broke at lunchtime and headed for the canteen, they toiled on. The toilets at the factory were forbidden to them; instead, a primitive privy was provided for their use in the factory yard, a privy that couldn't be visited except in the company of an SS guard, a privy that was horrendously inadequate for two hundred women.

Their weakened condition on arrival at the factory, combined with the overcrowding in the barracks, the inadequate water supply, the lack of food, their intolerably long working hours, meant that it wasn't very long before there was a death.

'A Russian woman died today,' Marta, who worked in a different part of the factory, said to them one evening as they shared out their paltry food rations. 'The guards simply dragged her body to one side and left it there and the foreman raised hell. He said he was going to report what had happened to the manager – which means both the foreman and the manager will probably be in Sachsenhausen themselves by the end of the week.'

The next day there was a very curious atmosphere on the factory floor. The guards seemed strangely edgy. When the factory whistle signalled the lunch break, the women too were given permission to have an hour's rest, and when work finished for the general workers at the end of the day, it finished for them as well.

Over the next few days, other changes took place. Second-hand clothing and clogs were distributed. The stinking makeshift privy in the yard was demolished. One of the indoor toilets was allocated for slave-labour use. When Hester and Detta were allowed into it for the first time, they entered it as nervously as if it had been a palace.

'There are *washbasins*, Detta,' Hester said unbelievingly. 'And oh, dear God, Detta, there is *hot water*!'

It had been too much for her. She hadn't been able to wash her hands in hot water for nearly four years and as the SS guard who had escorted them to the toilet had not entered it with them, they frenziedly washed everything else they could before he bellowed at them to come out.

That evening, back at the barracks, the Russian women told them that the owner of the factory had been visiting it on the day one of their number had died. 'And it seems he has clout,' a Russian woman said, 'even with those devils from hell, our guards.'

The factory owner's clout continued. The next day, there was bread and soup provided for all slave labourers at lunchtime.

'This won't have come from prison rations,' Detta said, between greedy mouthfuls. 'This will have come from his own pocket. Jehovah is providing for us, Hester. We're going to survive this war, just as I told you we would.'

Hester refrained from pointing out that it was the factory owner who was providing for them. If Detta chose to believe he was doing so because God had prompted him, it was fine by her. What she wanted to know was whether or not the factory owner was Claus.

She had the answer to her question two days later.

A batch of Wehrmacht uniforms had swung through on the overhead rail, faulty. The foreman demanded she leave the packing room to inform the foreman in the inspection room. For a slave labourer it was practically a task of responsibility and gave her a moment that almost felt like freedom. A moment marred by the presence of the SS guard who heaved himself away from where he had been sitting in order to accompany her.

This wasn't Sachsenhausen, though. In blessed wonder, she realized she was no longer in fear of being sexually violated, not while she was on factory premises. In the factory, things like that no longer happened.

The walk from one department to the adjoining one was short. Within yards of the inspection room, the inspection-room doors suddenly opened and a flurry of people came out.

They weren't workers. They were high-ranking officials. Terrified he was going to be severely reprimanded for escorting a slave labourer along a corridor used by senior management, the SS guard flung her flat against the wall and sprang to instant attention, giving a smart salute and a 'Heil Hitler'.

458

Hester felt the breath leave her body, not because of the impact, but because the tall, immaculately suited blond-haired figure in the centre of the group of men now walking past her, was Claus.

Her first reaction was that he looked ill. The skin was stretched tight across the high cheekbones he had inherited from his mother and a nervous tic was jumping convulsively at the corner of his eye.

And then he saw her.

His eyes widened, the blood leaving his face. In a beat of time that could not have been more than a few seconds, she saw outright disbelief, total horror – and the realization that it would be fatal if it became suspected that he not only knew her, but was related to her by marriage.

The group of men, with Claus still in their centre, moved on.

The guard gave a sigh of fervent relief and swung her in front of him, administering a clenched-fist blow to the middle of her back that sent her half falling through the doors of the inspection room.

Hester barely registered it.

Claus had seen her; recognized her. What would happen now? Would he make contact with her? Or, in order to protect his own reputation as a choice specimen of Aryan manhood who could not possibly have family-by-marriage links with a Jewess, would he ensure she was sent back to Sachsenhausen and the nightmare labour at the brickworks? There was no way of telling. All she could do was pray fervently for the best – and wait.

TWENTY-EIGHT

Berlin, June 1943

Claus's always tight self-control had never come so close to breaking. Hester alive and in his factory! Hester *alive*! As the men from the inspectorate finished off their tour of the factory, the super-human effort he was making to keep a lid on his feelings made him feel as if he were about to explode.

Hester alive – just. Jesus God. How many years had she been a prisoner? Three? Four?

'The changes you have made to the working conditions of the *Untermensch* will be reported, Herr Remer,' a member of the inspectorate was saying to him icily. 'Under the present system, your factory will not be able to fulfil its quotas.'

'My factory would not have been able to fulfil its quotas if the slave labour assigned to me had continued falling down dead as they worked, as the prisoner in the spinning division fell down dead,' he heard himself respond in a dispassionate, almost disinterested voice. 'Dead prisoners, or even half-starved and exhausted ones, cannot perform work. The lunchtime issue of soup is to enable them to work to full capacity. It does not infringe on their allocated rations. It is a cost the factory is shouldering to ensure there is no deplorable loss of labour.'

'It will be reported,' the member of the inspectorate repeated.

The entourage had stepped outside the factory now and the Adler limousines that had brought them were lined up on the cobbles of the factory yard, ready to whisk them away. The official speaking to Claus pulled on gauntleted leather gloves. 'The labour assigned to you is expendable. There is an endless supply. Your directive is to exploit these workers to the highest possible extent at the lowest conceivable degree of expenditure. That directive has come from the highest level. It is a directive you will ignore at your peril, Herr Remer.'

Claus gave a slight, acknowledging inclination of his head. The requisite salutes and 'Heil Hitler's were given. The men entered the cars. Chauffeurs closed the doors. Moments later, the cars swept out of the factory yard bearing the occupants back to their government offices in the Bendlerstrasse.

Beside him, Claus's factory manager said nervously, 'What now, Herr Direktor? Do you want me to rescind the instructions with regard to the midday soup and the working hours?'

'And have other women falling down dead?' There was no dispassionate disinterest in his voice now. It was so raw with emotion his factory manager winced. 'We'll instigate a night shift, Gustav. And Gustav, the woman who was in the corridor when we came out of the inspection room – without bringing it to the attention of any of the SS, bring her up to my office.'

His factory manager was just about to hurry off to do his bidding when he said as an afterthought, 'And have the photograph in my office – the one of myself with the Führer and Reichsmarschall Göring – put up in the most public place you can think of.'

His factory manager nodded understandingly. With a photograph such as that on public display, the SS guards within the factory would begin to tread more carefully.

Still exerting iron control Claus returned to his office. Only when he had told his secretary that he didn't wish to be disturbed and only when the door was finally closed behind him, did he begin to shake and, once he began, he couldn't stop.

Hester alive – and for years Hugo had lived believing her dead. The monstrous evil of it sent a judder through his body so intense he thought for a moment he was having a heart attack. How had a regime that had once seemed to be the best for Germany, a regime that had brought order and stability to Germany, metamorphozed into the present nightmare? He'd always considered himself to be a member of a civilized nation. He did so no longer. Five days ago, he had returned from the Ruhr and paid what had been intended as a fleeting visit to the Berlin factory, and when he had seen the condition of the women allocated to him as slave labour he had known that his country had abandoned all right to be described as civilized.

Their lack of adequate clothing and malnourishment had outraged him, but even worse had been the realization that when a woman collapsed through exhaustion the SS guards administered brutal punishment. It had been Gustav who had given him that information and, on hearing it, he'd been consumed with a rage he had thought was going to kill him.

His first act had been to demand a meeting, not with the relatively minor SS officer in charge of the guards who had come with the women from Sachsenhausen, but with Sachsenhausen's Camp Commandant. And then he had put in hand immediate changes, providing proper toilet facilities, even though it reduced the toilet facilities for his regular workers, doing so on the argument that the privy in the yard was putting his regular workers at risk of disease.

He hadn't troubled to explain away the bales of second-hand clothing and shoes he'd had distributed, and his argument for shortening the slave labourers' working hours and providing extra food at midday had been that not to do so would result in such exhaustion on their part that overall production would plummet and government quotas would not be met.

The senior bureaucrats from the Armaments Board, with whom he tussled, had had to take into account that he wasn't merely the owner of a not very important clothing factory, but that he was also the owner of the House of Remer steelworks. Perhaps even more to the point, that he was on speaking terms with the man Hitler had created Marshal of the Empire, Hermann Göring.

It was enough to ensure he wasn't suspected of holding subversive views where Jews and *Untermensch* were concerned. Where the Camp Commandant of Sachsenhausen was concerned, he wined and dined him lavishly, giving him as a careless gift his now never-used two-seater aeroplane. In exchange for this largesse he received the promise that as long as his factory's overseers and managers were able to adequately supervise the slave labourers, the number of guards at the factory would be reduced. At the prospect of more handsome gifts coming his way, he also agreed that punishments by SS guards, on factory property, would cease and be left to the responsibility of the overseers and general management.

All in all, it had been quite a coup. Aware of it, he forced himself into movement, walking unsteadily across to his desk and fumbling for cigarettes and lighter, wondering if Göring know about the conditions in the camps. As the camps came under the jurisdiction of Heinrich Himmler, it was possible that he didn't. Possible, but not probable.

He lit his cigarette, inhaling deeply. Where the miracle of Hester was concerned, it was not so much that she had survived those conditions and been sent to his factory, but that he had recognized her, for she was emaciated almost beyond recognition.

The tic at the corner of his eye began jumping wildly. How was he going to be able to help her? How was he going to ensure she remained in the factory, where he could at least make sure she was humanely treated? The prospect of the SS sending her back to Sachsenhausen, or to a factory somewhere else, made sweat stand out on his forehead. And how could he get word to Hugo that she was alive? Max might have known of a method, but he hadn't seen or heard from Max for over a year and didn't even know if Max was still in Germany.

He took another deep draw of his cigarette. Nearly everyone else in his family had seen the evil inherent in National Socialism almost from the very beginning. Apart from him, only his father and his uncle had embraced it – and from the day he had handed over ownership of the House of Remer, his father had lost all enthusiasm for it.

It was a division that had driven a deep wedge between himself and the rest of his family. He couldn't remember the last time he had seen his sisters and he knew why they were so chary of contact with him. It was to safeguard Nicholas. Nicholas, who, instinct told him, was actively working with others to bring about the Führer's downfall; Nicholas, who they respected as they had long since ceased to respect him.

The result of being so cut off from those he loved was a loneliness that had seeped into his very bones. The mask of dispassionate indifference that he presented to the world was one it had become increasingly impossible to lower. He certainly couldn't reveal his inner self to any of the glamorous, Hitler-fixated blondes who decorated his arm at public functions. And as if all that wasn't burden enough to live with, he now had the knowledge that he had become part of the system that treated human beings as if they were nothing more than raw material for labour, raw material that was totally expendable.

There came a knock at the door.

'Come in,' he said loudly, knowing who it would be. Knowing it would be Gustav with Hester.

If she had looked barely recognizable thrust back against the wall in the narrow corridor, she looked even less recognizable now that he could see her more clearly. Her once glossy cloud of soft dark hair clung lankly around a face that was gaunt. Her eyes had sunk deep in their sockets. Her shoulder bones were cruelly pronounced beneath one of the second-hand dresses that had been distributed to all slave-labour women within the last week. He could see the edge of a bruise at her neckline and wondered how far it extended. Worst of all, he could see terrible apprehension in her eyes.

'That is all, Gustav,' he said to the elderly manager he trusted completely.

Gustav inclined his head. 'Yes, Herr Direktor.' As overall manager of the factory it certainly wasn't one of his duties to ferry people around the building and in and out of Claus's office, but these weren't normal times. If Claus wished him to escort this particular member of the slave-labour force, then he wasn't going to quibble about it. 'Shall I wait outside, Herr Direktor, in order to escort this worker back to the packing department?' he asked deferentially.

'Yes.' Claus's voice was tautly abrupt.

It seemed to take a lifetime for Gustav to remove himself from the room, for the door to close.

He could see the apprehension in her eyes begin to thicken with fear, and that she should be afraid of him, afraid of the power he had over her, made his gut twist as if a knife were embedded in it.

'Hester . . .' he said thickly. 'Dear God, Hester. We thought you were dead. We were told you'd been executed within hours of your arrest.'

There were acres of carpeted space between them. He

couldn't move. He was terrified that if he closed the distance separating them and took hold of her she would turn to dust beneath his touch.

'What happened to you?' he said hoarsely. 'Where did they send you?'

'To Ravensbrück. And then to Sachsenhausen.' She licked her lips, trying to come to terms with the fact that for over three years Hugo had thought himself a widower.

'And were you always treated this badly? Were you always so ill fed? And if you were, how did you survive?'

She wondered how it was possible he could be so shocked by her physical condition. He was a man who socialized with high-ranking Nazis. Surely he knew what kind of atrocities took place in the camps? Surely he knew what kind of conditions she and her fellow prisoners were presently enduring in the camp they'd been moved to half a mile or so from the factory?

'I was given work in the Camp Commandant's kitchens,' she said, knowing now was not the time to tell him about the killings and the torture and the medical experimentation that had taken place at Ravensbrück. Knowing that if she told him now he simply would not believe her. Knowing that no sane, rational person could possibly believe her. 'And in the kitchens I was relatively safe.'

'Then that's what we must do!' At long last he was able to move. With sudden certainty he strode towards her and placed his hands on her shoulders. 'I will appropriate you for kitchen work, Hester. Kitchen work not here at the factory, but domestic kitchen work in the house on Unter den Linden.'

Relief that he had no intention of sending her back to Sachsenhausen in order to prevent their relationship from coming to light flooded her with such intensity that if it wasn't for his hands on her shoulders, she would have fallen.

When she could speak, she said unsteadily, 'And what

about the other women, Claus? How can I move into the house on Unter den Linden when they are living in conditions not fit for animals?'

'I'm rectifying all that,' he said swiftly. 'I've already got arrangements in hand for black-market bread to be delivered to the factory to supplement the soup. I've made it clear to the Armaments Inspectorate that the workers sent here from Sachsenhausen will be treated as regular House of Remer workers are treated.'

She swayed slightly, appalled at his lack of understanding. 'I'm not talking about working conditions. I'm talking about our living conditions in the factory camp. I'm talking about bunks with no pallets, some women with no bunks at all. A single water tap. Lack of toilets. No medical supplies.'

She saw the expression on his face and knew he hadn't known.

'Visit it,' she said. 'See for yourself.'

'I'll visit it,' he said, through clenched teeth.

The knowledge that things were going to change, that things were going to become bearable, was too much for her. Tears began to stream down her face and drip onto her dress.

Gently, almost reverently, he put his arms around her.

'When you've been assigned to me as domestic labour, you'll be safe, Hester,' he said quietly. 'The authorities will forget about you until this hellish war is over.'

It was all so much more than she had dared to hope for that she was beyond speech. Only when he finally released his hold of her did she manage to say clumsily, 'Thank you. Thank you, Claus.'

'Don't thank me. Forgive me for being so blind, for so long, but don't thank me.'

There was a long, emotion-filled silence and then she said hesitantly, 'I've not heard anything but rumours about the war for years, Claus. What is happening? Who will be the victor?'

467

'The Allies,' he said simply. 'The tide has already turned. Germany has just suffered a massive defeat in Russia. The war in North Africa is going badly. Though every armaments factory in the country is in production day and night we can't compete with American armaments production. The Allies will win the war, and when they do, Germany will claw itself back to sanity again.'

He didn't add that when the war was over, he would most likely be shot for his part in German armament production – and that if he wasn't shot on that charge, he would be shot because of his use of slave labour, even though that use was obligatory.

'You must go back to the packing department,' he said heavily, 'before the guards wonder where you are, and why. And don't breathe a word of our family relationship. If it comes to light, the inspectorate will ensure that all the changes so far in place will end instantly.'

She nodded, understanding all too well that she couldn't confide in anyone, not even Detta.

'Give me a few days, Hester,' he said in the moments before he opened the door for her to return to the packing department in Gustav's care. 'Then everything we have spoken about will be in place, I promise you.'

She knew he was speaking the truth. Once, in what now seemed to be another lifetime, Hugo had told her she could trust his brother Max with her life. Now she knew that the same applied to Claus – and that she would be trusting him with her life as far into the future as she could see.

TWENTY-NINE

Berlin, October 1943

Lotti lay in the bath, hoping her precious few minutes of soothing relaxation wouldn't be abruptly halted by the sound of sirens. There were air raids nearly every night now and though Lützowstrasse had so far remained unscathed, her former flatmates had all left the city for the comparative safety of doing war work elsewhere.

With the war going so badly, war work was now obligatory for everyone. The choice she had been given had been between working in an armaments factory or working as a street-car conductress. Without a second's hesitation she had opted for work as a street-car conductress. The hours were long and she was on her feet all day, but then the hours had been long and she had been on her feet all day when she had worked as a waitress, and being a conductress did at least mean that her days were full of incident, for she got to traverse the city on a regular basis and always knew where the latest bombs had fallen and what the damage was.

It was rare, though, that she could come home and enjoy the luxury of a bath. Like electricity and gas, hot water could no longer be relied upon and now that she had been miraculously able to run a tub full, she doubted if even an air-raid warning would persuade her to abandon it.

She slid lower down in the water, trying to ignore the fact that bath foam was now a commodity impossible to come by and that it was highly unlikely she would get any decent lather from her bar of soap. For months now, deprivation had been the name of the game. Food was rationed to a stringent degree. Everything needed coupons – and coupons did not go very far. She wondered what sort of rationing was taking place in England, knowing that whatever it was, at Shuttleworth Hall Vicky would be supplementing it with home-grown produce.

Shuttleworth Hall. She closed her eyes and conjured up its image. Even in wartime Shuttleworth Hall would be a haven of peace and comfort. It was too deep in the Dales for it to be anything else, for the Luftwaffe would certainly not be wasting time and bombs on village hamlets such as Little Ridding. It was October and the leaves on the trees down by the river would be beginning to change colour. She could see them in her mind's eye, gold and yellow and every shade of copper. The blackthorn bushes would be heavy with sloes – and no doubt Emily Elise would be picking them with gusto.

She wiggled her toes in the water, remembering how, whenever she had visited Shuttleworth Hall in October, Vicky had made sloe gin, pricking the sloes and dropping them into half-full bottles of gin until the remaining gin reached nearly to the top of the bottles. Then Vicky would add a wine glass of sugar and, over the next few weeks, would turn the bottles daily until, by Christmas, the gin was a rich magenta colour and ready for drinking.

It was only one of the many activities that would be taking place in Shuttleworth Hall's big, roomy kitchen, for every October Vicky launched into a frenzy of culinary activity, preserving jams and jellies, chutneys and pickles, all made with produce that either grew wild, like blackberries and crab apples, or that she grew herself, like damsons and plums.

At the thought of her aunt's spiced pickled plums, Lotti's mouth watered. Sometimes Vicky served her spiced pickled plums with home-baked bread and cheese, sometimes with cold meat. Both ways were equally delicious, and thinking of them now, when her lunch had been a mean portion of unadorned inedible meat and her dinner a sausage, was a torment.

The water was beginning to cool, and reluctant to emerge from it to the icy chill of the unheated bathroom, she focused her thoughts on Ilse's recent telephone call to her. 'An old theatre friend of mine who is now a pilot, Otto Schott, has just been awarded the Oak Leaves to his Knight's Cross for valour,' she had said in fizzing good spirits. 'He had to go to Hitler's HQ to receive the Oak Leaves from Hitler personally and you'll never guess, Lotti, *he wasn't asked to relinquish his handgun before going into Hitler's presence*! Isn't that amazing? If it had been one of Nicky's friends who had found himself in that situation, Germany's future would have been altered in an instant!'

Aware that the water was now too cool for comfort, she got out of the bath and hurriedly towelled her goose-pimpled body dry. She was going to go straight to bed for she had a five o'clock start in the morning, a twelve-hour shift to work and then, in the evening, she was going to Isle and Nicholas's to help them celebrate Nicholas's thirty-sixth birthday.

It was going to be a rather special celebration because Nicholas was now very rarely in Berlin. Staff from all the main ministries had been moved out of the city when RAF air raids had first begun making themselves felt. Ilse, who was still making films at Babelsburg, had been unable to accompany him. As an actress appearing in propaganda films, her work was classed as essential war work. Which, as Ilse said, was better than having to slog twelve hours a day in an ammunitions factory even if the lines she had to say did often make her want to vomit.

She was just getting into bed when the sirens went. None of the recent raids had been particularly severe and she hesitated for a moment, wondering whether the bother of getting dressed again and going down the street to the public shelter was worth all the hassle.

As flak barrage noisily erupted she decided that perhaps it was. Sitting out a raid when you had someone to sit it out with, was one thing. Sitting it out alone was quite another.

Hurriedly, she scrambled into layers of clothing, put the photograph of Max that stood on her bedside table into the small carry-all she now kept permanently packed and ready for such occasions and, gripping it tightly, rushed out of the flat and down to the street.

By the time she got to the shelter that served the street, it was already full. She squeezed past an elderly neighbour who was clutching a bag of documents to her chest – presumably precious family papers – and settled herself next to a young mother with two children.

The flak was now in full throttle and over and above it came the sound of the first approaching planes.

Lotti clasped her hands together. For her, the worst part of these nearly nightly scenarios was the knowledge that Hugo was a pilot and that he could very well be in the cockpit of one of the planes.

Even after four years of coming to terms with the fact, she still found it impossible to imagine Hugo at the controls of a bomber. He'd always been a quiet-spoken, bookish kind of person, not a man of action. Or he had been a quiet-spoken, bookish person. Hester's death had no doubt changed him drastically. He would no longer be the same Hugo he had once been, just as Claus was no longer the same person he had once been.

From the sound of it, the approaching planes were flying in low – always a bad sign. To take her mind off the bombs that would shortly be falling she thought about the rest of her family. Of Nancy, who had always been more of a sister to her than a cousin. Where was Nancy now? The last news she'd had of her had been when both sides of the family had still been able to communicate by letters sent via contacts of Paul's in America. That had been nearly two years ago. At that time, Nancy had been working for Reuters, but whether she was still doing so, Lotti didn't know. Somehow, because it was so easy to imagine Nancy in uniform, she rather thought Nancy might now be in the WRENS or the WAAF.

Bombs had begun to fall and the people around her fidgeted restlessly. One of the children began crying.

Steeling herself to remain calm, Lotti turned her thoughts to the one person who was never far away from them. Max. It was now a little over two years since they had been together. In the weeks after he had engineered her release from Gestapo headquarters they had been together constantly. Even despite the tensions of the war, it had been the most blissful period of her life. Then he'd received orders to go back to Munich.

'And from there, I rather think it's going to be a passage across Lake Constance into Switzerland and on to London and an entirely different kind of posting,' he'd said to her as they had lain in bed together in the glorious aftermath of love-making. 'It may be a long time before I see you again, Monkeyface, but I will see you again – and until I do, I won't fall in love elsewhere, that I promise you.'

He had kissed her long and lovingly and then he had taken her hand and kissed each and every one of the still swollen, malformed joints of her fingers. Since then she'd received only one communication from him, a hasty telephone call in which he'd said that his intuition had been correct. After that, there had been nothing.

A bomb fell so close that the shelter shook and plaster from the roof rained down on them. The crying child began to scream.

The noise was now deafening, the air pressure almost unbearable. A woman seated opposite her took out her rosary and began to pray. A little girl could be heard saying tearfully, 'Can't you make it stop, *Mutti*? It frightens me. Please make it stop.' There were no men in the shelter. Lützowstrasse had become a street of women. Some, like her, were engaged on essential war work, others had young children, others were elderly and infirm.

As another bomb fell near by and dust from falling masonry seeped into the shelter in billowing clouds, she wondered what Max's new posting had been. As an intelligence officer he could have been sent anywhere.

It never occurred to her that he could be dead. Somehow, she was quite sure that if he'd been killed she would know, that her sixth sense would scream the fact at her – and it hadn't done so.

The masonry dust was now so thick people had begun to cough and choke. The lady who had been clutching a bag of documents to her chest unearthed a bottle of schnapps from beneath them and, after taking a gulp from the bottle, generously handed it around.

When it was Lotti's turn to take a swallow she did so gratefully. Her love for Max and Max's love for her was still something that was secret. She had never spoken of it to Ilse, or to her mother. Claus she never saw now and assumed him to be no longer in the city but in the Ruhr, and living in his apartment at the steelworks.

Thoughts of Claus were obliterated as there came an explosion so ear-splitting she thought the shelter itself must have been hit. As she rocketed to her feet, there was widespread screaming and then someone shouted over the din, 'It's stopping! They're going away!'

The noise in the shelter subsided as everyone listened with bated breath. Sure enough, the massive overhead drone was a receding one. The raid was over. A little later, confirming what they now already knew, the all-clear sounded.

Lotti stumbled out of the shelter to be met by the sight of fire consuming what had been her end of the street. The air was scorching hot, thick with smoke and ash.

'I think,' she said to the woman who was still clutching a bag full of documents, 'that I've probably just lost my home.'

'I think,' the woman said soberly, 'that you've probably been very, very lucky. You could have been inside it.'

'And so Lotti has moved in here, with me,' Ilse said to Nicholas, winding her arm lovingly through his. 'And she arrived travelling very light. We went back to rescue what we could from her apartment yesterday and all we found was –'

'– the staircase leading up to it,' Lotti finished for her from where she was sitting on the sofa, her legs comfortably curled beneath her. 'And then nothing but fresh air and smouldering ash. No walls. No floors. Nothing. My entire apartment was simply wiped off the face of the earth.'

Nicholas sat down in a near by chair and drew Ilse onto his lap. 'Neither you nor Ilse should still be living in the city,' he said gravely. 'The raids aren't going to stop. They're going to get heavier and more frequent. You should move out to Wannsee. It isn't far out, but it's far enough to make a lot of difference where raids are concerned. Ilse would be even nearer to Babelsburg and it's within cycling distance, Lotti. The advantages would be that you would both be a lot safer.'

'It isn't within easy cycling distance, Nicky,' Lotti said wryly, 'especially not if there is a raid on.'

'And we're Berliners born and bred, darling,' Ilse said,

speaking for both of them. 'And Berlin is where we are going to stay.' She kissed him on his nose. 'So tell us both the latest news.'

'The latest news is that I may very well find myself in uniform and at the Russian front,' Nicholas said drily. 'Nearly everyone in the Foreign Service is now suspected of holding disloyal views and so they are replacing us with SS hardliners as fast as they can. My turn can't be long in coming.'

Ilse's arm tightened around his shoulders. For a moment, she didn't say anything and then she said hesitantly, 'Would it mean an end to your involvement in the conspiracy?'

'Probably.' He pinched the bridge of his nose. 'Even as it is, our particular conspiracy group is being blocked at every turn. There are very few occasions now when Hitler can be counted on to put in an appearance. Any city that's been bombed he avoids like the plague, as if his not seeing the devastation means the devastation hasn't happened. The schedules he has, he constantly changes. When he travels he does so at irregular times and unexpectedly. The only occasions on which he can definitely be counted to appear are his twice-daily military conferences with generals of the Army High Command. He would have to be killed at one of them, and though another conspiracy group has members who have access to such conferences, ours does not.'

'And does this other group plan to assassinate Hitler at one of these conferences?'

'Yes. But whether they'll be able to successfully do so is another matter. They intend smuggling a bomb into the meeting and bombs are notoriously unstable. We attempted something similar a few months ago – smuggling a bomb aboard a plane that was flying Hitler from Berlin to Munich. It failed because the detonator didn't fire. And another problem with bombs is that fuses make a hissing noise which it's difficult to cover up.'

Ilse slid off his knee and crossed the room to the cocktail cabinet that had been a wedding present from her parents. 'Do you know of any like-minded army officers or pilots who are due to receive a decoration for valour from the Führer?' she asked, pouring vodka into a glass.

'My cousin, Freddie. My father gave me the news only yesterday. He's brought down a hundred enemy planes – which means an addition of Oak Leaves to his Knight's Cross. He's to go to Rastenburg to receive them.'

'Rastenburg?' Lotti said, hoping Ilse was going to be equally generous with the vodka when it came to filling her glass.

'It's Hitler's latest HQ. As it's in East Prussia and in the middle of a forest, it's as far away from the bombed and burning rubble of our cities as our Supreme Leader can get.'

Ilse added vermouth to the vodka, her hand trembling slightly. 'Do you remember Otto Schott?' she asked. 'He had a small role in *Love and Intrigue*.'

'Vaguely.' He looked across at her, hardly able to believe that such an exquisite creature was his wife. Because it was his birthday she had dressed for the occasion, uncaring of the likelihood of an air raid. Her ankle-length white satin dress swooped low at the back, revealing creamy, flawless skin. Her pale blonde hair, light and shining, fell in a soft wave to jaw level. She was loveliness personified and out of all the men she could have chosen, she had chosen him. 'Otto was the good-looking young man Gründgens had intended grooming as a matinee idol, wasn't he?' he said, counting himself the luckiest man alive. 'Why do you ask?'

She recrossed the room and handed him his Martini. 'Because when Otto received his Oak Leaves to his Knight's Cross, he wasn't asked to relinquish his handgun before going into Hitler's presence. If he'd mentally prepared himself to do so beforehand, he could have shot Hitler then and there.'

For a long moment, Nicholas was silent and then he said regretfully, 'No. If that happened it was a fluke, Ilse. A one-off. It couldn't possibly happen again.'

'But it might!' She dropped down to one knee in front of him, taking his free hand in hers. 'It would be worth a try, wouldn't it? Surely it's a proposal you could put to Freddie?'

Nicholas looked from his wife to Lotti and back again and then he said slowly, with growing conviction, 'Perhaps you're right, Ilse. Perhaps it *is* worth a try.'

As the prospect of such an assassination attempt took on reality for him he put down his glass and rose to his feet, excitement building in him. 'It will mean a lot of very rapid coordinated planning. The plans have always been that within two hours of Hitler's death, army troops occupy and secure the national broadcasting headquarters and Berlin's radio stations. Their doing so is absolutely vital.'

'And will that be possible at such short notice?' Lotti asked, totally ignorant of just who, in the Army High Command, Nicholas and his friends could rely on.

Nicholas nodded. 'Yes. We've been in a state of readiness for months now, waiting only for the right opportunity. We have the support of General Olbricht, the deputy commander of the Home Army. He's in a position to rally the garrisons in Berlin and other large cities.'

He turned away from her, beginning to pace the room. 'And we have the support of Count von Helldorf, the chief of police in Berlin. With Olbricht and von Helldorf's help the radio stations and telegraph and telephone centrals will be immediately occupied. Once that is done, the commanders of the Home Army in other cities and the generals commanding the troops at the front and in the occupied zones can be immediately informed that Hitler is dead and that they are no longer bound by their oath of allegiance to him. In that way we'll get the support from all the generals who know the war is lost and want it to end, but who have been too cowardly to take action to bring that end about. Hitler's death will stop all vacillating.'

Lotti, who had not thought beyond the simple necessity of Hitler's death and had not taken on board the magnitude of the events that would have to follow it, rose to her feet and walked across to the cocktail cabinet. She needed a stiff Martini and Ilse seemed to have forgotten she was still without one.

'And I will need to accompany Freddie to Rastenburg,' Nicholas said, coming to a halt in front of Ilse, who was still kneeling by the side of his chair. 'There has to be someone able to inform other key plotters – especially Olbricht and von Helldorf – that the attempt has succeeded and that they must swing into immediate action. Unless a successful coup takes place in Berlin, Himmler will have the chance to seize the reins – and the result of that won't be a peace agreement with the Allies. It will be chaos and civil war.'

He picked up his glass and drained it. Then he said tautly, 'I know you've done a special birthday celebration meal for me tonight, Ilse, but I can't stay to enjoy it. I have only twenty-four hours in Berlin and I must speak personally to everyone who is going to be involved in this. First and foremost I must get in contact with Freddie.'

Ilse rose to her feet, her face wax-white. Her mention of Otto Schott's experience was putting in place a train of events that would almost certainly result in Freddie Schulenburg's death and could well result in Nicholas's death as well.

Lotti's nervous tension was almost as bad. Her long working hours traversing the bomb-battered city as a street-car conductress helped her to keep her fear under control, but didn't banish it. If the assassination attempt failed and Nicholas were perceived to have been part of it – and his accompanying Freddie to Rastenburg made such a conclusion almost certain – then not only would he be executed, but Ilse might very well be executed also. Of course, if the attempt succeeded, Nicholas's part in it would guarantee him a place in history and a key role in any future government acceptable to the Allies.

Sometimes, to make the tension bearable, she reminded herself that there was a third possibility. Statistically, the most likely outcome was that Freddie would be relieved of his handgun before going into Hitler's presence and in that event no assassination attempt, successful or unsuccessful, would be made.

The constant mental see-sawing between one scenario and another made her feel permanently sick. Adding to her feeling of nausea was the constant awareness of the destruction being wreaked on the city she loved.

It was blackened by soot, pockmarked by thousands of craters. One of the most important junctions on her route was strewn with the shells of so many burned-out buses and cars it was almost impassable. In some areas, entire streets had been obliterated. In others, house after house had had windowpanes blown to smithereens and doors torn off hinges. Nicholas's prediction was that raids would increase in intensity and number, not decrease. 'Hitler won't surrender,' he had said grimly. 'He will see Berlin and every other great German city razed to the ground, but he won't surrender. That's why he *has* to be assassinated. It's the only way to put an end to the hell he has plunged the Fatherland into.'

At night she and Ilse would sit in the kitchen in front of a small wood-burning stove, their hands wrapped around mugs of tea as they illegally listened in to the BBC's German language news broadcasts.

'Do you think we'll soon be listening in to an account of the assassination?' Ilse asked her one evening, nearly two weeks after the fateful evening of Nicholas's birthday celebration.

'I don't know. I hope so. But I only hope so if Freddie and Nicholas survive the immediate aftermath of it. Because if they don't –'

Ilse raised a hand in a mute, silencing gesture. The possibility of Nicholas not surviving was something she couldn't bear to contemplate. When she had married him, she had done so well aware she wasn't as deeply in love with him as she had been with Max. That was now no longer the case. He was the dearest person to her in all the world and the thought of losing him was one she wouldn't consider.

The next evening, as Lotti trudged homewards at the end of her long, arduous day's work, the sirens sounded and she had to clatter with hundreds of other people down the concrete spiral staircases of the enormous Potsdamer Platz shelter.

By the time the all-clear eventually sounded and she staggered in to Ilse and Nicholas's apartment, it was the early hours of the morning.

Ilse rushed to greet her in her dressing gown. 'God! I was so worried about you, Lotti!' she exclaimed, hugging her hard. 'Do you want a cup of tea? Soup? Where were you when the sirens went? Were you still working?'

'Tea. I'd love some tea, Ilse. And no, I wasn't still working.' She dragged a black beret off hair grey with ash and debris. 'I was on my way home. Word is the Ku'damm got the worst of it tonight. At this rate there soon won't be a department store left standing in the city.'

Instead of hurrying off to put the kettle on for tea, Ilse remained in the hallway, her eyes wide and feverishly bright.

'It's to be tomorrow at ten o'clock,' she said. 'That's when Freddie is to receive his Oak Leaves from Hitler. Nicholas got word to me a few hours ago.'

Lotti sucked in her breath and then said unsteadily, 'I need that tea, Ilse – and so do you. Come on, let's go into the kitchen and put some wood on the stove. All we can do now is wait and pray.'

Too tense to sleep, they waited and prayed all through the rest of the night. In the early morning Ilse telephoned the film studios saying she'd been taken ill and wouldn't be on set as scheduled. At nine o'clock, Lotti poured them both large brandies. At ten o'clock, the tension they were under was so excruciating Lotti didn't know how she was living through it. Five minutes past ten came. Ten minutes past ten.

At half-past ten, Ilse said in a cracked voice, 'Freddie must have been able to make the attempt. If he hadn't, Nicholas would have telephoned by now. And if he's made the attempt and it was a success there will be so many members of the High Command for Nicholas to contact that he won't have time to contact us for ages and ages. His not telephoning is a good sign, Lotti, not a bad one.' She was twisting her hands in her lap, her eyes imploring.

'Of course it is,' Lotti said staunchly, wondering how soon they would hear if the news was bad and who it was who would break such news to them. Would it be one of Nicholas's friends? Or would the Gestapo arrive en masse, breaking down the door as they stormed in to arrest Ilse and maybe to arrest her as well?

At eleven o'clock, she said, 'Let's put the radio on. There's bound to be some kind of news soon.'

There wasn't, or not the news they were waiting for with every fibre of their being.

At twelve o'clock, there was still no news. 'And why should there be?' Ilse said, struggling for optimism. 'The first hour after Hitler was shot would be complete bedlam. Nicholas would have to get in touch with men like General Olbricht and Count von Helldorf. There wouldn't be a second of time in which he could telephone here.'

She walked across to the window. 'After that, his first concern will be to return to Berlin and the Army High Command headquarters in the Bendlerstrasse. That's where von Helldorf and many others will have gathered. At this very minute, he's probably in the air. I'm sure it's *good* that we still haven't heard from him. Two hours is far too soon to hear anything.'

By two o'clock, aware that by her own calculations Nicholas was very probably now back in Berlin, Ilse was biting her beautifully manicured nails and Lotti was pacing the apartment, chain-smoking.

By four o'clock, their anxiety was almost at breaking point. On the radio, the regular news broadcasts were about everything but the Führer. There was no announcement of his assassination. No announcement of an attempted assassination.

'But Hitler *must* be dead!' Isle kept saying frantically. 'That's why there is no news. Communication with the outside world has simply been cut off until a new head of state and a new commander in chief of the army are ready to go on air to broadcast to the world what has happened.'

Lotti said nothing. Whatever was happening, Nicholas would know how deep their anxiety was. Even if he could not take the time to telephone them himself, she felt sure he would have detailed someone else to do so.

Suddenly, from where she was standing at the window, Ilse said urgently, 'Freddie's father has just turned into the street! He must have news!'

With feet scarcely touching the floor she flew from the room and into the hall, yanking the front door open.

Lotti didn't follow her. She couldn't. Terror was rooting her to the spot.

It was terror that was well founded.

Seconds later, Ilse's anguished scream rent the air, reverberating throughout all the rooms of the apartment.

Knowing only too well what Freddie's father's news had been, Lotti buried her face in her hands and, her legs no longer able to support her, sank to her knees.

Nicholas, handsome and good and brave, was dead – or soon would be.

And Adolf Hitler, devil incarnate, was still alive.

THIRTY

Berlin, January 1944

Zelda was doing something she hadn't done for years. She was entering a church in order to pray – and she was doing so as inconspicuously as possible.

Despite the mind-numbing cold she wasn't wearing a fur. Her coat was a shabby black-wool coat she had long since taken to wearing when making one of her rare forays onto the city's bomb-shattered streets. It was a coat that didn't attract attention. Worn with a faded wool headscarf knotted beneath her chin Babushka-style and pulled forward to hide her distinctively high cheekbones and the darkness of her eyes, it made her look like any other Berlin housewife out foraging for rations.

The church was quiet and empty, though from the smell of recently extinguished candles it hadn't been empty for long. Zelda lit her own candle and then went and sat in one of the pews nearest to the altar.

The nave was very dark. There was no light anywhere, save that of her candle and the dull, leaden light of the late winter sun as it filtered weakly through the stained-glass windows.

Trembling slightly, she knelt down and began to pray. 'Dear God,' she said aloud and in an unsteady voice, 'if there is a

God, please don't let Josef die.' She thought of the millions who, over the last few years, must have made similar prayers for their loved ones, only for their prayers to go unanswered. She clasped her hands even tighter, resting her forehead against them. 'Dear Heavenly Father,' she began again, aware she hadn't made the most polite of beginnings. 'Grant me forgiveness for all my many sins, and please don't let Josef die.'

Once again she couldn't get beyond that sentence. Please don't let Josef die. It was like a mantra running ceaselessly through her head. The doctor had said that Josef, struck down with pneumonia like so many other Berliners, had gone past the point when he might be expected to recover.

'I can do nothing more for him,' he had said tersely. 'You must come to terms with the fact that you will soon be a widow, Frau Remer.'

'I've been a widow once,' she had snapped back, hating him for his lack of determination to keep Josef alive, 'and I've no intention of becoming one again!'

Remer money ensured that even in these difficult days, Josef was receiving twenty-four-hour nursing care. The real nursing, though, the nursing that mattered the most to him, was done by herself.

'Don't die, my darling,' she pleaded ceaselessly, holding his near-lifeless hand close against her cheek as he slipped in and out of consciousness. 'Please don't die, Josef. Please stay with me. Please.'

It was a plea she took up again with her Maker. 'I promise I'll become a nicer person if only you let Josef live,' she said as her candle flickered and threatened to go out.

It was the prayer of a child, not of a sophisticated adult, and she knew it. The problem was she had never previously approached God for anything and she simply didn't have the language to do so. It occurred to her that perhaps she should have come when a service was in progress.

'Please, God,' she said yet again, tears rolling silently down her face. 'Please, God. Please . . .'

'Herr Remer is conscious,' the nurse on duty said brightly when she returned to their apartment. 'He is improving, I think.'

Zelda whipped off her headscarf and hurried towards Josef's bedroom without even taking off her coat. The instant she entered the room, all her hopes came crashing down.

Josef's eyes were open, but she knew immediately that he had reached crisis point; that they were open only because of his fierce determination to say a last goodbye to her.

She flew to his side, kneeling down beside the bed, taking his hands between hers.

'Z . . . elda,' he said with difficulty, his breathing so laboured it hammered in her ears. '*Liebchen*.'

'You're not to die!' Her throat was choked with grief. 'You're not to!'

He gave a very slow, dismissive blink of his eyelids. 'It's too late, *Liebchen*,' he croaked, 'it's already happening. I just wanted to say . . . to say how much I've always loved you. The miscegenate thing . . .'

He struggled for breath again and she wanted to scream at him not to remember such a thing at such a time, and then he said, 'The miscegenate thing . . . it always brought me a lot of pleasure. Your beauty. Your hair . . . so black. Night-black. You wouldn't have been you without the Iroquois in you, Zelda. All my life, every time I've looked at you, I've been unable to believe your beauty. Just the sight of you has always given me such pleasure . . . such pleasure . . .'

She tried to speak, but she couldn't because of the sobs in her throat – and then she knew it was too late for speech, for she was alone in the room and all her most fervent prayers had gone unanswered.

THIRTY-ONE

Yorkshire, March 1944

'Thank God we've both got forty-eight-hour passes coming up,' Hugo said wearily to Tony Walsh, his navigator, as he flew their Mosquito towards the blessed shores of England after a night raid on Aachen. 'What are you going to do with yours? Head home?'

'I doubt it. I don't have any family apart from a sour-faced aunt. When I have a forty-eight I usually hang around the base.'

Hugo looked towards him, appalled. Well known for being a loner, he usually didn't take the slightest interest in the lives of those he flew with, which was why he hadn't previously known of Tony's family situation. He tried to imagine what his own life would be like without Shuttleworth Hall as a sanctuary to retreat to every few months, and couldn't.

'I'm heading to Yorkshire,' he said, as they flew over the coast. 'My family home is a great rambling affair on the banks of the Ure. My mother turned it into a nursing home for wounded soldiers during the First World War and still fills it full of people at the least opportunity, evacuees and Jewish refugees at the last count. She likes guests and new faces. Why don't you come with me for the weekend? You'll be very welcome.'

It was such an unexpected invitation that Tony's jaw dropped. Being the oldest and most experienced pilot in the squadron, Hugo Remer's skill as a pilot was legendary, but he wasn't a man known for conviviality. He kept his private life private and didn't take kindly to jokes. When someone in the mess had made a harmless joke about him having the same name as that of a giant Ruhr steelworks he had bitten the poor guy's head off.

'Thanks,' he said uncertainly, hoping to God Hugo didn't want to get him into deepest Yorkshire in order to make a pass at him. 'Your mother sounds great. I'd like to come.'

When Vicky saw Hugo stepping out of a taxi in Shuttleworth Hall's daffodil-massed drive with a friend in tow, she was overjoyed.

'Hugo's here and he's brought a friend with him,' she said to Adam, hurrying away from the window and towards the door leading into the hall. 'If the meat loaf I've made for lunch is going to stretch to feed all of us, I'll need more parsnips and leeks digging up.'

'Then you're lucky it's a Saturday and I'm at home,' Adam said, as pleased as she was that Hugo was apparently beginning to socialize again, 'because the ground is as hard as iron.'

'And bring in some rhubarb,' Vicky said over her shoulder as she headed towards the front door. 'I'll make a crumble.'

Uncaring that the March day was bitterly cold she went out of the house without a coat, running to meet her beloved son as if she were a young girl and not a woman who had just celebrated her fifty-sixth birthday.

'How long are you home for?' she asked as he swung her off her feet, hugging her close. 'Twenty-four hours, or forty-eight?'

'Forty-eight. How's Grandpa?'

'He's frailer than he was the last time you were home, but he's still fiercely alert. He and Emily Elise have become jigsaw fanatics.'

Tony Walsh watched their joyous reunion in barely disguised astonishment. At the air base, Hugo never let emotion of any kind show. The general opinion was that he was a cold fish and it was rumoured that perhaps the reason for his taciturnity was that his wife, of whom he never spoke, had run off with either a Yank or a milkman.

'Tony, I'd like you to meet my mother. Ma, Tony Walsh, my navigator.'

'Pleased to meet you, Mrs Remer.' The sight of flawless skin, golden silver-flecked hair and eyes that were a deep cornflower blue, stunned Tony. It was simply something he had never expected. 'You've got a lovely place here. When we turned in at the drive I thought we were going to have to pay to enter.'

Compliments about her home always pleased Vicky and she laughed, liking the look of Hugo's friend. 'Thank you. Spring is always a good time of year at Shuttleworth Hall. The daffodils have been increasing for years now. Wait until you see them at the rear of the house. They stretch in a golden sea almost down to the river. And my name isn't Mrs Remer, it's Mrs Priestley. Though I'd prefer it if you used my Christian name, which is Vicky.'

'My pleasure, Vicky,' Tony said, relaxing into the spirit of the occasion and beginning to realize that the weekend was going to be far more enjoyable than he'd anticipated.

A pretty red-headed girl erupted from the house. 'And this is Emily Elise,' Vicky said. 'She's Hugo's younger sister.'

Emily Elise covered the yards between herself and Hugo like lightning. 'You *rotter*!' she said, hurling herself into his arms. 'Why didn't you tell us you were coming home? I've arranged to go to the flicks this afternoon with a friend from school, though I won't be going now. I shall cry off. It's a

489

Jimmy Stewart film, and as I'm not that mad about him it's no great loss.'

Having hugged Hugo to nearly an inch of his life she turned to Tony with a wide, sunny smile. 'Do you fly Mossies too?' she asked, tucking her arm into his as if she'd known him all her life. 'I think Mossies are amazing aircraft. Fancy building a plane of wood in this day and age – and Hugo says they fly like demons, far faster than metal planes. He says that Spitfires are dray horses in comparison.'

Tony laughed, relaxation seeping into his very bones. Whatever the reason for Hugo's unforthcoming personality, it certainly wasn't on account of his home life. Both his mother and his young sister – his half-sister presumably, considering her age and Hugo's mother no longer bearing the name Remer – quite obviously adored him.

It wasn't a situation that was familiar to him. His family consisted merely of an aunt and a scattering of distant cousins, none of whom could be described as being adoring.

'And this is Heini,' the red-haired live wire at his side said as they stepped into the hall and a big, clumsy-looking boy with a large round head came towards them with a rolling walk.

A split second later, as Heini grinningly greeted him, he realized Heini was mongoloid. He wasn't disconcerted, but it was yet another surprise. He looked across at Hugo, aware that some men would have felt the need to explain about Heini beforehand. That Hugo didn't think Heini needed explaining increased his new-found liking and respect for him.

'Wotcher, Heini,' he said, curious about Heini's name. Was it short for Heinrich and, if so, was Heini one of the Jewish refugees Hugo had spoken about?

'Heini's parents are in the West Indies and so he's living with us until they can all be reunited,' Emily Elise said chattily, confusing him even more.

From the hallway they entered a spacious, high-ceilinged

drawing room. There were two large cushion-filled sofas, several comfy-looking armchairs, a low table piled with books, another table with a half-finished jigsaw on it, a radiogram with a display case next to it stuffed with records. A log fire roared away in the fireplace. On the marble mantelshelf stood an array of silver-framed photographs flanked by two crystal vases of daffodils, and on every other available surface in the room were bowls of heavenly scented hyacinths. It was a room that managed to be both grand and cosy at the same time and, in the centre of it, a tall, broad-shouldered, red-haired man was shrugging himself into a leather-elbowed tweed jacket.

This was so obviously Emily Elise's father that Emily Elise's introduction was unnecessary – though she made it anyway.

'This is Hugo's friend, Daddy. He's a Mossie pilot and –'

'I'm a navigator, sir.'

'– and I'm not going to the flicks this afternoon,' Emily Elise continued blithely, 'I'm going to get out the Monopoly instead.'

Adam flinched forbearingly and shook Tony's hand.

'Adam Priestley,' he said. 'You're very welcome.'

'Thank you, sir. My name is Tony. Tony Walsh.'

'I'm just going out to dig up some extra vegetables for lunch, Tony. You're welcome to come with me, if you like.'

'I'd love to,' Tony said with alacrity. 'There are lots of allotments in south-east London and my old man used to have a huge one. He grew potatoes, carrots, leeks, parsnips and cabbage. As a nipper I helped him whenever I could.'

'And did your father grow fruit as well?' Adam asked with interest as they headed out of the room, Heini and Emily Elise hard on their heels.

The last thing Hugo heard, as the door closed behind them, was Tony saying, 'Only rhubarb – which he always called roobubbery.'

His mother had already left the room in order to put the

kettle on for a pot of tea and, glad to be on his own for a few minutes, Hugo walked across to the fireplace and lifted down the silver-framed photograph of Hester that had pride of place.

It was over four years since he had lost her and his grief was no easier for him to bear now than it had been in the early days. He knew his mother longed for him to fall in love again and perhaps marry, but he was certain he would never do so. Hester had been his life. He couldn't even begin to imagine anyone replacing her.

It was a photograph he had taken himself, in the Tiergarten. It had been autumn and the suit she was wearing was chocolate-brown with a small fur collar and neat fur cuffs. She was leaning against one of the railings that fronted the lake, laughing at something he had said, the breeze tugging at her shoulder-length dark hair.

Remembering the pure, perfect happiness of that moment he wanted to weep. The people who had told him that time was a great healer, had been wrong. His pain was constant and intolerable and as deep as it had ever been. Introverted by nature, he had become even more so. With immaculate politeness he shunned everyone who tried to get close to him. Only at Shuttleworth Hall did he come close to relaxing – and even there questions tormented him.

How had his beloved wife died? Had she been shot? Hanged? Beheaded? When had her execution taken place? Where? Nightmare images nearly robbed him of his reason. It seemed impossible to him that anyone could suffer mentally, as he was suffering, and yet still remain sane. The total concentration needed when flying had been his salvation. In the cockpit of the Lancasters he had flown on bombing sorties over German naval targets and north Germany, he had found some kind of bizarre relief, his hatred of all Hitler stood for superseding – for a short time at least – his grief.

With unsteady hands he put the photograph back on the

mantelshelf. The bombing sorties he had coped with, even welcomed. What was far more difficult were the kind of operations he had been assigned to since his move from Lancasters to Mosquitos. Mossies had initially been designed as fast, unarmed light bombers, but the Mossie he and Tony flew was part of an elite Pathfinder Squadron. Their task was to fly ahead of the main night-bombing force and to locate and then mark targets with flares for the bombers to home in on.

And the city now under almost constant attack was Berlin.

Still staring at Hester's photograph, he cracked his knuckles. When they had first married, Berlin had been their home. It was a city he had once loved just as passionately as he loved Shuttleworth Hall. It was his father's city – and his father still lived there. In all probability, Ilse, Lotti and Claus still lived there. So far none of the targets he had marked had been in Berlin, but that he soon would be acting as a pathfinder on a raid over Berlin was inevitable.

As he left the room and headed for the stairs, intent on spending time with his grandfather, he wondered bleakly how he would bring himself to fulfil such a mission. It was a question he had asked himself many times – and was one he was still unable to answer.

At lunchtime, with very little input from him, the conversation flew thick and fast.

'We did have evacuees,' Vicky said, passing a dish of roasted vegetables to Tony, 'but that was in the early days of the war. Once the heavy raids on the East End and the docks came to an end, they all went back home.' Her voice thickened with amusement. 'Some of the children liked the novelty of country life, but their mothers didn't. They couldn't get back to London quickly enough.'

'And Hugo said you had Jewish refugees living here as well?'

'We did have. We had two families who were allowed into the country as domestic workers and agricultural trainees but only on the understanding that they agreed to ultimate settlement elsewhere. At the moment, they are in Somerset and have been told that their final destination will be Canada. I miss them. Both of the husbands were Hester's cousins.'

'Hester?'

Vicky flashed a look towards Hugo, appalled that his friend knew so little about his private life.

'Hugo's late wife,' she said as Hugo's shoulders tensed and he kept his eyes fixed firmly on his plate.

Adam smoothed the moment over by saying, 'I'm glad you were impressed by the amount of vegetables and fruit Shuttleworth Hall produces, Tony. We keep the whole of Little Ridding supplied and most of the neighbouring villages as well.' He speared a Brussels sprout. 'Before the war, Shuttleworth Hall was famous for its roses, thanks to Paul, Vicky's nephew, who is a rose-breeder – or who was a rose-breeder before this bally war started.'

'He's a major now, in the American army,' Emily Elise said, 'and if you're wondering where Heini fits in, Heini is the one Jewish refugee we still have with us, though we don't think of him as being a refugee because he's been here since even before the war and so he's simply family.'

Tony grinned across at her, grateful that one mystery had been clarified, even if two more had been thrown into the ring. Why hadn't Hugo ever told any of the chaps at the base that he was a widower and that his wife was Jewish? It would certainly have helped their often difficult relationships with him if he had done. And just where did the American connection fit in? Adam had made it sound as if Vicky's American nephew had run his rose-breeding business from Shuttleworth Hall, which seemed a little strange unless Shuttleworth Hall was also Paul's home.

All in all, the longer he was at Shuttleworth Hall the more

intriguing he found the ramifications of Hugo's family life. It occurred to him, for instance, that Paul could well have been orphaned as a child, for if he had been there was nothing more certain than that Vicky would have taken him in and given him a home, just as she had given Heini a home.

He helped himself to more perfectly cooked vegetables, wondering what Vicky's reaction was going to be when she discovered that he too had no immediate family. Would she semi-adopt him, as well? The grin he had shot Emily Elise deepened. He could certainly think of worse fates. What he wanted to know now, though, was how long it was going to be before the next surprise came, because he didn't have a second's doubt that there would be one.

It came three hours later in the shape of Nancy and was a surprise not only to him, but to everyone else as well.

'I've had a bugger of a journey,' she said as she burst into the house and they all rushed to greet her. 'The London–Harrogate train took years *and* it was unheated *and* it was impossible to get even a cup of tea on it.'

She dragged a bright red beret from her hair and hugged Emily Elise tight. 'Getting from Harrogate to Little Ridding was even worse, and when I did get there, the taxi driver said he'd used up the last of his petrol ration by driving someone else here and that I'd have to hitch a lift or walk. Which I did – and let me tell you that it's far farther than it used to be!'

Emily Elise giggled, Vicky said she should have rung from the station as Adam always had an emergency can of petrol put by and Hugo said sheepishly, 'Sorry about the taxi, sis. I'm the someone else he drove here.'

'But he didn't drive you here by yourself,' Emily Elise said, eager to be centre-stage again for introductions. 'Nancy, this is Tony. He's Hugo's navigator and he comes from London and he used to work in his father's allotment.'

Seizing hold of Tony's hand she dragged him from where he had been standing a little apart from them all. 'And this is my half-sister, Nancy,' she said, pleased as Punch at the way the family party was so rapidly growing in numbers. 'She's spiffing. She drove an ambulance in the Spanish Civil War and is a war journalist and a communist.'

Vicky gave a howl of protest. Adam shouted with laughter and Hugo said in mortification, 'For the love of God, can no one shut this child up?'

'No,' Emily Elise retorted spiritedly as Nancy shrugged herself out of her coat. 'And I'm not a child. I'm twelve. And Nancy *is* a communist. She told me so.'

'I'm also about to be married,' Nancy said as Heini barrelled his way towards her for a hug. 'And before any of you ask, no, he is not a communist. He's a former newspaper editor who is now a Labour MP. His name is Leo Gunn. He's a Scot, from Caithness. He's ten years older than me and, as it's his idea that we get married, I guess it shows that he's more conventional than he thinks he is. Now, will someone please lead me into the kitchen for a cup of tea and will someone please tell me that, despite rationing, a miracle has taken place and there are curd tarts to eat with it?'

There weren't any curd tarts, but there were Yorkshire teacakes. Vicky toasted them and served them with some of the damson jam she'd made the previous autumn.

'And just how did you wangle the sugar for the jam?' Nancy asked, unused to such home comforts.

'I didn't have to wangle. I haggled. And as I had bucketfuls of fruit to haggle with, it wasn't too difficult.' She looked across to where Tony, Heini, Adam and Emily Elise were playing Monopoly and said: 'Let's go for a short walk before it gets dark. I want to know some more about this fiancé of yours.'

Nancy gave a heavy sigh and brushed teacake crumbs from

her chest. 'I knew you would. All right, then. Down to the river and back, but no farther.'

A few minutes later, as they made their way over the daffodil-crowded grass, she said, 'I'm sorry Leo isn't with me. Though I could get away this weekend, he couldn't. But I promise we will be here together at the very first opportunity.'

She was looking straight ahead, her jaw jutting pugnaciously, her hands dug deep in the pockets of her military-style coat.

'Has Leo been married before?' Vicky asked, assuming that a man of forty probably had been and not knowing how best to ask her prickly child the question she really wanted to ask.

'Yes, but not for long. There were no children.'

She stopped walking. 'We're living together, Mum. We've been living together for two years now. I know I should have told you about him before, but somehow ... after all that happened with Claus ... I just wanted to keep things secret this time.'

Suddenly, it was very easy for Vicky to ask the only question that was of importance to her. 'And you're in love with him, Nancy? Truly in love?'

Nancy's blue-grey eyes held hers. 'What you're really asking is, am I love with him the way I was in love with Claus?'

Vicky's silence was her answer and Nancy turned her head away, looking towards the river. She wasn't wearing her beret and her thick hair blew around her head in a mass of untidy curls. 'No,' she said starkly. 'I'm not in love with him the way I was in love with Claus, because that was an obsession. It was something I built up in my head from being a small child and when I became an adult – when I *thought* I was an adult – I simply carried it on. We never really had a single thing in common, apart from our family. Our passion for each other never extended to a shared passion for other things. With Leo it's different. We both know that this war is a defining, iconic moment in British political history. We're both passionate about working towards a new social order. In absolutely everything, we're a team.'

She turned back, her eyes meeting her mother's. 'I wouldn't want a repeat of the kind of love I had for Claus. What I want now is what I've got, because it's so much more. There's mutual respect. Total compatibility. Shared ideals. Shared goals. He isn't Greek-god handsome, like Claus. He's good-looking in a rugged, rugby-player-looking way. He's fiercely intelligent. Wildly funny. Immensely kind and, last but by no means least, he makes me happy in bed.' Her mouth tugged into a smile. 'So does that give you the answer to your question? And are you happy with it?'

'Yes, it does. And yes, I'm happy with it,' Vicky said, all doubts set to rest. 'And where will you marry? Here, or London?'

'London, if that's OK with you. It will be a Register Office wedding, not a church one.' There was impishness in her eyes that Vicky hadn't seen for years. 'Though I still have to break the news to Emily Elise that I'm no longer a card-carrying communist, just a very far-to-the-left socialist, a church wedding is still definitely out.' She began giggling. 'Did you see Hugo's face when Emily Elise said the word "communist"? I thought he was going to choke.'

'I thought *I* was going to choke,' Vicky said drily as, in mutual accord, they began walking again.

Nancy turned up the collar of her coat against the damp chill of the approaching dusk. 'It's nice to see Hugo with a friend in tow, isn't it?' she said as they reached the river bank. 'I wonder if Hugo has told him he's half-German? I bet he hasn't. I think I probably will, though. It'll be interesting to see what his reaction is.'

*

498

Tony's reaction was to drop his jaw and gape at her wide-eyed. 'You mean . . . Remer is a German name?' he said when he recovered his power of speech. 'You mean it really *is* a German name? It doesn't just sound like one?'

With coats buttoned up to their chins they were sitting on one of the terrace's wrought-iron and wood benches, watching Vicky wielding a pair of secateurs and cutting long sprays of delicate sunshine-yellow blossom from the winter jasmine growing against the house wall.

'No, it doesn't just sound like one,' Nancy said with all her old bluntness. 'It's very German. German as in House of Remer steelworks German.'

Tony stared at her. 'Please tell me you don't mean that literally?' he said, appalled. 'Please tell me you and Hugo aren't related to the House of Remer Remers.'

'Why? Because you'll refuse to even speak to us again if we are?'

'No. Because some joker in the squadron made a crack linking Hugo to the steelworks – not believing it for a moment, of course – and Hugo nearly bit his head off.'

'Well, he would.' The amusement in Nancy's eyes died. 'The German connection is far worse for Hugo than it's been for our older brother, Max, and me. Berlin is where our father, aunt, uncle and cousins live. We don't live in fear of having to bomb it, or, now that he's flying Mossies, having to locate and mark targets in order that other planes can bomb it. Hugo does. It can't be easy for him. It must be a nightmare on a par with the nightmare of his losing Hester.'

'Aah,' Tony said as Vicky transferred her attentions to a shrub abutting the jasmine and began cutting stems of greenery to go with it. 'That's something else I don't know about.'

'Don't you?' Nancy hesitated, but only for the briefest of

seconds. 'As I don't see why you shouldn't know,' she said, plunging straight in as usual, 'I'll tell you.'

When Hugo and Tony returned to their Lincolnshire air base, Hugo was just as untalkative and unforthcoming as he had been on their journey to Yorkshire. The difference was that this time the silences between them weren't strained or awkward. There was friendship between them now, albeit one that was more tentative on Hugo's side than Tony's. He knew, though, that the next time he went home he wouldn't be doing so alone and that Tony would be with him. It was a good feeling, one he hadn't had for a long, long time.

Later that afternoon, when the curtain drew back in the briefing room, his mood turned around in an instant.

'Tonight's target is Berlin,' his wing commander said. 'And it is to be a major raid. The biggest over Berlin so far.' He gave the details: 18 Mosquitos to act as Pathfinders for a total of 793 aircraft – 577 Lancasters and 216 Halifaxes. 'You're going to need your wits about you, gentlemen, so pay close attention to everything I am about to say.'

Hugo did so out of sheer habit, his face impassive. He wasn't feeling impassive inside, though. Inside he was feeling sick to his guts.

When the briefing was over he didn't join Tony and the other crews in the Mess. Instead, he walked out to the hangars, watching as an army of mechanics swarmed over the Mosquitos.

Berlin. Would his father, Ilse and Lotti still be in the city or would they have left it months ago, when the murderous raids over Berlin first started? And Claus? Would Claus be in the city or would he be in the Ruhr? He had no way of telling, but if they were still in the city and if they died in the raid, he knew their deaths would be on his conscience for the rest of his life.

He ground out his cigarette under his heel. He'd been flying sorties for longer than any pilot on the station. He'd seen crews blown apart and others die in flames. Throughout everything his nerves had remained rock hard. They didn't feel rock hard now. The fear that was natural before a raid – the fear that his innate courage always overcame – was fear that now had a different dimension.

It was a fear he successfully hid from Tony.

'Berlin,' Tony said two hours later as they pulled on their helmets and settled themselves at the Mossie's controls. 'You OK with that, H?'

Hugo nodded. 'Yep,' he lied. 'No problem.'

Tony, who was well aware that for Hugo their target was a problem of mega proportions, began checking Oboe, his radio navigation aid. If Hugo didn't want to open up to him about his personal situation where Berlin was concerned, that was fine by him. It was probably best that he didn't do so. Emotion of any kind wasn't what was needed now. What was needed now was one hundred per cent concentration on the task in hand combined with ice-cool nerves – and ice-cool nerves were something he knew Hugo had in abundance.

With other Mossies flanking them and the thundering herd of the main bomber stream behind them, they crossed the sea. The moon was far too bright for either his or Hugo's liking. The forecast had been for protective high cloud on the outward route, but high winds were fast dispersing it.

Once over enemy territory Hugo flew at low level to the south of Hamburg and then, climbing to 25,000 feet, headed for Berlin, still without any protective cloud cover.

The target he was to mark for the bombers behind him, was Hitler's Reich Chancellery on Wilhelmstrasse. The centre and symbol of all power in the Greater German Reich, it was a building of monumental grandeur and the task that night was to reduce it to rubble.

Once on the run-in audible radio signals would be constantly transmitted to him – through Oboe, directional control of his plane was in the hands of operators based in England, who were able to tell him, via the signals, just where he was in relation to the target. A solid tone indicated he was on course. Morse code dashes indicated he was too far to the left and had to correct to the right. A series of dots indicated he was too far to the right and had to correct to the left.

'Don't like the moon, H,' Tony shouted to him over the intercom. 'We're going to meet with heavy opposition.'

Mindful of the necessity of keeping the airwaves clear, Hugo merely nodded. He didn't like the moon, either. They were approaching Wannsee and the water shimmered beneath him like black silk. He fought to suppress images from the past. Family picnics when he'd been a small boy and Paul had taken him and Max out on pedalos and, when they were a little older, on sail boats. Swimming parties when he'd raced Lotti and Ilse across the small bay they regarded as their own private preserve. Evening walks on the lake's shoreline with Hester.

'Christ!' he heard Tony shout as they crossed the night-black woods that separated Wannsee from the city. 'Here they come!'

The ground defences opened with a storm of deafening, murderous flak and as they did so enemy fighters swooped towards them, guns firing.

The radio signals were still a solid tone. He was still on track and barely needed their guidance. Once over the city centre he could have pinpointed the Reich Chancellery with his eyes shut. His problem was that he wasn't yet over the city centre. He still hadn't released his marker flares and, until he did so, the bombers behind him couldn't release their loads to best advantage.

As a fighter dropped from seemingly out of nowhere, he turned in a steep, evasive climb. Despite the Mossie's superb manoeuvrability, it wasn't swift enough. The Ju88 came up underneath him with upward-firing cannon, hitting the starboard wing and pouring bullets into the fuselage with deadly accuracy. He peeled away only to face what seemed to be a solid wall of exploding shells and more fighter planes. Gunfire rattled all along Tony's side of the plane and he saw Tony slump; saw blood begin to course down the side of his head.

He knew Tony was dead. He knew the plane must be on fire. And he knew he was only seconds away from being directly over his target. Bailing out never occurred to him. Opening up the throttle he flew straight on as if the hell taking place around him didn't exist. He was still receiving signals from his Cat station, the station responsible for guiding him in on his run to the target. Only if he maintained the right altitude would the station known as Mouse kick in, signalling to him that it was time to release his marker flares.

The bomb-marker release order came. In the same second that he fulfilled his mission, releasing cascade after cascade of brilliant flares onto the Reich Chancellery, a Ju88 honed in on him, guns spitting.

A hail of bullets hit him. With the tail-fire now out of control the Mossie steepled into a deathly nosedive. Hugo didn't care. He was going to die and he was going to die in the city he had shared with Hester.

He could see a lake again and knew that this time it was the lake in the Tiergarten; the lake where his mother had taken him for picnics when he had been a small boy; the lake where he had photographed Hester when she had been happy and smiling, when her eyes had been full of love for him and when neither of them had had a care in the world.

The moon sailed over the water and as he dove down to it in a sea of flame, the lake rose up to meet him. Above, in the sky, the battle continued and on Hitler's Reich Chancellery bombs rained down, signalling to Germany's Führer that defeat was unavoidable and that victory for the Allies was now only a matter of time.

THIRTY-TWO

Berlin, February 1945

Lotti gazed around at her mother's drawing room in incredulity. Charlottenburg had not been bombed as heavily as the rest of Berlin and the spacious second-floor apartment bore not the slightest sign of damage. Lalique mirrors hung on the walls. A priceless collection of Ferdinand Preiss bronze and ivory figurines were on careless display.

'Don't you think you should pack everything valuable away?' she asked as Zelda handed her a cup of ersatz black coffee made from chicory beans. 'You're bound to either be hit or suffer a near miss eventually. And what about the vibration when hundreds of planes fly overhead? I would have thought that would be enough to bring everything crashing down.'

'That was your father's opinion as well, but I never shared it. Outside this room Berlin may be being reduced to ashes, but inside it I'm going to live for as long as I can as I've always done. With beautiful things around me.'

It was freezing cold and, as there was no heating, she was buried deep in her favourite sable coat. Though the world was falling around her and though she was rake-thin from short rations and stress, she was still exotically made-up, her sloe-dark eyes heavily mascaraed, her beautifully sculpted mouth a deep, glossy red.

Lotti, heavily enveloped in a miscellaneous collection of jumpers, cardigans, a far too-large military greatcoat that had once belonged to one of Nicholas's friends and with a headscarf tied turban-like over her hair, knew she was coming off badly in comparison. She took a drink of the so-called coffee, wishing her mother had served it in a mug and not a bone-china coffee cup. A mug she would have been able to warm her hands around.

'I thought that after *Vati* died you would leave the city, taking everything that was valuable with you. Nearly everyone else who has the choice has evacuated it. Even moving only as far west as Wannsee or Potsdam has to be safer than remaining here, especially now the Russians are so near to the city.'

She saw her mother flinch and knew that it wasn't because she had spoken of Russians, but because she had spoken of her father. Though she and Ilse had grieved for him, it had been nothing on the scale of their mother's grief. 'No one,' she had said at the funeral, looking like a carved effigy, her face heavily veiled, 'will ever know just how much your father loved me and of how much he gave up for me.'

'The only thing I ever knew *Vati* to give up were the steelworks,' Ilse had said to her afterwards, 'and he did that because he wanted Claus to inherit them sooner rather than later, didn't he? I can't see that it had anything whatever to do with *Mutti*.'

Lotti hadn't been able to see that it had, either. Her private opinion had always been that the handing over of the House of Remer to Claus had been something that had deeply distressed her mother, rather than being something she had wanted.

In normal circumstances, her mother's remark might have been one she would have discussed with Claus, but though Claus had attended the funeral, her conversation with him had been stilted. He had looked like a man under the strain of keeping a colossal secret and, considering his many close contacts within the Nazi hierarchy, she had not wanted to speculate as to what his secret was. Ilse had barely exchanged two words with him, either. It had been only months after Nicholas's arrest and subsequent execution and she had still been like a woman locked in ice. For reasons over and above their father's death it had not been a happy occasion and neither she nor Ilse had seen Claus since.

'I'd like you to do something for me,' Zelda said, breaking in on her thoughts. 'I want you to take Berthold with you when you go back to Ilse's. It was Claus's idea that he live here, but I can't endure it a moment longer. It was bad enough when your father was alive, but now your father is dead it's impossible. It's like looking after a child. He has no grasp of what is happening. He wanders the streets when air raids are in progress. He complains constantly at not having things like coffee and sugar and chocolate as if I were depriving him of them through spite. And he annoys me. He always has and now he's become so prematurely senile, he annoys me even more.'

Lotti thought of the intensely heavy bombing raids taking place over central Berlin, the British by night and the Americans by day. She and Ilse spent more time in cellars and air-raid shelters than they did in their own beds and the thought of having to shepherd a confused Berthold with them whenever they had to scurry for cover was horrendous.

'Central Berlin is no longer any place for Uncle Berthold,' she said, hoping the conversation wasn't going to end in an unholy row. 'He's much better off here and you probably see very little of him. It isn't as if it's a small apartment, is it?'

'It is when it comes to sharing it with your uncle,' Zelda said sharply. She wrapped her coat even closer around her. 'It would be just as bad if I were living in the Charlottenburg Palace. It wouldn't be big enough. Nowhere would be big enough. After the war Max or Hugo or Nancy will have to take care of him. For now, though, it will have to be you and Ilse. I've had enough.'

Lotti set her cup and saucer down on the art deco table that separated the chairs they were seated on. 'Why can't Claus look after him? I know I said central Berlin was no longer any place for him, but I was forgetting about Unter den Linden. The house there has vast cellars and is probably as safe as anywhere else in Berlin. Why can't he go back there?'

'Because Claus doesn't want him living there.' With unnerving agility Zelda sprang to her feet. 'God, but I'd like a little bit of cooperation from my children! All I'm profoundly grateful for is that I didn't know Berthold was older than Josef when I first came to Berlin, because if I had, I'd have spent the last thirty-six years married to him and would now be a complete mental wreck!'

Lotti stared at her, wide-eyed and open-mouthed. That her mother might once have married Berthold was something that had never occurred to her, nor did she imagine that it had ever occurred to anyone else.

Aware that she had let a long-hidden cat out of the bag and regretting having done so, Zelda rammed a cheap black-market cigarette into an ebony holder that had been accustomed to better things. 'As for Berthold . . . you can stop looking so panic-stricken. I've thought of a solution.' She lit the cigarette and inhaled deeply. 'Eva will take him in. He'll be company for her mother. And it won't be for long. According to last night's BBC broadcast, the British and the Americans are nearing the Rhine. Once they've crossed it, Hitler will have to capitulate and it will all be over.'

'He'll never capitulate.' Lotti's eyes glittered. 'A sane man – a man who cared for Germany and the German people – would have surrendered a year ago when it became obvious Germany had no hope of ever winning. But Hitler doesn't give a damn about Germany and the German people. He'll see the country destroyed beyond hope of recovery and every man, woman and child in it dead, rather than lose his precious pride and surrender.'

She rose. Talking about the man who had led Germany into hell was pointless. No one knew where he was, for the minute the war had turned against him he had ceased making public appearances. Rumours were he was in Berlin, conducting military operations from a bunker deep below the bomb-shattered Reich Chancellery. Wherever he was, he wasn't on the streets giving comfort, through his presence, to the thousands who had lost their homes in the raids or who had been left terribly injured and bereaved.

'I'm going,' she said to her mother, grateful her mother's nerves were still holding up so well. 'And I'm going home via the Tiergarten. It's become the biggest black-market centre in the city. A friend of Nicky's gave Ilse a half-dozen bottles of schnapps, so I'm in a good position to do some bartering. If I can get you some sugar, I will.'

'Never mind sugar,' her mother said tartly. 'Get me some decent cigarettes.'

Lotti grinned. 'Will do,' she said, admiring her mother's inbred American feistiness. 'And your idea about Eva is a good one. She's not only deeply compassionate, which is why she will take Uncle Berthold under her wing, but being a ward sister she's also implacably firm. And firmness is what poor old Uncle Berthold needs these days.'

Zelda nodded and for the first time Lotti became aware that there were strands of silver in her mother's blue-black hair. 'I wonder,' Zelda said in her cracked-ice voice as Lotti kissed her on the cheek, 'where Paul is now? I wonder if he's fighting with the American forces that are approaching the Rhine? I wonder how soon it will be before the war is over and he and Eva marry?'

'I don't know.' Lotti's voice was unsteady. 'Let's hope it's soon.' She flashed her mother a lopsided smile. 'And let's hope we're all still alive when it happens.'

As she let herself out of the apartment her thoughts weren't on Paul, but on Max. It was over three years since she had last seen him and in all that time there had been only one brief telephone call. Daily, she wondered where he was and what he was doing. As an intelligence officer there was no telling where he had been posted. He could very well be in Greece, or Yugoslavia. Or – and her nails dug deep into her palms – he could be attached to the British troops who, like the Americans, were forcing the German army deeper and deeper into a retreat there could be no coming back from.

She took a pair of heavy gauntleted gloves out of her coat pocket and pulled them on. The only reliable method of transport now was a bicycle and in February temperatures her hands would have frozen to the handlebars without the military gloves Nicholas's friend had left behind him.

As she wheeled the bicycle over the snow-covered pavement and onto the road, her heart and mind were still full of Max. They had been lovers for such a short space of time and under such extraordinary conditions that there were times when she wondered if their precious weeks together had been nothing but a figment of her imagination. The feeling of unreality about their relationship wasn't helped by everyone close to her being ignorant of it.

As she began the long bike ride towards the city centre she knew that not telling her mother or Ilse had been a grave mistake, for Ilse had submerged her grief by talking incessantly about Max. It had been then that the fear she always lived with, the fear for his safety, had been joined by another fear. Would Ilse seek to be reconciled to Max when the war was over? And if she did so, what would Max's reaction be?

The bitter cold wind stung her face and made her eyes smart. Her deepest fear was that it had been gratitude and relief that had catapulted him into her bed. Gratitude at her having saved his life and the lives of his friends, and relief at her having walked out of Gestapo headquarters with no worse injuries than broken fingers. What if, on returning to a Berlin in which Ilse was a widow, Max resumed his affair with her? Perhaps even married her?

She swerved to avoid a pothole and narrowly avoided falling off her bike. What would she do if, when the war was over and they were reunited, he was no longer in love with her? How would she endure it? How would she live with the pain?

She struggled to block the thought by focusing on the route she was taking. The streets she was now bicycling through were so bomb-damaged as to be unrecognizable and it needed a lot of concentration to ensure she was still heading in the right direction. Walls were blown in and blown out. Whole sides of houses were ripped off, leaving rooms and furnishings open to the elements. Rubble lay everywhere and every now and again there came a sinister smell of gas.

And amid all this devastation her fellow Berliners were courageously trying to carry on with their daily lives. A hairdresser's shop was open for business. A cinema was still miraculously unscathed and had a large queue outside it. Women were walking the streets with shopping baskets over their arms, stoically heading for a ration queue or a black-market food contact.

The bottles of schnapps in the bag hooked over the handles of her bike were her and Ilse's passport for a few extra rations. With luck she would be able to barter one of them for flour to supplement the meagre weekly bread ration. Another bottle she intended exchanging for real coffee and another for cigarettes for her mother.

On the fringes of the Tiergarten the sirens started wailing and howling. She skidded to a halt. The enormous Zoo–Tiergarten air-raid shelter was too far away for her to reach it before the planes came and she was unsure of where the nearest shelter to her was. Looking back over her shoulder she saw that the cinema queue was speedily dispersing, with nearly everyone scurrying in the same direction. Hastily, she wheeled her bike around and began peddling after them. They were locals who knew the area and, wherever they were going for shelter, she was going too.

As she swerved after them down a side street that had a large arrow marked 'Public Air-raid Shelter', the city's outer ring of anti-aircraft guns boomed into life. By the time she abandoned her bike at the shelter's entrance, the second ring of anti-aircraft guns was thundering.

Clutching her precious bag of bottles to her chest she clattered down narrow metal steps, knowing she had at least a two-hour hell of claustrophobia ahead of her.

From outside the shelter came a long screaming whistle and then a terrific, rocking explosion. The blast sent her flying to her knees, her arms still around her bag. An elderly woman fell against her.

'Dear God,' the woman said as they helped each other stagger to their feet. 'They must be bombing directly above us! What is left in this part of the city that they can destroy?'

As far as Lotti was concerned, the answer was nothing, but she couldn't say so, because the noise was now so intense the woman wouldn't have been able to hear her. Bomb after bomb was raining down, explosion after explosion shaking the shelter so that it rocked like a ship at sea.

Weak-kneed, she squeezed onto one of the crowded benches, praying that her mother's apartment hadn't been hit, praying that Ilse was safe, praying that the British and the Americans would speedily cross the Rhine and then the Elbe and that the nightmare they had been enduring for over five years would at last come to an end.

Hester stood in the garden of the Unter den Linden mansion, watching as hundreds of heavy bombers flew across the outskirts of the city towards its centre. They looked to be flying at a lower altitude than normal and in closer formation, and all of them seemed impervious to the anti-aircraft fire exploding around them. Had they flown in over Spandau? Had they already dropped bombs on the factories there? Had Claus's factory been bombed? They were coming in waves, the sky black with them.

With her mouth dry with fear for Claus's safety and for the safety of all the Jewish and Russian women working for him, she spun on her heel, running back into the house, reaching the entrance to the cellar only as the first bombs began to fall.

Whenever there was a raid through the day she was always alone, for Claus would be either at the factory or in the Ruhr, and shelter in a public air-raid shelter was impossible for her. The SS had grown even more maniacal as the war had gone from bad to worse and the slightest suspicion that she was a Jewess would be enough to ensure swift incarceration again at Sachsenhausen – and the barbarism at Sachsenhausen had plummeted to a depth hard for any sane mind to grasp.

'It's now not only a death camp because of starvation and torture and indiscriminate killings, it's an official death camp,' Claus had said to her not long after he had successfully established a camp for his Russian workers inside his factory's precincts. 'I've had the information from Göring himself.'

His face had been bloodless. 'He told me he'd just come back from the inauguration of a new installation at Sachsenhausen, one identical to installations that have been in operation for months past in the camps in Poland.' With shaking hands he had poured himself a large brandy. 'It's called "Station Z" and it enables large numbers of prisoners to be gassed all at the same time. Huge numbers. He told me as if it were something I must already be aware of. As if it were quite common knowledge.'

He had drained the brandy in a huge gulp and then, unsteadily, he had said, 'I have to work out a plan, Hester. A plan whereby none of the prisoners working for me ever go back to Sachsenhausen. And I have to work out a plan whereby I can have more workers allotted to me, because that's the only way they are going to survive.'

He had succeeded in both his aims. Whenever mention was made of any of his original workers being returned to Sachsenhausen he insisted that as they had all now become highly trained, he couldn't lose them without production levels plummeting.

And he had negotiated that large numbers of slave labourers be allocated to the House of Remer steelworks in the Ruhr. As at Spandau, the arrangement he negotiated with the Con-centration Camp Section of the SS Main Administrative and Economic Office was that for efficiency's sake there would be no daily transporting of slave labourers backwards and forwards from the camp they were presently imprisoned in, but that at his own expense he would establish a Forced Labour Camp within the steelworks perimeter. In that way, he had argued, the labour of those assigned to him could be more fully exploited.

Grudgingly, permission had been given. It was a camp whose fenced perimeter was still patrolled by SS guards – there had been no escaping that condition – but no guards oversaw the prisoners as they worked. There were no opportunities for casual beatings and no fear of starvation or torture. As at Spandau, his workers had the benefit of shower blocks and a laundry, his argument for them being that an outbreak of typhus would set essential war production back by weeks.

There were now three hundred women slave labourers in the

haven of the Spandau factory and eight hundred men at the Ruhr steelworks and both she and Claus knew they would all count against him when the war was lost and the Allies began their tally of war criminals. As an industrialist producing steel and armaments he would be on the list as a matter of course, but as a user of slave labour his name would be asterisked in just the same way as the names of those industrialists who had worked slave labourers to death in their thousands.

As the air raid took place above her, shaking the walls of the cellar, Hester felt sick at the thought of what would then happen to Claus. The most optimistic scenario was that he would be imprisoned. The worst, that he would be executed. If he were to be executed, she knew it was something she would never, ever, be able to come to terms with. Not only because she knew how unjustified it would be, when his reason for demanding as many slave labourers as possible was in order that he could save their lives, but because, next to Hugo, he had become the dearest person in the world to her.

As bombs continued to fall, the noise of explosions so horrendous she thought her eardrums were going to burst, she reflected that it was only due to his iron self-control that they weren't lovers, for ever since the moment when he had recognized her in his factory's corridor, he had behaved in a manner that had cut him off from meaningful contact with anyone but her.

No one else knew him as she did. In order to continue having influence with the bureaucrats at the SS Main Administrative and Economic Office and the SS commanders at Sachsenhausen and the camp from which his Ruhr workers had come, he'd had to continue acting out the part of a dedicated Nazi totally loyal to the Führer. No other option had been open to him. It meant that Ilse and Lotti and their friends – and anyone who thought like them – shunned and avoided him. He couldn't be his true self to them and he certainly wasn't his true self when with the

Nazi hierarchy he of necessity fraternized with. Only with her could he be the person he truly was and, as she could have no contact with anyone save him, it had meant they had become utterly necessary to each other.

Another terrifying crash shook the house and she hugged her arms even closer around her chest, shamed by the knowledge that though she still loved Hugo, she could barely remember her life with him. It was all so long ago – more than six years – and so much had happened to her in the intervening years.

Suddenly, there was a piercing whistle and an explosion so tremendous the entire cellar seemed to jar and tilt. The lights went off and she scrabbled to find the emergency torch. Just as she did so, there came an even more terrible sound. The rumble and roar of falling masonry.

Panic tightened her throat so she could hardly breathe. Of all her nightmares when enduring a raid, the worst was of the house being bombed and collapsing in such a way that all exits from the cellar – even the second exit Claus had made and which surfaced some twenty yards away in the garden – were blocked and that she would be buried alive.

The terrible roaring noise went on and on. Great billows of black dust swirled down the cellar steps accompanied by such a hurricane of sound that she knew it was the sound of the house collapsing in a mountain of rubble above her head.

'Please God, don't let me be buried alive!' she prayed, knotting her hands together, beads of sweat falling onto them. 'Please God, let me get out! Please God! Please!'

Clouds of dust continued to surge into the cellar. She was coughing. Choking. It was so obvious that exit via the cellar steps was now impossible that she didn't even attempt to mount them. Instead, uncaring that the raid was still taking place directly overhead, she made a run for the tunnel entrance.

It was so narrow and wet and dark and claustrophobic that

515

she'd only ever used it once before, and that had been when Claus had just finished excavating it and had asked her to test it out.

Now she scrambled her way along it, the torch slippery in her hand, engulfed by the fear that the house had fallen over the exit; that there was going to be no way out; that at the end of the tunnel, in the dark and alone, her life was going to come to an agonizing end.

After what seemed like an eternity the torchlight picked out the bigger excavation at the end of the tunnel, an excavation large enough to stand up in. It was here that the ladder was. As she grasped hold of it and shone her torch upwards she could see the steel square of the hatch that led into the garden.

The pandemonium above was no longer of explosions, but of hundreds of planes droning away and the piercing wail of the all-clear sirens accompanying the hideous sound of tons and tons of broken masonry shifting and settling.

With the torch in one hand and the other hand slippery with perspiration, she climbed the ladder and then, praying as she'd never prayed before, pushed upwards on the hatch with all her strength.

Nothing happened.

It didn't budge by so much as an inch.

'Please!' she prayed feverishly, freeing her other hand by pushing the torch between her legs. 'Please, God! *Please!*'

With her hands splayed against the metal she pushed until she thought every blood vessel she had was going to burst. Still nothing happened. There was a great weight on the other side pressing it down and she had no way of telling if the weight was merely rubble from the bomb-struck house or a gigantic piece of masonry.

Whichever it was made very little difference. The weight was more than she could move. She was sealed in and, behind her, choking clouds of black dust were already wafting down the tunnel towards the foot of the ladder, growing thicker and thicker as they did so.

'They've saturation-bombed Unter den Linden and the area around it again,' his overseer said to Claus with the air of a man who knew what he was talking about.

Claus didn't bother to retort that from way out at Spandau it was impossible to tell exactly which part of central Berlin had come off the worst in the raid. Hans Wolf's reputation for always being right was one that was well earned and, besides, Unter den Linden was so near to the government offices in Wilhelmstrasse and Vossstrasse that it came under attack far more often than it was spared.

So far, apart from the orangerie which had been blasted into extinction long ago, the family mansion had withstood everything that had been hurled at it and the cellars beneath it were deep and substantial. He had transformed one of them into a comfortable shelter, carpeting it and equipping it with a camp bed and bedding, an armchair, a radio, books, a first-aid kit and a plentiful supply of bottled water and biscuits.

Hester had assured him she felt perfectly safe there and, until now, he had believed that to be so. Now, as American bombers thundered into retreat, leaving an inferno of flames and devastation behind them, he had a gut instinct to the contrary.

'I've personal business to attend to,' he said to Wolf, and seizing hold of his overcoat he slammed out of his office and out of the factory.

As an Essential War Producer he not only had a Mercedes bearing a silvered swastika medallion that marked it out as an official car of the Nazi Party, but petrol for it. It was parked in the factory yard and he gunned it into gear, speeding out of the yard with such a scream of tyres that Hans Wolf ran to a window to see what on earth was happening.

As was often the case, Spandau hadn't been bombed and,

apart from the craters and potholes caused by earlier raids, the streets were clear. Considering the number of factories there were in Spandau, its relative good fortune where saturation raids were concerned was something he didn't understand, but was also something he was deeply grateful for. It meant not only that was his factory still undamaged, but that the women workers he now felt a personal responsibility for, were still unharmed.

As he sped from Spandau into Charlottenburg the scene was very different. A cinema had been bombed and as fire-workers fought the flames, other people were bringing out a steady stream of bodies. His stomach curled into a knot. Didn't the British and Americans realize that further bombing of Berlin was unnecessary? That the war was virtually over and that they were the victors? What point was there in continuing to create firestorms in a city that was now predominantly a city of women, children and old men? A city that desperately wanted the British and Americans to capture it before the Russians should do so.

In Mitte, the burning streets were mayhem and every now and again a shower of sparks rained down on his windscreen. Driving at any kind of speed was now impossible as people with scarves wrapped protectively across nose and mouth milled in the roads to keep away from the burning, collapsing buildings.

As he turned into the broad boulevard that was Unter den Linden his heart nearly failed him. Eddying clouds of soot and ash swirled amid monstrous mountains of smashed brick and twisted steel. Beyond the grand, gated entrance to his home stood a smoking, wrecked ruin he was barely able to recognize.

Though two of the four walls still stood, a third was semi-collapsed and the facade of the mansion had been blown out so that it had the appearance of an open-fronted doll's house. The vast slated roof had collapsed inwards, its weight shearing down through every floor. Beams, chandeliers, statuary, paintings, furniture – the entire contents of a house that had stood for three generations – lay tangled and splintered amid rearing blocks of granite and huge slabs of masonry.

He slammed on the Mercedes' brakes and hurtled from it, leaving the driver's door swinging open behind him. He didn't even attempt to locate the area where the entrance to the cellar was buried. Great slabs of pulverized marble and broken columns reared up over it, two storeys high. In the glow of a sky blood-red from the city's raging fires he scrambled over the lower slopes of debris covering the garden. Somewhere beneath it was the tunnel exit, but the wreckage around him was so total, so complete, it was hard to assess exactly where.

With every ounce of control he possessed he forced himself to stand still and to orientate himself. His breathing was harsh in his throat, his heart hammering loud and fast. He couldn't afford to make a misjudgement. He couldn't afford to spend time tearing away at rubble over the wrong spot.

It was now late afternoon and growing dark apart from the light from the fires raging farther down Unter den Linden and in Wilhelmstrasse. At his back, at the rear of the garden, were two birch trees and he scrambled over the rubble until he was in the same position in relation to them that, to the best of his memory, the steel hatchway was.

It lay beneath the outer limits of the collapsed building, deep beneath jagged masonry and bricks and slate, but not so deep that a squad of men with pickaxes and crowbars couldn't clear it.

The problem was that he didn't have a squad of men and he didn't have even a single pickaxe or crowbar. Indecision tore through him. Hester was presumably quite safe in her temporary tomb. There was lighting and water and food. She would come to no harm if he were to return to Spandau for men and equipment. On the other hand, she would know she was trapped underground and would be terrified.

His decision made, he flung off his coat and jacket and

launched himself at the rubble, heaving at blocks of masonry, hurling bricks away, choking on huge clouds of dust and grit.

'Hester!' he shouted, whenever he could spare the breath. *'Hester!'*

There was never any sound in response.

Up and down Unter den Linden there came the noise of fire trucks and water cannon, but they weren't directed in his direction. They were directed at the public buildings that were ablaze and he knew the men manning them wouldn't deviate to attend to a bombed house that wasn't on fire and in which only one person was trapped.

With maniacal strength he kept on wrenching at jagged blocks of stone, burrowing farther and farther down into the debris, terrified that when he succeeded in reaching the bottom of it, there would be only bare earth; that the hatchway would be elsewhere.

When, in blood-red flickering light, he glimpsed sight of it lying beneath the remains of a statue of Hercules, he gave fervent thanks to the God he hadn't prayed to since he was a child.

'Hester!' he shouted as he heaved and hauled at the broken marble head and torso. *'Hester!'*

With a last mighty effort he sent the heavy marble tumbling to one side and hauled up the hatch.

At first he could see nothing and then, as his eyes accustomed themselves to the blackness, he saw she was lying curled up in a comatose heap at the foot of the shaft.

It was then, as he slithered down the ladder to her side, that he knew what true terror was.

'Let her be alive! Please God, let her be alive!' he prayed like a mantra as he carried her to the surface over his shoulder, staggering with her towards the trees where there was still grass not covered by rubble.

Dropping to the ground with her, he began desperately

giving her artificial respiration. 'Breathe!' he shouted, labouring to bring air back into her body. 'For the love of heaven, Hester! *Breathe!*'

It was as if she heard him.

She made a great rasping sucking sound and then a choking noise.

He gave a sob of relief and her eyes fluttered open.

For a moment, she hadn't the slightest idea who he was. He was almost unrecognizable, his face grimy with filth and brick dust, his straw-pale hair as thick with dirt and dust as his face. What had once been an immaculately white shirt was now a torn, bloodied and filthy rag. Beneath its remnants she could see that his hard-muscled body was bathed in sweat, covered in bleeding gashes and cuts. His hands too were raw and bleeding, covered in mortar debris. And his eyes – eyes that were always so cool and impersonal – were ablaze with raw, naked emotion.

'Dear God, Hester! I thought you were dead!'

As he lifted her upwards, so that she was half sitting, half leaning against him, she began shuddering, tears streaming down her face. 'I thought I was dead too!' Her voice was hoarse, still thick with fear. 'The air was so thick with dust and grit that I couldn't breathe and then the hatch wouldn't open . . .'

She pressed herself against him, clinging to him as if she would never let him go, the memory of her terror totally overwhelming.

His mouth was hard against her hair. If he had ever previously had any doubts as to the nature of his feelings for her, he had none now. He loved her. And he couldn't tell her so. She was married to Hugo and, even more importantly, she still loved Hugo.

A judder went through him as he lifted his mouth from her hair, exercising more self-control than he had ever exercised in his life before.

In the darkness, the fires on Unter den Linden still blazed. Every few minutes or so the night breeze brought with it a peppering of ash.

'Can you walk?' he asked hoarsely, when he could trust himself to speak.

She nodded and he helped her to her feet, keeping one arm supportingly around her.

'Then let's go,' he said, and as she leaned heavily against him he turned his back on the monstrous wreck of what had once been his family home and led her past singed and blackened trees towards the Mercedes.

West of the Rhine, Max drove a jeep at high speed towards the building that was serving as the headquarters of the 1st Airborne Corps. He was in battledress, a green beret crammed on his thickly curling hair. The meeting he was about to attend as a senior intelligence officer was going to be one of the most vital of the war; one at which plans for the Battle of Berlin and its subsequent occupation were finally going to be revealed – and he was desperate for confirmation that he would be among those spearheading the drive on the city, for not until he was inside it would he know if those he loved were still alive.

As he swung in front of the building's entrance his nerves were at fever pitch. For days, rumours and counter-rumours had waged. The Russians were making such a spectacular advance across East Prussia that the possibility they would be the first to reach Berlin was very real. And his blood ran cold at the thought of Russian troops seeking retribution for all they had suffered at the hands of the Nazis. Berlin was now a city of women. Rape. There would be unrestrained rape. For that reason alone, let alone for political reasons, it was essential that the great British and American drive across northern France to the Rhine continued eastwards – that it continued eastwards until it reached Berlin.

He parked the jeep and hurried inside the building where he was met by an escorting officer.

The officer saluted smartly. 'This way, Major Remer,' he said, leading the way up a flight of stairs. 'I'm afraid you'll have to have your credentials checked before you enter the meeting room. It's obligatory for everyone – even the regimental commanders.'

They were met at the door of the meeting room by a military policeman and then, once inside the room, Max was warmly greeted by Colonel Joseph Dawson, a man he knew well.

There were only another dozen people present, all of them regimental commanders.

A general he had a lot respect for opened the proceedings. Standing by the side of a huge, curtained map, he said, 'Only those with an absolute need to know have been asked to this briefing. I don't need to emphasize that, until further orders, nothing you hear today is to go beyond this room. At long last, gentlemen, our goal is in sight.'

He drew back the curtain.

The map was of Berlin.

Max's nerve ends tingled.

'Our assault,' the general continued, 'will be part of a First Allied Airborne Army operation, calling for units from two other divisions: 82 Airborne Division, whose objective will be Berlin's Tempelhof Airport; 101 Airborne Division, whose objective will be Gatow Airfield, west of the city. Our objective will be Oranienburg Airfield, to the north-west of the city. Two regiments will hold the perimeters and the third will move towards the centre of Berlin. We'll hang on to this area until the ground forces get to us. That shouldn't be long – a few days at the most.'

Max let out a deep, heartfelt breath of relief. British and American intent was to be in the city well ahead of the

Russians, which meant he would be in the city almost ahead of everybody.

As if reading his thoughts, Colonel Dawson took the podium and said, 'We are also extremely fortunate to have had assigned to us Major Remer, who is Berlin-born and who knows the city intimately. His expertise is going to be invaluable to us. As to when we go – that depends on the continued speed of the advance on the city by our ground forces. Certainly, a drop won't be scheduled until the ground forces are within a reasonable distance of the city. And now, gentlemen –' he unrolled a transparent overlay from the top of the map, marked in heavy black ink with various objectives and drop zones – 'to the fine details of each phase of the operation.'

It was all Max could have asked and more, for as the plans unfolded it became clear that among the ground forces that would be making up the attack on the city was the Armoured Division Paul was fighting with. Though the chance of them meeting up while the battle for the city took place was nil, it did mean they would both be in the city and that at the very first opportunity they could track down their womenfolk.

Paul, he knew, was desperate to marry Eva the instant such a wedding could be arranged. And he too was desperate for a reunion with the woman he loved – the woman he'd always loved. As an intelligence officer he was aware of the failed attempts on Hitler's life and he knew that Nicholas had been executed. It meant that at his reunion with Ilse she would be a widow, and that would, he knew, once again drastically change the relationship between them.

Hurting someone dear to him was not something he was looking forward to, but he knew it was going to be a necessity. A necessity he was utterly prepared for.

The tense expectancy he felt at the prospect of so soon being part of the assault on the city buoyed him up all the way back to his field unit. It was there, four hours later, that he had a visitor who shocked him rigid.

'Sorry about this, Max,' Joseph Dawson said, taking off gauntleted gloves and slapping them together as his driver waited for him a short distance away, out of earshot, 'but I want to share my private feelings with you. And they are feelings you won't like.'

Max waited. A colonel who was Chief of Staff to a general didn't hare around a battle zone to share his 'private feelings' – especially not when there had been the chance for the two of them to talk together earlier in the day.

'I believe the information given out at this morning's meeting was given for political reasons, that it's the way General Montgomery would like to see things going. It isn't the way I believe things will go, though.'

A column of tanks trundled past them. From the distance there came the sound of artillery fire.

'And how do you think things will go, sir?' Max asked, a nerve beginning to jump at the corner of his jaw.

'I think the proposed Allied Airborne operation will be called off because, when push comes to shove, I doubt our ground troops will come within striking distance of Berlin. I strongly suspect they'll reach the River Elbe and then be diverted north and south, leaving the way open for the Russians to seize it. It's only a surmise, but I believe it to be an accurate one. Berlin may be the plum we've all been racing for, but my reading of the situation is that it will be yanked away from us at the last possible moment in order to keep the Russians happy.'

He gave a short, bitter laugh. 'And when it is – when the Ivans capture it – God help the city's Fräuleins inside it, because they'll be looking at one fate, and one fate only.'

And he made a coarse, ugly gesture with his fist.

THIRTY-THREE

Berlin, April 1945

'I'm going to Spandau,' Lotti said, pulling on the boots she always wore when cycling. 'I'm sure Claus is there, not in the Ruhr.'

It was early morning and through the closed windows of their apartment distant artillery fire could be heard. It was a sound far more terrifying than the familiar noise of British or American bombers. Artillery fire meant ground troops and, as it was common knowledge in the city that the British and the Americans were still forty-five miles away on the wrong side of the Elbe, ground troops meant the Red Army.

'You can't cycle to Spandau in this!' Ilse stared at her in disbelief. 'The Russians are only a bus ride away from the eastern outskirts! Artillery shells will soon be falling in the city centre!'

'And when they do, Russian troops will no longer be a bus ride away. They'll be in the city centre too. We have to have protection, Ilse. We have to have a gun and the only person I know who will be able to give us one, is Claus.'

Ilse blanched. Rumours as to what could be expected when the Russians captured the city had been rife for days. Some women were secreting razor blades in their handbags. Others were hoarding aspirin for suicide attempts.

'What will happen to Claus when the Russians arrive?' she asked, fear for his safety superseding all the hostility she had felt towards him for so long. His position as a key Nazi industrialist who openly flaunted social contact with men like Göring, was something she had always abhorred, but her abhorrence had hardened into revulsion with Nicholas's execution. After that, it would have been impossible to have ignored, or to have pretended not to see, the gold Hitler-autographed swastika pin in his jacket lapel and she and Lotti had avoided all contact with him.

Now, with the Russians on Berlin's doorstep, only the fact that he was her brother seemed to be important and no matter how fervently she hated all that he stood for, she didn't want to see him shot or marched off to Siberia.

'I don't know.' Lotti's voice was grim. 'If he's any sense he'll abandon the factory and head towards the American advance as fast as he can. That way, he stands a chance of keeping out of Russian hands. It may be something he's already done. If he has, it means I'll be coming back into the city empty-handed.'

Though the weather held a hint of spring in the air, she shrugged herself into her army greatcoat. With the Russians now so near, there was a lot to do before she and Ilse found themselves hunkered down in the middle of a blazing battle. For one thing, they needed to amass every scrap of food they could. Bread was still available, but it wouldn't be so for much longer.

'Go black-marketeering,' she said, as she paused at the apartment's door. 'Get bread, no matter how many hours you have to queue for it, and get the crisis rations that have been issued. Word is there's dried sausage and dried peas in them. Once you've got as much as you can, pack it all in a suitcase. That way, no matter what happens, we'll have food with us.'

She closed the door behind her. Cycling to Spandau was not going to be easy, for barricades and fortifications were being hastily erected at the end of nearly every street, but any form of public transport had long since been too unreliable for her to want to risk using it.

Two months ago, she had requested a release from her street-car war work in order to work at the Charité. Once there, Eva had appropriated her as a nursing assistant on her ward. Working with Eva had brought a measure of sanity back into her life. On their far too infrequent breaks, Eva would talk to her about Paul and the life he intended for the two of them when the war was over.

'Do you think I will like living in the Yorkshire Dales, Lotti?' she had asked, her lovely sea-green eyes earnest. 'Will I like Shuttleworth Hall? Will Paul's aunt Vicky like me?'

'Of *course* you will like living in Yorkshire,' she had said. 'Little Ridding is the prettiest village imaginable and the River Ure, where it flows past Shuttleworth Hall, is the most beautiful river in the world. As for Aunt Vicky . . .'

Her eyes had misted with emotion. 'Aunt Vicky will love you instantly and you will love her. It's impossible not to. Paul is like a son to her, not a nephew. In many ways she is far closer to him than to Max and Hugo, because they have the same interests. Aunt Vicky was attempting to breed roses at Shuttleworth Hall years before Paul was old enough to begin doing so. It's a passion they have always shared.' Amusement had crept back into her voice. 'And it's certainly not one Max shares with her. His interest in horticulture is nil.'

As she mounted her bike and began cycling off in the direction of the Tiergarten, she reflected on the deep comfort she had gained from talking about Shuttleworth Hall with Eva. For both of them, whenever she had done so, misery and fear had been blotted out. She had described Shuttleworth Hall in winter, under snow, when the rolling lawns and surrounding meadows glistened bone-white and shards of ice glinted on the Ure.

'And Aunt Vicky always has a huge log fire going in the drawing room and there is a great comforting Aga that keeps the kitchen warm as toast,' she had said, almost able to smell the delicious aroma of Vicky's home-baked bread and Yorkshire teacakes and curd tarts. 'It's a vast kitchen, the heart of the house, and it's where everyone eats unless it's a grand occasion, such as a birthday or an anniversary celebration or Christmas.'

But Eva wasn't with her now and there was no mental escape from the grim reality of streets packed with tense, frightened civilians scrounging for whatever food supplies they could lay their hands on. Tanks and troops were thick on the streets too, all heading eastwards in the direction of the approaching Russians.

She manoeuvred around a ruptured water main, entering the desolation that was now the Tiergarten with a heart so heavy she wondered how it would ever again feel light. The trees that had so far survived the bombing were blackened, their newly sprouting leaves shrivelled. In the lake, the tail of a British aeroplane rose from the water like a piece of avant-garde sculpture. It had been a small plane, one of the two-seater reconnaissance planes that led in the British bombers.

She averted her eyes from it, not wanting to think of the deaths of its pilot and navigator. Even though she was cycling towards the western half of the city, the incessant booming of big guns was still deafeningly loud. A squad of the Hitler Youth division, aged about twelve or thirteen, sprinted past her towards an anti-aircraft-gun placement in uniforms that were far too big for them.

She skidded to a halt, overcome by nausea. Was this who the defence of the city was going to be left to? Children? Ahead of her, where the path she had been cycling on merged with a main road, a stream of heavy-loaded limousines were high-tailing it out of the city southwards, towards the Obersalzberg and Austria, every car bearing a silvered swastika medallion marking it out as belonging to a high-ranking official.

Her heart began to slam against her breastbone. If men like these were fleeing the city, then time truly was running very short and there were perhaps only hours left before the Russians overran it. What on earth was she doing attempting to reach Spandau, in the uncertain hope of obtaining a gun when, even if Claus was in Spandau and able to give her one, she would have to return to the centre of the city with it, leaving her mother unprotected at Charlottenburg? She and Ilse should be at Charlottenburg with her; and as Charlottenburg was halfway to Spandau, once she'd left Ilse with Zelda, she could still continue with her gun-hunting mission.

She turned the bike around, beginning to retrace her route, appalled to see that the children were now helping to man the massive anti-aircraft battery.

Once clear of the park her way was hampered by the many rolls of barbed-wire standing in readiness for use as barricades. Barbed-wire that hadn't been there a bare fifteen minutes earlier. With growing panic she realized that nothing could be taken for granted any more. She might not be able to reach Ilse's apartment and, even if she did so, the two of them might not be able to reach Charlottenburg. As for Spandau, if there was street fighting by the time she set out for it, that too would be an impossibility.

She negotiated huge craters in the road, her hands sticky with sweat on the handlebars. Where would Ilse have gone for bread and the much-trumpeted crisis rations? Was it going to take Lotti an age to find her? Furious with herself for having made such a mess of things she pedalled past a seemingly endless food queue, and as she did so planes screamed in from the eastern outskirts, guns firing.

She slithered from the bike, running with it for the shelter of the nearest doorway. Gunfire ripped across the pavement behind her. Women who had been standing in the food queue were hit. Screams and gunfire and engine noise blasted her eardrums until she thought they were going to burst. Certain she was going to be hit, she pressed herself flat against a door leading to a dentist's, a door that bore the message 'Away Till Further Notice'. It was too late to find any other shelter. On either side of her, windows shattered beneath the storm of Russian bullets, flying glass embedding itself in the first soft flesh it encountered.

Instantly, she dropped into a crouch so that her heavy army greatcoat gave her all the protection it could.

'Please God, let it be over,' she prayed, protecting her face with her hands. 'Please God, let Ilse be safe. Please God, don't let them do this in Charlottenburg. Don't let my mother be in a food queue. Don't let any of us die now that the war is so very nearly over!'

As suddenly as it had begun, the raid came to an end, plane after plane peeling away to continue their murderous blast of gunfire elsewhere. Unsteadily, she rose to her feet and, ignoring her bicycle, ran across to the injured.

It was another two hours of being hampered by barricades and troops and tanks before she reached her and Ilse's apartment and it took another four hours for her and Ilse to make the nightmare journey by bicycle to Charlottenburg, a journey that in normal times would have taken them no more than an hour.

When they walked exhaustedly into the apartment it was to find Zelda standing tensely by the window, smoking. She was dressed in a vivid scarlet 1930s-style art deco dress, cinched at the waist with a flamboyant purple cummerbund. That her

531

mother was dressed as exotically as always, even when about to face the Russian onslaught, filled Lotti with both exasperation and admiration.

For a moment, she thought that Zelda was going to break the habit of a lifetime and open her arms to hug them tight, but instead, exerting a self-control that was visible, she cupped one arm with the other and said waspishly, having read the expression in Lotti's eyes: 'I thought red an appropriate colour under the circumstances and at least I don't look like a refugee.' She made an expressive gesture with her ebony cigarette-holder. 'You do. It's April. I smelled lilac yesterday. And you're still wearing that ghastly army greatcoat.'

'It's a good job I am,' Lotti retorted, unfazed. 'If I hadn't been, my legs would have been cut to ribbons by flying glass.' She lowered the suitcase they had brought with them with so much difficulty. 'And if you smelled lilac yesterday, you were lucky. All I've been smelling are burning buildings, rubble dust and the stench of dead bodies. Where shall I put this?' She nudged the suitcase with her foot.

'What's in it?'

'Food, mainly. Some medical supplies. A few items of clothing.'

'You've come to stay, then? This isn't just one of your flying visits?'

Before she could reply with equal tartness that they had risked life and limb to be with her in order to offer her what protection they could, Ilse gave Zelda a hug and a kiss, saying, 'Yes. We've come to stay. We thought it best if we were all together until the Americans and the British arrive.'

'The Russians won't overrun Charlottenburg,' Zelda said, holding Ilse a little closer than usual, knowing very well why the two of them were there and what it was they feared might happen. 'They'll fight their way through the eastern suburbs and smash into the centre of the city and storm the government buildings and the Reichstag, but they won't bother with the western suburbs. Why should they? There's hardly anybody left in them to offer any resistance.'

'They won't just enter the city from the east. They'll encircle it. The fighting here is going to be as fierce as anywhere else,' Lotti said, deciding that the best place for the suitcase was where it was always in sight and to hand. 'And there might be worse,' she added grimly. 'We need protection and so I'm going to try and get to Spandau. If Claus is there, he'll give me a gun.'

Her mother merely nodded and then, as a car screamed to a halt outside the apartment block, she looked out of the window again.

'You've been spared a journey,' she said drily. 'You don't have to go to Spandau in search of Claus. He's here.' She stiffened, leaning forward to see out of the window a little more clearly. 'And he's got someone with him. Either his secretary or a girlfriend.'

Lotti took a deep, steadying breath. Now, of all times, she didn't want to be faced with one of Claus's Hitler-loving girlfriends.

Neither did Ilse nor her mother. As the whirr of the caged lift could be heard, they instinctively grouped together. Zelda, still dramatically beautiful at sixty-two, was totem-pole straight, her silver-streaked hair wound in a knot high on her head, her mouth the same searing red as her theatrically distinctive dress.

Though Ilse's beige skirt had a rip in it from where she had caught it on one of the barbed-wire barricades, and though the skirt and her caramel-coloured jacket were creased and grimy, she still had an ethereal quality about her. Because of the lack of soap or shampoo her pale blonde hair was again braided, hanging in a long, heavy rope down her back.

Only Lotti looked utterly disreputable, her jaw-length hair

533

smoke-ridden, her face smudged with rubble dust and dirt. Her army greatcoat was now unbuttoned, revealing trousers, a high-necked sweater and a tight belt with a knife tucked into it.

The lift doors clanged open, seconds later the door leading into the apartment's hallway opened and then closed. There was a pause and then the door of the drawing room opened and Claus entered, alone.

He was wearing an overcoat and looked terrible, his handsome face ravaged by anxiety and stress.

'You shouldn't still be in the city,' Lotti said abruptly, making no move to either hug or kiss him. 'If the Russians capture you, you'll be shot or shipped off to Siberia.'

'I can't leave the city,' he said, halting yards away from the three of them. 'I have workers to protect.' He cleared his throat. 'I've brought someone with me,' he said. 'Someone I've been hiding, but who I will no longer be able to protect once the Russians arrive and, as Lotti has so succinctly put it, either shoot or imprison me.'

'Someone you've been hiding?' Ilse stared at him, noticing for the first time that he was no longer wearing his gold swastika pin. 'Do you mean a Jew?'

He nodded. His hair had fallen across his eyes and he pushed it backwards. 'Yes,' he said. 'A Jew, or, more correctly, a Jewess.'

He turned back towards the door, opened it – and a ghost entered the room.

Zelda sucked in her breath.

Ilse gave a cry of disbelief.

Lotti said incredulously, 'Hester? *Hester?*'

Hester moved forward, taking hold of Claus's hand as she did so, tears of emotion streaming down her face.

Lotti covered the distance separating them at the speed of light, seizing her, hugging and kissing her, saying over and over again, 'Hester! Is it really you? Is it really you? Oh, my God, but we thought you were dead! We thought you were dead years ago!'

Ilse was also hugging her and showering her with kisses.

Zelda had simply sat down abruptly, her near-black eyes disbelieving.

'But how did Claus find you?' Lotti was demanding. '*When* did he find you? What happened to you after you were arrested? Where has Claus been hiding you? In the Ruhr? At Spandau? Oh, God, Hester! I can't believe this is true. It's too wonderful. Too miraculous.'

'Claus didn't so much find me, as I found him.' Tears of joy at being reunited with them still streamed down her face. 'I was sent to his Spandau factory as slave labour.'

Ilse spun round to face Claus. 'And you didn't tell us? How could you not tell us? When was this? How long ago?'

'Two years ago,' Claus said, knowing exactly the reaction his admission was going to meet with.

'Two years ago?' Ilse's spellbinding Prussian-blue eyes opened so wide he thought they were going to pop out. '*Two years ago?* But we've seen you since then! We saw you at *Vati's* funeral – and you said nothing. Not a word.'

Claus again ran his fingers through his hair. 'I had reasons for not doing so,' he said, having no intention of revealing it was because, had he done so, she and Lotti would have demanded they hide Hester and he hadn't been able to bear the thought of being parted from her.

'Two years?' With her arm around Hester's waist, Lotti stared at him. 'But for these last two years you've been one of Hitler's key industrialists. You've been socializing with people like Göring. You've been someone non-Nazis have feared and avoided.'

'He's been someone hundreds of non-Nazis have owed their lives to,' Hester said quietly. 'I was sent as slave labour from

Sachsenhausen concentration camp together with a half-dozen Jehovah's Witnesses and nearly two hundred Russian Jews. All of those people are still alive. All of them would be dead if it hadn't been for Claus. And without him being who he is – a leading Nazi industrialist – he couldn't have saved them. He couldn't have organized a humane camp for them within the area of the factory. He couldn't have saved them from starvation by feeding them at his own expense. He couldn't have ensured their working days were free from beatings and fear. And he's done exactly the same thing on a much bigger scale at the House of Remer steelworks. He's insisted on having assigned to him as many slave labourers as possible in order to be able to save them from starvation and torture and almost certain death.'

For a long moment no one spoke and then Ilse crossed the room towards him and kissed him on the cheek. 'I'm sorry I ever doubted the kind of person you are, Claus,' she said simply. 'Forgive me.'

As he hugged Ilse close, Lotti's eyes met his. 'No matter how many lives you've saved, you'll still be treated as a war criminal,' she said, facing reality head-on as always.

'I know.' His deep-timbred voice was matter-of-fact. 'And where the Russians are concerned, my being here is of no protection to you whatsoever. Your best bet is to take food and water and barricade yourselves in the cellar until the worst of the fighting is over and the Americans and British arrive.'

He eyed the kitchen knife in her belt and was moved almost to tears by her gutsy bravery, knowing full well that if she was ever called to use it, whether on her own behalf or on the behalf of others, she would do so unhesitatingly.

'You'll need something more than a knife, Lotti,' he said, taking a pistol and a box of ammunition from his coat pocket.

As she took them from him, low-flying aircraft roared in. This time they weren't just over the centre of the city: they were over Charlottenburg as well.

The windows vibrated. The Ferdinand Preiss figurines on the display shelves rocked dangerously.

'I have to go.' It was the moment Claus had dreaded, the moment when he would have to leave Hester behind him, not knowing when, or if, he would ever see her again.

As the aircraft peeled away, there came another sound. The rattle of tanks.

'They may be ours,' Ilse said, reading everyone's thoughts.

'And they may not be,' Lotti said. 'Goodbye, Claus. Keep safe.'

Ashen-faced, Claus kissed his mother and Ilse goodbye and then turned to Hester.

Their real leave-taking had taken place before they had left Spandau, and now, for what might be the last time, he held her hands in his. 'Goodbye, Hester,' he said, longing to kiss her deeply and passionately and knowing it was now unlikely he would ever be able to do so. 'Take care. Survive. Be happy.'

'Goodbye,' she said, her voice little more than a whisper, her eyes brimming with tears. 'I'll always remember. I'll never forget.'

Somehow he turned away from her. Somehow he left the room.

Minutes later, they heard the sound of his car speeding away.

Ilse slid her hand into Hester's and Hester gripped it hard, asking urgently, 'Have you any news of Hugo?

Ilse shook her head, her lovely face sombre. 'No. The only news I can give you is that at the start of the war he joined the RAF. Since then we have heard nothing – and we know nothing of Max and Paul either.'

'And you, Hester?' Lotti asked, wanting to change the subject before thoughts of Max overwhelmed her. 'Tell us what happened to you. Tell us everything from the point where Ilse saw you being driven away by the Gestapo.'

537

'I can't,' Hester said quietly. 'Not now, Lotti. Not yet. Those horrors aren't for a moment like this, when we are finally together again.'

'Hester's right.' The agony of her goodbye with Claus, not knowing what his fate was going to be, had aged Zelda in a way years of remorseless bombing raids had failed to do. 'The present horrors are quite enough to cope with,' she said, so visibly distressed that Lotti crossed the room to her, putting her arm around her shoulders.

'Have you any schnapps hidden away, *Mutti*?' she asked, aware it was the first time in her life she had ever had to offer comfort to her indestructible mother.

'No, but I have something better. There's a bottle of good old American bourbon in the bottom of my wardrobe. Max left it with me the last time he was in Berlin. If ever there was a time to crack it open, now is it.'

As Lotti made a beeline for her mother's bedroom there came a sound she had never heard before. A low keening sound, it seemed to be coming from a long distance away. Full of foreboding, she rushed back into the drawing room, the bottle of Jack Daniels in her hand.

'What on earth –' she began as the sound rose into a terrible, ear-splitting scream.

As second later it was as if they were in the middle of an air raid, only this time it wasn't bombs that were dropping on them, it was artillery shells.

The four-storey apartment building juddered, the Ferdinand Preiss figurines toppled. Outside, there was mayhem. People ran in terror as tongues of flame ricocheted down the street, dozens of them mown down by shrapnel as if by a scythe. Cars erupted in balls of fire. The windows of the bedroom Lotti had just been in blasted into smithereens. The air pressure was terrific.

'*Down to the cellar!*' Lotti shouted over the deafening roar. '*Take the stairs, not the lift!*'

Thrusting the bottle of Jack Daniels towards Hester she grabbed hold of her mother with one hand and the suitcase with the other. Ilse grabbed hold of two of the bronze and ivory figurines and then, together, they sprinted for the stairs.

They weren't the only ones doing so. The family who lived on the floor above Zelda, a banker's widow and her elderly parents and teenage daughter, was also hurtling pell-mell down them. No one emerged from the floor below, for they had left the city long ago. From the ground-floor apartment a stooped figure emerged, swathed in shawls and carrying a canary in a cage.

'Into the cellar, Frau Menzel!' Zelda shouted at her as the woman paused bewilderedly in her doorway.

As the petrified Frau Menzel still made no effort to move, Hester seized hold of her hand, dragging her after them.

'What happens if the building falls on top of us and we can't get out?' Irmgard Diekermann, the banker's widow, asked as the cellar door clanged behind them.

'It won't,' Lotti snapped, knowing it was likely to do so at any moment. 'And if it does, we'll just have to hope we get dug out. There's nowhere else we can go. We can't reach a public shelter in this firestorm.'

'My little Pee-Wee is frightened,' Frau Menzel said waveringly as the canary beat its wings against the bars of its cage.

'We're all frightened, Frau Menzel,' Ilse said gently. 'Pee-Wee will settle down when the noise stops.'

Lotti looked at the bags and baskets that the Diekermann family had brought with them and was relieved to see that they seemed to be stuffed with food.

'And there's water,' Zelda said, reading her thoughts. 'Josef always insisted there was a large supply of bottled water down here. It's kept at the back of the cellar, under a tarpaulin.'

'How long is this likely to go on for?' Irmgard Diekermann's father rasped, directing his question at Lotti. 'I'm eighty-six. I don't have good bladder and bowel control and there are no proper facilities down here. Only buckets.'

'I don't know, Herr Diekermann, but there will be lulls, and when there are I'm sure Frau Menzel will be happy for you to use her ground-floor bathroom.'

The lulls, when they came, were few and far between. For the most part the shelling was incessant. Time ceased to have meaning. A day passed, and then two days.

Hester, with her nightmare memory of being buried alive in the tunnel at Unter den Linden, fought down crippling panic attacks, fortified by occasional swallows of the precious Jack Daniels.

Lotti and Herr Diekermann both occasionally left the cellar, Herr Diekermann to take advantage of Frau Menzel's bathroom facilities, Lotti to get the feel of what was happening on the streets.

'Russian tanks are in Bismarckstrasse,' she said tautly, returning from one such dangerous sortie. 'The fighting is still going on, but it looks as though resistance is crumbling. I saw lots of white flags.'

She didn't add that she'd also seen lots of dead bodies, many of them civilians who had been caught in the firing when they'd dashed from the Bismarckstrasse public shelter to get water from a near by street pump; or that there'd been looting, and that all the apartments, her mother's included, had been ransacked.

'I'm going out too!' Gertrud, Irmgard's sixteen-year-old daughter, said defiantly. 'I can't stand being cooped up in here any longer! If Lotti can go out, then so can I!'

'Not if there are Russians only streets away!' her mother shrieked, grabbing hold of her.

'She's more in danger of being ripped apart by shrapnel than of being raped,' Zelda said, weary beyond belief of their

540

mole-like existence. 'Russians aren't animals. Why should they rape every woman they see?'

'For retribution,' Hester said quietly. 'It will be done in revenge for all the atrocities and mass murders committed by German SS troops in Russia. It will be done in retribution for the extermination camps – camps where the SS were too impatient to wait for prisoners to die of beatings and starvation – camps where, with German and Polish Jews, Russian men, women and children were gassed in their thousands.'

They all stared at her, Zelda and Ilse and Lotti included, as if she were raving.

'There aren't any such places,' Irmgard Diekermann said scoffingly. 'Don't listen to her. She's making it up.'

'No, I'm not.' Hester's dark eyes burned in a face that had become bloodless. 'I know because I spent two years in Ravensbrück concentration camp and two years in Sachsenhausen concentration camp. I know about the gassings because Claus told me of them – and he got his information from Reichsmarschall Göring.'

No one said anything. Speech was beyond everyone. At last, it was Irmgard's elderly mother who broke the silence, her voice trembling with indignation. 'You're a Jewess, aren't you?' she said accusingly. 'My God, I've been holed up for two days and two nights with a filthy Jewess!'

Before Zelda or Ilse or Lotti could give her the benefit of hearing what they thought of her, Frau Menzel said, quick as a flash, 'You could always leave, Gerd. The air in the cellar, for the rest of us, will then be a little sweeter.'

'You must forgive my mother,' Irmgard Diekermann said hastily, terrified by the expression on Lotti's face. 'She's old. She doesn't understand that all that business is over with now. The rest of us don't care that your friend is Jewish. I have a little bit of cheese in my bag. Would your friend like a little of my cheese?'

541

'Hester isn't only my friend, she's family,' Lotti said icily. 'And no, Frau Diekermann. Please keep your cheese to yourself. We have provisions enough.'

A barrage of thunderous mortar fire deafened them all and then, as the reverberations rumbled away, there was heavy knocking on the cellar door and a woman's voice could be heard, calling for help.

'Don't answer her,' Herr Diekermann said as Ilse and Lotti sprang to their feet. 'It could be a ruse. It could be Red Army troops. They have women in their troops – women with sub-machine guns.'

The distress in the woman's voice was so desperate that neither Ilse nor Lotti paid him a moment's heed. As Lotti pulled back the bolts and opened the door, the woman half fell on her, covered in blood.

'It's my thigh,' she gasped as they dragged her inside. 'I've been hit by shrapnel. Please stop the bleeding. Please stop the bleeding before I die!'

Ilse ran towards the suitcase, scrabbling in it for the first-aid box. Gertrud Diekermann rushed forwards with a scarf. 'Here,' she said, thrusting it towards Lotti. 'Use it as a tourniquet.'

Zelda poured a generous measure of Jack Daniels into a glass, holding it ready for the woman to drink as Lotti began swiftly binding the scarf tight above the severed artery.

As she was doing so there came the sound of booted feet approaching. Zelda rushed to shut and bolt the door, but the soldiers were there before her, slamming the door wide and trapping her half senseless behind it.

There were four of them and as they entered the cellar, sub-machine guns at the ready, Lotti ignored them, signalling to Ilse to continue helping her with what she was doing, grabbing hold of Gertrud's hand and dragging her down so that she too was on her knees with her back to them, seemingly helping give the still-moaning woman emergency treatment.

Hester had been at the other side of the cellar and she remained there, perfectly still. Gerd Diekermann didn't remain perfectly still. She flung herself against her husband, screaming at him to protect her. Little Frau Menzel had her arms around Pee-Wee's cage, as if prepared to defend him with her life.

Satisfied that, apart from the aged Herr Diekermann, there were no men in the cellar, they kicked over bags, rifling through them, taking whatever easily edible food there was: dried sausage, a heel of bread, Irmgard Diekermann's cheese. One of them roughly took Herr Diekermann's watch from him, the others stood over Lotti, Ilse and Gertrud as Lotti continued in her task of removing shrapnel splinters.

For a moment, Lotti thought they were going to be left unmolested and then one of the soldiers yanked Gertrud to her feet.

'*Komm*,' he said, beginning to pull her towards the open door with one hand, while holding his sub-machine gun in the other. '*Frau, komm*.'

Lotti sprang to her feet. 'Let her go! She isn't a *Frau*, she's a *Fräulein*. She's only sixteen!'

The soldier stopped in his tracks and turned to face her. '*Frau ist Frau*,' he said, much to the amusement of his companions and then, as Irmgard Diekermann fell hysterically onto her knees, he dragged Gertrud out of the cellar.

There was nothing any of them could do. Lotti's pistol was in her greatcoat pocket and her coat was rolled in a bundle next to one of the plundered bags. Even if it had been within her grasp, using it would have been useless. One dead Russian would not prevent the other three from taking vengeance. The sub-machine guns would be turned on them and in a split second of time all of them, Frau Menzel's canary included, would be blasted into eternity.

The sub-machine guns were trained on them now. '*Frau, komm!*' one of the soldiers said, indicating with a wave of his gun Hester, Ilse and herself. '*Frau, komm!*'

It was something that was to become routine over the next few days. The cellar door would be stoved in and Russian soldiers, always in groups of three or four and always with guns at the ready, would haul her, Hester, Ilse and Gertrud up the cellar steps and into Frau Menzel's apartment.

The only way to survive was to try as hard as they could to mentally detach themselves from what was happening. It was something Hester had learned to do long ago when in Ravensbrück and Sachsenhausen, and it was an ability Ilse and Lotti swiftly acquired. Gertrud Diekermann couldn't acquire it, though.

'It's not your fault,' Lotti told her time and time again as the sixteen-year-old cried and rocked herself backwards and forwards ceaselessly. 'You've nothing to be ashamed of, Gertrud. It's not your fault.'

As she held the weeping girl in her arms she often thought about Eva, wondering if Eva and her fellow nurses were also suffering mass rape, or if their uniforms were serving as protection.

As their cellar-like existence lengthened into a week and the fighting in and around Charlottenburg continued, Gertrud Diekermann's agony came to an unexpected end. Instead of a group of filthy and bearded soldiers forcing a way in on them, a Russian officer, shaved and smartly uniformed, confronted them. There was a military decoration on his tunic and when he took his helmet off, he revealed a head of wiry fair hair.

'*Tag,*' he said pleasantly.

His eyes flicked over Helga, the injured woman they had taken in, and over Irmgard and her parents. When he surveyed Zelda, still in her flamboyant red dress with its purple cummerbund, his eyebrows rose slightly and then his gaze passed on, over Hester, Ilse and Lotti. When they reached Gertrud he spoke. '*Fräulein, komm bitte*,' he said politely – and held out his hand.

It was the kind of opportunity Lotti had never been faced with before. The officer was alone, and though he was armed with a pistol, it was in a holster on his hip, not in his hand.

Her pistol was within hand's reach, hidden beneath a pile of bloodied bandages. A hiding place that had, so far, served them well.

Very slowly, she moved her hand towards it.

Ilse, standing a few feet away from her, caught her eye, looked meaningfully towards Gertrud, looked back towards her again and shook her head.

Lotti, her hand on the bloodied bandages, did as Ilse was silently bidding her and looked towards Gertrud.

There was a very peculiar expression on Gertrud's face. It wasn't exactly compliance, but it was verging on it.

Reading the urgent message in Ilse's eye, she drew her hand back. This wasn't the usual situation. It wasn't a situation calling for the use of the pistol – especially when such use could put all of them in danger of retribution.

With a docility that had her grandfather despairingly burying his head in his arms, Gertrud left the cellar hand in hand with the young officer.

For the next hour no one said anything. Even her mother was silent.

When Gertrud returned to them she was composed, not crying. 'His name is Andrei Koniev,' she said, a defiant set to her slim shoulders. 'He wants me to be his war-wife for as long as he is in Berlin.'

Her mother let out a howl of protest and Gertrud squared her shoulders even further. 'And because I am now his war-wife, no one will now come here to rape us,' she said to Lotti. 'Andrei is a major and we are now under his protection.'

Her mother, who had never been forced with a sub-machine gun at her back to go up the cellar stairs and into Frau Menzel's desecrated apartment to be raped at gunpoint, began sobbing, gasping that she now had a daughter who had become shameless, a daughter who was no better than a prostitute.

They were accusations that, to Lotti's relief, Gertrud was indifferent to.

The incessant artillery fire had now become only spasmodic, and though none of them had any desire to leave the cellar for their shrapnel-damaged, plundered apartments – feeling far more secure when all together – they did begin to leave the cellar for forays on the streets.

'Don't head towards Spandau,' Lotti said after one such expedition, fearful that her mother might be considering trying to reach Claus's factory for word of him. 'There's what looks to have been a massacre at the bridge over the Havel. It's blocked on both sides of the river with burned-out trucks and tanks and bodies, and there's still shooting going on.'

Though Gertrud's protector was now supplying them with food, it was never enough for all ten of them and, as there were none of their original provisions left, Lotti and Hester had taken it upon themselves to do all the necessary foraging.

It wasn't easy, because everyone else who had been sheltering from the fighting and the storm of artillery fire was doing the same thing. Hunger was no longer the correct description for what Berliners were suffering. What they were suffering was starvation.

The gardens behind a near by bombed-out house had proved to be an excellent source of dandelion leaves and it was when Hester and Lotti were back-breakingly gathering them that they heard Ilse frantically shouting their names.

Lotti sprinted out of the garden in the direction of Ilse's

voice, vaulting a railing that still stood at its perimeter. Ilse raced to meet her.

'A Russian has taken *Mutti* into Frau Menzel's apartment!' she shouted. 'He's drunk. He's armed. There was nothing we could do to stop him. He was uncaring when we said we were under Major Koniev's protection. I offered to go with him in *Mutti*'s place, but he just laughed at me . . .'

Lotti sped past her, running in the direction of their semi-wrecked apartment block as she had never run before in her life.

She skidded into the hallway. Pulling her pistol from her belt, she stormed her way into Frau Menzel's flat and, as the half-naked Russian pinning her mother to the bed turned his head towards her in drink-befuddled consternation, she shot him between the eyes.

Blood, brain and bits of bone sprayed the room.

As the rapist's body slithered off the bed, Zelda rolled over and over until she fell off the other side of the bed and onto her feet.

'Are you all right, *Mutti*?' The pistol was now so heavy in Lotti's hand she didn't know how she was still managing to hold it. 'I had to kill him. There was no other way.'

'Don't apologize for it!' Zelda rasped, tugging her torn dress back down over her skinny hips. 'Just apologize for taking so long to get here!'

On unsteady legs she rounded the bottom of the bed.

'Now what do we do?' she asked, as they stood shoulder to shoulder eyeing the body. 'Even Gertrud's Andrei won't be able to protect us if it gets out we've shot a Russian soldier.'

Still holding the pistol, Lotti wiped perspiration from her forehead with the back of her hand. 'We get Hester and Ilse to help us, and we drop his body down the lift shaft. It will be found eventually, but as this apartment block is now uninhabitable, with luck not for weeks and perhaps not for months.'

Her mother nodded and then, as they heard Hester and Ilse racing pell-mell towards the building, she said, 'You might like to know there was a radio broadcast while you were out dandelion-picking.'

Lotti felt as if her heart had ceased to beat. 'Germany's surrendered? The war is over? The Americans are on their way?'

'No, but that news won't be long in coming now.' The exultation in Zelda's voice was euphoric. 'The Führer is dead, Lotti! Germany is free of the monster at last!'

THIRTY-FOUR

Berlin, July 1945

Major Paul Gould lit a Lucky Strike and watched as his men continued with their task of controlling and filtering the flow of refugees over one of the Elbe's bridges that was still intact. Initially, two months ago, it had been hordes of Wehrmacht soldiers they had been scrutinizing. With the war at an end and the surrender signed, the defeated German forces had been desperate to fall into American hands rather than Red Army ones.

His detachment's task had been to relieve them of their weapons and to identify and then detain any Waffen SS. Their fate – to be handed over to the Russians – was an unenviable one and they tried every ruse possible to cross the river undetected, often resorting to suicide if they failed.

Paul tilted his cap a little farther back on his head. The operation he was now supervising had become more of a mopping-up than anything else. A searching of civilians and the checking of their identity papers, with a close eye being kept for anyone who could possibly be SS.

It was a gloriously hot day and though his relaxed, easy demeanour didn't reveal it, he was taut with tension caused by intense jubilation mixed with extreme dread.

The jubilation was occasioned by the orders he had just received. With Berlin now neatly divided into American, British, French and Russian sectors, he and his men had finally been given the green light to put the Elbe behind them and head for the city the Russians had cheated them of taking.

His dread was of what he might find when there.

Would those he loved still be alive? After years of intense murderous bombing raids and after the firestorm unleashed on it when the Russians had fought for it, street by street, it would be a miracle if they had all survived. And then there were the reports of the treatment meted out to the women of the city when the fighting had abated.

'Mass rape,' his colonel had said, chomping on a cigar. 'Those are the reports we're getting. Every female from nine to ninety – and by the way, good work in winkling out that guy who claimed he was a forced labourer. He's not only SS, he's high-ranking SS. Keep it up.'

Mass rape. And not only was the woman he loved still in the city but, to the best of his knowledge, so were his mother and two half-sisters. It was a nightmare of such epic proportions he didn't know how he was managing to give concentration to the task in hand. Fleeing members of the Waffen SS were, at the moment, the least of his concerns.

During the early years of the war his anxiety on his mother's behalf had been kept in check by the knowledge that Claus's powerful position would ensure her safety. His half-brother was, after all, not only head of one of Germany's major steelworks, but also a man who had the ear of one of Hitler's closest henchmen, Hermann Göring. Hateful to him as that fact was, it had meant that, where his concern for Zelda was concerned, he had slept comparatively easily at night.

Those days had ended when the British had begun bombing the city by night and his own countrymen had begun bombing it by day. It was then he had learned to live with an inner tension quite at odds with his naturally relaxed, easy-going personality. Fear when in the midst of battle, he could – and had – coped with. Fear on behalf of those he loved was another thing entirely and it was a fear that had grown steadily as Germany had crumbled before the Allied onslaught. Claus would be no protection to their mother now. If he was still alive – and despite the yawning chasm that had divided them ever since Claus had first sported his gold swastika pin, he hoped with all his heart that Claus *was* still was alive – that he was Zelda's son would now be an extra danger to her, not a protection.

And then there were Ilse and Lotti to agonize over. Neither he nor Max knew if they were alive or dead.

He dropped his half-smoked cigarette and ground it out savagely beneath his heel. The possibility that they were dead was one he had stubbornly refused to contemplate all the years he'd been in uniform and he wasn't about to start contemplating it now. They would still be alive and he would find them. Just as he would find Eva. And the first thing he was going to do, after he had found Eva, was to get permission to marry her. That way, even before he was demobbed, she stood a chance of being able to travel to England.

The thought of her being at Shuttleworth Hall, waiting for him when his war service was over, made the nerves in his belly clench in knots. It was all he wanted in life. Eva, and a life far removed from the hell of the last six years – a life dedicated to the breeding of beautiful roses and lived amid the incomparable beauty of the Yorkshire Dales.

By the time Max finally got his orders to leave for Berlin as one of the scores of intelligence officers who were acting as interrogators there, there was no longer any question as to where the demarcation lines in the city had been drawn. The Russians had vacated half of the city, to the merciful relief of those who now found themselves in British, French or American hands. Everything east of the Brandenburg Gate was in the Soviet sector – and that included the Charité hospital and the house on Unter den Linden.

His aunt and uncle's home in Charlottenburg and the Remer clothing factory in Spandau were in the British sector, or were if they were still standing. And Lotti's flat and Ilse's apartment were both in the British sector, though only just.

'It's chaos,' said the young lieutenant who picked him up by jeep from Tempelhof Airport. 'We've only just managed to clear the runways of the remains of wrecked German aircraft. There's still no water or electricity in most of the city and every Nazi we interrogate is full of the guff that they've been badly misunderstood. They know nothing about extermination camps and every crime committed was committed by the SS.'

As they zipped as fast as they could down streets that were still full of craters, Max was staggered by the scale of destruction. He'd expected to see a city that had been bombed into ruins, but this was a city that had been annihilated. For the first time it occurred to him to wonder if it could ever be rebuilt.

'Detour to Lützowstrasse,' he said.

The lieutenant looked at him, startled. 'Colonel Hargrave is at headquarters waiting to brief you, sir.'

'I'm aware of that, Lieutenant, but Lüzowstrasse first.'

'Is it in the British sector, sir?'

Max nodded, his apprehension growing as he saw the extent of the almost unbelievable devastation.

He thought of his father who, when Max had last been in the city, had still been living in the mansion on Unter den Linden. According to the intelligence reports he'd read, Unter den Linden was now a wasteland. It was also in the Soviet-occupied sector.

'What is the situation for civilians with regard to movement between our sector and the Soviet sector?' he asked, wincing as he saw nothing but rubble-strewn ground where one of his favourite bars had once been.

'Everyone knows what the demarcation lines are, but there's nothing very visible about them. Just large notices on all the major thoroughfares, saying that you are now leaving the British – or French, or American, whichever it might be – sector of Berlin. It isn't hindering anyone's movements. People are wandering all over the city trying to trace family and friends.'

The nearer they got to the centre of the city, the greater the number of poorly dressed women they saw, working in gangs on the ruined buildings. Bent double, they ceaselessly salvaged bricks, knocking the mortar off them and then passing them hand to hand in a long chain until the woman at the end of the line stacked them into a horse-drawn cart.

'The Germans call them *Trümmerfrauen*,' the young officer said. 'It means rubblewomen, sir. They're paid in potatoes.'

'Yes, Lieutenant. I know what *Trümmerfrauen* means.' For a brief moment, Max wondered what the lieutenant's reaction would be if he were to tell him he'd been born in the city; that his father was a Berliner; that his cousin was Claus Remer of the giant House of Remer steelworks in the Ruhr.

They were approaching Lützowstrasse and his heart began hammering somewhere up in his throat. Was he right in trying to seek out Lotti before he sought out Ilse? All he really wanted was to get the awkward explanations over with. Instinct told him he wasn't going to be proved wrong in his reading of the new situation that existed now that Ilse was a widow – and that someone he still cared for so very, very much, was going to be savagely hurt was something that was crucifying him.

553

'Lützowstrasse, sir,' the lieutenant said, veering into the street that had once been so familiar.

It wasn't familiar now.

The houses and shops were mere shells, a mockery of what they had once been. The house in which Lotti and her friends had once shared a flat was blackened by fire, its top floor and a side wall missing.

His hands clenched into fists. It didn't mean Lotti had died in the conflagration. When the building had been hit she would most likely have been in a shelter. That's what he told himself – and he told himself with all the power of persuasion he possessed.

'Can we continue on to headquarters now, Major Remer?' the lieutenant asked, an edge of anxiety in his voice. They were going to be massively late meeting up with the colonel and he didn't want to be the one carrying the can for it.

'Yes, but I've another address I want you to drive to first.' With tension almost at breaking point, he gave the address of the apartment Ilse had shared with Nicholas.

At last he was going to see her again.

Nancy held on tightly to the bar on the jeep's dashboard as it swerved along the outside of a long line of heavily provisioned army trucks, dust billowing in its wake.

As a journalist she had fought tooth and nail to be in Berlin for its final drama, the moment when the instrument of surrender, signed on 7 May by General Jodl, at General Eisenhower's headquarters, was counter-signed on 8 May by Field Marshall Keitel in the presence of America's General Spaatz, Great Britain's Marshal Tedder, France's General de Lattre, and Russia's Marshal Zhukov.

It was a moment of history denied her. Though Western reporters and newsreel cameramen in their scores were there,

554

she had been refused a press pass and, without one, Reuters had insisted she stay west of the Elbe.

She had a press pass for Berlin now, though, and it was a strange sensation to be battling through war-devastated countryside towards the city she had always, as a girl, believed would be her lifelong home.

'Doesn't your husband mind you racketing around bomb-torn Europe by yourself, ma'am?' the American giving her a lift from Magdeburg asked, finding her sassy self-confidence a little unnerving.

Nancy shook her head. 'Nope. He knows it's my job – and he's a politician. Leo would be here in a heartbeat if he could be.'

'And what are you going to be reporting on when you get to Berlin? The supply difficulties? The political wrangling between Britain, America and the Soviets? The number of Nazis who'll be standing trial as war criminals?'

'Anything and everything,' Nancy said truthfully, not saying that she also had a lot of personal business to take care of.

Her first priority was going to be her father. There'd been no news of him since Max had last seen him in the summer of 1941 – and when she located him, she was going to have the terrible task of telling him that Hugo was dead.

The jeep bucketed around a pothole that appeared to be bottomless. Nancy braced her khaki-trousered legs against the front of the seat-well.

'Hang on, ma'am,' her new-found friend shouted cheerfully. 'Don't want to lose you now, when we've only another thirty kilometres to go.'

Nancy hung on as the jeep continued to bucket and bounce. Her generous breasts bucketed and bounced also, and a party of GIs in the back of one of the trucks they were passing wolf-whistled appreciatively.

Unfazed, Nancy grinned back and waved, her thoughts on what else she needed to do the instant she hit Berlin. As well as her father, she had Lotti and Ilse to locate and they too would have to be told about Hugo's death. And then there was Claus.

Though her companion wasn't aware of it, when he had asked if one of the things she would be reporting on were the number of Nazis expected to stand trial as war criminals, she had inwardly flinched.

When Max had last been in touch with Claus, Claus had been in regular social contact with many of the Nazi hierarchy and most especially with Reichsmarschall Hermann Göring. That fact alone would be enough to have ensured his arrest by the Allies, for an assumption would be made that he was a Nazi with political influence.

She pursed her lips. That such an assumption would be wrong was something she would stake her life on. Proving it would be another matter. There was also the question of whether or not he had used slave labour. If he had, that too could possibly damn him to years of imprisonment.

Though she was no longer in love with him, the prospect of his being imprisoned cut through her like a knife. Leo, from whom she had no secrets, had said to her, 'The Ruhr lies in the British zone, Nance. That means the House of Remer steelworks will be a direct British responsibility and it will be easier for you to get information about him. If the steelworks had been in an area of Soviet responsibility, there'd be no chance.'

Thoughts of the husband with whom she was so very compatible, cheered her. He always made everything seem possible. 'The Remer steelworks and factories may seem gigantic to you and to the rest of your family,' he had said, his bear-like bulk comfortably ensconced in a leather club chair, a whisky and soda in one hand, 'but in relation to the size of the Krupp steelworks and armaments factories, the House of Remer is small fry. You may well find that the Allies have their hands too full with the really big fish to pay him much attention, other than confiscating his personal wealth and razing the House of Remer steelworks and factories to the ground.'

Aware of how fortunate she was at having a press pass in her shirt pocket and of being in a position to ferret out information at first hand, she tucked her thumbs down her trouser waistband and, with all the undaunted optimism that was so much a part of her character, and out of deference to her companion, began whistling 'Dixie'.

Lotti slammed the door of the tiny flat in Waltraudstrasse that she, her mother, Ilse and Hester had been living in ever since one of the walls of the Charlottenburg apartment block had collapsed under mortar fire in the last days before the surrender. As it had collapsed on top of the lift shaft, burying the body lying at the bottom of it under tons of masonry, and as no one had been in the cellar when it had come tumbling down, she viewed the incident as an act of God, not an act of war.

It was a gloriously hot day and she was wearing one of the silk summer dresses Ilse had retrieved from the apartment she had lived in with Nicholas, an apartment that, being both spacious and central and in the British sector, had been requisitioned by the British. The feel of the silk against her skin and of the sun on her bare legs was a sensation of such pleasure it was almost sexual.

In the first few weeks after the surrender, even though Ilse had retrieved many items of clothing from the apartment, it was not the type of clothing they could wear. The Russian rampage had continued until the arrival of the Americans and the British, and the only way of trying to combat it had been to try and look as ugly as possible and to dress in heavy shapeless sweaters and baggy trousers. Even after the threat of rape had begun to fade, silk summer dresses had been way out of the question because she and Hester had, out of necessity, become *Trümmerfrauen*.

Ilse had been spared such manual labour. An old friend of hers from the film studios had contacted her, telling her that the studios in Babelsburg were already up and running again.

'It's true,' she had said, sheer delight on her face when she had returned from checking out the information. 'A man from Poland is shooting his first production there. It's being financed by the Americans and he nearly fell over himself when I turned up.' She had twirled around their tiny Waltraudstrasse flat until she'd fallen in a dizzy heap on their shabby sofa. 'He's given me a lead part. It's incredible and unbelievable, but I'm a film star again!'

Neither she, nor Hester, had begrudged her her good fortune.

Working on bombsites in unflattering old clothing, her hair protected by a headscarf grey with rubble dust, her hands calloused, her nails broken, while Ilse set off for Babelsburg each day, her golden hair shining, her hands manicured, hadn't helped her nervous tension where Max was concerned.

Her fervent hope had been that he would be among the first British officers to enter the city. He hadn't been. Though the British sector was now up and running, its headquarters staffed to overflowing with intelligence officers, Max was not one of their number. There had been no communication from him. She didn't even know if he was in Germany.

Still thinking about him, she crossed the Waltraudbrücke to Argentinische Allee, continuing on her way to the American headquarters opposite the Oskar-Helene-Heim U-Bahn station, which was where she was now employed as an interpreter.

Two weeks ago, when the British and Americans had first arrived, she had dressed herself as smartly as possible in a grey flannel dress of Ilse's and had visited both British and American headquarters. The British officer who had interviewed her had, speaking perfect German, declined to engage her as an interpreter. The Americans had snapped her up as if she were gold.

She'd been assigned to a tall lanky major with a close-cropped head, who came from Kansas. He had an easy, relaxed way about him and in looks and manner reminded her of Paul.

As she approached the grandiose facade of what had once been the District Headquarters of the Luftwaffe and was now officially the Office of the Military Government of the United States, she made a huge mental effort to put to one side her anxieties about Max – and whether, when he returned to Berlin, he would still be in love with her or not.

Her job as Major Chuck Gleeson's interpreter was a responsible one, and that it required her full concentration was something she was deeply grateful for. She showed her pass to the guard at the entrance, knowing a full day lay ahead of her, planning that she would, at the end of it, visit her uncle, Berthold, who was still living in close companionship with Eva's elderly mother.

'Hi,' Chuck Gleeson said with typical American informality as she walked into his office. 'Sit down, Lotti. I've some news for you that you may, or may not, like.'

Banishing all thoughts of Berthold she sat down, hoping against hope he wasn't going to say he no longer needed her. If that was the case she would, with luck, simply be assigned to someone else; but whoever that someone might turn out to be, he was unlikely to be as straightforward in his dealings with her as Gleeson. Nearly every uniformed American she had met had made a pass at her. Major Gleeson, who had a photograph of his wife prominently displayed on his desk, had never done so.

'I've been given another posting,' he said without preamble. 'I'm being shunted down to Frankfurt and I leave this evening. It's not much notice for you, but finding another interpreter as free of Nazi connections as yourself may not be easy and I'd like you to consider either coming with me, or joining me there as soon as possible.'

She shook her head, not having to give his offer even a moment's thought. Leaving Berlin now, when Max could well show up at any time, was unthinkable.

'I'm sorry,' she said, hating the feeling of letting him down, 'but I can't leave Berlin. I have family here and I'm hoping that someone close to me will be arriving in the city very soon.'

His disappointment was obvious. 'Think about it,' he said. 'I'm leaving on a military flight from Tempelhof at seven-thirty and I'd like not to be leaving alone. While you're thinking about it, here's today's agenda.' He passed her a typed sheet of paper. 'My first meeting is with the newly appointed waterworks superintendent. That will take place here. My second meeting is with the manager of the Domäne Dahlem dairy farm and we'll be going to Dahlem by jeep. And until the waterworks guy shows up, what about coffee and cookies?'

At the end of a working day that took in not only meetings with the waterworks superintendent and manager of the dairy farm, but meetings with a dozen other Germans, who had all been screened as being free of Nazi Party connections, Lotti set off for Eva's home in the French sector, her jaw aching from the endless repetition of sentences in German beginning, 'The Herr Major says . . .' followed by, in English, 'The Superintendent says . . .'

Wedding had always been a predominantly working-class

district and Lotti found it strange to be visiting Max's father in surroundings so different to the grandeur he'd previously been accustomed to. To his credit, he had acclimatized remarkably well. He and Bertha, Eva's mother, had settled into a relationship that was almost marital in its comfiness. Bertha, who was in her sixties like Berthold and who, like him, was vague and confused to the point of irrationality, was happier in his company than in anyone else's, including Eva's – and Berthold seemed unaware of anything but the minutiae of his and Bertha's almost childish daily routine.

'Yes?' he said, peering owlishly at her through his pebble-thick lenses, as if he couldn't quite place her and didn't particularly want to. 'Yes?'

'It's me,' Lotti said, kissing him on the cheek. 'Lotti. I've come to see how the two of you are. Eva tells me you've begun butterfly-hunting again.'

His eyes brightened and Lotti wondered if anyone else in the whole of Berlin had spent the war as oblivious to its horrors as her uncle had. The scurrying down to the local shelter during air raids had annoyed him intensely, but he had never seemed aware that he risked incineration, or that fellow Berliners were being incinerated in their thousands.

It was the same when the city had fallen to the Russians. The only Russian to have crossed Berthold and Bertha's doorstep was a soldier still in his teens who, when Bertha offered him a cup of mint tea, declined politely, helped himself to a clock that had taken his fancy and, the clock under one arm, a Kalashnikov under the other, had disappeared, carefully closing the door behind him.

'There are lots of butterflies on ground where houses once stood,' Berthold said now as Bertha began making tea for the three of them. 'Buddleia grows there easily and butterflies love buddleia.'

Lotti prayed for patience, wondering how Eva endured

Berthold's inanities when her days were spent in a medical centre treating the injuries of women who had suffered gang rapes, women who desperately needed an abortion as a result of rape, and raped women who had been infected with venereal disease.

'There is still no news of Claus,' she said, trying to turn the conversation to something pertinent. 'Hester is now spending all day, every day, making inquiries at all the Allied headquarters. None of them is willing to release names of captured war criminals, and that he has been captured we know from some of the Russian women who are still living within the precincts of the Spandau factory. They say they're staying there until they're given a chance of testifying as to how he saved their lives.'

'Hester?' Berthold blinked. 'Isn't Hester the Jewish girl?'

Lotti gritted her teeth. 'Yes – and she's also your daughter-in-law. If Claus is ever traced, it will only be because of her Herculean efforts.'

Berthold wasn't interested in Herculean efforts. 'I found a Marbled Skipper the other day,' he said, only really interested in talking about butterflies. 'At least, I think it's a Marbled Skipper. Would you like to see it?'

'Only the fact that he's family – and more especially that he's Max's father – enables me to keep my patience when I'm with him,' she said to Eva that evening when they met up for a pre-curfew drink. 'The war might as well not have happened, Berlin might as well not be in ruins. It all passes Berthold by.'

'It passes my mother by as well,' Eva said with a weary grin. 'They are both suffering from premature senility, and in a way it's a blessing. The world may have become a disaster zone for millions, but they've been spared much awareness of it.'

She tilted her head a little to one side, eyeing Lotti curiously.

'What's troubling you, Lotti?' she asked, concerned. 'There are times when you look more strained now than you did when the bombing was at its height. What's the matter?'

Lotti pushed her cup of coffee to one side. 'It's Max,' she said simply. 'I'm terrified that when he returns to Berlin it will be because Ilse is a widow. I'm terrified of her throwing herself into his arms and of his keeping her there.' Her voice wobbled, her eyes overly bright. 'I'm terrified he won't be in love with me any more, Eva. I'm terrified that when he knows Ilse wants him back – and she does, I'm sure of it – he will barely remember the weeks when he and I were lovers.'

Eva frowned. She had never been able to understand why Lotti and Ilse constantly skirted the subject of Max without ever admitting to each other what their true feelings for him were. 'If Ilse does throw herself into his arms, it will be your own fault,' she said reasonably. 'After all, why shouldn't she, when she doesn't know you're in love with him and that when you were last together he was in love with you? As far as she is concerned, the way is clear and there is no one to hurt. Tell her differently and she'll act differently.'

'I don't want her to act differently.' Lotti's voice was taut with tension, her lemur-like eyes fierce. 'I want Max to know that if he still wants a life with Ilse, he can have one. And then I want him *not* to want a life with her, but to want a life with me. Does that make sense, Eva? I don't want him to return to me because he can't have Ilse. I don't want to be second best. And I just want this awful uncertainty to be over. I just want him to return to Berlin so that I will know what my future is to be.'

'And if he does decide that Ilse has always been his love and that it's Ilse he wants to spend his life with, what then?'

Lotti's face was ashen. 'Then I'll go to Frankfurt and see if Major Gleeson can find me a job there as an interpreter,' she said, her heart feeling as if it were being squeezed into extinction. 'And I shan't come back to Berlin. I'll do what Nancy did when she knew there was no future for her with Claus. I shall build a life for myself without him, but I'll never fall in love again. I couldn't. Max is in my heart and soul. He's my other half – and without him I shall never be complete again.'

The American who had given Nancy a lift into the city dropped her in Potsdamer Platz. 'If you ever want a night out, ring me on this number,' he said, taking a card out of his shirt pocket. 'That husband of yours need never know.'

Ignoring the proffered card, Nancy stepped out of the jeep. 'No,' she said with a cheery grin. 'But I would. Bye. And thanks for the lift.'

He gave a good-natured shrug of his shoulders to show there were no hard feelings and seconds later was zooming out of Potsdamer Platz, tyres squealing.

Nancy shifted the heavy bag she was carrying over her shoulder into a more comfortable position and set off in the direction of the Brandenburg Gate. It was shell-pocked and charred, but still standing. A huge placard informed pedestrians and motorists that it was now the entry point to the Russian sector. There were no Red Army guards checking identity papers and no one else seemed to be bothering and so Nancy didn't either.

Walking through it and on to Unter den Linden was a strange sensation. On its corner, the Café Krantzler was a burned ruin. The Hotel Adlon, near by, was still open for custom, but badly bomb damaged. What had once been a magnificent boulevard of neoclassical mansions and palaces was a wasteland of ruins, with hardly a linden tree remaining.

The sun beat down strongly as she walked with increasing slowness to where her father's family home had once stood. Two walls were still standing, windowless and roofless, a third wall was half demolished and the fourth wall, once the pillared facade of the mansion, had been obliterated entirely. All that remained was rubble over which chains of women were clambering, buckets in hand, scavenging the good bricks from the broken ones.

She went no nearer. She simply looked and turned away. That her father had died in the devastation was not something she even considered. Ever an optimist she was sure he was still alive and that, with a little patience and a lot of detective work, she would find him.

Her next two ports of call were Lotti's flat in Lützowstrasse and the apartment Ilse had shared with Nicholas.

One was as ruined as the house on Unter den Linden, the other was occupied by a British official who had no idea where the original occupier now was.

Deciding that her best plan of action was to book into whatever hotel was still standing and offering accommodation to the press, she began walking in the direction of a bar in the British sector that she knew would be a hot-spot meeting place for her fellow reporters. As she did so she became aware of a long queue of battered-looking women. At first she thought they were queuing at a public kitchen, for soup. Then she saw that the building was an air-raid shelter and that the sign above it, written in Russian, said 'Typhoid'.

With all her journalistic instincts aroused she crossed the road towards it and, ignoring the queue, walked straight in.

It was a medical centre. There was a reception desk. A dozen or so examination cubicles. A larger screened-off area that looked as if it was for minor surgery and a half-dozen nurses who looked to be run off their feet.

In her usual direct manner she strode towards the reception desk. 'Hi,' she said, flashing her press card and ignoring the fact that the woman behind the desk was speaking to a very malnourished and deeply distressed young girl. 'The typhoid sign outside. This isn't really a typhoid clinic, is it? And why is the sign written only in Russian?'

'Just a minute,' the woman said, annoyance in her voice. 'I'm dealing with someone.'

Unfazed, Nancy continued looking around her with interest. Behind a screen she caught sight of a woman being examined as she sat in an obstetric-looking chair with stirrups.

Though habitually insensitive, Nancy was never stupid. 'This is a rape clinic, isn't it?' she said suddenly, realization dawning.

'Yes, it is,' a voice said from behind her.

Nancy turned around. 'Hello. I'm from the British press,' she said, and flashed her press pass again.

The woman she was facing was about her own age. Though delicately boned, with a lovely heart-shaped face and sea-green eyes, there was something about her that indicated great inner toughness.

'I came in because of the sign,' she said, liking the cut of the other woman's jib. 'We're in the British sector and it's written in Cyrillic. I wondered why.'

'It was put up before the British – or the Americans and the French – arrived. It ensured Russian soldiers gave us a wide berth. It isn't necessary now, but I've never had the time to take it down.'

It was a red-hot human-interest story. Nancy said swiftly, 'Will you tell me about it? Most of what has so far been written in the British press is rumour. A first-hand account from someone running a clinic such as this will have great impact.'

The mesmerizing sea-green eyes held hers. 'Are you wanting a first-hand account of the setting up and running of the clinic?' she asked. 'Or of the way that around ninety per cent of rape victims who became pregnant came here desperate for abortions? Or are you wanting me to give you a first-hand account of my own experience of rape?'

It wasn't often Nancy was thrown off track, but the idea of the woman in front of her having endured the same experience as the wretched women she was offering treatment to, threw her completely.

Well aware that she'd finally penetrated the other woman's thoughtless bumptiousness, Eva said conciliatingly, 'Let's go outside to talk. I'd like British women to know what the women of Berlin have suffered. Do you smoke?'

Nancy nodded. 'But don't share your cigarettes with me,' she said as they walked outside. 'They must have been hard to come by. I've got a full pack of Lucky Strikes, a gift from the American who gave me a lift here.'

The street was busy, the traffic heavy with British army vehicles.

With a look towards them, Eva said, 'We were so grateful to see them, there's hardly any animosity towards British troops.' She accepted the cigarette Nancy proffered. 'Most Berliners regard them more as liberators than conquerors.'

It was the feeling Nancy had already gained and she knew she would do another story from that angle. 'What's your name?' she asked, offering Eva a light.

'Ketzler. Eva Ketzler.'

Nancy had been in the act of lighting her own cigarette. Now her hand froze. Her eyes widened.

Eva quirked an eyebrow. 'What's the matter?' she asked, realizing that the woman she was with couldn't have hidden anything she was feeling, even if paid to do so. 'It isn't an unusual name.'

'Neither is mine,' Nancy said, joy bubbling up in her throat. 'It's Remer. Nancy Remer.'

For a moment, Eva simply stared at her and then she said weakly, 'You're Paul's cousin?'

Nancy nodded, her grin nearly splitting her face in two. 'And you're the woman Paul's told everyone he's going to marry.'

It wasn't a question, simply a statement of fact.

'Oh, God!' Eva began to tremble, hardly able to believe that so suddenly, so out of the blue, she had contact with the English side of Paul's family. 'Do you have news of him? Is he safe? Is he in Germany?'

'Last I heard he was uninjured and with the US Ninth Army. Which means he's in Germany and likely to show up any time. And what about my father and Lotti and Ilse? Are they safe and uninjured?'

Eva blinked tears of emotion away. 'Your father is living with my mother and me. He's fine physically, though mentally he's become very vague and not too aware of what's going on around him.'

'He never was aware of what was going on around him. What about Ilse and Lotti? I checked out where they were living before the war, but the house where Lotti once had an apartment no longer exists and the British have requisitioned Ilse's old home.'

'They're living in a tiny flat not far from the Ku'damm with their mother and Hester.'

'Hester?' Nancy stared at her as if she'd taken leave of her senses. '*Hester?*'

Eva nodded, her smile radiant. 'Yes. Thanks to your cousin Claus, Hester has survived the war too. There can't be many families in Berlin who have emerged from the last six years so intact.'

There was a band around Nancy's chest so tight she could hardly breathe. 'Not completely intact,' she said. 'My brother Hugo was shot down on an RAF bombing raid. He died thinking Hester was already dead. We all thought Hester was dead.' She paused, steadying her breathing, and then she said,

568

'How did Claus help Hester to survive? Where is Claus? Does anyone know?'

'Claus hid her,' Eva said succinctly. 'And no one knows where he is, though as he was in Berlin when it fell to the Red Army, we're assuming he's been arrested and is being held as a war criminal.'

Nancy sucked in a deep breath, marshalling her thoughts. 'I need to make contact with Ilse and Lotti,' she said, scrabbling in her bag for pen and paper. 'Can you let me have their address? And will they be there now? What are they both doing?'

'Lotti won't be at the flat now. She's working as an interpreter for the Americans. She'll be here about six or six-thirty. We always meet up for a drink before curfew. Ilse may be home. She has a part in a film being produced at Babelsburg and is there at the crack of dawn, but home by late afternoon.'

'Okey-doke.' Nancy slipped the piece of paper with Ilse and Lotti's address on it into her army-shirt pocket. 'I'm going to find somewhere to lay my head. Ilse and Lotti's flat is obviously packed to capacity and so is your home by the sound of it. Then I'm going to see if Ilse is back from Babelsburg. After that, the two of us will come here to join up with you and Lotti.'

In mutual accord they dropped their half-smoked cigarettes to the ground and grasped hold of each other's hands.

'I'm so glad we've met,' Eva said, her eyes brimming with emotion.

'So am I. Paul has told everyone his plan is that Shuttleworth Hall is to be your home. You'll love it. And my mother will love you.'

Eva gave a shining smile. 'That's what Lotti tells me as well.'

Nancy, who wasn't usually given to kissing people, kissed

her warmly on the cheek and, as she parted from her, her spirits were sky-high.

At one fell stroke she'd met Paul's future wife, ascertained that every member of the Berlin side of her family was still alive and knew where all of them were, apart from Claus. Only as she walked into the bar she'd been heading for did she remember Eva had made no mention of her uncle. She paused for a second and then shrugged her shoulders. Josef's austere personality had always meant she'd never been over-fond of him. If he were dead she would, for her aunt's sake, be sorry, but his death wouldn't throw her into deep grief.

Amalia's was, as she had known it would be, smoke-laden and jammed shoulder to shoulder with reporters in army uniforms and British servicemen.

She'd pressed only a few feet into the crush when she knew that God wasn't just giving her a spectacularly good day – He was giving her a bonanza of a good day.

'Max!' she shrieked. '*Max!*'

He pushed the drink he'd been holding into the hand of the person he'd been talking to and shouldered his way towards her.

'Nancy!' He gave her a brotherly hug, not remotely surprised at seeing her. 'I might have known you'd beg, borrow or steal a press pass here. Are you doing what I'm doing? Trying to track down the family?'

'No. I've already done it.'

As his eyebrows shot high, she giggled. She always liked scoring points off him and this time she'd done so big time.

'Seems army intelligence isn't quite up to a par with ex-*Yorkshire Post*, female-journalist intelligence,' she said, gleeful satisfaction in her voice. 'Our father is living with Paul's girlfriend and her mother. He's OK, but more ga-ga than ever, apparently. Aunt Zelda, Lotti and Ilse are sharing a flat together. I have the address in my shirt pocket. The big news, though . . . the *really* big news . . . *is that Hester is alive and living with them!*'

He stared at her, goggle-eyed. It was the first time in her life she had seen him so staggered and lost for words and elation zipped through her.

'I ran into Eva, Paul's girlfriend,' she said as they continued to be jostled by people on all sides. 'She brought me up to date on everything. The only thing she couldn't tell me was Claus's whereabouts.'

'You have Ilse's address?' He took hold of her elbow and began marching her smartly towards the door.

'Yes.' She took it out of her shirt pocket and handed it to him. 'I was going there straight after I sorted out a room for myself.'

Once out on the street he began striding down it so fast she had to run to keep up with him. 'Where are you going?' she asked breathlessly as he reached a parked jeep and vaulted into the driving seat. 'I'm meeting up with Eva and Lotti at six. I thought you'd want to come with us.'

'I do,' he said, revving the engine into gear. 'But I'm going to see Ilse first.'

'Not without me, you're not!'

Tossing her bag into the rear of the jeep, she scrambled into the passenger seat. 'God, but you've got a high-and-mighty attitude!' she said, falling into the old pattern of sibling bickering. '*I* discovered her address. It should be *me* taking *you* there, not the other way around.'

He shot her a grin, his hair, beneath his major's cap, as thick and curly as that of a Medici princeling's. 'You can't, sister dear,' he said, loving her to bits, 'because *I'm* the one who has the jeep!'

As they veered down potholed streets still filled with rubble, she said suddenly, 'We're going to have to tell her about Hugo.'

'I'll tell her.' He swerved round a burned-out tank that still hadn't been removed.

There was something in his voice that made Nancy frown. 'Do you think the news you were able to give us – the intelligence news that Nicholas had been executed for being one of the plotters in an attempt on Hitler's life – is going to prove correct? Do you think she's going to have bad news of her own to give?'

'I know it.' He turned out of the street and into the even busier Kurfürstendamm. 'That news wasn't speculation. It was hard fact.' He sped past the ruins of the Kaiser Wilhelm Memorial Church. 'Ilse is a widow. Has been a widow for over a year.'

There was something in his voice that sparked intuition even as latent as Nancy's into life.

'You're not thinking of –' she began as he swerved off the Ku'damm and into a side street, about to ask if he was thinking of resuming the affair Ilse had broken off in order to marry Nicholas. It was a sentence she never finished.

'Sweet Christ!' he said savagely, ramming on the brakes and bringing the jeep to a screaming halt. 'There she is!'

She was stepping out of a black Opel car.

Nancy sucked in her breath. Berlin's streets were full of malnourished-looking women dressed in pathetically shabby clothes and down-at-heel shoes. If Ilse was also malnourished, it didn't look like malnourishment; it looked like ethereal slenderness. Her ivory-pale hair was worn shoulder length in a gleaming pageboy bob. Her dress was cream and exceedingly simple. Her shoes were wedge-heeled and a highly polished nut-brown. She looked as Ilse always looked. Cool and elegant and heart-stoppingly beautiful.

Before Nancy could catch her breath, Max was out of the jeep, sprinting towards her. She saw Ilse gasp. Saw her eyes fly wide open. And then saw the flaming smile of joy that lit her face.

Nancy had been all set to run in Max's wake. Now, as Ilse

572

flew into his arms, she hesitated. What was taking place wasn't merely a family reunion, one in which she would be an equal partner. It was something different, something at which she sensed she would be exceedingly *de trop*.

As she had never understood why Max and Ilse's love affair had ever ended in the first place, she wasn't remotely surprised at what was now taking place only yards away from her.

Heaving her bag from the rear of the jeep she slung it over her shoulder. She had waited for a reunion with Ilse for six years. Another few hours wouldn't make any difference. Rather relieved she wasn't going to have to be the one to break the news of Hugo's death, she began heading back on foot the way they had come.

Once back at the bar, a reporter she had known during her *International Herald* days gave her the address of where he and a clutch of fellow reporters were staying. Ten minutes later, she was comfortably installed and hurrying to keep her six o'clock appointment with Eva and Lotti.

The second she put in an appearance, Lotti nearly bowled her off her feet. 'Nancy! I *knew* you'd wangle a way to get here at the first opportunity!' she said ecstatically. 'Eva says you got a lift here from Magdeburg. I'm surprised you didn't simply parachute in!'

Their mutual euphoria was so overwhelming they were laughing and crying at the same time.

'And I've just met up with Max,' Nancy said when at last she and Lotti were no longer in a bear-hold with each other. 'I don't know how long he's been in the city, but he was desperately searching for your and Ilse's address when I met him.'

'Max? He's here? In Berlin?' Lotti's dark eyes flashed past her, expecting to see him in her wake. 'But where is he, Nancy? Why isn't he with you?' The urgency in her voice was so acute that Nancy laughed.

'He'll be meeting up with us the minute his reunion with Ilse is over. I've never seen two people so desperate to be reunited with each other. I don't think it's going to be only Paul and Eva's wedding we'll soon be celebrating. The way they flew into each other's arms, I think we'll soon be celebrating Max and Ilse's wedding as well.'

Lotti stood as still as a statue, the blood draining from her face.

'What's the matter, Lotti?' Nancy was totally bewildered. 'Are you ill?'

'No.' Lotti forced the word through frozen lips. 'No. I just need to be on my own for a bit, that's all.'

And ignoring Eva's sympathetic move towards her she turned on her heel and rushed out of the clinic, her eyes blinded by tears, her heart broken.

THIRTY-FIVE

Berlin, July 1945

'Max! Max! How glorious to see you again!' Ilse clung to him as if she would never let him go.

Overcome by relief at having positive proof that she had survived and was uninjured, Max laughingly unwound her arms from around his neck.

'You look amazing, Ilse,' he said truthfully. 'Are you sure you've really just been through a war?'

'Oh, I've been through a war all right.' As they walked with arms around each other's waists into the house in which she and her mother and Lotti and Hester had their little apartment, her face and voice were suddenly sombre. 'And horrific as all of it has been, the last few weeks of it were the worst.'

'I know.' He looked at her in deep concern, wondering if she wanted to talk about it; wondering if it would be a healing process if she did so.

She read in his eyes what he was thinking. 'No,' she said. 'Not now. There's another nightmare that was far, far worse than anything that was done to me by revenge-seeking Ivans.'

'You mean Nicholas's execution?'

She stood still for a moment outside the door of the apartment, her eyes holding his. 'You know?'

He nodded. 'I'm an intelligence officer, Ilse. I knew practically the instant it happened.'

She opened the door. 'I don't know where my mother is,' she said, leading the way into a minuscule sitting room. 'Lotti is working for the Americans and won't be home for another couple of hours and Hester spends all day, every day, trying to find news of Claus.'

'It's you I wanted to see,' he said, not wanting to talk about Claus yet, knowing that what Hester had so far failed to do, he would be able to do with comparative ease. 'Before I'm reunited with Lotti, there's something I want to tell you.'

They sat down together on a sofa, hands clasped.

'I know what you're going to say,' she said, her voice soft and low. 'I know you love Lotti. I once saw the two of you having dinner together on the terrace of a restaurant overlooking the lake at Wannsee and the way you were looking at each other left me in no doubt of it. It was then I decided to marry Nicholas. Not because I didn't love you. I did.'

Her bluebell-blue eyes held his. 'I still do. When, after I married Nicholas, nothing happened between you and Lotti, I thought perhaps I'd made a mistake – and that I may have made a mistake about other things. And then, after Nicholas was executed . . .'

Her voice shook. 'After Nicholas was executed I thought that perhaps when the war was over . . . when the world was a sane place again . . . that we might . . . that what we'd once had we could have again. But you've come to tell me that we can't, haven't you?'

'Yes,' he said gently. 'What we had will always be very precious to me, Ilse, but what I have with Lotti is something else entirely. It's something you had with Nicholas, even though it was something that only grew after you were married, and it's something you will one day have with someone else.'

'But not with you?'

'No,' he said, his voice still gentle. 'Not with me.'

He rose to his feet, drawing her to hers.

There were tears in her eyes and he brushed them away. 'Nancy is with me,' he said. 'She arrived in the city a few hours ago and it's thanks to her having met Eva that I got your address.'

'Nancy?' Incredulity replaced the disappointment and sadness in her eyes. 'But where is she? Where did you leave her?'

A smile tugged at the corner of his mouth. 'I think she had the sensitivity to realize I wanted to speak to you alone and so stayed in the jeep.'

'Nancy? Sensitive?' She gurgled with amusement at the very idea. He cracked with laughter and everything was suddenly easy between them again. They were cousins and friends, and that there had once been anything more was something relegated to the past.

'Lotti is meeting up with Eva at six o'clock.' He glanced down at his watch. 'It's already fifteen minutes past.' He shot her his familiar down-slanting smile. 'Do you think you can squeeze into the back of the jeep with Nancy?'

'Just try and stop me,' she said, convulsing with laughter when, a minute or so later, they discovered the jeep to be empty and Nancy long gone.

The instant they walked into the medical centre, now empty of patients, Max knew something was wrong. Not only was Lotti not there – a disappointment so crushing he hardly knew how to handle it – but the expression on Eva's face was almost hostile and Nancy looked extremely sheepish.

As Ilse rushed towards her and hugged her, Nancy hugged her back, saying to Max as she did so, 'I'm sorry, Max. When

I told Lotti about your reunion with Ilse she took it badly. I can't think why.'

Eva had already told her why, but it wasn't something that could be spoken of in front of Ilse.

Ilse gave a gasp of distress, well aware of the assumption Lotti had come to. Max, equally well aware of it, swung away from Nancy – who he could have cheerfully throttled – and said urgently to Eva, 'Where might she have gone? Which bars? Which cafés?'

'She doesn't go to bars and there are no cafés yet to speak of.' Understanding now that things may not have been as Nancy had thought them, she tried hard to be helpful. 'She said she wanted to be on her own, so she may have gone to the Tiergarten.' Another thought struck her. 'And there's another possibility.'

'Yes?' Max demanded in a fever of impatience. 'What is it?'

'Major Gleeson, the American officer she's been acting as an interpreter for, has been posted to Frankfurt. He wanted her to go with him – as his interpreter, nothing else. He's due to leave from Tempelhof at seven-thirty. And it's just possible, if she really thought Nancy's assumption was correct, that she's heading for Tempelhof to go with him.'

He didn't waste a second. That Lotti was capable of leaving Berlin if she thought he had returned there for Ilse, not her, he didn't doubt for a moment.

As they heard the squeal of his jeep's tyres, Nancy said miserably, 'I've rather messed up this family reunion, haven't I?'

It was true, but neither Ilse nor Eva had the heart to say so.

'You weren't to know, Nancy,' Ilse said consolingly, giving her another hug. 'And once Max catches up with Lotti, everything will be fine. Even though there's a non-fraternization rule, he's got permission to marry her. A perk of his long years with MI6, I guess – that and his having been born in

578

Germany, which rather knocks the non-fraternization thing on the head.'

Max roared out of the British sector and into the American sector, where the airport was situated. Only once was he stopped and asked to show his papers. 'Major Max Remer, British Intelligence,' he snapped, returning the salute he was given. 'According to the agreement of our high commands, Allies in uniform don't have to produce papers.'

The American lieutenant nodded his head in agreement. 'That's right, Major Remer,' he said, insolently resting his hand on the pistol at his hip. 'Just wondered where you were going in such a hurry.'

Max breathed in hard through his nose, his nostrils whitening. 'Tempelhof. On urgent military business.'

'OK, Major,' the lieutenant said, having had his moment of fun annoying one of the Brits. 'You may proceed.'

Max did so, churning a cloud of dust that would, he hoped, choke and blind the officious Yank.

By the time he got to Tempelhof, he knew he was too late. It was seven fifty-five and there was nothing on the runway waiting for clearance to leave. His barked inquiries as to whether Major Gleeson, of the United States Army, had already left for Frankfurt, were met in the affirmative.

When he asked if a woman had been among Gleeson's party he was met with a steely gaze. 'I can't give that kind of information, Major Remer,' the captain he was questioning said. 'Major Gleeson left with two members of his personal staff, that's all I can tell you.'

Once back in his jeep, Max slammed the steering wheel hard with his fist, cursing himself for being so foolish as not to have anticipated what Nancy's assumptions might be; cursing Nancy for never exercising the least caution in anything she said.

Somehow, in his blood and in his bones, he knew Lotti was now well on her way to Frankfurt. He also knew he was going to have a devil of a job getting permission to travel there.

It took him three days and when permission was finally and grudgingly given it was on the understanding he was back in Berlin within twenty-four hours. 'And if you're not,' Colonel Hargrave snapped, 'it won't help that you're a blue-eyed boy where the powers-that-be in London are concerned. You'll find yourself in a military prison and with the key thrown away. Is that understood?'

He managed to cadge a lift on a US transport plane. It was an uncomfortable, freezing-cold journey and when they landed in Frankfurt the rain was coming down in buckets.

Another hitched lift, as uncomfortable as the flight and through a city with streets as ruined as Berlin's, took him to US Military Headquarters.

'I'm here to see Major Gleeson,' he said when his identity papers had been inspected.

'Is he civil affairs or military government affairs?' the Magnum-toting officer asked.

'Civil affairs,' Max snapped, having done his homework on Chuck Gleeson before leaving Berlin.

There was much scrutiny of US paperwork before he was eventually advised that Major Gleeson was in Zone 2.

'He's only just arrived here,' said the officer who tracked down the information, adding with a grin, 'and he brought his own little German girl with him. He says she's his interpreter.' He gave Max a knowing wink. 'If she is, she's a darn sight prettier than the Brunnhilde battleaxes we've been foisted with.'

Max clenched his teeth, knowing that now was not the time and place to be entering into a confrontation and drawing undue attention to himself.

Taking his cap off and shaking the rain from it, he

proceeded to follow the directions he'd been given for Zone 2.

There was a maze of annexes and corridors to navigate before he came to an office with 'Major Charles Gleeson – Civil Affairs' on it. The placard bearing the name had been taped to the door with what looked to have been more speed than care, and the door was wide open. Beyond it, a crew-cut American was unpacking boxes of documents.

Max eyed the pips on the American's shirt and tucked his cap beneath his arm, well aware that the next few minutes might be a little tricky.

'Major Gleeson? Major Max Remer, British Intelligence.'

Chuck Gleeson straightened up and faced him, an eyebrow quirking perplexedly.

'Yes, Major. What can I do for you?'

'This isn't army business, Major Gleeson. It's a personal matter,' Max said, wondering who it was Chuck Gleeson reminded him of. 'I believe Fräulein Lotti Remer, who acted as your interpreter in Berlin, is acting as your interpreter here, in Frankfurt?'

'That's correct.' Chuck Gleeson frowned. 'I don't understand this "personal matter" stuff, Major. Could you be a little more explicit?'

Max breathed in hard, hoping to goodness Gleeson wasn't going to cause waves when he knew why he had come. 'Lotti Remer is my cousin,' he said. Seeing no reason to beat about the bush, he added, 'And she's also the woman I shall be marrying in a few days' time.'

Chuck Gleeson's eyebrows rose in bafflement. 'Your cousin? She can't be. She's German. Her file was very carefully checked over before she was engaged to work for me. She's a Berliner, born and bred, though a Berliner with no background of Nazi activities. She was never a member of the Nazi Party. She wasn't even a member of the girls' section of the Hitler Youth.'

'I know that because she is, as I said, my cousin. I was born in Berlin too.'

'You were?' Deeply intrigued, Chuck Gleeson forgot all about the boxes he'd been unpacking. 'And so you're the person Lotti was expecting to show up in Berlin? The person who was the reason for her originally refusing to transfer down here with me?'

Max nodded.

'So what happened? When you showed, was there a row? I couldn't get a word out of her when she turned up at the airport.'

'There wasn't a row, because we never met up. There was a misunderstanding before we could do so.'

The deep interest in Gleeson's eyes wasn't prurient and Max added, 'She thought I'd arrived intending to marry someone else. It wasn't true.'

'And she doesn't know that yet?'

'Nope. That's why I'm here.' He took a docket out of the breast pocket of his jacket and handed it across. 'Before I flew into Berlin, I obtained permission to marry. Having a German father and having been born in Berlin, there's a loophole in the non-fraternization regs that my superiors have been able to take advantage of. The thing is, I have to be back in Berlin by eight o'clock tomorrow morning. Needless to say, I want Lotti with me so I can take advantage of the permission to marry before some busybody hotshot rescinds it.'

Chuck Gleeson knew all about busybody hotshots and he knew all about being in love – as the silver-framed photograph on his desk testified.

'I think,' he said affably, handing the marriage-permission docket back to Max, 'that we need to do a little negotiating. I'm happy for you to whisk Lotti off to Berlin and make an honest woman of her, but I'd like her to return here and continue working for me until I find a suitable replacement for her. If such an arrangement suits Lotti, are you happy with it?'

Max nodded.

Chuck Gleeson grinned. 'There's just one little hiccup in your plans so far,' he said. 'And that is, you haven't yet asked her to marry you. She might say no.'

'She might,' Max said, 'but I'm pretty sure she won't.'

'Well, you're just about to find out, Major,' Chuck said, amusement thick in his voice, 'because here she comes.'

Max spun round to face the door.

At first, she didn't see him. She was carrying two enamel mugs of coffee and was concentrating on not spilling them.

It was four years since he had last seen her and though there were hollows beneath her cheekbones that hadn't been there before and though she had lost weight and her petite figure wasn't as voluptuously curvaceous as it had once been, in other ways she hadn't changed at all.

Her hair, almost as dark as her mother's, was still defiantly worn in a style distinctly her own. Instead of being shoulder length so that it could be worn in a smooth pageboy bob or, more practically, drawn away from her face and pinned in a roll at the nape of her neck, her thickly waving dark hair swung jauntily at jaw-length. She was wearing a cream cotton dress brightly patterned with scarlet poppies, the V neckline emphasizing the curve of her breasts. Her curiously foreshortened face was still as beautiful to him as it had ever been, her mouth still as generously wide, her nose still as pleasingly small.

He cleared his throat.

She looked up.

The mugs of coffee went crashing downwards.

With a nonchalance Max was always to remember, Chuck Gleeson took not the slightest notice of the steaming liquid swilling around on the floor. He simply sidestepped it and exited the room, closing the door behind him.

583

Neither of them moved.

The expression in her large dark eyes was a tumult of mixed emotion: unspeakable joy at seeing him again, sheer terror that he was about to tell her that the love of his life was Ilse.

When he spoke his deep voice was husky with emotion. 'I love you,' he said, knowing he loved her with every fibre of his being. Knowing that if her feelings for him had changed, it was a catastrophe he would never recover from. 'I went to see Ilse first so that if she had hopes we could rekindle things, I could let her down gently.' His voice thickened. 'Nancy got things wrong, Lotti. I want to marry you. I want to marry you at the first opportunity. I want to marry you within days.'

She sucked in her breath, swayed unsteadily for a second and then catapulted into his arms.

He rocked her against him as if he would never let her go. The four years of separation were over. Four years of not knowing if she was still alive. Four years of not knowing if he would ever see her again.

'I've got permission from the British authorities for us to marry,' he said, his mouth close against her hair. 'But we have to marry in Berlin.'

She released her hold on him fractionally enough to be able to look up into his face. 'Of course we'll marry in Berlin,' she said, her arms around his neck, her face radiant. 'I'm a Berliner. Even though the city is in ruins, there's nowhere else I'd rather be married.'

'I love you, Monkeyface,' he said fiercely in the seconds before his mouth came down on hers. 'I always have. I always will.'

With a deep, rapturous sigh her mouth parted, her tongue sliding past his.

It was a long, long time before either of them spoke again

– and it was an even longer time before Chuck Gleeson tapped queryingly on the door bearing his name.

In the days before their wedding, Max traced Claus's whereabouts. He was being held by the British pending transfer to Frankfurt, where it was intended he would be held until his trial, the charge against him that of having plundered and exploited the occupied countries and of having enslaved their citizens.

'In simple English, he's accused of using slave labour,' Max had said to Hester. 'Because of the circumstances of his use of slave labour – because of your testimony and the testimony of the German Jews and the Russians who worked for him – it's a charge that isn't going to stick. He's going to have to remain in custody, though, until all the evidence has been presented.'

'You're sure he won't be found guilty?' she'd asked urgently. 'You're quite, quite sure?'

'Absolutely.'

Her relief had been total. 'Thank God,' she'd said shakily, clasping her hands in her lap to prevent them from trembling. 'I couldn't have borne it if anything terrible had happened to him – not so soon after learning of Hugo's death.'

Her eyes were red-rimmed and there were deep shadows beneath them. She had been crying ever since Ilse had broken the news to her that Hugo had been shot down over the city he'd once been so happy in. Though the Tiergarten was now a wasteland, its trees decimated by enemy bombing or by having been cut down by Berliners for much-needed fuel, she was drawn to being there.

There had been fierce fighting in it during the last days of the war, but now all the burned-out tanks had been removed and there was no longer any sign of the British aeroplane that had, for so long, lain half submerged in the middle of its lake.

There were no cultivated flower beds left and hadn't been

for years, but self-seeded flowers had grown and she would sit on the grass overlooking the water, her arms encircling her knees, remembering her life with Hugo and knowing she would carry her love for him in her heart for always. Having loved so completely once, she knew the love she and Claus now shared would be just as complete; that it hadn't been born only out of extreme circumstances and extreme need, but was a love that would last them the rest of their lives.

Lotti also knew she had a love that would be lifelong. Permission had been given for her and Max to marry in the chapel of the St Andrew army barracks and it was going to be as much of a family occasion as they could manage. Nancy, because of her married status, was to be her matron of honour. There were to be no bridesmaids, as she couldn't very well have Eva and Hester as bridesmaids and not Ilse, and asking Ilse to be her bridesmaid would, she felt, have been crassly insensitive.

Her wedding dress was one all four of them had worked on like beavers. Made out of white parachute silk, it had a sweetheart neckline, a dropped Basque waist, narrow sleeves that tapered to a point over the back of her hands and a long flowing skirt that reached to the floor.

'By rights, you should be carrying a bouquet of red roses,' Nancy said as she helped her to dress and do her hair on the morning of the ceremony. 'Ilse has tried everywhere to find some, but it's an impossibility.'

'I don't mind,' Lotti said. 'Eva has made me a bouquet of purple buddleia and daisies. She's tied it with white silk ribbon and it looks beautiful.'

'Happy?' Nancy asked unnecessarily as she stepped away from her to admire her handiwork.

Lotti's radiant smile was her answer. 'Ecstatic,' she said, taking a last look at herself in the mirror and picking up her bouquet.

In the small chapel her mother, Hester, Eva, Eva's mother, Berthold and Max were all waiting for her.

The British army chaplain who was to perform the ceremony, smiled at her from where he was standing in front of the altar. Her mother, who was to walk with her down the aisle in lieu of her dead father, took her place next to her. Max, who had no best man, flashed her a heart-stopping smile and then turned to face the chaplain.

With her hand tucked lightly in the crook of her mother's arm, she had barely gone a yard when there came the sound of running footsteps approaching the chapel.

Seconds later, the door burst open and all heads turned, including her own.

'Hi,' Paul said breathlessly, striding towards her to give her a kiss. 'Someone told me there was wedding taking place here without a best man and so I thought I'd help out.'

His uniform was dusty, his boots caked with dirt and he was still carrying a pistol on his hip. His mother threw her arms around him and hugged him tight, tears streaming down her face.

Eva pressed the back of her hand to her mouth, hardly able to believe that they were being reunited in such a special place and at such a special time.

Once his mother had released her hold of him, he moved swiftly down the aisle to where the woman he loved was waiting for him.

'Sorry it took me so long, sweetheart,' he said, his voice cracking and breaking with emotion as he took her in his arms.

The kiss they shared was deep and passionate and no one, not even the chaplain, suggested that it should come to an end.

When at last it did so, he said tenderly, 'I've business to attend to, *Liebchen*,' and in a couple of swift strides was at Max's side.

Max slapped him on the back, overcome with emotion.

'OK, buddy,' Paul said, grinning broadly. 'Give me the ring and let's get this show on the road.'

It was then, as Max handed him the wedding ring, that he finally knew who it was Chuck Gleeson reminded him of.

'Dearly beloved,' the chaplain said, doing as Paul had suggested. 'We are gathered together here in the sight of God and in the face of this congregation, to join together this man and this woman in holy Matrimony . . .'

A few minutes later, after they had exchanged vows and as Max slid the wedding ring on her finger, an azure butterfly came out of nowhere and fluttered onto Lotti's bouquet.

'An Osiris Blue!' Lotti heard Berthold whisper in awe. 'They are so rare, I've never seen one before!'

'With this ring,' Max said, his eyes holding Lotti's as the butterfly hovered on the buddleia's purple blossom, 'I thee wed, with my body I thee worship, and with all my worldly goods I thee endow. In the name of the Father, and of the Son, and of the Holy Ghost. Amen.'

As the chaplain joined their right hands together the butterfly remained with them and when they walked back down the aisle as man and wife, it danced ahead of them, leading them out into the sunshine.

'A photograph,' Nancy demanded, holding up her hand to bossily prevent them from moving a step farther.

The butterfly was again on her bouquet and as they happily posed for a photograph, Lotti was aware of Berthold edging nearer and nearer to her. Her eyes took on a determined glint. On this day, of all days, her uncle was not going to add to his collection.

Bending her head, she softly blew on the delicate blue wings and then, her hand tucked in the crook of her husband's arm, watched elatedly as it shivered and shimmered and then flew high, dazzlingly, gloriously free.

THIRTY-SIX

Yorkshire, June 1946

Vicky tied an apron around her waist to protect the oyster-silk dress she had married in twelve years earlier and that she still wore on special occasions, and began checking on the salads she had made earlier that morning.

'But when will they be *here*?' Emily Elise demanded, her coppery-red hair held away from her face by a velvet headband.

Her school's regulations demanded that when she was at school her mane of hair was tightly plaited, something she bitterly resented now that she was fourteen. Today, because it was a family occasion – and a very special family occasion – her waist-length hair cascaded in a pre-Raphaelite torrent of curls and waves.

'If the London train is on time reaching Harrogate, the train they are likely to catch from Harrogate to Little Ridding is the eleven-ten.' Vicky tweaked a lettuce leaf unnecessarily.

'Can I go with Lotti and Max and Daddy to meet them?' Emily Elise took a raspberry from a bowl piled high with them.

Vicky, expectation and nerves wound to a fine point,

tapped her hand. 'Please do not do that,' she said admonishingly. 'You'll get raspberry juice on your fingers and then on your dress. Where is Zelda? Is she still sunning herself in the hammock as if there's all the time in the world before they arrive?'

'Aunt Zelda says that if you're in such a state today, what are you going to be like tomorrow, when it's the wedding day?' Emile Elise said, adroitly avoiding answering the question. She wasn't a grass and she adored her exotic and unconventional aunt.

'If the cake doesn't arrive as promised from the baker's and if Leo has to return to London because there's an important vote being taken in the House of Commons, I shall be in a flat spin.'

It wasn't true. Nothing put her in a flat spin, not even caring for Berthold and Bertha who were now living in the west wing and had become quite a feature of Little Ridding as they happily ambled the countryside around it, searching for butterflies. A flat spin today, though, wouldn't have surprised her in the slightest, for she couldn't remember any time in her life when it had been so important to her that everything should be perfect.

'Are Lotti and Nancy still setting the trestle tables on the terrace?' she asked, her mind half on the table setting and half on the gooseberry fools she had made and which were still in the coolest recesses of the larder. Had she made them too early? What if the London to Harrogate train was late? What if Claus and Hester didn't arrive when they were expected to arrive?

'They are, but they're squabbling again. Lotti thinks the napkins should be in napkin rings and Nancy wants to do something fancier with them.'

There came the sound of a baby crying. 'It's all right,' Emily Elise said, before she could query who was looking after her

590

precious grandson. 'Max is doing his devoted-father bit and Jonathan Hugo never cries for long when his daddy is holding him.'

Adam entered the kitchen from the cellar door, a bottle of wine in each hand. 'This is the last of the Sauternes that your father laid down in 1937,' he said, triumph in his voice. 'I knew there were a couple of bottles left somewhere. And speaking of your father, he's asked not to be disturbed until everyone is here. He wants to be as sprightly as possible and so he's conserving his energy.' He cocked an ear in the direction of the terrace. 'Does that baby need feeding? Where's Lotti?'

'Laying the table for our grand family celebration lunch,' Emily Elise said, pitching in as usual before the person spoken to had a chance to answer. 'Do you think I'll recognize Claus and Hester? I haven't seen either of them since Ilse married Nicholas and I was only six then. Do you think that having been in prison for so long, Claus's hair will have turned white?'

'I don't want to disappoint your sense of the dramatic,' her father said drily, wiping the dusty wine bottles with a damp cloth, 'but Claus has been in prison for eleven months, not eleven years, and it was a prison under British jurisdiction, not the Bastille.'

Emily Elise took another raspberry, caught her mother's eye and decided it was time to exit back to the terrace, where it was likely something more interesting was going on.

'That child is growing more and more like Nancy,' Adam said in pretend despair. 'Let's just hope that somewhere in her future there's a Leo waiting.'

'She'll be very fortunate if there is.' She took her apron off and checked that her pearls were lying as they should on the softly draped neckline of her dress. 'I think I've got everything as prepared as I can. Claus hasn't been to Yorkshire for eleven years. Not since Nancy finished her relationship with him. Do you think he's going to find it all a little disorientating? Especially after having been held in close confinement for so long?'

'You're beginning to sound like Emily Elise,' he said, love thick in his voice. He stood the two wine bottles on the kitchen table and closed the distance separating them, putting his arms around her. 'Everything is going to be fine,' he said comfortingly. 'It's a measure of how strong his Yorkshire ties still are, that he and Hester have arranged to marry in a Register Office here, and not in Berlin.'

She rested her head against his comfortingly broad chest. 'I thought that when it came to it, I might feel a little strange about their marrying, but I don't. I'm just grateful that she'll still be closely within the family circle. I couldn't imagine our family without her.'

He tilted her face up to his and kissed her. 'And I couldn't imagine anything without you.'

They smiled at each other, two people who knew what love was all about.

From the terrace they heard the baby give another little mewl and she said, 'I'm going to check on my grandson. He's only three weeks old and babies need feeding every few minutes at three weeks old.'

When she stepped onto the terrace Lotti stopped arranging the glassware on the table and said in mock exasperation, 'You're checking up on me, aren't you? You think I'm being a bad mother.'

'Of course I don't think you're a bad mother. I just thought he might be hungry, that's all.'

Jonathan Hugo was no longer in Max's arms, but was lying in his pram, wrapped in a shawl as fine as lace.

'He isn't hungry,' Lotti said, indulgent of Vicky's ceaseless new-Grandma concern. 'I finished feeding him only fifteen

592

minutes ago.' She put a water glass next to a wine glass on the white napieried table, saying as she did so, 'Max says it's nearly time to go to the station to meet Claus and Hester. Adam is driving, taking Eva, Ilse and Max with him and, if you'd look after Jonathan for me, I'd like to go as well.'

Vicky adjusted the parasol shading the pram. 'Of course I'll look after him for you,' she said unnecessarily. 'Where's Paul? Why isn't he taking Eva?'

'He's gone to collect Violet. With luck they'll be here by the time we all get back from the station.'

Nancy, who had been attending to the glassware at the opposite end of the long table, suddenly said crossly, 'One wine glass with a water glass isn't enough, Lotti. We're having red *and* white wine. The red wine, care of Leo. The white wine, whatever Adam has rustled up from the wine cellar.'

Lotti raised her eyes to heaven. 'Lord, Nancy. Don't you ever stop quibbling? I don't know how Leo stands it.'

There was no real exasperation in her voice and Nancy grinned. 'He stands it because he thinks I'm wonderful – which I am.' She finished putting additional wine glasses on the table, stood back to admire her handiwork and said, 'Where's Eva? She went off half an hour ago to cut some roses for the table.'

'With Ilse.' Lotti flopped down on a sun lounger within hand's reach of Jonathan Hugo's pram. She was wearing a halter-necked scarlet sundress and high, wedge-heeled sandals. Her bare legs were suntanned, her toenails painted the same vibrant red as her dress.

Nancy, who was wearing a cotton shirt with the sleeves rolled up and wide-bottomed linen slacks, regarded her with grudging admiration. 'You don't look as if you've just had a baby,' she said. 'And now you're a mother, don't you think that embossed silver toe-ring looks odd? Shouldn't you be more conventional – all sensible sandals and buttoned-up cardigans?'

'Only when the last nail has been knocked in my coffin,' Lotti retorted, much to Vicky's amusement. 'I don't smoke any more, if that's a comfort to you. Max has suddenly taken against it.'

She screwed her eyes against the sun, looking towards the steps leading down to the lawn. 'Here come your roses,' she said, as Eva and Ilse approached, their baskets laden. 'Did you say you only wanted enough for table decorations? They're carrying enough to start a flower shop.'

Eva was pregnant and Vicky walked swiftly down the steps to meet them, relieving her of the basket she was carrying.

'It's only flowers, Vicky,' Eva said with amused affection. 'It isn't heavy.'

'Yes, well, a basket of any sort can throw you off balance when you're walking up steps. Are these small pink buds for the table and the full-blown white roses for the house?'

Eva nodded. 'Those were the instructions Paul gave me. The red ones are for Hester's wedding bouquet. Paul has asked me to put them in a dark place with water up to their necks. The white roses are Madame Alfred Carrière. I don't know the name of the red ones, do you?'

Ever since she had married Paul eight months ago in Little Ridding's village church, Eva had been intent on learning all she could about roses.

'The red one is Mrs Anthony Waterer,' Vicky said helpfully.

Ilse slipped her arm through her aunt's. 'I love the names roses are given, Aunt Vicky. Who was Madame Alfred Carrière, do you think? And who was Mrs Anthony Waterer that she should have such a lusciously beautiful rose named after her?'

'I don't know about Madame Alfred Carrière,' Vicky said as Max walked across the terrace towards them, tapping his wristwatch meaningfully as he did so, 'but the gentleman who bred Mrs Anthony Waterer was named Waterer, so perhaps he named it after his wife.'

'Time to go,' Max said, his voice taut with the excitement he was feeling. That Claus had been released so soon from British custody was due largely to his efforts. That he had been released with a commendation from the Joint Distribution Committee, the international Jewish relief organization, was due solely to Hester's efforts.

In part, the commendation said:

As the owner of a Ruhr Nazi steelworks and a Berlin Nazi labour factory, Mr Claus Remer preserved the lives of the slave labourers employed by him, ensuring that Jewish men in his Ruhr steelworks and Jewish women in his Berlin factory, were spared death in Sachsenhausen concentration camp and other concentration camps. Witnesses have testified that no Jew employed by Mr Claus Remer was ever beaten, starved or suffered death at his hands, but every Jew was always treated as a human being.

Coming from the source it did, this testimony was enough to ensure he could face the future with his reputation untainted. Life would never be the same for him, of course, but Max knew from his meetings with him that Claus had no desire for anything approaching his old way of life. The Allies had razed the House of Remer steelworks and armaments factories to the ground. Steel production and armament production would never again play any part in his life – and nor did Claus want them to.

'The Berlin factory is to be left in my possession,' he had said, his relief at the fact obvious, 'and I shall continue to operate it as a clothing factory. With luck, I might even be able to do so in close alliance with Adam's woollen mills in Yorkshire.'

He hadn't said what his plans were for the future with regard to Hester, but Max had been able to guess.

As the holder of a British passport and the widow of a British officer, Hester could have returned to England at any time once the war was over, but she hadn't done so. Instead, she'd remained in Berlin, hunting down all her fellow Jews who had survived the war thanks to Claus, ensuring the letters they wrote reached the right people, visiting him as often as she was allowed, keeping his spirits up when no one else could possibly have done.

And now they were to be married, and he couldn't have been happier for them.

'Time to go,' he said again. 'Is Emily Elise coming with us? Because if she is, she'll have to go in Leo and Nancy's car. Heini's so terrified of not being there on time he's been at the station since nine o'clock and he'll want a lift back. It's going to mean her sitting on either Claus's or Hester's knee on the return journey.'

Vicky rested the shallow basket laden with roses on the balustrade and looked down over the lawn to where the hammock was strung between two trees. Zelda was still lazily stretched out in it and Emily Elise was sitting cross-legged on the grass near by, in animated conversation with her.

'Emily Elise!' she shouted. 'The cars are about to leave for the station!'

Emily Elise scrambled to her feet, sprinting for the terrace steps, the sun glinting on her torrent of fiery hair.

'The only other person I've ever seen with hair like that is Rita Hayworth,' Ilse said to Vicky. 'And that's only been on film.'

'You'll probably be seeing Rita Hayworth in real life soon,' Vicky said, referring to the fact that Ilse was leaving almost immediately for Hollywood, where there was a contract waiting for her to sign at MGM. 'And, more interestingly still, you'll be meeting people like Clark Gable and James Stewart.

Emily Elise would love it if you snapped up someone like Clark Gable as a husband.'

'So would I,' Ilse said with a chuckle as Emily Elise ran breathlessly up the steps to where everyone was waiting for her. 'But establishing myself in Hollywood is going to be hard work. It won't give me much time for husband-hunting.'

She was wearing a coffee-coloured silk dress patterned with white polka dots, the skirt swirling mid-calf around legs sheathed in nylons so sheer they took Vicky's breath away. Her white kid shoes were peep-toed and she was carrying a large white straw hat, decorated with a coffee-coloured silk rose. Her barley-gold hair was swept high into a timelessly elegant chignon and her eyes were the blue of a summer sky.

Looking at her, Vicky was sure that not only was she going to be a huge success in Hollywood, but that if ever a woman would never have to husband-hunt, that woman was Ilse.

'Time to go,' Max said for the third time and then, to Vicky, 'I'll explain to Claus that there wasn't enough room in the cars for everyone and that you and his mother preferred staying behind in order to greet them when they arrive here. Now come on, everyone, for the love of Pete, let's *go*.'

There was a mad scramble for the two cars, a flurry of doors slamming, the revving of engines.

Throughout it all, Zelda never stirred and neither did Jonathan Hugo. As the two cars careened off down the drive in the direction of Little Ridding, Vicky stood for a moment at the top of the terrace steps, so deeply happy there was no way she knew of expressing it. For the first time in years her family were around her again in the home that meant so much to her.

It was very hot, very still.

At her back, against Shuttleworth Hall's walls, the roses her father had planted forty years ago still grew. Veilchenblau, a mass of tiny bunches of dark magenta flowers fading to lilac, reaching to the bedroom windows. Zéphirine Drouhin, rose-pink and wonderfully fragrant. At their roots lavender grew the length of the house and the slumberous air was heavy with scent and with the sound of bees.

Beneath the two trees there was movement.

Zelda swung her legs over the side of the hammock, her feet as naked as if she were a young girl.

'Have they gone?' she called. 'Are we on our own?'

Vicky looked towards the pram, saw that beneath his parasol Jonathan Hugo's eyes were fast shut and called back, 'Yes. Apart from the baby, and he's sleeping.'

She walked down the steps well aware of just how special this moment was. Not for six years had she and Zelda been alone together – and it was thirty-seven years since Zelda had last been at Shuttleworth Hall.

'Let's walk down to the river,' she said, as Zelda walked to meet her across the grass. 'The last time we did so must have been just before we left for Berlin in 1909.'

Companionably, they linked arms.

'I can hardly remember back so far,' Zelda said frankly. 'I was very much an American then, wasn't I?'

'You could be very much an American again if you wanted to be.'

Zelda shook her head, light shining on hair that was once again a defiant blue-black.

'No. That's not on the cards at all, Vicky. I'm a Berliner – and once a Berliner, always a Berliner.'

'Even now?' There was incredulity in Vicky's eyes. 'Even after all that has happened?'

Zelda's mouth, glossily scarlet, curved in a wide smile. 'I've been a Berliner since the day the two of us walked with your father into the mansion on Unter den Linden as Harald Remer's guests. That transformation never happened to you, did it? Not even in the early days of your marriage to Berthold?'

They were at the river bank now and the Ure flowed and rippled past them over its rock-strewn bed, its surface glittering in shades of green shot through with grey and silver.

'No,' she said, knowing that it had been her inability to become a Berliner that had led her into the deeply satisfying life she shared with Adam. 'I was never a Berliner. Not even for a moment. I've always been a Yorkshire girl. I'm a Yorkshire girl through and through.'

Their eyes held, their smiles deep, and then, in mutual accord, they joined hands, just as they had been in the habit of doing when they were children, and together began to walk back up the long grassy slope to the terrace where, in just a little while, their much-loved Yorkshire and Berlin family would be gathering for the celebration of a lifetime.

ACKNOWLEDGEMENTS

My thanks to my editor, Claire Bord, to whom I owe an awful lot – not least the book's title. Clare Parkinson was a wonderful copy-editor and a job that can often be tedious was enlivened by much laughter. Thanks are also due to my agent at A P Watt, Sheila Crowley, and also to Linda Shaughnessy. I would also to acknowledge my indebtedness to the stories told me as a child by my grandmother, great-aunts and great-uncle, who survived the difficulties of being a half-British and half-German family throughout two world wars.